When Gregory the Grey, head of the Magickers, and Brennard, the leader of the Dark Hand, dueled for the future of the world, it split the space-time continuum, paving the way for the Age of Science while at the same time most sources of magic were lost in our world. All the Magickers and the members of the Dark Hand alive at the time fell into a magic-induced sleep from which they did not begin to awaken until the early 1970s.

Since then the Dark Hand has hunted the Magickers, determined to steal their power and destroy them. And legend has it that both Gregory and Brennard survived their duel, and are hidden away, slowly regaining their strength and awaiting the moment of their own awakening.

Now the Magickers' only hope for survival is to seek out children with "talent" and train them to use their abilities for the good, and to find the hidden gateways to strongholds where the sources of magic still exist.

THE
MAGICKERS CHRONICLES

**DAW BOOKS PRESENTS
EMILY DRAKE'S
*THE MAGICKERS CHRONICLES***

VOLUME ONE:
The Magickers
The Curse of Arkady

VOLUME TWO:
The Dragon Guard
The Gate of Bones
(coming October 2010)

THE
MAGICKERS CHRONICLES:

VOLUME ONE

THE MAGICKERS

THE CURSE OF ARKADY

Emily Drake

DAW BOOKS, INC.
DONALD A. WOLLHEIM, FOUNDER
375 Hudson Street, New York, NY 10014

ELIZABETH R. WOLLHEIM
SHEILA E. GILBERT
PUBLISHERS
http://www.dawbooks.com

First Printing, July 2010
1 2 3 4 5 6 7 8 9

DAW TRADEMARK REGISTERED
U.S. PAT. AND TM. OFF. AND FOREIGN COUNTRIES
—MARCA REGISTRADA
HECHO EN U.S.A.

PRINTED IN THE U.S.A.

THE MAGICKERS

Dedicated to Michael Gilbert:
Remembered for his artistic talent, dry wit,
and keen sensibilities, and missed by many friends.
He won the battle, but lost the war....

Contents

Once Upon a Midnight

THE moon hung like a silver lantern in the midnight sky; white sand below his feet made a soft shushing sound as he moved. His sneakers sank with every step, and he pulled his T-shirt closer around him as the sea mist fell like a cold, cold rain. The sea looked like black glass, except where the tide broke on the shore in glowing foam and hissed into silence.

The castle stood before him on broken stone, as though the sea had pulled most of the shore from under it, wearing away the land. It looked more like a ruin than a castle; the dark jagged tears into the walls and towers were like shadowy breaches of despair. Jason stood for a moment, staring at it. A cold wind pressed around him. He'd gotten this far before. . . .

He walked widdershins three times around the castle, a long walk for his eleven-year-old stride although he stretched his legs as far as he could. Then, and only then, did he approach it. He could feel the stone sense him, awakening.

Putting his hand out to the great gate surrounding the castle, unlike a moat or drawbridge, he passed his palm over the immense brass door knocker and the lock sculpted as a dragon's head and tail. He snatched his hand back from the metal, knowing what would happen, and even then he almost

wasn't in time! Flames sprouted from the opening jaws and
flared nostrils. The air smelled hot and brassy.

"Sssssssson of wizardsssss passssssss . . ." the door knocker
hissed.

The gate creaked open with a howling screech.

Jason dashed through the opening gate before the knocker
could do anything else. He tripped on rubble immediately
and fell to his knees with a cry, his yelp echoing harshly back
at him. He rose quickly, dusting himself off, and cast a look
around. A broken roof overhead still blocked out most of the
sky, but moonlight came through in razor rays, looking sharp
enough to cut. As it illuminated the area, he saw where he
stood. A fallen tombstone lay in front of him, half in moonlight, half in shadow, with another one tilted not too far ahead
of him. Jason whirled around.

Out of the shadow, something grabbed at him. He spun to
face it . . . a cold marble angel with her hand outstretched, a
pleading look on her face, and her wings folded at her back.
He took a deep breath and stepped away. This was no castle . . . it was an immense tomb. Stone walls built around a
decaying burial ground. He took a deep breath to steady himself. Although he knew what he sought, he'd never been this
far before.

"Don't stop me now," he beseeched quietly. His voice
echoed back in a mutter he could not understand. Jason edged
around a chunk of granite. As he passed by, the moonlight
struck the letters R I P, engraved in a Gothic style.

The gate clattered and shuddered behind him as the wind
shivered through harder and faster. He could feel it cutting
through his clothes as though it came out of the dead of winter. Moonlight skipped across row after row of headstones and
beyond them, a shadow-dark doorway into the castle wall . . .
if indeed it was a castle at all. Perhaps a crypt! At the far side
of the graveyard, a blackened stick of a tree twisted out of the
ground, its gnarled branches and twigs like grasping arms with
contorted hands reaching out to him.

He had to get to that doorway—had to. What he needed to
know, what he had to find must lie beyond there. Jason steadied
himself as he walked between the rows of headstones, many
blank, some with their carvings worn away except for a letter

here and there, others fallen to unreadable rubble. The wind tugged at the dead tree's branches and its stiff twigs pounded at a tombstone like skeletal fingers. Tap . . . tap . . . tap.

A yellow-eyed crow sat on the top branches, watching him. The immense bird seemed to soak up all the shadows of the graveyard and grow larger with every movement it made. It ruffled its wings.

Jason hurried past, his sneakers sending up puffs of ashy dust. He pinched his nose to stifle a sneeze, not wanting to wake whatever might sleep here . . . if anything did. The shuffle of his steps and the tap-tap of the tree branch were more than enough noise for him! Not everything here was dead, he thought . . . he hoped! And he had to hurry to find out if he was right.

A single splinter of moonlight pointed a way through the door. He stepped through it.

Inside, moonlight danced almost as if it were sunlight coming through a window. He stood in . . . a room. It was nearly bare, but there was a rocking chair and a window and a small writing desk up against the wall, and Jason thought his heart would stop because he *knew* this place! Oh, it wasn't the same, but he knew it and he hurried farther inside, because someone sat in the rocking chair. Could it be the person he'd hoped to find? The someone he could barely remember no matter how hard he tried?

"Mom?" called Jason softly as he drew near. Warped wooden floorboards creaked ominously under his weight. His heart thudded in his chest like a great drum beating. His hand went out to the shadowy woman's shoulder. He could just see the back of her head, her body as she sat resting in the chair. Only in a dream could he get this close—

Ker-ACK! He plunged downward as the floor gave way, tumbling him into total darkness. When he hit, it was on cold stone, and he lay for a moment, breathing hard, his pulse skipping erratically. The moonlight had followed him down, pooling around him like a puddle of spilled milk, sour spilled milk, and he stood up slowly.

Cold, icy stone was all around him, pressing close. At the other end of the narrow passageway, he could see a solid, long, yet tablelike object. He rubbed his eyes and took a cautious step forward, no longer sure what was solid and what was not. As he moved toward the object, he could see what it was. A stone sarcophagus, a coffin, like the ancient Egyptians had used. He turned around to go back, but the passage had narrowed to a mere slit behind him, and he had nowhere to go!

"I'm all right," he said to himself. "I'm fine." Like a chant, he repeated it over and over as he was forced toward the coffin step by step. He'd gone as far as he wanted to. Enough was enough; memory or dream, he didn't care, he did not want to go any closer.

But he had no choice as the passage continued to narrow behind him, nudging him forward. The stone coffin became clearer, a man lying on its top, arms crossed over his chest, himself granite or as still as stone. Etched into the side were two words: Jarred Adrian.

His father's name.

Jason could feel every inch of him raise in goose bumps. No! This wasn't what he wanted. He wanted to see them both alive! Alive and warm, and his. . . . He stopped in his tracks. He wanted out! Out or . . . he put his head back, looking to where the moonlight rayed through from above . . . out or up! He could hear the tap-tap of the dead tree in the cemetery overhead. Looking into the shadows, he could see black roots, twisting down, splitting the stone. There had to be a way out. Up! Yes . . . up! He jumped, grabbing the roots, and began to pull himself up hand over hand. The tree felt slimy and slippery, bark and stubs catching at him, snagging, but he shinnied up stubbornly as the tree tried to wrap itself about him. The roots surged around him like giant wings, trying to hug him and hold him. He swore he could see yellow crow's eyes in the winged darkness pecking and grasping at him. He fought back. Up! Up!

"Wake up!"

Jason bolted upright in his bed, blankets twisted around him, gasping. "Wake . . . up."

He took a deep breath. Sharp moonlight sprayed across his bed, as white as the bright sun, striking his face. He shook, then drew in another deep breath.

He rarely slept through an entire night. Jason sat there for a moment, forcing himself to calm down. He turned his head, trying to read his clock despite the dark, shifting shadows that filtered through his room in the still of the night. Rays of light like silvery swords guided his glance. There in the corner was a wooden rocking chair, the only thing he had left of his mother. His soccer gear sat neatly folded on the seat, his backpack hanging from its arm. Bookshelves stretched across one entire wall. He could read some of the titles: *The Sword in the Stone, The Dragonriders of Pern, The Last Unicorn, The Dragonbone Chair,* and others. Too many to actually see, but he knew them all well.

They were braced in their places on the shelf by stuffed animals here and there. Three teddy bears, a fat stuffed cat, and two bunnies. In the sunlight, all would look rather well loved and with a bare spot here and there. On the top shelf lay a squadron of toys from *X-Men* and *Star Wars,* squared off to contest one another. There was a small CD player on the nightstand next to him with a collection . . . well, a stack, of CDs, two of which needed to be returned to Alicia. A book lay folded back on the nightstand, too, its chapter heading reading: DRAGONS BARRED THE WAY to the kingdom of the dead.

So that's where he got that nightmare from this time. He should know better.

Everything was familiar. Jason felt a little better and prepared to scrunch back down in bed.

Then . . .

Tap. Tap. Tap.

He froze in place. From the north end of the house came the light, fluttering snore of his stepmother. Punctuating it like a big kettledrum came the booming snore of his stepfather. The McIntires slept in what Jason referred to as the Heavy Metal part of the house. Of different blood, he apparently didn't have the snore gene. Or, at least, if he did . . . he slept through it.

Ker-ack! At the window again. Jason peered down the length of his attic bedroom, gloomy in the deep night. No trees reached this high. Something was at the porthole window, the only one in the odd-shaped attic that had no screen. It wasn't really meant to be opened and shut, although he could . . . and did.

He slept in the attic, undeniably the best room in the house, with its porthole window that faced the dimly seen ocean, and its second bay window facing the foothills. The door to his room was in the floor, not the wall. Jason rather liked the idea that he could pull up his ladder and lock himself away from the world. He didn't really belong here, not really. He was here by default.

Not that he could get away with hiding for long. William "Dozer" McIntire would stand in the hallway and bellow until the ladder was lowered.

"Boy," he'd roar. "Come down here and join your family!" Then Jason would risk having his teeth shaken out of his jaws by one of his stepfather's enormous bear hugs.

William "Bulldozer" McIntire stood tall enough that his thinning brown hair threatened to scrape the ceiling that led to the attic. His great tough hands felt like catchers' mitts on Jason's shoulders and he looked like he could carry a building on his back. Jason's stepfather was in construction. He tore things down, so he could rebuild them twice as big and four times as expensive.

Then there was Jason's stepmother, Joanna. Dainty, petite, with wide blue eyes and a seemingly innocent stare. She could wrap the Dozer around any of her slender fingers. Daughter Alicia took after her mother, with quick, small hands and eyes that looked at you while she made secret plans.

Yet once he'd had two parents like everyone else. It was so long ago, he didn't remember his mother dying. He remembered being alone with his dad, the two of them together. After a while, his father had married Joanna, giving him a stepmother and a stepsister. Then his father had died, and Joanna had married William McIntire. She liked to look fondly at her third husband and declare, "Third time's the charm!" Which, although it seemed okay to say, always made Jason feel funny deep down. It wasn't his father's fault that the second husband hadn't lasted. Jarred Adrian would have lived if he could have!

McIntire had thrown open his home, his heart, and swept all of them inside without even asking if it was what they wanted. But how could they not want it? McIntire enjoyed life. Hale and hearty, loud and laughing. Even Alicia seemed happy. At any rate, she was the darling of both now, and he was . . . what was he? A leftover? If he was loved, it was rather like a stray cat, he thought. And if he sometimes thought that Joanna had married awfully quickly after losing his father, he never said anything. It would not, he knew, have made a difference. Everyone else was happy. What did it matter if there were great, yawning gaps in his own feelings? What did it matter if he remembered, although dimly, far happier times?

Ker-ack!

It sounded as though the window itself had split! Jason rolled out of bed, his sandy blond hair sticking out all over. His pajamas were rumpled from the restless night. His feet stuck out like great clumsy things, and he stared at them and his bony ankles in dismay. He'd grown again?

A weed, Jason Adrian, he told himself. *That's what you are. A stray weed that wandered into the McIntire garden. . . .*

Jason dragged his desk chair over to the window and knelt on it, pulling aside the shutters. Silver light shot through, practically stunning him with brightness. It flared up from the brilliant moon outside and . . . he leaned on his knees. Someone was down below. Someone with a mirrorlike flash in her hands, gazing back up at him.

He rubbed his eyes to clear them. It looked like . . . Mrs. Cowling . . . his English teacher. Jason squinted down at the neighborhood street and the woman, whoever it was, disappeared, briskly walking down the sidewalk, behind trees and out of his view. One last bright flash illuminated his window. What the heck? Jason leaned his chin on the brass sill, nose almost to the glass.

Ker-ACK! Yellow-eyed blackness swooped at him! Crow! His heart jumped in his chest. Was it? How could it be?

Black wings fluttered; shadow filled the window, then disappeared. He pushed his face back to the window again.

Silently, it came at the glass and swerved away at the last moment before smashing into it. Frowning, Jason unscrewed the great brass clips that held the window firmly in place, and swung the glass out. He leaned out, looking. Warm spring air washed across his face as though the yellow moon hanging low in the sky exhaled at him. He wasn't still dreaming . . . was he?

Pain slashed through his scalp. "Ker-aw!"

"Yeow!" Jason swatted wildly. His hand jabbed at the air, then connected heavily. Feathers flew, followed by a dull thump on the roof.

Now what had he done? Killed it? If it wasn't dead, just hurt . . . well, he couldn't leave it there. With a grunt, Jason levered himself out the porthole and onto the rooftop. Crouched barefooted on the shingles, he swept his gaze about and saw nothing.

Streetlights glowed a soft yellow, muting the nearly colorless colors into drab beige. Nighttime cloaked the entire neighborhood. The walking woman could not be seen anywhere. His head stung. He was almost a hundred percent positive he was awake, yet . . .

He leaned away from the porthole window a bit more. His pajama sleeve caught on the framing and, as he yanked his arm to free it, the window swung shut. With a hollow sound, it fell into place.

Jason groaned. Locked out, and on the roof! What mischief he'd get blamed for, he wasn't quite sure, but he was definitely in trouble.

The brass frame to the porthole window rattled coldly under his hand, refusing to budge. Jason stifled a groan. He'd have to get in through the front door somehow. He'd done this in reverse once before, up the back of the house, inching up on a rain gutter which was scarcely used in Southern California, and swinging across the roof gable. And where was the bird anyway? Nowhere. It had probably flown off, cackling at waking him from a deep sleep and making him fall out of his nest of a bed.

Jason took a deep breath and began to scramble sideways until he reached the gutter. As the metal took his weight, it creaked and swayed in protest. It threatened to bend away from the house entirely and send him crashing down.

Jason bit his lip, looking down. Was a jump out of the question? The faraway ground suggested that was the case. Maybe a mild thud into the flower bed of creeping charlies planted in this shadowed side of the house? He might even be able to do it without waking everyone. He might make it back to bed and sleep without getting a stern lecture and Joanna watching him sorrowfully as though she had somehow failed in her duties. He might even do it without hurting himself so badly he'd miss soccer tryouts, providing he hadn't been grounded. He hung his head over, considering the options.

No, at this point, a climb at least partway down seemed best.

The roughened metal of the rain gutter scratched his bare feet as he climbed, scraping his toes raw. The warm night hung over the neighborhood, and the sinking yellow moon could now barely be seen over the rooftops. Something black and swift darted at his head!

"Ow!" Jason twisted his head around. Back again! He glanced up. Scalp smarting, he shinnied down the gutter a little more carefully. Where the eaves jutted out and the second story began, he had to stop. Bare feet and ankles wrapped tightly around the coarse, pitted metal, he lifted both hands to pull himself over.

Then it came at him again, as intent as if protecting a nest of eggs or fledglings.

It sailed back, yellow eyes shining and talons outstretched. Jason ducked, smothering his yelp of alarm. His whole body swung wildly away from the house. The gutter moved with him, creaking horribly. With a *skkkkrink* and a *skkkkronk,* it tore lose. For a moment, he swayed wildly as though on a single giant stilt. It swayed toward the house. He scratched at the siding, trying to catch hold. It swayed away. His heart pounded. Back. Forth.

The rain gutter shuddered like a wild beast and then tossed him. He soared downward through the air, arms and elbows flying, and crashed into the hedge surrounding the yard with an *oooof!*

Good news. The hedge stopped his fall. Bad news. It prickled through his pajamas with a hundred nasty little thorns and forced the air right out of his solar plexus. The wind fled his lungs for a moment or two. He lay faceup, looking at the night sky and the golden eye of the huge moon and gulped for air like a beached guppy. After long moments, he finally inhaled deeply. Once he could breathe, he lay still, both his heart and his head pounding, and worried whether the crash had been heard.

With no dog or cat in the house, there was nothing to sound

an alarm but the sharp ears of the McIntires themselves, yet the only sounds reaching him were a thunderous snore chased by a faint one.

He sighed. The gutter wobbled in the night air, waving at him, but it looked as if it would stay partially attached, now that his weight was gone. However, there was no chance he could shinny up it again.

Jason was done for, as far as sneaking back in the house. The moon hung over him, and as plain as could be, a shadow glided across the face of it. Glistening blackly with spread wings, it turned and came for him.

Jason sat up abruptly, gathering his feet under him.

The creature dove right past his eyes, stalled in mid-flight, and landed. It folded its wings about its body, an immense crow, as yellow-eyed as if it had absorbed the moon. The bird cocked his head, then hopped forward. It blinked and studied him. Took another crow-hop nearer.

Jason tensed.

With a gleam in its yellow eyes, the bird darted forward, pecked the back of his hand, and launched itself into the air with a great "Ker-aww!" Feathers and something white were shed as it soared skyward.

He snatched his hand back, but the bird's peck hardly amounted to anything compared to the stinging assault of the hedge's prickles. His hand was a mass of scratches already and his skin crawled with itching. Stupid hedge.

Strange crow.

He stood cautiously, eyeing the night sky to see if the shadow had come back. Nothing.

He bent over to see what the crow had dropped into the dewy grass. A scrap of paper. Jason retrieved it. The moon seemed to sit on his shoulder, illuminating spidery writing:

You May Have Already Won . . .

Jason scratched his head, the only part of him which did not itch abominably. He muttered quietly, "I've never won anything. And I am locked out with a thousand bloody scratches all over me, thanks to you . . . stupid bird."

He squinted. It must have been ripped off some junk mail

contest entry, thrown in someone's trash, gilt edges attracting the bird's eyes. He shoved it in the pocket of his pajamas. He had no luck. His present predicament proved that.

Jason stared at the rain gutter again. Well, there was no sense putting it off any longer. He would have to ring the doorbell and awaken someone to get back in. With any luck, it might be Alicia. She could be bribed.

Jason limped to the corner of the house. A slow, dark cloud moved over the face of the golden moon, plunging the whole neighborhood into immense, purple shadows. He stumbled into the hedge (Ow!, again) and it exploded with a splitting hiss. He sprang back as leaves flew in all directions. A great ginger tomcat burst out, green eyes gleaming and bounded off, his crooked tail flipping in disgust with every leap. The cat stopped, turned, flashed a defiant flag of his tail, and dodged into a hole under the fencing.

With a deep breath of resignation, Jason sidled around the corner of the house. The front door opened as soon as he touched it, and Alicia stood on the threshold, looking at him, framed in glaring light.

"Oh," she said with a smile. "Are you going to owe me."

2

Rut-Roh

"ALICIA crossed her arms and said, 'This had better be good.'"

Sam danced in the early morning light as he hiked his backpack up on his shoulder. "She said that? Really?" His best friend stood, alert, awake, and listening.

Sam had been patiently waiting at the corner just before school. He'd dropped his battered backpack and was playing with a Hacky Sack, bouncing it up and down between his hands and his feet. He snatched it out of midair as Jason joined him. Sam was small, wiry, and brown all over—brown hair, brown eyes, and a dark brown tan. He made up for it by wearing bright yellows and reds.

"Oh, she said that and more."

They stood in a river of students making their way toward Jefferson Middle School. The sun, which had seemed incredibly bright earlier, now hid behind a clump of hazy, smoggy clouds. Leaves skittered and scattered away from his shoes as if worried they might be crunched underneath. Skaters boarded past, their wiry bodies poised in sleek balance over their skateboards, despite their baggy shorts and often untied sneakers. Jason watched them soar past, surfing the concrete walkways. He'd been trying to learn on his own, difficult to impossible without a decent skateboard. Anything with wheels could be guaranteed to draw a concerned look from Joanna. Even headgear and elbow pads would not appease her.

"Really," Jason answered. He paused and shouldered his books as a skateboarder whizzed by, nearly careening into both of them. By the time he struggled back into balance, the skater was long gone, around the corner, snaking in and out between other walking students. Voices rose in laughter. A group of girls passed, bursting out in giggles as they swung by, and he wondered if it was aimed at him or not. He watched them. A pack of girls? A gaggle of giggles?

"You're road kill." His best friend tugged at his pack again, the lumps and bumps and weight of his folded-up scooter bulging from inside.

"Well, not exactly." Jason had recounted the same story to Sam that he'd blurted out to Alicia. The difference had been that Sam had listened, believing, while Jason's stepsister had watched him with a mocking light in her eyes.

"A bird at the window, a big crow or something. It kept pecking at the glass. It wouldn't stop! I opened the window to get a look at it . . . and I fell out."

"You fell from the attic window?" Her eyes had widened, then narrowed.

"Right into the hedge," he had answered, limping forward.

"Right." Her eyebrow had raised slightly. "Two stories?"

"I tried to shinny down the rain gutter." She still had not let him past and his body itched, his hands moving everywhere scratching. "Give me a break, Alicia, okay?"

She'd moved over then, letting him in, saying, "You owe me, big time."

Sam sighed as he pocketed his Hacky Sack. "That's bad."

Jason nodded. They started forward again. A small shadow darted overhead. He looked up. The crow winged its way into a neighboring tree, then vanished after giving him a yellow-eyed stare for a moment. A shiver went down his spine.

"What are you going to do?" asked Sam.

"With any luck, Joanna will make brownies this week. If I fork over my share, I should be off the hook."

"Man. And I thought *my* sister was a monster." He grinned. "What about your parents?"

"Nothing much." Jason shrugged stiffly. Everything hurt, but not as much as it had when he first woke to morning light clobbering his eyelids, streaming in through the window like a flashlight aimed directly at his eyes. He had rolled over in his creaking bed. There was nothing in his body that did *not* hurt. And the tryouts for soccer camp were today! It was bad enough he didn't play on the local teams yet, like most of the guys, or that he had chicken legs in PE shorts, but now he was going to have scratched chicken legs!

Jason had punched his pillow before getting out of bed, wishing he didn't have to face this day at all! With a sore grunt, he had grabbed a pair of jeans and started to dress. He wasn't very good at telling lies. He didn't believe in it, and he wasn't quick enough to think of good ones. Honesty served him best, even if it could be painful.

Sam's face scrunched up. "You're kidding? You came downstairs looking like you lost a cat fight and no one said anything?"

"Well . . . Joanna didn't have her contacts in. And the Dozer . . . he sat behind his paper and read her the sales ads and then . . . he looked at me." Jason stopped on the sidewalk. His breakfast did a flip-flop in his stomach as it had then, William McIntire looking at him over the top edge of the newspaper, and then his stepmother considering him vaguely.

"Jason, I have told you time and time again. If you have good manners, you can sit and eat with anyone in the world. Even the Queen of England. How can you come to breakfast without combing your hair and washing your face?"

Jason's teeth clicked as he closed his mouth.

The Dozer let out a low rumble that could have been in agreement or just clearing his throat as he looked, really looked, at Jason. He felt his scratches grow hot and itchy.

"Son," vibrated William slowly. He leaned over. His brown eyes squinted as he stared into Jason's face. "If you think you need to shave, come and see me. Dull razors hurt. I know this is the sort of thing a father should show you, but I'll stand in as well as I can."

"Oh, my." Joanna glanced at her husband.

"Don't worry." The Dozer squeezed her hand tighter. "I've got it handled." He nodded at Jason. "You might want to splash some of my aftershave on your mug. It'll sting, but you'll heal faster."

Jason exhaled.

Sam exhaled, too. "Man, you're only eleven. And he thinks you were trying to *shave?*"

"At least he didn't ask me what happened."

"So you're still going to tryouts for soccer camp?"

"You bet."

Sam heaved a sigh of relief. "Partners, right?"

Jason slapped his hand. "Definitely!"

The fact he'd been okayed to try out for soccer camp had faintly surprised him. Evidently his stepmother thought that shin guards would protect him, although she had questioned him a few days ago about the difference between rugby and soccer, as if to reassure herself she'd made the right decision. She'd looked at him, her sunglasses tilted back on her forehead like a hair ornament, repeating his words now and then, faintly ending up, "And no tackling?"

"No, ma'am. No tackling. This is soccer." He pressed his mouth shut firmly on what was not exactly a lie.

"Well." She put her reading glasses on as she pulled out her organizer. "Work hard and make the team! You know we approve of summer camps. They build character."

Early bell sounded through the air as the stucco buildings of the school loomed in view. The flow of students had slowed to nearly a trickle, Jason's tale delaying them. The bell's echoes faded as two snickers came from behind.

"Partners, huh? Well . . . partner this!"

Movement too swift to duck grabbed him up, pulling his sweatshirt jacket over his head, blinding him. As he kicked and fought to get free, his feet and body suddenly left the ground. For a moment he was flying blind, hands on his arms tossing him through the air. He hit with a fragrant thump, Sam letting out a grunt beside him as he landed also, and then a thunderous clang as the dumpster lid slammed shut over them. Darkness fell even as Jason clawed his sweatshirt off his head.

"Oh, man," said Sam. "I'm going to stink all day."

They both struggled to stand on the heaps of garbage under them, and push up on the heavy metal lid overhead. It wouldn't budge. The noise of students moving past had stopped as everyone now was probably inside the classrooms, or at least the school gates.

Something tapped at the metal lid. Tap, tap.

Sam tilted his head. "Hello? Get us out!" He knocked and rattled loudly. There was silence. Then something walked across the lid: tick, tick, tick.

Jason listened. What on Earth . . . ?

They held their breath, listening. Someone was teasing them, toying with them.

Tap. Tap. Tap.

Then, "Kerr-awww." And a rattling "CAW!"

A crow! He'd had it with crows!

Jason made a fist and punched at the dumpster lid. There came an explosion of wings and caws as the crow took startled flight off the top. It came back with a heavy thud, CAW-ing even more loudly.

Both Jason and Sam put their hands up and rattled the dumpster lid, yelling at the top of their lungs.

Bright sunlight flooded in as the lid suddenly opened. Mrs. Cowling, Jason's English teacher, stared in, her big, fluffy brown hair in a sunny halo about her round face. "Goodness," she said. "What are you two doing in here?"

She helped Sam out and then Jason. The stench of the dumpster floated about them like a cloud, and then slowly faded. Jason looked back in the trash bin. They were in luck, it seemed, most of the rubbish seemed to be old boxes and dry stuff. The reek must be a permanent odor stuck inside. He shook himself, pulling his backpack and sweatshirt jacket down.

"We got thrown in," Sam answered sulkily. His dark hair stood out in wild thatches.

"Do you know who?"

"Didn't see a thing."

Jason traded looks with Sam. He had a wild guess who it might have been, but it wouldn't do any good to say anything. He shrugged. Mrs. Cowling nodded. "Well, off with you, then.

Tardy bell is about to ring." The two sprinted off to the school gates and their first period classes.

Overhead, a crow rattled another raucous "CAW!"

SPRING, nearly summer, sang hotly through the late afternoon air, muted by the schoolroom window. The cries of boys already suited up for soccer team tryouts and running around the green field could barely be heard. He could see Sam's blazing red jersey and more than once, the faraway figure had turned and looked toward his building. He had to be wondering where Jason was.

Jason's fingers cramped around his pencil. If he looked at the wall clock one more time, Mrs. Cowling would spot him. Outside of cheaters, there was nothing she hated more than clock watchers. It would hurt her feelings that he wasn't paying attention, especially after her rescue of the morning.

His eyes watered with the effort of not looking. He needed to be out on the field warming up. Would class never end?

Mrs. Cowling returned to the front of the class and stood, her fluffy brown head tilted to one side. Thankfully, the school clock was just behind her, above the chalkboard. She smiled and said cheerfully, "To repeat, this final essay must be five hundred words long, in ink, and due by Friday. I want to see your best effort! This is your final grade of the year, and I am hoping to hear that many of you qualify for Honors English next fall!" She glanced toward Jason and smiled slightly. They'd talked about that after class. He liked writing, and she liked what he wrote.

Immediately, Martin Brinkford's hand shot up. Someone at the back groaned even as Jason bit his lip. Brinkford could talk for hours, endlessly, about nothing, and Mrs. Cowling had to let him. It had something to do with Brinkford's father being a generous donor to the school's many needs and charities.

"Yes, Martin?"

Tall, with cold blue eyes, and surfer-blond hair, Brinkford

sat at the back with the big square boy called George Canby. "Will a computer printout be accepted?"

Mrs. Cowling smiled brightly. "Although a typed paper would be easier on my eyes, no. I want to see the essays done in your very own words, thoughts, and handwriting. I know you all have it in you to be very interesting and original."

Brinkford sank down into his chair. "I don't get my papers off the Internet," the blond-haired boy said, his mouth twisted sulkily.

"No, of course, you don't," Mrs. Cowling said. "But others may be tempted, so I've decided this is a fitting way to handle it. I want only your best thoughts!"

Jason resisted the notion to out-and-out stare at Martin. He was all but certain it was Brinkford and Canby who'd trash-canned him and Sam. Brinkford gave him a mocking look back.

The buzzer went off, as if punctuating her words. "See you tomorrow," Mrs. Cowling ended. "Oh," she added. "Tommy and Jason, please stay after a moment."

Jason, poised to leap from his desk chair as if shot from a cannon, deflated and fell back onto the seat, staring at her. If she was going to ask about the dumpster again, he still couldn't say anything.

"Silence is golden," Canby said as he passed by. He made his sneakers fart on the linoleum floor as he headed to the classroom door.

Jason rolled his eyes and slumped farther down in his desk.

The other students left in a blur of motion and a thunder of noise, until the classroom stood empty but for the three of them. "Jason, I'll be just a moment with Tommy," Mrs. Cowling said, and drew the thin, lanky student aside at her desk.

Jason got to his feet, slowly. The sun and grass called from outside. The soccer tryouts fairly screamed. Sam passed by again, jogging around the end of the field. He looked out the window with a longing so intense it hurt somewhere inside of him. Average, ordinary Jason—but out there he could show them what he was made of. Tough, long legs for speed and cornering. Quick eyes. The ability to angle downfield and wait for a pass. A kick at the goal. A noun is the object of the sentence. . . .

Jason blinked, as Mrs. Cowling's soft answer to Tommy penetrated his thoughts. A whole year of this and Tom "No Neck" Spears whose head was shaped like the football helmet he wore nearly year round had no idea what Mrs. Cowling was repeating to him. Jason stifled another groan. He'd be here all afternoon if she wanted him to wait until Tommy understood grammar. The asphalt just outside the windows rippled in the afternoon heat looking like a slick black sea. Beyond it, the green grass of the athletic fields lay like paradise. He sighed.

She gave him a look past Tommy's ears and put her hand on the boy's thick shoulder. "Just a moment, Tommy. Jason, I'll be right with you. Take a look on my desk and see what you think?"

He shifted.

"Well . . . okay. Sam's waiting for me. Soccer tryouts and everything." He thought of distracting her. All he could think of was the soccer sign-up table, dressing, warm-ups, stretches.

"I suppose you have your heart set on that camp," she repeated, her eyes behind her spectacles big and owlish. Her fluffy brown hair puffed out slightly on its own.

"I'm going with Sam. If we make it. Which we will."

"I'll be right with you, then." She turned her back on him, not seeing his disappointed fidget as he drifted to her desk.

She was not the English teacher they'd started with at the beginning of the year. That had been Mrs. Ervin, but she was going to have a baby and had left in February. He'd gotten along all right with her, but Mrs. Cowling was another matter. They'd gotten along *great*. She was fun in the classroom and shared a lot of neat things she brought in for them all to look at and, even better, she liked to read almost as much as he did.

He leaned on her desk, impeccably clean, as always. He'd never seen a teacher without piles everywhere. If there was something on her desk, it was always a neat something to touch, examine, ponder about. Once she'd brought in a miniature sarcophagus with a fake mummy inside and everything.

Today, a crystal ball sat on the battered wood top. He reached for it without thinking, and turned its coolness over and over in his hands. He looked into its clear, colorless depths. Could he see his fortune in it? Could anyone? He turned it again. A wave of color rippled through it and he looked around to see if he had sent a prism of rainbow light on the walls anywhere. Nothing.

The crystal ball warmed to his touch. He cradled it. *Give me luck,* he thought. For soccer! He stared into it and saw a warped image of himself. Scratches across the nose, lopsided mouth, eyes peering curiously.

Jason held the ball closer. How could it reflect like a mirror? He narrowed his eyes to examine the crystal ball better. A dark shape welled up inside. Grasping, a five-fingered hand seemed poised over his reflection, about to snatch him up. He blinked.

His hands trembled slightly. The dark hand shifted, turned, sailed about and became an immense black-winged bird that soared through the inner Jason, and then everything went clear—

"Jason?"

He jumped. Mrs. Cowling caught the crystal ball as it sprang from his hand. "Did you see anything?"

"I . . . I . . . I'm not sure." He shut his mouth firmly.

Her mouth twitched. "This is what I had for you."

She picked up a bound notebook from the desk. It had been resting under the ball. He flushed as he realized that, and she handed it to him.

"It's your story, the one I entered into the state Imagination Celebration. I thought it was something you should keep, always."

"Wow." He held the notebook. The cover was embossed with a dragon breathing flames. "Thank you."

"Thank you for letting me read it, and enter it. I hope—" She paused. "This isn't a good time to talk about it, is it?"

He shook his head.

"Run to tryouts, then."

Backpack in hand, Jason bolted for the classroom door. He skidded through the polished hallways and out the door. Waves of heat hit him as he emerged, blinking. He turned the corner of the building and slowed, trotting to the locker rooms to change. The sound of cleats on asphalt clattered behind him and he turned to see a wave of boys engulf and swerve around him. They were gone in a moment, jogging back to the field and its edge, a cloud of sweat following them.

Jason spotted the temporary tables dragged under the breezeway for sign-ups and darted over. Two men sat behind it, smiling at him, one of them a big square man who looked as though he had never run a step in his life, and the other a crew-cut, thin man who was wearing a faded soccer shirt and running shorts. "Little late."

"Sorry, teacher wouldn't let me go. I signed up at the pre-sign-up," Jason said, words tumbling out.

"Did you? We should have you on our list, then."

The big man eyed him. "Got to have good grades. Can't have poor students on the teams. Rules."

"It wasn't for that." Jason craned his neck, trying to read the lists upside down. He stabbed his finger at his name. "There. That's me." His name was squiggled next to Sam's.

"Is it?" The skinny man squinted at the list. "You don't look like you're headed for middle school."

Jason shifted under his backpack. "Well, I am. That's me."

"Ever played team soccer before? Get coaching?" The big man scratched his eyebrow vigorously.

"Just at school last year before I moved here. But I'm fast."

"Takes hard work, not magic, to make a team."

"Yes, sir, I know."

The skinny man cleared his throat. "Well. You'd better change clothes and get out and warm up. They're already running sprint trials. Take this, clip it on, and see Benny . . . he's in the dark blue Rovers suit, all right?"

"All right!" Jason grinned and took off for the locker rooms.

Once on the field, his small regular school locker jam-packed with his clothes and backpack, he felt better. Sam cornered him outside the lockers.

"Where have you been?"

"Mrs. Cowling kept me after. She had my story put into a book, it's really cool." He tugged his soccer shirt into position. "Help me find Benny."

"That's him." Sam pointed downfield. He spotted a

harried-looking guy with frazzled red hair and a stopwatch in one hand and a clipboard in the other. Benny looked at him as they jogged up. "What do you need?"

"I was late getting on the field. Where do I go?"

"Right here. What age group in the fall?"

"Starting middle school."

Under Benny's frazzled red hair, shocking blue eyes stared at him. "Middle school?"

Jason nodded.

"All right. I run you two at a time. Brinkford! Got your running partner." Benny waved a hand. "Stretch, warm up, and wait. It'll be a few minutes. If you see someone walking around dressed like a soccer ball, that's our mascot. Get a rules handout from him."

"Okay." Jason turned away from Benny, his heart sinking as tall, weedy Brinkford stared at him over the tops of the others' heads. Sam nudged him.

"Brinkford's such a slime."

"Suppose he makes the camp, too?"

Sam shrugged. "You, me, we'll bunk together. Brinkford can go ooze somewhere else."

Jason bent over to stretch. Blood pounded in his ears as Brinkford sauntered up.

His classmate lifted the corner of his lip. "Running against me? You wish." He turned his back and said something to his shadow, and laughter echoed. George Canby glanced at him and made a remark back, and both boys bent over in glee.

Jason felt his ears pound. He trotted over to the edge of the grass, circled by a running path, Sam in his wake. "I've gotta make camp. Otherwise, it's a summer with Grandma McIntire. I won't even be able to see you!"

"You'll make it. Just remember, you don't have to beat Marty. You're running against the stopwatch time. He's the fastest kid here. Even being second to him, you'll probably beat a lot of other guys' times. Okay?"

"Okay!" He nodded at Sam.

Martin Brinkford stood a good head taller than Jason, with longer legs. He might not be able to stay even, but that wouldn't matter. It didn't matter if he won. It mattered only if he ran faster than a lot of the others. Even if all he saw were

Martin Brinkford's heels, it was the stopwatch he had to worry about. But the laughter stung.

Jason hung at the back of the group, watching boys split off two by two and grunt and thunder their way across the field to where another soccer coach stood with a stopwatch in each hand. Old, weathered wooden bleachers framed the imaginary finish line. From time to time, girls sat there watching, or finished runners sprawled there, waiting for their turn to take the passing tests which involved dribbling a ball through a cone obstacle course using only their feet to keep the soccer ball in line, to an odd adult or two who just seemed to be there to cheer on their son. Just such a person perched there now and although Jason watched him, he could not quite clearly see who sat there, although the agility with which he leaped to the very top row of the bleachers almost certainly knocked him out of the parent category.

A sharp whistle split the air.

"Okay, to the line . . . Brinkford and Adrian. Let's go, hustle, hustle!"

Jason moved over to the coach's side. Brinkford looked him over slowly, grinned, and moved into position.

Jason almost closed his eyes. *It didn't matter who won. What mattered was the time on the stopwatches.* He took a deep breath and shook his hands loose. Martin Brinkford made a noise almost like a cat snarling. Jason rolled his neck and shoulders, trying to calm a suddenly jittery stomach.

"On your mark."

He fixed his gaze on Sam standing across the field.

"Get set."

Jason inhaled.

"Go!"

Martin Brinkford took off like a shot, Jason barely half a step behind. He dropped his chin, concentrating on pumping his legs faster, driving him after Brinkford. The gap between them widened, then closed.

His feet pounded the grass and ground. He narrowed his eyes. Martin grunted slightly and began to draw away again, but they were close, so close to the coach already! Breathing hard, Jason focused on the goal line.

Sam began jumping up and down and waved his arms.

Urging him on. Jason dug in. His lungs were on fire. Brinkford sprinted barely ahead of him. He was catching up!

Something blurred in the corner of his eye.

WHAM! Hit and hit hard, Jason tumbled. He felt a sickening crunch in his ankle that did not stop until his body screeched to a halt on the grass. He sprawled, heart pounding and leg screaming in pain. Sam bent over him. "Oh, man!"

Jason writhed on the ground. The hot, heavy smell of another body hit him.

"Little body check," Canby noted. "Didn't you see me coming?" The chunky boy stood up, smirking. Divots of grass and dirt fell from his body.

All Jason could do was grab his leg and try not to cry.

"Canby!" yelled the coach. "You're not supposed to tackle the runners!"

"Oh, yeah?" Canby looked down at Jason, who tried to sit up and then lay flat with a groan. "He wasn't in the drill?"

"You know he wasn't!" Sam stood nose-to-nose—well, nose-to-chest—with Canby.

Canby looked at Sam. "Prove it." He backed off as the coach reached Jason.

"Come on, son, get up! Walk it off. Let's go."

Jason rolled to his side. He tried to get up. He put all he had into it. "I can't!"

His ankle shot lightning bolts of pain through him, and all he could manage was to kneel there, holding onto his right ankle, hot tears at the corner of his eyes. He shook his head, gasping for words.

The coach bent over him. "Sit back and let's have a look, then." He probed Jason's ankle thoroughly, each examination bringing gasps and grunts of pain from Jason. The coach squeezed Jason's shoulder. "That's a pretty bad sprain. I'd say soccer season is over. Might have some ligament damage. Anyone at home who can come pick you up?"

"Shoot," Sam muttered. "There goes everything."

A shadow fell over Jason as he began to recite his stepmother's cell phone number. Martin Brinkford looked down and smiled thinly, his slender face hardly even heated from the run. "I had you beat anyway."

The coach looked up sharply. Brinkford pulled his face

into a concerned expression. "We'll have to match up again. There'll be tryouts for winter league. I'd like to beat your butt fairly."

"Brinkford!" the coach snapped. Brinkford shrugged.

"Yeah. I'll see you then." Jason stared into the other's face, the sheer pain of the ankle gone for a moment. Brinkford and Canby drifted away as the coach got an answer on the cellular phone and even Jason, sitting on the ground, could hear Joanna's brisk and excited responses. He was not to be moved. She'd be right there to pick him up.

"Oh, man," repeated Sam, his face wrinkled with worry and upset. "Tough luck."

Tough luck. Crystal ball or not. . . . Was there any other kind?

3

You May Have Already Won . . .

JOANNA frowned, then quickly relaxed her face as though worried she might create a line there. "I thought you said no tackling?"

"Well, it wasn't a tackle, exactly."

She put a glass of milk on the kitchen table and stood to watch as Jason fooled a bit more with his air splints. "Then what was it?"

"Not like a football full-body tackle. It was a sliding tackle. Like . . . hmm . . . when a runner in baseball slides into base and takes out the second baseman? They can knock you off your feet, and that's what he did to me." He could only be thankful they hadn't gone through this dialogue at the Emergency Room.

"But this is soccer, dear."

"I know, but . . ."

She looked at him, one eyebrow perfectly arched.

Jason inhaled. "You're right. But this is a soccer move, only I wasn't in the drill with him and never saw him coming. I was in a running trial. Sam waved at me. I thought he was trying to get me to run faster." He sighed.

"That sprain can be worse than a break." Joanna set a plate in front of him, heaped with potato chips and a freshly made tuna salad sandwich on fluffy white bread. "You're going to have to wear that splint for a few weeks. You're going to need care and watching." She sighed.

"I'll be careful."

"Once it heals, you can think about soccer in the fall."

"You'll let me try out again?" He remembered to shut his mouth before she asked him to. His jaws ached with the surprise, though.

Joanna smiled. "Well, if they have to carry you out on a stretcher a second time, I think we're going to have to find a new sport. But, yes, William and I think sports build character. However, this leaves us with a quandary."

He filled his hand with the enormous sandwich. Someone at one of her many club meetings must have told her about growing appetites. He tried not to wolf it down while he thought of worrisome things.

Alicia had been remarkably quiet. She assembled some carrot sticks on her plate into what looked like a Chinese symbol. Carefully, she picked all around it till, suddenly aware that she was being watched, she looked up, blinked, then smiled.

"Mom?"

"Yes, dear?" Joanna answered as she sat down with a bowl heaped with salad greens and a sprinkling of dressing. Dozer was evidently off at one of his late meetings. She straightened the country gingham place mat, smiling brightly at her daughter.

"Did Jason screw everything up?"

Jason looked from one to the other. Why did he suddenly feel guilty? "I didn't mean to." His ankle throbbed in agreement. He crunched some chips to avoid saying anything else. His mouth filled with a burst of salt and potato flavor.

"I know, dear, and I know you're going to miss Sam all summer. Anyway, Mrs. Cowling phoned. She asked to come over."

"She did? What for?"

"She heard about your leg. She has something to discuss with us." And Joanna made a slight face which meant the subject was closed for the moment. Curious, he devoured the last half of his sandwich, under which he found a haystack of carrot sticks as well. Munching, he sat back in his chair, his foot propped up on the spare chair. His air-filled soft splints were nothing less than radical looking, and in a day or two he could wear shoes again. In the meantime, he got to wear sandals a week before anyone else at school, until classes let out for the summer. It was poor compensation for having his summer ruined, though.

"Mo-om," prompted Alicia. "Am I still going or not?"

Joanna jumped up and went to her daughter, hugging her. "Of course you're going!" She squeezed Alicia tightly. "The summer in Colorado at film camp! You're going to have such fun and learn so many things!"

Jason watched them. A mixture of feelings went through him. He sat silently for a moment, thinking. Camp had sounded neat. It really had. Playing soccer every day, doing camp stuff with Sam. Belonging in a certain place, day in and day out, without wondering if he was only there 'cause the others were just so darned polite!

He shifted in his chair. Something crinkled in his jeans pocket and he drew it out. *You may have already won . . .* He looked at the scrap of paper. How had that gotten there? It seemed to migrate through his clothing without any help from him! He buried it before Alicia could notice.

"And, of course, William and I have plans." Joanna frowned slightly. "That is, Jason, if we can find a place for you. Mrs. Canby offered, you know, to make amends by watching you for the summer. Now, her husband is a big supplier for William, but I don't trust that boy. He has always had a kind of mean look. Squinty eyes. So, I thanked her and said no. You don't mind, do you?"

Jason snorted. He almost inhaled his milk. Neither Canby nor Brinkford had made the team because of "bad sportsmanship" in the tackle on Jason, which the two had evidently planned. Alicia watched him as he put a napkin to his face and coughed. When his nose and throat seemed to have settled down, he said, "No, that's fine. So now what? What do I do?"

"I know you don't want to go to Grandma's, but most camps are already filled. We haven't much of a choice." Joanna's voice trailed off, and she looked at him thoughtfully.

It was torture. Like having your toenails pulled off one at a time, watching Joanna ponder. Were they going to send him to geekville or retirement city? Because it was obvious he was getting sent off *somewhere.*

Both looked at him now. Alicia seemed to have finished building whatever it was she was building with her food instead of eating it.

Jason stared at his plate as if Mrs. Cowling's crystal ball rested there and could give him a hint of what was going on. He waited hopefully. His eyes blurred and for a moment, the barest moment, he thought he could see the gleaming eye of that midnight crow looking up at him. He blinked and stared hard at the shiny porcelain plate, littered with bread crust crumbs and a broken potato chip. The image, if it had been there at all, was gone.

"There is an alternative to staying with Grandma McIntire, but it's last minute and you'll be on your own, not going with Sam. I don't think you'd like it, but I'm open to what Mrs. Cowling has to suggest."

He waited to hear more, his curiosity roused. What had Mrs. Cowling said?

Alicia wrinkled her nose. "C'mom, Mom." She squirmed impatiently.

Joanna tapped her butter knife on the table. "Did Jason make fun of your camp?"

Alicia's mouth snapped shut, and she sank back in her chair. Her bottom lip pouted out silently.

He shifted in his chair. "I don't want to stay with Grandma."

"It would kill two birds with one stone. She always gets terribly lonely when her nurse takes her vacation, and it would be nice to have someone there. And you have to have someplace to go. I don't want to cancel our plans, this is . . . well, it's our honeymoon. We delayed it, but now it's all planned and paid for." Joanna blushed faintly as she put her napkin to her lips.

"But Grandma . . . She's . . . she's dotty!"

"Eccentric," corrected Joanna. Behind her mother, Alicia rolled her eyes and mouthed, "D'oh." He pretended he hadn't seen her.

"She won't take cable television because she's afraid they're spying on her. The only thing she can still cook is Jell-o and I'm sick and tired of that. I have to mow and trim the lawn twice a week—"

"She has fast-growing grass. And that's only a tiny area around her little home." Joanna patted his hand. "I know she has strange ideas, but she's very fond of you. You need to try, Jason, to think of all of us as your family. Sometimes, I don't think you do."

He stared at the table. Sometimes, he didn't. Sometimes, he didn't think they thought of him as anything other than a guest. A guest they were now trying to pawn off, very politely.

"There is a swimming pool there," Joanna said helpfully.

"I have to have a special pass to use it. They don't like kids there. Right, Alicia?"

"It's a retirement park. They have lots of rules." Alicia shrugged. "You've got to go somewhere. Maybe you could make money mowing the other lawns."

"Nearly everyone else has gravel." He stared at her. She was being no help at all. What did she care? She had *her* wish for the summer. He could feel the corner of his mouth turn into a surly curve as he opened it to protest again when the doorbell rang.

Joanna got up quickly. "That must be Mrs. Cowling now. Come into the living room with us. Alicia, clear the table."

He wrinkled his nose at her as he trailed his stepmother from the room. At least he didn't have kitchen duty.

His English teacher came into the house in a flourish of peacock-blue fabric. She hugged both of them and took up residence on the edge of the couch, a wide smile shining from ear to ear. "How's the ankle?" She watched as he sat down and propped his foot on the coffee table. Joanna smiled at Mrs. Cowling.

Jason looked around, found the ottoman and used that instead. "It hurts," he admitted. "I have to take some Tylenol every couple of hours. It'll be better tomorrow."

"Broken? That is a splint?"

"Bad sprain. That's really to keep some pressure on it and to keep me from twisting it more. I even have to wear it at night." Jason looked at it proudly.

"Good idea." Mrs. Cowling settled her long, sweeping blouse about her. "I am sorry you were hurt."

He shrugged. "It's all right."

"All may not be lost." She took a deep breath and spoke

to his stepmother. "As you know, the school participates in the statewide Imagination Celebration. I like to assign essays. Other classes do skits, artwork, and so on. It all goes on display at the mall. But, of course, you know that. You were there for the ribbons and things." She gave Jason a proud glance.

Jason fought off a blush and sat straighter in his chair. Mrs. Cowling had been ten times prouder of him than either Joanna or the Dozer. Alicia had had a dance recital for that same celebration. She had a gold trophy sitting somewhere in her bedroom.

"Jason, a gentleman by the name of Gavan Rainwater wrote the school. He was very impressed by your essay, it appears, and he's sent in an offer of a scholarship to his camp. I confirmed it yesterday as soon as I heard about your accident. I have brochures—information—all right here. I looked into it. They are new, but they have references. I mentioned it to your mother when I called to come over, and she said it was your decision." Mrs. Cowling dipped into her rather large purse and produced a handful of colorful papers.

"Camp Ravenwyng?" noted Joanna thoughtfully. She spread a brochure open. "They don't mind taking him with that ankle?"

"Oh, no. This is a creativity and leadership camp, although there're activities of all kinds." Mrs. Cowling watched Jason.

"I'm not going to be crippled *all* summer. Maybe I can still go to soccer camp in a few weeks?"

"We already asked, hon. It's full. They can only take so many boys." Joanna looked back down at her brochure, then added, "I'm so proud of you, but I honestly don't think that you feel you've done anything." A soft smile flickered at the corners of his stepmother's mouth. "Your father was just like that. Quiet and modest, even when he'd done something great."

She rarely talked about his father, which made her words even more important. Jason stared, suddenly hungry for something that was not a sandwich or potato chip or waiting cookie.

"He would do these remarkable things yet seem so humble about it. . . ." Her voice trailed off and she bit her lip. She sighed and looked down at the brochure. "Well, I see there's a deadline here. Midnight tonight to accept. That doesn't give us much time to think about it. I'm not happy about this, letting him go when he's hurt and all. My husband's mother has offered to take him."

"From what I heard, it's a grand opportunity." Mrs. Cowling smiled brightly at them. "The references are good, and the program seems very interesting."

"You've checked it thoroughly?"

Mrs. Cowling smiled so brightly her cheeks glowed like polished apples. "I think Ravenwyng would be just perfect for Jason."

"A camp for geeks?" His voice squeaked and he shut his mouth.

Mrs. Cowling studied him. "A camp for bright, interesting people."

He ducked his head, slightly embarrassed.

"Unless, of course, Jason, you'd rather not consider it. It's up to you. Grandma or . . . geek camp." Joanna watched him.

Put that way, he didn't have much of a choice.

Camp. Be careful what you wish for . . .

4

Straight on Till Morning

"GOT everything?" Joanna asked for the tenth time that morning.

"I think so. Clothes, extra shoes, sleeping bag . . ." Jason paused, tugging on a fastening strap. In addition, the staff at Ravenwyng had sent her a list, and she'd promptly taken Jason in hand and gone off to find the several rather odd items at the bottom. *A Field Guide to Herbs*, a book on Celtic mythology (any book, the list had stated), a jeweler's loupe, and a handful of star charts.

Ever resourceful, his stepmother had had no trouble in finding any of the items. She'd been unfazed by the oddity, as well, even when the shop selling the star charts had also tried to sell her a deck of tarot cards. Jason rather regretted that she hadn't given in and bought those as well. The colorful designs and intrigue of the deck caught his attention with a delightful curiosity.

"Fortune-telling?" the shopkeeper had commented, with a shake of her dangling coin bracelet and a wink at Jason. He hovered over the card with a magician brightly painted on it until Joanna clucked her tongue and dragged him out of the shop.

"It's not scientific," she'd explained briskly, before hauling him down to the Wal-Mart to buy new shorts and socks.

Lots of things were not scientific, Jason thought, as he piled the sleeping bag and duffel near the front door and checked his watch. What was it that kept you hanging around the kitchen for a few minutes, without knowing why, until the phone rang? Or just knowing you were gonna be it the second before your name was called? He hadn't argued with her then, and he wouldn't now. Instead, he wondered how neat it would be if the laundry ink pen they'd used to mark his clothing could be invisible ink that wouldn't show at all till wet. Then it could read: Jason Adrian . . . someone remarkable.

"You're sure you have everything? Flashlight?"

"I have everything," he said firmly. In fact, he had one or two things beyond everything, having sneaked back to that store and bought the deck of tarot cards which was still in its wrapper, unopened, only that front card on the box which held it visible, the rest of its wonders to be savored later.

Alicia leaned against the doorjamb. "I hope there won't be this much fuss when I go," she remarked.

"That will be different, dear. We'll have to drive to the air-port and put you on the plane." Joanna sighed slightly. "You'll only have two carry-on bags, and your camcorder and vio-lin. Dear, dear, we'll have to do some more planning on that. Perhaps a trunk would be better, insured, of course. Going by plane is much more complicated than going by van." She moved away from the door and Jason's bags, as she frowned and took out her folio to start making some notes. She drifted off in thought.

He took a deep breath, grateful for the recess.

Alicia took a step to follow her mother off, then stopped, considering him. "I didn't say this before." She tucked a blonde strand of hair behind her ear. "I think it's neat, actually. You winning and everything. I mean, we're all astonished you could do something like that. I hope you have fun."

"Thanks. Me, too. I mean, I hope you have fun."

"Oh, I will." Alicia smiled and she sounded as if she had no doubt whatsoever in the world. She bounced a quick step down the foyer and after her mother's disappearing form. "Mom! I think I need new shoes, too. . . ."

McIntire had already crushed Jason's hand in good-bye be-fore going off to his latest construction site.

So he sat alone in the small foyer, looking out the arched doorway, waiting to leave. The bus would be parked at the school grounds for precisely one half hour to gather students. He still didn't know exactly where he was going. The brochure had promised "clean air, cool water, newly renovated campsite in the Sierra Nevadas with all the amenities but phone usage and television prohibited to promote creativity among the campers." Cellular phones would not work because of the remote location and mountainous surroundings. That was something he could not imagine here. A faint haze of dirt and smog shimmered over the horizon as far as he could see, and even the foothills had towers to transmit signals. You'd think Northern California was like faraway Tibet or something.

How far away could it be?

How far did he want it to be?

A crow winged past, with a raucous caw.

Startled, Jason jumped to his feet, wincing as his ankle pulled. He blinked and leaned out the doorway. As quickly as it had flown over, the dark shadow was gone. The hairs at the back of his neck prickled. His eyes stung, and he looked at his watch. He'd gone to sleep sitting in the doorway! He grabbed his duffel while yelling toward the back of the house, "Mom! We've gotta go."

He hefted his sleeping bag and was out to the curb, loading the family van without waiting for an answer. Alicia and Joanna came out in a few moments to find him perched and ready.

The high school parking lot had filled. There were three camp buses—two, long, yellow, and shiny, each with a name stenciled boldly down the side. Sam had already left for soccer camp, so there was no sense looking for him there. Campers and parents circled around these buses, the luggage bays open, and sleeping bags and suitcases and duffels being tossed in by tall, tan camp counselors in white shirts, khaki shorts, and well-laced hiking boots. He took in the sight of a campus that awed him a bit, and the milling crowds of kids, counselors, and parents with cameras. It was definitely camper day, and this was definitely the launch point for any number of camps in the area.

Joanna drove past very slowly, searching. "That's not it," she said, peering at a bus.

"Nor that one." Alicia rubbed her nose thoughtfully.

Jason stared across the school. At the end of the lot, a battered, short bus sat with its sides painted white, a large coal-
black wing outstretched in flight adorning it. "There!"

"Are you sure?"

"It has to be," Alicia said loftily. "Ravenwyng. How obvious. Bet you're glad it's not called Crow's Toes." Jason snorted
at the teasing.

Joanna parked a few slots away, a tiny frown line between
her eyes. "Not many here."

Alicia wrinkled her nose. "Old bus."

His stepmother did not look much happier as she stepped
out of the van. "Do you think it's safe? It doesn't look very . . .
very . . ."

Jason got out quickly before Joanna could mention
Grandma McIntire again or think those second thoughts he
could see settling in like wispy clouds. He grabbed his bags.
"It's fine! New tires and everything, Mom. Look." He kicked
one as he passed, headed to the curb where he'd spotted a pile
of backpacks and bags. A tall, older boy smiled faintly as he
approached, and pointed at the stack.

"Throw it anywhere for Ravenwyng." He watched as Jason
did so, then turned his attention back to the Gameboy in his
hands.

The man at the fore of the bus came around to meet them,
smiling.

He stood and watched as the driver swept a baseball cap
off his waving, dark brown hair and bowed.

"Gavan Rainwater, at your service." He looked at Jason
then, his vivid blue eyes shining with laughter. "Said your
good-byes? Have all your gear?" He wore a tie-dyed shirt that
brought out the brightness of his eyes, and faded jeans, and his
hair curled down to his shoulders. He leaned on a cane, the
carved silver wolf's head cupped in the palm of his free hand
although he did not look the least bit crippled. The wolf's jaws
held a large crystal in its teeth.

Jason stared, a little uncertain.

"I am speaking to Jason Adrian?"

"Ah. Yes, sir."

"Ready to go?" Gavan tapped the side of the bus gently,

knocking the wolf's snout against the raven wing. "Hello and
well met!" He beamed at Alicia and her mom as they came
around the side of the bus. He bowed with a flourish. "Your
sisters drove you?" He smiled past Jason at Joanna, and he
could hear his stepmother make a flustered noise as they shook
hands and Joanna explained that, no, she was his mother.

Rainwater answered, "No? Really?" as he shook hands all
around. Joanna's face pinked, and Alicia rolled her eyes while
Jason looked over the other campers. Barely a handful waited.
The tall boy was quite clearly the oldest, by several years. A
long-haired Asian girl, her face intent on a paperback book
held in her hands as she sat cross-legged against the school
grounds fence seemed to be waiting by the Ravenwyng gear;
he wasn't sure. He could not catch the title of her book, but
the cover looked like it was a fantasy of some kind, a flowing
white horse and a minstrel or someone leaning against it. She
looked up, smiled faintly, then went back to reading.

Two boys his age or a bit older sat on their sleeping bags,
bolstered by the chain-link fencing, steadfastly ignoring everyone around them. They were playing cards, attention riv-
eted on the colorful squares in their hands, looking up once
and then back to their game as though nothing else were more
interesting. One had flaming red hair and the other looked as
wide as he was tall, but in a muscular way, and grunted every
now and then over a card.

A car chugged in next to the bus. With a battered fender
and dings all around, it smelled hot, and before it was fully
parked, the girl inside had the door open. "Wait for me! Wait!"
she cried out, all arms and legs, and dark golden-brown hair
bobbing in a ponytail. Her hair caught the late afternoon sun
in streaks of platinum. Her camping gear left the car in an ava-
lanche, her body caught in the middle. Breathlessly, she kissed
her mom good-bye. "I'll write! I promise! Lots and lots."

Her mother seemed an older version of the girl—heart-
shaped face, no freckles, though, her own golden-brown hair
pulled back at the nape of her neck. She laughed. "Slow down,
Bailey, they're not even loading yet!" She laughed again as
Gavan Rainwater took her hand. "I really recommend you
keep her away from caffeine for a day or two," she said to the
counselor.

He smiled. "Madam, your daughter is enchanting."

"That's one word for it." She tugged on Bailey's ponytail in a fond way. "I talked with an Eleanora. Isn't she here?"

Gavan Rainwater gave a slight bow. "She is most definitely here. She left in search of drinking water, I expect her back any moment now." He produced a small slip of paper out of nowhere. "Well. One lad still expected, one Henry Squibb, and then we're off!"

Jason bent to help Bailey. She bent over at the same time, knocking their heads with an audible clunk. He staggered back a step. Bailey's face turned red as she stammered an apology and they both reached for the same bag, her hand grabbing his wrist instead. She jumped back as if burned, and practically fell over the young woman who had appeared by the front of the bus.

"Good heavens." She caught Bailey by the shoulders and steadied her, dusting her off. "Everyone here yet?"

Gavan bowed. "Even as promised, the incredibly talented Eleanora Andarielle."

The young woman flushed slightly and gave the group a little curtsy. She wore black from head to toe, although her skirt had small white flowers sprinkled on it, and the gauzy material looked thin and light. She wore a barely seeable white underblouse, a billowing long-sleeved black blouse over it. "Not incredible, just a bit thirsty." She wore a very large and apparently heavy music case over one shoulder. She put a slender hand out to Bailey's mother and then to Joanna. "So pleased to meet everyone."

Bailey leaned close and whispered, "What did we get for counselors? Rejects from a Grateful Dead concert? He's in tie-dyes and she's a Victorian Goth."

He glanced at the counselors. Indeed, they seemed a world away from the khaki-and-sandal-dressed adults standing at the other end of the parking lot, clipboards in their hands and whistles round their necks, tanned legs showing under their shorts.

The noise of one of the sleek buses firing up and preparing to pull out at the other end of the lot almost drowned out her soft voice. As it passed them, Jason could hear voices already raised in a chanting song, punctuated by cheers and laughter.

"Not everyone has to look alike!" he shot back at Bailey.

"True." She nodded sagely. "You don't look like anyone I've ever seen before."

As if overhearing, Eleanora apologized. "Forgive my attire. I was giving a dulcimer concert earlier." She tapped her music case.

"Oh, dulcimers!" Joanna clapped her hands together. "What a beautiful instrument to master."

"I'm afraid I've far from mastered it, but the tea seemed to go well. I may not look ready to be a camper, but I'm sure we're all eager to hit the road. Thank you for trusting us with your children."

Gavan knocked on the side of the short bus and threw open the luggage bay. "It's getting late, ladies and gentlemen. Let's start loading while we're waiting." He stood by while those sitting got to their feet, stretched, and began to toss their bags into the bays.

Bobbing for sleeping bags and duffels, both Jason and Bailey went to work, while he watched her out of the corner of his eye to avoid another skull rapping.

His stepmother loomed over him, her eyes glistening. He paused, holding his breath, and straightened. She actually looked sad to see him off. He wondered at that. Would she really miss him? More than just politely?

Joanna tried to smile. "Have a good time, then! We'll write you from the islands. If there're any problems, Grandma McIntire will come and get you."

If he had to eat gruel, he would not come home to Grandma McIntire. Whatever other doubts he might have, he was firm on that one. "I'll be fine," he said confidently.

Alicia waved smugly. He waved back. His stepmother pressed some bills into his hand before giving him a hug and walking away quickly, Alicia in her wake. He hardly dared breathe till the McIntire van disappeared in the distance. Then he let out a whoop, and ducked his head when Gavan turned, raised an eyebrow, then grinned.

"Dibs on the back seat," the two cardplayers said. The one with flaming-red hair and blue eyes squinted against the sun, adding, "Anyone have a problem with that?" The other, square, muscular, with dark eyes and dark hair buzzed around the ears, looked around for a challenge. He didn't get one.

Bailey hugged her mother good-bye fiercely. "Be safe driving home."

"I will." Her mother hugged her back, not letting her go for many moments. Then she got in her car and drove away quickly, without looking back at her daughter standing in the school parking lot. The car let out a small cloud of smoke as it turned the corner, disappearing.

Bailey rubbed her nose. "She's got a long drive. I hope she'll be okay."

Eleanora Andarielle moved to the girl's side in short, gliding steps, and put her hand on her shoulder. "I'm sure she'll be fine."

Without a word, like a shadow, the other girl passed by them, got on the bus, chose a window seat, and curled up, book in hand.

Rainwater tugged on a long silver chain, pulling a pocket watch out of his jeans. He clicked it open. It chimed softly as he read the watch face. He looked at Eleanora. "We can't wait much longer for young Master Squibb."

"Of course." She ushered Bailey on. With a solemn nod back, she gathered her skirts and got into the bus in the front passenger seat, setting the dulcimer case near the dashboard.

Jason started toward the bus door, but the two players brushed past him, one of them accidentally kicking his splint. He stopped, wincing. They clambered aboard without a look back. The small bus shook as the bigger boy mounted the steps and disappeared inside.

The tall older boy passed by as well, turned, and put his hand out to Jason. "Don't mind them," he said. His dark hair gleamed like the blue-black paint on the Ravenwyng.

"Oh, I don't." Jason got up the steps. Who could be worse than Brinkford and Canby?

He stood in the aisle and watched as the older boy picked a seat by himself, settling down his backpack.

Someone tugged on his sleeve. "There's room here. Come on! Misery loves company."

Jason looked down into Bailey's freckle-dusted face. He didn't think she meant quite what she said, but she did have a faintly unhappy look on her face, as she glanced out the window. He slid into place next to her as she pointed out the ends of the seat belt.

Gavan pulled his baseball cap into place. It had *Wizards* embroidered across the front in rainbow thread. Jason tried to remember which team that was, and couldn't.

"I'm Bailey Landau." She stuck out her slender hand.

He rubbed his forehead gently. "I think we've met. Jason Adrian."

She looked around and then said conspiratorially, "Are you nearly a winner?"

It took him aback for a moment. Then he grinned. "Yeah. You?"

"You bet!"

She seemed normal enough. He didn't quite know what to expect. Alicia had regaled him with stories of past camps she'd attended. Short sheeting, snipe hunts, shoes tied together and filled with unspeakable swamp goo. Maybe Bailey was already setting him up, in a good-natured way, for a prank.

"What happened there? Scooter?"

"Here?" Jason pointed at his splint, and shook his head. "Soccer."

Her eyes widened. "How?"

"Sliding tackle. At tryouts." Jason looked out the window.

"Who won?"

Jason grinned at Bailey. "Neither of us made the team. I was too injured, and he was too mean." He looked at his leg. "Only a sprain. I get to take these off in a week or so."

"Cool beans." Bailey leaned over, looking at the air splint. "If you have to wear something, those are radical. IMac bandages." She sat back with a giggle. She took a Gameboy out of the knapsack. "Want to play Monopoly?"

"Sure."

In a few moments, Bailey had them set with electronic tokens going round and round on a miniature electronic Monopoly board. She was beating him soundly when they both looked up and saw that the Ravenwyng bus was the only one left.

The empty parking lot suddenly came ablaze with headlights and a honking horn. The headlights blinked frantically in the late afternoon sun as they pierced the gathering shadows.

Doors opened. A jumble of family members popped out like bees swarming out of a hive, depositing their charge at the bus steps, he red of face and panting. He seemed to be Jason's and Bailey's age. His short, spiked brown hair, glasses, and round face gave him a slightly bewildered owllike expression.

"You're late," Eleanora said quietly from her corner of the front seat.

"But not very!" Gavan countered cheerfully. "And, look, it's almost the cool of the evening." He opened the passenger door to the front seat. "Need a hand?"

The camper huffed and puffed on board, trailing bag after bag, slung from his hands, around his shoulders, waist, and neck. The owlish lad plopped down next to the older boy although the bus was still half-empty. "I'm Henry," he said cheerfully and stuck his hand out. "Henry Squibb."

The other smiled faintly. "Jonnard Albrite," he said, and shook Henry's hand. "Call me, Jon. You just barely made it."

"Got that right. Dad wouldn't stop for instructions!" Henry let out a rolling laugh, and Jason instantly liked him. Bailey grinned, too. He waved cheerfully at the reading girl. "Ting!"

She looked up, her mouth curved, and she waved back.

"That's Ting Chuu," Henry announced cheerfully. "Ting is Chinese for graceful. I met her at the Imagination Festival." He tugged his windbreaker around his chunky form, getting comfortable on the seat as the bus engine started with a roar and began chugging. "Is everyone a winner?"

A snicker came from the back of the bus. "I see a bunch of losers."

Before anyone could protest, Gavan called out, "We're off!"

With a lurch and a hum of tires, the vehicle shot forward, and Jason saw the beige blur of his hometown slide past. The vehicle surged along the highway as the sky darkened in a blaze of pink-lemonade clouds and a layer of blues, deepening where it touched the foothills.

Eventually tired of Monopoly, both Jason and Bailey put their heads back and must have dozed. He woke and stared, disturbed. The countryside seemed to be flying past, but a look over Gavan Rainwater's shoulder showed the speedometer well within the speed limit. The crystal in his wolfhead cane caught the slant of the late afternoon sun and sent prism light dazzling into Jason's eyes. He sat back and rubbed his right one a little.

They could not possibly be headed the right way. Nor did any other car or truck seem to be on this highway. And that was truly incredible. Roads in Southern California simply were not empty. Not unless they headed off across the bleak desertlands or something but that would be headed east, not north to the mountains. And, by his calculations, they wouldn't arrive till the middle of the night or later.

Bailey had a small denim knapsack and hugged it to her, before loosening the flap. "Hungry?"

He shook his head. She pulled out a granola bar, unwrapped it, and began to pick at it delicately. While crinkling the bright foil, she bent her head and said, so only he could hear, "This trip has a time of its own."

He looked at her. "That's impossible."

"Cross my heart, hope to barf." Bailey finished half her bar, rewrapped it, and neatly put it away. "We're going nowhere fast."

Bailey saw the worry on Jason's face and looked out the window, too. She frowned and whispered, "Told ya." He didn't like the fact she'd been reading his mind.

Bodies to the rear shifted uneasily as well. "Hey, man, we're in the middle of nowhere."

A small green sign appeared, coming into view. Roadrunner Way off-ramp, it notified, 3/4 miles. There was no way of determining if the sign was correct or not, as the highway itself was turning in and around small golden hills, browned by the sun and summer heat. As he peered toward them, he thought he saw a small, dun-colored dog trotting down the road. It swerved and dashed away as the car roared past. No homes out here, it could not have been anyone's pet. Coyote? His glimpse was too fleeting to tell.

As they turned down a gradual slope, the off-ramp of a much smaller road forking off came into sight, along with a faded and battered sign proclaiming: Gas Food Lodging. Someone had X'd out Food and Lodging.

Eleanora frowned. "We're lost," she said softly to Gavan. Jason could barely hear her.

"Nonsense. There's nothing out here to get lost on."

Her head came around sharply and she whispered something that sounded like Dark Hand that made Gavan look thoughtful. But Jason was almost sure she couldn't have said that, because it made no sense.

It immediately became very quiet. Jason found himself nearly asleep again, his chin jerking as he almost tumbled into a dream. His eyes did not want to stay awake. He pinched his kneecap and, though it smarted, the pain flung his eyes wide open. He found himself staring into a great dark mountain and the road ending abruptly at its foot.

Gavan murmured something to Eleanora. She answered back softly and leaned out of her seat to put her hand on the wolfhead cane. The car shuddered as if on rough road. Gavan struggled with the steering wheel. They bumped from side to side. The vehicle's lights beamed yellow rays into inky shadows. Jason found himself holding his breath.

Bailey jerked at Jason's elbow. Her eyes opened wide. "We're gonna die!" She covered her face with her hands and let out a squeaky shriek.

Eleanora looked around at them. "It's just a tunnel." But her voice seemed strained as if she could barely find the strength to say another word. Her hand quivered, and the wolfhead cane trembled in her hold. The bus danced and swerved on the dusky road.

Jason stared into the night. He could see no tunnel's edge in the massive rock ahead. Only pitch-black mountain dead in front of them. He took a deep breath.

They plunged into a cold darkness.

5

Camp Ravenwyng

THE tunnel swallowed them whole. The car bucked and tossed in the coldness. Jason scrubbed his eyes against the nothingness. It flowed past him, slimy and cold. Bailey shivered against his shoulder. He inhaled.

"Come on, Eleanora. Forget about your shoes and give me all you've got," Gavan muttered. Eleanora gave him an annoyed look, then frowned. The crystal in the wolfhead cane seemed to be the only light left. The silvery head seemed to glow with warmth, and the crystal flared. It let out a tiny flash and then, suddenly as if ejected, they shot forward and out of the tunnel.

Bailey hiccuped. Henry Squibb let out a shaky laugh as pale light flooded in through the windows. Someone whooped from the back of the bus.

Not only was it not total darkness . . . it was no longer evening, though close to dusk. Gavan slowed, dirt and gravel crunching under the tires, as he turned down a lane edged by wilderness. Thick with evergreens and other trees, and a jagged ridge of true mountains off to the east. A very blue sky with lowering purple clouds. A cardinal winged past in a streak of scarlet.

Bailey said, "Go tell Dorothy we're not in Kansas

anymore." Her head swiveled about, taking in a forested area that obviously got far more rain than any forest in Southern California.

Jason was beginning to understand what she meant. He sat on the edge of the bus seat.

Eleanora settled back with a sigh, dropping the wolfhead cane. Gavan called out cheerfully, "We'll be just in time for the first campfire!" He drove in under a swinging white sign over a sagging metal gate, white paint flaking and edged with rust. Faded dark letters read CAMP RAVENWYNG, with another version of a bright-eyed soaring raven. The gate didn't look as if, even closed, it could hold fast. The terrain itself sloped gently as the road wound uphill. He could spot large cabins, roofs peaking through small clusters of trees and shrubs, the buildings grouped by twos and threes. The road broke into a very big clearing with three very large buildings, and Gavan pulled to a stop next to several other battered but evidently reliable old buses, their sides white with dark-winged logos.

They piled out, as Bailey would say later, like rats off a stinking ship. The redhead punched his friend in the shoulder and said, "Hey, Stef. This is a dump."

"You're a dump, Rich." Stefan thumbed his nose. He stretched his chunky body. "At least we're finally someplace." He ran his hand through his spiky brown hair. "Maybe we can pan for gold or something." He snickered.

He ignored the small crowd of campers and adults standing outside what appeared to be a large barn, the buildings old and weathered. "Although I gotta admit it doesn't look like much."

Gavan swept his hat off as he helped Eleanora down the bus steps. "Ladies and gentlemen, welcome to Ravenwyng. Dinner will be ready in a bit. After dinner, we will be meeting in the Lake Wannameecha Gathering Hall to go over cabin assignments, and tomorrow we'll start our first full day of camp! Gather up your things and put them in the Hall for now. In the meantime . . . toilets are in that building there. One side is for the ladies, one for the gents. Ladies' cottages are around the curve of the lake. Most, if not all, will be explained on the morrow!"

Eleanora dusted herself off before heading away to the distant building, moving with a graceful, gliding step, her shoes hidden by the sweeping hem of her long skirt.

"Platforms," muttered Bailey.

"Hmmm?"

"Platform shoes," she added. "She walks funny, huh?"

"Oh." Jason nodded.

Bailey rubbed her nose. "Sounds like a good idea!" She dashed off after Eleanora and caught up with her, headed to the restrooms.

Jason reached for his stuff and Bailey's, nearly locking elbows with someone—again. As he pulled loose, the other grabbed his arm. The boy looked up, revealing a thin face, darkly intense blue eyes, and curly hair that fell over one eyebrow. He smiled, and it lit up his dark eyes.

"Heya," the other said. "I'm Trent."

"Jason."

"Glad you guys finally got here. We've been holding dinner." Trent gave a lopsided grin.

"You look like you can't afford to miss a meal."

"Got that right!" He hefted Bailey's bag over his shoulder with a grunt. "This yours?"

"Nah. My friend Bailey's. She went to the bathroom."

"Figures. Girls pack a ton. I had to throw out half the stuff my mom used to put in . . . when she was alive to pack." Trent strode with him toward the Gathering Hall. He looked down at Jason's leg, noticing the limp, then back up. "Broken leg, huh?"

"Sprain. Almost healed."

"Neat splits. Those plastic?"

"Sorta. You pump air into 'em. They're lighter, softer."

"Cool. Kinda geeky looking, but all right."

Jason looked up at the Hall door as they passed through. Someone had nailed a piece of wood, shaped rather like a lopsided and sideways figure eight, to it and painted it blue.

Trent tapped the object. "That's Lake Wannameecha."

"Seen it?"

"Not yet. So you came in with the big kahuna, huh?" Without waiting for Jason to nod, he added, "I drove in with Crowfeather. He's way cool, this Native American guide. Knows all sorts of stuff about wildlife." He dropped his voice. "Camp's not quite what they expected, seems. They just bought it. Bath-room's in good shape, though."

"What's wrong with it?"

"Supposed to have been remodeled and updated. Only about half the work was done, I guess."

Inside, electric lights burned, but low and weak, with a wa-very yellow light. Trent dropped his bundles near a neat stack. "This's my stuff. Just park your stuff here, too."

Henry came chugging in, struggling with his things. Rich and Stefan were on his heels. Stefan smirked and said, "Let me help you with that, Squibb."

He reached out and tugged on the strap holding the bloated sleeping bag together. With a sharp yank, it came un-done, exploding like a giant air bag. It all but swallowed Henry from sight. Suddenly blinded, Henry tripped and fell, skidding across the Hall's floor. He came to a stop looking somewhat like a sausage stuffed into a fluffy brown roll. The two boys strolled off, shoulders shaking with laughter.

Henry sighed and rolled out of his sleeping bag. Trent leaned over and gave him a hand up. He looked thoughtfully at the massively fluffy sleeping gear.

"Big . . . ummm . . . bag," he said.

"Down. Best kind, but once those feathers get air in 'em and get all poofed up . . ." Henry sighed again, and pushed his glasses back into place on the bridge of his nose. He leaned over and began to squeeze his bag down to size. Jason got on his knees and helped him gather the straps.

"Next time, pick on somebody your own size," Trent said to Stefan's back.

The two turned slowly. The square kid looked across the end of the Hall at Henry Squibb. "He is my size."

Trent grinned. "I meant intellect." He let out a hearty laugh before grabbing one strap and helping Henry and Jason pull the bag tight. "What is this thing, anyway? An air bag for a humvee?"

The three of them couldn't help smirking, Henry's round face going red in both humor and embarrassment. "My mom . . ." he sputtered finally.

"My mom," Trent said, "would have put a pillow on a skateboard, if she could have figured out a way. And I think she taught my dad how." He wrinkled his face up ruefully.

Henry fell over laughing. Bailey trotted up, watched them all silently for a moment, and then joined them. Jason pointed at her. "Trent, this is Bailey, Bailey, this's Trent."

She nodded even as she looked about the cavernous and well-worn Hall. "Thank goodness the bathrooms are modern."

"See the lake from there?"

"Wannameecha? Oh, yes. Looks nice. There's racks of canoes and kayaks stacked behind the mess hall."

"Speaking of mess hall!" Trent took a deep breath and beamed. "Smells like dinner!"

Jason could smell a savory scent as well.

"Wait'll you meet the cook. FireAnn. She has this big cloud of red hair and this cool Irish accent. We all had to go pound on pots and pans in the mess hall. She's got a crew coming in, but they're late."

"Why pounding?"

"We had to chase the raccoons outta the kitchen." Trent grinned again, merriment flashing in his dark blue eyes. "She was yelling at them that the slowest one out would be pot pie tomorrow!"

Jason laughed.

FireAnn did indeed have fiery red hair, held back by a dark blue bandanna that seemed as if it might burst open. She stood at the back of the mess hall while they sat and ate, and her green eyes flashed with satisfaction as the campers scarfed up every bite and a few came back for seconds.

"Tonight's free night," Trent said, as he wiped up the last of his gravy.

"How so?"

"Tomorrow they assign kitchen duty, toilet duty, camp duty. And they'll have us scheduled for classes till the cows come home." Trent's thin face considered him. "Never been to camp, huh?"

"First time."

"For every action there is a reaction and chore," Bailey said. She dropped her fork with a clink.

"Something like that," Trent agreed. He glanced at Jason. "She always like this?"

"Sometimes," Jason said. "Only more so."

By the time they left the mess hall, darkness had fallen once again. Little moon stayed out, a thin shivery sliver in the sky. The sound of music carried to them, and they set out in search of it. The smell of woodsmoke filled their nostrils, and a thin, gray funnel could be seen wafting up to the night sky. The melody grew brisker and brisker until they nearly ran to catch up to it.

The three found themselves in a clearing. Gavan Rainwater stood, surrounded by the orange sparks coming off an immense bonfire, fiddling away, a short black cape hanging from his shoulders, his body in motion as he danced and strode to the music he bowed. With his dark hair curling about his face, and the fiddle alive in his hands, he looked rather like a Gypsy.

Other campers and the counselors began to gather. Eleanora came in last, silently, and took a seat on a stump, looking up at Gavan as he reeled off the last of the air, and stood for a moment, inhaling deeply, becoming still. He bowed solemnly. "Time to meet some remarkable teachers."

He pointed with his bow. "Tomaz Crowfeather."

A short, thin man stood, his face weathered, his eyes dark, his hair parted in the middle and pulled back into a twist anchored by a shining feather. He wore a vest over a faded denim shirt and jeans that looked as if they had indeed been beaten into worn softness by rocks. Beaten silver disks set off by turquoise nuggets in his braided leather belt and bracelet flashed in the firelight. He gave a half bow of acknowledgment.

"Anita Patel." The shadows yielded a slight, graceful woman who wore a sari and pants, and as she turned and waved at all of them, tiny bells on one anklet pealed.

"I will show you how to breathe and move," she said softly, but everyone seemed to hear her. A crimson dot accented her forehead between dark brows.

"Adam Sousa!" Gavan pivoted on one heel and pointed his bow at an intense young man sitting on a log at the fire ring's far end. Sousa jumped up. His long, slender fingers tapped a rhythm on the silver cornet hanging from his belt as he flashed a grin. "Mathematics and Music," Gavan said and bowed to Sousa.

Trent and Bailey and Jason all looked at one another. "Do you think ... ?"

They shrugged. "But I bet he plays Reveille in the morning."

"Eleanora Andarielle. Literature and Mythology."

Eleanora raised her hand and waved.

"Elliott Hightower and Lucas Jefferson, Sports and Crafts."

Across the bonfire from them, Jason could do little more than spot the two men by their gestures.

"Cook FireAnn! An enchantress with herbs and food." FireAnn danced into the gleaming bonfire light, her hair freed, and did a turn of an Irish jig around Gavan before bowing and dropping back into the shadows.

They all cheered FireAnn.

"Plus, we have one or two guest lecturers who may drop in from time to time! Now, I am done talking. Sit. We have marshmallows to roast and names to exchange and bedtime coming all too quickly."

So they sat, and Tomaz Crowfeather passed out green sticks he'd whittled for roasting spits and FireAnn passed out marshmallows and they sang camp songs and cheered until the flames grew smaller ... and smaller ... and smaller.

In the Gathering Hall, the campers assembled at their gear, faces weary, voices now quiet. Bedtime seemed a good idea. "I want to sit on something soft," Henry declared. He tugged his bag over toward the seating area.

Henry Squibb tugged and tugged, seemingly unable to get the bag open now. Jonnard went over and the two wrestled with it for a moment before it suddenly burst open, flattening both of them. While Henry turned red and apologized a thousand times to Jonnard, Jason looked his gear over.

Trent frowned. He leaned over to Jason. "Someone's been in my stuff."

"What? How can you tell?"

"Special knot my dad taught me. It's tied different."

"Anything missing?"

"I can't tell yet."

Jason looked at his things. He opened his duffel. Things that he knew had been packed first now lay on top, as though someone had neatly turned his bag inside out. He looked up, saw Trent watching him in the dim light. He nodded.

Gavan and Eleanora came to the front of the Hall, and the tired campers fell silent, watching.

"Ladies and gentlemen," he said. "It's late and we're all ready to turn in. But in what cabin, in what bed? What companions shall share your adventures with you in the coming weeks?" Gavan shook his head and tapped his cane on the floor. "Too difficult a problem for a mere mortal to solve. So we have called upon the Wishing Well, and a ritual older than any of us here! You'll be led out, and given words to speak. Remember them! Repeat them precisely! Your very future depends on it!"

He pointed his cane at Jonnard and then Stefan. "Crowfeather, Sousa, take your first victims!"

"Eleanora and Anita, take those two hostage!" He pointed at Ting and Bailey. Bailey went with a giggle, but Ting's eyes were very big as they were led out the door.

Gavan rapped on the floor. "Hightower, Jefferson—those two!" And the wolfhead cane pointed at Trent and Jason.

Outside, the lights seemed very thin against the darkness of the evening. The others shuffled through the grass and dirt to an old structure he had not noticed before. It seemed to be a genuine stone wishing well, complete with a great wooden crossbeam that had a bucket hanging from it. The roof was littered with pine needles. He could hear whispering voices ahead of him, but nothing clearly. Bailey suddenly bounced in excitement and started to bolt back to the Gathering Hall. She slid to a stop beside Jason.

"Kittencurl! I'm at Kittencurl Cottage!" Almost before she had stopped, she was off again.

Trent shook his head. "Better her than me," he muttered.

Jason laughed.

Hightower curled his strong coach's hand about Jason's arm. He bent down. "Now listen to what I say very carefully when you get to the well's edge. You'll be repeating after me."

"Mmmm . . . okay." Jason felt a little foolish. Ting passed them without a word, but her mouth curved in a secret smile.

The stone-walled well looked very old. A small sign, firmly fastened to its roofing said **Water Not Potable.** Trent hissed in his ear, "Means you can't actually drink from it."

Jason nodded. He put his hands on the rim of the well, the cold stone clean and firm to his touch. Dark water lapped below and reflected back the thin gleam of the moon.

"Now repeat after me," Hightower said quietly, and gave Jason the lines one at a time. He took a quick breath and blurted them out to the well. His voice echoed very faintly.

> *"Brick and Mortar, Stone and Stick,*
> *Which roof and walls*
> *For the summer call?*
> *Wishing well,*
> *It's time to tell!*
> *Which cabin shall I pick?"*

The last echo dropped away and for a moment, there was total silence. Then, breathily, in a voice that was neither male nor female but very odd, it answered:

> *"No matter where you roam*
> *Your heart holds your home.*
> *In my waters, the answer true*
> *Of the cabin meant for you."*

Jason sucked in his breath at the eeriness. Maybe someone was hiding in the trees behind them talking, maybe someone wasn't. He looked down into the well. The waters seemed to stir, and then the voice sighed a word he was not sure he caught.

He looked up. "S–starwind?"

"Good choice, lad! Nice cabin." Hightower thumped him on his shoulder. "Go get your gear, I'll be taking you and the others going that way in a bit."

Halfway back, Trent bumped into him. "What was that, d'you think? Throwing their voices?"

"I dunno. I'm just glad to get a place to sleep. Where are you going?"

"Someplace named Starwind. You?"

The chill of the cold from the Wishing Well warmed instantly. "Me, too!"

Trent pushed him slightly. "Now I know it's a put-up deal." But he grinned broadly.

Henry rushed past to roll up his sleeping bag in a hurry. They called after him, "Where're you going, Squibb?"

"I got Cabin Skybolt, with Jonnard!" He let out a chuckle before ducking off and tackling the mountain of gear he'd brought with him.

Jon, a tall shadow against the darker night, waited silently outside the hall for Henry to join him before heading down the pine-edged pathway toward the boys' cabins.

Their cabin, when they reached it, crested a small hill. From its front porch, Lake Wannameecha could be easily seen. Carved into the front porch eave was a large shooting star, with an immense comet tail, STARWIND etched under it.

"Too cool," Trent said. He lifted the latch and went in, Jason holding the flashlight behind him. It was deserted, dusty, with leaves littering the floor despite the shuttered windows, but no varmints lurked there as far as they could tell. They threw their bags on bunks.

"In the morning," Trent muttered, "I'm going to find out who was going through the stuff."

"Right." Jason slipped his shoes off. The two of them shook out the sheets, blankets, and towels they had rolled in their sleeping bags and tried to pull their cots into some kind of order. He threw his bag down like a comforter over the top and slipped in. He smelled faintly of woodsmoke as he drifted into sleep. The campfire Parting song had been neat, all the counselors chiming in and wishing them safe till morning. The morning would bring a shower, breakfast . . . and a mystery.

The cabin had grown very quiet when Jason woke. He lay there uncomfortable with the knowledge he should have hit the restrooms before he went to sleep. He tried ignoring it, but there was no way he was going to get back to sleep if he didn't hike down to the bathroom. And there was no way he was

going to wake Trent or anybody else to go with him, despite
the counselors' instructions to be careful at night.

Jason crawled out on hands and knees. His eyes adjusted
quickly to the darkness and he found the doors easily, slipping outside, flashlight in hand. He twisted it on. Nothing happened. He shook it. Batteries rattled dully inside. He twisted
it on and off a few times. Nothing. His body ached, and he
decided to forge into the night anyway!

Down through the path of evergreens, the halo of lights
surrounding the Gathering Hall and facilities drew him. He
paused as he heard the soft murmur of adult voices head his
way.

"It's not what I expected."

"It'll be fine. It's worn out, but there's magic in it. There is
no doubt there's an Iron Gate about. If we can find that, can a
Haven be far behind?"

"That's the good news, and the bad news. The Dark Hand
will be as attracted as we were. We've time, but not much."

"We've done more with less."

"True . . ." the voices moved off.

Jason rubbed at one eye. Nothing they said made any sense.
He waited three long heartbeats until his bladder told him he
could wait no longer, and then he walked quickly, desperately
across the grounds. The facilities were dark and chill, and he
danced about a bit trying to stay warm, finishing as quickly as
he could. Coming out, he breathed a sigh of relief that he had
not been detected.

Halfway across, Jason stopped as he heard something
nearby. He turned and saw a glint of moon reflected in green
eyes. A large form moved through the shrubbery, leaves crackling. Something large and hot and wild growled. He froze.

He could see it slink past the wall of the mess hall, pause,
and then trot his way.

Furred. It snarled, and Jason caught a flash of white teeth.
Coyote? No. He stared at it and it stared back as it slunk closer.
It crept forward a step at a time on clawed paws, eyes fixed
on him, glowing green in the night. It looked like an immense
jackal, ivory fangs dripping. His yell of disbelief stuck in his
throat. He tried to force it out. Help! He needed help! He could
smell the creature's hot breath as it growled menacingly.

Then it sprang. Jason fell back, the thing covered him, and he felt a sharp pain in his hand. Its weight forced him down into the soft dirt, and he did two things instinctively. He kicked hard at the underbelly. His hand, caught in the beast's jaws, tore open as he shoved it, punching deep into the mouth.

The beast gave a strangled, surprised snarl as Jason forced his hand deeper into its throat. It let go abruptly, leaping aside, and Jason struggled to his feet. He could feel the hot spit sting as it rolled down his torn hand. With a growl it circled, and Jason knew it would leap again.

White light floated across the ground. FireAnn stood in the mess hall doorway, a broom in her hands. "Who goes there?" she called out, her red hair a mass of flames licking about her head.

The creature sank back on its haunches in the shadows. Its green eyes flickered as it turned away. It paused. With a low growl, it said, "You're mine!" and then disappeared into the deep shadows by the lakeside.

Jason stood stock-still in shock. He shuddered after a moment. "It . . . it's just me."

FireAnn stood in the glowing doorway. His teeth clattered. "I . . . I . . . it bit me!"

"What?" She came out and bent over him. "What happened?"

His hand stung, and he could feel the blood dripping off it. He didn't think he could stay on his feet. "Something . . . big . . . it bit me. . . ."

She shook his hand gently, cradling it. Blood dripped into her palm. "Take a deep breath now. You're going to be all right. What happened?"

Bush prickles stuck all over his pajamas, and he felt their dull stings. "Am I gonna get rabies?"

"Did you fall in the bush? Coming out of the bathroom?"

He nodded. "It jumped me and I fell, and it went for my hand and . . ." He could hardly talk, his teeth chattering.

She smoothed his hand out in hers, eyes narrowed, looking closely at it in the golden rays of light falling from the kitchen doorway. "It doesn't look like a bite. Are you sure?"

"I . . . it . . . it said . . ."

"It said?" Her eyes looked into his.

He clamped his jaw shut tight. She didn't believe him. Or if she did, she'd think he was crazy. He shivered.

"Go wash it, and come into the kitchen, and I'll have a better look. I've some ointment, too."

He could feel her eyes on him as he scuttled back to the restrooms.

Water felt good on the bite. He scrubbed it with soap for long minutes, wondering what to do, leaning heavily against the sink. The beast had spoken. Could he tell anyone? Would they even believe him?

He patted paper towels over the back of his left hand a few times. Jason took a deep breath, trying to push away the sick feeling in his guts.

On the way back, FireAnn waved him in. He stepped into the warmth, still shivering, still scared. She took his hand again, saying quietly, "Ever been camping before, Jason? Out in the wilderness?" Her voice had a slight Irish lilt to it.

He shook his head. She smoothed her fingertips over the wound. He stared at it in disbelief. The ragged tear had already settled into place, sealing, looking more like an angry red welt. "This is no animal bite," she said. "I think maybe one of my kitchen varmints frightened you. The bush tore into you when you fell. Bites look entirely different, you see. You should not worry yourself." She smiled in reassurance and spread some salve on it. Instantly, the fiery hurt faded. "You'll be fine. But you should see Dr. Patel, all right?"

"But—but ... rabies ... ?"

"Bushes canna carry rabies, but believe me, if they did, my ointment would kill it." FireAnn gave him a reassuring pat. "Now, off to bed with you." He stood, feeling wobbly, and headed back to Starwind. He turned once and looked back to the mess hall. Beyond, in the bright kitchen, he could see a great, deep shiny steel cauldron and FireAnn over it, stirring. The smell of fruit and sugar being cooked wafted toward him. Then, as he passed Lake Wannameecha Gathering Hall, she closed the door.

He crossed the darkness quickly, every hair at the back of his neck standing up. Was it following him? Did it trail him? Would he make the cabin in time?

Finally, hardly able to breathe, he tore up the steps of

waiting Starwind and threw himself inside. Trent stirred, mumbled something, and rolled over. Jason took a deep breath, then latched the cabin door and lay down on his bunk. How could the wound seal up so quickly? Why the strange crescent? It had bitten him, hadn't it? Hadn't it?

His hand on his chest, sore and throbbing slightly, he fell into a deep, troubled sleep.

Lanyard Ho!

"**G**ET out! Get out! GET OUT!"
Lids clanged like gongs. Pans thundered like drums. Shrill cries of fury pierced the morning.

With a yelp, Jason sat bolt upright in his sleeping bag. Images of feral eyes glowing in the dark still danced in his mind as he ran out the cabin door. Were they under attack? Across the way, Henry Squibb had not only gotten to his feet, still wrapped in his immense sleeping bag, he ran around trapped inside it, wailing. Others milled around.

But it was not Henry's loud cries that shook the camp.

"Out, I say! Out, out, OUT! And stay gone!" the loud-speakers bellowed.

"Something's wrong with breakfast!" Trent cried. He lit out for the mess hall, Jason at his heels. Doors to the building flung open, campers shooting off in every direction.

As they peered at the commotion, FireAnn appeared in the mess hall kitchen. She brandished her broom, laying about her with every cry. Her hair lashed around her as she danced in anger. A small herd of chipmunks bolted from the kitchen. In a wave of chitters and chatters, they dodged across the open ground and into the grasses and tall trees down by the lake's beach. A raccoon lumbered out of the kitchen, a pot lid caught on a hind paw that it kicked aside, and then it broke into a gallop just ahead of FireAnn and her broom. Its bandit face mask looked squinched up unhappily.

Trent rolled against Jason, laughing so hard he could barely stand. Behind them, other campers pushed forward to see what was going on.

"Excuse me."

Jason turned as he heard Eleanora Andarielle's soft voice at his ear. She passed by as he moved aside and he blinked in confusion. She was taller than he was, wasn't she? He seemed to have remembered that from yesterday. But today the top of her softly curled hair would have brushed under his chin. Before he could think any more about it, she had joined FireAnn, just as two more raccoons left the mess hall kitchens in a lumbering hurry, grumbling unhappily at being woken up. Eleanora bent over to collect pot lids, and joined FireAnn clashing them. "Well done! I'd say the enemy is in retreat!"

The cook gave a last triumphant wave of her broom in the air before disappearing into the kitchen. Her voice then wailed in dismay, "What a mess!"

Eleanora turned, her skirt swirling in a dark cloud about her ankles. "I'll need five campers this morning to help Fire-Ann clean up, so breakfast can be made." She pointed quickly, catching a sleepy-faced but already dressed Bailey with the sweep of her hand.

Bailey looked at the two of them, shrugged, and trotted down to the kitchens, her sneakers swinging from her hand. She dodged a last chipmunk barreling through the doors, little tail flipping with every leap and bound.

"The rest of you get changed and report to the crafts area down by the lake. I've buckets, mops, and brooms to give out. It's cabin cleaning time! You'll shower before lunch because you've got some real dirt pushing to do." Hightower shooed them toward the bathrooms. Jason stared at him a moment. The counselor was incredibly tall and lean, a shock of thin black hair standing almost straight up. He had a long, thin nose with a crooked bent to it. "Let's get a move on!" He picked up the whistle hanging around his neck and shrilled a note. Everyone raced off to get ready.

Jason winced as someone pushed past, hitting his hand. He

ought to find a nurse or something, just in case. He waited till everyone went by on their way toward the lake before looking at it in the full morning sunlight. Lifting his left hand, he stared in surprise at a thin, purple line, like that of a crescent moon. Healed yet sore.

He traced a fingertip over it. Very sore. Yet seemingly nearly healed. But how . . . ? Would the camp doctor even believe him?

A sharp whistle jerked Jason's head up, as Hightower beckoned for the latecomers. He'd think about it later. Right now, he was awake, dressed, and hungry with no breakfast till some work got done.

Trent pushed a mop at him and swung his own over his shoulders with a bucket hanging from either end. "Look at it this way," he said, as they hit the winding pathways leading to the clusters of cabins. "At least we're cleaning up our *own* mess."

They trotted through the evergreens to the chatter of blue jays. The cabins seemed to come in twos. The first two were more like lodges, one roofed with dark green shingles, the other with dark blue. The second pair were rustic, actual log cabins, the windows storm-shuttered and with screens leaning up against the porch, covered with leaves and pine needles. Starwind and Skybolt. A jagged white lightning bolt marked the other cabin, where Jonnard was patiently peeling Henry out of his humongous sleeping bag.

"What did we miss? What was the racket all about?"

"FireAnn chasing raccoons and chipmunks out of the kitchen."

"Ah," said Jonnard. He smiled. "I bet it'll take a few days for them to decide to stay out. They've probably got comfortable nests in there."

"I think Cook lit a fire under 'em," cracked Trent. He swung his own mop. "Cabin cleaning time," said Jason, in case the other two didn't catch the drift. Trent took the steps in a leaping bound, more dried leaves flying away from his shoes.

"Can I see your place?" Squibb asked. He had turned red in the face, and a tiny trickle of sweat ran down his neck, which he wiped at uncomfortably. Jonnard nonchalantly threw the sleeping bag back inside the domain of Skybolt.

"Sure. Come on."

The rusty latch lifted with a small complaint. He was not sure what he had expected as light from the front door streamed in, not having seen it in anything but wavering light from his old, dim flashlight. Henry came puffing in behind them, muttering, "Better not be any spiders. I hate spiders." He stood in the middle of the cabin, looking around, pushing his glasses back up his nose from time to time. "Yeow!" He jumped as Trent sneaked up from behind and tickled his ear with a broom straw. He whirled around, then sputtered, "I guess I asked for that."

Jason laughed. "Never tell the enemy your weakness!"

Jonnard said mildly, "I keep telling you, Henry, spiders are good. They'll web the mosquitoes and gnats for us."

"I don't care. Don't like 'em! They give me the creeps." Henry shuddered all over. "This is sorta like our place and sorta not."

"What's different?"

"Well, you've got four bunks, like we do. But we don't have a window seat with a cabinet or bins—" he pointed across the room.

"We have," Jonnard said quietly, "a built-in writing desk. The top comes down. Rather primitive but nice. And a closet."

Henry said, "And you've got windows on three sides. We've got 'em on all four." He spun around. "But yours is a cool place, too."

Trying to work around the two with his broom, Trent muttered, "Hightower said no breakfast till your cabin was cleaned."

Henry jumped. "We'd better get going!"

Jonnard laughed as Henry turned and hustled out the cabin door. He waved and followed.

Working quickly, the two got the storm windows open, and cleaned screens in place, letting sunlight flood in so they could mop down the floor. By the time a cornet call floated through the air, they were done, dusty, and starving. Hightower and Jefferson met them at the boys' side of the bathrooms with towels and soap.

Soon, they were scrubbed and dressed and still starving, lined up at the mess hall doorway. Jason's stomach rumbled, as he smelled delicious aromas of breakfast ahead of them. Jostling to get trays, plates, and utensils, Jason could see a line of eager campers ahead of them. The hall was only a third filled, though, built to hold far more campers than their numbers.

Finally, they made it to the front of the line. The wait was worth it. There were piles of fresh, fluffy biscuits. Bowls of butter and homemade fruit jams to go with them. A dish of hot, steaming sausage gravy to pour over the biscuit, if you'd rather have it that way. Jason couldn't decide, so he split his in two and had one half with jam and the other with gravy. Down the line were scrambled eggs and crisp bacon. Nectarines and grapes and melon. Milk and individual boxes of cold cereal. Jason trailed after Trent and watched as the wiry boy heaped helping after helping onto his plate. By the time they headed to the tables, Trent carried a small mountain of food in front of him. Even Henry Squibb and Jonnard dropped their jaws in astonishment as he passed by.

"My theory is," Trent said, "you never know when you're eating next."

"This, however, is camp food," remarked Jonnard. He sat, his back straight, his dark hair neatly combed back, his plate consisting of two pieces of toast, a neatly dissected poached egg and several pieces of melon.

Trent paused with a forkful of fried potatoes halfway to his mouth. "And your point is . . ."

Jonnard quirked an eyebrow. "Never mind," he said. With two precise cuts of knife and fork, he skinned the rind from both slices of melon and proceeded to cut them into bite size pieces.

Actually, Jason was beginning to wish he had taken two whole biscuits as Trent had. The hearty flavor burst in his mouth as he gobbled his down. The bacon was crispy with a slight smoky flavor and the eggs creamy and fresh tasting. He polished off a just right, juicy nectarine, and looked for a paper napkin to wipe his chin. Jonnard passed him one.

Henry and Trent finished eating at about the same time. By then, Hightower and Jefferson had moved to the front of the mess hall.

"All right, ladies and gentlemen. I hear almost all the cabins are in tiptop shape! Well done to the dirt crews. This morning, you ate wherever you felt like it, but starting tonight, you'll be eating at the table that matches your cabin. And showering and so forth on your schedules. So keep in mind that your cabin mates will be with you a lot.

"Headmaster Rainwater and Jefferson and I will be looking you over throughout the day, seeing what you're made of and throwing together regular schedules according to your ages and abilities. We've campers here from ten to fifteen, so we want to make sure everyone's having fun. Okay, now. The day's schedule will be posted at the front of the mess hall. The schedule for tomorrow will be posted after evening meal. It's your job to read it and know what's going on, and show up for activities."

Hightower rubbed his bony hands together. "Any questions?"

Trent's hand shot up.

Elliott Hightower looked at him.

"Did you play basketball in school?"

Hightower's eyes widened in surprise and then he let out a chuckle. "A little. All right, then, turn in your trays. Be sure to scrape and clean your plates and sort out the recyclables. Be kind to the kitchen crew, your turn is next week!"

As they carried their plates to the cleanup area, they spied Bailey sitting on a stool in the kitchen, wearing an oversized white apron and a poofy white hat on her head. She was eating and, catching a glimpse of them from the corner of her eyes, she waved cheerily. Then she turned away, watching something across the kitchen intently. Jason edged up to the counter to see what it was.

He could hear someone's edgy voice. "I tell you, I have allergies. I need to know what's in some of these things or I can't eat them. It could kill me!"

FireAnn stood, a great frown making sharp lines between her vivid green eyes, her arms folded across her chest. "And I am answerin' you, lad. We are all aware of allergies and there is nothing in my recipes that will bother you. But my recipes are mine and likely to stay that way!"

The two redheads stood, nose to nose. "I could get deathly ill!"

"Not iffen your mum filled out your papers correctly. Think

I'm daft, lad?" She raised her wooden spoon in emphasis. "There isn't enough tea in china or gold in Fort Knox to pay me for teaching a lad with poor manners. I am here because I wish to be, not because I am paid to be! Now, run along with you before I assign you kitchen duty for the next two weeks and you discover my cooking from the pot scrubbing up!" FireAnn brandished the wooden spoon.

Rich sputtered as he took a step backward. "We'll see about this."

"Indeed we will."

He turned, his face redder than his yellow-red hair, and stomped his way past Trent and Jason, headed outside.

The cook shook her head. "Temper, temper. He should try peppermint and chamomile tea."

Jason could not help but shoot FireAnn a big grin before leaving as well. Trent right behind him, they found the posted schedules and jostled their way to the front to read them. "Canoes!"

Jason scanned down the rest of the schedule. He tapped a class after lunch. "Lanyards?"

"Sure. Crafts, you know."

"What . . . ?"

"You've seen those braided key chains?"

Jason scratched his head. "Yeah, I think."

"Those are lanyards. Like roasted marshmallows, you gotta do lanyards at camp, man." Trent nudged him. "You'll like it. Sounds lame but it's fun."

"You wouldn't be kidding me, would you?" The blue edge of the lake looked far more inviting. The sound of waves lapping against the rocky shore and soft silt beach carried through the scattered trees.

"No, seriously, it's fun. Once you know what you're doing, you go on to leather crafts. I had a friend make this cool braided belt once. Of course, it kept stretching out and his pants would fall down. . . ."

Jason laughed as they trotted down to the beach, and the cooling breeze off Lake Wannameecha hit him. Crowfeather was already there, squatting next to the racks of canoes, running his hands over them in inspection. There was a weathered, wooden bin with its lid open. He waved at the bin. "Life vests. Grab one. Buckles and straps are pretty easy to figure out.

Help each other if needed." A man of few words, he turned
back to his examination of the boats and paddles.

"Know anything about canoeing?" Trent looked at Jason.

"Not a thing. They do float, right?"

"They're supposed to."

Crowfeather straightened with a slight grunt. "In fairly
good shape. I'm sure you guys will give them a bang or two."

Dust rose in the landing as the rest of the group shuffled in.
Crowfeather watched them silently, his arms crossed over his
chest, till they all fell silent as well.

"Line up however you wish."

Trent muttered, "Uh-oh," as they bumped shoulders getting
into some semblance of order. He grabbed Henry Squibb who
came up, panting and red-faced, and thrust him between them.
Jason looked at Trent, bewildered, then just shrugged. As soon
as the last straggler fell in, Crowfeather went down and counted
off, pointing at them. "One, two, one, two," until he'd ticked off
the last boy. "Two-man teams, ones with ones, twos with twos."

Trent punched Jason lightly in the shoulder. Both, of course,
had been counted off as twos. Henry pushed his glasses up, frowning until another boy headed for him, tanned hand stuck out in a
grabbing handshake. "Alfaro," the other said. "Daniel, but everyone calls me Danno." Relieved, Henry pumped his hand.

"Henry Squibb . . . and everyone calls me Henry." He
beamed in welcome. Clad in a bright orange life vest, he looked
rather like a rotund orange. Jason snagged some faded yellow
vests for himself and Trent, which was an improvement, even
if slight. They looked more like lemons.

Lake Wannameecha lapped serenely at the beach. Crowfeather turned as though following Jason's gaze. "Let the wind
come up," he said, "and that lake will be as rough as the Atlan-
tic in a storm. Or it will seem that way."

He pivoted on one bootheel, the silver-and-turquoise linked
belt around his waist chiming slightly. "All right. This session
is short. Remember your partners, remember what I am going
to show you about paddling. Then you'll be dismissed to write
a letter home and let your folks know you got here in one
piece. After lunch, at the swimming classes, we'll get an idea of
your skills in and on the water. Tomorrow, we'll launch these
canoes." He smiled slightly. "Be prepared to get wet."

He spaced them apart, handed them paddles, and ran them through what he called dry land exercises, all the while drilling safety rules into their heads. Jason liked the feel of the oar in his hands, but felt a little silly paddling at dry air. Until, when told to switch sides, he and Trent clapped their oars together with a loud smack. He staggered back just in time to see Danno hit the dirt, avoiding Henry's long swing.

Danno lay there laughing, even though his coffee-brown eyes grew large as Henry's oar swished back over his head a second time as Henry bent over, saying, "I'm sorry! Oh, no . . . I'm sorry again!"

By the time the session ended, they were all sore in the shoulders but switching from side to side without threat of beheading their partners.

They retreated to their cabin gladly, wrote their letters, and no sooner turned them in at the Gathering Hall office to Gavan Rainwater than Adam Sousa swooped down on them.

"Orientation hike!" he announced, with a flourish of his silver cornet. "Three in line, marching formation!"

Bailey skidded into place between Trent and Jason, her freckled face rosy. "Hey, guys! How's it going?"

"Canoeing looks awesome."

"Yeah? How's your cabin?" Without waiting for an answer, she prattled on about her cottage, Kittencurl, until most of the campers had fallen into formation and Sousa blew a blast on his cornet, quieting everyone. Bailey switched breathlessly into a whisper. "But there's this cabin on your side that no one ever camps in—Dead Man's Cabin. It's . . . haunted."

"Well, d'uh," Trent returned. "If it had a dead man in it!"

They all fell silent as Adam Sousa signaled for the marchers to follow him. He counted off their brisk strides before breaking into song:

> "Well, I don't know, but I've been told
> Ravenwyng Campers are awful bold!
> Sound off, One, two
> Sound off, Three, four
> Sound off . . . One, two,
> Three, Four!"

With grins on their faces and the sun beating down, they made up verses that grew sillier and sillier as the marchers snaked their way through the grounds of Camp Ravenwyng and ended up in front of the mess hall just as FireAnn sounded the lunch bell.

As they fell out to wash their hands and faces, Bailey grabbed their arms.

"Did you see it?" she asked.

"That blackwood cabin with the shuttered windows and the great black slash over the doorway?"

She nodded solemnly.

"Nope."

She shoved at Trent. "You two! Beat you to lunch!"

As it turned out, she did. The Kittencurl Cottage table butted up end to end with the Starwind table, so she scooted her tray over as they sat down and they talked excitedly about their different mornings. Full of food and a little sleepy, they finally headed to lanyards.

Trent nudged him in the ribs. "See? It'll be nice to sit down and do something with our hands."

Jason picked at a splinter in his thumb. He stifled a yawn as they sat down at the craft tables, trays of colorful plastic strands in front of them, and silvery metal pieces like key chain loops and hooks in plastic bins next to them. Gavan Rainwater sat on the end of the head picnic table, watching as fifteen or so campers stumbled in, faces sunburned, and took their seats.

"Nice quiet afternoon on the lake," Gavan said. He smiled at them. "Now, as you take up the strands you choose and braid them in some of the patterns I'm going to be showing you, I want you to think behind the simplicity of the object. Beyond square knots and braids. I want you to think of the flow of the color, the energy that you are moving, back and forth, over and under." He leaned on his cane. "Just let your thoughts go."

Jason combed his fingers through the long plastic strands, finally settling on a cobalt blue, dark and mysterious, offset by a lighter blue that had a touch of redness in its tone. Gavan had gotten off his table and was strolling by. He stopped. "Only two strands, Jason?"

He pondered. He looked at the instruction sheets weighted down by the supply trays and then nodded. "To start with."

"Not stretching your limitations?" Gavan watched him, watched his hands.

Jason was careful to leave his left hand mostly palm up, for the moment. The crescent scar on the back of his hand ached and throbbed briefly, then subsided. "Not yet," he answered.

"Very well, then." Gavan nodded curtly and moved along.

Trent had five colors he wove skillfully in and out, while Jason struggled to braid his two which did not seem to want to cooperate. When he finally had his lanyard completed, he tied it off with a sigh of relief. He looked up to see that Gavan had made a design as well, a complicated, great knot of color.

Everyone got up to go and look at it.

"Anyone tell me what this is?" Rainwater asked, sitting back, a sparkle in his blazingly blue eyes.

No one answered. Finally Trent shrugged. "A Gordian knot?"

Rainwater's attention snapped to Trent. "A Gordian knot? Why would you say that?"

"Looks like one. I mean . . . a great, complicated knot."

Rainwater tilted his head, gaze sweeping across all of them. "Anyone else? Anyone know what a Gordian knot is?"

Jason shifted. He'd heard of it before, but couldn't quite remember.

Gavan pointed the wolfhead at Trent. "Tell us all what kind of knot that is."

Trent stared at the ground gathering his thoughts, then took a breath. "Well, this is the short version. It was a very complicated knot tied in ancient Greece. Whoever could untie or unravel it, would be worthy of conquering those lands. When Alexander the Great began his career, a bunch of wise men figured to stop him. They brought him to the knot. His advisers couldn't figure it out either. Alexander had no intention of being stopped. He took his sword out and sliced the knot in two. His solution was quicker, more direct, and much more forceful. He did pretty well what he set out to."

"And this knot? Would you slice it in two?" Gavan tapped the lanyard woven display.

"I'd have to be pretty sure I was ready for whatever the reaction would be," Trent said. He gave a lopsided grin.

"An excellent point." Gavan bowed to Trent. "Ladies and gentlemen. Now that your bodies have rested and the afternoon has grown to its hottest . . . I think swimming is in order."

They made their way to their cabins to change clothes. Jason said to Trent, "That was cool. You knowing that and all."

"I know a lot of stuff like that," Trent answered. "Mythology is my life." He grinned. "Last one to the lake gets turned into a frog!"

7

Red Jell-o

DINNER found Jason famished. He hit the line in front of Trent, just barely, and this time he took everything that looked good plus seconds. But as they moved to the end, where the desserts were set out, he shied away from the great sparkling heap of red Jell-o squares. If he had wanted to be buried in gelatin, he'd have stayed with Grandma McIntire. In fact, he was willing to swear that was the main staple of her diet. Alicia told him once that wasn't true, it was just that she thought kids really liked Jell-o. Well, he had . . . once. Now . . . Jason shuddered.

"Don't tell me you're not going to get any?"

"Nope."

"You're kidding? Well, get some for me, then."

Jason rolled his eyes. Dutifully he reached out and scooped up a dessert dish of the shivery cubes and set it on his tray. He opted for a cup of chilled fruit cocktail as well. FireAnn smiled at him as he carried his tray off to their table. "A hearty eatin' lad! More power to you."

Henry had already finished his dinner, and was sitting crosswise on the nearby bench, discussing the merits of chess with Jonnard who looked extremely interested, as opposed to his normal look of polite faint interest. Bailey scooted over immediately, a frown darkening her face.

"Hey, what's wrong?"

"Someone," and she lowered her voice so no one else could hear, "has been stealing things from our cottage."

"What? Who? What kind of things?"

"We don't know. Everyone is missing something. My favorite set of barrettes is gone, and one of my hair scrunchies. Ting is missing her best purse comb. Even Jennifer says she is missing something." Bailey sat up straight as Jennifer approached them and went to sit at the far end of the table next to the wall. Pale and blonde and lovely, Jennifer hadn't said a word to Jason in the two days their tables had been joined. She sat down carefully, and tossed her long hair back over her shoulder. She was clearly older and the type of girl Alicia would refer to as "high maintenance." He wasn't sure what that meant exactly, but if she was at all like Alicia, she spent a lot of time in the bathroom getting presentable.

He leaned over to Bailey. "You think it's Jennifer?"

She shrugged. But her actions spoke differently as she viciously stabbed her fork at some grapes rolling around in her dessert cup.

Jason considered. Then he said quietly, "It may not be. Someone went through my things before we even got our cabins."

Bailey looked at him. Then she nodded. A slow smile returned to her as Trent sat down. Then she asked brightly, "How'd everyone do in swimming?"

Henry broke off talking to Jon and swung about completely, positively glowing. "I passed! I made intermediate swimmer. Never swam in a lake before."

Nor had Jason. The sensation of the silt beach bottom under his feet and the rockiness of the lake bottom had been different. But he was a good swimmer, or so he liked to think, and had enjoyed the afternoon session. Warmer, then cool waters as the lake deepened, felt great against the heat. Emerging had made his skin tingle in the breeze. "I did all right," he said.

"All right?" Trent sat down and ate half his meatloaf before expounding. "Boy's a fish in the water."

"C'mon." Jason stared at his dinner tray, too embarrassed to look elsewhere.

"I kid you not. He's a dolphin." With a swoop of his fork, his thin friend devoured the rest of the meatloaf.

"Dolphins are sea mammals. Saltwater."

Trent shook his head vigorously. "There's freshwater ones in China. Endangered, too. Ugly things, for dolphins." He pointed at Jason, grinning. "And he swims like one!"

"Eat your Jell-o!" Jason got the extra dish off his tray and pushed it over to muffle Trent. That seemed to work. Trent looked rather like a chipmunk for a few moments.

Bailey giggled. She jumped to her feet. "I'll see everyone later at the campfire!" Passing Trent and Jason, she whispered, "I'm setting out a trap tonight." Then she was gone with a smell of vanilla as well as dinner. He looked after her.

Henry and Jonnard returned to their discussion on chess. Ting and Jennifer watched one another while they both ate alarmingly small portions of their dinner and said nothing. Jason thought guiltily of Sam and how he had hardly missed his best friend with Trent and Bailey around. 'Course, it had only been a few days.

"Sure you don't want any?" His buddy circled the last bowl of dessert.

Jason had to admit the cherry gelatin did look pretty, crowned by fluffy clouds of whipped topping. But even the sight of it brought back stifling memories of Grandma McIntire and his narrow escape for the summer. He shook his head.

"Your loss," Trent commented cheerfully, before diving in and polishing off the dessert.

By the time they left the mess hall, dusk had started to fall. Bailey caught up with them as she had promised. "Let's think of a ghost story to tell tonight," she said excitedly.

"Oh, I'm not any good at that." He didn't have a tale he could make up, though the beast that had tackled him would scare anyone.

"I am," Trent offered. "I mean, I've read a lot of 'em." They sat down at the fire ring with nobody else in sight. As Bailey and Trent put their heads together, deciding to tell a spooky legend about Dead Man's Cabin, Jason caught a hint of movement. Almost as if his thought had summoned it, something moved in the growing twilight.

He turned his head slowly.

Something a little darker than the shadows made a gliding

movement, then disappeared. He gathered himself, ready to leap to his feet, then told himself it was nothing. He heard nothing.

Then, again. In the deep trees ringing this end of the lake, something very dark, low to the ground, moved.

He fastened his gaze on the copse of trees and shrubs that hid whatever it was. The back of his hand throbbed slightly. Green glowing eyes flashed at him from the twilight. His breath froze in his lungs.

By the time he could move again, the narrowed eyes had retreated into the shadows. He had seen something . . . or had he?

"Trent."

"Hmmmm?" His friend looked up. He'd been laughing at something Bailey said.

"See anything out there? I mean." Jason cleared his throat. "Ever wonder if there is anything to see. Deer and stuff."

Trent gazed across the clearing toward the lake end. "Too early, isn't it? I mean, they come out at sunset." He turned his attention back to Bailey.

Jason watched the forest, half listening to them, half nervously searching for that which he could not quite see. Was it out there? Or did he imagine it?

A branch snapped. His friends didn't notice it, but he jumped to his feet. From the shadows of the trees, a figure stepped out.

"Well, well. Bailey. Trent, isn't it? And Jason. Already waiting?" Eleanora smiled. Despite the heat of the summer evening, she wore a long soft dress, and a filmy, floating cloak draped from her shoulders. She had a basket hanging from her wrist. "A little early for the bonfire, isn't it? How about I save your places if you'll run these raspberries down to Fire-Ann for me?" Smiling wider, Eleanora held out the basket, brimming with fresh picked raspberries.

Jason took the basket, amazed that his heart hadn't stopped in his chest from fright. He walked nervously back to the mess hall while Bailey and Trent chattered away at his heels.

He knew that whatever he had seen in the darkness, it hadn't been Eleanora.

FireAnn beamed in delight as they handed her the full basket. "Berries! Just what I needed, darlins."

"I don't think they've been washed," Bailey offered. "Eleanora just picked them."

"Oh, aye, I'll clean them and cull them before I put them in the big pot." Behind her, in the kitchen that was already spanking clean even though dinner had hardly been finished, the singular huge pot simmered away. It smelled more than ever like jam. The pot seemed more like a cauldron to Jason, from what he knew of pots, which admittedly was little. Still . . . he eyed it curiously.

"Eleanora is a grand lass to think of me! Just wait till you take your Poetry and Chants class from her. A lively one, that girl is."

FireAnn dumped the basket into a bright, brass collander and put it in the sink. "Better run, you three, or you'll not get a good seat." Still smiling, she tucked her red hair under her bandanna and began to wash the berries for cooking.

Dismissed, the three of them strolled back through the camp as the tall lamppost lights came on, and the thin strings of flickering outdoor lights that graced some of the buildings. Jason was wondering what a poetry and chants class could be, when Bailey sighed.

"It's rather like Christmas," Bailey said wistfully. Her breath seemed to catch for a moment.

Jason looked at her. "Homesick?"

"Nope!" She kicked a pebble across the dirt and grass pathway. "Well, maybe a little. It's usually Mom and me. But, as Grandma always said, home is where you hang your clothes!" She skipped down ahead of them to where Eleanora did indeed hold their places amid a growing crowd of campers.

"That actually made sense," Trent remarked.

"Strange, huh?"

They sang "Captain Jenks of the Horse Marines" with Sousa leading the lively chorus. They listened to Trent's and Bailey's ghost story with avid attention, laughing and gasping in most of the right spots. Tomaz Crowfeather told them one of his many tales (or so, he said) of the Trickster Coyote. That one had the hair standing on the back of Jason's neck. But it wasn't a coyote that had attacked him. That, he knew. What it actually was, he didn't know.

"Almost time to head for your cabins," Gavan said, with a

look at his pocket watch in the fire's glow. He took the poker and stirred the logs apart to settle their ashes down for cooling. One of the logs broke apart into bright red coals, then immediately cooled to feathery gray ashes. Out of its depths crawled a small lizard, hissing, tongue tasting the air.

Jennifer gasped. "It'll burn up in there!" She flailed her arms about in distress. Her pale face grew whiter in anguish.

The lizard, hardly visible in the darkness but for the faint glow of the dying flames, crawled over another log, tail slithering behind it, and disappeared.

"It'll be all right," Trent said. "That was a fire salamander. Flames can't hurt them."

"Do you think, Master Trent?" Gavan said brightly. "The stuff of legends, after all."

He shrugged. "Some legends are born from facts, although misunderstood ones. Chances are he's really just moving too fast for the coals to hurt him."

Gavan rubbed the wolfhead on his cane and nodded. "Naturally." He lifted his voice. "Lights out in twenty minutes, ladies and gentlemen!" Without further ado, he broke into the song known only as Parting, and his deep voice swirled around them.

> "As Parting we take from one another,
> Let Life and Luck surround you
> Keeping you from harm and hopelessness
> Till once again our eyes meet in greeting . . .
> Hand in hand and heart in hope,
> We stand as friends always
> Wherever the road takes you
> Take strength in our Parting
> Till once again our eyes meet in greeting."

Eleanora stilled her dulcimer as the last notes faded.

Most of the campers got to their feet and began to make their way down the path to the cabins and cottages. Jason didn't join the crush because resting across the top of his sneaker was the coiled lizard. It hadn't disappeared at all. Its warm red underside glowed against his shoe and he could feel its heat, just like that of the fire ring. The creature seemed quite content to rest there. Jason took a deep breath and started to tuck his feet under him as others crowded past. The lizard lifted its head, gold eyes seemingly examining his face, before it skittered off and slid into a hole under the log they sat on.

Jason got up, dusting himself off. Some things were strange. And others, stranger.

The lights were off and they had settled in their bunks when a frenzied shout from across the way brought them to their doorway. Henry Squibb danced about on the porch, white foam flying with every step. Squealing and howling, he finally came to a stop and bellowed, "I'll get you for this! Whoever you are!"

He stooped over to pull off his socks and flung them over the porch railing where shaving foam continued to drizzle off them.

Jason saw two hunched-over forms sneaking away, but the light was not so dim he could not recognize Rich and Stefan.

Henry danced one last shivery jig before going back inside Skybolt, slamming the door shut behind him.

Jason grinned in spite of himself as he latched their door shut. Trent was already back in his bunk and breathing deeply as he settled in.

An hour later, Jason was wide awake, sitting up in his bunk, breathing hard, and rubbing his eyes. His heartbeat drummed in his ears.

A nightmare of nightmares still danced behind his eyelids and he blinked hard, to fling it away. A dead man, lying on a stone platform, waiting for him. Beckoning with one whiterthan-death hand. Stretching his hand out to Jason. Silent pleas drawing him closer. The castle, the boneyard of his worst nightmares faded slowly.

His hand had writhed with pain. He had stared at it, his left hand, and the wound from the attack had opened up again, and streamed blood. It was the only color in the whole, awful place.

Stone had imprisoned him. He took no steps and yet moved closer though everything in his body fought it! The fingers curled . . . reached out for him— The last thing he wanted was for that dead man to touch him!

He'd awakened, his throat aching with a scream he couldn't force out. Now he fell back, shaking.

Jason gulped breath after breath. He couldn't close his eyes without the nightmare wavering before him. He had to think of something different! It seemed to take forever to conjure up something pleasant and sleep was far away. He had almost drifted off when he heard soft footsteps by the cabin. Voices murmured.

"Everyone sleeps?"

"Like charmed. And you?"

"Restless. I had the dream again, decided to walk it off. Do you think they're dreaming, too?"

"I hope not. If I can get them to sleep through the witching hour, they should be fine. Better they don't know yet. . . ."

"Tomaz says the storm may be gathering strength. He seems worried."

"So I heard. I can't catch a glimpse of it myself."

"You think he's wrong?"

"It's possible. He is not, after all, of our generation."

The voices blurred, moved away, and his sleepy mind could not follow the almost sense of what they had said anyway. Jason tumbled into a deep, dark, dreamless night.

8

Tomes and Tombs

HE rolled out of bed, hit his hand, and stifled a groan. For a moment, he thought it had all been some kind of dream, but no . . . there it was . . . plain as the gash on his hand, which looked angrier than before, puffy and red. It could be infected. He had no choice but to see the camp doctor.

The sky was still gray and no one else seemed awake as he washed and then went to the office inside the Gathering Hall which belonged to Dr. Patel. Her door, however, was cracked open and as he peeked inside, she looked up from her desk, saw him, and smiled.

"Come in, come in! You're up early. Not sick, I hope?"

He shook his head.

She gestured a slender dark hand at a chair next to her. "Sit and tell me, then." Her eyes smiled on him as well, dark as chestnuts, but lively.

"Well, it doesn't look too bad today . . . it happened the first night, but I got to thinking. Well . . . I don't want an infection or anything." How could he tell her it was an animal bite? Dare he?

"You are hurting yourself? Let me see." Her words immediately became a little brisker.

Shyly, he put his hand out and she took it in hers. She probed him quickly about the healing wound, feeling him wince as she touched the tender spots. "How did this happen?"

"I fell. I tripped over something by the bathrooms and my hand went sliding into the bushes and just got ripped open. Is it infected? Am I all right?"

"Night before last, you said?"

He nodded. She frowned slightly. "And who am I talking to?"

"Jason. Jason Adrian."

She smiled. "I was going to see you today anyway, to ask about your ankle. How's it coming?"

"Oh . . . fine."

"Still a bit sore?"

"Not really. I mean, a little now and then."

"Excellent." She pulled out a pair of glasses that looked more like miners' headgear and looked at the back of his hand again. "This seems to be healing cleanly, but I'll give you a bit of salve to put on it. Your shots are up to date, correct?"

He nodded. "I can't get lockjaw then, or . . . or anything?"

"Highly unlikely." She slipped her glasses back on her forehead. "You look a little worried."

"Well, you know. Rabies, that sort of thing."

Dr. Patel looked at him, her Indian face smoothed in a careful nonexpression. "Is there something you're not telling me?"

He fought back a squirm. "No. It's just that, well, you know. It was awful sharp when I fell. And I couldn't see. I thought maybe . . ." He felt his face grow hot. "I thought maybe I'd stuck my hand into something that was sleeping and it bit me."

She slid her glasses back down, great grotesque-looking things that covered half her face, and peered at him intently, the lenses making her eyes blurred and buglike. "Nnnnno," she said finally. "This is a slice, although there is a small puncture mark at the top, here," she tapped his hand lightly and he tried not to jump because it *hurt*. "Looks like a thorn grabbed you and then sliced around as you fell into it." She pushed the goggles back up and blinked as she refocused. Dr. Patel added, "Unless there's something you haven't told me."

"Oh, no. No."

She smiled then. "Only thing you'd have to worry about

around here would be a wild animal, like a raccoon or possum, but they're pretty healthy. Spoiled, in fact, from the looks of them being chased out of the kitchen! And there hasn't been a recorded case of rabies in this area for over thirty years." She pulled a log out of the desk. "Just use that ointment and let me know if it doesn't keep healing."

He pocketed the medication in relief and stood. The loud-speaker sounded with the announcement for breakfast, and the doctor said, without looking up as she recorded something, "Don't miss breakfast."

Dismissed, he hurried out of the office, suddenly famished. Quick as he was, there was a line snaking ahead of him, and tables were filling as he got his tray and sat down.

"Catch anything with your trap?"

Bailey stabbed her spoon at a bowl full of cornflakes. "No." Droplets of milk splattered onto the tabletop and she wiped them up with her white paper napkin before crushing it. Next to her, Ting hardly missed reading a page while eating a dish of cottage cheese and fresh fruit.

"Better luck next time. Want us to help in setting it up?" Jason chased the last of his eggs around with a corner of toast.

She considered that, wrinkling her nose slightly. The dusting of freckles over her heart-shaped face crinkled. "Maybe. I'll have to find out about the guest rules."

"Guest rules?"

"Yeah. You know. Boys on this side of the lake, girls on that side of the lake." Bailey twirled her spoon. "Guest rules."

"Ah." Jason felt faintly foolish. "Probably best."

Henry leaned over from his near empty table. "Hey guys, guess what?"

Trent shot a look at him. "Your sleeping bag is full of shaving cream?"

"Ha. Not anymore. But that's not it! Jonnard got pulled aside for a special conference."

"What for?"

Henry tugged his glasses back into position, his owl-round face bewildered. "Don't know. Nobody would tell me. They just came and got him."

Jason and Trent and Bailey all looked at each other. Bailey said slowly, "Jennifer didn't come to breakfast this morning."

They glanced down the table. Ting sat, book in hand, but Jennifer's corner was indeed empty with no signs of the tall blonde girl ever having been there.

"I didn't even notice," said Jason.

Bailey beamed at him. She was still glowing when she left the table a few minutes later to go straighten her cabin and go to her first session.

"What did I say?"

Trent shrugged at Jason. "Something right, evidently. Who knows?"

Neither of them did. They finished off their trays and then trotted back to Starwind to straighten up. They spotted Jonnard hurrying in to the mess hall before it closed, a look of mild amusement on his face. He smoothed his dark hair back just before entering and ducked inside the doorway just in time to miss Trent's faint snicker.

"If I get like that in a few years, just shoot me."

"You mean, I'm tall and sure the girls will like me, like that?"

"Yup."

"I promise." Jason took Trent's hand and shook it firmly. He turned back to the day's agenda tacked to the bulletin board. "Tomes and Tombs with Eleanora?"

"No kidding? When's that?"

"Right after mail call." Jason shifted weight uneasily, thinking of his nightmare. "What is a tome?"

"That's an old word for book. Makes it sound ... I dunno ... more important."

Jason looked at the location, in the Gathering Hall. Sounded like the class was being held with all the campers at once. He shrugged. "We'll find out, I guess."

Indeed, they would.

But they almost didn't. Eleanora stood at the front of the lecture room, listening to the restless shuffle of desks, looking over the sea of campers alertly. "A minute or two longer," she said briskly. "While the stragglers trail in." She pulled at the light laced cuffs of her jacket and took a step or two to the side of the blackboard. Even in the heat of summer and at camp, she still dressed as she had that first day, coming from tea and a musical recital. She moved with a gliding grace that made him think of dancing, somehow. Once again, even though Jason was sitting now, she looked taller than he was. He blinked in thought.

The lecture room door burst open and Bailey came bolting in. She stopped just inside the threshold, as everyone turned to look, and her face turned red.

"Nice of you to join us, Miss Landau," Eleanora noted.

"I—I'm sorry." Bailey moved sideways, her gaze finding Jason and Trent. She found the empty desk chair next to Jason and sidled into it. Her golden-brown hair stuck every which way out of unmatched braids.

Under his breath, Jason whispered. "What happened?"

"They stole my brush and comb while I was at breakfast! You can't imagine. I turned the cottage upside down looking." Bailey tugged at one braid unhappily.

Eleanora cleared her throat. "All right, ladies and gentlemen, shall we begin? I want you to take notes, but I want them to be mental ones. I don't expect you to carry around scraps of paper with you your whole life to remember this class." She smiled.

"Most of you were asked to attend Camp Ravenwyng because of your writing skills. You showed creativity and imagination and a certain talent that caught the judges' eyes, whether you thought you had or not." Eleanora drew up a tall stool. "I am not here to turn you into English geeks, but I am here to teach you to appreciate the ability to know and use verbal and written language. There is power, you see, in naming things. A rose is a rose is a rose by any other name . . . but is it?"

"A tome is a dusty, musty old book and a tomb is a dusty musty old burial plot, but both are very different. We are empowered by knowing the difference and the names that separate them. Anyone have any other examples they can think of?"

Bailey's hand shot into the air. "A lion who mews into the night is not the same as the lion who roars."

"Ah, but both are lions . . . or are they?" Eleanora smiled in response. She perched on her stool, bracing her feet on the crossbar. Her long skirt fell in graceful ripples about her legs. "A lion named a lion has no other voice but a roar, wouldn't you say? Just as a kitten must mew because that is what a kitten does."

She tapped the blackboard. "More power in names. An emperor, a king, and a president. Each rules in quite a different way, wouldn't you say? Each evokes a different response: the time, place, and the manner in which they ruled, even though all are indisputably rulers."

From behind him somewhere, Stefan snickered lowly. "*X-Men* rule."

Eleanora lifted her gaze as if she had heard it, but she did not remark on it. Instead she turned around, picking up a piece of chalk, and moving off the stool. "Now. If a name has power, then a spoken name has even more. You can think Rose to yourself all you want, but until you name it aloud, its only power resides with yourself. Are you following?"

Trent put his hand up. "What if you're wrong? I mean . . . you can't call a wren a Phoenix. It doesn't work that way. One's a small bird, the other a legendary creature who is reborn through fire. The wren's in trouble if you think it's a Phoenix."

Laughter ran through the room. Eleanora smiled. "That's Crowfeather's class! Hopefully, he'll have taught you the difference. In this day and age there aren't many things which have not already been recognized and named by someone, unless you're into computer sciences. But you're right, Trent. The talent lies in recognition of the object's qualities and abilities. You have an obligation to think about it before you Name something." She paused. "I want you all to think on that. You'll realize its importance shortly."

"For now though, I am going to talk a bit about poetry. Why poetry? Because it celebrates the power of naming things for what they really are, and what they can mean to you."

Eleanora turned back around and for the next long time, she wrote about meter and beat and rhyming on the blackboard. They decided that nothing rhymed with orange, and that limericks were silly but fun, and that some poets were absolute geniuses. They made up more verses for Sousa's camp marching song and the hour fled as if it had wings.

Stefan showed, much to everyone's surprise, a talent at songwriting poetry. He still pushed his way out of the hall belligerently after giving Henry a wedgie, redheaded Rich tailing behind him muttering something about lunch and FireAnn's cooking.

"Hey!" Henry danced around for a moment or two, tugging his shorts and underwear back into the comfort zone. He sputtered one or two more times getting out the door.

Trent clapped him on the shoulder. "Just think, Henry. When you figure out what it is you're going to do to get even with Rich and Stefan, you get to Name it!"

"Hey," repeated Henry. He smiled slowly. "I will, won't I?" His smile spread as he left Lake Wannameecha Gathering Hall.

Outside, the brilliantly blue sky had become dotted with white-and-gray clouds. Jason could almost smell the incoming storm. Bailey tugged at one of her frazzled braids. "That was my grandmother's brush and comb set," she said. It looked as though a storm cloud had settled on her brow.

"How are you going to get it back?"

She shook her head bleakly. "With no idea who's been taking them, I can't complain or accuse or anything."

"Trap didn't work at all, huh?"

Bailey sighed.

"Tell you what. After Lights Out, Trent and I will come over and help set up a trap. You don't have time to wait on Guest Rules. Something else will be missing by dawn."

"You will? Really?"

Jason nodded. Trent looked away and he got the sense his friend disapproved. "You'll have to get rid of Jennifer somehow."

"Oh, she's got a counselor-in-training meeting, that's why she didn't make breakfast. Lights Out are an hour later for her."

"Great! We'll be there then."

A small smile replaced the unhappiness on Bailey's face. She waved.

Trent bumped shoulders with Jason as they trudged along the campground pathway. "That," he said quietly, "was dumb."

"Why?"

"It's after Lights Out."

"Well . . . it seemed the best time."

Trent rubbed his hand through his hair. "I know, I know."

"Don't you want to find out what's going on?"

"Yeah, but . . ." He shut his mouth.

"What?"

Trent shook his head. Something else was bothering him, but he said not another word, just pressed his lips together tightly. When Jason punched him lightly, saying, "You've got to help me think of something," he merely nodded.

After dinner, though, Trent seemed to loosen up. He dragged Jason with him into the kitchen and waited patiently for Fire-Ann to give her staff and the student assistants instructions on cleanup and preparation for the next day. She turned around, wiping her hands on her apron. The smell from the always-bubbling tall pot was next to heavenly. "Well, well. Waiting patiently. What can I do for you, gents?"

"We were wondering if you had some empty jars. Like . . . pickle jars or mayonnaise jars."

"Me? Lord love a duck. We've not been here long enough t' empty jars." She wrinkled her nose for a moment. "Tell you what. Have a look-see in the pantry, see if there's any under the bottom shelf." She pointed toward the storage area of the kitchen, an immense area nearly as big as the kitchen itself. As they entered it, Jason was awed by the size of the sugar and flour sacks, and containers of this, that, and the other.

"We must eat a lot."

"Are you kidding? Of course we do!"

They got down on their hands and knees, brushing aside empty battered old pots that had been stored there by Fire-Ann's staff when they brought in all her bright, new cooking pans. Behind them stood a row of dusty jars, with lids. Trent beamed. "Just what the doctor ordered!" He took three out, blowing the dust off.

Jason sneezed. Rubbing his nose, he asked, "Now what is this for, really?"

"Tonight. Later." Trent stood, carrying a jar in each hand. "You'll see."

·   •

Passing through the kitchen, he enthusiastically hefted his trophies for FireAnn to see. She smiled, tucking her wild hair back under her bandanna, and waved back.

Whatever it was, Jason hoped it wasn't supposed to be a surprise.

9

Glow in the Dark

"IT'S going to rain tomorrow."

"Feels like it." Jason looked at the sky, though it was dark. But clouds hid the stars and fleetingly covered the moon from time to time. The wind had come in, and the trees rustling around them sounded like high tide in the ocean. It was a noise both soothing and restless. He contemplated the velvet darkness. It rarely rained in the summers he was used to, and he wondered just where it was they were. In the low mountains, but not so low that the air wasn't just a bit thinner, and not so high that there weren't much higher mountains ringing the horizon. The crickets were singing loudly and quickly from the day's heat, but their noise began to slow as the evening cooled.

Trent gave him a jar. "We'll go down by the lake. I know where a patch of lightning bugs are."

Jason examined the jar lid. Trent had carefully poked a number of small airholes into it. "We're going to catch them?"

"Sure. Keep 'em for a day or two, and then let 'em go. They'll be fun to look at tomorrow. 'Sides, they're our alibi." He winked at Jason. "Come on, Bailey is probably chewing the end of her braid off!"

Quietly, they left Starwind. The cabin door forgot to squeak at all as they eased through it and left the porch from the side, rather than down the steps. He had already mapped out the way in his head, off the beaten path, and headed toward the far end of the lake where the girls' cottages were located. Like the boys' more rustic cabins, they were built in groups of twos and threes, resting among the curving paths that toured the lake. Thick forests shrouded the other side of the lake, and Crowfeather had promised them a kayak tour in a day or two, saying that the rest of the lakeshore was fairly rugged.

Trent trotted at Jason's heels as evergreen branches tugged on their sleeves. Lights from cabins along the way went out, one after another, leaving only the campground overheads on, and those by the lodges and the hall. The wispy white zigzag pattern of the flying lightning bugs could be seen more clearly in the dark. Like tiny stars hanging by the small coves and eddies of the lake, the bugs swung back and forth. Jason stopped to point out a gathering spot where the bugs seemed to move in hazy clouds. Trent stopped and watched, then nodded.

Jason heard a panting behind them. He turned on his heel and looked quickly . . . to see nothing. The camp lay in black shadows around them, except for faint patches of light that seemed far away. Yet he could almost smell the hot breath hanging on the air. He turned completely around, searching the night.

"What is it?"

"Do you hear something? Feel something?"

Trent paused, then shook his head. "Something wrong?"

Jason felt the back of his hand twitch. He swallowed tightly before managing, "Guess not." He hugged his jar to his rib cage.

There was a noise, which he did not recognize, and then he looked aside to see Trent unscrewing the jar lids on the two he held. "Let's get our jars filled before we get to Bailey's."

He nodded, and let Trent lead the way down to the backwash cove where the bugs seemed to have gathered. The hair at the back of his neck prickled as he felt, rather than heard, something trailing him through the darkness. He rubbed hard at his hand and felt the tenderness lying under the skin like a bruise. Only a thin welted line remained, but the pain underneath was like a warning to take the injury seriously, healed though it seemed to be.

They scooped the bugs out of the air on the fly. It was harder than it looked, but eventually they had four or five buzzing in each of their jars, soft flashes of light, captured. Trent kept his two jars after examining them, his hands filled with their glow through the glass walls. He stifled a yawn as he stowed his jars inside his windbreaker.

Jason watched the bugs crawl around inside their small prison. Up close, the faint green cast to their flashing was stronger. Watching them was like watching tiny fairies flitting back and forth. No wonder people believed in them once. "This won't hurt them, will it?"

"Nah. They'll be fine till we let them go tomorrow." Trent looked around. "Which way from here?"

Jason pointed. He backed away from the cove bank carefully, shoes slipping a little. Trent clambered after, branches bending from their passage through. They emerged on a side path, scratched and breathless, bugs humming noisily inside their jars. Stealthily, they approached Bailey's cottage. Built a little larger, with a porch that wrapped around, and a sloping roof, the cutout of a stretched-out cat, with its paws hanging down and curled about the door's threshold, was nailed overhead.

At their footfalls on the porch's edge, the door yanked open. Bailey peered out. "Jason? Trent?"

"That's us."

"Get in here!" She reached out, grabbing Jason's wrist and pulling him inside. Trent tumbled after. "It's almost Lights Out!"

"We won't take long," Jason said as Trent pushed a jar of lightning bugs at her.

"Hold this and don't drop it."

"Bugs?"

"Fireflies. Our alibis. So don't shake it, drop it, or put it down." Trent grinned and waved at Ting, who sat cross-legged on her bunk, reading yet another book. She smiled briefly and waved back.

Trent rubbed his hands together. "What do we have for bait?"

"Not much." Bailey sighed. "I've got a CD. Not that I want anyone to take it, it's my favorite. But my name is etched into it on the blank part." She opened the plastic case and showed them the faint spidery lettering. "It'll be easy to identify."

"All right, then. This is what we're going to do. . . ." Trent took the CD from her and told her about the trap as he and Jason quickly assembled it.

Bailey admired it when they were done. "Simple."

"Ought to make enough noise to catch anyone, if you're nearby. If you're not, they'll still be marked." The two boys stood and admired their little trap.

Bailey checked her watch. "It's past Lights Out!" She signaled Ting who made a face of disappointment as she set her book aside, and Bailey led them back to the cottage door. The cottage had two small nooks, and closets and a window seat. There were also two big chairs done in rose-hued, patterned upholstery to curl up in. Around the top of the walls just below the ceiling, was a bright wallpaper strip of cats and kittens, parading, sitting, curling, cleaning, and tumbling. She scooted them outside. "I'll let you know at breakfast what happened!"

Yawning, she closed the screen door on their heels and the cottage lights snapped off. Jason nearly slipped off the last porch step, his shoes still slick with lakeside mud and silt. Trent caught him as his ankle turned slightly. He bent to straighten his air splints and as he did, he caught the glint, the flash, of a green eye in the bushes behind the second cottage across the way, watching.

"We need to get back," he said tightly. He turned and fled across the campground.

Thunder rumbled across the dark sky. It was far away yet, like a low growling, and the lightning that had set it off was hidden behind the clouds and mountains. Trent leaped and ran after him, branches whipping around their bodies as the wind picked up. He did not stop to breathe till they were in front of their own cabin door, and then he doubled over, lungs aching. The fireflies in his jar rattled a bit angrily. He set them down on the rough wood of the porch. One of them glowed, and another answered.

Trent turned his jar around in his hands. "Makes you wonder, sometimes, how they came about doing it."

"Doing what?"

"Making light. I mean . . . did dinosaurs see fireflies, do

you think? Or was it later . . . like woolly mammoths?" Trent leaned over and set his jar next to Jason's. The glass walls clicked against each other.

"Gentlemen," a voice said quietly from the porch's edge. "A little late for you, isn't it?"

Trent jumped in mid-yawn. Jason looked through the shifting shadows to see Gavan Rainwater leaning against the porch posts. He moved forward a little, to catch what moonlight managed to sneak out from behind the clouds.

"We're just going to bed now, sir," Jason answered.

Gavan glanced at their jars. "Out collecting?"

"I thought it would be fun," Trent said. "They don't have fireflies where he's from." He jerked a thumb toward Jason.

"No? This is a good area to study all kinds of wildlife and phenomena," the camp leader continued. He tapped his cane on the steps. "I suggest, however, that you hit the hay now. Plenty of time tomorrow to take on studies."

Jason listened to Trent drift off into regular deep breathing, almost a snore, as thunder rumbled dully from far away again. Too restless to sleep, he turned on his side. He didn't want to sleep, even if it was the only way he hoped to catch a glimpse, a memory of his father. All too often it was the cold tomb, and he couldn't bear that again, he couldn't.

After long, long moments, he thought he could hear steps outside, and the brush of a tree branch. He caught Tomaz Crowfeather's words from somewhere nearby, "You're right, Gavan, these are tracks here . . . circling. Fresh, too."

"Any idea what it is?"

"What I think it is, you don't want to know." There was a long pause during which Jason felt himself sink that much closer to sleep. "Not that I haven't seen them in a long while, but I was hoping it would be a longer time before I spotted any. Wolfjackal. Has to be."

A hiss of breath. "No. . . ."

"Gavan, I have not yet found a way to secure the entire campgrounds. A warding of that type takes more manpower than I have."

"Dark Hand . . ." Gavan muttered something before adding, "Do what you can. I won't have anyone at risk."

"I can put a few charm bags down, maybe throw it off the scent. I can't give you more than another day or two, even at that." A pause in Crowfeather's voice. Then, "You need to take care of matters. This is an undertaking greater than the handful we have here."

"I know. Believe me I know." Gavan sighed. "I'm up against a lot, Tomaz. The Council thinks we're too brash, this is too soon, and they won't throw their support in yet. They want to see what happens before they take a risk."

"Well, then. We'll just have to show them the potential, won't we?"

"Yes. Yes, we will."

He held his breath, waiting to hear if there were other words, but nothing came. Either they had moved away or lowered their voices so much he could not hear them any longer.

Wolfjackals. Jason's eyelids fluttered. He held his right hand over his left, palm down over the scar. *Gavan and Crowfeather knew what it was that had attacked him.*

The thought somehow comforted him. The danger was real. He had not been imagining things. He would not have to fight ghosts. In the morning, he would think of a way to deal with it. Maybe he could say something now.

10

Lightning in a Bottle

"THE Rain in Spain is Mainly a Pain . . ." Bailey recited. "But it does make mud," she added, as she turned away from the window.

"What's that got to do with anything?" Jon peered at her from his corner of the arts and crafts table, elbows resting on the newspapers spread from one end to the other. Big plastic bags of clay were thumped down in the center of every table in the great hall, and their voices seemed muffled. Every camper was here, swimming and boating lessons having been canceled, and although the rain had been interesting the first day or two, it wasn't at all now, nor did it cool the weather off. Each raindrop had been as hot as if there were teakettles in the clouds spitting them out.

"We'll be working with mud." She tossed her head, golden-brown ponytail flipping vigorously.

"Ceramics clay is not mud. Well, it is . . . but it's not."

"Indeed it isn't!" a brisk voice rang throughout the hall, and campers all over looked up from reading the cartoons which seemed to be the only thing printed on the many newspapers. A plump, apple-cheeked older woman swept into the hall, her silvery hair in many, many curls, wearing a paint-stained smock over an interminable set of clothes. Her dark eyes fairly sparked as she looked about and pulled a stool over to perch on, its wooden legs screeching against the floor. Jason blinked. She almost looked familiar, yet he hadn't met her . . . had he? He stared in fascination.

"This clay," and she thumped a heavy gray plastic bag with the back of her hand, "is much different. It's called Steve's white and it's . . ." she let out a mirthful chuckle, "highly sanitized and refined mud!" She, too, glanced out the windows at the drizzling sky. "You will find, if you study the histories of the world, that long ago empires rose and fell on the quality of their mud." She smiled. "It takes the finest mud in the world to make quality porcelain, for instance! Today is an excellent day to find out what you're made of . . . I mean, what you can make of clay." She smiled sweetly.

Stefan thumped on the bag of clay left on his table. He also smiled . . . slowly. "We're gonna get dirty."

"Only if you smear it all over yourselves." The woman added cheerfully, "My name is Freyah Goldbloom, Aunt Freyah to all of you. Not that I'm your aunt, but . . . well, it seems to suit me."

Jennifer put her slender hand up. At her nod, she asked, "Will we be throwing or just modeling? And will they be glazed and fired?"

"Aha! Someone who's done more than make mudpies. Believe it or not, there is a wheel and a kiln, but I haven't had a chance to inspect them to see what kind of shape they're in. No, I think this is a just dig in and do it session." Freyah's apple cheeks reddened even more. "Today, I think we'll stay with pinch pots and basic figurines, whatever you feel like doing." To demonstrate, she troweled out a handful of clay, rolling it between her palms until she had a thin snake, then coiled it into a pot. "Of course, if you come up with anything outstanding and want to have it fired, I will be happy to set it aside for you." Her hands manipulated, pulled, and pinched until she finished forming her pot.

But not just any pot. As Jason watched, she gave it ears for handles and then sculpted a cow's head and muzzle for a pouring spout. "A creamer," she said, as she finally finished.

Ting, Bailey, and Jennifer applauded. Jon considered the item in faint bemusement as she then proceeded around the

tables, troweling out clay and dropping it in lumps on the papers in front of them. Jason dug in. Cool, pasty, hardly wet.
He worked it through his fingers to get a feel for it and an
idea of what he wanted to do. Now the battered mugs and old
jars partially filled with water also made sense, as he dipped a
hand into one and got his clay a little moister, easier to work
with. It squished wonderfully.

Trent immediately went to work, humming and drumming
his fingers as he paused now and then to rework his artistry.

Aunt Freyah stopped by Jason's elbow. She watched as
he worked a bit more water through the clay. "What are you
working on, lad?"

"Nothing yet. Just trying to get a feel for it."

"It needs to be a bit dry, you know, to hold its shape . . .
whatever shape that may be."

"Okay, no more water. I just wanted to . . . you know . . . feel
it. All the way through. Not just shape the outside."

"Interesting," Freyah said, with a shake of her many silvery
curls, and a pursing of her lips, and a blaze of her dark eyes.
"Very interesting. I'll check back in later to see what you've
come up with."

He nodded without looking as she moved away, his attention on the material in his hands. He wasn't quite sure what
he was going to make as he hadn't had any idea, brilliant or
stupid, pop into his head yet.

Across from him, Bailey already had a cunning mouse resting on the newspaper and she was busy adding a coiling tail.

Trent had made a reclining dragon of sorts. He looked up.
"Hey, Bailey. Can my dragon devour your mouse as soon as I
make his jaws bigger?"

Bailey made a snuffing noise. "I think not!" She turned her
newspaper about, pulling her creation closer to her, out of his
reach.

All around him, campers worked busily. Stefan and Rich
worked on a common project which looked to be some kind
of low, sleek car, which even then he wouldn't have recognized, but Aunt Freyah had crooned, "Oooh, an automobile,"
as she'd passed them.

Henry worked on what looked to be a squat owl, with spectacles on its beak, although Jason wasn't really quite sure . . . it could be a bust of himself.

Ting made a teacup, with a clever handle.

And all over the room were a number of pinch pots, in various stages of being and uprightness (the clay seemed to have a tendency to sag).

He looked down at his clay, which seemed to be waiting patiently for him to decide what to make of it. From his observation of the sagging, and knowing how much water he'd added, he knew a stand-up piece was impossible. He flattened the clay in front of him, and after long moments, had a great seal or plate with the sculpture of a spread winged raven upon it, thinking of the creature which had awakened him one night, seemingly long ago.

"Know him, do you?" Freyah smiled at his elbow.

"It seems like it, but . . ." Jason shook his head. "It's a wild creature. How could I?"

"Perhaps that's why you made him flat. You know the one dimension."

Jason looked down, then into her apple-cheeked face. "Maybe," he agreed. He thought a moment. "Do I know you?"

She smiled. "I don't know . . . do you? Perhaps you know just the one dimension of me."

He shook his head, his face warming slightly. "I mean, I know I don't know you, but I feel like I should."

"Take a good look." Aunt Freyah watched him, her expression light, and he tried not to feel uncomfortable as he took a good look at her. Take away the faint wrinkles about the eyes and mouth. Make the eyes lighter. The hair with a soft and fluffy mind of its own . . . he blinked.

"Mrs. Cowling?"

"Why, of course! How could you miss it?" She clapped her hands together softly. "You must be one of the students my niece recommended! Sarah has quite an eye for a bright mind. How wonderful to meet you." She grasped Jason's hand warmly, her skin firm yet slightly gritty with clay not quite washed off.

"Then you are an Aunt Freyah." How could he have missed

the apple-bright cheeks, the cheery smile? The more he stared now, the more obvious the resemblance was.

She beamed. "Well, of course, I am."

"Are you a teacher, too?"

"A developer of talent, we call it. Indeed. Sometimes it skips a generation or two, but in my family, what's left of it, we appreciate discerning minds. I was very pleased when Sarah decided to follow in my footsteps." Chairs behind them scraped impatiently across the floor, and he became aware others were waiting.

Freyah clapped her hands. "Finish up, everyone. We can leave everything out for a few days to dry. It will be in what we call the greenware stage. Then, if the kiln is working, we'll get them glazed and fired, those of you who want to save your efforts." She laughed gently.

The sight of the clock caught his attention. He stared, his jaw dropping open. Two hours had gone by with hardly a notice. Outside, rain continued down, and now he heard it, pounding the rooftop continuously, and the sound of the dripping from the drainpipes of the building. Everyone filed out, heading to clean up and then to their cabins for letter writing, with the sky darkening over them.

He had gotten three postcards. Two from Joanna and the Dozer, from two different ports (the Dozer's card showed building cranes and skyscrapers in a faraway city) and a scribbled message of two or three lines each, and a third one from Colorado of the camp Alicia was in. It looked nice, although he thought Ravenwyng was probably prettier and much less crowded. He read them each, carefully, three times, in case he might have missed part of a message. They might have been sent to anyone, nothing particularly personal on any of them. Sam hadn't written yet, and Jason wondered how he liked soccer camp. If it were any more ... normal ... than this one. With a sigh, Jason tucked them inside his folder and backpack and dutifully sat down to write his grandmother who would pass on his words to his stepparents when they called, and a second letter to Alicia who at least had an address.

He wore his backpack to dinner so that he could drop the letters off at the office. Jennifer bumped into his shoulder as she was leaving, and his backpack shifted, letters and something else tumbling out. She bent to get it, blonde hair swinging about her shoulders and handed everything back but the pack which had fallen out, still in its colorful box.

"Tarot cards! Are they yours, Jason?"

He shrugged. "I guess."

She sat back down with her tray and pushed it aside. "Do you know how to use them?"

Bailey stared, hard, over Jennifer's shoulder. Dumbstruck, Jason just shook his head.

"Ah." She smiled slowly. "Mind if I open them? I'll read your fortune for you. There is the cutest little store in my mall, the New Cave, where they sell these. One of the ladies who works there taught me how to read them."

"No, ummm, go ahead." Jason shifted uncomfortably. Realizing how much Aunt Freyah reminded him of Mrs. Cowling also made him realize how much Jennifer reminded him of Alicia, tall and cool and always seeming to judge him a little.

Bailey rolled her eyes and then stubbornly stared back down at her dinner. Ting leaned forward on her elbows. She said quietly, "I use I-Ching sticks."

"Do you?" Jennifer shuffled the deck of oversized, colorful cards carefully. "You'll have to read for us sometime. Okay, Jason. Cut the cards and think of what it is you want to know." She selected a card and laid it on the table faceup. "This represents you. The cards I'll place around it will be the answers to your question."

He looked at the deck as she put it in a single stack, facedown, in front of him. He wanted to know . . . what he was doing here . . . what was going to happen to him. Did he have a family or not . . . what he was supposed to do about anything. Questions whirled through his mind.

Trent chewed in his ear. "Going to finish your potatoes?"

Without turning, he answered, "No, but that apple crisp is mine. Touch it—and you die."

Trent snorted.

Jason put his hands on the card, looking into Jennifer's pretty face. She smiled slightly. He cut the deck into three portions, and she gathered them up and prepared to deal the cards around in a pattern, the charm bracelet on her wrist giving a gentle chime as her hands moved. The first card . . . he gulped . . . as she snapped it over and said, "This covers you."

She frowned at the picture card of the High Priestess. "Se-crets," she said. "Mystery yet to be revealed."

She flipped another card over, placing it crosswise. "This crosses you."

Trent sucked in his breath, choked, and coughed for a minute. Henry was so busy thumping Trent's back that Jason could study the card alone for a few moments. "The Nine of Swords." It showed a terrified man sitting up in his bed as if awakened by a nightmare or disaster, nine sharp swords hanging over his head.

"You know," said Jennifer, reaching for it, "we can do this some other time."

"No." Jason took a deep breath. "Go on."

"Of course go on," Jon put in smoothly. "The reading can't be done till all the cards are on the table. That may not be as bad as it looks."

"True." Her bracelet tinkled. "This crowns you." The Ace of Swords, a triumphant card, went down. Jennifer's face brightened. She quickly laid out the rest of the pattern and looked over it, frowning. In the position designated to reflect himself again, showed the Seven of Wands, a young man on a hilltop with a quarterstaff in his hand, fighting off others. She tapped it. "A fight for what you want, and it may seem the odds are against you, but you have the advantage."

"This is the most important card of the near future," she added, and turned the final one.

Jason's heart skipped a beat.

The Four of Swords.

"Cheerful card," cracked Trent. But he put his hand on Jason's shoulder and squeezed it.

Jason looked at a still figure lying atop a tomb. Three swords hung above him, one decorated the side of the coffin below. A stained-glass window in a corner of the card gave the scene a feeling of being in a church or mausoleum. He breathed in and out slowly, forcing nightmares from his mind. It was only a card. Only a card.

Henry squeaked out, "Jason's gonna die."

"No, no. This is not the Death card. Although . . ." Jennifer's voice trailed off. "Difficulties," she added.

Jonnard leaned over her shoulder then. "An interesting life

of mystery and trial. And deception, perhaps. But this card," and he tapped the High Priestess again, almost at the beginning of the whole pattern. He looked at Jason, his own expression calm and quiet. "This card tells us that all that follows may be untrue, if She does not wish to reveal your future to you."

Jason managed to exhale, and Jennifer gave him a weak smile. "True. Very, very true." She picked up the cards and handed them back. "I think the cards decided to have a bit of fun with us."

Unconvinced, he put them back in their newly opened box and turned around to eat his apple crisp as everyone trailed off but Trent.

Trent watched him as he took a bite. "Just some paper and paint," he said.

"I know." Jason shrugged, still feeling eerie. "But weird."

"No kidding. Maybe you should check the deck later, see if there's any good cards in it. Maybe you bought a defective deck."

Jason laughed in spite of himself. "I can always hope."

"Sure you can!"

Trent brightened up even more as Jason pushed the apple crisp his way, saying, "I don't feel like eating any more anyway." He watched his friend a few moments, thinking that the cards had shown him everything he knew—and nothing he didn't know, and nothing he understood. Jason sighed.

After dinner, he sneaked back into the Hall's crafts room, just to look at his raven again, wondering if he'd done as good a job as he remembered doing. He felt like he had to touch it, hold it in his hands. Firing, Freyah had explained to them, sometimes cracked a clay piece beyond repair or use. Golden light gleamed from the door, and he knew the room was not empty. He froze in the hallway, ready to head back in the other direction, not wanting to be found. He could see shadows of people moving about the room, hear voices.

"Take this one. Animal spirit. Bailey went right to it, without hesitation. She's got nimble fingers, that one, to go with her brashness. And this one? The teacup? Not only indicative of her cultural background, but of her understanding of herself as a kind of cup, waiting to be filled by life. Very Zen, don't you think?" Aunt Freyah's crisp, mirthful voice spilled over, as golden as the light filling the corridor.

Jason sidled a step or two sideways and froze when the floor creaked a bit.

"Any indication of what we really need? A Gatekeeper?" He knew that voice: Gavan Rainwater.

"Alas, not yet, but that talent is rare, as you know. And it doesn't always manifest itself early or easily."

Gavan sighed.

"Now, now!" exclaimed Freyah's chipper voice. "You can't give up, and you haven't even found the Iron Gate yet, so don't be putting the cart before the horse! Things will fall into place."

Gavan answered quietly, his voice sounding far away as if he had moved to the other end of the room. "We are short on time. There may be a mana storm headed this way. If it is mild, we can use it to aid us. If not. . . ." His words trailed off altogether.

"What about this one? A copy?" Eleanora sounded keenly interested in something.

"Oh, no, no. No, that is not a copy of the camp logo, at all. And, it's fairly well done. But even more interesting is how he went about it . . ." Freyah's voice dropped for a moment. He could not hear the rest of what she said, although he could hear it punctured by a questioning sound from someone who sounded like Dr. Patel as well. His ears burned as they talked about his work, his art, and his hand ached.

The hair went up on the back of his neck. What were they doing looking at the clay work like that? He felt as though he'd just been put under a microscope! It was too late to make something different from the clay, but he felt as if he had somehow shown his most secrets thoughts by what he'd made.

He crept away cautiously, his throat tight, until he made it to the rainy outside and stood in it for a moment, clearing his thoughts.

Bailey sat down and slumped over her tray, eyes weary and puffed. Without a word, she looked at them, and then shook her head. She trimmed the leather scrap she worked on, shaping it into a merit badge which could be embossed later to show Swimming or Archery or Herbs or any of the other classes they were attending. Trent looked very disappointed as he laid out some hide strips to weave a belt. The thief was still on the loose in the camp. Breakfast had been dreary and dull, the rain without letup.

Outside, it drummed on the ground and against the mess hall roof. It ran in gray rivulets down the windowpanes. Far off, thunder could still be heard, but that part of the storm never seemed to move any closer. They had run throughout yesterday dodging a downpour, and now it looked as though the drizzle would never end, although the rain itself was a summer rain and far from cool. Jason trimmed off the badge he had made and stamped, running his fingers over the raised emblem of a canoe. Rain or not, it was a neat idea to have them make their own merit badges.

Jennifer sat at the table, her long light blonde hair neatly combed and pinned back, with a notebook by the side of her crafts tray, pen clipped to it, and looked ready to take notes. She wouldn't quite meet Jason's smile. Ting also had a notebook by her tray, but it looked as though she had been writing a letter in it. In the upper right hand corner, she had sketched a bird from the look of it, although Jason tried not to stare. Letters were private, after all.

Maybe there would be some more coming in tomorrow. He'd just sent his second letter off to Sam.

Danno Alfaro came over from his table to sit next to Henry Squibb. Henry looked pale, the leather cutting shears dwarfing his plump, dimpled hand. Danno thumped him on the back. "Hey, no canoeing again. Wonder how they're going to keep us busy today."

Henry let out a groan. "I just want to go back to bed."

"That bad, huh?"

"Bad? I hardly slept." Henry lowered his voice slightly. "Waiting for the next prank." He said not another word but began picking pieces of leather as if trying to decide what to make. He had his choice of a pouch, a belt, or badges, but the mess in front of him hardly resembled any of them. His shoulders hunched as if waiting for Danno to make fun of him.

"Hey, at least you know who's after you and it's real. In my

dreams, it's like the Dia de la Muerta . . . Day of the Dead."
Danno shook his head slowly.

Jason shot him a glance. "What are you talking about?"

"Nothing." Danno shut his lips firmly. He glanced around
as Gavan Rainwater, passing quietly between the tables, a coffee mug in his hand, slowed slightly and then went on by.

Then Danno only said quietly, "This place has secrets."

Jason felt his jaw drop and then carefully closed his mouth.
Did Danno have nightmares like he did?

"What kind of secrets?" Ting asked.

Danno shrugged. "All kinds, you know?" They all looked
at each other.

Henry, however, brightened a bit. He said softly, "If only
there was something I could think of to get even."

"We'll get 'em. Don't you worry."

Trent shifted on the table bench next to Jason. He brought
out his jar and set it on the table. The fireflies moved around
the jar, glowing and dimming like lights being turned on and
off. He grinned at Jason. "I think I'll make a bug badge." Outside, the skies got very dark.

"Lightning in a bottle," Jonnard said from behind them. He
gestured at the glass jar, and they made a buzzing sound, like
hornets. His voice seemed to echo.

The room darkened. The lights went off and came back
on, fitfully, sputtering. Lightning struck outside, its light blazing off the lake surface, and thunder boom-CRACKED right
overhead, the whole mess hall shaking. The lights went off to
a flurry of screams. The fireflies made short, darting flights in
their glass prison, their white-green spots the only illumination for a moment.

Gavan and Eleanora got to the front of the hall at the same
time. "Everyone sit and stay quiet,"he said calmly. "We'll have
power in just a moment." He glanced at Eleanora. "I think it's
time." She took a deep breath and then nodded.

He tapped his wolfhead cane once, as if to steady himself.
Then Gavan bowed his head, and lifted one hand slowly. As he
raised his hand, the lights came up.

Trent leaned back. "Woah," he said softly, echoing the
sounds of awe.

Gavan leaned back on his cane. "We have everyone here

this morning?" His gaze swept the hall. "Because we believe the time has come to make an explanation. Because you're who you are, a number of you have noticed some odd occurrences around camp. And because you're who you are, there will be more. We had hoped to have more time for evaluations, but this has never been an exact science." He laughed then, and smiled.

"Ladies and gentlemen. You were all chosen to attend camp because you showed us a certain talent, an aptitude. Like calls to like. We hope we recognized what we were shown."

The lights flickered again, and he frowned. This time he spat out a word, and if anyone doubted he was doing something to restore the power, all doubt fled. At his word, the lights blazed.

"How did you do that?" a shy voice asked from the second row of tables on the other side.

"Because I have the Will and Talent to do so."

Gavan rubbed the wolfhead on his cane in thought a moment, before looking up into the silence.

"What was once thought Lost forever is now known to merely have been Sleeping. This camp is intended to show you how to use your talent and develop it. To respect what you are and will become. Magick is alive in the world again, and you are its heirs. You can create it. Wield it. Welcome, ladies and gentlemen, to the world of Magickers."

Bailey's eyes went saucer big. Into a room of quiet, she dropped, "Wow. That is letting the cat out of the hat!"

11

Things That Go Bump
in the Night

ELEANORA drew herself straight, her gaze raking the mess
hall. FireAnn had come out from the kitchen, and crossed
her arms, wooden spoon still in her hand. Even though breakfast was long gone, and they were buried in leather crafts, she
was busy getting ready for lunch. Gavan indicated them.

"All of us here are Magickers, in one way or another."

Eleanora added gently, but in a voice that carried to the far
back corners of the room, "And because we once came from
your world, we understand what you must be thinking now."

Stefan let out a rude sound, echoed by Rich.

She nodded in their direction. "Of course. I'd do the same
in your place." She tugged at her flowing skirt, lifting the hem
a bit. As the bottom of the skirt rose to expose her ankles, it
also revealed another sight. Eleanora floated a good five
inches above the floor, her shoes resting solidly on . . . nothing.
As if to emphasize that, Gavan swung his cane under her.

Her face glowed faintly pink. "I don't like being short," she
added softly.

Gavan snorted. "Waste of energy."

"It's my energy," Eleanora returned loftily. She looked back at them. "Even if you don't believe me now . . . you will." She stepped back with her usual grace, her shoes moving silently above the floor. She let her skirt fall back around her ankles. "Don't think we're going to hand you a magic wand and teach you to wave it. Magick doesn't come from a wand. Nothing is as simple as that."

"The first thing we need to teach you," Gavan said solemnly, "is how to stay alive. That may take a great deal of doing, seeing as how the enemy already knows we are here."

"Enemy?" echoed Jonnard.

"Of course," muttered Trent. "The balance. Where there is Light, there is Dark. Always." He leaned on his elbows, his fascinated attention on Rainwater and the others.

Gavan nodded toward Trent. "There is most definitely Dark. Although we didn't know it at first, and that is where our story begins." Gavan pulled up a kitchen stool and sat on it. Outside, the rain stopped, as though finally worn out. "Nearly three hundred years ago, Gregory the Gray met Antoine Brennard in combat over a disagreement on the basis of Magick. Because of that, all Magick was ripped out of the universe. It was not, then, a war of Good against Evil, although events afterward changed all of us. The shock of that incident killed many Magickers. Stunned others.

"Some of us were lucky to fall into a deep, deep sleep. Sheltered somewhere and miraculously left alone till we could awaken and find ourselves in a new world, a new century. Struggle to find ourselves at all." Gavan cleared his throat.

"Most of us who would awaken began to sometime in the last century. Because we are what we are, we found each other. Realized what had happened. Realized what we had won, and what we had lost. Decided on a course of action that, eventually, brought us to this day.

"Each and every one of you have exhibited enough Talent for us to decide you could use training and our help. We ask nothing for it. Most of us have spent the last decade or two finding other Magickers and working toward a day like today. The Circle increases; that is our only reward. Some of you here today will fail to learn. It is not a failure to be someone of worth. Magick is fickle. In some of us, it can come and go unless we learn how to steady it and use it well.

"So. In the meantime, we ask that you spend your days here with an open mind, and a closed mouth. What we do must be secret. I've no desire to find myself in a lab somewhere being dissected to see what makes me tick or why Eleanora is on invisible stilts.

"Everyone take the hand of someone standing next to you. I want everyone in this room joined." His gaze swept across them, and Jason moved to take Bailey's hand on one side and Trent's on the other. Their hands felt as his did, a little dry and rather nervous. After a moment of stirring and commotion, they all fell quiet again.

"Repeat after me," Gavan commanded. His voice started quietly, and as they echoed his words, rose to a thunder on the last.

> *"By hand, by touch, by sight, by mind*
> *By heart, by soul, this vow does bind.*
> *Of this circle and magical ways*
> *Locked in my body, the secret stays.*
> *I so swear!"*

He smiled. "Now. There will be some of you tempted to test this binding. I recommend you don't. The disease tetanus was famous for its symptom of locked jaws, but in my time, not all those who had locked jaws had caught that dread disease. Some were merely oath-breakers."

Trent's hand shot up. Eleanora nodded to him.

"What about our parents? They're not part of the Circle."

"No, they're not." She brushed a long dark curl from her forehead as she frowned. "We need your silence this summer, while we can train you to know yourself and learn how to protect and deal with your families. They did send you here, knowing that this is a camp for the talented. How extraordinary . . ." She paused, with a slight smile. "It might be a real shock for them."

Gavan added, "Now, while we set up classes for tomorrow in the Gathering Hall, there is an afternoon movie, a mud-bowl tug-of-war, and an early night so you can catch up on your sleep. Tomorrow our setup for phone conferences will be working and everyone has a call home coming. Also, we will be having a Talent Show that we are going to videotape and send to all the parents, since we are not having visits. Look for that on the schedule, so you can start practicing. As far as being a Magicker, you'll have lots of questions to ask, and we'll have some answers. But not all. Many answers are for you to find on your own."

The mudbowl tug-of-war was as messy as promised. But no one minded, for at the end of the free-for-all, the sky opened up again and drenched them all so thoroughly there was little mud left for the indoor showers to take care of. Bailey preened at being on the winning side, declaring she was "happy as a pig in mud."

Trent scratched his head. "I think she got that one right on the nose." He watched as Rich and Stefan thudded past, grumbling at poor calls and weak wrists. "Nothing like sore losers," he commented when they'd disappeared. He bent over to help coil up the immense rope with Jason.

"Going to the movie? I hear it's optional."

"I didn't catch the title, did you?"

Trent's eyes shone in glee. "It's one of Jim Carrey's, should be a scream."

Jason considered the idea of some gross-out slapstick comedy, then nodded. It stopped raining as they made their way to the long line at the showers.

"I think it's a still," Bailey said quietly, as she joined the two waiting for her at the back of the mess hall after dinner.

"What's a still?

"That bubbling pot FireAnn is always fussing over. And they're going to make magical elixirs from it. We couldn't possibly have known that before, but now we do."

"We do?" echoed Trent.

"A still?" Jason stared at her.

"Did you get mud in your ears? Both of you?" She put her finger to her lips as they ducked through the flaps and went outside. The moist air of the summer night hit them, and a firefly floated lazily past, a brief white zigzag lighting their way.

"A still," she said confidentially, "is a contraption people use to make their own liquor with."

"I've seen those. That's a cauldron. It doesn't look anything like a still. They've got tubes and distillers and all sorts of things wired together." Trent sounded openly doubtful.

Bailey shot them a look. "She's gotta start somewhere," she retorted. "Now that we know she's using Magick."

"Well . . . yeah . . . maybe. I still think she's making jam."

"For days? And days and days?" Bailey made a huffy noise.

Jason shrugged. When Joanna wanted good jam, she went to the gourmet food market. What did he know about making your own? Still, he did know that the back of the kitchen around the great stewpot smelled of berries and sugar. Spelled fruit something or other to him. He said as much.

"Don't be silly. Cook is up to something. She kept shooing me away. You don't fuss like that over some jelly."

"Did you try to get a spoon to taste or something?"

Bailey looked forward. "I did." She looked around.

"What happened?"

She made a funny face. "The spoon melted."

They spoke in unison. "It what?"

"Went all wobbly and then . . . nothing! Just flat disappeared in my hand. Started at the bottom and worked all the way up till I dropped it!" She waved her empty hand in the air and then frowned. "Maybe that's why Cook always uses wooden spoons."

"I," said Trent firmly, "don't want to eat anything that dissolves spoons."

Jason thought. "Maybe it's vanishing cream."

They stared at him a moment. Then Bailey grinned. "Cool! I'll have to check it out when she's done cooking it!"

From the great shadowy hills which loomed pitch-black in the summer night, something howled. It echoed down the mountaintops, cold and stark. All three of them stopped in their tracks.

Trent frowned, then rubbed his nose. "I've heard that before. Usually in the middle of night though."

Floating notes shivered through the air.

"It's a wolf."

He shook his head at Bailey. "They don't have wolves in this part of the States. It's just a coyote, like Tomaz Crowfeather talked about. Lonely, though . . . you should hear others. There should be a pack, you know?"

Jason had goose bumps on his arms. He swung them vigorously. "I'd just as soon not hear a pack all night. It's hard enough to sleep around here with all the noise."

Bailey stopped in her tracks and tilted her head to look at him. Trent bumped into her and caught himself, hanging off her shoulder. Both of them stared at him.

"I don't hear anything."

Trent muttered, "I sleep like a log."

Jason scratched his eyebrow. "But there's people coming and going all night. I mean . . . they try to be quiet, but—"

"They? You went out and checked it out, right?"

"Ummm . . . no."

"Jason!" Bailey stared in disbelief. "Maybe it's that thief who goes through our cabins."

He shifted his weight. He didn't want to admit he intended to, but not with them. "I know, I know. With curfew and all, I don't want to get in trouble. But I will."

"When? I want my stuff back."

"When I have a little bit better idea of what's going on here. I mean . . . Magickers and all . . ." He paused. "There's a lot to learn. It's all pretty amazing stuff."

"You can bet," Trent offered, "that we've only seen the tip of the iceberg. I bet there's all sorts of stuff they're hiding from us."

"Has to be. We're just not ready for most of it yet."

"But how much do they have to teach? Has to be tons, Jason."

Trent said softly, "You could probably spend your whole life learning to be a Magicker."

"Exactly. Now's the time to learn it. Once we go home . . . we're back in a world of mundanes. I don't know about you two, but I want to learn everything I can while I can!" Bailey looked from Jason's face to Trent's.

"You don't want to make any enemies, Bailey."

"Enemies schmenemies. Aren't you curious?"

Jason cleared his throat. "Very. But I don't want to get sent home either. Tell you what. I'll see what's happening tonight. And then we'll have a meeting and decide what to do."

"Sounds good to me," Trent said. He put his hand out. "Buddy shake."

They all piled their hands on his and gave a team shake with a grunting "Huh!"

More fireflies were gathering as they escorted Bailey to her cottage and then sprinted to their own as another lone howl drifted out of the northeastern mountains. On the way, Trent explained seriously to him about the increase of coyotes even in city areas. "Very smart," he finished, as they trotted inside. "Sometimes they trot through your block, and you don't even recognize them as coyotes."

The air reeked of fresh popped popcorn from Skybolt. Trent pointed and said, "Charge!" They took the porch by storm and as soon as they entered, Danno and Henry began pelting them with hot fluffy kernels. Trent dodged, laughing, but Jason stood and caught them, and stuffed the salty-buttery kernels into his mouth. He grinned. Jonnard sat at the chessboard, looking tall and calm, but his eyes were fixed on the game.

He sat on the bunk and grabbed Henry's back-scratcher. Gingerly and yet with a noise of utter contentment, he slid it inside his air splint and scratched away.

"When do you get rid of that, anyway?" Henry slid his bishop across the board, eliciting a howl from Jonnard, and looked back across the room.

Jon sputtered. "How did you—how could you—what—" He ran out of air. He glared down at the board.

"Next week, I hope," Jason answered Henry. "Feels pretty good, actually, even if I do itch. Sprain. Only been about three weeks."

"It's the heat," Danno commented. "Makes you itch." He scratched his torso as if in sympathy, his unruly thatch of dark brown head hair practically standing on end. He frowned at the chessboard and muttered. "Henry, you got him again."

"I know," said Henry. He grabbed a handful of popcorn and munched it confidently. "Give up?" He watched Jonnard.

Jonnard grunted, before adding, "Not yet."

"Never give up!" Trent said, throwing himself on Jonnard's bunk and digging out a stack of comic books from his backpack.

"Easy for you to say. He's only beaten me like a zillion times. It's my turn!"

"Everybody," Jon said quietly, "has to be good at something." No one else said anything. How could they argue with that? Jason watched Henry rub at his eyes. The sun had gone down, finally, it was late and they were all yawning by the time Jonnard heaved a sigh and pushed the chessboard back at Henry. "I give." Danno swept the fallen popcorn out with him as he sprinted to his own cabin down the lane.

Henry beamed sleepily as he gathered up his pieces into his felt-lined, folding chessboard case, packing everything away neatly before crawling into his bottom bunk in the corner. Jonnard raised an eyebrow and said, finally, "Well done."

Trent and Jason wandered back to Starwind.

Everyone but Jason was nearly sound asleep by then.

He lay down on his cot. Something skittered across the cabin rooftop, pausing now and then. Probably a squirrel, raccoons were heavier. Pine branches rustled as the wind picked up a little. He looked at the gnarled beam, not that far overhead from the top bunk, reminding him of his attic bedroom. Moonlight snaked in through each and every crack in the boards, just a dot here and there, light fanning across the wooden floor.

He took a deep breath, rolling onto his side. He should sleep. If he could. But he wasn't sleepy. Everyone else already seemed deep in their dreams.

Something tapped on the roof. Jason sat up. Tap, tap. A crow? Then a branch cracked loudly as something or someone stepped on it. A muffled "oof," and then a smothered protest, then quick footsteps headed down the slope.

He swung his legs out and slid carefully out of the bunk, still clothed in shirt and long pants. He quickly shoved his feet into his sneakers before slipping out the cabin door. Jason clung to the shadows, letting his eyes get used to the night again. A sliver of moon hung over the sharp, jagged peaks to the northeast. With little moon out, the night was very dark with an immense field of stars, stars whose light was usually drowned out by city lights.

Then something bumped into him, yeowched faintly, and grabbed at him to keep from falling over. She clutched once she caught hold, and swayed. Jason squinted into Bailey's face.

"What are you doing out here?"

"Investigating." She yawned and wobbled in her tracks.

"You'll get us both caught!" He grabbed her elbow, steering her away from the cabin.

"I didn't think you'd do anything." Bailey rubbed at her freckled nose. "After all, it wasn't your stuff that got taken."

"You didn't think I had the guts."

"Well." She shrugged. "Guess I didn't." She yawned again, and he nearly joined her. "Aren't you the least bit sleepy?"

"No. Well, I wasn't." He pointed down the slope. "That's where they went."

"Who?"

"People. Unless raccoons giggle."

Bailey blinked at him. "I . . . don't think they do," she said slowly. She swayed in her tracks. Carefully she massaged her eyelids.

"Why don't you go back to bed?"

"And miss the fun?" She took a deep breath." 'Sides, if we get caught, we can say you were escorting me to the bathrooms."

"You're around the end of the lake!"

Bailey rolled her eyes. "Come on! I'll be right behind you."

If only he'd realized that would be half the trouble.

Jason spotted the empty cabin down the hill, hidden in a small grove of evergreen, one window glowing yellow against the night. He started down, carefully picking his way in the dark.

A few pebbles rolled his way as Bailey stumbled and caught herself. He put his hand back to steady her. She bumped heavily into him. "Sorry," she said in his ear, then giggled.

He pointed at the window. "Someone's in there," he said. "If we can get close enough, maybe we can hear who."

"Good idea," Bailey whispered back. Her breath smelled faintly of peppermint toothpaste, sweet and clean.

Moving carefully, for the hill was steeper than it looked—or could be seen, in the nighttime—Jason led the way down. Pine needles went slick under his shoe soles. He slid a ways before catching himself. He could hear the soft murmur of voices.

"Is she almost done?" A man's voice, faintly familiar.

"I think so. We know it takes time." This one, soft, barely above a whisper. Jason could hardly hear it.

"We haven't much more time. We need to start weeding them out."

Jason swallowed hard at that. One of the answers they would find out on their own? Not everyone would make it through camp?

"Patience," said Eleanora quietly.

"I've no time for patience! The Council was happy finding Magickers one by one. They are not happy we're trying to train a camp full of them. You know that. The only reason we have their backing is the faint evidence that a Gate might be close." Gavan made an impatient sound. "Any findings in here? I don't like having a cold room like this, without reason."

"It's haunted," answered Eleanora faintly.

Someone snorted in derision.

Almost to the abandoned cabin now, he straightened and prepared to take a step leading to the cabin's window. What were they looking for? What did they mean by a cold room?

A loud yawn rumbled behind him. Then a stumble. Then Bailey barreled into him like a huge snowball rolling down a mountain, sweeping him off his feet and crashing them both into the cabin.

Lights went on everywhere. Jason lay on his back, staring upward at white flashes.

"Well, well. Mr. Adrian. Miss Landau." Gavan leaned angrily over them. "Have you anything to say for yourselves?"

12

Thin Air

"AN explanation would be nice." Eleanora bent in as well. The bright light behind her head shone a little like a halo, but it would have to have been one for an avenging angel. She looked rather irate.

"Or even necessary," echoed Tomaz Crowfeather. The normally silent man leaned one shoulder against the edge of the cabin as Jason sat up. His blue-black hair glinted darker in the shadows, pulled back and tied at the back of his neck. He held a circle of turquoise beads in his hands and they went click-click-click as he fingered them. The silver disks on his watch glinted.

Jason cleared his throat. "We ... ah ... were ... well, she had to get to the bathrooms."

Eleanora turned the flashlight in her hand toward Bailey. Bailey lay peacefully on the ground, softly snoring, eyes closed. "She appears to have forgotten that."

Jason stared. "She's ... asleep!"

"Apparently."

"But ... but ..." He stood up, raining pine needles and dirt. Bailey stayed sprawled, blissfully dreaming. He pointed. "She wasn't asleep when—" His mouth snapped shut.

Eleanora looked at him, her eyes softening somewhat. "Everyone in camp is asleep, Jason, except for you."

He stared at the three of them. He did not drop his gaze until Gavan shifted. "And the three of us, too, it seems. Well. I cannot prove you a hero, nor can I prove you a fool." He gestured, and Tomaz knelt down and carefully picked up Bailey. "Follow Eleanora back to her cabin, and she'll tuck Bailey in. She won't be pleased in the morning to hear about another week's assignment on mess hall duty, but at least she'll have her friends with her."

Jason sighed, and nodded.

The two moved away as Rainwater stared down at him. "I can say this." Gavan moved next to Jason and looked into his eyes. "If you were meant to know, you'd have been invited to the meeting."

Jason's face went hot, even in the cool night air. He struggled back up the slope alone, his ankle a bit tender but not terribly sore, combing pine needles out of his hair with his fingers. By the time he got to the top of the slope and crawled into his own bunk, he was as sleepy as anyone in camp . . . and he probably snored louder.

Bailey dropped her breakfast tray next to Trent's and Jason's. "How did you sleep last night? I slept like a sack of bricks and woke up with my hair looking like a squirrel tried to nest in it!" She grinned as she grabbed a spoon and prepared to dig into her cold cereal.

Trent and Jason swapped looks. Her hair looked okay now, sleek and wet from the showers, and braided back neatly.

"I slept, uh, fine," Jason answered.

Trent took a moment to roll a pancake up and swallow it whole. "Never heard a thing." He speared another pancake to duplicate the feat.

"So when are you going to investigate?"

Jason's fork dropped with a clatter. He slapped his hand palm down, trapping it on the tabletop. He grabbed it up as snickers floated toward him, and Stefan could be heard saying something. Not what, but he didn't want to know. He could feel Stefan's cold eyes on the back of his neck.

Bailey elbowed him. "How'd you get yourself on duty with me? That's too cool. Now we can find out what Cook is doing in that stewpot for sure."

His jaw dropped. She didn't remember a thing about last night. And not only didn't she remember a thing, she didn't care about getting stuck with another week of mess duty.

"Not telling, huh? Some day, Jason Adrian, you're going to be too clever for your own good." She crunched down happily on raisin bran. "Trent, why don't you take next week, too? Cook likes volunteers, and it's not so bad, really."

Trent scratched his head. "Actually," he considered. "It could be fun."

"Great! I'll tell Cook. Now all we have to do is vote and see who gets to vanish first." Bailey grinned and dug seriously into her breakfast.

He could have used disappearing cream last night. The only question was—whom would he have used it on first?

Trent drummed his fingers on the tabletop as he demolished his stack of pancakes and began to work on a pile of crispy bacon strips. He dipped his chin now and then as if bobbing his head in time to a tune no one could hear. He looked up to see Jason watching him with a sideways look, and grinned. "I hate it when the voices in my head get louder than the music."

Jason laughed. He pulled his plate of what seemed to be nicely scrambled eggs with chopped bits of ham and French toast closer and dug in. Bailey finished her breakfast, took the tray off to the cleanup counter and came back with a glass of juice. "What's up today?"

"Arts and Crafts at ten. Lanyards again."

Trent cracked his knuckles. "Hey, don't knock lanyards. That's weaving. Probably for dexterity or something."

"Dexterity? Are you crazy?"

He shook his head at Bailey. "Think about it. Finger agility. Who knows what we need to cast spells and such? They didn't pass out any magic wands, you know."

"Cabin," Jason got out, still chewing and swallowing.

"Cabin?" Bailey arched her brow, staring at him.

"Cabin cleaning is first."

"Oh, yeah. Right."

All three of them sighed.

"It's not so bad," Bailey said finally. "I mean everyone pitches in."

"Maybe you'll find your stuff."

She considered that a moment then shook her head. "I didn't lose it. It just disappeared." She stood and finished her juice. "See you guys later. I might as well go get started."

Trent got a second stack of pancakes and sat down, rolling them and eating them like breadsticks, syrup and strawberry jam tucked inside.

"Where do you fit it?"

Trent laughed. "That's why I roll 'em up. Easier to stack 'em inside!" He licked at a dribble of jam. At last he pushed his tray away. "Ready?"

"Sort of. I want to look at Dead Man's Cabin first."

Trent wiped his hands on a paper napkin, aimed, and made a basket into the trash can as they walked out the mess hall door. "How come?" he asked when they were outside and headed down the gravel path.

"Bailey and I went down to see it last night."

"You did?" Trent scrubbed one hand through his hair, spiking it up. "She didn't say a word. Keeps a good secret."

"I don't think she remembers."

"How could she not remember?"

"She fell asleep," Jason replied simply. He paused at the bottom of the path, which curved around through evergreens and snaked its way toward the empty cabin. Last night they'd come from above, and he swore he could see slide marks down through the carpet of old pine needles and leaves.

Trent kept a lookout while they approached the cabin and watched it for a moment or two, to see if any noise or movement came from inside. Then both boys dashed inside. For a moment, the total darkness blinded them, and then the thin ray coming in from the door was enough to see by.

Dusty, empty, not even a chair. Jason squinted.

"Nothing," said Trent.

"Not a thing," Jason agreed. "Except . . ." He took a deep breath. A faint aroma lingered on the air. It smelled faintly familiar.

Trent inhaled. "Cook's stewpot," he said.

"That's it! But why . . . ?" Jason took a step or two deeper into the cabin. His sneaker kicked something, and it clattered into the corner. A half-eaten spoon rocked in the corner, its silvery, jagged edges catching the light rays. He stared at the evidence.

Trent jerked. "I hear something outside."

He didn't want to be caught again. He'd have to think about this later. "Let's go!"

Later, hiking through the camp behind Sousa, picking up strays as they went, Bailey joined them, her face pink with frustration, muttering to Ting who also looked very unhappy. Their explanation, however, could not be heard over Sousa's spirited marching music.

The two boys could only wonder what had happened. They watched curiously, though, unable to figure out what the problem seemed to be. Sousa marched down the winding pathway, cornet in hand, trotting them across the grounds, then leading the campers out in a parade behind him as they wound through Ravenwyng's acres. Bailey bumped shoulders with them finally, still frowning, and muttered under Sousa's happy tooting, "Someone took my candy money this time."

"Your candy money?"

"A shoe full of quarters, in case we ever find civilization again. I had it in my old, stinky, swamp waders. Someone had to be desperate." She wrinkled her nose.

"No kidding!"

Trent dodged her elbow.

"How much did they get?"

"Close to three dollars. Not a fortune, but enough for a handful of candy bars." She sighed. "I'm going to set a trap!" The cornet peeled again, and they trotted after the paraders. After working their way across a meadow of summer flowers, even Bailey seemed cheered, all of them following Sousa as if he were the Pied Piper. Trent fished around in his pocket and came up with a kazoo. He started a lively tune that had Bailey in red-faced giggles by the time they got to the craft tables by the small lake.

Although it was midmorning, the sun reflected hotly off the lake and the small breeze felt good as they scattered to their various tables. Gavan and Eleanora stood to one side, quietly talking. It looked as if a thousand diamonds had been scattered over the tabletops but there was an immense banner hanging from the old oak's branch. DO NOT TOUCH.

Trent glanced at Jason. "Looks like they mean business." He slipped his kazoo into a pocket and sat down.

Jason considered the crystals and quartzes shimmering in front of them. Bailey sat down across from them, uttering a small word of awe. Her dusting of freckles paled on her face. She put a finger out and a tiny arc of lightning zapped forth, snapping.

"Ow!" She yanked her hand back, pinking.

Eleanora's gaze swept the campers. "No touching," she said quietly.

No one else dared. Bailey sat for a moment with her finger in her mouth, as if burned, before sheepishly leaning back. Her eyes, though, stayed on the glittering objects.

Sousa gave a trumpeting flourish on his cornet, saluted Gavan, and marched off, his tailed coat swinging as he walked.

Gavan moved to the center of the craft area and waited. In just a moment, there was an absolute hush. "Ladies and gentlemen," he said. "Welcome to your first lesson as a Magicker."

Jason sat straight. A chill ran down the back of his spine.

"You've had fun these past few days as campers, but you all know now why you are here and I'm sure you're more than ready to learn. Today Eleanora and I will introduce to you what will become your closest friend and ally, your closest bond as a Magicker . . . your crystal. The crystal you choose will probably not stay with you more than a few years as you grow, but most Magickers never entirely put theirs aside. It remains as a talisman to those first, exciting, hazardous years learning your crafts.

"We will lose some of you over the years as Magickers," he added solemnly. "There can be accidents in this world as in any other. I want you to take your time this afternoon, as we work with you. If your life does not depend on your crystal today . . . it *will*."

Eleanora began to walk between the tables. Not too far from them, Jonnard ran his fingers through his hair and commented, "No crystal is alike, just like fingerprints."

She looked sharply at him. "That is correct. So today, what we will do is something as simple and complex as picking out your crystal. Needless to say if, after study and observation, the crystal you reach for shocks you . . ."

Rich snickered, and Bailey blushed again.

Eleanora patted her on the shoulder. "It is not meant for you." She leaned down and whispered to Bailey, but not so quietly that Jason could not hear her say, "Don't worry, dear. Someone had to make the mistake of touching them. It just turned out to be you. I did the very same thing, way back when."

Bailey smiled gratefully as Eleanora floated down the aisle. She took a place just behind Jonnard although even standing she could scarcely be seen behind the tall, seated youth.

Gavan nodded at Eleanora. "All right, then. As you look at the crystals, I want you to consider each one. I suggest not making a choice unless it is clear to you that there is no other crystal that appeals as much to you. Stand up, Magickers, and begin your first lesson."

Trent rolled his eyes as he clambered to his feet. "Just what I need," he muttered to Jason. "Belted by a piece of rock."

"Hmmm?" Jason answered. He leaned over the table, intrigued by the walnut-sized gems. They all seemed to want his touch. How could he choose? And there wasn't just this table . . . there were seven other tables. How could only one become his?

With a snort, Stefan scooped a rock off the ground and tossed it onto the table in front of him. "This one's for you, Jason." He looked at Rich, and their shoulders rocked in mirth, which they smothered as Gavan looked over at them, and said, "I suggest you find your own matches."

Still chortling, the redhead shrugged and reached for a pale yellow quartz across the table from him. There was a crackle, a pop, and a yell, followed by a dust cloud as Rich sat down abruptly. He shook his head, eyes round and blinking.

Gavan cleared his throat. "I also suggest you all take this a bit more seriously."

Trent slowly put his palm out over a pale blue stone. There was a rustling rather like the crackle of static electricity, and he pulled his hand back quickly. His brow knit in a expression of concentration.

Jason decided to look at all the tables before even thinking about a stone. Most looked as if they had just been chiseled out of their quarry or vein, not polished or even cleaned, but they were still beautiful. The edges were sharp or brittle. As he leaned over, he could see the shadowy hint of the planes inside, the facets that made them the kind of stones they were.

Bailey had evidently followed him. Her freckled arm darted past him, as he paused, and without hesitation she plucked a large amethyst from the table and cradled it triumphantly in the palm of her hand. He smiled at her as she threw him a wide, beaming grin.

"Well done," Eleanora murmured as she passed them by.

Bailey retreated to their table in the shadow and stood, turning the crystal over and over in her fingers. "Jason, look at this," she breathed in a voice full of soft wonder.

"I'm trying to find my own," he answered. He drifted farther away.

"But I can see inside . . ."

He found himself drawn to a rough quartz of nearly flawless clear beauty except for a rough vein of gold and dark blue chips. He started to do as Trent had done, hold his hand over it to see if the warding energy inside would react to him. Inside, a cooling warmth drifted up.

Gavan was behind him. "Not," he began to say, but he was too late, as Jason picked up the quartz and a welcoming thrill went through his entire body. "That one," Gavan finished. Jason twisted around to look at him.

"Why?"

Gavan instead looked at Eleanora. "I thought we decided not to put that one out."

She looked back, a defiant expression on her face. "I agreed to no such thing."

Gavan met Jason's curious stare. "You may pick another if you wish. I will Unbond that."

"No." He shook his head quickly. "I like it."

"Yes, but . . ." Gavan paused. "I'll discuss it with you later."

"Come look at mine, Jason," called out Bailey persistently.

"Hold your horses." He took a moment to look at his crystal closely, turning it over and over on his palm. It was both a fine and rough object, beautiful and ugly.

Jason heard a muffled shriek. He turned back to Bailey impatiently, only to see thin air where she had stood. Thin air and a crystal hanging in it. Then it quivered and plunged to the ground. His jaw dropped, and he blurted, "Bailey's gone!"

13

Now You Tell Me

"THE absolute first rule of Magicking is never drop your crystal." Gavan sheathed his cane inside his short cape and then added briskly, "No one move."

Too late. Jason had already jumped the bench and scooped up the amethyst before the words left Rainwater's lips. The purple gem felt warm in his hand as its rich facets twinkled up at him. No wonder Bailey had picked it, he thought, cupping the crystal. As to what had happened to Bailey . . . he looked up as Gavan reached him and gently took the crystal from his hand.

With a shake of his head and a knotting of his brow, Gavan rolled the object between his palms. The camp leader seemed to blink in and out of focus for a moment. Jason rubbed the corner of his eye and tried to fix Gavan firmly in his sight as Rainwater glanced toward Eleanora and shook his head, once. She paled.

"As you may note," Gavan said dryly. "The crystals can help you unlock any number of abilities. It is important, mortally important, not to attempt to do anything with them until you've been instructed how to handle them. Bailey is fine, that much I know. That is not always the case."

"What do you mean mortally important?" Rich leaned on

his elbows, tossing his crystal up and down, up and down. A faint sneer curled one corner of his mouth. He seemed very unconcerned about what had happened. Jason felt a glower creeping over him.

"He means," Eleanora said, frowning, "your lives will depend on it." She moved quickly, sweeping the unchosen crystals into trays and setting them aside, covered. Although every move was briskly efficient, her usually bright eyes seemed shadowed with an expression of worry.

"It didn't zap me," Jason murmured, as he realized something. His hands itched vaguely in memory of holding Bailey's crystal.

"No, it wouldn't. It's been attuned to Bailey." Gavan turned the crystal over and over. Afternoon sunlight gleamed throughout the purple walls tumbling through his fingers. "It's imperative we find her as soon as possible."

"But . . . what happened?" asked Ting faintly.

"Miss Landau is gone," Eleanora said.

"D'uh," commented Rich. He nudged Stefan's thick shoulder.

"Once you have learned a bit," she returned smartly, "you will realize there is a world of possibilities that could have happened. This is the most dangerous time in any Magicker's life, the beginning, when you first learn how to handle yourself. It's when you make the most mistakes, of course . . . and when you are first hunted."

At her last words a hush fell over the campers. Jason looked at her pale face. He should put his own crystal in a pocket, he knew, or some place safer, but he felt better with it in his hand where he could grip it, feel it. Ridged edges pressed sharply into his fingers as he curled his fist tightly about the object.

"Hunted?" echoed Jon.

She nodded to him. "By those who can't understand or are jealous. And by those on the Dark side, whose nature it is . . . to hunt." She glanced at Gavan who stood very still, cupping the amethyst, and who looked back with a faint frown, and shook his head, again, very slightly. He pocketed the amethyst.

Ting stared with wide, dark eyes. She held her faintly pink crystal at her throat, and stared at the blank space where Bailey had vanished. A cold shiver ran through her slender figure.

Jason put one hand over the other, covering his mark, his own crystal still in his fingers. Who were the hunters? Of what and why? And was he now marked forever as prey? Was he hunted? He tried to hide a shudder, echoing Ting.

Jennifer moved over next to Ting and rested her hand on the girl's shoulder. "They'll find Bailey."

"Of course we will!" Eleanora nodded emphatically and added, "Because Gavan and I will be busy, I'm going to dismiss the class today, with homework. All of you were asked to bring a jeweler's glass or loupe to camp. I want you to take a look at your crystal with it and see if you can draw what you discover under the lens. There will be facets, angles, and chambers. Let's see what you can translate to paper, if you can, those of you who have studied geometry. Even more importantly, I want you to note the colors in your crystals and see if they have a feeling for you. Color is the result of light energy, and energy is what we Magickers draw on." Eleanora clapped her hands lightly.

"And most importantly, do not look too deeply into your crystals or try to enter them . . . or we will lose you as well. There will come a time for that, with training," Rainwater added tautly. Eleanora's slight form dipped for a moment as if she lost altitude suddenly, and she put a hand out to Gavan to steady herself. They exchanged a low word or two that Jason could not catch. She then inhaled very slowly. "This is not as serious as it looks. We'll have Bailey back by dinner."

Stefan snorted. "The question is . . . in how many pieces?"

Gavan shot the boy a hard look. Stefan and Rich backed into each other, suddenly silent, and milled around as if both were trying to leave quickly.

Trent shook Jason's shoulder as they trudged back to the cabin. "Bailey will be all right."

"You can't be sure of that. They aren't." He rubbed his hand again. "I wonder what happened. Do you think something took her?"

"I think they have some idea, but they're not going to tell us, at least not yet. They don't need anybody else disappearing. That thing still bothering you?"

"Yeah. It's sore, like a stone bruise or something." Jason rubbed his hand again.

"Just let me know whenever you decide to brush your teeth, so I know when you're foaming at the mouth for real."

"Great. Thanks."

His buddy grinned. "You're welcome." Trent tossed his crystal up and caught it. Jason had a glimpse of the opaque, frosted gem. The thought of losing touch with his own, at the moment, made him slightly queasy. He frowned and fidgeted.

"Aren't you afraid of dropping yours?"

"And vanishing like Bailey?" Trent scratched the corner of his eyebrow. "Nope. At least not yet. I can hardly wait to get a closer look at it though. My dad had fits trying to find one of those jeweler's glasses. What about you?"

"My stepmom is very organized. If she doesn't know anything about something, she knows how to find someone who does. She bought me a very nice one."

"Wait a minute. You've got a stepfather . . . and a stepmother?"

"Yup."

"Okay, I don't get it."

Jason brushed his hair from his eyes. "It's complicated. First . . . my mom died. A long time ago, I don't really remember her. For a while it was just my dad and me. My aunt helped, then she married and moved away, and my dad got married to Joanna. Then he—" Jason's throat tightened, and he looked away, across the twisting trails of the camp and to the brief, blue glimpse of the lake. "Then he died. So I just had Joanna." He took a breath. "Then she married William McIntire, or the Dozer, as a lot of people call him."

"Wow," said Trent. His friend looked at him. "Here I am bunking with you, and I had no idea how twisted you are. You've got a lot of potential to be really screwed up. You could get away with a lot."

That made Jason laugh in spite of himself. As they pushed inside their cabin and threw open the shutters to let the light flood in, and the fresh afternoon air stirred through the pools of heat inside, he said, "What do you think happened to Bailey? Seriously."

"No way of knowing."

"*They* know."

"Well." Trent pulled his chair up. "They probably have

some ideas, but if they absolutely knew . . . they'd have gotten her back already. They're probably figuring out how to track her." He opened his backpack, rifling through it, before getting out pencil and paper and his small, closed-up magnifying glass made especially for gems.

"Track her? I don't like it. Anything could have happened to her. Stuck in her crystal like a genie in a bottle?"

"Sure. Don't you think Magick leaves some kind of trail? Maybe an aura. Something. I bet they're in conference right now, mulling it over."

"Maybe." Feeling a little better, Jason stared out the screen door. He tried to imagine a comet tail of sparkling motes left behind Bailey as she vanished. What convoluted saying of astonishment would be trailing after her? Across the way, Danno and Henry tumbled into Skybolt, with Jon trudging up the steps after them, in his older, more dignified way. A moment later he came bolting down the steps, pillows flying through the air after him. He laughed once, then straightened and shook his fist at the cabin. "Don't you have any place to go!" Fits of giggles welcomed him as he gathered up the pillows with the dignity of being older, and went back inside.

Jason's air splints felt hot and heavy on his leg. Reaching down, he let the air out and then unfastened them, putting them aside on the tabletop while he laid his crystal down on a piece of crisp, white paper. His own jeweler's loupe was folded up in a neat, black leather case. It was almost like opening up a Swiss army knife, bringing out the tear-drop shaped lenses. He set his crystal down and looked at it with his own eye first. It was a stone of flawed beauty, but the flaws themselves were intriguing and beautiful. The bands divided a third of the stone into a chamber which had a quartz texture all its own. The most serious flaw, though, was cold and hard granite, nearly shearing the stone in two. It wasn't supposed to have been out on the table, yet it had called him. What did that mean?

Across from him, Trent hummed as he looked his frosted stone over, tumbling it between his fingertips. Again, for a slight moment, Jason felt horribly queasy at the movement, then looked away and gripped his pencil. What did Trent feel trying to look into the foggy depths of the rock he'd chosen? What had Bailey felt? What *had* happened to Bailey? He frowned at his crystal. The sooner he had some understanding of it, the sooner he might have a hint. He wished he had not let Gavan take the amethyst . . . surely there was something there which could tell him what she had done, or had had done to her. This was going to take some time. The cabin creaked slightly, wood against wood, as the afternoon wind began to pick up.

Something tickled the back of his ear, and he scrubbed at it, scratching the itch. After a moment or two, the other ear tingled, and he brushed at it. Trent looked up as the table wobbled.

"Problem?"

"I'm worried about Bailey. And there's a gnat or something in here."

"I'm worried, too. As soon as it gets dark, I figure we need to find her crystal and look at it. I mean, they're not telling us everything, and we might know more than they do anyway."

Jason grinned at Trent, pleased to have found a coconspirator. "Great. We'll plan later."

Trent's face split in a lopsided smile. "I'm always scheming." With a laugh, he brought his jeweler's loupe back up to his eye and peered through the magnifying lenses at his quartz. "Pretty rocks, you know? Easier to carry about than a crystal ball."

Jason ran his finger over the bands. "Gavan didn't want me to get this one, did you notice?"

"I saw that." Trent stood up and came over, peering over Jason's shoulder. "That almost looks like a crystal melted into an agate or something, the way it's banded. I like it. It's neat looking."

"My dad used to say that it was a person's flaws that made them interesting." Jason shifted in his chair. "How do you suppose these are used . . . and for what?"

"I imagine they're just a focal point, for discipline or meditation or such. So you can concentrate on whatever and learn to harness it." Trent sat back down after twisting his chair around so he could face Jason.

"Why do you say that?"

He shrugged. "Well. Rocks in themselves can't be magical, or anybody could just pick one up and use it. I doubt they're batteries or channels. I mean, don't you think that what makes you a Magicker is inside you—not the crystal?"

"I haven't had much chance to think about it. It all hit so quick." Jason sat back in his chair. "It's like . . ." He paused to scratch at his ear tickle again. "It's like someone said to me, okay, you're everything you ever wanted to be, now—what are you going to do first? And there's so much to do; you can't decide what to do first . . . only there's a catch. You have to know how to do it." He hung his arm over the chair back. " 'Sides, I'm worried about Bailey right now. What about you?"

"Bailey worries me, too."

A slight breeze caught at Jason's sketch paper and began to waft it off the table. He grabbed at it, anchoring it down with his left forearm as he began sketching again. "No, what I mean is, what do you think?"

Trent didn't say anything for a long time. Jason looked up to see his friend sitting quietly, eyebrows knotted together. He put his pencil down. "You don't believe them."

"It's not that. Although, you've got to admit, it's a hard one to swallow. They could all be conning us. What better way to make a kid think he's special than to tell him he's Magick? Hey, you! Ever wanna be one of the X-Men? Darn right I do! But . . . do I want it to be real? Yeah. Every book I've ever read, every computer game I play . . . is something like this." He let out a soft sigh. "But is it real? I don't know yet, and I don't feel different."

"But you want it."

"Of course. Don't you?"

Jason looked at the back of his hand. The crescent there had healed into a thin, pale ridge. It still hurt if touched or bumped accidentally, and he thought of the snarling, green-eyed beast which had left it. "I'm not sure," he answered slowly. "I think there's a lot more to this than any of us can guess."

The bug that had been tickling decided to bite, in a quick, hot pinch. "Ow!" Jason leaped to his feet, swatting at the curve of his ear. He whirled around and saw nothing, but the hot sting of his ear told him *something* had definitely just taken a bite of him!

"Quit rocking the table!" Trent threw a colored pencil at him. Jason threw one of his splints back. In moments, the fight had carried out onto the pathway between the cottages with Henry and Danno joining in until Jon came out and threw a bucket of water on all of the participants, grumbling about a nap. Trent looked at Jason who looked at Henry who looked at Danno who promptly tackled Jonnard into the muddy puddle and in a few more moments, no one could tell anyone apart except for his height and general eye color in a mass of mud. Bailey would have loved the mock fight, providing them with teasing remarks and laughing at them.

There was no Bailey at dinnertime either. Nor at the campfire. Ting sat miserably, a handkerchief twisted in her fingers. She leaned close to Jason. "I miss her," the slender girl said quietly. "And to top it off, someone took my favorite watch."

"Trap didn't work?"

She shook her head at Trent, her long dark hair falling forward over her shoulder. "I can feel her. Can't you? I'm scared she's lost somewhere and can't get back."

Trent just shrugged. Jason held Ting's wrist for a moment, her skin soft but slightly cool to his touch. "We'll find her, and that's a promise." A log split open with a loud pop, sending a shower of orange sparks up into the night. When the Magickers gathered everyone and held hands to sing the Parting song, Jason was already planning what he wanted to do about his missing friend.

"You're sure," Trent said into his ear, "it's the red Jell-O."

"No, I'm not sure . . . but you're still awake, right?" Jason paused in the darkened corridor of the Lake Wannameecha Gathering Hall, and he could all but feel Trent's hot breath down the back of his neck.

"Yeah."

Jason inched forward. This back way smelled of dust and old wax, and musty still air that hadn't stirred in a long time. It felt like the mummy wing of the great museum he'd loved when he was younger, when he still had a father who would take him, and still lived in a great city that had a huge, stuffy museum. The air tickled at his nose, and the fine hairs on his arms.

"This," remarked Trent quietly, "is dead."

Jason nodded. It did, indeed, feel lifeless, as though they

had stepped into a huge mausoleum or tomb, though it was far different from the tomb that haunted his dreams. He inhaled. Their very presence ought to be enough to wake the Dead. He gritted his teeth. Something nudged at him, an insistent thought. Nothing could be this quiet . . . unless it were a trap. It could be Magick . . . it *had* to be Magick. He stopped in his tracks. "Don't breathe, Trent. Don't think. Be as . . . lifeless . . . as the Hall is."

Trent sucked in his breath. "Of course!" he answered in a low voice, as if Jason had discovered something basic, something primal. And so, quietly, scarcely breathing or thinking, they inched toward the doors to Gavan Rainwater's office. A tiny band of light fell upon them, and they froze in their tracks. Trent slipped to his knees as Jason leaned over Trent's shoulder, looking in, and he peered in as well.

Eleanora sat on the edge of a great, cluttered desk carved of dark gleaming oak. Her shoed feet dangled a long way from the floor. Gavan sat back in an immense leather chair, his face creased, one hand rubbing his brow. The bright purple amethyst filled his other hand.

"At least we know she is alive," Gavan said. He passed his open hand over the crystal.

"It's almost as if she doesn't want to be found."

The two stared at each other. "Sometimes they forget . . ." Gavan said slowly.

"Oh, no. No! Don't say that."

"Eleanora, she could wander lost until it's too late, you know that. Once she's forgotten, we've little chance of getting to her."

"Is she trapped . . . inside?"

"I can't tell. Damn me, but I can't tell!"

Eleanora leaned over and put her hand on Rainwater's knee. "It's not your fault."

"It is. I should have warned them first. But the moment is so wonderful . . . that first bonding, that first crystal . . . I didn't want to cloud it for them."

"You didn't know."

He shook his head. "And I should have known! Gregory would have known. . . ." Still clutching the crystal, he leaned back heavily in the chair. "They'll begin to panic if we can't rescue her soon. We'll lose some of them, they'll call home, we'll have to let them go."

"FireAnn is ready with the Draft."

He shook his head, an expression of profound loss settling on his features. "What a waste. What a dreadful, horrible waste."

"We do what we can. Look at all the lives we've touched here. Nearly fifty, Gavan! Fifty with the strength to be a Magicker in them. . . ."

He looked at her. "Not enough," he commented. "Not enough for what needs to be done, not enough for what we all face."

"You always were impatient," Eleanora said softly. "It's a beginning. The toddler does not begin to walk without a first step."

"Yes, well . . . we've had to fight for this step. If we stumble, the Council won't fund us for another session. We'll have to return to training one by one . . . and watching the Talented slip through our fingers or be lost to the Dark Hand. She must be frightened, and she's hiding. Hiding so well we can't find a trace of her. In the crystal or out." He sighed and rubbed his forehead, then paused as if listening. Gavan turned his head, staring toward the door. "Do you feel something?"

"Me? Yes, but my nerves have been jangled since we came through the pass!" She twisted around on the desk. "Who's there?" she called out sharply.

Gavan stood up quickly.

But Jason had already pulled back, retreating, hauling Trent behind him. He did not dare even breathe until they were in the normal areas of the Hall. They both gasped for breath, dodged out the side door and into the shadows. Even at that, Jason thought he could hear something moving with them, breathing, and pacing their steps.

They moved slowly, so as not to frighten the crickets into silence or fall over a branch. Back at the cabin, lights having been long turned out all over the camp, they dropped their clothes on the floor and slipped into their bunks. Jason let out a sigh of relief that they had not been short sheeted . . . yet.

He could hear the rustle of Trent settling into his blankets. "What now?" he asked.

"Sleep. See what the morning brings."

If it did not bring Bailey, he would have to do something drastic. Wherever she was, she shouldn't be there. And with every passing moment, it got more dangerous for her. If the Magickers themselves were worried, she should be terrified.

To Catch a Thief

THE brassy sound of Reveille woke them. Jason stretched in his tangled blankets, blinking sleepily at the cabin roof. He could hear Trent grunt as he pounded his pillow and tried to settle back in, but it was hopeless. Gray morning seeped in as did FireAnn's morning yell and pot clanging at those who had invaded her kitchen during the night. He grinned in spite of himself. If not scared away permanently after days of this, the varmints must almost certainly be half deaf by now!

It was Trent who got up first, then smothered a curse as he bumped the table in the near dark of the cabin. "Very funny," he muttered, swiping at the papers which covered the table-top. "Who moved the table? And lookit this." Jason, throwing the shutters open to let what little light there was into the cabin, turned.

"What?"

"Spelling out SOS with my drawing papers! Funny guy." With a half smile, Trent swept up the papers and shuffled them into a short stack.

"What?" Jason stared at his friend.

"SOS. At least, that's what it looked like." Trent looked back, and then in realization, added slowly, "You didn't do it, did you?" He stared at the wooden tabletop. "Maybe I didn't see it the way it was."

"Maybe you did." Jason reached for his clothes uneasily.

Trent snorted. "And maybe if we stand around here all morning, we'll miss hot water and then breakfast!" He grabbed a stack of clean clothes and began shoving them on before dashing out the door a length ahead of Jason. The mess hall was half-empty by the time they sat down at the tables to eat, their hair still wet and slicked down around their ears.

A fog lay over the surface of the lake, and low clouds made the day sullen, but it looked as if the sun would win through shortly. Trent dove in, eating as if he were starved, as usual. Jason stared at his tray. Everything had looked good when he'd chosen it, but he wasn't really all that hungry. The table at the other end was horribly, terribly empty. Not to mention ominously quiet. Someone tapped him on the shoulder. He swung around on the bench to where Henry sat, scraping his fork around his plate.

"What?"

Squibb looked up. "What what?" He squirmed halfway about, and pushed his glasses into place on the bridge of his nose.

"Thought you wanted something."

Henry shook his head. They must have bumped shoulders accidentally. "You're sure?"

Henry ran his hand through his fuzzy black hair, then brightened a little. "Well, actually, yes. I was supposed to tell you Jennifer and Ting already had breakfast and left."

"Is Ting still upset?"

Henry nodded sadly. "Not only with Bailey gone. She says there's a ghost in their cabin."

"Besides the thief?"

"A thief and a ghost? Ting couldn't sleep all night, they said." Henry's eyes got rounder. "Woof." He stood up, tray in hand. "Catch you later," he got out before hurrying off.

"You think there's both?" Trent asked, snapping a crisp piece of bacon in two and devouring it. "Or one making enough noise for two?"

"I don't know. First of all ... the thief has been going through our things, too. But not stealing anything . . . so why just steal

from Kittencurl? I don't get it. And as far as a ghost goes . . .
well, I think it's just nerves, but I don't blame her. I mean, Bailey just vanished. Where did she go? What happened?"

Trent waved his fork around. "Beam me up, Scotty?"

Jason elbowed him. Someone a table or two down snickered, as though they'd heard that also. He lowered his voice.
"We already know there's a lot they haven't told us yet, and
probably a lot they can't tell us. Not yet. And what if we went
home, bragging about camp and why we're so special? They
can't risk that."

"So they're gonna keep us here forever? Camp Brigadoon?
We only wake up every hundred years?"

"No. Of course not. But . . . something."

"We'd cook our own gooses by talking. Someone, somewhere, would want to dissect us for sure. Or burn us at a
stake."

"That won't shut everyone up, and you and I know it. So we
learn, but we're in danger. In danger from what?"

"Ourselves? Other Magickers?"

Jason thought of the whispered comments about the Dark
Hand. Someone or something worried Eleanora. Was it a good
thing or bad thing they had all been gathered into one place
at one time? "Could be both, Trent. Why would only the good
guys survive, you know?"

Jason sat in thought a moment, pushed his French toast
around, had a bite or two, then pushed his tray away. "I've got
an appointment with Dr. Patel before I start classes."

Mouth full and munching away, Trent managed a nod.

Jason felt a little odd going into the back office area of Lake
Wannameecha Hall, unable to detect the quiet heaviness
they'd felt last night. Of course, a lot of things seemed different at night, but he was fairly certain they'd run into a warding
or something magical. He was relieved the eerie and menac-
ing atmosphere was gone this morning.

Anita Patel looked up with a smile as he leaned in the
doorway and knocked, her dark hair smoothed into quiet
wings about her small face, her sari and jacket in soft blues,
tiny mirrors sewn on them reflecting slightly as she shifted her
weight. "Ah, Jason! Come in. Right on time. How is that ankle

feeling?" She patted the cushion next to her as he sat down. He swung his leg up on it, and she unfastened the splints, pulling down the cuff of his sock.

He watched as she probed the mottled flesh with gentle fingertips. The color had gone from purplish to greenish and now was mostly yellowish, and the bruised area was shrinking quickly. It didn't hurt at all.

"You're healing very well."

"Can I take 'em off?"

"I'd say so. Wear them only if you're hiking with Sousa or Jefferson, or maybe canoeing . . . use them when you're doing something really strenuous where you might need the support. Otherwise, I'd say, do your flex exercises, and you should be fine." She smiled. "About time?"

He nodded. "Seems forever. Only four weeks though."

"You heal quickly," the doctor and yoga teacher said quietly. "It is a good thing, and equally lucky you didn't tear a ligament or tendon. Nasty to repair, those are." Her almond eyes considered him. "Now, your hand please."

"My . . . hand?"

"Yes. I'd like to see how that scratch is healing." She paused, waiting.

Reluctantly, he laid his hand on the desktop. She raised a hairline-thin eyebrow, then gathered up his hand. "Healed," she remarked in a very doctorly voice, looking the thin white crescent-shaped scar over carefully. She probed it gently and although he managed not to hiss his breath inward, she must have felt him tighten. "Or is it?" She felt again, gently, and he winced. "Strange. It is still tender, no?"

He nodded.

"I would not worry for another few days. Then, if it still hurts . . . you may have a thorn or splinter from the bushes under there. I will get out my special glasses and take a look, all right?"

"Special glasses?" Lenses with Magick, he wondered?

She pulled open a desk drawer and tapped her goggles headgear. He remembered them, then. She smiled. "Gives me bug eyes!"

He let out a quick laugh in spite of his worry. Would she be sitting there laughing with him if she thought he was seriously

wounded or infected? He tried not to think about it anymore.
"Dr. Patel . . ."

She closed her desk again, still smiling slightly, and tilted
her head, indicating she was listening to him.

"Did you become a doctor before you found out you were
a Magicker?"

"That is quite a story, and one you should hear, but I think
I will save it till some evening at the campfire, now that you
all know what we share." A white envelope shifted on the
desk slightly, skittering close to her hand, and she said, "Oh!
Jason . . . would you mind taking this down to Ting at Kittencurl Cottage? She has a bit of a headache, and these are some
pills for her."

He took the crisp envelope, felt two oblong pills bulging inside it. The phone rang, and with a nod to him, she picked it up.
After listening a moment, she said, "Poison oak? Oh, that can be
nasty. I know there's a big patch of it around here somewhere,
I should ferret it out and mark it. The kids keep getting into it.
FireAnn has cooked up a nice little ointment for that, though,
which should take care of it in a jiffy." She waved at Jason who
got to his feet and began to edge sideways out the door.

While she gave instructions for applying FireAnn's ointment, he ducked his head and left, wondering if that was what
had been cooking in the great pot in the mess hall kitchen for
days. If so, it had to be the best smelling medicine he'd ever
sniffed! The envelope rattled in his fingers as he began to trot
down the path toward the girls' side of the lake. The clouds
had lifted some, leaving the air heavy and damp. Swimming
later would feel good. For that matter, so would canoeing, with
a splash or two.

"Jason! Hey! Wait up!" Jonnard's deep voice rang after
him, and as he paused, the tall boy loped up.

"Trouble?"

"No. I just have something to take over to the other side for
one of the counselors." He shook his envelope.

Jonnard nodded. "Someone not well?"

"Ting's upset over Bailey. Dr. Patel sent her something."

Jonnard nodded. "Let me know if I can do anything."

"Sure thing." He watched as Jason trotted on down the
path, and stood there for a long time. The back of Jason's

shoulder blades prickled for a moment with the knowledge he was being watched. When he reached the far end of the lake and looked back, the other had finally gone.

Ting opened the door very slowly. "Oh, Jason!" She let out a long breath.

"Dr. Patel sent you these." He passed the envelope through the crack in the screen door. "Are you okay?"

She wrinkled her nose. "No, and I'm worried sick about Bailey and . . . something is here." She stepped outside onto the porch, her dark hair swinging about her shoulders, and shivered despite the summer heat. "Well . . . it's not here now. It comes and goes."

"Anything else get stolen?"

"No."

"Look, I'm sorry our trap didn't work."

"Oh—it did. But there was no one there when I got up to check it!" Ting waved a thin hand in puzzlement. "Not a sight of anything. No doors closing, steps, nothing. Just the trap and tin cans scattered everywhere."

Jason beamed. "It worked? Cool. Cookies still there?"

"Gone," Ting said dramatically. "Not a crumb."

Jason blinked. "Gone?" he echoed.

She nodded, and then had to push a wing of raven-dark hair from one eye. Behind them, the screen door banged in the slight breeze, and the Kittencurl sign thudded gently against the cottage. The porch itself creaked as if the wind could walk over it. Ting shivered. She looked back over her shoulder nervously, and her fingers crumpled the envelope he'd given her. "I keep hearing . . . noises," she said hesitantly. "I think the cottage is haunted."

"Can't be. Only place we've heard about is Dead Man's Cabin. Listen, I can't stay, but if you need anything, we'll help all we can, all right?"

Ting nodded slowly. Then she said, "I know you must think I'm foolish. I can't help it. Ghosts are part of my ancestry." She sighed.

"You're not foolish. We'll figure out something to do!" He waved, leaving her standing alone on the porch, hugging one thin arm about herself.

What he was going to do, he had no idea.

* * *

Scheduling at the camp kept him so busy, he almost gave up the idea of thinking. That evening, he plunked down beside Trent at the campfire, tired and yawning. He waved away a charred marshmallow and picked up a stick to toast one for himself.

Trent sneered as he said, "I like mine browned, not burned."

Eleanora was playing her dulcimer as everyone settled in. Then, in the back, Lucy, a stocky girl with brown hair bunched in stubborn pigtails, asked, "Why did Gregory and Brennard fight, anyway? Why did they ruin everything?"

She stilled her strings with the palm of her hand. "No one is quite sure, actually. No one was there but the two of them. It happened something like this...."

"Once upon a time, hundreds of years ago, when civilization was still rather young, two wizards met in a discussion over their beliefs: an old fool, and a young fool."

"Teacher and student," Trent blurted out. Then he twisted his hand on the knee of his jeans.

Eleanora turned to him, the firelight making her face glow as it played over her skin. "Yes," she said, nodding. "That is often the way of it, isn't it?" She smoothed her skirt again. "The young fool claimed Magick was finite. To demonstrate his belief to the master, he held up a pitcher of water and emptied it. 'When it is gone, it is gone!' he claimed triumphantly. His teacher took the pitcher from him and looked into it. 'Of course it is gone,' he said. He took his student by the hand and took him down to the riverside. 'Here is where it is. A pitcher cannot make water, it only holds it. But the seas, the rivers ... are of water themselves, and make water as well as hold it. Although there may be a day when all rivers and oceans dry up, I do not think it will happen for thousands of years, no matter how many times we may dip our pitcher into it to refill it.' And the teacher stepped back, feeling very wise indeed."

Eleanora took a soft breath. "But the student said, 'Then you are still a fool, for if Magick were like water, then any fool could have it and use it!' And he left in a fury. He did not hear the old teacher saying after him, 'But not any fool can see those rivers or fashion a pitcher to carry the element we call Magick.'" Her face creased in a faint wrinkle. "That was not the first of their arguments, nor was it to be their last, but it was perhaps the argument that defined both. It had become clear that Magickers disagreed over the source and care of their ability, and two camps formed. Now, you must understand that the two had been good friends as well as teacher and pupil so the old fool was very hurt by the sudden turn of the other. He had long preached that care must be taken of Magicking for its consequences were not always readily seeable. He worried about Brennard's view of Magick and what it might lead to, and in the years to follow, what he heard worried him even more. Brennard and his followers had found a way to leech the Magick out of a person, draining them dry forever. The shock of it left many near death. And why do it? Could Brennard not find the ley lines? Could he not sense the mana which lay about for his use? True, the pockets and troves of mana were not always easily findable, but they *were* there. No need to steal and harm another! Gregory grew deeply troubled. As teacher, and generally regarded leader of the Magickers, it was his duty to stop misdoings. So he challenged Brennard to a duel."

A murmur of surprise ran through the campers. Eleanora waited till they quieted before continuing. "They met in a remote area so as not to harm others by their actions but—" She paused, then shook her head. "No, that is getting ahead of myself. Just remember what I said about . . . consequences."

She inhaled, lacing her fingers together and sliding them over one knee. "A great duel commenced. It became clear that all Brennard had been accused of, and more, was true. He attacked Gregory vigorously, first trying to weaken him enough to drain his Magick and then, when that failed, launched an all-out attack to kill him.

"Dark deeds and disdain were bad enough, but murderous intents shook Gregory down to his core, and soon he knew he was in a fight for his life . . . and the lives of all Magickers who opposed Brennard. Gregory, it is supposed, decided that it was kill or be killed, though killing was beyond his beliefs."

Someone let out a tiny gasp. Eleanora paused but did not stop talking. "Because he would not murder another, he did something more . . . interesting. He bonded himself to Brennard, bonded himself so closely that whatever Brennard did to

Gregory returned on himself, hoping he could stop his pupil that way.

"But Brennard would not be slowed. He had a mission, you see, to keep Magick from being burned out and becoming extinct forever. He would take the fight to the end!" Eleanora inhaled deeply again, her face pale, her eyes very bright. "Then Brennard lashed out with all of his strength to fell Gregory, once and for all! With that blow, he destroyed the Magickers as we knew them."

A hush fell over the gathering, disturbed only by the snap and pop of a pine cone or two amongst the bonfire logs.

"The shock of that attack slew Gregory and sent Brennard into a deep, deep coma. Magickers all over felt the final attack. Some died of the echoes of that blow. Most fell into a coma themselves from the shock, and many died from that, their families unknowing of where they were or how to protect them. Some were thrown across time, those that were closest to both of the wizards. Whatever happened to them then, one thing has become clear now. Magick was lost for centuries. Only now is it being reclaimed, and the same two factions still argue about its properties. We do know this . . . there are those on both sides who will stop at nothing to prove themselves right, and the others wrong."

She paused, as Tomaz Crowfeather stepped forward to scatter the coals of the burned-down campfire. "Nothing," she repeated.

15

White as a Ghost

JASON woke at midnight. Shivering despite the summer heat, the camp quiet except for crickets and katydids, his blankets were knotted and thrown aside as if he'd been wrestling with them. He took a deep breath, then sat up. His pulse roared in his ears like high surf at the beach. He could not remember the dream this time. Only that he had fought it. Across the room, Trent breathed hard and moved about restlessly, but did not awaken.

Jason watched him briefly in the dim light. It looked as though Trent might be having nightmares as well, dreaming just like he did, but not remembering the next day. Or perhaps not fully dreaming the terror. Was there something about the other campers that kept them safe from what he had just gone through?

He rubbed sleep from his eyes, not willing to lie back down just yet. He stood up and went to the door, and opened it, just leaving the screen door shut. The porch creaked slightly. He put his nose to the screen to see out. Nothing could be seen in the moonlight-streaked night . . . or at least, nothing but the porch with its heavily shadowed corners. He heard a grunt.

Jason squinted through the cross-grained screen. Two

hunched-over figures passed, not on the walkway, but through the fringe of trees and shrubbery bordering it. He couldn't see their faces clearly, but he recognized the heavy-shouldered one by the way he walked. What were they even doing up? Where were Stefan and Rich going this time of night? They'd already bypassed Squibb, their favorite target. Stefan seemed to be carrying something heavy, pressed against his chest.

"You're sure that's what this is?"

Rich laughed low. "You can't tell? I can smell it through the wrapping paper. Soon as we get there, we'll look it over, but I can tell you . . . my cousin sent me what he said he would!"

"You're going to need to hide this."

"Everyone around here is too nosy. I've got an idea anyway."

"How much farther?" A yawn muffled the rest of Stefan's words.

They disappeared into the brush, but the crackle and heavy breathing told Jason which way they were headed. He hesitated, then grabbed a pair of hiking shorts and shoved his feet into his tennis shoes. He wanted to know what they were carrying about. What could be smelled through its wrapper? Food? Candy, perhaps? The thought made his mouth water. He slipped into the night after them.

Like grasping hands, shrubs and branches seemed to grab at him as he wiggled past, hoping for silence. A twig snapped under his foot, and he froze, but from the heavy breathing and grunting of Stefan to Rich, he did not think they'd heard him.

But something else had. He heard a movement behind him. Quiet. A soft panting. It stopped when he did. Jason looked back over his shoulder uneasily. He saw nothing but shadows and brush, and yet. . . .

Stefan and Rich trundled off again, in another direction, this time with a wavering yellow beam in front of them. It barely cut through the thickness of the night, but he knew where they were heading, the old boathouse down by the landing in the shallow end of the lake. He set off after them, not wanting to be discovered, but knowing that if he were being trailed in turn, he dared not stand around alone in the dark. Feeling jumpy, the hairs standing up on his arms, he trotted after the two, not so quietly as quickly now. He thought he could hear something trailing him even as he slowly caught up to the other two.

. With a last pulse of their fading flashlight, the boys disappeared into the weathered boathouse. Jason glanced up at the overhead string of tiny white lights, barely enough to outline the building. He crept to the door that hung permanently ajar, its wood warped by many summers and winters near the lake. The light inside was pale and rippled as though underwater. He scrubbed at his eyes to see more clearly. Rich was tearing off string and paper, exposing the long, deep cardboard box.

"Wait," he said, his copper hair gleaming in the half-light. "Wait until you see these babies!" Paper crackled about his ankles as he dropped the box and leaned over it.

Stefan let his breath out in a long hiss. "Oh, man," he breathed. He hunched his heavy shoulders as he squatted down, broad face split in a wide grin.

Jason squinted, unable to see into the box. What was it they had?

Rich rummaged around and then brought up a string of tiny cylinders hooked together. Jason blinked. Firecrackers?

Rich grinned. "I'd like to set these babies off now . . . right under Rainwater! Snap, crackle, bang!" He gave a low laugh.

"Bottle rockets, fountains . . . and—*sweet,* cherry bombs!" Stefan sounded as if he could hug the box. "You've got a treasure here."

"One we need to hide."

Jason watched the two as they continued to paw through their booty until even he could smell the faint aroma of sulfur from the fireworks. The two he watched drew closer together and their voices became muffled as they discussed their plans. He leaned a bit more. He could almost . . . but not quite . . . hear.

Something spidery brushed against him. Jason spun around! He sucked his breath in as he looked—and saw nothing.

But something had been there. Maybe for the barest of moments. He breathed in slowly. Could he smell it, if it had been animal? Nothing but the vaguely sweet smell of the night-blooming flowers, and the crushed scent of the needles and greenery about him. He inhaled again, and pressed himself back to the building. Suddenly the door swung open.

Jason dropped. Chin buried in the dust, fighting to keep from sneezing, he lay on the ground as the door banged wide open in front of him. All he could see of Stefan and Rich were their battered shoes.

"That's agreed, then?"

"Best place to hide something is under their noses," Rich said smugly. "And no getting into it early. Either one of us sets 'em off early, we'll get caught. I've plans," he cautioned. "Big plans."

Jason watched them shuffle past. So did he. He got to his feet when they were just out of earshot and followed quickly. Something snatched at the pockets of his shorts as he brushed past a gnarled tree and he dropped his hand to shake off the branch, only to find nothing there. With a frown, Jason hurried to catch up.

With the strung lights growing ever more dim as if the night itself were trying to snuff them out, the three boys made their way back to Lake Wannameecha Hall, Jason only a few steps behind and still in hiding. He caught his breath as he saw them enter the hall near the rear offices. Should he warn them? Should he follow them in, knowing the wards that stood on guard duty?

After a long second, Jason ducked inside warily. He heard the crisp sound of paper and headed in that direction, rounding a corner nearly skidding into them, but he caught himself in time. Scarcely breathing, he plastered himself to the wall. The brown, paper-wrapped package crinkled again, echoed by a grunt.

"There," Rich whispered loud enough for Jason to catch. "In the emergency supplies. Unless there's an emergency, no one would even think of looking there."

"Good enough." Another grunt, then the creak of a door being shut stealthily. "I can hardly wait!"

"Me neither. Let's get out of here. This place is giving me the creeps."

Jason slipped down the hall and around another bend, into the shadows. He waited until they had gone before creeping out. With a quick look around, and the dread of the wards on him, he found the supply closet marked "emergency" and opened it slowly. The plain brown package had been shoved all the way into the back, on the bottom shelf. He crawled in on hands and knees, opening it carefully. Four strings of fire-crackers lay among the goods. He eased one out, tucked it inside his shirt, closed the box up again, and crept back out.

Low words caught his attention. He hesitated, knowing that he could be caught at any moment. He dipped his fingers in his pocket, to stroke the crystal that had already become like a friend to him, and found his pocket empty. He caught his breath, then remembered he'd left it out to switch it to clean clothing in the morning. Another word, louder, and one he knew: Bailey.

That gave him little choice. He *had* to know who was talking about the missing girl. Pressing close to the wall, he edged closer and closer to the speakers until he could distinguish the voices beyond just vibrating tones: Tomaz, Eleanora, and Gavan.

". . . time is now the enemy."

Jason peeked through the office window. The blind had been drawn, but there was a tiny slit of light showing through. He put one eye to it, seeing Tomaz's sleeve, and part of Eleanora's worried face, and the restless wolfhead of Gavan's cane, moving up and down and back and forth like his teacher might tap a pencil nervously.

"I'm open to suggestions." Gavan sounded weary though his cane stayed active.

"I haven't any." Eleanora rested her chin in her hands. It seemed to be her desk she sat at, the chair behind her was plum velvet and winged slightly. It fit her. "With every moment, we lose hope of tracing her through the amethyst."

Tomaz said, "What if she does not wish to be found?"

Eleanora's face tilted up. "Don't even say such a thing."

"It would explain why we can't."

She shook her head. "Yes and no. The crystals are complicated . . ."

Gavan interrupted, saying, "That's why I asked for your help, Tomaz. Because we're awakened, we know a bit more about the crystals. But you've spent your whole life as a Magicker, and you know this world—" He tapped his cane, "—better than we ever could."

"I think she's gone home," said Eleanora. "But she's afraid

to show herself because she knows she hasn't got a good explanation. Bailey is sharp and Talented. And she loves her mother dearly. It's just the two of them."

"So, then. I need to go and coax her out, it looks like."

Eleanora said faintly, "If I'm right."

"And if you're not?"

Eleanora had held something in her hand. She laid her hand on the desk and slowly uncurled her fingers. The amethyst lay on her palm. Its brilliant purple color had begun to dull. She tried to speak, choked, and could not.

"If she's trapped in the crystal itself, Ellie, I'll bring her back. You know that." Gavan leaned into the tiny frame of Jason's view. He hugged Eleanora.

"But will it be in time?"

He shook his head. "We can't know that. All we know is if I go in there looking for her and she is *not* trapped within, with my strength, I could pull her in and she'd be even more lost."

Tomaz said mildly, "Perhaps we should have introduced the crystals later in the summer."

"No. No, if Magickers are to grow and learn how to protect themselves, they must learn their crystals. It comes before anything else." Eleanora sighed. "And there are other matters. Two. One, there is a thief about the camp. A petty, annoying thief."

"What?" The wolfhead cane was tossed in the air and caught by a tight-knuckled hand. "Why wasn't I told earlier?"

"Because virtually nothing has been stolen; things have just been rifled through . . . disturbed. Except for the Kittencurl and Rosebriar Cottages, which are on my side of the lake, right next to each other. Small personal items of little consequence were taken from each. The only thing of any real value was Ting's wristwatch, and it's an inexpensive one from what I understand."

"Of no importance, then." Gavan sounded impatient. "Set up a charm or two, the thief will be deterred."

Tomaz shifted, and for a moment, his denim-clad back hid Eleanora from view. "I differ on that."

"Why? We've worse problems to deal with."

"Maybe, maybe not. Personal items can be used to make fetishes and such. That is a magic in the world I come from.

It is like stealing a bit of yourself, to turn against you." Tomaz moved again, and this time Jason could see Gavan, looking in Tomaz's direction, then biting his lip in thought.

"Interesting."

Eleanora echoed, "Very."

"Well, then. We can't have that." Gavan rubbed the bridge of his nose. "Can it wait until after you look for Bailey?"

"As long as the thief doesn't leave camp, sure." Tomaz nodded, his ponytail bobbing like liquid black smoke upon his back.

"All right. We'll deal with that, then. What else, Eleanora?"

"We've a Ghost."

The cane thumped the floor like a gunshot. "Now that, I will not allow. Not here, not now. We're working hard enough to shield them from the nightmares, and their own stray abuses of Talent. I will not tolerate a noncorporeal presence here, leeching on them before they're strong enough to know what they're dealing with!" Gavan leaped to his feet. "That, you and I can deal with."

"A Ritual?"

"A Ritual indeed. There will be nothing left of that Ghost when I'm through with him!" He tucked his cane under his arm. "Tomaz, come with me to my office. I'll give you the particulars on Bailey, and the sooner you leave the better." He kissed Eleanora on the forehead. "I'll see you in the morning, and we'll have the Ghost done for by midnight tomorrow." Gavan began to stride toward the door and Jason.

He sprinted for the exit door of the Hall, and gulped for breath once outside. Now he had a hiding place of his own to find.

Ducking his head, Jason hurried back to the cabin. He ran with the strength of old, his ankle barely tender, swift and sure through the darkness. It felt good to stretch out, as though he had been cramped and contained for a long time. His footsteps fell in a quiet rhythm and he imagined himself a ghost, running unseen through the cooling summer air.

Fingers pinched at his sleeve. Jason twisted his head, swerving. Nothing but air around him, and evergreens with heavy-needled branches. He swerved again, with a cold shiver snaking down his spine. What was it? Was Ting right? Did a ghost indeed haunt this camp? A ghost powerful enough to worry Gavan and the others? He spun around and saw nothing, not a thing. He gasped for breath and stood very still, shivering.

Then, off to his left, toward the lake, he spied the gleaming reflection of a green eye. Jason inhaled, turned, and ran for his life. He gained his porch in one leap. His ankle gave a slight tweak as he fumbled at the latch and then shut the cabin door heavily behind him. He thought he heard and felt a thump as a heavy body hit the door after him. Panting, he dropped the latch bolt into place and waited to see if anything else could be heard.

A shuffling, dragging sound came across the porch. It stopped. Started. Stopped again. Rather like Jason's heartbeat. He took a deep breath, went to the nearest shuttered window, and opened it.

It did not notice as he looked out, a gray-and-silver possum, with two tiny babies clinging to her underbelly. She had part of an orange clutched in her front paw, and her crabbed movement across the porch was hampered by her treasure. He heaved a sigh of relief as he fastened the shutter back into position.

Trent stirred in his bed. Jason quickly pulled the string of crackers from his shirt, and tucked them between the mattress and platform. Depending on what Gavan and Eleanora did, his theft might be useless. Or it could be just what the doctor ordered.

He fell onto his bed and slipped into a long, dreamless sleep.

In the morning, Jefferson took over the canoeing class. He waded into the lake, his skin shining darkly in contrast to his white shirt and shorts, and picked Henry Squibb up by the scruff of the neck at least twice, righting the canoe and putting him back in. Then, with a splash and a laugh, Danno and Henry finally managed to paddle away from shore without capsizing. Trent grinned and led Jason in a circle with their canoe, the two of them paddling gracefully in tandem in their craft, while Henry and Danno, laughing, flailed about in theirs. At the last, Henry discovered he could splash with his oar, if not guide the canoe well, and everyone ended up as drenched as if they'd capsized, too.

Jefferson stood on the beach, his muscular arms folded across his chest, and smiled.

Then they had another Crystal Class.

Eleanora paused at the front of the tables. "First," she said, "I would like to talk to you about the care of your crystals and quartzes. We had selected a wide variety for you to choose from. Most are rock crystal, which gives you a nice arrangement of planes and facets to focus through. Like anything you use constantly, they can get dirty, oiled from coatings on your hands, and so on. We recommend using only plain water to clean them. Occasionally, water with sea salt. Nothing stronger or different. Your crystals can react with certain other liquids in some cases, or even be dissolved by them. Understood? Plain water, a soft cloth." Eleanora smiled.

Rich's hand shot up, and she nodded at him. "Can we be allergic to our crystals?"

"Not in this state, I believe. Are you having any reactions?"

He shook his head slowly, looking dubious.

"No welts or itching?"

Rich shook his head again.

"Then you're fine. Any other questions?"

Rich's hand shot up again. Eleanora looked at him again.

"Can they make you do things? Like, you know, have strange cravings?"

"Like chocolate, for example?"

Jason grinned as the girls all giggled. Rich squirmed. "Not like that, but—"

"Like what?"

"I don't know, but . . . what's to keep us from disappearing like Bailey did?"

"Common sense, I hope. We'll have Miss Landau in hand very shortly. In the meantime, nothing should go amiss."

Trent muttered out of the side of his mouth. "Little late for that. We've already got a miss missing."

Jason bit the inside of his mouth to keep from snorting and drowning out Eleanora's talk.

"My suggestion is that you copy down all the strange things

you're worried about and make an appointment to meet with me in my office later."

Rich paled and shut his mouth tightly. He squirmed as if he wished to say more. Eleanora watched him silently with one eyebrow arched. Evidently deciding not to take the dare, he kept quiet.

"Now, then." She smiled brightly. "Today we're going to learn one of the fundamental benefits of having a crystal, one of its nicest functions." She held hers up, smiled, spoke a word, and a soft golden light flared out, visible even in the sunlit day.

Ting leaned forward on her elbows. "Wow," she said softly.

"You wouldn't be afraid of the dark," Jennifer said to her. She patted Ting's shoulder.

"How do you *do* that?" Trent breathed at Jason's shoulder. He had his crystal out, but his gaze was fixed intently on Eleanora, and he was rolling his stone through his fingers without noticing it.

The light spilled through the Magicker's fingers like a waterfall of gold, cool to the touch, Jason guessed, but glowing as warm as firelight. He looked at his crystal, wondering how she did it.

"Focus," Eleanora said. She moved her hand over her crystal, and the light went out. "Focus into your crystal, find the plane you feel most comfortable on . . . the facet you can see easiest and you can handle . . . and I want you to build a flame there. Think it, imagine it." She passed along the tables as Jason got his out and palmed it. "That's it, Jason." She raised her voice. "Hold your crystal to Focus on it. It's bonded to you and attuned to you. Setting it on a table or desk and looking at it will not activate it."

There was a stir all around as the others got out their crystals, digging into pockets everywhere. Henry dropped his with a dismayed squeak, bent over to pick it up, let out a howl when Stefan gave him a wedgie, danced around a bit getting his underwear unknotted, and dropped his crystal a second time. Finally, he stood somewhat quietly, round face very red, hair sticking up all over, and eyes blinking behind the round lenses of his spectacles. He cupped his crystal fiercely, moving to put Danno and Jon between him and the rest of the class.

Ting and Jennifer bumped shoulders, trying hard not to giggle, as they held their crystals, hands wiggling as they suppressed their laughter with a muffled snort. Ting's rock crystal held a pleasant pink tinge to it. Jason could not help but notice the two girls, their noses wrinkling in concentration as they stared. Jennifer's blonde hair swung forward, like a fine golden curtain, covering part of her face as she ducked her chin and looked down at her hand.

A pang went through him for the missing Bailey. Trent's comment aside, he fretted over the fact that the Magickers seemed to have no idea what had happened except that they seemed somewhat unconcerned in front of everyone but sounded worried when they thought they were unobserved. Crystals and *poofing* Magickers did not seem to be entirely unexpected though. Wishing he knew what they did, he stared down into his crystal and tried to keep to the subject at hand. Or, in his hand, as it was. Having an object that could light up like a flashlight, with no batteries needed, would be great, he had to admit.

The cool depths of his crystal seemed an unlikely place to hold fire or light, though. He tried to project a spark onto its surface, only to lose the glint over and over. Like a snowflake melting, it would fade before he could build it into a larger glow, even as he frowned and stared until he could feel a dull, throbbing headache pain between his brows. Pressure descended till he felt like he had an elephant standing on his head.

Looking away, Jason rubbed his eyes. Across from him, Ting's crystal hummed in a rosy glow, her face rapt as she stared at it. Jennifer's pale rock also glowed, with a strong, silvery light that rayed brightly across her hand. Ting's almond eyes widened slightly. "It's . . . getting warm . . ." she said, alarmed. Her hand jerked as though she might toss it, but before she could, a ker-RACK! split the air, and her crystal shattered into pieces. She let out a startled squeak.

Jennifer immediately grabbed her wrist. "Oh, Ting!" she said in dismay. "Your crystal."

Eleanora hurried over, saying, "Don't worry, these things happen. We can find you another—" and she stopped, staring at the pieces in Ting's hand. "Well," she said finally. "I've seen that before but not often." She stirred through the fragments with a gentle fingertip. "Usually they darken, and go lifeless. However, yours, Ting, still hold the light." She smiled. "Keep them, they might be useful someday. In the meantime, we've got to get you a replacement! Jennifer, why don't you snuff your lantern and take her to Master Rainwater's office in the Gathering Hall, and he'll pick out another." She looked around. "Is anyone else having success in getting their lantern focused? Don't be discouraged. It takes time."

Jon held his palm up, where his green citrine cast an eerie light green light over the table. She nodded at him, unsurprised.

Jason rubbed his nose, hard, where an itch seemed to be succeeding far more than his concentration on his crystal. He scrubbed it again, to keep the itch from coming back, and stared down at his crystal. A little twinkle flared and flickered about, almost like a fairy light. Like a small spark in a heavy wind, it threatened to go out. He cupped his hands about the crystal, sheltering it, willing it to just *be. Stay . . . stay!*

Danno, at his back, let out a startled exclamation, "Madre de Dios!" and Henry Squibb gave an excited yelp.

Jason whirled around just in time to see Henry's crystal flare like a nova with light and then shoot into skyrocketing flames! He leaped onto one foot, howling, then dropped his crystal into the dust. The light immediately went out but it took all three of them—Jon, Danno, and Henry—to kick dust over the flames and put the crystal out.

Eleanora stood in puzzlement a moment, her face white. "Now that," she said, "is something I've never seen." She went to Henry and took his hands. "Are you burned?"

"I . . . I . . . don't think so." Henry shook all over, then straightened. "Well, maybe a little."

She nodded, looking over his reddened palm. "Not badly, but I still think you should see Dr. Patel. Off with you . . ." She paused as Henry trotted off a few steps. "Henry."

"Yes'm?" He turned around, blinking owlishly through his glasses.

"Your crystal, Henry."

He took a deep breath and came back to a dirty lump. "What if it . . . what if it . . . ?"

"You are its master, Henry, not the other way around."

He nodded, and picked it up, dusting it off. Not a singe on it. With a half-smile of relief, he pocketed it, then turned again to trot down to Dr. Patel's quarters.

She let them Focus for another ten or fifteen minutes before holding her hands up, saying, "I think that's enough for today, class. You may have some headaches and crossed eyes from the concentration, that's normal. A nice walk in the brisk air should take care of that! Good work, everyone."

Nobody else had gotten his or her crystal firmly glowing yet, although Jason felt he was very close. Eleanora paused by the end of their table. "How did you do, Trent?"

He shrugged. "Not very well. I mean, it got clearer on me, more transparent, but that's about it."

"Interesting. Actually, with that stone, it's quite a bit. It's . . ." she paused. "It's stubborn."

"Good! 'Cause I am, too."

She nodded, and then her gaze fell on Jason. "Jason, you look unhappy."

"It just kept slipping away." He flexed his hands, surprisingly tense and tight after cradling his crystal.

"It'll come. It shouldn't be easy, making cold fire, don't you think?" She smiled slightly, then glided past to the next group of students.

"Nothing," whispered Trent in Jason's ear as they hurried for break and to make it to FireAnn's herbal class, "is easy about this."

Jason nodded, matching strides with Trent's lope. The only great thing about the afternoon was knowing that Bailey, at least, hadn't disappeared in an eruption of flame!

At dinnertime, Ting came late, and slid into line between Jason and Trent, a worried look on her face.

"What's wrong?" Jason said softly.

"Something very strange," she whispered back. "Our thief left a note. Or, at least, I think he did."

"What?"

"Cookie crumbs. I stumbled over them, but . . . but I'd swear they spelled out 'Help me'."

Trent coughed. "A thief who asks for help?"

She nodded. "I know it sounds weird."

"Why not a pen and ink?"

Ting shrugged. "I don't know. I don't even know if . . . if the crumbs really spelled anything out. It just looked like it to me."

"Can you show us after dinner?"

With a faint blush, Ting shook her head. "Gone. Something ate them. It was while you guys were at canoeing, and I came to get you, but you were out on the lake. By the time I got back to Kittencurl, everything was gone."

Jason let out a sigh of regret.

Trent shuffled ahead in line and waited till they caught up before remarking. "There are people like that, you know. People who can't keep from stealing. Maybe it's someone like that."

"And that's why they asked for help?" Ting looked at him, doubt in her almond eyes.

"Won't know till we catch him, will we? But it's something to think about."

"Well . . . I set the trap again. I added a few more tin cans. We ought to catch *something*," Ting vowed. "Only I'd rather you guys were there when it happened."

"What about Jennifer?"

"She's got another counselor meeting tonight." Ting looked around then ducked her head, her voice getting even more quiet. "I took a look at her notes. She's getting advanced Magick training in those sessions, too."

"Oh, really?"

"That's what it looked like."

Trent looked almost as interested as Jason felt. The corner of his mouth went up. "I'll ask Henry about Jonnard. Squibb couldn't keep a secret if his life depended on it." As Jason and Ting laughed, Trent found himself at the head of the serving line and boldly went to pile up food on his plate.

Ting shook her head. "I don't know how he does it," she murmured to Jason. "He eats so much!"

"He's got one of those bodies that burns it up. He doesn't even lie still at night," he told her.

She nodded before stepping forward herself to get plate, utensils, and napkins.

Jason got some carrot and raisin salad and regular green

salad before stopping in line and looking at a great tray of
Mulligatawny. It looked like nothing he'd ever seen before, its
aroma intriguing and spicy. He stared at the dinner selection
in fascination while, ahead of him, Ting swerved past it to get
some spaghetti which looked ordinary compared to the fragrant dish. Trent beckoned to him.

"Get some rice and spoon that over. It's like a . . . a spicy
stew. Try some!"

Jason hesitated again. Then, he took Trent's advice, and
added bread and fruit as well as dessert (no gelatin of any
kind, thank you!) in case the Mulligatawny was awful. Once
spooned over the rice, he could see chunks of meat and onion
and some other vegetables in a rich, golden brown broth more
clearly. It smelled intriguing. Behind him, he could hear equal
discussions of fascination over the dish, including Rich who
said, "God! She's trying to kill me."

Stefan snickered. "Then you don't hafta eat it, do you? Just
get the chicken noodle soup or something. Jeez, what a wuss.
Looks good to me."

"Stef, anything looks good to you. If it doesn't gobble you
down first, you gobble it down." Rich grumbled another word
or two before Jason left the crowd behind as he headed to
their table.

Jennifer was just finishing and standing up. She leaned
over to give Ting a half hug. "I've got sessions tonight, don't
forget!"

"I know."

"Want me to send someone over to keep you company?"
Jennifer asked, her well-glossed lips turned up in a hesitant
smile.

"I'll just read for a while. I'm kind of tired, actually."

"Okay. I'll try to come in quietly, in case you fall asleep."
Jennifer allowed herself to smile then, and was gone with a
toss of her blonde head. Trent watched her leave before digging into his dinner.

"Interesting," was all he said.

Jason knew better. He knew what kinds of wheels were
turning when Trent said something like that. "What is?"

"She's wearing her crystal like a pendant, around her neck.
Didn't you see?"

Jason shook his head, but he felt a touch of envy for a moment. As Ting had noted, advanced lessons. Not that he wanted to wear his stone in a girlish necklace about his neck, but ... what was she learning that they hadn't had a chance to yet? What wonders of Magick?

Caught up in his own thoughts, he scarcely noticed the first few rich bites of the Mulligatawny stew. Then, his mouth bursting with the flavor, spicy and rich, and the warmth of the tender meat and gravy, toned down by the rice, he noticed his dinner and dug in. The chilled salads cooled his tongue back down, but he decided he liked this markedly different food.

While they were all eating, Sousa appeared at the doorway, cornet in his hand. "No campfire tonight," he announced, much to the dismay of everyone who enjoyed the nightly meets. He put his hand up to quiet the protests. He looked about the mess hall. "It's important tonight that you be safely in your assigned housing so we know where you are. I promise you that tomorrow night, we'll have a tale of adventure to tell you and I think FireAnn promised fresh-baked chocolate chip cookies and brownies for all."

The campers cheered at that. Sousa tooted a cheery bar or two in return and left, while the murmurs of the curious rose again.

"What do you think that was all about?" Trent mopped up the last of his Mulligatawny with a slice of bread.

Jason thought he knew. The Ritual that Gavan had promised Eleanora ... by midnight, and whatever that Ritual was, it must be dire, even dangerous. He couldn't say, "I don't know," so he just ducked his head and concentrated on finishing his carrot and raisin salad.

Ting chewed on a fingernail. "You two are still coming by, aren't you?"

Trent and Jason swapped looks. "Sure," Jason returned even as Trent said, "Better not."

They looked at each other again.

"But—" they said in unison.

Her face crumpled slightly in worry.

"All right," they said together.

Ting managed a smile.

*   *   *

Outside, after dinner, Jason punched Trent in the shoulder. "What was that about? I thought you were fearless."

Trent screwed up his face a bit and shrugged. "I've got my reasons. This isn't just any camp, you know? This is one you can't afford to get thrown out of, if you want to know who you are and what you can do." He stopped in his tracks. "Listen, I'll see you later. I've got some laundry to do before bedtime." He headed off in the opposition direction, leaving Jason standing baffled and alone.

He was still alone when the time came for Lights Out, because Trent had come in and gone to bed without a word and now snored lightly. Jason fidgeted a moment, remembered what he had promised Ting, and withdrew the string of fire-crackers from under his bunk, tucking them inside his wind-breaker jacket. He took the box of matches from the window seat drawer, left there to light candles in an emergency. How long they'd been left there, he had no idea. He hoped they would still strike and light quickly.

Like a slim shadow, Ting waited for him in the corner of the porch, her back to the cottage outer wall. "Where's Trent?" she asked quietly, her eyes turning down a bit in disappointment.

"Fell asleep. I couldn't wake him."

"Oh."

"Hey. I'm here."

She smiled slightly. "Yes, you are!" She dropped her voice to an even lower whisper. "Sessions were cancelled tonight, Jennifer is reading. What do you think is going on?"

He shook his head. "All I know is . . . you need to go to bed, with Lights Out. Everyone needs to be quiet and seemingly asleep before he makes his move. I'll be out here. I've got something guaranteed to scare off your Ghost . . . and probably your thief, too!"

"What?" Her eyes widened.

"Don't worry about it. But I guarantee, you'll know it when it happens, and it's in the best Chinese tradition."

Eyes still wondering, Ting moved back inside the cottage and there was a faint click as she slid the bolt into place. Jason moved around to the rear of the cottage, where he sat down in a bush and tried not to think about the various things that crawled about, whether it was night or day, and waited. Even as he tried to ignore it, it felt like a dozen of them were crawling over his ankles or arms. He fought not to scratch. Instead, to keep his mind off the tiny creatures tickling across his skin, he began to think about the thief, the Ghost and the strange things that had been happening.

He heard the Magickers as they came up the back slope of the cottages, chanting. Jason bit his lip. They would catch him, for sure. He wasn't certain what they'd do for catching him a second time, but it couldn't be good. He hugged his arms around his legs and tried to feel invisible.

The words sang out and caught Jason, pulling at him. He could hear Gavan's pleasant tenor tones, and the lovely voices of Eleanora, and Dr. Patel, and the slightly off-key and deeper voice of FireAnn. They paused a moment, and then Eleanora said, pleased, "That wards the cottage. Nice harmony. The girls should sleep right through." They ringed the clearing nearest Kittencurl, and then the dark seemed to mask them from sight. He rubbed his eyes as they began to recite strange words again. Their chanting made him sleepy and he fought to listen, to keep his eyes open. When he finally understood their words, what he heard chilled his blood.

The Ritual was irresistible. It tugged at his own thoughts and soul, threatened to send him away—except he belonged here, *he did,* and Jason anchored himself to that while a cold, hard Banshee wailed about and plucked at him. Tugged at his collar and sleeve, promising, then threatening to take him away, or to banish him.

He blinked, hard, as they stood in a circle, candles in their hands, their voices growing louder and faster. He tried to breathe, and could not, unless it was in time to their chanting. He felt dizzy.

"Be gone!" commanded Gavan.

Jason's heart thumped hard in his chest. He put a hand out to the ground and dug his fingers in. He was no Ghost! Yet . . .

Eleanora began chanting again. He was able to take a breath. He curled his other hand about his crystal, and as its edges pressed roughly into his skin, he felt a bit better.

"Be gone!" commanded Gavan again.

Jason's whole body quivered, in spite of himself. And then,

and then, out of the corner of his eye, he saw a pale scrap. A wavering glimpse of . . . something . . . being pulled out by the Ritual.

He stared as he saw it flicker.

"Come no more to this reality, this plane, this time, this earth!" recited Gavan. He took a deep breath. He was going to chant, "Be gone!" for the third and last time. Jason knew it. And that would be the last of the Ghost.

He blinked as it paused by him, stretched out an imploring hand. He knew that wisp, that scrap of existence!

His body felt like lead, fastened to the earth, anchored there so the Ritual could not sweep him away. He'd chained himself there. Jason took a breath, tried to stand, and couldn't.

"Wait!" He gulped for breath and yelled again. "No! Wait!"

Then, as the Magickers turned to look at him, and Gavan Rainwater frowned in a thunderous expression, he blurted out, "Stop! Bailey's the Ghost!"

16

Lions and Tigers and Bears, Oh, My!

"WHAT?" Eleanora turned on him, candlelight reflecting her pale, shocked face.

But nothing was as pale as the wispy being before him. He grabbed at it, feeling something spidery tingling across the skin but not Bailey's hand . . . if it was Bailey, and it had to be, he could think of no one else!

"Gavan! Quickly, the crystal! Before we drive her into the other plane and lose her entirely." The flame on her candle shook as Eleanora's hands trembled.

"Don't be taken in, Eleanora. Haunts can be very devious." Gavan frowned heavily.

Jason stood still, watching the ethereal mist gather round him. "Bailey?" he asked quietly. The wind sighed around him.

"If it be our lost lass," FireAnn said softly, "she might be forgettin' who she is. A Ghostly existence is not an easy one." She reached over and gently took Eleanora's candle from her, adding, "Before you spill wax all over or burn yourself."

Dr. Patel watched Jason with a slight frown. She wore her sari with a matching shawl covering her sleek head, its edge hemmed in silvery thread that sparkled in the moonlight. "Are you all right, Jason?"

"Yes. It—it just made me feel very weird for a moment or two."

"Understandable. This is not a Magick for the unprepared." She smiled slightly, and he felt a comfort emanating from her, cool and dry and efficient. "You'll let me know if you worsen?"

"I will." He thought a moment, then dug his hand into his windbreaker. A chocolate chip cookie came back out. Slightly stale, from dinner before last, he'd forgotten he'd put one aside for later. He held his hand out, palm flat. "Bailey, I know you've gotta be hungry."

"Jason—" Eleanora said in warning, then halted as Gavan unwrapped the amethyst crystal from his silk handkerchief. He took her hand and cupped it with his, their warm flesh enveloping the purple stone. She let out a soft sound of dismay.

Gavan shook his head as he looked into her face. "I can't tell if it's her, and we can't afford to be wrong. To stop the Ritual now means we may not be able to deal with the Ghost later, it will have grown too strong."

"But if it's Bailey, we can't banish her!"

The pale fog shimmering around Jason seemed to thicken, gathering, until the outline was about his height, and definitely that of a person. He bounced the cookie on his palm. "It's chocolate chip," he coaxed.

The night gave a soft moan.

The sound made the hairs on the back of his neck stand up straight, and he fought not to shiver.

"Poor dear," said Anita Patel, looking about with concern. She pushed her shawl from her head, dropping it around her shoulders. "I think the boy is right. I can sense her aura."

FireAnn held her two candles high. After a moment, disappointment rode her face. "I canna tell."

Gavan took a deep breath. He looked down into Eleanora's face as she wavered a bit, bobbing slightly up and down as if her strength were taxed. "I'll do it," he said. "But if it is not Bailey . . ."

"I'll do what I can for you," she said quietly.

He nodded. Then Gavan Rainwater closed his eyes, and

tightened his hands over hers and the crystal, and a look of intense concentration crossed his face. The tiny lines at the corners of his eyelids deepened, as did the ones near his mouth. His jaw tightened.

A wind picked up, off the lake, chill and brisk. The trees around them ruffled. Jason stood uncertainly, as the fog near him seemed to grow colder and colder as the night breeze whirled around it. It grew thicker, too, but instead of becoming more distinct so that he could see Bailey's face, it did not. It flapped its arms at him, and he felt an icicle touch on his face.

Gavan jerked suddenly, one hand flying off the grasp of the crystal. His eyes flew open in surprise and dismay. He reeled back almost as if he had been hit. Eleanora cried out, and Jason could see she tightened her grip on the amethyst crystal. He staggered back another step, his one remaining hand on the crystal shaking, his arm outstretched to its fullest length. He brought his other hand up, and, gritting his teeth, once again cupped his fingers about Eleanora's hand and the stone. "There is more at work here than we know," he managed to say, his voice tight in his throat. "I'm not sure I can . . ."

"Don't even think that, Gavan!" Eleanora tilted her face up to look into his eyes.

Jason shivered. The Ghost wavered again, and this time when it moaned, he could see the cloud of its head open, dark night shining through, as it wailed in eerie tones. Its eyes shone like two dark spots. The Ghost floated nearer. Its chill struck him to the bone, and his teeth began to chatter in spite of himself. Dr. Patel shrugged into her silk shawl while FireAnn chafed her hands. The temperature continued to drop until his nose went numb and frozen.

"Bailey . . . take the cookie?" His hand shook as his whole body seemed to dance with cold shivers. He thought the cookie would surely pop off. Something even icier touched his fingers and slid off his skin. The cookie lurched sideways suddenly and he pinched his hand shut to keep from dropping it.

"Keep trying, Jason! Don't let her think we've given up on her!" Eleanora called to him, even though her gaze remained locked on Gavan, who had grown paler even than the ghostly apparition before them.

He took a breath, expiration frosting on the air as though it were the deepest of winters, and held the cookie back out. Something slimy ran across his hand again, a wispy tendril, and he tried not to make a disgusted noise. He held steady and, instead said, "Come on, Bailey. You can do it!"

The wind died suddenly. The air all around them grew still and frosty. Gavan shuddered.

Through tight lips growing blue, he said, "Come to me, Bailey. You've got to find the way to do it. Come . . . NOW!"

A sound split the clearing, like that of a scream, yet almost too high to hear. Jolted, Jason felt his hand, his whole body jerk. The cookie flew into the air as he staggered back on his heels. Gavan dropped as though he had been pole axed and, unbalanced, Eleanora nearly toppled over on top of him. The candles FireAnn held snuffed out. With a cry, she dropped them in surprise.

Only Dr. Patel seemed unmoved. Her almond eyes fixed on the cloud of white as if she could see what moved there.

With a tremendous WHOOOSH the fog left.

Jason grabbed for the cookie, out of habit, and found . . . nothing.

"I've lost her," Gavan said, as he rolled over onto his back and took a few deep breaths. "Eleanora, she's gone." As soon as the color came back to his face, he stood, and steadied Eleanora.

"No." She shook her head. "Oh, no."

"I won't give up, but . . ." He paused, and leaned on his cane as if he actually needed it to bear his weight. His deep blue gaze swept over all of them. "We know that once lost like that, retrievals are . . . difficult, at best. If not impossible."

Dr. Patel said softly, "It *was* Bailey. I saw her clearly, though only for a moment."

Jason only half-listened, because he already felt sure he knew who the ghost was. What he didn't know was . . . where had the cookie gone? If he'd missed snatching it back, where was it on the ground? He shuffled his feet a bit in the night and saw . . . nothing.

Gavan nodded. "I won't give up easily."

Jason stood stock-still, as something brushed the back of

his ear. The evening breeze had come back, and the trees stirred around him, but he heard something ever so faintly. He thought he heard someone say, "Saves mine . . ."

His blood went cold. Or was it . . . you're mine? As the creature had promised him.

FireAnn picked up her candles and said briskly, "Everyone should be in bed. If you can't sleep, I'll send a draft of chamomile by. Tomorrow, as they say, is another day, and now that we know it's our missing lass, we can take steps."

"Are you all right, Jason?" asked the doctor softly. Standing beside him, she was hardly taller than he was, and the faint smell of incense clung to her silken sari.

"Yeah." He shivered. He'd have to think about this later, when he was warmer, and the night wasn't pressing on him. The back of his hand twitched and as he covered it with his other, he winced at new tenderness. "We can't lose Bailey. She's . . . she's . . . special," he finished lamely, for want of a better word.

"You're all special," Gavan said. He bowed to FireAnn. "I think we should follow our own advice, and this time, young man, I won't ask why—"

A howl tore his words in half. Another one followed it, sharp and coming nearer. The noise swirled down on the clearing like a whirlwind, and he could almost hear the running of the pack, the gnashing of their teeth as the howlers bore down on them. The throbbing in his hand quickened as though keeping pace with their thundering strides. Jason wobbled, nearly overwhelmed by it.

"Wolfjackals!" Gavan swung about, his cane in his hands. "I should have known they'd sense the breach. FireAnn, get Eleanora and Anita back to the Hall, quickly!" He pulled at Jason. "You, stay with me." He seemed not to notice Jason's pain as he took the boy's elbow and tucked him in close.

FireAnn linked arms with Eleanora and Anita Patel. "Back to back," she said to Gavan Rainwater, and to the others, she added, "Here we go, duckies. One step at a time. They'll not take us all on at once!"

Gavan stepped in behind the women, turning, and they moved as one unit, FireAnn leading the others ahead and

Gavan and Jason walking backward, on alert, watching the
woods fringing the campground.

He would ask what wolfjackals were, but he already knew.
Sweat beaded Jason's forehead.

"Got your crystal on you?"

"I—yes," Jason got out. His throat creaked as he tried to
talk.

"Good. Take it out. Hold it tightly. And, mind you, don't
drop it!"

"No, sir."

"I'm going to draw on you. If you get to feeling really faint,
call out. Otherwise, just stay with me, stand firm, and I'll keep
us all from harm, no matter what it looks like is going to happen. Understand?"

"Yes, sir," said Jason faintly. He already felt weak. How
could he give any strength to Gavan? But if he said anything,
if he showed him the mark, how much more trouble would he
be in? He clamped his jaw shut and took a deep breath. The
backs of his calves ached as they walked backward faster and
faster to keep up with FireAnn leading a brisk retreat.

"Our energies are spent, but the wards on the cottages
should hold. We're the only ones in danger for the moment,"
Gavan muttered to Eleanora as they trotted toward the main
hall. His hand gripped Jason's shoulder tightly.

Then came the moment which he knew, if he lived beyond
it, he would never forget. From the darkened sky itself, they
seemed to come, running down out of the clouds and iron
mountain peaks and alighting onto the common ground of the
camp, their eyes shining green, their teeth like white, sharp
slivers of the moon. With howls and growls, they emerged one
by one and fanned out into a pack. Five of them descended
onto the pathway and slowed to a stop, their tails wagging low
and stiff from side to side, their jaws agape. The wolfjackals
lowered their heads, and he had not a doubt they could rip his
throat out whenever they wished.

A sharp tear went through the back of his hand. It felt
damp, as though bitten, but he could not look at it. He could
not do anything but stare at the hunting pack just as they
stared down their prey.

"Away with you. You are denied," Gavan called out. His statement might have been more convincing were they not backing up quickly, to keep at the backs of the three more vulnerable women.

The pack trotted slowly to keep even. The air smelled of them, hot furred beast, coppery blood tang, musk, saliva, sharpened teeth, eagerness to run them down.

The leader's head twitched, jaws widening, crimson tongue lolling. His head jerked about again, as though birthing a voice with great difficulty. "This is open land. We hunt."

"No. No, this is our land, and you know it. Our mana seeps into the very earth joints here."

"I know nothing. We hunt here. If you would deny us, close the Gate."

Gavan muttered something under his breath. He cupped his left hand, clutching Jason's fist where he held his crystal tightly. He inhaled. "You are denied! Leave now!"

"Or . . ." The wolfjackals trotted closer yet. "Your threatssss seeeeem empty."

Gavan raised his cane. A searing blue beam shot from the end of it, blackening the ground. Dirt and crushed grasses sizzled. With a yelp, the beast jumped out of range. Gavan inhaled tightly, and a second bolt shot from the cane. It zapped one of the beasts. The wolfjackal rolled with a yelp, and the smell of burning fur filled the air.

The pack leader whirled about, snapping. Then he lowered his head, facing Gavan again. "For that, I will have blood-dddd," he grimaced and snarled out of ivory-toothed jaws.

Gavan jumped forward with a great stamp, and two of the wolfjackals bolted away in sheer reaction. They circled and came back to the rear of the pack, heads down as if embarrassed. Their packmates snapped sharply at them for their cowardice.

Fiery pain crept up Jason's hand to his arm and into his neck. He concentrated on breathing, on Gavan's words. He felt as though he were leaking. As though everything inside of him faded away . . . They continued to walk backward, one slow steady step at a time. A soft glow behind told him they were close to the building.

But he had been close to the building when bitten. So they weren't afraid of the lights and such. They weren't entirely wild. They were . . . beyond his knowing. The one spoke. The others milled about with a savage intelligence. His heart thudded in his breast as though the only thing in a vast, hollow drum. It hurt to feel it pounding so hard.

Something pale and white flitted past them. Jason barely caught sight of it, but he felt it. The wolfjackals did as well. The pack wheeled about in sudden confusion, smelling new prey and yet not quite sighting it. "What is thissss?" the leader snarled, and snapped at empty air. Hot saliva dripped from his jaw in eagerness.

With a fear for more than himself, Jason thought he knew. They saw, sensed, what he could not. And alone, she was in even more danger than he was! He yelled, "Run, Bailey!" with all the air left in his lungs.

The wolfjackals scattered, leaping after the faint ghostly apparition. They howled in fierce joy at the new hunt. The white wisp darted away, out of reach. It bobbed back and forth, almost frantic seeming, just in front of the snapping wolfjackals. The beasts whirled and spun and lashed out again and again.

Gavan called out, "NOW!" He bodily picked up Jason by the waist and they all lunged for the Lake Wannameecha Gathering Hall.

Once inside, FireAnn bolted the door, and Eleanora let out a sharp, crisp curse before heading to her office. "I can't leave the Ghost to them!" She came back with a very large, clear crystal in her hands. "Now," she said firmly. "They'll be sorry." She took her place near Gavan who gently set Jason back on his sneakered feet.

Wobbly, Jason sat down.

Eleanora tossed her head and linked her arm with Gavan's. She threw the door back open and the two of them stepped into the golden courtyard as the five wolfjackals lunged into sight.

Jason saw only a brilliant flash of light. He heard the yelps and snarls and then—nothing. He didn't know if it was because they'd won . . . or he'd keeled over as he felt his mind go blank and his body slump down. The only feeling he had anywhere was in his hands . . . pain in the left one where the scar felt newly ripped open, and pain in the right one where he held his crystal so tightly it cut into his palm. Then the dark snarled around and enclosed him.

Scars and Scares

ICY cold. He woke up shivering, teeth chattering, as if he'd been dunked in a tub of ice water. Dr. Patel was gently unfolding his fingers from around his crystal, saying softly, "Just relax a bit, Jason." He tried to, but his body reacted on its own, jerking about like a puppet on loose strings. It took him a moment to realize he was staring at the ceiling of Lake Wannameecha Gathering Hall, and not the sky, or his own cabin, or even his very own attic room, so far away. She frowned at the bruising and tiny cuts around his crystal, but only said, "We'll have to wash the grit out of those. Your crystals aren't polished and cleaned yet."

Dr. Patel leaned over him, and so did FireAnn, a worried look knitting her cinnamon brows together. Her hair had come unbound again, and surrounded her face in a hazy, burnished cloud of red. "You're tough, laddie," she said quietly. "Just take a deep breath."

Jason nodded.

FireAnn shook his shoulder. "Dinna nod at me, laddie, breathe!"

He inhaled deeply. The warm air burned inside his lungs. He knew he'd never be warm again. Why was he so cold? Dr. Patel laid her silken shawl over him and despite its lightness, it seemed to blanket him with soothing heat as she tucked it about him with a few words of a language he did not recognize, then added, "What happened?"

"Ah, well." FireAnn looked up briefly. "We're nay sure yet! It's a battle of wills out there."

"What happens if we lose?" Jason forced words out through teeth determined to chatter.

Anita Patel hissed, and then gently added, "We can't be losing. This is not the kind of battle we can afford to lose." She helped him sit up.

He dared a glance at his scarred hand, saw nothing and tucked it under him. He could have sworn the skin had broken anew, the blood freshly running down his hand and trickling off his fingers from a jagged gash. But he saw nothing in his quick glance.

Not too quick for Dr. Patel to catch, though. She grabbed his wrist firmly. "Let me see that hand, Jason."

He yielded to her because he had no choice. Fire began to creep through his body as the feeling came back, prickly heat pinching and poking numb places. He clenched his jaw tightly to keep his teeth from chattering. She spread his fingers to examine the scar carefully.

"I think it's time you told me the truth about this, Jason."

He couldn't meet her level gaze.

"What is it?" asked FireAnn.

"A bite or scratch. He wasn't quite sure when he came in at first. Scratch, we decided, and it looked like it, though deep but closing quickly. He had babbled a bit about a wild animal first, then let it go. Do you remember the night?"

The cook rubbed her head, fiery hair moving about her like smoke. "Without a crew to help with the kitchen, I was a mite distracted. Gavan was hounding me to get the Draft concocted. There was someone lost near the toilets . . . I canna say I remember that being you, though, Jason. Lad, we're a chain that's only as strong as the weakest link. If there's something we need to know, you should be telling us."

He squirmed. Dr. Patel smoothed her fingertips over the crescent scar. She already knew, he sensed. He sighed. She let go of his hand.

"I didn't know what it was then. It jumped me . . . you scared it off." He stared beseechingly at FireAnn.

FireAnn let out her breath in a gust. She smelled faintly of spearmint. "Oh, lad."

Dr. Patel frowned. "They've been here since the first night? That's not good, FireAnn. I had no idea, and I don't think anyone else did."

Cook laid a hand gently on his shoulder. "What happened?"

"It took hold of me. I . . . well, I couldn't pull loose, so I shoved my fist down its throat. It let go in surprise, I think. Then it heard a clatter from the kitchens, so it growled at me and left."

"Well. I was scarin' more varmints than I knew, eh?" Fire-Ann looked faintly pleased.

"I washed up. It hurt a lot but by morning, the gash had nearly healed up. Just looked like a bad scratch, but still, I was worried. I mean . . . rabies and stuff. I didn't know what to think, but you seemed very calm about it, and it didn't look that bad in your office. Maybe I had jabbed it into a branch when I fell."

She nodded solemnly.

He exhaled. The moment had come, he knew it. With all that he had been through, he would be sent home. "I'm sorry to have been so much trouble," he said.

FireAnn poked him gently. "The most Talented are often the most troublesome. Dinna you think Gavan Rainwater knows that? Why, as a lad himself—" She rolled her green eyes.

"Don't give him false hope. It's bad if he's been marked, very bad. You worried about infection, but I can tell you that you've no idea what a wolfjackal can sink into you." Dr. Patel sighed. "Regardless of what Gavan wants, he may not be able to help, this time." She stood, straightening her sari. "And he drew blood, don't forget that, FireAnn."

She sucked in her breath, and looked sadly at Jason. "A blood pact?"

"Not quite, but . . ." the doctor's voice trailed off.

Jason shivered. "You have to tell?"

"Do you think it wise to keep a thing like this hidden?"

After a long moment, he shook his head. The thought that he might be the weakness that would get Bailey or someone else hurt, or bring the wolfjackals back, knifed through him. "No," he said quietly. "I wouldn't wish this on anyone!"

"That's a good lad," returned FireAnn soothingly. She wiped her hands on her apron as she straightened. "Wonder if they need help out there."

"I imagine they could use a bracing cup of tea when they're done."

Cook nodded. "Fix a cuppa, I will, then." She hurried down the corridor to what must be a small kitchenette off the offices because shortly thereafter, he could hear some pans rattling, although a great deal quieter than the usual clatter and bang at the mess hall.

Dr. Patel leaned against the corridor. She studied her own hands a moment, before meeting Jason's gaze. "There is no way I could not tell."

He sighed. "I know." Finally, he felt warm again although it might be with shame. Standing up, he handed the shawl back to her, the silken fabric shimmering for a moment between his fingers. Magical? He would not doubt it, if she told him. "Sometimes, I ask myself, why me?" He rubbed his hand again. The slight tenderness that had almost gone was back, as painful as it had ever been.

"Perhaps, in that, we are all lucky. Another young Magicker might not have handled it. Do you think just anyone could have stood against the wolfjackals now, marked as you were?" Whatever else the doctor might have added was cut off by the sharp, piercing whistle of the teakettle and FireAnn's cheerful voice calling them back for tea.

Before either could head down the corridor, the door banged open and Gavan blew in, pulling Eleanora behind him. He kicked the door shut, grinning ear to ear, his hair mussed as though he'd been standing in a high wind. Eleanora cleared her throat, as she patted down her clothes, and tried to put some order back in her dark, tangled hair.

"Well," he said, in a deep, pleased tone. "I think we showed them what we can do." He looked at Jason then. "And it appears to be time for a talk with you, Jason. You know both more . . . and less . . . than you should."

Eleanora walked on her shoe soles, and she was so diminutive that she barely came to Jason's throat. She drew her shoulders up, but could not levitate, and it was then he knew the toll it had taken to stand off the wolfjackals. Magick demanded a price. She looked as pale as alabaster. The thought scared him. She put a hand up on Gavan's shoulder to steady herself.

Before Gavan could utter another word, however, Anita interrupted. "FireAnn," she said, "has tea ready. Shall we all have a bracer before we discuss anything?"

"Most excellent idea," breathed Eleanora. Gavan moved down the hall, pacing himself to her unsteady steps. He murmured something toward her ear that Jason couldn't catch, but it brought two bright dots of color to her cheeks.

FireAnn not only had a huge, steaming pot of tea ready, but she'd also set out a plate of cookies and a second plate of little jam tarts. Jason slid into his chair with a rumble from his stomach that said food would be very welcome. He helped himself to one tart and two big gingerbread cookies, their tops crackled from baking and sprinkled with sugar. No one said anything but, "Please pass the cookies," or, "Cream and sugar, anyone?" and "Thank you, I will have another," for several long minutes.

Then Gavan put his cup down, and as the doctor refilled it for him, he mopped cookie crumbs off his mouth and remarked, "We chased them off with their tails tucked between their legs."

FireAnn cheered. "Well done!"

He nodded. "It taxed us more than it should have. They were very strong. That lends credence to Tomaz's worry that a mana storm is approaching. They're drawing on it already. How, I've no idea. The Dark Hand has ways I'm not familiar with."

Anita stared at the tablecloth thoughtfully as FireAnn rocked back in her chair. Then the doctor looked up, gazing at Jason. "Before more is said," she remarked quietly, "there is something you should know."

"Yes?" Gavan arched an eyebrow.

Jason waited uncomfortably, then as the silence dragged on, he realized she would not say it, and she waited for him to. Tart halfway to his mouth, he put it down on his plate. "I was bitten," he told Rainwater and Eleanora, putting his left hand out, palm flat on the table, so that his crescent scar would be clearly seen on the back of his hand. The thin white scarline had gone purple and angry looking. That did not worry him so much; he knew it would be faded by morning.

"That's not from tonight." Eleanora looked at him, and the worry in her eyes made him feel awful.

"No. It happened the first night. I ran into this beast coming out of the restroom."

Gavan rubbed the side of his nose. "And no one knew? You told no one?" He threw his linen napkin on the table. "Damn it, how can we keep safe if we're too weak to even know when the Dark Hand is among us?"

Eleanora reached out and laid her hand over his. "Gavan," was all she said, a note of warning ringing in her voice.

He inhaled and looked to Jason. "Go on, Master Adrian. I sense there is more."

"It grabbed me. Its teeth . . . tore me. I pushed it away, and it heard FireAnn in the mess hall. It backed away and just disappeared, then."

"Said anything, did it?" Rainwater's clear blue gaze rested on him.

Unable to trust his voice, Jason shook his head. How much worse could it be? Would they deny him the chance to be one of them? Perhaps much, much worse if he repeated what the wolfjackal had said to him. *You're mine . . .*

Gavan also nodded in agreement. "Talking does not come easy to them. They are not made for it. I imagine it causes them pain, but I doubt their maker cares. What did you do then?"

"I went back to the restroom. I washed, over and over. It hurt. It was this bloody gash."

Eleanora gave a muffled sound. He looked up to see her wringing her hands, musician's hands that it would be a crime to hurt or scar.

"I'm . . . I'm all right now," Jason told her. "When I got up in the morning, it was nearly all healed. I went to see Dr. Patel anyway. The pain went all deep inside, like a bad bruise or something. I was worried. Well . . . rabies and stuff, you know?"

"They are from beyond the veil," Gavan said. "They do not carry our diseases, nor are they vulnerable to them. They carry plagues of their own, however, and we do fall to them."

"He didn't tell me," the doctor interrupted softly, "that he had been bitten. I should have pressed him a bit. He was worried about infection, so I cleansed it and gave him some ointment for it."

FireAnn had only been listening, leaning on one elbow, and sipping her cup of tea. Now she commented, "Perhaps that is why Jason doesn't sleep like the others. One Magick outweighing the charm? He doesn't succumb to the Parting song and blessing."

They all stared at him. He shrugged. "I don't know why I don't sleep. I wake up at home, but I don't have trouble going back to sleep."

"Another mystery," Gavan sketched a fingernail on the tablecloth. "You have a nose for them," the camp leader said. "You keep showing up."

Jason flushed with embarrassment. "I don't mean to," he answered slowly.

"Nonsense!" FireAnn stood and freshened all their teacups. "Of course you do! You've a large curiosity bump, nothing wrong with that. Me mum and you would get along right well."

Eleanora smiled wistfully. "I haven't seen Beulah in years," she responded. "How is she?"

FireAnn nodded. "She's doing well enough. Now, lad. Keep talking." She settled back at the table.

"I don't know what else to say."

"Have you seen wolfjackals again, before tonight?"

"Once or twice, I thought . . . could have been something else, in the brush." His own voice sounded funny to his ears, and he stopped short of telling them he thought he'd been followed several times. They probably thought he was coward enough.

Gavan scratched at his chin. "Not good news, but then, not unexpected either. We knew they would come hunting, I had just hoped we'd have our defenses up first, our Iron Gate shut. Now we'll have to step up our efforts to locate it. We're going to start mapping the ley lines tomorrow."

"Lay lines?" Jason looked about in confusion. "And what do you mean about a Gate?"

"L E Y," furnished Eleanora. "Trust me, you will know far more about them than you want to know. A more boring task,

I cannot imagine, but it has to be done. Ley lines are natural bands of Magick, or mana, the energy that Magick uses, rather like magnetic fields that occur in the earth naturally, and we're going to be identifying our network in the next few days. Think of them like power lines, cables, buried deep within the earth for us to discover."

"As for the Gate." Gavan rubbed his palm over the top of his cane. "Imagine that we can fence in this camp with magical wards. There are Havens that were fenced like that centuries ago, and Gated. The Gates move a bit, on ley lines, but we're fairly sure one is here. We can move that fencing to surround the camp and merge into a Haven, we believe. It won't be easy, but it can be done, and then we can have a safe place to learn and teach."

"It must not be easy to be a Magicker." Jason picked up his tart and began to nibble before his stomach could let out a rumble of hunger loud enough to be heard by everyone else. Smiling, FireAnn nudged the tart plate a little closer.

"Never has been, nor does it ever seem to be destined to be." Gavan tapped his cane upon the floor. "I must ask you, Jason, to hold your tongue about what you've seen and heard. I can't explain everything to you now, and even if I could, you don't know quite enough to understand it. Be patient with me?"

"Can I ask you a question?"

"One, and let us pray it is not longer than what is left of our night, for me to answer."

"Do you know about the nightmares?"

He threw a look at Eleanora, then glanced back to Jason. "Yes," he said quietly. "We know a bit about the nightmares."

"Who is the man in the tomb?"

"We're not sure. Do you remember well enough to tell us?"

"He's very, very pale. Sometimes he has short, dark curly hair. He wants me to come to his side. He reaches out with his hand. I used to think—I used to think it was my father. I had dreams of him like that, before. Now I don't know anymore."

"Sometimes?" echoed Eleanora. Her teacup shook slightly in her hand.

Jason nodded. "Sometimes, I would swear, it's a different man. Long, silvery-gray hair. He seems . . . older. He doesn't reach for me, though, and he doesn't scare me so much."

FireAnn sucked in her breath and then coughed several
times as though she'd inhaled a cookie crumb. She put her
napkin to her face and turned away.

"Perhaps, Jason, on another night ... you'd do a bit of dream
exploring for us? Until then, I really haven't any answers I can
give you." Gavan smiled lightly. "But those nightmares are
why we try to give everyone a good night's sleep, even if they
don't want it."

Jason nodded. "One more?"

"Only if it is exceedingly short."

"You're not going to throw me out?"

"No," said Gavan Rainwater thoughtfully. "At least, not
yet." He rolled the silvery wolfhead sculpture on his cane between his palms. "Don't think that some of you won't be sent
home, because some will. That's why FireAnn here has been
cooking up a Draft of Forgetfulness for days. Not everyone is
cut out to handle the Talents we've been given, and we cannot
send them home remembering what has occurred."

"You just ... take their memories?"

"The potion does."

"You'd mess with their minds like that? What about the
oath we swore?"

"The Draft makes it easier to live. If you don't know you've
lost something, you can't mourn for it or search to get it back.
The Oath keeps them safe, even though they've forgotten. We
have no choice, Jason. There is a vast world out there that would
love to ... mess with our minds ... if we are ever found out. I
don't know about you, but I'd not care to be on the Internet in
an autopsy finding out what made me tick!" Gavan stood.

"All right then. New agenda, items of import. Mapping the
ley lines so the Gate can be located and closed against the
coming storm. Getting Bailey Landau back. General training
must be sped up a bit; we've a lot to teach them and the days
are flying past."

"Bailey will be found," Eleanora reassured him.

"Master Rainwater," Jason got out as Gavan started to
leave.

"Yes, Jason?"

"Do you think anyone could ever go back to ordinary after
seeing a Magicker?"

"Like anything in life, sometimes you've got no choice." Gavan pivoted in a swirl of dark cloak and then was gone down the hallway, his footsteps echoing.

Dr. Patel stood smoothly. "I'll walk you back to your cabin, Jason."

He nodded, then could not help smiling as FireAnn put two great gingerbread cookies and two tarts in a napkin, folded the ends over and handed the package to him. "Roommates," she explained, "can sometimes get horribly grumpy if they find out you've been somewhere without them . . . and you've had good things to eat that they haven't."

Jason tucked the package inside his shirt gratefully as he thanked her. They all left the building a bit cautiously, but other than the fact that the night was later and darker, nothing seemed untoward.

The doctor hugged him about the shoulders before letting him go into his cabin. She waited outside in the shadows until he dropped the latch into place, and he stood, listening to Trent's soft, deep breathing.

He should fall into bed and sleep, but he didn't think he could. More than anything, he thought of the Ghost. What had he heard the second time . . . "saves mine" or "you're mine"? And how could he tell Gavan his fears that the enemy somehow had a hold on him he didn't know about and could do nothing about? And what was the Dark Hand, and why was it the enemy, and what had happened to all the other Magickers, once upon a time?

And how could he help Bailey before she was lost to them all forever or the wolfjackals got her? When he finally drifted off, it was into a tangle of half dreams and nightmares, none of which he could escape from or wake up from, until he remembered none of them at all. Even the ones which might have held clues.

18

A Stitch in Time

J ASON woke to the sound of crunching. He couldn't quite place the noise as he craned his head from his pillow and rubbed his eyes. The night, as Gavan Rainwater had predicted, had been much too short. He yawned.

The crunching grew louder and as he sat up, he saw Trent at the table, elbows propped up, happily consuming one of Fire-Ann's cookies.

"If you're going to sneak out," Trent stated, "at least you brought back goodies!" He imitated a contented purr.

Still muffled by sleep, Jason answered, "Glad you like 'em." He swung his legs out and stretched. If FireAnn had beaten her pots or Sousa blown the camp-rousing melody on his cornet, he'd slept right through it. "Everyone else up yet?"

"Nope. Thought I heard something at the door, so I woke up."

"Something?"

"Yeah, the screen door was rattling and bumping. Must have been the wind."

Or . . . Jason concealed a shudder. He didn't want to think what else it could be. He padded over to the table and sat down. Trent had already eaten the little tarts, according to the pattern of crumbs on the table. He stifled another yawn. "So . . . wanna know what happened?"

Trent licked a finger. "I figure you'll tell me sooner or later." He hummed slightly.

"Maybe." Jason leaned back in his chair, stuck his foot on the table, and looked at his ankle. Despite last night's doings, it seemed to be even more healed, the colors fading. He decided not to wear his air splints again.

"Do you *mind?*" Trent pushed his foot off the table. "I'm eating here!"

"You," observed Jason, "are always eating somewhere."

"True. So, did you catch the thief?"

"No, I ended up Ghost hunting instead."

"Wow." Trent sat up. "No kidding? I missed that?"

Jason shrugged. "You didn't want to come," he pointed out. "Anyway, I caught the camp leader and Eleanora and Dr. Patel and FireAnn doing some kind of ritual, to send the Ghost away. Only, it hit me ... and I don't know why we didn't think of this before ... Bailey is the Ghost!"

Trent dropped his cookie. "Bailey is dead?"

"Oh, no. No, no no. But she's neither here nor there. She's been leaving clues or trying to." He frowned heavily, wondering what he was going to do to help her now.

"How can she be a Ghost? What did the crystal do to her anyway?" Trent left his cookie on the table and took out his own crystal. Cloudy, it looked more like a frosty snowflake than any of the other crystals Jason had seen. It could be looked into, Trent had shown Jason that, but it was like looking into a very dark, shadowy chamber.

"I don't know. They haven't told us much about them yet. I don't know how they figure she could have gone home either, unless ..." Jason fished his out. "Unless ..." He tumbled the crystal about in his fingers thoughtfully. His jeweler's loupe lay on the table, next to his sketches. He picked it up and held it over his gem, looking at it ... into it ... each facet of the quartz like a chamber or door, opening, leading. ...

Jason stared deeper. He could, if he concentrated hard enough, see something. A crack. No, not a crack, an edge of something opening, like a door. An image forming. His own home's doorway inside, wavering, growing more distinct the harder he looked. Home ... The doorknob turned as if he reached for it, the door opening inward slowly and he leaned forward, eager suddenly to see if it was home, eager to be back—he could feel the cold brass of the knob between his fingers, turning, turning, the tumblers clicking as the door opened wider.

"Jason!" Trent knocked the crystal out of his cramped fingers. It shot across the cabin, and Jason sat back, dazed and blinking. The feeling of being home faded slowly. "Man!" Trent glared at him. "They said not to do that! What were you doing?"

"I'm . . . not sure." He stretched his fingers, got up, and retrieved his crystal, checking it over for nicks or fractures. Then, with a sigh of relief, he set it down on the tabletop, where it rested. It seemed a bit different, somehow, for all that. He poked at it. "What did you see?"

"You, staring like a geek, into that." Trent seemed unnerved. He paced about the cabin, back and forth, back and forth. "I thought it was going to suck you in."

"Suck me in?" Jason stared.

"Like a vacuum cleaner. I figured you were just going to get sucked in headfirst and disappear like Bailey."

"I think I could have gone there. . . ."

"Where?" Trent threw his hands up.

"Oh." Jason drew his crystal back and pocketed it. "Home. I thought I saw home for a second there. I could have walked through the front door. You know how there are planes inside? Just like doors."

His friend stopped short. He shot a glance at his own crystal. "Transportation? Or, more correctly, teleportation? No brooms or magic carpets? Just walk through a crystal door?"

"Maybe."

"Then what happened to Bailey?"

"She dropped the crystal? She hasn't been trained? The crystals don't really work that way? I would think that Gavan and Eleanora tried that already." Jason got to his feet, and further words were cut off by the sound of brass bugling throughout the camp, Sousa's homage to morning. He snatched for the last half of a cookie, but Trent beat him to it. The sight of the disappearing cookie tickled his mind. He almost thought of something. Almost. Trent grabbed his bath towel and snapped

him in the butt, before turning and running. Racing, they
bolted toward the showers and breakfast.

Tomaz had returned. He stood in the hall posting the day's
schedule, but looked up as Jason walked over, and their eyes
met briefly. The man gave a silent nod, before returning to his
chore. The turquoise and silver on his rings and heavy bracelet
flashed in the light from the wide, mess hall windows.

"What was all that about?" Trent whispered.

"Darned if I know." Jason felt as though something important had happened that he had no inkling of. Behind him,
Jonnard and Danno and Henry shuffled into line, Jon looking more than ever like a scoutmaster in charge of an unruly
troop as they headed to the restrooms. He also looked quizzi-
cally at Jason, who could only shrug in reply.

Henry, however, fairly bounced in excitement. "I can't
wait!" His rosy face glowed from the hot showers and the
corners of his glasses steamed faintly. He took them off and
wiped them dry. "I can hardly wait," he said for a second time,
no one having responded immediately.

"What's happening, Squibb?"

"Best news ever. The computer room is opening later.
Three brand new 'puters. No Internet, but some good soft-
ware, I hear."

"Computer room?" Trent's face brightened. "You're kidding me."

"Absolutely not."

"That's great! I was beginning to have the shakes!" He
put his hand up and high-fived Squibb who nearly dropped
his towel and whose round face beamed in joy anyway. For
the next few moments, going through the line, they swapped
nearly incomprehensible statements about speed, memory,
RAM, monitor sizes, and sundry other computer speak
which Jason only understood vaguely and neither Danno nor
Jon seemed to understand at all. In fact, Jason thought that
Jonnard's eyes had glazed over slightly by the time Trent and
Henry started discussing mouse types versus tracing balls
and other devices.

By the time they got inside the building, the two were lost

deep in the subject of computer gaming and the rest of the world might as well have disappeared.

Jon waited patiently for both of them to take a deep breath at the same time, then interjected mildly, "Yes, but why do they have computers *here?*"

Everyone stopped and looked at him. "I mean, you can't expect they have them so that the two of you can play games, can you?" He paused while Henry and Trent sputtered a moment. "I mean. Think about it. Three brand-new machines, so that you can play super Gameboy on them? I don't think so."

"This is technology supreme," Trent argued. "What would a Magicker be using them for? I can only guess. For taping and editing the Talent Show, if nothing else."

"Exactly," Jon said as if he'd made a point. "We can only guess, and I suppose we'll find out soon enough."

Somewhat disappointed, Trent and Henry quieted, but Jason for one was glad for the sudden silence. He had begun to drown in a sea of computerisms. Then a shadow fell over him.

Tomaz Crowfeather stood patiently, waiting to be noticed. The Magicker dropped his hand to Jason's shoulder with a firm pressure.

"I hear you have been busy," Tomaz said.

"Ummm . . . I'm afraid so."

Tomaz winked, his tanned face wrinkling about his eyes. "There is nothing wrong with a young Magicker casting a long shadow. Many of us here have been waiting years in hope for such signs of Talent. But you draw troubles as well. Wear this. It should help."

He dropped a small bag in Jason's hand, a carefully plaited string of yarn to hold it. Blanket weave designs decorated the small, plump fabric bag.

Jason cradled it. It crunched slightly, and a fragrant but odd smell came out, as though the bag was full of herbs and leaves. He put it around his neck and dropped it inside his shirt. "What's that for?"

"That, young master, is for the wolfjackals."

"Oh." He looked around, afraid that the others might hear, but they did not seem to notice.

Tomaz stayed silently by his side, smiling slightly, and Jason realized that no one but the two of them could hear the words he spoke. "What's in it?"

"What you think is in it." Tomaz smiled slowly. "Dried things. Powders. Herbs. Magic of my own. Do not get it wet, but wear it otherwise. Will you do that for me, young master?"

Jason nodded. "Thank you," he said, and meant it. The touch of the little bag against the hollow of his throat helped lighten the worry about the crescent scar on his hand. He did not know how it did, but it did.

Tomaz nodded. "I will see you for canoeing," he reminded Jason before he left. "But not wearing that." He winked and strode away.

Jason touched the lump under his shirt.

Trent fidgeted as though waking up. He stared at Jason. "What's that?"

"Tomaz gave me something." True to his impression, Trent had apparently not heard a word that had been said.

"Oh, yeah? What?"

Jason hooked his finger about the cord, withdrawing the bag from beneath his shirt and taking it off so Trent could get a look at it. Then he dropped it into his pocket so it would stay with his clothes and safely dry while he showered.

"A fetish. Cool."

"A what?"

"Fetish. Like a . . . charm or talisman. Herbs, feathers, fur, made out of that sort of thing."

"Oh." Jason momentarily pulled it out of his pocket to look at it again. "It is cool."

Then the line moved again, and Trent rushed him into the finally open showers. "Come on, I want a look at the computers before we have to go to another activity."

Jason let the other's enthusiasm suck him in and draw him off after breakfast. True to Henry Squibb's word, there was a classroom lab open at the Gathering Hall. Inside it, computer desks, tables, and chairs reigned among the debris of many cardboard shipping boxes and a tangle of cords that looked quite complicated, leading from the various machines in stages of being unpacked. Trent walked among them, looking but not touching.

"They're going to be networked, apparently," he said. He looked up to see Jason watching him, and grinned. "Hooked together. So I can, like, type a file on my machine and you can access that file."

"Can't I do that anyway, if you send it to me?"

"Yeah, but that means I have to send it to someone outside like an agency or site which may or may not see it before he sends it to you. Or the cows may come home before traffic slows enough that he *can* send it. Networking is instantaneous. What's mine is yours, what's yours is mine. Straight from me to you." Trent tapped a computer connecting cable.

"Ah." Jason looked the units over. He used computers at school, but they didn't particularly fascinate him, although he did vaguely wonder, like Jon, what they were doing here at camp. Finally, fidgeting, he tugged at Trent, not wanting to be late to calisthenics. That would mean extra push-ups and hiking, and he had other things on his mind.

Lucas Jefferson met them with a big grin on his face and long iron rods with an end bent for a short handle. Trent and Jason fell in at the back. Ting turned around and waved at them, drawing Jennifer's attention who also turned and waved. They did a quick roll call, and then Jefferson tapped on a camp table, rattling a stack of clipboards.

"All right, ladies and gents, you are mine for the rest of the morning. I want you to listen up, because Mistress Eleanora is going to cover the book learning and lore of much of what it is we're going to be doing today. This morning, we are going to do the grunt work." He flashed a wide, ivory smile.

Stefan grunted, on cue. He lumbered up to a table and sat down heavily, arms crossed. Rich thumped him on the back of the head, a playful hit which Stefan scarcely seemed to register.

"As soon as I'm done explaining a bit, I'm going to have you break into pairs. What we are going to do today is mapping. It's not fun. It's hot. And it's boring. But it's essential because it has to do with where a Magicker gets his Magick from."

"Ooooh," breathed Danno softly. Henry took his glasses off and cleaned them solemnly.

"Magick is sunk into the earth itself. It can lie there, deep and dormant, as though lost under a great ocean. Or it can surface, like a pretty shell we can easily pick up off the sand. It is everywhere . . . and nowhere. It is a power that comes from the land and its elements, and although it is everywhere, it tends to run in deep streams and patterns. We call them ley lines. Know where your ley lines and power nodes are and you can . . . if it's your Talent . . . do quite a bit of Magick. You're going to hear more about this from Miss Eleanora later. Now, you're going to help me find the ley lines." Lucas hefted a fistful of metal rods. They looked like straight rods, with a handle or grip bent at the ends at right angles. Very simple. A long letter L in metal. "Anyone ever seen one of these before?"

Danno put his hand up. "I have."

"What's it called? What did you use it for?" Jefferson smiled broadly at Danno.

"My grandfather calls 'em witching sticks. He used peeled wood branches with a fork to hold. Those are metal, though, and called dowsing rods. They're used to find water. He digs wells where they tell him."

"Ever use one? Or just watch him?"

Danno looked uncomfortable. "I used 'em."

"Did they work?"

After a long moment, Danno ducked his head in a nod.

"Excellent! Because they can work, and do. I know contractors and builders, who even use them to find power lines, sometimes building studs."

Jason blinked. He'd seen a pair of those rods in the Dozer's big tool boxes. He knew they'd looked vaguely familiar!

Lucas separated a rod out and held it in front of him. "Now, with power lines, cables, and such, there are better tools. But for dowsing ley lines," he winked, "we have to do it the old-fashioned way. We use them in pairs." He pulled another rod free from a stack. One in each hand, he held them side by side, the short ends disappearing into his large hands. He held them easily in front of him, pointing straight out. "You hold them parallel, like this. You squeeze 'em kind of easy so they can't swing around as you walk, but you hold 'em gentle like. We'll be walking in rows, side by side, step by step. If the rods feel like swinging apart, you let 'em. Or the points dipping down.

When they stop moving, you stop! You freeze, right there. Your partner, the one with the clipboard, is going to mark the spot, best as he can, on the topography maps we have printed out. The reason the rods move is they are sensitive to fields of energy we can't find easily otherwise. We'll be spread out, but you'll be able to see campers on your left and right. If your fellow campers are stopped as well, you wait till their rods are in position again and they're ready to walk again, before you move out. Any questions?"

Hands shot up and voices peppered the air, but Trent stepped to the stack of clipboards and grabbed one up. He pointed at Jason. "You're dowsing. I'm mapping."

Lucas patiently answered a number of questions before he said firmly, "Get your gear, and follow me, and we'll have a try at it. Then I think you'll understand it a bit better."

They hiked to the edge of the campground where wilderness pressed heavily and the fencing, if any, seemed broken down. Jason touched his charm bag against his neck uneasily, feeling chilled although the summer sun burned down hotly on them all. Jason held his metal rods, one in each hand as he'd been told. He stepped forward and felt nothing, absolutely nothing, with Trent trotting along behind him, humming and drumming his pencil against the clipboard until Jason wanted to yell. With each step dust puffed up from drying grass and pine needles. Suddenly, the rods in his hands slowly began to swing apart. He slowed, then stopped as they moved all the way to each side, his jaw dropped in astonishment.

Jefferson jogged up. He held a single rod in his hand and it swung wildly as he drew even with Trent and Jason. "Well, well. Looks like you've found a strong one. Let's see if the others can catch the stream."

Pleased, Jason stood very still. The sun beat down on his head. He could see Henry and Jonnard, of all people, mapping, off to the right. Way to the left, past several groups, Jennifer and Ting worked. Soon, all halted. It was an uneven wavering line of campers. Trent shaded his eyes, then began to sketch, quickly, on a second piece of paper.

"What are you doing?"

"Well. We've got our spot here." Trent tapped the pencil on

the map he had. "And the whole line here." He flipped the first sheet up and tapped the second page. "Otherwise, someone's got to go through and coordinate everyone's spot, see?"

Jason didn't quite, but he nodded as if he had. Jefferson bellowed, from somewhere over a small hillock to Jason's left, "Move out!"

Jason righted his dowsing rods and began to stride forward again, slowly. They'd gone maybe the distance of the school-yard at home, when his rods began to swing in his hands again. He stopped as they suddenly flung open to each side, making a wide vee, and quivered.

There was a shout or two next to him, and Trent once again began sketching quickly, his face furrowed in concentration.

As the morning wore on, the momentary excitement of having the rods actually move seemingly on their own wore off. Jefferson had the area laid out in grids and once they worked one direction, they came back and worked the other at right angles. When they finally turned in their clipboards and rods, he was hot, dusty, sweaty, and scratched. Jefferson thumped him on the shoulder. "No guts, no glory," he said, grinning.

Stefan looked as if he'd fallen headfirst into a hedge as the pair of them trudged up to turn in their gear. The heavy boy shuffled about as Rich piled his metal rods into Jefferson's stack.

"What happened?" Trent stared in fascination.

"Nothing." Stefan grunted and shrugged away. Rich, though, snickered. "Fell into a brier patch," he said.

"Didn't see it?" Jason thought that even Stefan must be smart enough to avoid a brier patch, if he knew it was there.

Stefan grumbled and scrubbed at his nose, where a long angry scratch ran across it. "Long story." He lumbered off, Rich in his wake.

Trent whispered in his ear, "Ever try to figure out what it is that makes those two Magickers?"

Jason nodded thoughtfully. At the cabin, he packed his fetish away as he got towels and trunks and they went to swimming class gratefully, letting the cooling waters of Lake Wannameecha wash away the dirt and grit and the heat of the sun. The promised lecture from Eleanora, however, did not materialize as that class was canceled and instead, Dr. Patel led them all in yoga and breathing exercises, which was okay, but had Jason wondering.

Where was the glory in being a Magicker? When was he going to see something wondrous done? What good was it if they couldn't even find Bailey?

After dinner, they sat at the fire ring. Jennifer was reading notes in her notebook by the last of the sun, her face hidden by a curtain of long blonde hair, her legs tucked under her. Trent lay flat on his back, watching the last of the daylight catching the clouds drifting overhead. Henry sat miserably, having failed at dowsing. Jonnard was off somewhere and Danno had kitchen duty. Ting sat on the log, needle in hand, expertly sewing back on a pocket that had been ripped free earlier.

And Jason leaned against Trent's knees, angry and unhappy that Bailey was still gone. She had depended on *him*, and he'd failed her so far. All the clues meant nothing to him. She had vanished into thin air just like that cookie he'd tried to hand her. . . .

"Do you think we'll have Bailey back by the Fourth of July? We need her for the big game. Not to mention her mother will be frantic with no letters and no calls. How do you tell someone her daughter is a Ghost?"

Ting shivered. "At least I know it's a friendly Ghost."

"We could cover, I guess," said Trent thoughtfully. "But not for long."

"We shouldn't have to cover," said Jason firmly. "There must be a way to find her."

Ting pulled on her needle and thread quickly, and a small smile crossed her face. "There!" she said in satisfaction, and held her shorts up. "A stitch in time saves nine!"

Jason's head snapped around. "What was that?"

"Sewing," said Ting. She waved her needle and thread about. "Mending? You do know that things can be repaired?"

"No . . . no . . . what was that you said? I only half heard you."

"A stitch in time saves nine?" Ting looked at him through curious almond-shaped eyes.

"That's it! That's it!" Jason leaped to his feet and did a war dance around the fire ring, scattering chipmunks and sending blue jays winging off, and drawing stares all around. "A stitch in time saves mine," she'd whispered in his ear. It could only have been Bailey twisting that saying about. In time! "That's why they can't find her! Bailey's isn't some*where*. She's some-*when!*"

19

A Cheese to Catch a Cheese

JENNIFER flung her hair over her shoulder and peered at Jason. "Whatever are you talking about?"

Jason stopped dancing, slightly out of breath. "I know where Bailey is. She's right here. Only, she's out of time somehow, offtrack. Out of sync."

Ting put away her sewing things neatly, mulling over what he'd suggested, before saying, "I think he's right. He has to be. Too many things have happened."

Jennifer clipped her pen to her notebook. She stood. "What are we going to do about it?"

He stopped still. "I've no idea," he answered slowly. "I have to tell the Magickers, of course."

Jennifer snorted. "We are all concerned, but I think that's the wisest course."

"We're also on probation," Trent said. He dug the toe of his sneaker into the dirt around the fire ring.

"We don't even have a plan. Yet," Jason answered.

The sun lowered behind the mountains, dusk settling in, and the clouds Trent had been watching turned a fiery pink and gold in the sky. Its heat lingered behind, though, blanketing the whole camp, and another swim sounded great, but no one was allowed in the lake after late afternoon. That did not mean no one went swimming . . . they had all heard of swimming trips sneaked in, but Jason did not feel like venturing out tonight. Other campers filtered in, and whatever plans were being thought of, were quickly put aside.

Eleanora joined them. "Nice evening," she said quietly. She carried her dulcimer. "No bonfire tonight."

Sighs of protest greeted her, and she smiled faintly. "All is not lost. FireAnn and her staff have been cranking at ice cream, and I hear they're serving sundaes in the mess hall."

"Ice cream!" Henry Squibb jumped to his feet and trotted off without another word.

Cool, creamy ice cream sounded too good to miss for any reason, but Jason hung back till they were all alone. Eleanora smiled at him. Trent stayed in the background, almost close enough to overhear, but too far away to participate in the chat. "Not screaming for ice cream, Jason?"

"Oh, it sounds good, but . . . I think I know about Bailey."

Eleanora had let her hand fall upon the dulcimer, and its strings chimed very faintly. "Tell me," she said, after she stilled it.

"She's out of sync."

"Out of sync? Synchronization?" Eleanora watched his face.

"Exactly. She's out of time with us. Either a step or two ahead or behind. I don't know for sure which way and I don't think she knows either, other than she's almost but not quite here."

"And you figured this out for yourself?"

"Not exactly. She managed to tell me something. I only heard part of it, and it didn't make sense. Bailey gets things twisted around sometimes."

Eleanora laughed softly. "I have heard a saying or two she's put into knots."

Jason grinned. "This one was 'a stitch in time saves mine.' I only heard half of it and just realized a few minutes ago what she was saying, and what she meant."

"That does have a ring of truth about it." Eleanora sat down on a tree stump, gathering her skirts about her. "That would explain what we've done wrong trying to track her. Even why she dropped her crystal."

"Why?"

"Well, if she's fallen a step behind, she had not even chosen it yet." Eleanora made a slight face. "Time is very difficult to deal with. We don't, usually, unless there is an accident of this sort. It takes a lot of mana and discipline. And we can't alter Time. But Bailey is like . . . well, let me think of a way to put it. If Time were a stream, a river, Bailey would be a stone put into it . . . a stone that didn't belong there, then. We can retrieve her. We can't change the tide or flow of the river in any way whatsoever."

Trent edged closer. "Can't . . . or won't."

"Both." Eleanora considered him. "Sets off too many ripples, don't you think? And every one of us, for some reason or other, would want at least one small moment in our timelines changed. The final effect would be like, oh, a covered pan of popcorn kernels being heated up and popping more and more rapidly until the pan is one big explosion. No." She shook her head. "I don't think any of us wants that."

"Removing Bailey won't harm anything?"

"No. But the longer she stays, the more potential harm she can cause. She is not meant to be there, and not only will Time fight her, her own body will begin to fight her. The Bailey we know will cease to exist. We have to rescue her, and I fear we've only one or two more chances to try." She stood. "How about we head to the mess hall? I think I can persuade Fire-Ann to put some ice cream aside until later. With any luck, Bailey can join us."

Trent trotted a little behind them as they went down the gentle sloping trails toward the bright lights, muttering to himself. Jason cast him a puzzled glance over his shoulder, wondering where the "I'll try anything" Trent had gone to. Cheers and the happy clattering of spoons in dishes greeted them at the mess hall.

Three silvery and frosted kegs sat on the counter, with FireAnn's crew dipping out great spoonfuls of ice cream from them. There was vanilla, with flecks of the savory bean in the ivory cream; chocolate, deep and rich looking; and fresh berry ice cream in swirls of pink and purple fruit. Everyone licking his or her spoon looked extremely happy. Jason slowed down unhappily. Despite Eleanora's suggestion, it didn't seem that there would be any left for later! That chocolate looked as if it were meant for him. He sighed.

Eleanora looked about. "I don't see Gavan yet. I think perhaps ice cream now is in order," she said in sympathy.

Without further urging, Jason and Trent dashed to the small line still waiting for the frosty desserts. Up at the front, Stefan growled a bit, saying, "No chocolate. Just the berries. I want the berry ice cream."

Rich's jaw dropped. "But, Stefan, my man. You're crazy about chocolate."

"I said . . . berries. I want berries!"

"And that you shall have," FireAnn said joyfully. She towered his bowl and smiled as Stefan shuffled out of line, a blissful smile on his broad face, Rich trailing behind with a look of disbelief plastered all over his.

Jason was able to get his bowl heaped with a good helping of all three, FireAnn winking at him as she dolloped the last bite of vanilla on top. Behind him, Trent broke out into a happy hum, back to normal. Eleanora settled for fresh berries only, with just a bare spoonful of the fruited ice cream on top.

She looked at her dish with a wry smile. "Diets," she remarked, before joining them. "Although," she added, with a faint purr after the first taste, "this is quite a treat!"

Jason had just finished, and Trent had gone back to beg for seconds, when Gavan came in. He searched the hall before spotting Eleanora and heading over. She spooned up a last mouthful of fresh berries, offering them to him as he sat down.

"Yum." His blue eyes sparkled with appreciation. "Think I could get FireAnn to save me a bowl?"

"I'm sure you could."

He nodded, and then ran his hand through his hair. "Well, lads." He smiled at Trent and Jason. "The lot of you did some nice work earlier today. There are some good mappers about. You, in particular." He patted Trent's shoulder.

"Thank you," Trent mumbled around the bowl of his spoon, his words muffled and half-frozen.

"Another day or two of mapping like that, inputting into the computer, and we should have a good idea of what immediately surrounds the camp. We'll have to go farther afield, of course, to get the whole area done, but . . . well, it looks promising."

"Is it safer away from camp?"

Gavan looked down at his cane. "No, Eleanora, it won't be. This is a project I have to take, literally, step by step. They have us at a disadvantage, and they know it, and they'll harry us."

"Bad news with the good, then."

"Aye, it is." He took a deep breath, straightening his shoulders.

"I've some more good news, then. Jason here has solved the conundrum of Bailey's whereabouts."

"What?" The sparkle returned to his blue eyes as he looked upon Jason. "Spit it out!"

"Well." Jason set his dish aside. "She's not lost somewhere, but somewhen. She's a step or two out of time. I'd guess behind, but I'm not sure about that."

"In time. Of course, of course! I should have thought of that . . . she's parallel." He frowned. "We'll get her back, then, but it'll take a bit of planning. Someone with a definite link to her will have the best shot, someone who can go in, get in rhythm with her, and bring her back."

"That would be me," Jason said firmly.

"You?" Gavan arched his eyebrow. The wolfhead crystal seemed to glow at him.

"As Bailey would say, 'Send a cheese to catch a cheese.' I've heard her, once or twice. She's been able to leave a hint or two for me, and I'd have thought of where she was sooner if I'd been smarter." He took a deep breath and said, "I don't know what to do, but if you show me, I'll do it."

Gavan nodded solemnly. He said to Trent, "Sorry, lad, but I think Jason had better go this alone."

Trent nodded back, but Jason thought he saw an expression of relief cross his face quickly before he ducked his head and finished off the last of his dessert.

Something pinched his ear again, leaving a fleeting feeling behind of cold fingers, tweaking to get his attention. If only it *was* Bailey. Perhaps she already knew what they were going to try and do! If only things could be that easy. . . .

* * *

The three sat around Gavan's desk. He cleared it with a sweep of his cane, papers flying and Eleanora settling with a slight frown on her face as if she realized she might well be the one picking up the mess. He fetched Bailey's amethyst crystal out of his drawer, unwrapping it from the silk handkerchief and setting it in the center of the desktop. "Yours next to it, but comfortably within reach," he directed Jason.

"Yes, sir." Carefully he placed his crystal next to Bailey's. His was larger, he hadn't realized that, but either was small enough to cup in the palm of his hand.

"Cover both."

He stretched his arms out and began to do that, his left hand over her crystal, right hand over his, and his crescent moon scar gave a sudden throb. He jerked his hands back, wincing.

"What's wrong?"

"Nothing." Jason touched the fetish bag at his throat and put his hands out again. He switched the crystals first, then settled his left hand over his own. No lancing pain. He relaxed a bit and settled into position, Eleanora and Gavan trading glances over his head. He squirmed in his chair a bit and Eleanora hooked her foot over the chair rung, scooting him close to the desk. He shot her a grateful look as he rolled his shoulders and got more comfortable.

"Now," said Gavan firmly. "If anything goes wrong, you're to find us and return immediately. Close your eyes."

He did so. He felt a hand settle on each of his shoulders.

"This is where we shall be, Jason. Find us there."

A bit bewildered, he answered, "I can feel you."

"Not with your everyday senses. Find our Magick there, anchoring you."

He didn't know how! Jason clenched his eyes shut, till his lids crinkled together. How did they expect him to know something like that? He couldn't do this! He had no way of knowing; what had they shown him of Magick really? And yet . . . and yet . . . on his right shoulder, he could feel a steady warmth, like a banked fire. And on his left, well, it wasn't a feeling at all, it was a sound. He could hear the very faint chime of music rippling past his ear. Slowly he said, "Eleanora is music. And you are fire."

"Very good. Now, open your eyes. Focus on your crystal first and when you feel good about it, you're going to look into Bailey's. You're going to see if you can find that door she disappeared through, and follow her."

Jason nodded carefully. "Yes, sir." He looked at his crystal, seeing in his mind's eye the way the jeweler's glass showed it to him, magnified into all its various layers and angles. He loved the look of his stone. Even the flawed part of it. With reluctance, he shifted his attention to Bailey's amethyst and looked at it intently.

A spiky crystal, with many, many facets and sharp edges, like a dozen or so brilliant purple gems stacked up unevenly and fused together, it was still a beautiful cluster. He could see why Bailey had chosen it. It would have looked pretty in a setting for a necklace, he supposed, or some piece of jewelry. With a faint pang of homesickness, he thought of his stepmother and how she loved to shop for jewelry. She rarely bought any; her taste was expensive, but she used to talk to him and Alicia when they were along. He hadn't listened then and wished now he had. He looked sharply into the gem blanketed under his right hand.

He thought he saw a faint line, stretching and then opening, like a door slightly ajar. He knew that vision and plunged forward toward it eagerly. It was a door, it was Bailey's, and he had to catch it!

Honeycomb

HE dove through into a threshold of stunning cold, like plunging headfirst into an icy pool. He sputtered in surprise, shaking his head vigorously as it pounded with the sensation. Jason stood for a moment in purple shadow and looked about, then saw a fleeting glimpse just ahead of him. He ran after, calling, "Bailey! Wait!"

The wispy nothing turned about, then became solid. It was Bailey in all her freckled and golden-brown-haired glory. She spun around, her jaw dropping in surprise, and then she let out a cry of joy. "Jason!" She started to bound toward him.

He stopped short, as a loud grating noise came from in front of him. A deep black crack opened up as the crystal under his feet vibrated for a long moment, rather like an earthquake. He stared down into it. Was it breaking up around them? Time did not seem to be on his side. "Come on," he said urgently, and held his hand out.

"I can't." Her voice trailed off, and she came to the edge of the chasm and stood hesitantly. "I've tried and tried." She shivered and hugged her arms about her ribs. "I'm cold. I'm hungry. And I'm sleepy."

"Sleepy?"

"I don't dare nap. I doze off now and then, but . . ." She looked at him, her face pleading. "Please help me, Jason!"

He leaned forward across the darkness, stretching closer. "Bailey, you've got to meet me halfway."

"I can't."

"Bailey, you can't stay. You're going to . . . you're going to die in here." As he spoke, the chill settled around him like a cloak, until its numbness went right to his bones. His ears felt brittle, like icicles that might break off. The only part of him that stayed warm was a small spot on his right shoulder.

Gavan, he thought. He shrugged his shoulder high, putting his ear and cheek to the warm spot for a moment. It heated him right through, as though he'd spread his body near a fireplace, and he managed to shake off most of the cold.

She just stood and looked at him, her heart-shaped face pale and afraid behind her freckles, her hair tangled and disheveled. She lifted her hand to her face and nibbled on the corner of a nail. "I . . . can't."

" 'Course you can!" He stood on the brink, and stretched out both hands. "Come on! You can't get home from there."

She turned on one foot, pointing into the shadows behind her. "The camp is that way."

"The way back to our camp is this way." He jerked a thumb over his shoulder. "You're out of step, Bailey. Just a Ghost. You've got to come with me."

"No one saw me." Bailey frowned. "I'm so hungry! All I've had is that cookie. And I want to sleep in my warm bed and . . ." She took a step backward.

"Bailey!" Jason sharpened his voice. "Listen to me. I'm here. Take hold of my hand and come with me." Music played softly in his ear, as if Eleanora tried to remind him of something. Was she hurrying him? Encouraging? He couldn't tell; all he knew was that Bailey was balking and he couldn't lose her. "We don't have a lot of time anymore, Bailey." He couldn't understand why she hesitated, why she just looked at him. Why she seemed so pale. Then he realized that she was fading, gradually. She was not the Bailey he knew, not quite, not altogether. And it would only get worse. He *would* lose her. "Come on," he coaxed. "FireAnn made ice cream. More cookies than you can eat."

"I want a hamburger."

"Those, too. And your own bed at Kittencurl waiting for you. Ting has it all ready. Jennifer has letters from your mom. Everyone is this way." He half-turned, showing the way.

She stood on tiptoe. She looked down into the dark crack between them, then back up at him. "I'll have to jump."

He stifled a mutter. "I'll catch you!" He stretched his hands out again.

"I don't think I can do it. . . ."

"Bailey," he said firmly. "You can do anything." He wiggled his fingers. "You're just a long step away. Not far at all. And I won't let you fall in, I promise!" She looked into his eyes across the dark chasm. "Come on. We've got things to do. Canoe races. Helping Henry get even with Stefan and Rich. Learning our crystals. Catching that thief."

"That thief!" Bailey cracked a grin. "I've a plan."

"Trent and I will help, just . . . take my hand . . . and jump."

She took a deep breath. She looked back over her shoulder, to something only she could see in the purple shadows. "Maybe I should go home instead. Mom must be so worried. I think I can make it from here," she said wistfully.

A sinking feeling hit him. He was losing her. "Someday, Bailey. But not from here, and not without help."

She swung around. Without another word, she leaped.

It caught him off guard. She came at him, arms and legs akimbo, golden-brown hair streaming, hands grasping desperately for him. He waved frantically, trying to catch her flying hands. In an awful moment, as she hung in midair over the darkening gap, he knew she wouldn't make it.

"No!" Leaning farther forward than he dared, he locked wrists with her. She cried out and tore her right hand away from his left as though stung. Jason fell to his knees, off-balance, and gave a great pull, yanking her on top of him, and they both went tumbling.

But she was on his side of the awful gap. He got to his feet and pulled her up. Bailey leaned on him, and took a great gulping breath. "I can't see," she whispered. "It's all . . . dark and purple shadow."

"I can," he reassured her. He linked his right arm about her arm, tucking her close to his side. He turned and looked and saw only mirrorlike walls facing them, tinted with the inner glow of the crystal.

Jason pondered. "Ummm."

"Anything to eat?" Bailey's voice sounded wispy and weak.

"Not on me."

She giggled faintly. "Should have sent Trent. He's always got food on him, unless he's eaten it first."

"Hey!" said Jason, mock-insulted. Without trying to worry her, he examined the area around them, searching for the way out. There was none. Now they were both trapped. He stopped in his tracks. Bailey shivered next to him and he could feel how cold she was, how lifeless this crystal was becoming. She was running out of time.

He closed his eyes, thinking. The fire on his right shoulder seemed to flicker. The music in his left ear tinkled faintly. He couldn't lose them! Without them . . . Jason's eyes flew open. He looked ahead. As long as he had the two Magickers anchoring him, he was not lost. He couldn't be. The planes ahead of him might look solid, but they had not shut away Eleanora and Gavan. He hugged Bailey. "One step at a time," he told her confidently. He moved forward into the purple shadows, his friend leaning on him.

From behind, a howl sounded. It echoed and resounded off the crystal walls, rising and falling.

Bailey gasped and clutched at him. Jason fought the impulse to spin around. "There's a canyon between it and us," he said. He moved another step closer to the heat, the music.

"It followed me in when I tried to keep them from getting you. One of them tracked me. They can see me. Smell me. That's why I can't sleep, I've been running and running ever since. I ran in here to hide, and I've been trapped. I couldn't find a way out!" Bailey's voice trembled.

"I won't let them catch us. Just hang on to me!"

The wolfjackal howled again, louder, closer. He though he could hear triumph in its throat. He had no doubt it could jump the canyon. But he was almost home, and of that, he had little doubt as well.

He could hear the chimes, like a waterfall of notes, cascading about him. Heat washed up against them, banked warmth from an unseen source, but he knew who it was. On his heels, he could hear the noise as the running beast gathered itself, and jumped.

"This way, Bailey!" He grabbed her and pushed her ahead into . . . nothingness.

"Next time, I want pillows," she said. Contentedly, she licked off her spoon, leaning back in the great winged back chair in Eleanora's office, because Gavan's was undeniably still a mess . . . what with papers and objects from his desk toppled everywhere, not to mention overturned chairs from when Jason and Bailey had hit ground.

"Next time?" Both Gavan and Eleanora looked at Bailey.

She blushed. "Well. You know. If I ever have to fall out of a crystal again . . . once burned, twice careful."

Jason took a small tart from his plate and passed it to her, saying, "Still hungry?"

She snatched it up with a muffled "Thank you," crumbs dribbling from the corner of her mouth. Finally, she sat back, empty bowl on her lap, a cat-who-ate-the-canary pleased look on her face. Her eyelids drooped.

"I think," observed Eleanora, "that a good night's sleep is in order. And then, tomorrow, young lady, we will listen to your adventures and reacquaint you with your crystal . . . from the outside!"

Bailey nodded slowly as Eleanora reached forward to take the dirty dishes. Gavan leaned over the chair, then picked her up in his arms, as though she were a small child. "To Kittencurl and bed," he said.

Jason watched them go. Suddenly, Bailey peeked from around Gavan's arm.

"Thank you," she got out sleepily. He beamed.

Ting and Bailey sat chatting away, laughing and giggling, with an occasional smile and thrown-in laugh from Jennifer as Bailey devoured a breakfast fit for either Trent or Henry Squibb. She grinned at Jason and Trent as they slid into their seats. "I'm almost all caught up!" she announced, pointing at her tray.

"Good." He didn't like the image of a quiet, lackluster Bailey.

She seemed to be back, in more ways than one. She sidled over and whispered, "Have I got things to tell you!"

"I don't know," he whispered back. "Have you?"

"I'm serious! You won't believe what I heard, ghosting about." She glanced around the mess hall. "For instance, Tomaz is looking for a skinwalker."

"A what?"

"I'll tell you later!" She giggled and put her elbow in his ribs. "Later!"

"Okay."

She slid back to Ting, and they exchanged some more words, quietly this time, except that Ting looked up, over Bailey's head, at the two of them, before ducking back down and the two girls burst into loud laughter. Was it something he'd said? Puzzled, Jason studied his breakfast.

"Girls," muttered Trent. "Can't live with 'em, and can't live with 'em."

That made Jason laugh. "Now," he said, "you're beginning to sound like Bailey." He started to eat his Frosted Flakes before they got soggy.

Back at their cabins, with some spare time to clean up the area because inspection would be tomorrow, they found Jonnard marching Henry about the small clearing and path, dowsing rods in his hand. Henry's round face looked more owlish than ever, huffed and puffed up with frustration.

"I can't do it! I just can't." Henry shoved his glasses back to rest properly on the bridge of his nose.

Jon looked down on him, saying mildly, "If you can't, that's perfectly all right. Magickers have all kinds of Talents. There are all sorts of perfectly capable people who can't dowse. But you *are* the one who asked for extra practice."

"I can't do anything!" Henry began to wail and then stopped short. He sighed instead. "I'm going to be drummed out, I just know it."

"You're here at camp. Meanwhile . . ." Jon glanced at the two of them standing there. "Anyone have a clean handkerchief or bandanna?"

"Bandanna in the cabin!" Trent shot off and came back with a bright red bandanna in his hands. He handed it to Jon.

Jon stretched it out between his fingers. "Okay, Henry, one

last try before I let you give up on dowsing." He held out the bandanna as a blindfold. Henry fidgeted while he fastened it about his eyes. Stefan and Rich sauntered up, and stood, smirking, at the path's edge. Jon eyed them, then decided to ignore them as he bent over to retrieve a line of pennies he'd laid out on the ground. After a moment or two, he had them laid out in a new line.

"All right. In the same general area we were before, there's a line. Find it, Henry," Jon said quietly.

Henry's hands flexed around his dowsing rods. Before he could bring them into position and start, both Stefan and Rich darted to his side, saying, "That's too easy." Grabbing him, they began to spin him round and round in circles, till—when they halted and stepped back—his glasses had slipped all the way to the end of his nose and he wobbled in his shoes. "Now, try it!" They stepped back, chortling at their cleverness.

Jonnard shot the two of them a dirty look before saying, "It's all right, Henry. Let me know when you're ready."

"N . . . now," Henry quavered. He stumbled, then righted himself as he walked forward.

With Trent, Jason, and Jon all encouraging him, his path snaked all over the small clearing dizzily. Even when he steadied, not once as he neared the line of coins did his metal rods even twitch. Rich and Stefan snickered and smirked till even they were tired of it and wandered off. Squibb finally halted with a sigh, tugged the blindfold down around his neck. "It's no use. I'm just an idiot."

Jon took the rods from him and patted him on the shoulder. "No, you're not. When's the last time anyone ever dug a well hoping to hit pennies? At any rate, you're a whiz on the computers, I hear."

"But that's not Magick."

"It is to someone like me." Jon smiled. "Come on, let's play chess a bit before class." Without another word, he turned and went into their cabin, his long legs taking him up two strides at a time over the steps and porch. With a sniffle, Henry took off the bandanna, tossed it to Trent, and followed. Trent watched them disappear thoughtfully.

Inside, Jason remembered something.

"Hey, Trent. You ever heard of a skinwalker?"

Trent stopped in the middle of making a basket with a pair of rolled-up dirty socks. "A what?"

"A skinwalker?"

He scratched his nose and shot the socks into the corner from across the room anyway. "I don't know if this is what you mean ... but I think it's like a Native American term for a shapeshifter. A skin changer, like. Like ... I dunno ... a were-wolf. Where'd you heard about one, anyway?"

"Bailey told me. She heard stuff while she was walking around, half here and half not. She says Tomaz is looking for one."

"Whoa. That's pretty heavy." Trent stood up. "Someone who sprouts hair and claws and stuff in the full moon." He bared his teeth and began to stagger across the cabin at Jason.

Jason wound up and thwapped him with a pillow, and Trent fell over, laughing. When he stopped, he asked, "What do you think?"

"I don't know. She said she had a lot to tell me. We'll see." He shrugged.

"May you live in interesting, weird times," Trent said, as he got to his feet and began to knot his socks up so he could pelt them at Jason.

"Thank you!" Jason beamed at him.

21

Gimme Some Peanuts
and Crackerjack

"ARE you sure you're up to this?"

"'Course, I'm sure!" Bailey yawned and stretched. "I'm almost all caught up!" She grinned, then hid her mouth. "'Sides ... this is get even day! And it's the Fourth! Who could miss a baseball game on the Fourth of July?"

Ting hugged her. Jason eyed Bailey. She still looked a bit pale behind her freckled nose, but all in all, much better. He crossed his arms as Rich and Stefan snickered.

"No way is she gonna be on my team," Rich said. Stefan lumbered across the baseball diamond, putting on his catcher's gear as he moved, strapping the protective padding across his chest and bulky thighs.

"No way I'd ever want to be," Bailey shot back. She pressed her lips shut thinly as Jefferson came round the corner of the backstop, clipboard in hand.

"All right, ladies and gentlemen. It's been a fine day. Are we ready to hold our vengeance match this late afternoon?" He smiled broadly as though he had been listening. "Let's get teams picked."

The warped wooden stands thundered dully as campers

who weren't playing settled themselves down with colorful paper sacks of fresh popcorn from the kitchens. The aroma wafted deliciously over the baseball diamond, and Jason almost opted to go sit and watch as well. Trent's stomach gave a faint rumble, but he put his hand on Jason's wrist, frowning.

"We can't let 'em get away with this," he whispered.

Jason nodded. He pushed the desire for popcorn to the back of his thoughts and squared his shoulders as Jefferson asked, "Do we have both captains here?"

"I'm here," said Rich, the corner of his mouth curling back unpleasantly. "Dunno what happened to Fred, though."

"He's still at the swimming relays. He should be here any second," Ting shot back.

"With dead arms, if he's swimming," said Stefan gleefully. He gave a grunt as Jefferson eyed him a moment. He shuffled around and found himself, somehow, standing behind Rich.

Bailey stood with her arms folded. Jennifer leaned over and whispered something in Bailey's ear.

"I don't think that was the least bit funny," said Bailey. "And you guys are going to lose."

Jennifer smiled. She pulled her hair back into a ponytail and tucked it up into her baseball cap, looking as if she meant business.

Fred came loping up, hair all slicked back from swimming, pulling a sweatshirt on over his clothes. He grinned and slapped Trent's upheld hand. "Okay, let's get this grudge match going!"

Jennifer sniffed, casting a glance Stefan's way, who despite being all bundled up in catcher's equipment, looked more rumpled and dustier than ever. "Grudge or grunge?"

Even Jefferson laughed while Stefan just scowled and rubbed his stubby nose. Jefferson tapped his clipboard again. "Okay, you two, let's pick teams."

In just a few moments, with bodies scrambling to keep up as the team captains chanted names off, two lines of players soon faced each other. Fred and Rich quickly did the hand over hand on the bat Jefferson held out to them, with Fred winning. He smiled. "We'll be the home team."

Rich's lip curled. "You'll need last ups," he warned. "We're gonna knock you outta the ballpark!"

Fred looked at Rich's players, and then up and down his line at Jason and the others. He smiled slowly. "You're going to need more than luck," he promised. "Okay, huddle up for field assignments!"

He looked Bailey in the eyes. "First base."

"M . . . me?" She stood on one foot and then the other.

"You. You're fast, you think fast. Ting, you're pitching." Fred rattled off everyone's assignments and they gathered gloves and trotted out to the field to enthusiastic cheers from the rest of the campers in the stands. After a rousing rendition of "The Star Spangled Banner" led by Sousa, the game was on!

Jason took his place in right field. Trent was shortstop, Jonnard center field, Jennifer second base, Henry was catching, Danno was at third base, and Fred in left field. Ting did some stretches, then narrowed her eyes and glared down at home plate, sizing up the first of Rich's batters. She wound up and threw, dead on, and Jefferson loudly called "Steeee-rike!"

She beamed.

Her second pitch sailed past the home plate, down and a little outside. George Anders swung his bat at it threateningly, but held up, and Jefferson called out, "Ball one!"

George hit the fifth pitch, popping it up, and Trent came in a little, catching it neatly. The stands wildly cheered the first out. The smell of popcorn had faded, or maybe Jason was too far out in the field to catch it, but the thought stayed at the back of his mind. Stefan came up to bat and with one swing, he sent the ball sailing over the weathered back fence of the field. Campers came to their feet screaming as it sailed into the bushes and Fred went trotting after to retrieve it. Ting sagged on the pitcher's mound.

Jason and Trent both came in. Trent thumped her on the back. "Good going!"

Bailey walked in, just in time to catch that. Her face went pinched. "What do you mean by that?"

"I mean . . . good going. Every pitcher is gonna lose a pitch like that. Ting got it out of her system early, no harm done!" Trent thumped Ting again, who staggered a little.

"Oh." Bailey looked back and forth. "Well . . . that's good, then!" She hugged Ting.

Ting let out a small sound. Fred showed up, ball in hand, cleaning off the dirt with his sweatshirt before dropping it into her hands. "Got that out of the way. Now let's play!" He grinned. She took a deep breath and nodded.

Ting struck out one and walked one, but the team came to her aid and made the other outs on good plays. By the time they took their ups at the plate and then returned to the field, Jon's line drive had sent Fred across for a score, and the game was tied 1–1.

As the day trudged into dusk, it was 7–7, clearly not a pitcher's duel. Tired, Ting went to sit on the bench, happily munching popcorn, and Fred took her place, drafting Christopher Bacon out of the stands to replace him in center field. And so the day went. Jason had two good hits, a strikeout, and two pop flies. Trent had solid hits but only got around the bases one more time, and as the sun went down in the sky and the mosquitoes began to gather, everyone came to a tired huddle before taking their at-bats.

Jefferson consulted his clipboard. "Listen up, everyone. Because this is the Fourth of July, and FireAnn has a special dinner cooking, and there's going to be a big bonfire after, with some special effects . . ." He winked at this. "Game will be called at the end of this inning."

Everyone cheered even more wildly. Hunger rattled around inside Jason's ribs. He looked longingly at the bench where Ting now sat with a cone of red, white, and blue cotton candy in her hands. She saw his look and waved back happily. His stomach growled.

Positions had been rotated and new players volunteered from the stands. Stefan was now pacing around heavily in center field, stopping occasionally to lean mockingly on the drooping fence. No one else had hit a home run.

Jason waved his bat, pointed it at the new pitcher, and took up a stance. Not that he thought he'd get a home run, but just to rattle him a little. Tran's face was, as always, closed and unreadable, but Jason thought he saw a flicker in his eyes. He moved on the pitcher's mound and Jason got ready.

He met the ball squarely with the bat. He could feel the impact and followed through on the swing, knowing it was a good one. He sprinted for first base, dropping the bat on the way, head down, digging in his heels, ankle twinging only the barest bit. The ball shot between first base and second base, but he had no time to make it to second and stayed at first on a good, solid hit.

Fred put his hands up over his head and applauded. Jason caught his breath and waited to be brought home. He slapped at a mosquito at the back of his neck, muttering. The sky had gotten very dark, and the hanging lights that festooned the campgrounds twinkled in golden winks, intermingled with lightning bugs imitating them, in slow lazy swarms by the lake's edge. He waited while Trent popped out and then Danno got hit by a pitched ball, so they both moved forward. Then Tran struck Fred out, and Bailey stepped up to bat.

She took her cap off, smoothed back her golden-brown hair, and then put her cap on backward, and settled down at the plate like she meant it. Rich was catching now and grunted something at her Jason didn't quite hear. Bailey's response was to kick a cloud of dirt over the plate, making Rich burst into sneezes and coughs. She tried to look apologetic as she dusted him off. Jason hid a smirk. He tagged up at second. Behind him, he could hear Stefan grumbling about something from his position in center field.

Bailey stepped back into the batter's box. Dusky shadows hid her face except for the determined expression on it as she waggled her bat and settled into a hitter's stance. A lightning bug whizzed by as she began to sing, "Take me out to the ball game, take me out to the crowd, buy me some peanuts and Crackerjack, I don't care if I ever get back . . ."

"C'mon, Tran, let's get this out before Bailey disappears on us again," Rich sneered.

Bailey wrinkled her nose and tightened her hands on the bat. Out in front of the stands, Henry orchestrated an animated cheer. For which team, Jason couldn't quite tell from the yelling, but it was spirited. The audience sensed a game about to end . . . which meant a dinner about to be served!

Tran pitched. Bailey hit. The ball—soared.

Jason stood and blinked for a moment, then touched the base as Danno ran his way, urging Jason. "Move, move, move!"

The ball seemed to whistle through the twilight air as it

passed. Jason slowed his stride a bit as it arced overhead. Stefan gave a grunt as he began to run. He could see Bailey from the corner of his eye, pounding down the right field line, from home plate to first. It wouldn't . . . couldn't . . . be a home run. Jefferson had straightened from his umpire's stance, taken his mask off and stood, watching the hit ball.

If Stefan caught it, the game was over. If he dropped it, the game was over. Either way, Jason knew he could round the diamond and cross home plate. He dug in happily.

Behind him, there was an immense crash. Jason crossed, then turned around to see that the back field fence was . . . gone . . . and Stefan with it. Danno and then Bailey joined him. They stood, looking at center field. Bailey bounced. "Did he catch it? Did I hit a home run?"

"I dunno," Jason told her. Jefferson looked at her and shrugged, saying, "I don't know either."

Grunts and growls came from the thick, prickly bushes on the other side of the fence, as something heaved around in them. Then, slowly, Stefan stood and raised his glove in the air, the baseball nested firmly inside it. The crowd cheered madly and stampeded toward the mess hall.

Bailey rubbed her nose. Then, with a sigh, she turned away. Jason grabbed her wrist. "Hey! That was some hit anyway."

Jefferson waited till Stefan jogged slowly in from the brush, then he declared the winners.

Bailey cheered up at the bonfire when Lucas sang, "Casey at the Bat," and then, with a startling boom and snap, fireworks began out on the lake. Jason could see the profile of Hightower on a flat raft, setting them off and standing back.

Flowers and sparks of color shot up and bloomed in the dark skies until their ears ached from the noise, their eyes were dazzled, and the smell of the smoke stung their nostrils.

Jason heard Rich as he leaned over and whispered to Stefan, "Not as good as ours are gonna be!"

Gavan Rainwater heard also. He turned his head, and leaned into the conference. "Actually . . . those *are* your fireworks. We cannot thank you boys enough for contributing to the holiday." He winked before walking off to join Eleanora and Dr. Patel.

Rich's jaw dropped and he blinked in disbelief as he stared at the lake. "Oh, man. . . ."

Stefan scratched at a welt and prickle and thumped his friend on the shoulder in sympathy, a tangle of brush still hanging from his shirt. "Hey, at least we got to see 'em. And we did win the game 'cause I jumped the fence an' caught that ball." He reached at the weed in distraction, scattering leaves and grass and dirt all over both of them.

The night ended in a great burst of fountains, big and little, and sky rockets zooming all over the lake. Ting let out a contented sigh as they said good night before heading off to their cottage.

In the morning, Rich and Stefan were first in line at Dr. Patel's door, scratching and broken out in blisters from head to toe. Bailey sailed past them with a wide ear-to-ear grin.

"I," she said triumphantly to Jason, "hit the ball that put him in the poison oak patch!"

Bailey caught up to the crystal class quickly. In the blink of an eye, she had a cold flame centered in her amethyst. Crystal in the palm of her hand, she smiled at the lantern light within as she showed Ting. Ting's crystal flickered with a heart-shaped pink glow while Bailey's had almost a cat's-eye gleam to it. Trent lit his quickly and snuffed it just as quickly, before even Jason could catch a glimpse of it.

Eleanora stood behind Jason as if she'd also been hoping to see what Trent warmed inside his strange crystal, but she said quietly, "Some Magickers are not comfortable with Fire. Water is more their Element," before she moved away.

Henry pulled an oven mitt out of his backpack. Rich looked at it and let out a roaring laugh. Henry's face went pink. "What?" he said, waving his bemitted hand about. "Fire-Ann let me borrow it."

Rich tried to contain his chortles. "G . . . good thing," he managed, "it's already singed!"

Henry sighed. Danno gave him a slight shake of encouragement. "I'm ready," he said. He toed the bucket of water from under the picnic table.

Squibb didn't look all that confident. He pushed his glasses back onto the bridge of his nose and ran a hand through his bushy hair before taking a deep breath. Jon stood to the side, eyebrow arched in interest, his tall, slender body poised alertly as Henry fetched his crystal out and placed it in the center of the oven mitt's palm.

Frowning, he spoke a single word and the crystal flared up like a Roman candle. One single flame shot upward with a WHOOSH! Birds took wing with cries of startlement, filling the sky. Henry choked and the flame shot down into the crystal and extinguished. The oven mitt appeared none the worse for damage though the air stank of charred hair. When Henry turned to look at Jason, his face stricken, Jason could see why. The hair had been burned right off his forehead!

Gavan cleared his throat. "Better control this time, Henry. In no time at all, you'll have that tamed."

Stefan grunted. "It'll be like having a flamethrower in your pocket."

"Useful." Rich nodded.

"Stuff a sock in it, you two." Danno took the mitt off Henry's hand and put it back in his pack. "Another day or two and you'll have it." Henry stood blinking, looking a little stunned.

"Indeed," said Jonnard. "A bit more practice, is all. Fire is clearly your Element."

"It is?" Round-eyed, Henry looked around him.

"Well, of course it is. It's eager to answer you. A little too eager, that's all." Jonnard smiled slightly.

Gavan nodded at Jonnard. Jennifer tucked a strand of hair behind one graceful ear. "Perhaps," she said, a little shyly, "I could help them read their Elements."

Gavan looked at her thoughtfully. "That might be very helpful, Jennifer. Think you can do it?"

"I've been studying." She touched Henry on the shoulder as she came and stood by his side, and paused for a moment, her crystal pendant in hand. "Oh, definitely Fire." She smiled at Henry.

"Oh." Henry relaxed slightly, and a lopsided grin came to rest on his otherwise harried looking face. "I'll have to try harder, then."

"I think," Rainwater said smoothly, "the key is in trying a bit less." He winked and moved on between the students.

"Oh," said Henry. "Right. I can see that." He reached up,

removed his glasses, wiping the steam from them before replacing them on his forehead. A dry, crinkled hair fell as he did so.

"Henry," suggested Eleanora. "I think you should retire for the day, and return that mitt to FireAnn as her staff will probably need it." She smiled encouragingly.

With another poke aimed at stabilizing his glasses on his sunburned nose, Henry nodded and trotted off in the direction of the main buildings.

Nothing else as interesting happened in any of the other classes although Bailey seemed to need little catching up. She watched and listened with intent interest, sitting or standing back with a faint already-knew-it expression on her face. During break, as they trotted to wash up for lunch, she repeated to Jason, "Have I got things to tell you!" Then she frowned slightly and rubbed her freckled nose. "If I can remember them all."

"I don't have any free time till after dinner," he said.

"That's fine. Come over and take a look at the trap. I have some changes to make."

"Did you see who it was as Ghost?"

"Not . . . quite. I have an idea, though." She winked and headed off for swimming, her ponytail bouncing behind her.

Jason watched her thoughtfully. The old Bailey was back. Nearly. Neither of them had spoken much about what she had felt when grabbing for his left hand, his marked hand. She had only said that "it hurt," and a small flicker of fear gleamed in her eyes before she changed the subject quickly. He sighed. The crescent twinged a little as it always did when he thought about it.

After dinner, the sun still hung brightly over the western hills, although the sky deepened to a dark, clear blue. It was a perfect summer evening and they all sat around on her porch waiting for it to get dark. Sousa had promised a singalong for later.

Bailey sat with her ponytail pulled over her shoulder, curling the end of it round and round her finger. "First of all, I saw things."

Trent let out a whoop, making her blush after she thumped him. "Not that kind of stuff! I stayed away from the showers!"

She rolled her eyes. "If you're not going to listen, I won't tell."

He pulled his face into serious lines. "I'll listen. See? I'm looking like Jason."

"Hmmpf."

Ting tapped her pencil on Jason's knee. "Both of you stop it. I want to hear, even if you don't!" She balanced her notebook on her lap, poised to take notes. Bailey shot her a grateful look.

"Now . . . if there are no more interruptions?" She looked around. Feet shuffled restlessly, but no one made a sound as she settled herself on the steps of Kittencurl Cottage. "Good. First of all, I couldn't eat. Everything was half a step ahead of me. If I reached for it, it was gone. The only thing I managed to get was a cookie which Jason stubbornly kept out for me, and I barely got that."

Trent looked at Ting. "Make a note: take food."

Ting giggled, but her pencil wiggled as she jotted something down quickly. Jason peered over her shoulder. It read: Make sure Trent has food at all times. He covered his grinning face with a well-aimed scratch at an eyebrow.

"But I heard things, and could read things left out, and saw things, although I couldn't do anything about them till later. By then, it was usually too late." Bailey sighed. "First of all . . . not everybody is going to make it as a Magicker. Being here doesn't mean everyone has enough Talent or ability to make it. That stuff FireAnn has been brewing for days now is called the Draft of Forgetfulness." She looked about and lowered her voice a bit more. "And it works. Anyone leaving isn't going to remember much of anything. And . . . some of us have been working with Magickers for a year or so already, like Jennifer and Jon."

Jason let his breath out in a hiss. "Doesn't sound good."

Trent shrugged. "When you think about it, what choice do they have? They can't send someone home who will talk about it, if they remember. By the time we're ready to go home, we'll have a stake in being a Magicker. That means we'll keep it quiet. As far as Jennifer and Jon go . . . well, they've always been like counselors and stuff. I always got the feeling they knew a lot more than they let on."

"Some idiots will talk about anything." Ting shook her head, looking worried. "They'll ruin anything, just to get attention. The Draft is the only way to go."

Bailey nodded. "The Magickers have a plan for that."

Jason said, "What are you saying, Bailey? That we can't trust them?"

She looked solemnly at him. "There are Magickers in and out of here all the time we haven't even *seen*, let alone met. There's a whole Council that meets at night."

"There is?"

She nodded at Trent. "You'll never see them. They come in late at night and leave early."

Jason did not mention that he *had* seen them, or at least heard them.

"You get a look at them, Bailey?"

"Well . . . sorta. I was kind of seeing everybody a half step behind what they looked like." She sighed. "I know they meet to talk about us, and make plans, and there's a storm coming that has all of them awfully worried."

"Mana storm?"

"That's the one."

Ting stopped writing again. "What is that? Is it like a hurricane?"

"It's a storm of power, from what I hear," Jason told her. "It turns everything upside down. It's like Magick goes uncontrollably wild, I think."

Ting and Bailey shivered together. Trent said quietly, "If we don't know what it is, we can't jump to conclusions."

"Right. What else, Bailey?"

"The Dark Hand is thought to be behind those nightmares we have."

"How?"

She shook her head. "No idea. And Tomaz is looking for a skinwalker in camp. That sounds really bad. They don't know if he's from the Dark Hand or one of us. That's all I heard about that, I couldn't get into the rooms. Doors." She sighed. "I had to sneak into the toilets when I could. Not much sleep. I slept one night in the chair here, but Ting almost sat on me. I didn't want to scare you." She grinned at her friend. "No. I didn't see the thief. Almost, but, well, being out of step and all, not quite. Still, I know what time the thief comes by and I think we can catch it tonight, after Lights Out."

"You think so, Bailey? I want my watch back."

Bailey shrugged and added, "Won't know till we try!" She paused, as Stefan and Rich sauntered by, hiking around the lake, but also giving them the eye. Rich particularly looked them all over as if memorizing who was in what place. He snickered. "Double-dating?"

Trent muttered as they nearly passed out of earshot.

Jason's eyes narrowed as he watched them laugh and lumber past.

Ting ignored them totally. "Have a trap for the thief in mind?"

"Well. As my grandma always says, you can catch more bears with honey than vinegar—"

A noise came from the other side of the cottage before Bailey's emphatic words even faded. There was a crash as something heavy plowed through the underbrush near the cottage's edge, the side that fronted into a lot of the wilderness near the lake.

A big burly shape went by, with Rich trotting at his heels, red hair sticking out. "Oh, not again. One of you guys stop him!"

Trent glanced at the big bear cub headed deeper into the woods that fringed the cottages and answered, "And I should stop him . . . why?"

"Because he'll get in trouble, that's why!" Rich tried to tackle the bear, and it shook him off, bawling and snuffling. It kicked off what looked like tennis shoes before loping away on all fours. Ting's jaw dropped.

Rich threw his hands up. "Get back here!" he bellowed.

The bear seemed to whine "Hun-eeee" as Rich tried to catch up with him.

Jason stood up. "What's going on? That's a wild animal . . . isn't it?"

They all traded shrugs.

He said. "I guess we should help." He started in the general direction of Rich and the bear. After a few moments of hesitation, the others followed him.

They tromped to where they could hear a low, grunting

voice, and Rich's higher one, pleading. They rounded an ever-green tree and then stopped in astonishment.

A brown bear wearing the shreds of Stefan's shirt and trousers sat on the ground, contentedly and repeatedly scratching his back against a stout tree trunk, over and over and over. They stared at the young bear and then at Rich. Rich looked at them. He sighed. "Well. Now you know. At least it's not another brier patch, and don't any of you dare mention the H word or I'll be chasing him around the lake."

At that, the bear stopped scratching and tossed his head a bit, rolling his eyes. He gave a most Stefanish grunt and looked at them with beady brown eyes.

"Good grief. Is that . . . ?"

Rich glared at them. "Who do you think it is?"

Trent swung on Bailey. "There's your skinwalker."

The bear let out a half-growl, and pawed at his nose.

Jason looked at the creature sitting in the remains of Stefan's gear. "No doubt about it."

Dust Bunnies

THEY all stared, fascinated, as Stefan-bear cradled something in its paws, eating and slurping. Bailey pointed up, overhead, at a beehive that was drizzling honey from one of its broken sides. "Good thing it's almost dark."

Rich signed again. He began picking up shreds of items and tucking them in his backpack. The sneakers appeared to be intact and he thumped Stefan-bear on the shoulder, saying, "Good boy! Atta boy, you remembered to kick your sneakers off!"

Ting backed away a step, glancing at the bear as he grunted and chewed at his honeycomb. "Is it *safe* to do that?"

"Well." Rich considered his hairy friend. "I'm not really sure. He knows me." He shrugged. "All I know is, I can't go where he goes. And sometimes he can't even go there." Ruefully, he picked brambles out of his sleeve.

"Brier patch," Jason said suddenly.

Rich looked at him mournfully, then nodded.

Trent squatted down, staring into the bear's face. "How does he turn back? How long does he stay a bear? He doesn't look full grown either, somewhere between a cub and an adult."

"Last couple of times, right away. Now . . ." Rich looked as Stefan happily continued to grunt, slurp, and munch. "Got me."

Bailey giggled. "At least not until he's done, I should imagine. He's really enjoying it."

The chubby cub tossed his head about, eyed her, grunted again, and shifted the honeycomb in his paws. He had a white diamond-sized patch on his russet-brown chest, and droplets of honey drizzled down into it.

"I'd say that was a yes."

Trent stood. "I'd say you're going to have to hose him down."

The bear made a bleating sound, pinning his ears back. His long pink tongue curled around an end of the honeycomb, scooping out more amber honey. His ears flicked forward again in sheer pleasure.

"Actually," Rich shifted from one foot to the other. "He likes bathing in the lake. Listen, you guys, you can't tell anyone."

Ting looked uneasily from Stefan-bear to Rich. She said slowly, "I don't see how you're going to hide it. I mean . . . he's pretty big . . . and noisy. And he smells like a bear."

The bear rolled his eyes about. He crunched down the last waxy bit of his honeycomb and tried to lick his chest off before getting to his feet. A last shred of T-shirt fell from his back as he did. He looked terribly odd with trousers still on, although they scarcely fit him as they hit his knees. He reminded Jason of a very old Smokey the Bear stuffed toy he used to have. Another thought occurred to him. There might be an advantage to having Stefan and Rich owing all of them for keeping a secret. "Tomaz is looking for a skinwalker," he mused.

"They'll kick us out, man." Rich's pale complexion went to pasty white. "He's a freak. We can't leave before he finds out how to . . . how to . . ." He seemed at a loss for words.

"How to deal with it?" Jason nodded. "Okay. We won't say anything. That doesn't mean you won't get found out, though. Eventually . . ."

Rich twisted his backpack in his hands. "All we need is a little time. I hope." He grabbed an ear and tugged on it gently. "Come on, Stefan. You can be seen!"

With a low bleat and a grunt, the bear followed Rich deeper into the shrubbery. Trent shook his head as the two disappeared temporarily. "Tomaz is already on their trail."

"Maybe. Maybe not. Anyway, maybe we can get Squibb some peace and quiet."

Trent leaned on him. "A little blackmail? I see you've learned from me, grasshopper!"

But Ting only shivered as they walked back to Kittencurl.

"What's wrong?" Bailey asked.

"What if he's not the one Tomaz is looking for. What if Crowfeather is looking for something worse? Something dark and dangerous?"

"Then let's hope he finds out quickly. I haven't heard anything, though, have you? I mean, the wolfjackals are bad enough. . . ." Bailey kept chattering as they walked back.

Their voices trailed off as the sky turned night dark and they climbed their porch steps. Sousa's rendition of Lights Out sounded throughout the camp, oddly faint on this side of the lake. Trent and Jason could not follow, so they stood at the trail and waved as the girls disappeared inside. Trent waited for the screen door to bang shut, then said, "What if she's right?"

"Something dark prowling around?" He didn't want to think of it. He rubbed his hand. "Trust me, Trent. Wolfjackals are bad enough."

"I'm not saying they aren't. But sometimes your worst enemy is the one inside of you." Without waiting for an answer, he started toward their end of the lake.

With a funny feeling in the pit of his stomach, Jason trotted after Trent. He wanted to ask just what Trent meant by that but he was afraid he knew. The thought of being imprisoned in a body that wanted to hunt, to hurt, was animal wild . . . without being able to change or control it . . . made his blood run cold. The nightmare memory of the chill, silent tomb and the being that wanted to draw him always closer rose unbidden. What did the being want to tell him? What would he do if he got his hands on Jason? Was that what made a skinwalker out of you? How much longer could he even resist?

A shiver ran down the back of his neck clear to his feet.

A faraway howl echoed down from high jagged peaks that the night almost hid. Coyote. Or wolfjackal? He spun around on the path, grateful that it seemed a long way off, yet wondering if that was a lie. He heard Trent's fading steps and turned around to hurry and catch up.

Something dark and big reared up in front of him. It reached out and caught his elbow. Jason let out a squeak and tried to dodge. His ankle turned, sending a ping of pain all the way to his nose.

"Yeowch!" Jason flapped his arms for balance.

"Hold on there," Tomaz Crowfeather said quietly. His hand tightened around Jason's arm, steadying him on the pathway. He waited till Jason caught his breath, then said mildly, "Out a little late?"

"We walked the girls back to their cabin. Ting is a little nervous, and Bailey is, well, Bailey," Jason finished lamely. He didn't like lying, and he was almost certain that Tomaz could see right through him. He shifted his weight uneasily.

Tomaz watched him. "I have not decided if trouble sniffs you out, or you sniff trouble out. You're safer back at the cabin."

Jason nodded as Tomaz released him and helpfully pointed him in the right direction. "Wolfjackals?"

"Many things travel the night," Tomaz said. "Some evil with their quarry in mind, others . . . more confused than anything. But a frightened animal is as dangerous as a mean one, remember that." He raised his hand and waved it in farewell.

Before Jason could take the hint and bolt for home, a scream split the night. Before the terrified wail stopped, both Tomaz and Jason were in motion. Jason led the way. "That's Ting," he said, vaulting up the steps at Kittencurl.

Tomaz reached for the screen door, interrupted by a horrible jangling and clanging of bells and cans. Jason slowed down. Their trap had just gone off! "The thief! That's Bailey's thief trap!" Squeals and yells filled their ears as they entered the cottage.

Ting, still dressed, her pajamas clutched to her chest, stood on a chair, dancing and yelling, "It's a rat! A rat!"

Bailey, on her hands and knees, dove into the strings of cans and bells, trying to catch something that was scampering about wildly. Both Tomaz and Jason watched in total bewilderment.

"Thief?" the Magicker said to Jason.

Jason nodded. "Someone's been taking things." His further explanation was cut short by Bailey's triumphant yell.

"Gotcha!" She stood in a jangle of sound and string, looking rather like an odd Christmas tree. There was something in her hands, a small ball of soft charcoal-and-white fur. Its long tail hung through Bailey's fingers, a little black tuft at the end, with a puff of dust and cobwebs dangling from it. Whiskers flicked back and forth desperately. Amber eyes stared at them, blinking rapidly as the creature searched for a way out of Bailey's clutches.

Ting stopped yelling. "It . . . it's a dust bunny." She stared at Bailey who smoothed a fingertip over the frightened animal's head.

"Some kind of mouse," said Bailey. She cooed to it. "Poor thing's scared to death."

"It's a rodent," corrected Tomaz. "Kangaroo rat, actually, although more related to the mouse part of the rodent family. This particular variety of kangaroo rat is often called a pack rat." He eyed the creature trembling in Bailey's palms. "Missing items, you said? Small things, often shiny?"

"Well . . . yes." Ting climbed off the chair.

With a smile, Tomaz began to walk about the cottage carefully, treading on each board. Everyone followed but Bailey who couldn't move in her tangle of traps. He listened to every moan of wood as he stepped carefully, until he stopped in a corner of the porch. Bailey and the pack rat were out of sight in the main cottage. There he knelt down and, with one hand, gently pried up a warped board.

Bailey called out, "What's going on? What's happening?"

"He's looking for something," Ting answered.

Jason peered over Tomaz's shoulder, then added, "And he's found it!"

They looked into a little nest of strawlike twigs and colorful lint. In it lay a silver-toned watch, a shiny barrette, a handful of quarters and one cat's-eye marble, and a dainty silver-handled brush and mirror. "I think," Tomaz announced, "we've found your thief." He quickly collected everything and stomped the board back into place.

Bailey waited with a most perturbed look on her face. Ting laughed and began to carefully untangle her. The pack rat had settled down in Bailey's hands. Tomaz looked at her thought-fully. He spread the booty out on the table. "I think everything lost can be found in here. They like to take and store pretty things in their nests."

Bailey let out a sigh of relief as Ting unwound the last noisy string from her.

"That is a wild creature."

"A very frightened one." Bailey rubbed her thumb over the pack rat's head again. The creature relaxed her soft, folding mouselike ears and let out a soft chirr. "Can't I keep it till we can release her somewhere safer?"

"Safer?"

"Well." Bailey nibbled her lip. "She could get eaten out there." She stared out their screen door.

"Yes," agreed Tomaz. "It is a dangerous world out there. Perhaps you should keep her safe for a while. I suggest some-thing hard plastic or rubber or metal. She'll chew her way out of anything else. Something soft for a nest, something shiny to keep her happy." He smiled slightly.

Bailey fairly beamed. "Thank you!"

"Do not thank me," the Indian shaman said quietly. "The animal has made her own choice, I think." He nodded to the creature who had settled comfortably on Bailey's palms and now groomed her whiskers carefully, much like a cat making herself at home. "Sleep well," he said, guiding Jason to the door. "And remember," he added, with a wink. "Unlike the rest of us, pack rats are nocturnal."

Jason took the hint and headed back to the cabin where Trent was already in his cot, reading a book by flashlight. He sat up. "I figured you stopped by the restroom."

Jason shook his head. "No, first I ran into Tomaz . . ."

"Really? What was he doing? Did he spot Stefan?"

"No, but I bet he was out scouting and patrolling. Any-way . . . the trap went off at Kittencurl! You should have heard the noise."

"No kidding? We caught the thief? Who was it?"

"Bailey caught it."

"It?"

"Yup. A wee little mousie thing, about this big. Tomaz said it was a pack rat."

Trent rolled his eyes. "Pack rat? Don't they squirrel stuff away?"

"Anything and everything!" He described the nest while he stripped down for bed and tucked away his dirty clothes and laid out clean ones for the morning. As he lay down, they could hear muffled footsteps outside.

Rich's voice said, quietly and unhappily, "Next time I tell you to stay away from something, do it!"

Stefan let out a grunt. Then, miserably, "Bears like skunks, I guess."

The noise of the two of them shuffling past faded, with a bold distinct odor left behind. Stefan was obviously back in human form.

"Skunk!" repeated Trent, snickering.

The two of them sank into their cots with peals of laughter. The last thing Jason remembered hearing was Trent, every now and then, echoing, "Skunk!"

23

Crystal Clear

"THEY took my amethyst from me," Bailey whispered, as the group came together for Crystal Class.

Jason's hand went to his crystal in his pocket and he wrapped his fingers about it quickly before asking, "Why?"

She shook her head. Jennifer reached over and patted her hand. "I'm sure it's nothing. The sea salts and tubs are out. I bet we're just going to learn how to cleanse our crystals." She smiled. "Once we know how to do that, and know our auras, then I can start showing you how to make items from them." She touched her pendant, which consisted of her crystal wrapped in a spiral of silver wire and hung from a chain.

Bailey looked a bit happier. "Cool."

Trent leaned on his elbows. "Ever get everyone's aura read, Jen?"

Blonde hair swung as she shook her head slightly. "Not even close. With forty-nine campers here, I don't even know everyone yet. But I'm going to try!"

Jon had been showing Danno something, with Henry and Tran looking on. It appeared to be a diagram of chess moves. He looked up with a slight frown. "But what if you're wrong?"

She gave him her attention. "What if I'm wrong?"

"You can make mistakes. You're not that far into training."

"Anyone can make mistakes."

Jon looked at her steadily. "But what if someone depends on what you tell them. Say . . . Henry here. He needs to know what his Elemental nature is, as far as his Talents are concerned, and you tell him . . . Water. You can see how dangerous that would be."

The older girl smiled slightly. "Anyone can tell Henry is Fire."

Jason stirred, saying, "I can't. I mean, it seems reasonable, but I can't."

"It takes training, like anything else."

"Tell me what I am," Jon said quietly.

Jennifer paused, her face coloring slightly. "You know I can't. I've tried before. You've been working on Shielding."

He shrugged as he turned away. "It's dangerous to rely on anyone but yourself."

Jennifer bit her lip slightly but did not argue with him. She bent her attention to the small tubs on the tables in front of them, filled with clear water and little else. Campers milled around curiously as the heat of the day settled in and a splash here and there sprayed across the rocks. Crystals caught the sunlight and spiked it about in a rainbow of colors.

Stefan swiped his big paw of a hand across the surface of one tub, sending up a tidal wave of water right in the pathway just as Gavan walked into the clearing to start the class. Even as Ting gasped and Rich let out a cry of warning, he raised his cane, unconcerned, a brightness catching the water in midair, droplets splattering into a fine mist and raining down onto the dirt as though hitting an unseen barrier. Grinning, Gavan gave his cane a playful shake and growled before lowering it as he stepped to the front of the tables. He leaned on it, cape folded back on his shoulders, at ease in his light shirt tucked into faded blue jeans.

"Not that that wouldn't have felt good," he said, glancing up at the sun overhead. "All right. We've been handling the crystals for a while now, learning the one that is bonded to you, and everyone is generally doing quite well." His attention swept over his students, even Henry Squibb, who flinched as though he could duck behind Jonnard or somehow make himself invisible, and he drew something out of his pocket and laid it on the table. A great white quartz sparkled in the light, its many crystals shining almost completely clear. He tapped it. "This is an ordinary rock crystal, found quite commonly, although not always in this size or clarity. You've all been working with your bonded crystals, but a Magicker can use a master crystal such as this or bond with any number of crystals if his Talents are inclined that way. So, while we urge you never to drop your crystal," and his clear blue eyes fastened on Bailey a moment, "it is possible to find and use a master like this if you have real need."

"What's the catch?" asked Trent.

"Catch?"

"Why use a bonded one if any will do?"

"Ah." Gavan picked up the quartz. "The catch is the performance. Let me think if I can put it another way." He scratched the side of his crooked nose. "A bonded crystal would be like a race car, high energy and tuned to do one job, with one driver, quite well. A master crystal would be like a small subcompact economy model. It may get you where you're going, but much slower and without as much flash. Or it may be unable to get you where you really want to go but it will keep you safe while you figure out a plan if you're in trouble."

"How will you know if you're in trouble? Other than the obvious?" Gavan pulled Bailey's amethyst out of his pocket and held it forth on his palm. The once brilliant purple crystal sat, dulled and dark, a shadow of its former self. Bailey sighed.

"Oh, Bailey," breathed Ting. "I didn't know it had gotten so bad!"

"I didn't want anyone to know," Bailey answered, her voice miserable. She sat down at one end of her table and cupped her chin in her hands as she leaned forward on her elbows.

Jennifer eyed the object resting on Gavan's palm. "I don't know," she said slowly, "if cleansing will help that."

"Nor I," the Magicker responded. "I want everyone to take their crystals and get a feel for their aura. We've done this before," he added as he began to walk slowly among them, "so you already know what your crystal probably feels like to you, but I want you to refresh that knowledge. Take a few moments, and then we're going to cleanse our crystals and see if the aura feels stronger or different."

Trent grinned. "I hope Stefan's crystal is cleaner than his socks, or we'll be here all day cleaning." He ducked his head as Stefan let out a growling mutter and laughter rolled through the others. He rolled his own misty crystal through his hands, closing his eyes in concentration and trying to look innocent as Gaven passed him by.

Jason cupped his. Gavan paused, and put a finger out, stroking the band of granitelike material that divided the crystal. "Ever give you trouble?"

"I don't think so. What kind of trouble?"

"When you're Focusing on it, ever go cold or feel blocked?"

Jason shook his head. "Never."

Gavan looked searchingly into his face a moment, then commented, "Good," before moving away. Jason looked after him, wondering. None of the Magickers had ever explained why his crystal was not meant to have been bonded. He gripped his crystal tightly, feeling its energy wash over him. Never had he felt it divided. If the band were a barrier, it had always been open, not locked. Perhaps this was one of the things he was meant to discover for himself. Or perhaps not, if he found the right question to ask.

Trent bumped him. Jason peered at his friend. "What?"

"Something wrong?"

"Nah. Just thinking."

"You do that a lot." Trent nodded to himself as Bailey giggled faintly and Trent looked happy to have made her do so.

Gavan took a small bag of white rocks and filled his palm, then scattered it into the tub of water in front of him, and swirled his hand around, dissolving them. "Sea salt," he said. "About half a handful for each tub. Only one crystal at a time should soak and be washed in this, so take turns. I want you to swish the crystal about, then hold it in the water, and I want you to think it clean. Tell it to be pure and clean, if you will. Then let it sit for, oh . . . five minutes. Take it out and dry it with one of these rags laid out here, and then I want you to Focus on the aura. Let me know what you think." He pointed at Bailey. "Come here and let's do yours, but don't Focus first."

Trent dropped his crystal into the small tub, elbowing Jason into a short line behind him. Jason didn't mind as Henry and Danno tussled each other to fall in after Jason. After what seemed a very long time, he fished his up and moved aside, drying it off. Bailey was already holding her crystal and looking at it in dismay, the color still cloudy as she rubbed and rubbed at it.

"Hey," said Trent. "It works." He tossed his polishing cloth back on the table and turned his about, admiring the newly shining surfaces.

Jason swished his crystal in the cool water, smelling the very faint aroma of salt. His crystal seemed so much clearer and vibrant underwater. He waited five long minutes before fishing it out to dry.

Holding it, feeling the water-cooled mineral warm to his skin, he felt its aura build and run through him, a clean light tinted ever so faintly with a soft green. To his relief, the aura felt even stronger than before, and he pocketed it without realizing he had a big grin on his face until Jennifer smiled at him.

"It's always nice if it's done right," she said.

Slightly embarrassed, he mumbled "Yeah," before moving away from the table. Bailey caught his eye again. She sat in an unhappy heap at the table's end, watching Gavan closely.

As he drew near, all he could clearly hear her say was ". . . don't want another one. Can't we do something? What's wrong with it?"

Gavan put his hand on her shoulder. "Before I go on, I want to say this. We rarely stay with one crystal our whole life. They have different properties and we have different needs and abilities. We often outgrow the first and move on."

"I don't want to move on. I'm not ready to!" Bailey looked at the Magicker with her soft brown eyes. Lacey, the packrat, poked her head out of Bailey's shirt pocket to let out a nervous chitter before diving back in, her tufted tail hanging out and twitching now and then.

"Isn't there anything we can do?"

Gavan shrugged at Jason. "Not that I can think of. The crystal is attuned to Bailey, but once we got her back here, and her well-being was assured, it should have returned to normal. Instead, it's dying out. She's not going to be able to use it as a Focus."

Bailey rubbed at her nose.

Jason sat down next to her. "I'm sorry," he said to her. "After it kept you safe even with the wolfjackal that followed you in, and all."

She nodded, and looked even more miserable.

Gavan tilted his head. "What was that you said?"

"When I went in to get her, she had a wolfjackal who'd followed her in. We were only one step ahead of it when we came out. We told you . . ."

Gavan looked as if he could smack his forehead. "You did, that's right. At that moment, I didn't quite catch what you meant. I thought . . . we all thought . . . you were talking about the Ritual. That's it, then. The wolfjackal is still trapped inside, and it's poisoning the crystal."

"You can do something?"

"If that's it, yes. But Tomaz will be best to handle it. Shall we try, Bailey?"

She nodded rapidly.

"Good. If it works, I'll have it back to you by sundown!" Gavan tossed the crystal in the air and caught it, tucking it away in his cape. He considered her. "You shall have to tell me how you managed that. It could be a useful trick someday."

Bailey wrinkled her nose. "I didn't mean to, but if I remember, I'll let you know."

"Do that." Gavan straightened then, to give his attention to the others. "Anyone have any changes to report?"

Danno said nervously, "Mine went to orange."

"But that's excellent, Danno. An excellent aura color . . . it usually reflects joy, and an energy coming out of that." Gavan pointed at Stefan. "How about you?"

Stefan grunted. "Nothing changed, I guess. Is this class gonna run all afternoon, or can we get a break? I'm hungry." Even from across several tables, now, Jason could hear the boy's stomach rumble. Like Trent, he was always hungry, only Trent stayed wiry while Stefan just seemed to get broader and taller. "No change at all is better than losing the aura. Anyone else have any changes to report? Anything unusual happen?"

"I," said Henry quickly, "got zapped."

"Zapped?"

He nodded, his round owllike face reddened from the sun despite the bar of sunblock across his nose. "Zzzzapped."

"Hmmm. We may have had a double ward on it for the Choosing. If so, that could be half your problem." Gavan took out a small notebook and jotted something down. "Remind me to check it later?"

"Yes, sir." Henry sighed.

As it turned out, most of the crystals improved, and while Gavan was checking and looking at them, Tomaz appeared. One moment the wide dirt path to the craft area seemed empty, the next moment he was there, slapping the dust from his denim jacket, his turquoise-and-silver bracelet jangling softly. Gavan did not look at all surprised as he passed him the amethyst and they conferred, their voices not carrying to the campers. Tomaz nodded once, then patted Bailey on the shoulder before returning down the path, his blue-black hair gleaming in its pulled-back ponytail.

"Almost like Gavan had called for him."

Trent nudged Jason in the ribs. "What makes you think he didn't?"

"Hmmmm." Before he could say anything further, the loudspeakers rang out for break, and Stefan nearly plowed them over as he headed out.

After break, they had short sessions on using the master crystal, then FireAnn came to get them for Herb Class. Bailey didn't brighten until the late afternoon session of Frisbee pitch, where sailing the cheerful plastic disk across the marked field and trying to score points for longest toss, and highest toss, and most accurate toss gave way to the joy of simply leaping around the field and catching whatever Frisbee they could.

At the fire ring, long into the night, Tomaz appeared at Bailey's elbow while she was singing, took her hand, and put her crystal in it. The purple colors, even in the dim glow of the flame, shone with all their old brilliance. Bailey gasped.

"You did it!"

He nodded. "It taught me a valuable lesson, too, one which may be of help to us all someday. I need to strengthen it a bit, though. I had a difficult time." He chuckled then, dark eyes snapping with his laughter. "You are full of surprises, Miss Landau."

"I bet that wolfjackal was surprised when you caught up with it!"

He inclined his head, saying nothing else, before falling back into the shadows at the edge of the bonfire's casting, and Bailey clutched her crystal tightly, throwing one arm around Ting and the other around Jennifer before returning to sing.

Jason fished out his crystal and looked at it. Had he ever looked beyond or behind that band? Was it as open as he felt . . . or could something be locked away inside, and he not know it? He held his crystal thoughtfully for a very long time before putting it away, as the fire burned down to crackling embers.

24

Wanda

"TALENT Show!" breathed Ting. "They finally posted it! It's been days and days since they said watch for the announcement." Her hand eagerly tapped the camp calendar.

"Really? No kidding? When's it set for?" Bailey tried to push closer to see through the crowd of campers buzzing around the calendar.

"Saturday night. That gives us six days to finesse our rehearsing."

Jennifer, who had no trouble seeing over both Ting's and Bailey's heads, smiled faintly. "Just like karaoke."

Ting bounced. She tugged on Bailey's hand. "Are you ready!"

Bailey hung back a little. "Well . . . I dunno. The shower is one thing, up on stage is another. . . ."

"We'll be fine," Jennifer said coaxingly. She tucked a long strand of blonde hair behind her ear. "We might even scrounge up some matching costumes. I have things I haven't even worn yet."

"That would be too cool," pronounced Ting. "Let's do the Fifties."

"But I'm not ready!" With Bailey protesting faintly, her roommates towed her away, chattering eagerly. She cast a wild-eyed look at Jason like a skittish pony, and he grinned.

Trent scratched his nose as the girls left. "Think we could do something?"

Jason looked at him, shrugging. "Maybe. It's not like we've been practicing or anything, though, and I know a few who have."

"Yeah, but it's for the video. I want my dad to see it."

Henry eagerly began taking notes as he turned away from the calendar, talking Danno's ear off. "Looks like Squibb has something planned."

Trent snorted. As the two backed up to leave, they nearly bumped into Stefan and Rich. Trent eyed Stefan. "I bet you could have a puppet show," he said to Stefan. "Those dirty socks of yours probably walk and talk all on their own."

Stefan grunted. "Very funny."

"I thought so." Trent watched them boldly, relishing the knowledge they held over the two boys' heads. It had been days since they'd watched Stefan's incredible transformation, and yet they seemed to be the only ones who knew of it. Rich was getting worry lines as he desperately tried to keep the secret.

Rich stared. "We'll see who laughs last." He folded his arms and ignored Jason and Trent, his yellow-copper hair standing in stubborn thatches.

As they left, Jason said thoughtfully to Trent, "I don't think we've seen the last of trouble from those two, and I don't think you should be teasing them like that."

"You're no fun either." Trent lightly punched him in the shoulder. He sprinted off, leaving Jason sputtering.

"No, no, no," said Jefferson as he paced the beach. "It takes teamwork to move a canoe swiftly. Decide where you're going to go and then work with each other. Don't paddle against each other!" His voice echoed from his cupped hands as he waded through the shallow water. The canoes on Lake Wannameecha seemed determined to conduct a demolition derby, bouncing into and off of each other despite the frantic paddling of their occupants. They were all capable of canoeing with basic strokes, but Jefferson's attempt to teach them racing strategy had gone wrong . . . horribly wrong. Canoes thudded back and forth and paddles cracked against each other sharply, amidst the yells and laughter of the campers.

Water slapped and splashed everywhere as the campers quawked and warned each other and ducked, but everyone eemed to be dripping wet from head to toe and not really nhappy about it. A hot July sun blazed down. Even when canoe tipped over, dumping everyone in it and drenching thers, no one seemed unhappy. Heads bobbed up from the ake, grinning, as the unlucky canoers grabbed their boat in an ttempt to push it back to shore and right it. As usual, Jason ad left his fetish in the cabin for this class, knowing he'd end p soaking wet.

Jefferson waved his arms about. "What are you all doing?" e bellowed. His sunglasses hung on a cord about his neck, and e looked to be almost as wet as everyone else. He laughed.

Jason stopped, oar in midair, lake water sliding off his face, ooling him as it dripped. "Having fun?" His shirt clung to is body, and water squished in his tennis shoes, and he felt reat.

The tall, dark instructor looked at all of them and finally hrugged. "Well . . . good. But try to learn to paddle while ou're at it. This could be a skill you'll need one day! Swim-ning is later!" But he smiled widely as he yelled it out over the vater. He then turned and ran for his life as a capsized canoe umped out of the water, seemingly headed right at him. He overed the crystal on his wide bracelet and a flash dazzled he lake water a moment, catching the canoe in midair and ettling it back onto the water calmly. The campers let out an hhhhh of wonder. He grabbed an oar as it floated past.

Trent tossed a look back at Jason. "Shall we show them ow it's done?"

Jason countered, "On the count of one-two?"

Trent nodded. "One," he called out, stroking strongly from he front of the canoe.

"Two," called Jason, paddling. And so they worked, one, wo, one, two, the canoe shooting away from the beach and the ther canoers. It glided smoothly across the water, creating a reeze as it moved that ruffled their hair and cooled their skin. n moments they were beyond earshot of Jefferson, and even he gleeful shouts of the other campers seemed faint. Lake Vannameecha flowed under them like glass with scarcely a vave or ripple except for that trailing from the rear of the

canoe. Jason felt the pull in his shoulders as he paddled behind
Trent, but it felt good and in short order, they sailed into a part
of the lake they'd never been, beyond the silvery beach coves
of the campground. They kept paddling to where the water
was deep blue and clear, and they were all alone.

Of a single mind, both of them put their paddles across
their knees, and let the canoe skim to a halt. It bobbed gently
on the tiny waves. Trent leaned out of the bow to point. "That's
all wilderness," he said. "I don't think we've even hiked back
in there."

Jason eyed the thick greenery and rugged coastline at this
end of Lake Wannameecha. The wonder of open land, still
relatively untouched, struck him. Anything could be in there.
Perhaps even the Iron Gate that bothered the Magickers
so much lay hidden in there, its whereabouts waiting to be
discovered.

Something splashed behind them. Both turned to look at
the deep-blue water, where circles of ripples spread out, then
faded. "Fish," said Trent. "Jumping at a bug." Tiny lines spread
across the lake. Trent dipped his hand into the water. "Don't
you wish you could see underneath? Like with a waterproof
camera? All the stuff happening down there we have no idea
about?"

Jason carefully leaned his weight the other way to keep the
canoe balanced. He eyed the lake. "Probably," he said slowly,
"just a few fish. Grasses. Maybe a turtle or two? Water isn't
clear enough to see through very deep. Not like a crystal or
anything."

He looked up.

"Maybe." Trent nodded. He played his fingers through the
water. "I guess we'd better get back before Jefferson has a
cow. We're not supposed to be out of sight of the beach."

Jason's hand ached. He lifted it to look for blisters from the
paddle, but it was the back, the scar that burned. He dropped
it back into the soothing water again. Something stirred below
and there was another splash, louder, from behind them.

"I wish I had my pole with me!" Trent turned around in the
canoe, and squinted over the lake's surface, looking for the
fish wistfully. "They sure are jumping."

Jason peered back, his arm up to his elbow in the water.

Something cold and slimy tickled past his fingers. He jerked his hand out with a yelp and peered down.

"What's wrong?"

"Something . . ." Jason said. He looked at his fingers. They seemed fine. "Something touched me."

"Cool."

"And . . . icky."

"Just a fish. Or maybe some lakeweed." Trent picked up his paddle. "You city boys are wusses. You should have caught it with your bare hand! Tickled it close and snatched it up."

"Me? Are you calling me a wuss?"

"If it doesn't have concrete or plaster at the bottom, you don't want to swim in it!" teased Trent.

"Yeah, well, if it doesn't plug in and surf the Internet, neither do you!" He plunged his arm back into the water, leaning over. Tickle a fish into his hands! Who did Trent think he was, Henry Squibb? He wiggled his fingers in annoyance. From the corner of his eye, he caught a glimpse of a long, dark shadow moving under the canoe and then, something caught his arm and YANKED! Jason was pulled overboard.

He hit the water with a very loud splash and went straight down, his arm in the grip of two cold, wet hands. Water bubbled up around him. He tried to keep his eyes open and his mouth shut but neither seemed to work the way he wanted. Bubbles flew all about his face, and the dark lake water, as something towed him under, lifejacket and all, tugging hard before his jacket stubbornly refused to let him be dragged under any more. He had a wild glimpse of the lake surface and canoe overhead, bubbles flowing upward from his nose and mouth, and something . . . someone . . . pulling at him.

Not a fish. He saw her—dark and shadowy, hair flowing about her like a storm adrift. Not human. Scales. Mermaid? No, she had legs, kicking to try to pull them both down to the lake bottom and failing. Slender, willowy form hardly taller than he was. He twisted his arm in her hands, but she was strong, far stronger than he. She let go suddenly, shoving him away and disappearing into the murky depths of the lake.

Like a cork, Jason bobbed to the top, sputtering and coughing. He rose to the surface like a breaching whale. Something slapped the water as he inhaled, coughed, spit, and inhaled again.

"Jeeez, doofus. I said to catch a fish with your hands, not your teeth!" Trent slapped the water with his paddle again. "Come on, grab it! Grab hold!"

Still choking, Jason thrashed over to the paddle and gripped it. Trent hauled him to the side of the canoe and braced his weight while Jason clung to the side and tried to breathe regularly. "Okay, that was not fun." He inhaled and only gargled a little bit that time.

"No kidding. Warn a guy next time? Good thing you had your jacket on."

"I saw . . . I saw . . ."

Trent looked down at him. "You saw what?"

"The underside of the canoe, for one." Jason wolfed down another gulp of air. He thought he felt a faint tug on his sneakers and did not dare look. He didn't want to capsize the canoe. She must be teasing him, because she was certainly—whoever and whatever she was—strong enough to yank him back under. And he had a feeling Trent would not believe him when he told what he'd seen.

"Breathing okay? Let's see if we can get you back in." Trent took up the proper position as taught them by Jefferson and braced himself.

Jason shook his head. "No way we can try that."

"Hang on, then. I'll head for the shore and pull you out there."

Despite the heat of the day, Jason felt chilled. He didn't want to stay in the water, but knew he had no choice. The canoe might capsize and they would both be overboard if he tried to climb back over the side.

Trent grabbed a paddle and began to propel the canoe. Jason hung on as tightly as he could, but as the cool water of the lake pulled at him, he thought he could feel fingers around his ankles. Trent looked behind and yelled, "Something is there!"

"I know!" panted Jason. He hit the water around him, splashing wildly in hopes of scaring whatever it was away.

Cold fingers tugged at his sneakers. Jason felt as if he were going to be pulled under again at any moment.

Trent slapped his canoe paddle on the water. The loud noise echoed like a gunshot around the lake. White foam shot everywhere. But the tugging on his sneakers got harder. Jason held on for all he was worth. He kicked, struggling. She bobbed up besides him, blue hair wild in the spray, giggling and blowing bubbles. She thought he was funny! She disappeared under the canoe again and he felt her cold, wet arms wrap around his knees.

She'd drown him. He had no doubt of that. She didn't understand, or without Tomaz's fetish about his neck, he'd drawn something Evil. . . .

"Almost there!"

"Hurry!" gasped Jason. She pulled at him. If she was from the Dark, taking his life would mean nothing to her. His insides went cold. He could barely hang on. His hands burned with the effort, his arms and body were being stretched too far. Did his hand throb or was it all part of his desperation? She was pulling him under. . . .

Trent grunted with effort. The canoe skewed about wildly as Jason's weight threw it off-balance. His hand slid over the molded rim. "I can't hold on!"

"Almost there." Trent panted, breathless.

Jason tried to kick, but she had a firm grip on his legs. One good yank and he would go under again—

Then he felt a tickling at the buckles on his life jacket. No . . . no . . . she was trying to free him from the jacket. One side suddenly slipped lose. "Hurry!"

Trent laid into it, paddle dipping strongly into the water. The canoe shot forward in spite of Jason's dragging pull on it. The water warmed slightly as it became shallower. Jason closed his eyes. His hands were slipping. His arms felt numb. She began to apply steady force. He was going to go under. . . .

The canoe bumped into the rocky shoreline. It rocked madly as Trent leaped to solid ground and then lay down on his stomach, grabbing Jason by the wrists. "Come on. Pull on me!"

He gave a twisting kick and then, suddenly, the hold on him broke away. The rocks on the shoreline met his feet and he scrambled up them, braced by Trent until he stood on dry land. Well, nearly dry land. Water streamed off him in an immense puddle. A huge strand of grass was tangled about his sneaker and ankle. Bending, it took him a few moments to unwrap it and shake it off. Was this what had gripped him? He turned and looked back at the canoe as he gulped to catch his breath. It waggled once, as if something struck or pushed at it, then it bobbed quietly in the deeper water near the rugged shore.

Just off the point where they stood, a big boulder poked out of the waters like an iceberg. It was split, and in that crack, a tall pine grew stubbornly. Water frothed about it suddenly.

"What was that?" asked Trent. He stared at the lake water.

"I don't know." Jason looked away. He did not feel like telling what he'd seen or felt. "Something."

Trent dusted himself off. "Wanda."

"What?"

"Loch Ness has Nessie. Lake Wannameecha has ... Wanda." Trent grinned. "Any tentacle marks on you? Sea dragon bites?"

Jason shot him a look and Trent just punched his shoulder. "Wuss."

"Yeah, maybe." He took a shaky breath. He put his hand to his throat, where the fetish bag usually snuggled. He thought of finding a way to wrap it, keep it dry, so that he never had to take it off again.

"Ready to head back?"

"Give me a minute." Jason stood in the hot sun. Rattled, he hardly knew where on the lake they were. He began to dry out a bit. Something glinted in the woods a few paces away. "Where are we, anyway?"

"No idea. We could be inside or outside the campgrounds. I just know which way we need to go to get back." Trent shadowed his eyes. "I don't think we've been this way with Sousa, though."

"I'm turned around." Jason spun on one heel as if to prove his point. "I can't tell north from west here."

The sun, just about directly overhead, was no help that way although, soaked as he was, he felt grateful for its warmth. He looked at the almost spearlike glint shining through a patch of green. "I want to see what that is. You hold on to the canoe."

Trent stared at him blankly. "Like the canoe is going anywhere."

"If it drifts off, we've got a very long walk," Jason pointed out. *Or was pulled out to the lake's center.* She could very well drag it off out of disappointment or spite. Or by design. He wasn't anxious to climb back in right away, either, but knew he would have to.

Trent reached into the bow and got the mooring line. He wrapped it around one of the heavy rocks edging the shoreline and then dusted his hands off. "If you're going to look at something, I'm going with you," he said firmly.

"I can almost guarantee they don't have cookies." But Jason grinned as Trent caught up with him. They cut through the deep piney forest in search of whatever the sunlight was reflecting. Branches reached and grabbed at them. After a very short trek, they bulled their way through onto a . . . road. A sagging overhead signpost creaked in the slight breeze, and a rusting gateway sat open on the land. Jason blinked.

Trent laughed. "It's the front gate," he said.

Jason looked at the dark mountain range looming over where the road disappeared. He doubted that the tunnel they had come through was in those mountains. He doubted that their bus ride had taken them anywhere near those mountains, but he did not doubt that wolfjackals ranged them. He shivered, as his still damp T-shirt cooled on his torso. "Can't be. Would have to be the back gate, if anything. Let's get out of here."

"Sure," Trent agreed. "I think we've found enough trouble for the day." As quickly as possible, they made their way back to the lake. Jason tugged his life jacket back into place, tightening the buckles. Trent waited till he was seated before casting off and jumping into the canoe. They brought it about quickly and started paddling toward the camp. Once, Jason looked back.

"Should we tell anyone about her?"

"Her who?"

"Wanda." Trent grinned at him over one shoulder. "We never saw her, but something was there. She'd make a good campfire story."

"You can tell it," Jason said firmly, "but *only* if you leave me out of it!"

"Deal! You get too much glory anyway."

Jason aimed a paddleful of water at Trent's back and managed to hit most of his target. Laughing, Trent said, "I'd get you back—but you're already all wet!"

"Just get me home. I'm probably grounded for the rest of camp." Jason stretched his shoulders, then began to paddle strongly in rhythm with Trent. The canoe shot ahead, gliding silently over dark blue waters . . . and he thought he could see a darker, small shadow pacing them till it tired and darted away. He put his hand to his neck again, his left hand, and felt a dull pain knife through the back of it. He frowned.

When they paddled into the cove, Jefferson was still wading among a few of the canoes, trying to straighten them out. Bailey and Ting flew by, waving their paddles. Jefferson checked his watch and frowned.

"Two days beached," he said, pointing at them. "And get that cabin in shape, you've got inspection coming up as soon as I break classes for lunch."

Trent groaned. That meant no swimming or canoeing. In the heat of early July, that was cruel punishment. Jason was almost glad, though. He was not sure he wanted to go back into the water just yet!

They jostled shoulders heading back. They'd left the clean laundry lying every which way, and it looked as though it had rained socks. Other than that, it didn't take them long and they had just finished when they heard Stefan lumbering past outside, Rich at his heels, sneering something they couldn't quite hear. Trent went to the window. He motioned for Jason.

"They've got something." Trent eyed the pillowcases slung over their shoulders.

"What do you mean?"

"They're up to something. Somehow I don't think that's their laundry."

Jason watched the two disappear down the trail toward the main buildings. "He didn't say we were confined to the cabin, did he?"

"Nope." Trent slipped out the screen door. "Let's see what they're up to."

Staying just far enough behind, they stalked the two down to the restrooms. There, Rich handed his bulging pillowcase to Stefan and took up a casual watch at the corner of the building. He looked around, then motioned to Stefan who did a mad dash into the girls' side of the building.

"What—"

Trent shushed him. "This is going to be good," he said. "Whatever it is."

Jason shifted uneasily. "We ought to do something."

"Do what? We don't even know what it was they did!"

They watched intently. A long minute dragged by, then Stefan rolled out of the girls' toilets and joined Rich, trying to look nonchalant as he stuffed two empty pillowcases into his shirt. And waited.

In a few moments, the trio from Kittencurl came around the curve of the lake. Jason could hear scraps of singing and chatter as they headed for the restrooms. Rich looked at Stefan and smirked as they moved back in the shadows.

"Whatever it is," Jason said, "I think we should warn them."

Trent started to shake his head, then muttered, "Too late anyway," as the three girls went into their half of the building.

A moment later, Ting screamed. Jennifer burst out of the building in long-legged strides, her blonde hair flying behind her, before she turned and stood, pointing wordlessly. Rich doubled over in laughter, leaning on Stefan.

Trent and Jason went to see just what it was. As they drew closer, they could hear . . . frogs.

Frogs croaking, ribbiting, and making whatever other noises they could. Ting stood in the open doorway to the bathroom, surrounded by green bodies of all sizes, hopping and croaking. Big frogs, little frogs. Ting seemed frozen, mouth half open. Bailey picked her way through, color blazing over her angry expression.

She pointed toward the doorway. "Out! Out! Everyone out!"

The frogs and toads began milling around, jostling each other. Ting looked at her and shook. "I . . . can't . . . move," she wailed.

Bailey put her hands on her hips. "Oh, really!" She took Ting by the wrist. "Follow me!"

She led the helpless girl out of the bathroom. There was a moment of silence as they emerged into the sunlight. Then, in a rippling ocean of green, the frogs and toads followed. Hop, splosh, hop, gr-beep, ribbit.

With a squeak of her own, Ting lunged away from Bailey and ran across the lane to where Jennifer stood. The pursuing frogs crowded in around Bailey. They ribbited hopefully. She stepped away.

Hop, hop, they followed. She moved again, trying not to step on anything.

The frog chorus eagerly hopped after.

Bailey threw her hands up. "Somebody do something!"

Stefan and Rich fell over laughing. Tomaz Crowfeather appeared on the pathway next to Jason and Trent. Trent could hardly stand up for laughing and hung onto a pine tree. The sapling bent and wobbled, waving its branches wildly.

"What's going on here?"

Everyone looked at Tomaz and shrugged.

He raised an eyebrow in gentle disbelief.

"Bailey is . . ." Rich caught his breath. "Frog herding." He doubled over in another fit of snickers.

"I am not!" Bailey tossed her head, ponytail bobbing. She marched off a few steps in a huff, following by a rippling, croaking, trail of green. The big ones hopped and plopped. With gleeful chirps, the little tree frogs pinged high out of the herd, soaring above the others. Jason watched them parade. Hop, plop, ping! Hop, plop, ping!

"Interesting." Tomaz crossed his arms across his chest, turquoises and silver glinting in the sun. "I think we need to talk, Bailey."

She opened her mouth to say something, but an immense toad plopped across her sneaker, puffed up, and beat her to it. "Rrrrrrribbit!"

Ting giggled and clung to Jennifer who laughed so hard a tear slid down her cheek.

"That . . . that's a lot of potential princes," Trent managed. He fell back into the pine tree in a shiver of branches and mirth. "You going to kiss all of them?"

"At least I won't draw flies!" She glared at them. "More than I can say about all of you, standing around with your mouths open!"

She stepped away. Hop, plop, ping! The frogs followed in adoration. Jason could not contain his laughter any longer. It bubbled out gleefully. Bailey looked at him, and then the others. Even Tomaz's mouth twitched although he tried to keep a careful lack of expression on his face.

"Am I amusing everyone?" Bailey looked around.

"Not quite," Rich snickered. "But if you wait a minute, I can get the rest of the camp here."

She snorted and flounced off then, down to the lakeside, her chorus line of frogs hopping and gurgling quickly after her. Every once in a while, she waved behind her, yelling, "Shoo!"

With a thoughtful look, Tomaz followed as well. They could hear his voice drifting back as he informed her that she had somehow summoned them, and only she could send them away. Bailey let out a groan, echoed in croaks loud and small from her adoring audience. When last seen before duty called them away, she was sitting on a boulder by the lake, frogs croaking in chorus to her, plopping in and out of the water, little tree frogs pinging high in the air to punctuate the deeper ribbits with cheerful chirps.

Snipe!

BAILEY'S amphibian audience still had everyone laugh-ing at dinner. Having finally gotten rid of them, she took the joking with good humor, wearing a T-shirt she and Ting had decorated in Crafts Class which read DANCES WITH FROGS across the front.

"At least," Trent said to her when he caught his breath, "they didn't try to pull you back into the lake like Wanda did Jason."

To a chorus of "What?" Trent then had to tell Jason's story. Jason ignored him and picked on a meatloaf that, quite unlike FireAnn's usual fare, seemed rather tasteless and uninterest-ing. Jennifer, Ting, and Bailey all slid their food trays down to hear Trent, and Jon, Danno, and Henry swung around on their table benches to listen as well.

He made a well out of his mashed potatoes and gravy and hoped that would taste better. He really didn't want to think about the thing that had played with him in the deep Lake Wannameecha waters and whether he'd actually seen any-thing like what he thought he saw. Or if something about him or his hand, that cursed scar, had set it off. Was he now a door-way, drawing things through that should not be? And if he was . . . were they evil?

Trent drew oohs and aahs from his listeners as he spun the yarn out. Jason, catching a sentence every now and then despite trying not to listen, felt his ears grow warm and the back of his neck begin to itch. He squirmed on the cafeteria bench as Ting giggled at something, then scraped his fork over his plate loudly and rattled his cup. When he finally heard Bailey laugh, repeating "Wanda!" he exhaled, knowing the story was over. The fetish bag rested inside his shirt comfortingly, but he didn't like knowing that he would have to remove it again.

"That's a good one," Danno praised. "Tell it for the Talent Show!"

"Maybe." Trent grinned. "I have a certain roommate to live with, though!" They all laughed.

"I," announced Jon, "have a tale to tell at the campfire tonight." His tone drew Jason's attention. He gave up on his meatloaf and turned around.

Henry beamed in approval and pushed his glasses up his nose to their proper resting spot. Eagerly, he leaned forward on his elbows to listen, quite unaware of a puddle of gravy spreading around one of them.

Jonnard nudged a paper napkin across at Squibb before continuing, "It is the tale of the snipe bird, a rare bird which is most often seen at night, unlike other birds. Its feathers are coveted for charms and talismans. Shapechangers particularly value them." He smiled secretly.

"But a snipe hunt is a wild goose chase," Bailey said, looking at all of them. She wrinkled her nose, freckles dancing.

Jon continued smiling. "Precisely. However, the common snipe does exist, and I shall have a computer setup indicating that on its Web site."

Trent tilted his head. "I sense a plot."

"I should hope so." Jonnard pushed his tray away. "Shall we discuss it later? Much depends on secrecy. Tonight, before dinner."

They all nodded. It was time, it seemed, to get even with Rich and Stefan.

Ting took a bite of her oatmeal cookie before breaking it into crumbs and then showering them into Bailey's cupped hand.

Bailey looked about, then stuffed the crumbs into her

pocket, which began to wiggle with a life of its own as Jason stared in fascination. As it jumped and moved, a long tufted tail snaked out and hung, twitching in satisfaction as its owner munched on cookie crumbs.

Jason grinned. "Your . . . erm . . . tail is showing."

Bailey blushed and swept the packrat's tail back into her pocket. "She keeps doing that."

Ting considered her friend. "I should think she wouldn't like being pocketed up."

"Oh, Lacey sleeps most of the time. She only gets wiggly when she's hungry or at night." Bailey joggled her elbow into Ting. "That's when she makes all her noise!"

Ting rolled her eyes. "It's a good thing I'm a sound sleeper. I heard Jennifer complaining about all the scrabbling and squeaking earlier. Maybe we should let Lacey go free?"

As if knowing her name, the little kangaroo rat poked her head out, shell-like ears opening up attentively. Her dark eyes sparkled brightly and she seemed to show no fear, unlike the night when captured. The past few weeks had been good to her, and her coat glowed with health. She scrubbed at her whiskers busily, little paws shedding extra crumb bits like tiny dust motes.

"Lacey," said Bailey firmly.

The packrat glanced up, then dove back into the shirt pocket. The tufted tail gave a defiant flick before disappearing after the rest of the creature. Ting laughed. Bailey squirmed a bit, then giggled. "Ticklish," she explained.

"I should think." Trent stood, empty tray in hand. "If Jon is going to try to set up anything in the computer room—" he gave a lopsided grin, "he'll need help! Henry is good with a PC, but he doesn't know half of what he thinks he does." He checked his watch. "I have just enough time before we're scheduled. I can set it up so all he has to do is push a button."

"Even that might be too much," Ting commented wryly as she trailed Bailey out of the cafeteria.

"You know," Bailey murmured. "When I talk to Mom tonight, I bet she'll have some ideas for our costumes. . . ."

Trent snorted at Ting's last words. He bolted out of the cafeteria ahead of Jason who looked after him, then shrugged. The two of them seemed to be going in opposite directions more and more these days, and he couldn't shake the uneasy feeling that something was wrong with Trent. It was nothing he could put his finger on, but just a nagging tug. If only he knew what it was he'd done, or hadn't done. He sighed and left the mess hall.

Dark clouds hung above the jagged peaks, but they seemed to be moving quickly, and the hot summer day was unaffected except for the humidity. Maybe rain at midnight or so, he thought. He rather liked storms, and lying in bed listening to one would be far better than lying in bed trying to forget another nightmare! Lightning and the boom of thunder would be welcome compared to the specter of a cold tomb and its occupant reaching for him. . . .

A shiver ran across the back of his neck.

"Are you feeling all right, Jason?" Dr. Patel asked kindly, behind him.

He jumped. She stood next to him and he had not even heard her approach. She put her hand upon his brow, a quick touch, before he moved away. "I'm fine."

"All right." She did not sound convinced and had a faint expression on her face that reminded him of his stepmother when she was about to lecture him about being careful.

"Really. I'm okay." He made a face. "Can't go out on the lake for a couple of days, but other than that, fine."

"Too bad. The lake looks pleasant in these hot days. But you don't look warm to me, Jason. You look rather chilled." Dr. Patel's brown eyes continued to watch him in concern.

He shifted. "You don't need to worry about me."

She smiled gently. "The Magickers are a big family. Like all families, we quarrel, even brawl a bit, but heaven help the outsider who tries to hurt one of us. In short, Jason, if you need us, we're here." She patted him on the shoulder and then moved off to her yoga class, sari wrapped about her slim figure.

He waited till she was out of sight before reading the schedule over again. Marked in bold handwriting next to the printout was his grounding from the lake for the next two days, and Trent's as well. It didn't seem fair somehow in the heavy summer heat that hung over the camp, yet he knew they'd probably earned it. But he hadn't told anyone what he thought he'd seen. Had he seen anything? Or had he just panicked in a brush snag? Or if he had seen something, what would happen to her . . . it? Would they rush out on the lake to net her? Even worse, with the mark of the wolfjackal on him, and not wearing his protection . . . had he drawn it somehow? Could he bring evil down on the camp simply by being here? He didn't quite know what to do or think. He had the uneasy feeling it was a secret he should keep, but he didn't know or understand why. He moved away from the schedule, sighing.

"That's a heavy sound."

Jason let out a squeak. He turned and looked up into Tomaz Crowfeather's weathered face. "Do you guys always sneak up on someone?"

"Us guys? Meaning Indians or counselors or . . ."

"Magickers," answered Jason.

Tomaz chuckled. "It is not hard to be silent when someone else is deep in thought. Care to walk with me? I have some tracking to do. I see your canoe time is canceled for a few days." He read over Jason's shoulder a moment.

"Sure." Jason didn't feel like he had a choice but to volunteer. Tonight was family calling night, and as he had no real burning desire to talk to Grandma McIntire, he had plenty of time. As Tomaz moved off, he fell into step. "What are we looking for?"

Crowfeather rubbed his heavy silver-and-turquoise bracelet. Then he answered slowly. "I am not quite sure, Jason. Let us hope I will know it when I see it." He paced slowly and deliberately and they walked in silence until they reached the edges of most of the cabin clusters. Once or twice he knelt to look at paw prints.

The third time, Jason fidgeted, then asked, "Wolfjackals?"

"No. See here?" Tomaz indicated the pad and toe imprints. "This is a lighter animal. Small pad. But, also larger toes. That is the sign of the coyote." He smiled faintly. "The yellow trickster has spent most of the last century spreading across the continent. Where we hunted the wolf, and drove him near to extinction, the little wolf sneaked in to take his place. The coyote is very smart, very quick." Tomaz straightened.

"If you know it's only coyotes, why do you patrol every day?"

"Because I don't know it's always coyotes." The Magicker

faced into the wind and inhaled deeply as though he could catch scents carried on it beyond the norm. "The mana here is rich and heavy in spots. Other things could be carried in."

Jason repeated slowly, "Other things?"

Tomaz only said, "The world is full of many things, Jason, wonders that long ago took refuge in, for them, a safer place. Sometimes the tide carries them out, however." He spread his arms and chanted a few words, and stood, palms turned upward and cupped slightly as if he could catch the wind.

Jason stood quietly and just watched. For a moment, he wanted to tell Tomaz what he'd seen in the lake. But he hesitated. If only he could feel the Magick like that. If only he could inhale it and hold it deep inside, making it a part of himself. If only he could feel it in his bones. Did the bite keep him from that? Or the granite band in his crystal? Was he flawed too?

"Takes a long time to know yourself," Tomaz said quietly.

"Is that what we're doing here? Really?"

Tomaz studied him for a moment. Then he gave a slow nod. "Yes, mostly. We can use mana. We can bend it, even shape it, to our will. But if we do not know ourselves, do not know what we might be capable of, we do not know if we *should* do what we *can* do."

"Is the Dark Hand deadly?"

Tomaz scratched his brow. "Perhaps," he said quietly. "Based on what I have seen in my lifetime, yes, perhaps. One thing I know for sure, is that they must be treated seriously and cautiously. My view, however, is not popular."

Jason skirted a thick gorse bush as Tomaz strode the other way, his sharp gaze scanning the dirt and even the prickly bush leaves for bits of fur. "It's not?"

Tomaz shook his head. "There are many who say we are all Magickers. All one family. Even the black sheep. I say . . . they are not black sheep. They are sidewinders, snakes in the grass. Treacherous and deadly." He paused, and squatted next to a wild berry bush, its pickings lean, still greening in the summer sun. Instead of berries, he plucked a thick black tuft of hair off it. He rolled it in his fingers, then smelled it as Jason watched. Then Tomaz dropped it, stood, and dusted his hands off. "Bear," he said.

"Goes with berries, huh? They really have bears around here?"

"Yes. A young bear, from the print or two I've seen. Adolescent. But I've not seen any adult prints about, which is what I find baffling." Tomaz tugged on his vest. "A bear will stay with its mother, two, three years, even if another cub is born."

"What does that mean?"

"I am not sure . . . yet." Tomaz surveyed the edge of the wilderness fringe. "Tell me, Jason, can you feel it?"

He looked around. It was hot. He could feel the bright sun's rays streaming down, and a slight breeze off the lake fighting with them, but he didn't think that's what Crowfeather meant. He thought a moment, and then thought of the ley lines they'd been mapping. Like a glowing net over the grounds, they shimmered, but only in the computer simulation done of their positions. He shoved a hand in his pocket to curl his fingers around his crystal.

Without thought, he swung to his right, took a step or two forward, and put his free hand out, grasping at a ribbon of nothingness in the air. He felt . . . he felt a surge . . . like a quickening heartbeat, or the effort he put into a fifty-yard dash. His jaw dropped.

"There," said Tomaz. "You have it. Let it go, because you're not going to be using it."

Jason blinked once or twice, wondering how. Nothing worked until he held a mental image of simply relaxing his hand and dropping it, empty. The sudden, sharp moment faded. "That was . . . that was it, wasn't it?"

"A mana stream, and you went right to it. From the way you homed in on it, I doubt you even need dowsing rods to find them. Some people have that instinct."

"I did good!"

Tomaz grinned. "You did great. However . . . finding them is one thing. Using them, another."

"Why can't everyone be a Magicker, then? If they could only sense the mana? Like singing. Most of us can sing a little. Some of us can sing pretty well. And a few can sing well enough to break glass and stuff."

"It's far more complicated than that, and it's not an ability like singing. Truthfully, few of us have it. Think of it like the gene for pole vaulting. Most of us wouldn't even know we had it or try it out. But those of us who do, can vault so high ... and maybe land safely, or maybe not. It's a rare few who can jump high enough to set records. Landing safely is still dangerous."

Jason thought of Henry Squibb, getting more and more nervous and clumsy and unsure of himself. Did he have the Talent to jump high and land safely? Would he be sent home like the campers last week, ten suddenly so homesick they left camp, each after drinking the feared Draft of Forgetfulness, and the others watching them go, knowing that the homesickness had been charmed on them. The only thing wrong with each of them was that they hadn't been enough of a Magicker. Could Henry survive much longer? He leaned more and more on Jonnard's power rather than his own. Jason tried not to sigh in worry.

Tomaz clapped Jason on the shoulder. "The senses are a wonderful thing, Jason, yet they can deceive you. I wish I could tell you to trust your heart, if your eyes and your mind worry about something. But I cannot. Sometimes the heart is the easiest to deceive, and that is why I fear the Dark Hand. Deception is their greatest ability." The sun glinted off the turquoise-and-silver inset watch he wore. Tomaz consulted it, and said, "If I don't get you back, I'll be grounded, too."

With that, they trotted back into Camp Ravenwyng.

They met behind the mess hall in the twilight. Neither of the girls was there.

"All right." Jonnard looked about. "Bailey and Ting can't sneak out after Lights Out, they've decided. Too risky. Jennifer is involved in some project with Eleanora, so she's in and out. She might catch them. So, it's up to you two while Henry, Danno, and I run the Hunt. It's too bad we didn't know the girls weren't going to help sooner. We could have done this back at Skybolt."

He handed Jason a paper sack. Jason looked in it. Two large cans of shaving cream sat in it. Jonnard glanced at him. "Do I have to tell you what to do with that?"

"Nope!" Jason grinned and handed the bag to Trent, who looked inside, with Danno peering over his elbow.

"Good." Jon scrubbed a hand across his chin. "My mother

thought I might sprout a beard this summer, and she likes to be prepared." He shrugged. "I didn't, and it would be a shame for those two cans to go to waste. Anyway, they took the bait. Rich and Stefan are meeting us at eleven thirty."

"If anyone can stay awake."

Jon looked at Trent sharply. "You can do anything if you prepare and plan for it. Jason?" He looked at Jason then.

"I'll be up."

"Good. We probably won't have much time out there. They're sharp, they'll guess they've been taken pretty quickly."

"Where is Henry, anyway?" Danno said.

"FireAnn kept him after herb and botany class. He was having some trouble identifying poison oak, kept trying to do it by touch. He'll catch up in a few."

"Gah." Danno shuddered, then began to rub and scratch at his hands in sympathy. "Henry always learns the hard way."

"Hopefully, after tonight, Rich and Stefan will learn not to mess with us." Trent stowed the paper bag under his elbow, and added, "I took a look at their cabin earlier. Even if they lock the door latch, they usually leave a window wide open. We'll get in, one way or another."

"All right. Good luck to everyone." Jonnard saluted them before moving off into the growing darkness.

"Good plan," said Danno.

"Yeah. The only thing that can go wrong is if Stefan bears out. Then, we've all got a problem." Trent scratched his nose. "Or maybe not. He can only chase one of·us at a time!"

Jason grabbed Trent's sleeve. "Come on, bearer of great news. It'll be Lights Out soon enough."

Inside their cabin, they hunched over his flashlight and sketched out prime areas of attack. The beds and closet, of course, though Trent voiced a whispered opinion that Stefan was likely never to have used a closet in his life. Snide Rich was equally likely to have his things folded within an inch of their life and put neatly away.

"The object here," Jason mulled, "is to trash them without trashing them too much and getting in trouble with Rainwater."

"It's a challenge, but I think we're up to it." Trent stifled a yawn. "As long as we're awake."

"I'll be awake."

"Good. I'm gonna . . . lie down . . . for a minute or two." Trent crawled onto his bed and in seconds, the cabin filled with his soft snoring.

Jason crawled into his bed, cradling Trent's flashlight in his hands under the covers, reading one of his cabin mate's many *X-Men* comic books. Not the least bit sleepy, his duty was to watch the time for the appointed hour. He heard soft steps go past the cabin several times and then a heavier tread, which might be Hightower, Jefferson, or Crowfeather patrolling yet again. Finally, he heard an exclamation from Henry Squibb, high-pitched and excited, quickly smothered. He checked his watch and saw it was nearly time. He crawled out and woke Trent. They both hurried, putting their shoes on in the dark. Trent grabbed up the paper sack of shaving cream plus a few other goodies they'd found and waited by the shuttered front window, peeking through a slit in the slats.

Trent beckoned to him. "They're here."

Jason clicked off the flashlight, not wanting anything to give them away. He joined Trent and peered through the wooden slats. Even for Henry, the boy looked pale, and he paced nervously about in front of Skybolt. "I hope Jon knows what he's doing," he muttered. "I don't think Henry's up to this."

"Why?"

"I think he's scared, and not of Stefan and Rich. He wouldn't go at all, but he trusts Jon."

Before Trent could answer, Stef and Rich came up, and grabbed Henry by the elbow.

"We have to hurry. Someone's out patrolling. I heard them pass by the cabin."

"Move out, then," Jon ordered and Jason watched them go. He could barely see the group, pillowcases in hands, as they trotted off. Stefan took up the rear in the lumbering run he'd developed. He even *moved* like a bear most of the time.

Trent nodded, and yanked open the door. "They're gone, let's roll!"

They sprinted through the dark to the cabin occupied by

Rich and Stefan. Later, Trent would claim he could find the cabin by the stench alone as he spun the yarn out. As they reached the steps though, it seemed no different than any of the other cabins although it seemed to be set apart from the rest, evergreens and bushes hugging it close. The door was latched firmly, but as Trent had predicted, the side window was wide open. He easily slipped the screen down and boosted himself through, then stuck his head and hand out for Jason.

"Hold your nose," he advised. "It reeks in here."

And it did, as Jason hung over the windowsill and then swung his legs over. It smelled strongly of old sneakers and something else, musky and animal. The next cabin inspection was only a few days away. Open windows or not, Jason did not see how Sousa or the others could not fail to notice it. Stefan-bear had a distinct odor that hung over nearly everything in the cabin.

Trent took the flashlight from him and aimed it at the bunks. Jason got out his crystal and concentrated until its golden lantern light flared. Trent tossed him a can, saying, "I'll get started on the bunks."

Jason played his crystal lantern over them. "Too messy . . . no way to short-sheet them."

"Ah, never fear, I have a plan." With a grin, Trent opened up the pillows and began to fill the cases with shaving cream. "Niiiice and fluffy."

Jason quickly began finding the worn sneakers scattered all over the cabin floor, filling them with quick squirts of shaving cream that seemed to explode into clouds. As a finishing touch, he tucked the scraggly laces into each billowy cloud. The two of them moved quickly through the cabin until first one, then the second can of shaving lather sputtered empty. Trent hummed off-key as he moved from window to storage cupboard. A can rattled as he shook it.

"I thought all the shaving cream was gone?" Jason peered at his silhouette.

"It is. This is silly string." And with a chuckle, he began to spray the plastic string through the air, enwebbing the door latch, the cupboard pulls, anywhere that had a knob or pull or latch. Satisfied, he stuffed the can inside his shirt. "I think our work here is done."

Jason lifted his crystal lantern high, spilling golden light throughout the entire cabin. The pranks were not obvious. Stefan and Rich could fall into any number of them, and even once they discovered that their cabin had been visited, there were secret, hidden traps of lather and other goodies which should befall them all night. He nodded in satisfaction. They slipped back out the window and fastened the screen in place when they heard heavy footsteps.

Backs to the cabin, they squatted down and held their breath. Needles cracked and branches rattled, and then the figure, whoever it was, passed by. They waited long moments, till they gulped for air, then stood and sprinted back to Starwind. Once inside, they grabbed each other by the wrist and did a fierce little victory dance.

"That," Trent said when they finally stopped, "felt great."

"We got 'em good," Jason agreed. "Now," he added, pulling up a chair, "we listen."

"To what?" Trent dragged the other chair over and joined him at the window.

"To the noise of discovery, which ought to be any second. They've been out thirty minutes. I bet they've found out by now...." He sat back in his chair and watched as Trent pulled over one of his favorite comic books and began to read by flashlight.

"Why don't you use your crystal? No batteries to worry about."

"Like Eleanora said, some people can't work with Fire that well. I must be one of 'em. I can hardly do that bit." Trent flipped a page. "Could be worse, I could be lighting up like Squibb does."

While he read, Jason watched the night activity. A possum sauntered past looking in the moonlight like an odd, hunched-over cat, with a ratlike tail trailing after it. Just a step or two behind came Hightower who paused to look at the tracks, then went on down the camp pathway toward the main buildings. Jon and Henry would be safe coming back for an hour or so, at least. An owl hooted as if to echo the lateness of the hour. Trent yawned as he turned a page.

Jason heard something. He put his eye to the shutters, watching. He saw Jon and Henry come stumbling back to their cabin. He put a hand out and shook Trent.

"Something's wrong."

"What? What is it?"

"I can't tell." He stood. It looked to him as though Squibb had been hurt, leaning on Jon as the tall boy helped him up the cabin steps. He could hear Henry's moaning voice. "Come on!" He wasn't going to stay there and guess, Lights Out or not.

Trent jumped to his feet to follow and they thundered across the wooden porches of both cabins. Inside, Jonnard had a switch on, and Henry sat on the floor, face in his hands, crying. Jon looked almost as distressed as Squibb, his face pale and his dark hair going in every direction.

"What happened?"

"He'll be all right," Jon said slowly. He sat down heavily on the desk chair, dropping the two pillowcases. "Did you get their cabin?"

"Yes, but—"

"He'll be all right!"

"No, I won't." Henry sniffled, looking up through his fingers. "It's gone, gone, all of it."

Jason stood, baffled. Trent stared. "What's gone?"

"He'll be all right." Jon sounded as if every word were an effort. "We took them everywhere. We had them looking in every prickly bush and disgusting hole around the lake." He took a deep breath.

Henry made a loud snuffling noise and dragged his sleeve across his face. "It's gone," he repeated, very muffled.

"Henry," said Jonnard. "Shut up and go to sleep, you'll be fine tomorrow."

Squibb shook his head mournfully.

"What's gone?" Trent shot looks from one to the other. "And where's Danno?"

"Danno didn't show up. We took Rich and Stefan out for snipes without him. Henry, it'll be all right."

"No, it won't." Henry stopped sniffling and instead sat on the cabin floor and began to shake. Pale and shivering, he looked absolutely miserable.

Jason squatted beside him. "Tell me what's wrong?"

Henry looked up into his face. "It's gone. My Magick. Look. . . ." And he pulled his crystal out of his pocket. The vibrant, sometimes fiery crystal had gone soot dark. It looked absolutely lifeless. Henry poked a finger at it. "Blasted," he said. "Like me." He sniffled again.

Jason touched the stone. Colder than ice. No matter what Jonnard said, Henry was in trouble. Deep, deep trouble. . . .

"What's going on here?"

The boys all turned. Hightower stood in the doorway, waiting for an explanation. He did not look happy.

Shouts and yells of surprise and anger from several cabins away did not lighten the solemn atmosphere, despite Stefan's loud bellow cutting through the night. Rich shouted threats in his high-pitched voice, although of what they could not tell. Despite the commotion, Hightower's attention stayed fastened on the boy in front of him.

Henry stood up, and held his crystal out on his palm, hand wavering. "My . . . Magick . . ." he said, and looked at the Magicker hopelessly.

Hightower frowned heavily as he reached out and dropped his hand on Henry's shoulder. "I'm sorry, son," he said. "There isn't anything I can do."

Henry fainted.

26

You're Off the Island

ONE huge golden topaz, rough-shaped and unpolished, sitting on the corner of an old wooden filing cabinet like a
crystal lantern, lit Gavan Rainwater's office. It looked like a
fallen star, Jason thought, as he sat miserably next to Jon and
Henry, who could not stop sniffing. Trent stayed on his feet,
one shoulder to the bookcase that overflowed with books and
scraps of paper that looked very much like parchment, and
even a few rolled up scrolls. Magickers stuffed the office until
the only real room left was the chair behind the desk and that
stayed empty for the moment as they waited for Rainwater.

Henry rubbed his nose dry, or attempted to. "I'm sorry," he
said for the hundredth time. He shredded the damp tissue in
his hand.

"You didn't do anything wrong," Jason told him, for at least
the tenth time. Trent leaned forward and pounded on Squibb's
shoulder.

Bailey and Ting shared a desk chair, leaning close together,
their faces very pale. Lacey scrambled out of Bailey's pocket
and down into the palm of her hand, where the packrat sat
very quietly, her tufted tail hanging out, a tiny spidery strand
dangling from it. "It was just a snipe hunt," Bailey said quietly,
to no one in particular.

Tomaz shifted at a sound in the hall, and opened the office door, holding it for Rainwater, who swept in with FireAnn at his heels, a goblet in her hand. Jason instantly recognized the tantalizingly sweet smell. Despite the wonderful aroma, every Magicker she passed seemed to shrink away from FireAnn and the goblet. Tomaz did not shrink back, but turned his face away. Gavan pulled his chair out and sat down, FireAnn at his elbow, his brow knotted. He looked as if he'd just been awakened, his hair slightly rumpled, his eyes not quite their usual brilliant blue. He leaned his cane against the desk.

"This is not good news."

"Gavan," began Eleanora, and then she stopped and tightened her mouth. Her dark hair had been pinned up for the night, in a mass of curls about her head, and she barely floated above the floor.

FireAnn shook her head at Eleanora. "It has to be done," the fiery-headed cook insisted.

Jason realized the Magickers had been arguing. They had that look as they traded glances. Maybe there was hope for Henry yet....

"Well, Henry," Trent said loudly. "Looks like you've been voted off the island."

"No ..." Henry whimpered slightly. He stared at his lifeless crystal.

Dr. Patel put a slim brown hand on Trent's shoulder and squeezed. Trent rolled his eyes but shut up as if she'd said something into his ear. Bailey and Ting shifted even closer together.

"This is not an easy thing to do, for any of us, Henry." Gavan nodded at FireAnn and took the goblet from her hands. He rolled the pewter chalice between his hands. "In the morning, you'll have good memories of camp. And a case of poison oak, I'm afraid, from tromping through all that brush. Dr. Patel will have called your parents, telling them she's sending you home early for better treatment, and she'll drive out with you."

Henry stared through his spectacles at the goblet. "But I won't remember Magick," he said. "The . . . the binding . . . and . . . that."

"No. You won't."

A lone tear dropped from Henry's already red eyes, and

slid over his cheek. He wrung his hands together and, then, slowly, nodded. Jonnard said, "I'll go with you in the morning, Henry, ride in the van with you."

Dr. Patel moved slightly, looking at Eleanora and Gavan. But it was Eleanora who said, "I think that would be nice of you, Jon. It would be good for Henry to have someone with him, and I think his parents would appreciate it, too."

Squibb scratched at one arm. He dug in his pocket to get out a small jar of ointment, and Tomaz leaned over and took it from him. "You're going to have to suffer through this one," he said quietly. He gave the jar to FireAnn who sighed as she tucked it away in her apron.

"Oh," said Henry. "I really have poison oak?"

"Afraid so. It'll be a mild but stubborn case. You'll be fine in a few days although nothing is quite as good as what FireAnn cooks up."

Henry pushed his round-lensed glasses back up his nose. "I'll do anything," he declared. "Don't make me go! Please?"

"We've no choice. We have to protect ourselves, Henry. Your . . . Talent . . . as a Magicker has been on the edge your whole time here. And now . . . this." Gavan picked up the dead crystal. "We've all seen it before, and it strikes fear in our hearts, because it could, possibly, happen to us as well. You've burned your power away and you're empty. It could come back, I've heard of a rare case or two where it did, but here and now . . . you've lost it, Henry. Without it, you're at risk here at camp, and there's little we can teach you. It becomes a matter of protecting you, and ourselves, against outsiders. The Draft of Forgetfulness is a kindness, really. You won't remember what you've lost. It's the best we can do." He extended the goblet to Henry. "Drink it all down."

Jason jumped to his feet. "No! Don't let them do it to you."

Tomaz put his hand around Jason's elbow. "Jason," he said, in warning.

"No, you can't do this. This is the best thing that's ever happened to him, to any of us. Don't take it away from him."

Gavan Rainwater said sadly, "We didn't take it away. He burned it out or lost it. All we can do is protect him, and the best way to do that is to return him to the ordinary world where he belongs."

Jason struggled. "But he doesn't belong there! Anyone can see that. You can, can't you?" He looked at Eleanora, then Anita Patel, then Jonnard. No one would meet his eyes. "Look, I'll protect him. I'll do whatever I have to do to keep him safe."

Bailey offered, "You didn't send me away when I goofed."

"This is different. This isn't to punish anyone, it's to protect them, and ourselves."

"I don't want to be protected like this."

"This is all my fault," Bailey blurted out.

Eleanora moved to the girls, murmuring, "It's no one's fault. It's the way things are."

"I dared them to get even with Rich and Stefan." Lacey raced up Bailey's arm and dove into her pocket headfirst, tucking her tail in after, quickly, as though sensing all the upset.

Eleanora gently brushed a loose strand of hair from Bailey's brow and tucked it behind her ear. "I think that was a given, regardless." She glanced at Gavan. "May I take the girls back, Gavan? I think they understand the seriousness of our situation here."

He scratched at his chin before agreeing, "Good idea."

Ting stood and pulled something from her pocket, a light pink stone wrapped in a bit of wire. It glowed faintly. She gave it to Henry, who stared at it a moment. "It's a good luck charm."

"A little late," commented Trent.

Henry curled his plump fist around it. He smiled nervously at Ting. "Thanks. I think I'm going to need a lot of luck." He watched as Eleanora led the two girls from the crowded office.

Jason shrugged against Tomaz. "Henry, don't let them do this to you."

Tomaz pulled Jason back against his chest and held him. "No, Jason. This is the best way."

"I did it to myself, I think." Henry shrugged. He put his charm into his pocket.

"If you do this to him . . . you could do it to any of us. To

Jon or Trent, or . . . or me." His heart felt like it would explode in his chest.

Gavan Rainwater leveled his gaze on Jason's face as he answered, "Only if it were absolutely necessary. But, yes, if we had to, we would. Magick has dwindled through the centuries. We are nearly all that is left of it, and yet, even beyond our wish for self-preservation is the belief that we have Magick because we are destined to help with it. So saving ourselves is not as selfish as it appears. But it is necessary."

Jason thought of his own crystal, with the band of stone through it, edged by fool's gold. Was his already half dead? Was that why Gavan had not wished him to choose it? Would he be sitting at this desk tomorrow or the next day, with that goblet in front of him? "Why wait? Do it to me now!"

Henry reached for the goblet. He took a deep breath, then blurted out, "It's okay, Jason."

Jason let out a wrenching protest as Henry lifted the Draft and gulped it down, swallow after swallow, as tears streamed down his reddening face. Jon turned away and looked at the wall, as if it were too much to watch. Trent stared down at his sneakers.

Horrified, Jason could not look away as Henry set the goblet down. He belched, then colored brightly. Henry reached inside his pocket and pulled out three computer diskettes and gave them to Trent. "Better keep these. If I forget everything, they won't make any sense, anyway."

Trent pocketed the black squares. Henry had neat labels on them. The one in front read: Important! FireAnn's Herbs. Henry had put all his notes on disk.

Squibb scratched his other arm, tiny marks already beginning to welt. With a sigh, he glanced at the doctor. "Am I going to itch all night?"

She smiled softly. "I've something conventional that will help, although it's not near as good as FireAnn's ointment. You'll sleep soundly."

He nodded and stood, wobbly. He took a deep breath. "I wish I didn't have to forget you all."

"You won't, exactly. There will have been a camp. Canoeing. Lanyards. Baseball games. You'll have had a great summer." Gavan stood, as well. "You'll sleep in the infirmary tonight, and Jon will have your things all packed and ready to go in the morning."

Jon nodded.

"What about Danno? Won't he get to say good-bye?"

"Danno is sound asleep. I'll explain things to him tomorrow, as well as to the rest of the camp."

Henry nodded mournfully.

Gavan picked up his cane. "As for the rest of you, we are not done with tonight's activities. We will deal with all of you tomorrow."

Trent sighed and slipped out the office door. Tomaz squeezed the hard and callused hand he held on Jason's arm before letting him go. Whether it was meant to comfort or caution, he could not tell. Jason and Jonnard left together, paused in the doorway, and waved good-bye to Henry.

Henry brightened a bit behind his glasses. "Nice guys," he said to Dr. Patel. "Did we have fun together?" He smiled at her pleasantly before yawning hugely.

"Yes, Henry," she said softly. "You had a lot of fun with them."

Jason bolted from the office doorway. He did not stop running till he leaped up his cabin steps and threw himself through the door. Even at that, Trent had beaten him back. They did not speak to one another as they sank into bed and an uneasy sleep.

Jason woke early, but not early enough to see Henry leave. One of the buses was missing when he trotted up to the bathrooms, and he stood for a moment, looking at the small lot off the Gathering Hall. He remembered how they had all tumbled out of the buses that first night, tired but eager. The fear that had knotted in his chest last night would not go away. He could understand, for the first time, Trent's growing disenchantment. Although they were all here for the summer, the time was rapidly passing and could end abruptly for any of them. Maybe Trent was used to even harder knocks than Jason, for he seemed to have been expecting this all along.

One uneasy thought had been with him through his restless sleep. Up till now, he knew that he was accepted, mistakes and all. He had never asked why. He had never wondered what it was the Magickers wanted of him. Now, he did. It had become clear that something was wanted of each and every one of them, and it had gone unspoken. And, equally clear, if they could not deliver it, they would be shipped off and forgotten.

He shivered. He was never sure at home how long he'd be welcome, despite their cheer and smiles. He wasn't one of them, not really. Here he was one of them—or was he?

27

Unbearable

"HEEEEY, batta, batta!" yelled Bailey. She stared from the warped and weathered bench to the home plate where Ting tried to look mean and waved her bat in answer as she settled into a stance. On the pitcher's mound, Dr. Patel tried to look equally mean as she held the ball and read signals. It was the master Magickers against the new Magickers and the masters were ahead, 5 to 2.

Trent stretched his legs at second base, edging away, with a wide, knowing grin on his face. With another wave of her bat, Ting fidgeted in the batters' box again. Jason stood firmly on first, thigh smarting a bit where a wild pitch had winged him, before Sousa had pulled himself as pitcher and put himself in the outfield, sending Anita Patel in for him. The master Magickers all looked a bit overconfident as well as tired and dusty. Jonnard sat in the on-deck circle, waiting for his turn at bat.

Nearly four weeks of play on the baseball diamond had run the grass down to browning stubs. Dust flew into the air more often than baseballs, and the outfield fence had been moved several times, both closer to home plate and farther away. Today it sat a tad bit farther away, with Gavan roaming center field snagging any well hit ball that even looked like it might be a home run. Eleanora had been assigned to play first, but then everyone had protested as she levitated to catch balls slightly out of reach.

The counselors split down their ranks to play on one team or the other, so Jennifer made noises at him as she guarded first base. There was a whole raft of campers sitting in the main stands, cheering one side or the other. FireAnn had made cotton candy and everyone sat eating off their sticks, cotton spun in glorious colors that just also happened to color their tongues the same vibrant shades. With every cheer they made, a rainbow bloomed from their open mouths.

Dust rose as Jennifer shuffled her sneakers. Jason took a short lead off the base, just in case Ting got a good line on the ball. Dr. Patel wound up and pitched.

"Steeee—rike one!" bellowed Jefferson. He pounded his mitt with the baseball before throwing it back to the pitcher. Ting flipped her long dark hair over her shoulder and narrowed her eyes, staring Dr. Patel down.

It seemed to work because the next two pitches were balls. Ting dug in at the plate and look back at Jonnard for advice.

He gave her a signal that meant, swing away. So she swung at the next pitch and the ball popped up in a high, high arc that landed just out of reach of catcher Lucas as he came out of a crouch and ran for it. Two strikes. And then three balls.

Jason limbered up. If she hit it at all, on a full count, they were going to have to tag and run for it.

Dr. Patel touched the faint mark on her forehead as if for luck, wound up, and then pitched. Ting swung with all of her willow-slender strength, and the ball shot low and away from the bat. It sizzled between first and second base before hitting the ground and still moving like a cannonball, rolled to the back fence.

They were all a little slow to react, so Trent ended up on third base, Jason on second, and Ting on first. Bailey screamed and yelled at Ting, her tongue a brilliant cherry red. Rich and Stefan stood near third base, trying to distract Hightower and everyone looked at the scoreboard as Jonnard came to the plate. It was their last chance to score. Trent did a little warm-up dance on third base as if he might try to steal home.

Jonnard looked across the entire baseball field as if calculating his chances. He looked unruffled, as usual, and slightly cool, as usual. And his tongue was a normal pink as he stuck it out at Lucas who said something unheard to him in the batting box. Lucas grinned before settling into his catching stance.

The last batter of the last inning of the last game. The next two weeks after the Talent Show, the master Magickers had already told the campers, would be spent in intense courses on the crystals, and making individual plans for home study. Oh, the canoe races and relay races were yet to come and some Hoedown Barbecue or some such, but the end of their time drew near. And depending on the coming storm, they might be out of time altogether.

Jason looked at the mountains. It was a hot, crystal-clear day, not a cloud in sight. He had no idea what a mana storm would look like. Would it start like summer lightning, with nothing but heat shivering across the sky? Would it boil up in huge, dense white thunderhead clouds? Would it crawl out of the dusty lands and snake crawl through the camp like some growling beast?

Eleanora slapped Jason on the shoulder with her mitt. "Don't go anywhere!" she said, trying to sound gruff. He smothered his worries and concentrated on watching the pitcher and batter staring each other down.

Dr. Patel took a deep breath, wound up and threw hard, coming down off the pitcher's mound with the effort. Her slim strength snapped a fast ball at home plate. Jonnard stepped into his swing.

KER-ACK! The bat connected with the ball. It took off, rising, rising, arching over the infield, gaining altitude. Jason watched it go overhead. It flew against the blue sky, a white blur.

Bailey yelled, "It's going . . . going . . . it's GONE!" She spun around, ponytail flying like a pennant. "Home run!"

The ball sailed over the makeshift barrier in the outfield and thudded to earth somewhere out of sight. Jason crossed home with Ting panting right behind him, slapped hands with Trent who crossed ahead of him, but everyone charged the field to capture Jonnard as he circled the bases. Yelling in victory, they hoisted him up on a sea of shoulders and trotted around the baseball field chanting in mad confusion. They danced around

the master Magickers who laughed and tried to pull Jon down
from his victory perch and did not quite manage it.

They all ended up at the mess hall where FireAnn and her
crew made more cotton candy and shaved ices, flavored with
sugary, colorful syrups that turned tongues even more bizarre
colors as they spooned the cold treat down. Danno and Jonnard cheerfully stuck their tongues out at each other, comparing the colorful stripes and blazes as they ate, and no one
seemed to miss Henry.

When Gavan dropped an easy pop fly out behind second
base, no one but Jason heckled him, saying that he'd pulled a
Henry.

When Tomaz and Jennifer each ran for a slowing line drive
and trapped Bailey between them in a sandwich, no one but
Jason said, "That could only have happened to Squibb."

And when Bailey led her cheering section, there was no
Henry to lead the other side, owlish face red with enthusiasm,
hair sticking every which way out of his cap. No Henry to beg
for an extra splosh of cherry syrup down his shaved ice, and
no Henry to be squeaking back and forth on the mess hall bench,
joking with Danno and teasing Jonnard.

"What's wrong?" asked Trent. He'd picked blue raspberry
syrup and was working on getting his tongue a deep electric
blue. He licked his spoon.

"I miss Henry."

Something went out in Trent's face. "So?" he shrugged and
answered, looking down in his dish. He vigorously stirred his
ice into a melting slush, picked up the bowl and drank it, his
lips going blue as he did so.

"So . . . it could happen to any one of us."

"Yeah, but it didn't. And he asked for it, screwing around
like that."

"We don't know what he was doing."

"Look, all they had to do was lead Rich and Stefan around
in circles. I could have done it. There's no Magick in that. But
he didn't, he screwed around with his crystal and he burned
his nerves out. His own fault. It's been weeks, and if you went
to see him, he wouldn't even hardly remember you. Yeah, I'm
sorry, but . . . But I'm here right now, and so are you." Trent's

expression stayed closed and he said nothing more. He got up and left without another word.

Jason looked over and saw Bailey watching them both. She slid her bowl down and scooted over on the bench. She fetched Lacey out of her pocket and held out a bit of cherry-flavored ice on her finger. The packrat sniffed curiously before eating the fruity coldness. She shook her head several times, whiskers wiggling furiously.

Bailey giggled. "I don't think she likes the ice."

"Bet she's never had any before." Jason watched the packrat scramble up her arm and dive into the pocket of safety. "She sure seems tame."

"Tomaz says I have animal sense." She let out a rich chuckle. "Better than no sense at all!" She looked down at her pocket, where the long tufted tail swung lazily, almost catlike through the air. She stroked the tuft affectionately. The tail stayed out, though it jumped and danced as if Bailey tickled its owner unbearably. The sight made Jason squirm. She looked at him. "What's wrong?"

"I'm . . . not sure. You ever feel disconnected from everything?"

"What do you mean?"

"I mean . . . no one seems to care about Henry. Or anyone else who's gone, you know?"

Bailey made a little face. "Well. I guess it's like . . . we're happy it wasn't us. And it's like . . . who wants to see Henry suffering cause he lost his Magick? It's not right, but it was a relief to see him go. He was so miserable!" She looked down, somewhat ashamed, and traced a finger on the tabletop. "No one really wants to think about something like that happening."

That didn't explain Trent's attitude, though. Not good enough. Jason sighed.

Bailey looked up. "You don't have to agree. I just don't think anyone wants to think about it. Maybe you're just a little braver than we are."

"Maybe." He didn't like the sound of it, knew it wasn't true.

"Give it a day or two. It's tough thinking about all this, all at once, you know? It's a big kettle of fish to catch."

He nodded. Bailey flashed him one of her big grins before getting up to leave. The little tufted tail hanging from her shirt pocket gave a wiggle like a good-bye wave. Jonnard was deep in conversation with Danno when he left as well. It was as though Henry had never existed.

The day dragged, in dusty shimmering heat waves off the campgrounds. Trent abandoned the craft project he and Jason had been working on, a pair of neat boxes with marquetry designs on the lids, leaving Jason to piece the inlay together. Instead, Trent started work on a silk flag design of some kind, sketching onto the fabric, and then brushing paint onto it quickly. Jason caught a brief glimpse of what looked to be a spread-eagled raven carrying a lightning bolt in its claws before Trent hid it away.

He stayed behind in Herb Class, volunteering to weed Fire-Ann's bountiful herb and vegetable garden while the others sprinted off to swimming. Trent stood on one foot and the other.

"I think . . ." Trent said slowly, "I'll go to the computer lab."

"Fine."

"There's work I can do there. The ley line map is almost finished. Some files should be backed up."

"We could get this done early and then go to the lab."

Trent scratched his chin. "I'd rather go alone, you know?"

"No. No, I don't know." Jason pulled out a weed and threw it across the garden. "What did I do?"

"Nothing."

"You won't even hardly talk to me anymore."

"I've got stuff on my mind."

"I can listen. Sometimes it helps to have someone listen."

Trent did not look at him. "Not this kind of stuff. Okay?"

"I can help."

His friend said harshly, "No, you can't, Jason. Just keep your nose out of this, all right? If I wanted your help, I'd ask for it!"

"I just wanted you to know I care."

"Jason, you can't solve everything, okay? There are lots of things you just can't help, and sometimes trying just gets in the way of everything."

"But—"

"No," said Trent firmly. "I don't want to hear it!" He stalked out of the garden, shoulders stiff.

Jason stabbed and dug at the weeds heatedly for long minutes. Bits of dandelion and errant grass and scrub brush came up in chunks. Dirt packed the nails of his hands and colored his knuckles as he used the hand tools to dig and turn the earth. By the time he finished, the garden had never been so well weeded. The earth looked wet and crumbly and rich, and his stepmom would have been proud of it . . . for the gardening. His hands, well, she would have handed him a scrub brush and told him to clean up!

He dusted himself off, swatting at the clods of dirt. The sun had begun to slant low in the sky, and dark purple shadows angled through the camp. Clouds rolled in, pushed by the wind, and the sky became dark. He'd missed Sousa's hike, but his legs nagged at him. He wanted to get out and run a bit, angry energy still boiling in him and aching for a workout. He put FireAnn's gardening tools in the old wooden bucket she kept for them, and left the fenced-in garden.

He stretched first, calf muscles loosening slowly after the hours squatting over weeds. Then he stretched his arms and torso before heading toward the hiking trails.

At one time, this camp had had horses, and the trails had been cut by hours of hooves moving over them as campers rode. Now, the dirt was pounded by sneakers and hiking boots. A quick jog would feel good, he thought, as he broke into a slow run.

He ran until the clouds mounding up over the mountain peaks looked black and angry as though they had inhaled his cast-off energy. He ran until he had to stop, bent over, and breathe deeply. He ran until he knew that his ankle was finally, completely healed, and only as slightly sore as the rest of his body from the exercise. But he couldn't quite outrun his thoughts.

Jason ran his hands through his hair, smelling the sweaty heat rolling off his body, then turned and looked back at the camp. Four more deep breaths, and he would head back. He looked skyward, wondering if it might rain before he got back.

He did a stretch again to keep his legs from tightening and launched into a slow trot. It seemed to be downhill going back, the sprawled-out vista of the camp and lake ahead of him, and he picked up speed easily. As the trail entered the main part of the camp and its dirt lanes, he could hear loud voices and the bleating cry of Stefan-bear.

Jason slowed, approaching the cabins through the evergreens. Stefan-bear sat on his rump, snuffling and bawling. A shredded shirt lay on his shoulders, and a pair of shoes had been kicked off to the side. It seemed that the bear side of Stefan had made a surprise visit. Gavan and Tomaz were arguing with Rich nose-to-nose, and a dozen or so campers stood around watching. What had happened, anyway?

Trent joggled his elbow as he took it all in. "Way to go, friend," he said. "Way to not be there when you're needed."

"What are you talking about?"

"That." Trent pointed. "But it doesn't matter now, does it?"

"I didn't do anything!"

"I guess that's the point, isn't it. You were all over me earlier with offers to help, but when you were needed, you were nowhere."

"What happened?"

"Someone spilled the beans on Stefan, looks like. And we're getting the blame. You disappeared conveniently." Trent wheeled around and walked away, leaving Jason sputtering for words. The evening lights came on with a sparkling golden blur, dazzling his eyes for a moment. When he stopped blinking, Gavan had Stefan-bear by the ear and Tomaz had Rich by the arm, leading both back to their cabin.

There was nothing for it now but to shower for dinner. The swimmers had finished showering, and it was foggy and steamy and empty when he went in. He scrubbed for a long time, working on his hands and looking at his scar. Would it ever fade away to nothingness? Maybe he could have it lasered off, like a tattoo or something. When he came out with clean skin, clean hair, and clean clothes, Ravenwyng seemed eerily quiet except for the noise of the mess hall, which blazed with laughter, clatters, clinks, an occasional cheer, and lots of chatter. Not really hungry, he headed for it anyway.

From the shadow, someone called his name.

He stopped in his tracks. Had he even heard anything? The skin on the back of his hand crawled. He stepped forward, aware of the trees and shadows and cloud darkened sky as deep as night.

"Jason."

He took a shaky breath. Man or woman, he could not quite tell. But not beast. Of that he was certain. He stood still. "Wh–what?" The wind shivered through his damp hair, chilling him. He rubbed his scar as if he could ease the sudden lancing of pain through his hand. Would it never heal? Could it heal?

"Help you need, help I would."

"Me? Why?" Jason listened, but he could hear nothing behind him. No steps or breathing. The voice was older, but he couldn't quite recognize it. He shifted as if to turn around.

"No, no. Better in the shadows to stay." The air smelled of crushed pine needles. "You worry about those sent away. It is good you do. There is much they don't tell you. Much that can go wrong."

"You know about Henry?"

"I know many things. Many answers. Ask yourself how, if the mana is everywhere, Henry could lose his powers? The others? Perhaps they have not told you everything, the way it is. Perhaps they are not telling themselves the truth."

Jason took a breath. He *had* wondered. "Who are you?"

"A friend. A helper. Someone who needs aid. We can help each other, perhaps."

"How?"

"From time to time, I might need you to answer a question. And I, of course, would answer any of yours. Lend you my knowledge, my training." Shadows billowed, dark and quiet, around Jason.

He might be a kid, but he knew nothing was as simple as that, as his left hand throbbed with urgent pain. He thought of the wolfjackal's low declaration, "You are mine." The shadows didn't hold that creature . . . but . . . something wasn't right. "What do you want from me?"

"A simple understanding. I can help you . . ." The voice trailed off.

A habit now, Jason put his hand into his shorts pocket and cupped the crystal. A wrongness shoved at him, from the outside, from the gloom enveloping him. "No," he answered.

"No? A generous offer I make. And you say no?"

"Why should I trust you? You're hidden."

The person behind him took a hissing breath. *"You're mine,"* it said. "And I will have what I want, one way or the other. Trust me, you will live to regret this."

A force like a shove hit him in the small of the back, sending him to his knees. And then his hand abruptly stopped its pinching hurt, and the trees rattled as if a furious wind raced through them, and he lost his appetite.

When he slipped into the mess hall, dinner was nearly over, but FireAnn brought the entrée tray back out and scooped up some lasagne for him personally. He picked at it, not saying much.

All he knew for certain was that his scar drew trouble. Evil. And he was a danger to just about anyone as long as he wore it. He sat miserably through dinner, and the song circle, and the bonfire, knowing that. Trent had not said another word to him, and perhaps that was even wise. He finally headed back to his cabin before it was over.

28

Duel

JASON opened the cabin door, wondering what he'd done to lose Trent's friendship. He didn't know where the old Trent had gone, so he hadn't the slightest idea how to find him. He only knew that he was missing. The old Trent he could have talked to. Could have found some way to shake off what seemed to be happening. Was it his fault? He didn't know. And there was no way to get Trent to listen!

He had no need to even turn on a light. After all these weeks, he knew the cabin by heart, and the mess he'd left behind and the mess Trent was likely to leave behind. He took off his shoes and dropped them in his corner before heading to bed. He'd peel down to his underwear, as he always did, just before crawling inside the covers.

A feeling swept over him. The hairs at the back of his neck prickled and his crescent scar grew chill. Had the whisperer followed him? He turned around slowly, thinking that he was not alone in the cabin. Too far from the light switch, he pulled his crystal out and focused the lantern light and held it up to see. A tall, indistinct silhouette shape froze across the room. It became clearer as his crystal gained strength.

His crystal flared with a white-blue light, picking Jonnard

out of the shadows of the cabin. The tall boy made a face, a slight curve to his mouth, a bitter smile.

"What are you doing here?" Jason held his hand higher.

Jonnard held something in his hands, and he turned away slightly, letting it fall back to the tabletop. Trent's duffel of his prized possessions clattered to the surface.

"That's not yours."

"None of this," Jon replied smoothly, "is mine." He let papers cascade through his hands carelessly, as though not caring at all now that he had been found out.

"What are you doing?" Jason repeated. His voice caught slightly in his throat. He had no doubt that if Jon wanted to run over him to get out of the cabin, the bigger, older boy would. He wanted to know what to think, how to understand why Jon was in his place, looking through his and Trent's things.

"Getting caught, it seems. After all these weeks, I must have gotten careless. I was beginning to think there was no reason to be cautious. Certainly Eleanora's wards were nothing to fear."

"You're the thief."

"Oh, no. Bailey's packrat is the only thief. I am merely a . . ." Jon paused, then smiled slightly. "A spy."

"Spy? What for?"

"Secrets, of course. Many, many secrets. Everyone has them. Don't you ever wonder?"

Jason watched him. "Sometimes." The uneasy feeling at the back of his neck shivered down his spine.

"I wonder all the time. Secrets can be so useful." Jonnard looked at him, his face even paler by the crystal lantern light. "Henry's secret was that he wasn't nearly as good at the computer as he said. He fumbled at that as he fumbled at most of his Magick. Talented, but undisciplined and untrained. Trent did most of the hard work for him, was always there with help and tips. Trent's secret . . ." Jon looked down at the table where the things he'd been looking through were spread around. "I'm not quite sure yet. His dad's a single parent who writes often. They seem to have a good bond, if a frugal life." He looked up. "What about you, Jason? Have you secrets I haven't been able to find out? Oh, I don't mean your strange family with its stepmother and stepfather, and the fact you get very little mail other than cheerful postcards from them. Off traveling, are they? Freed of your burden for the summer? No . . . I mean the real secrets. The ones you have pinned away in darkness."

He felt something shrink inside him, knowing that the other had been through his letters, his notes, then told himself that Jonnard was just trying to psych him out. "Like you said, everyone has secrets."

"And do you keep them?"

"I won't keep this one. I don't know what you're doing, Jon, but it's creepy. And I think Gavan needs to be told."

"Oh, he'll learn soon enough." Jon tilted his head as though listening. "Storm's coming, can you feel it?"

"The mana storm?"

Jonnard arched an eyebrow. "No other storm would catch my attention." He lifted a hand. "Wild mana. There for the taking, bringing with it high winds and rain, lightning and thunder, as violent as it can be. Some storms are mild, some very powerful. I intend to drink deeply of the power, and it will be great. The storm grows every day. I don't think anyone in this camp can stand against it."

Jason listened. He heard nothing, and the heaviness settling over him could have come from anything that had happened in the past few days, but he wouldn't let Jon see it. He remarked instead on the other's lack of emotion. "Don't you even care?"

"No," answered Jonnard, slipping his hand into his pocket. "Not really. I won't be here." He brought out his crystal. "Shall we see just how good you are?" He held his crystal high and dark amber light blazed out like a sword, piercing the white cloud of illumination from the stone Jason held. It angled through; touching him, slicing like a knife with a pain that made him let out a high keening sound.

Jason stumbled back as it hit him. One breath, two, and then he realized he was under attack, as his own stone faltered, the light thinning and breaking up. It spun away, scattering about the cabin like a thousand tiny stars before winking out, one by one. He took his eyes off Jon and Focused on his crystal, pouring his thought into it. No time or breath to ask why. The life of his crystal depended on what he did, as Jonnard continued to attack.

The light of each crystal sharpened, Jason's flaring out until he was shielded by it. The amber sword cut at it, bounced off with a humming sizzle. Jon frowned. He took a step across the room, raising his crystal in his hand. As he moved, the crystal rang with a pure, clear note, and its light darkened. It thinned, widened, and began to descend on Jason. Wide and winged, like a great dark cloak, it hovered overhead. Then, slowly, both boys breathing hard, it began to envelop him.

Part of him wanted to scream at Jon. He stuffed that part away so that he could concentrate, or he would lose his crystal . . . and who knew what else. He furrowed his brow and thought as hard as he could into his precious stone. The bond between them warmed steadily, yet he could feel the cloak start to wrap its icy wings around him. It sucked at the light, absorbing it. Something in him began to realize that Jonnard knew exactly what he was doing, and had done it before.

Every muscle in him tightened. Where was Trent? Should he shout for anyone else? And even if he did, would they get here in time before Jonnard did . . . what?

Jason shuddered. He drew on everything he had inside him to keep his crystal light without firing up or going empty. The stone grew warm in his palm, faceted planes shimmering. Yet still Jonnard's dark cloak fell over him and began to wrap him tightly, its coldness sinking into his very bones. Jason reacted instinctively.

He dropped and rolled. As he did, he clenched his hand around his stone, cutting off all light, and the cabin went dark. The icy shroud disappeared. Jason rolled again, into the far corner, and lay in the shadows, clutching his crystal under him. He wasn't quite sure what had happened or had worked, but the attack stopped.

A long moment ticked by. Then Jonnard said carefully, "Jason?" A board creaked as he took a step. "That was really very clever. Yes, I need to see you to target you. At least . . . now I do. When I get stronger, we shall see."

Jason held his breath. His crystal felt hot against his chest, and his marked hand twitched as if to toss it aside. He clenched his teeth, fighting himself, to stay down and quiet and unseen.

"A coward's way out. But clever, yes, I'll remember that. Is that your secret, Jason? You're a coward?"

Another board creaked, closer. He could almost feel the wood vibrating in his ear. Jason tried to decide what to do next. He was trapped, and they both knew it. The only thing he didn't know was what Jonnard intended to do with him.

He would have to try to make it to the door.

The screen door banged, loudly. Jason flinched and he could hear Jonnard jump, startled.

"All right, you two. It's payback time. It's time to get even for you narcing on Stefan." Rich's thin, unpleasant voice snaked through the air. Behind him on the porch, something heavy shuffled and lumbered up and let out a bleating whine. The smell of bear filled the cabin.

Jonnard let out a curse. Moonlight streamed through the opening door, outlining his tall body. He raised his crystal and then, in a blink, disappeared.

Jason stood slowly. The cabin door flung open and Rich turned on the light. "What are you two, mushrooms?" He stood in the threshold, hands on his hips, mouth curled unpleasantly. At his back, the bear that was also Stefan stood up and filled the entire doorway.

"You won't believe this but, number one, am I glad to see you! Number two, we didn't tell anyone about Stefan, and number three, I have to see Gavan." He uncovered his crystal and white-hot light shot out. Like a small star, it went nova in the cabin.

With a surprised yell, Rich and Stefan scrambled for their lives, rolling off the cabin porch in their haste. Jason watched the flare with eyes that immediately began watering. He shoved his crystal in his pocket, bolted out the doorway, did a leapfrog over Stefan-bear who was whining on all fours at the bottom of the porch steps. He hit the ground running and did not stop till he skidded into the bright lights of the Gathering Hall, the other two pounding on his heels and they all ran full tilt into Tomaz Crowfeather as he came around the corner.

29

Storm Warning

ALL three of them barreled into Tomaz. The Magicker rocked back on his heels with an *ooof* collaring Rich with one hand and Stefan with the other. No longer a bear, but a stocky boy again, Stefan rolled his head around and let out a low bearish grunt as though he might turn, and Tomaz said warningly, "None of that, now."

"Jon—in my cabin—spying," Jason blurted out.

"Now? It's late. Everyone's at the bonfire, and it's nearly Lights Out." Tomaz directed that last in a stern voice at the two he held in his grasp.

He had caught the sleeve of Jason's T-shirt, but he wriggled around and got loose, standing up as Tomaz added, "What's the story with you three?"

"He's a troublemaker," said Rich sulkily. Stefan only grunted unhappily.

"I told you—we didn't tell on Stefan." Jason cast his gaze on Tomaz. "I've got to see Rainwater. He's got to know what happened with Jonnard. Please."

Tomaz gave Rich and Stefan a little shake. "You boys will have to sort this out later. But it wasn't Jason who gave you away. Do you think I could track you all over camp for a week and not know?"

"Well." Stefan shuffled about. "Guess not."

"All right, then. Back to the cabin. I'll see you in the morning." He leveled a look into Stefan's face, and the other grunted and backed up, almost bearlike, before turning around and following Rich down the camp lane as Tomaz released him.

"Now . . . what's this about Jon?"

"I caught him in the cabin. He was going through everything. He said he was spying, had been, all along. And then he came at me with his crystal."

"Came at you? He attacked you?"

Jason nodded, still a little breathless.

"You find Rainwater, I'll check camp for Jonnard."

He bolted into the Gathering Hall corridor, uncaring of quiet or wards or anything else. The alarms went off with a howling screech as he skidded into Rainwater's office, startling Gavan. Amid bells and whistles, he skidded across the floor and thudded into the desk, panting, "Jonnard is spying . . . on everyone! I caught him, and he attacked me with the crystal, and he almost killed mine like he killed Henry's, and he said it was too late!"

Gavan narrowed his blue eyes and stilled the alarms with a wave of his hand. The office fell suddenly silent. "Explain yourself, and do it slower this time." He pointed at an empty chair.

Jason fell into it, and told the story again, this time from the beginning to the spy's vanishing end. As he told it, he realized what he had blurted out about Henry's crystal. Jon had been with Henry. He had no doubt and no proof that somehow what had happened to Henry had been something Jon had done . . . and Henry had not even been aware of it. Henry hadn't lost his power on his own . . . Jon had done it to him. How could they all have been so blind?

"Jonnard?" repeated Gavan again, tapping his cane on the floor. Disbelief filled his face. "Damn me for not catching it."

Tomaz came back in the doorway, a bit out of breath. He tugged on his vest as if to compose himself. "He's gone, not a trace."

"But how—" Jason looked from one Magicker to the other. "How could he do that?"

"His crystal." Tomaz stared at Gavan.

"But . . . but . . . he walked inside it, like Bailey?"

"No, Jason, he knows how to use it to move." Gavan sat down again, heavily. "I'm a fool, Tomaz. He has to be one of the Dark Hand."

"No more a fool than I."

"But so young . . ."

"He's obviously been recruited, taught. Did we not recruit him ourselves? Dr. Patel brought him in. No doubt they placed him where she would run across him. They knew enough of us to infiltrate and spy effectively. I didn't catch him either, and who knows . . . there might be more here."

Gavan buried his face in his hands for a moment, then looked up. "We haven't long."

Infiltrated . . . Jason thought of the dark voice in his ear, the smooth coaxing promises. They'd reached for him, too! Caught by the shock of it, he stood speechless. He stared at the back of his hand. Had he any choice?

"All right, then." Gavan took a deep breath. "First things first. The Dark Hand knows we're here, can attack from inside as well as outside, whatever element of surprise we hoped to have is gone." He stood again, as if gathering his energy. "We need to find the Gate."

Tomaz gave a slight shake of his head. "Send them home."

The two stared into each other's faces. Gavan said slowly, "I refuse to give up like that."

"FireAnn has enough Draft for all."

Jason's eyes widened. Give them all the Draft of Forgetfulness and ship them home?

"Crowfeather, I can't bundle up thirty-some campers and send them home this early. The others who have gone were a big enough risk. This camp . . . this *school* has to stand. It has to, if we're to have any future. There is Haven beyond the Gate."

Tomaz hooked his thumbs in his concho belt.

"What kind of haven?" Jason asked, almost certain neither would answer him. He could feel the tension in the air. He understood then, that the Magickers were still fighting for survival, still unsure of what path to take. Older than him by far and yet, in some ways, no more the wiser.

"The Borderlands," said Tomaz shortly. "Think of them as pockets of free manna. They are next to us, but are not us. As the world changed, many things that were Magick fled there. For most, however, it was too late, and they died anyway, or so my people tell it. Coyote was once thought to be a Gate-keeper, and sometimes he is, but mostly he is a Trickster. He lives off the delusions of others."

"This is not a delusion."

"No, of course not." Tomaz answered Gavan. He set his jaw stubbornly.

Jason scratched his temple. Something nagged at him to be remembered. What would they have to do to be safe? Was Gavan going to try to hide all of them? What was it Bailey had said . . . hide in plain sight? He shifted his weight, tangled in his undone shoestring, and nearly fell over. Stooping over, he retied his shoe. The one lace, still frayed badly where the lake dweller had tugged and pulled at him, looked as if it could give at any time. Memory rushed in.

He blinked as the blood rushed to his head. "Excuse me . . . tell me about the Gates."

"The Borderland Gates? There is a long and dark history to them, Jason. I had planned to cover that in next summer's class, if not a bit sooner. The Iron Gate is the closest to us right now, and the easiest to traverse, named for the great Iron Mountain and its valley just beyond. The others . . . the Fire Gate and so on . . . well, some are even thought to be sheer mythology, and of course, it doesn't help that strange and odd things happen near the Gates, because of the mana that seeps through. Not to mention an occasional denizen the likes of which haven't been seen in modern man's world."

Jason waved his hands. "No, no. I mean the camp's gates, front and back. Why can't we just shut the camp's gates against the wolfjackals and everything?"

"Most of the camp is not fenced, just staked out to show the boundaries," Tomaz began, "And with the mana sweeping in for them to use as they will, ordinary gates won't stop them—" Gavan stopped him sharply

"Wait a moment." Gavan stared at Jason. "Did you say, front and *back* gates?"

"Well, yeah. The ones under the sign at the front road coming in, and the old ones by the back of the lake."

"Ravenwyng has no back gate." Gavan reached out for Jason. "What did you see? Tell me."

"When Trent and I took the canoe way out that time we got grounded, we had a . . . a problem . . . I went overboard. We had to beach the canoe for me to climb back in. Anyway, I found the back gate there, just off the shore. There's a rough lane crossed by this huge, swinging gate. It's already open, though."

"That makes no never mind," said Tomaz. "What you saw may not be what actually *is*."

Gavan repeated firmly, "There is no back gate." He stared at Jason. "Could you find it again? Have you marked it in your mind?"

"I couldn't forget it."

"All right then. I'll get Eleanora, and we'll all take a look at it. Tomaz, get Lucas, Sousa, Hightower. Tell them about Jonnard and see if . . . well, see what you can do? He's probably covered his tracks, but you might be able to back trace him. Secure the camp against the storm if you can."

Tomaz nodded.

Eleanora was in the music room, practicing, stroking her fingers over her dulcimer and coaxing out beautiful strains of music. Gavan and Jason stood quietly in the doorway till she looked up, sighting them. She put her palm across the strings of the dulcimer to still it. She smiled faintly. "We each have our own way of dealing with things. I like my music."

"And it is no wonder, that." Gavan tried a smile. "I need a word with you, though I hate to interrupt."

A frown replaced the smile. "Sounds serious."

Gavan strode in, drawing Jason with him. In quick, terse words, he told her of Jonnard's betrayal and attack on Jason. Her face paled and her hands shook slightly as she slipped the instrument into its tapestry case. She reached for Jason's hands.

"Are you all right?"

He nodded.

"But that's not all," Gavan added, with a dramatic flourish of his cane. "He saw a Gate."

"Really?" Eleanora considered Jason. "Well, it's about time."

"About time?" Gavan's brows shot up, and he stared at Eleanora.

"Well, I should think it is, don't you?" She stood up and put her instrument away on a deep shelf. She looked over her shoulder at Gavan. "You didn't know?"

"Blast me for being blind," Gavan grumbled. "I was almost certain it was Bailey. Brash. Always rushing ahead to explore . . ."

Eleanora smiled faintly, and shook her head. "Bailey's power is with animal lore, that is plain."

"Know what?" Jason asked.

Gavan coughed. "Of course, there was a possibility . . . but with forty-nine of them to look over—"

Eleanora turned around with her hands on her hips. "The signs were all there. He was always about and around at night, restless, couldn't sleep. Looking for something, never quite sure what. It took me a while, too. He is very circumspect."

"Well." Gavan cleared his throat a bit. "I've been busy. There's no doubt we all recognized he is Talented. . . ."

Tomaz agreed. "I would have missed it, too, with the Council on my back. In fact, I did miss it . . . till now. Now it's as obvious as the nose on your face."

"Know what?" demanded Jason.

"That you are a Keeper of the Ways. In short, a Gatekeeper. I would bet my dulcimer on it." Eleanora tossed her head. "And I thought Gavan was keeping his eyes on you, because he knew that, too. I should have realized other things had you distracted, Gavan." She took out her crystal and began polishing it in the deep folds of her brocade skirt.

The Magicker muttered something darkly. He leaned on his cane. "I don't intend to waste more of it. The Gate is at the far end of the lake."

"You've seen it?" Eleanora smiled sweetly at Jason.

He nodded.

"It's marked well in your mind?"

He nodded again.

"Then we won't be canoeing there." Eleanora took up Jason's hand again, and said briskly, "Hold on to him, Gavan." She raised her crystal in her free hand. "Picture it in your mind. Absolutely, firmly, no wavering. Focus on it!"

"What are we doing?"

"We have been practicing moving objects with the crystals. Now we are going to move ourselves," said Gavan flatly. He took up Jason's other hand. "Do as she tells you."

Eleanora held out her crystal to Jason. "Look in. This is a door, and it is opening. When you see, on the other side, that picture in your mind . . . just as sharp, just as clear . . . I want you to step through that door and go there. Don't worry about us, we'll follow."

"But . . . but it's your crystal."

"Yours isn't quite trained yet. Trust me, Jason." Eleanora leaned closer. "Think on it. Quickly now. Make it true and clear."

He looked into the pale rose quartz, thinking of the rugged shoreline, the split boulder just off the lake with the pine growing stubbornly out of it. He tried to think of the gate, too, but it would not stay in his mind. But the beach where he'd finally scrambled to safety, that he had. The gate would only be a few strides beyond that. The plane of her quartz began to open, like a door swinging inward, and beyond it, the vision of his thoughts lay. With a squeeze of their hands he stepped into the gemwork.

There was a moment of nothingness. It was dark and cold, and his whole body stopped as though he had sneezed violently. Then he stepped onto firm ground, stumbled, and Gavan and Eleanora tumbled out of nowhere next to him. All three of them went sprawling.

"I shall have to teach him about landings," Gavan said dryly. He bounded to his feet, and helped Eleanora up.

Eleanora winked at Jason. "Just remember it's like parachuting," she said. "That first step is a long one!"

"You've parachuted?" Gavan considered Eleanora with an odd expression on his face. "Wonders of the modern age."

She did not answer but adjusted her skirt and blouse and bent to tighten the laces on her high-button shoes. When she straightened, she rose in the air her customary elevation of three or four inches as though nothing could be amiss.

Jason stood up. They faced the lake, with its deep waters like a mirror, reflecting the rain clouds mounding up over the hills, silver and black in the moonlight. He turned round. He could see the metal glint through the underbrush. "There," he said, and pointed.

They hurried to keep up as he went to it, his face all knotted in a frown because he *hadn't* been able to focus on it clearly and that worried him. Even as he approached it now, it seemed to have moved a bit from where he'd seen it originally . . . yet how could it? Rusting metal gateposts buried in the dirt, and fencing fading off into the heavy underbrush, and a huge swinging gate fastened back among the evergreens couldn't move on their own.

"Impressive." Gavan tapped his cane on the ground.

"It's rusting." In fact, the more Jason looked at it, the less sturdy it appeared.

The Magicker shook his head. "No, lad, not that. You landed us practically on top of it."

Eleanora put her hand on Jason's shoulder. "Gates, you see, shift in time and place. That's why we can't hope to find them without help or Talent." Her ruffled blouse moved restlessly in the strong, cooling wind off the lake.

"It *did* move, then."

"No doubt."

Gavan reached out with his cane, probing. "And it is on Ravenwyng property, or within a jump of it." He smiled thinly. "I think even Tomaz would agree we ought to be able to get the Border to take the camp in." He tucked his cane under his elbow. "All right, everyone through for a quick look-see, and I'll leave word what we're trying to do with the camp, and then we go batten the hatches."

The moon was engulfed by clouds. A dark shadow fell across them, as the wind howled up, cold and harsh. Eleanora turned as a wailing howl broke the air, followed by another and another.

"Too late!" she cried.

Harsh clouds hid the sky and the moon's light boiled in shades of black and gray. Lightning split the clouds as the wolfjackal pack touched down in triumph. Ivory fangs flashed, and pewter claws raked the ground. Dull thunder rolled behind them. The very air seemed to shiver and dance as they materialized out of the nowhere to the now.

Eleanora drew her crystal, and Gavan brought his cane up to face the pack. "Stay behind us, Jason."

He drew his own stone and cupped it. Uneasily, he waited for its welcoming glow, worried that the battle with Jon had harmed it. The unpolished edges jabbed him as he held it tightly. The wolfjackals paced and stirred around behind their leader, just as the clouds in the sky seemed to rise and fall and boil behind one immense thunderhead as it grew over the mountains. The beasts snarled and snapped at the darkening air, their eyes flashing with an eerie green glow.

"Now we both know where the Gate is," Gavan said grimly.

"They would have found it anyway."

"Yes . . . eventually. No time to set up wards."

Eleanora did not look at Gavan but kept her gaze leveled on the wolfjackals as they stopped, then circled and fanned out into an attacking stance. Ivory fangs gleamed in the scant moonlight left. He counted a pack of seven, larger than before, and the wolfjackal in front loomed the size of a small pony. "They're bigger," he stammered, surprised.

"Feeding on the mana storm." Gavan braced himself. He focused his wolfhead cane so that the immense crystal held in the wolf's jaws aimed less than a few feet away. "That's far enough," he called out.

The wolfjackal pack slowed to a stop, and the others began to pace back and forth behind the leader, who seemed momentarily content.

"A Gate," growled the wolfjackal leader. "We but seek to pass. We have that right."

"Not here and not now."

"Our rights!" The pack leader threw his head up, letting out a baleful howl.

"You have none."

"The Gate is as much ours as yours." The packleader snarled and snapped at thin air.

"I deny it to you. Later, perhaps, when I've talked with the Hand."

The wolfjackal grinned, his tongue lolling out of his sharp jaws. "Sooner!" he promised, his thick tail low and moving from side to side, but it was not a canine wag. Every move the dun-and-silver beast made was one of menace. Jason found he was holding his breath, and tried to relax enough to get some air.

A bolt of pale green light shot from the cane Gavan gripped tightly in his hand. It struck the ground in front of the pack, sending up a puff of scorched dirt. The wolfjackal jumped back with a startled yelp. He reared back against his followers, then shook himself indignantly. His ruff bristled up, and he lowered his head as he paced forward. "You shall pay for that."

"Here they come," Gavan warned needlessly, and the three of them braced themselves.

With a snap and snarl, the pack launched itself. Jason froze. His marked hand twitched so hard, he could barely grip his crystal. His breath caught in his chest as he tried to bring up a shield of light from his stone, but all he could manage was a pale, quivering glow.

Gavan abandoned the crystal embedded in his cane, and drew forth one hanging from a thick-linked gold chain about his neck, drawing it out of his collar. Instead, he used the cane like a wooden sword, parrying, thrusting, and sweeping. The wolfjackals yelped as he rapped sharply at their heads and limbs. Froth flew from their snapping jaws as they bit at the cane and caught only air.

The pack leader crouched and lunged at Gavan. Rainwater parried with the cane, catching his jaws, but unable to stop the body from ramming him. Both fell and tumbled. The wolf-jackal ended up on top, jaws spread wide as Gavan shoved the cane crosswise into them. The wood clattered against ivory fangs.

Eleanora let out a small sound, as three battered at her shield, and she retreated a step, coming up against Jason. "Run," she said. "We're outnumbered!"

"I can't leave you."

Gavan gave a loud grunt and yell and shoved the wolfjackal back onto his haunches as he scrambled up, panting. "I think retreat is advisable."

"Where?" Jason backed up, as the pack re-formed and began to slink close, their hot breath filling the air.

He pointed toward the open Gate. Jason turned to lead the way. Something hot and heavy hit him full tilt, sending him rolling through the gateposts. It snarled and snapped as he threw his hands up to protect his face, and the crystal flared weakly. He shoved the beast away and clambered to his knees, but the wolfjackal jumped again, jaws snapping. Jason fell back.

His head snapped against metal with a stinging, slashing jolt. He cried out as pain lashed through his scalp, red hot and pounding. Dazed as the beast drove at his chest, teeth gleaming, he rolled over and managed to stagger up. He clung to the gatepost, evergreen branches whipping around his body. Sickened to the pit of his stomach by the sudden pain, Jason fell against the Gate. Hot blood poured from his scalp, into his eyes, and over the metal framework. The Gate moved as he clung to it, swinging inward. Double vision wavered in front of him. Jason groaned as the Gate dragged him through the dirt, a vast great Iron Gate of intricate scrollwork and heaviness that he clung to desperately, his hands and face slick with blood.

As he hung on it, stomach heaving with the pain shouting through his head, the Gate shut with a heavy clang, all of them on the outside.

Eleanora and Gavan swung around. "Oh, no!" she cried in dismay.

"We'll make a stand here," Gavan said grimly. He swung out and slashed the wolfjackal away from Jason's ankles. "Hang on to me, lad!" He reached out, and slipped an arm under Jason's shoulders.

"We can't hold out here, Gavan."

"I won't lead them back to camp. Not yet." Holding Jason on his feet, he parried, then slashed at a wolfjackal slinking close.

"I know where wolfjackals won't dare to follow."

"Oh . . . no . . . Eleanora . . ."

His words did not slow her. She linked elbows with Jason and cupped her crystal close, crying out a single word: "Auntie!"

Before the word faded, Jason felt his guts wrenched yet again and they were snatched into chill darkness, then dumped unceremoniously in a patch of clover in front of a small, thatched cottage.

Jason blinked.

Aunt Freyah came out, brandishing a broom in her hand. Then she stopped. "My, my. A visit is always welcome, I say. Can't look a gift horse in the mouth! Up with you before those foul beasts track you in!" With that, she swept them to their feet and into her home.

30

Always Eat Dessert First

SHOOING them inside to a sunny and cheerful parlor with huge overstuffed chairs covered in bright fabric with immense sunflowers on it, Freyah sat down and watched them sharply. "Unexpected, but always welcome," she said and beckoned for them to sit.

"A warning. This is a Haven only so long as no unpleasantness enters. Whether in Evil as those who chased you to my Border, or in your thoughts and hearts." Freyah folded her hands.

"Aunt Freyah, you know we'd never—" Eleanora looked appalled.

"I find it is always better if a guest knows what to expect."

Gavan plopped Jason down in a chair, before turning away a bit, whispering, "She is a true Magicker. She pulls all this out of herself. Enjoy it . . . as she grows older, she is losing the strength to do much else. We'll try not to upset her if we can." He turned his back completely and walked away a pace or two.

She watched Gavan sharply. "How much trouble are you in?"

"No one said anything about trouble."

Freyah raised her eyebrow. "I doubt you are here to ask

me about firing the greenware in the kiln. All that wonderful artwork is finished, is it not? And with a pack on your heels, there is always trouble."

Eleanora bobbed up and down a moment as though having trouble holding her height. Jason watched her until he grew a little queasy, and his stomach complained. Gavan took out a handkerchief and pressed it to the side of his head, which throbbed horribly, although it no longer felt as if hot blood oozed through his hair. He wiped the blood off deftly before pocketing the handkerchief.

Freyah's sharp black-eyed gaze was on him instantly. "What's wrong?"

All he could think of was Gavan's warning not to upset her. "Well, I . . . I haven't eaten . . ." He faltered. He couldn't remember since when. Or where, for that matter. Well, he could remember where he was when he usually ate, but not where this was. They'd gone from stormy night to sunny day. *When* were they, and *where?* It was confusing to think, so he stopped. He caught sight of himself at a mirror's edge across the room and saw that his wound did not show, although he looked rather pale.

She rocked back in her chair, color flooding her already apple-bright cheeks. "Not eaten! Honestly, you two, what sort of heathens are you?" Without waiting for a response from either Gavan or Eleanora, she fished out a huge wicker picnic basket from behind her chair. Nearly the size of a clothes hamper, its woven sides glistened a pine yellow. "The stomach is directly responsible for the well-being of the rest of the body. Particularly at his age. Eat now, talk later."

She flipped open the hamper top, and wonderful aromas filled the air. His knees went weak. He could smell freshly roasted turkey. Cherries. Chocolate fudge.

Gavan made an impatient movement with one hand, but Eleanora gave him a look that could have dropped a wolf-jackal in its tracks.

Freyah put a napkin over his knee, snapped her fingers, and a dining tray came scampering over on aluminum legs to stand by Jason, supports quivering.

Freyah looked at the serving tray. "George," she said firmly. "Do stop that."

The tray bobbed in a quick curtsy and froze into position as Jason stared in amazement. Freyah sighed as she reached into her picnic hamper. "He loves company," she said apologetically. "The more food I can heap on him, the prouder he is. Never dropped a crumb, he has! Just like his sainted father whom I finally retired into a picture frame." Freyah glanced across the room at a picture with an ornately braided metal frame, a fond expression crossing her face.

Gavan drummed his long fingers. Turned away from Freyah, he studied the other end of the room. Jason peeked but could not see what Gavan was eyeing.

Eleanora found a height she liked and stuck to it, the hem of her skirt shimmering about her ankles. She smoothed her outfit down over her knees as if she'd meant to come to tea and not retreat from a full-blown attack. "Aunt Freyah. Would it be a bother if we ate as well? I know I haven't seen a meal in quite a while, and I'm almost certain Gavan here—"

"Can do very well for himself, thank you!" Gavan interjected.

". . . is famished as well," finished up Eleanora smoothly. She smiled brightly at Freyah.

"Well." Freyah's chin dimpled as she looked into the basket. "Well, well. I hadn't really planned for more than the lad here. . . ."

"You planned for him?" Gavan found something interesting on Aunt Freyah's face to stare at.

"I, well. Hrmmmm." The rounded woman stirred uncomfortably on her plush armchair. "That is to say." But she didn't say it. Instead, "I sensed a Gatekeeper had begun to test his skills."

Eleanora shot Gavan a look as she leaned forward and hugged Freyah. "Now, Auntie. I've seen you pull all sorts of wonders out of that basket before. You could easily feed four, no doubt. We won't impose, but if you've anything extra at all, I know we could use a bite or two. Before we talk about things necessary and a bit odd."

Jason found himself looking down at a small tag affixed to the side of the reed hamper basket where it nudged his knee. It read "Feeds 5–6." He blinked. The serving tray in front of him gave itself an impatient shrug.

Freyah took a deep breath. "Well, then. Let's see what I can muster up! Eat dessert first, I always say! The rest of the meal may be uncertain at best." And with that, she dug her dimpled hands into the picnic basket's interior and began to pull out china dishes covered with food. An ivory china plate with crimped edges came out, filled with fresh baked cherry tarts. Then an etched crystal dish piled with chocolate fudge cupcakes, their icing creamy and swirled into little peaks. Both Jason and George fairly shook with delight as she set them down on George's tray.

"Help yourself. Milk over here." She pointed, and the little sideboard behind them bloomed with four chilled glasses of frothy milk.

Eleanora sighed wistfully, her hands empty, as she settled into a chair. She stared wistfully at the pastries. "Aunt Freyah."

Jason grabbed a cupcake and devoured it in two gulps. Never had anything more wonderfully chocolate melted on his tongue. He washed it down with half a glass of milk before sitting back happily, eyeing the plates. Another cupcake or a tart? The throbbing in his head had nearly disappeared.

"Both," Aunt Freyah said to him, smiling as if she could read his thoughts.

"Good idea." Gavan filled his own hands with both, his golden-brown hair falling over his brilliant blue eyes, heedless of the mournful look Eleanora gave him.

Eleanora sighed. "Aunt Freyah."

"Now, eat your fill, but don't eat too many. Vegetables and main course to come, you know!" Singing happily to herself, a wordless and nearly tuneless tune, Freyah sat back with a tart in her fingers and nibbled delicately at the edges.

"Aunt Freyah," said Eleanora yet again.

Freyah blinked. "What, child? What, and what again? Spit it out!" She wrinkled her nose. "Oh, you can't. You haven't eaten a thing. But I thought you said you were hungry."

"Vegetables and main course to follow . . . which would be what?" Eleanora asked primly.

"Oh." Her aunt leaned forward to rummage around in the picnic basket, saying, "You would ask before he's quite ready, and you know it makes him ticklish." A faint giggle from the depths echoed her statement before she looked up in triumph. "Aha. Carrot and raisin salad and turkey sandwiches on squaw bread. Not ready yet, though."

Jason managed to gobble his cherry tart a little slower than his cupcake. The cherry was both tart and sweet, juicy in its filling and the crust buttery light. He chewed, his whole mouth delighted by the flavor, and his stomach growing happier by the swallow. He looked up to see Gavan licking the top frosting off his cupcake, before popping the cake part in, a pleased grin on his face.

Eleanora crossed her arms. "Well, really." She looked pointedly away from all three of them as they ate.

"What's wrong?" Jason peered at Eleanora.

Gavan speared another cherry tart with his long fingers. He ate half before saying to Jason. "You know. Diet. Girlish figure, all that."

"I know?" Jason began to repeat, puzzled. Then, "Oh." He grew quiet. He looked at the back of Eleanora's head in sympathy.

Freyah snorted. "She wouldn't have to worry about her weight IF she ever walked with her feet on the ground instead of in the clouds. Got some decent exercise."

"I don't have to. I choose to. It's important I carry myself well, or else everyone else towers over me."

Taking her linen napkin off her lap, a shower of chocolate crumbs falling to the floor and then mysteriously disappearing, Freyah dabbed the corners of her mouth. "Of course, I made them nonfattening, but if she wants to be a martyr—"

"Oh!" Eleanora's head swung around like a shot. "Auntie! Bless you!" Eleanora dove onto the plates, her quick, neat little hands easily outsprinting Gavan for the last cherry tart and cupcake.

"Indeed? Bless me? Now, there's a thought!" Freyah sat back, patting her silver curls into place about her face, with an enormously pleased expression. A tinkle of china came from inside the basket, ringing like a bell, and she leaned forward to peer inside. "Second course!"

With that, she pulled out saucers heaping with carrot, raisin, and pineapple chunk salad, followed by a simply enormous platter of turkey sandwiches. Gleaming silverware shot out of the wicker picnic basket like a fountain. George leaned sharply right and left to catch all of it on his tray top, the utensils clattering noisily into place.

Freyah and Jason clapped. "Well done, George!"

The tray quivered with pride.

"Graceful and strong," Eleanora cooed and patted one of George's few open spots. The tray sidled a little closer to her in the gap between Jason and her chair, whereupon she took advantage of the shorter reach to snag a sandwich plate and balanced it on her knee.

Jason grinned as Gavan frowned, then took a slightly smaller sandwich, its multigrained bread and thick crust nearly overwhelmed by thick slices of turkey, lettuce, and a cranberry sauce filling. He managed it in three bites. Jason took his time with his, savoring every juicy and tasty bite of the turkey, slices of white and dark meat neatly layered, and coated with a tangy white mayo. Every mouthful tasted like the best, warmest memories he had ever had of Thanksgiving. When he finally sat back, it was with a very full and happy stomach.

Freyah gathered up all the empty plates and put them back in the wicker picnic basket which immediately began a crunching and crackling sound. She smiled fondly. "His favorite part," she said. "He does love to eat the china." The basket churned and bobbed as it consumed the remnants of their lunch. She closed the lid, patting it. A muffled burp ensued.

Jason smothered a laugh.

Eleanora dabbed her napkin at the corners of her mouth, her eyes sparkling as she smiled at Jason. Freyah, however, smoothed her face into seriousness. She pinned her sharp gaze on Gavan. "Now, then. Trouble. Explain it."

"We didn't say there was trouble . . ." Eleanora protested faintly.

"No, no," Gavan added. "Nothing about trouble, at all."

Freyah stared.

"That is to say," Gavan continued. "Not that each of us doesn't face adversity in some small way, every day." He brushed a lingering tart crumb off his cloak, avoiding her unblinking dark eyes.

One eyebrow rose, punctuating the black stare which threatened to become a cold glare.

Gavan cleared his throat. "That is."

"Nothing important, Aunt Freyah, really," supplied Eleanora. Gavan shot her a grateful look as Freyah now began to stare at Eleanora.

The room chilled. Jason shivered slightly, drawing his legs up to curl into his armchair. George darted to the side and came back with an afghan curled on his tray. Jason took it, and tucked it about him. "If no one wants to tell her, I will."

All three Magickers looked at him.

"Someone with spunk," Aunt Freyah remarked.

He shook his head. "No," he said slowly. "I think it is mine to tell because I was the one who did it." He put his hand to the side of his neck and rubbed it slowly, still feeling a sharp pain ebbing away. Eleanora's mouth curved sympathetically as she watched him. Gavan muttered something in a low voice, as he wrapped his cloak about himself, sinking into his chair, long legs jutting out. He did not, however, move to stop Jason from speaking.

"I found the Gate."

"Excellent. However, that does not explain the three of you being dumped on my doorstep, does it?" Freyah looked to Gavan sharply, her silvery curls bobbing. "Pleasantries aside, I warned you. I told you there would be trouble if you pursued this course. You stubbornly did as you wished."

"There is a massive mana storm sweeping our way."

Her eyes snapped. "Again. Do you presume me to be an old fool or just old? Of course, I know a storm is headed our way."

"I intended to use it, if I could, to bring the camp inside the Gates. Barring that, to open up Iron Mountain Academy again, if I can free it."

Freyah sat back in her chair, and Eleanora stared at Gavan, openmouthed. Her hand went up to wipe away a crumb from lips parted in surprise.

"A bold move."

"We need our children, our future. We need to educate and protect them. How many of us died because we had no warning and no shelter when . . ." Gavan paused. "Well, the past is history. Let the lad continue."

"I found the Iron Gate. Accidentally. It's at the far end of the lake, and I thought it was just, you know, the back gate to camp."

She beamed at him. "Smart lad. And, while coincidence is rampant, I don't think that was any accident. You were meant to find it! Still . . . that is not the problem?"

"The Gate is closed."

"Oh, dear. My, my. That is a pretty kettle of fish."

Jason wondered for a moment if Aunt Freyah had ever talked at any length with Bailey, or vice versa. She took a napkin and pressed it exactly upon the scalp wound hidden in his sandy hair, and took the napkin away to examine it. Old and fresh blood stained the crisp white linen. She frowned at Jason. "Closed with blood?"

Gavan pursed his lips and looked nonchalantly at the ceiling. "Aye. Likely it was. The lad *is* wounded."

"And you let him sit there, in pain?"

"It doesn't hurt so awfully. It's the camp that's important," Jason said faintly.

Freyah stood up. She flipped the lip down on the picnic hamper and shoved it back behind her chair again. There was a faint crash inside as if someone had dropped something breakable.

"No help for it, then. If the Gate is closed, it's closed."

Eleanora folded her hands on her lap. "None? Are you sure?"

"I am certain, and none." She unclipped a brooch watch from her vest and looked at it. "My advice is to hurry home, and make whatever plans you can to ride it out. I'll notify the Council, but I think we'll all be nailing our windows shut." She refastened the watch. "It will be a rough one."

Gavan nodded. He extended one hand to Eleanora, and the other one to Jason. "My thanks, then, Aunt Freyah, for the refuge." He lifted his cane to focus on his wolfhead crystal, and Jason noticed the teeth marks and notches in the wood.

Freyah reached for both shoulders and drew him close in a big hug. She whispered in his ear, "Only you can undo what has been done," before letting him go. She kissed his temple lightly, and the pain and throbbing of his wound dropped away immediately. Jason blinked.

He had scarcely a moment to wonder when the door in the crystal opened and he fell through, and they landed at Lake Wannameecha Gathering Hall.

31

Wild Magick

JASON managed to stay on his feet. Sandwiched between Gavan who smelled faintly of chocolate and vanilla, and Eleanora who smelled of roses, the three of them alit in the courtyard of Ravenwyng. The faint coppery smell of blood still clung to him, though the wound seemed to have closed. It was his hand that hurt now. Fretting, Jason rubbed the back of his left hand.

Tomaz stood, his arm outstretched, sending a raven into flight from his fist. He turned and looked, his arm still in the air, the raven an ebony blur. Jefferson was there, watching, his muscular arms crossed over his chest. And FireAnn and Sousa came running from the mess hall across the way, her face pale with alarm and fiery red hair wild about her face. His cornet rattled from its chain on his belt.

The storm began to pelt rain, hard and heavy, on all of them. The raven circled once overhead and disappeared into the swirling clouds, with a loud cry.

"It has started," Tomaz said heavily to Gavan.

"So I can see. We've a day or two, no more. The rain has begun moving in, and it will only worsen." Gavan appeared to make a decision. "Tomaz, you and Jefferson, come with me. We've been outrunning wolfjackals at Iron Gate."

Tomaz's face reflected his surprise. "You've found it? Good. We need the hope."

"Not unless we can get the Gate open. Eleanora . . ." Gavan took her by the elbow, steadying her. Winds buffeted at her and she bounced slightly in the air away from them, unsteadily, like a ship that had lost its rudder in a heavy sea. "Send the children home."

"All right. What will we tell the parents?"

"Tell them . . . tell them . . ." Gavan looked around the grounds. Evergreens had begun to creak and bend, their branches brushing the ground. The lake itself rippled in high, icy waves as the light wires overhead danced furiously in the wind. "Tell them the camp is old and the electric system went out in the rainstorm. It will take several weeks to make repairs and update the camp, and by then summer will be over."

She said softly, "If this storm hits us as hard as I think it's going to, we'll lose Ravenwyng."

"Then it won't be a lie, will it?"

"No. It won't." She leaned on FireAnn. "Let's make the camp announcement. I'll have to talk to them, make sure that . . . that they understand." The two women helped each other cross the courtyard, the screaming wind pulling and tearing at them. Eleanora gave up her levitation, dropping to the ground as if it could anchor her.

Gavan dropped his hand on Jason's shoulder. "Thank you, lad, for all you've done." He leaned over, looking into Jason's face. "You're a Magicker, lad. Never let that go. No matter what happens here, I'll be back for you someday. Understand that?"

"You will?"

"It's a promise," Rainwater said. "You are one of us. If not me, then Tomaz, or Eleanora, or whoever can come, will come."

Jason felt a tightness in his chest. He nodded.

Gavan straightened. He shook his wolfhead cane at Sousa and Hightower. "Drive them out, as soon as everyone is ready. Take their crystals, mark them . . . make sure they've had the Draft."

"Gavan!" It was one thing to leave, another to have to drink the Draft.

He dropped his hand on Jason's shoulder again. "It's all we can do, lad, for now. The promise is not broken, only dimmed. Have faith in me, for now!" He turned on his heel, beckoning to Tomaz and Jefferson and in a blink, was gone.

He looked at Sousa. The Magicker looked back with gentle dark eyes. "It wasn't meant," he said, "to end this way."

Jason nodded. That barely helped. To have come so far and lose it all hurt.

Sousa added, "Better go pack." Before he stopped speaking, Eleanora made the same announcement over the loudspeakers. Jason headed to his cabin. The cabin across from Starwind stood, its shutters closed, and the screen door battened shut. He stared at it a moment, thinking of both Henry and Jonnard, before going inside. He did pack. He set aside his backpack, leaving some critical things until last. Trent came in.

They looked at one another. Trent went silently to his side and began to pack, thunking his things into his bag as though punching his fist into a mitt.

Finally, Jason said, "I have a plan."

Trent looked up. "You think you can fix this?"

"I don't know. What I do know is that I don't want to drink that stuff and go home. I don't want to lose this summer. I don't want to lose my friends. I don't want to lose anything that's happened."

"They're not just taking us home . . . they're taking everything away?" Trent's expression changed. "What are you going to do?"

"Stay and fight. Or shield. But I intend to stay."

Trent considered him for a long moment. Then he went to the small closet in the cabin that held their few cleaning supplies. He brought out the broom and his knife, and sat down.

"What are you doing?"

"You'll see." The bright red Swiss army knife flew as if it had wings. In moments, Trent had whittled off the broom head and instead had a wicked, wooden point on it. Then he reached into his duffel and brought out his painted silk banner. He fastened it to the other end of the broomstick. The white silk background brought out the vivid black raven, its wings outspread, and the gold paint used for the lightning bolt it carried glittered with flecks of mica. "This is a lance. And I'm ready."

"That's awesome."

Trent rested it on its point, and leaned back to look at it. "It is, isn't it?" His face stretched in a grin. "I don't intend to go easy."

They marched out of the cabin, down to the Hall, where Bailey and Ting had already climbed into a bus, and looked out at them with worried faces. Bailey hung out the window.

"Jason, you're hurt!"

He touched his scalp with gentle fingers and winced. "Yeah."

"Aren't you coming?" Ting watched both of them.

He shook his head. "Come out, I want to talk to you." They climbed past the hustle and bustle of campers loading their things on the bus.

Bailey held her packrat in her hand. As she stepped down, she smoothed her thumb over the little creature's silky head. "I don't know whether to keep her or leave her. I think if I left her ... she might ... well ... something awful might ..."

Trent stroked his hand down Lacey's back. Her tufted tail twitched in happiness. "She's not a wild animal anymore, Bailey. You might as well take her. Like a ... a hamster or something."

She smiled at Trent. "That's what I was thinking!"

"I only hope her mother does not mind," Ting said. "I don't want her at my house." She eyed the pack rat a little suspiciously.

"Can you believe it?" Bailey added excitedly. "We live across the bay from each other. It's not such a horribly long drive. We can visit."

"If you remember," said Jason quietly.

"Why would we forget?"

He just watched her face.

The two girls looked at him. "Oh, no." Bailey frowned. "They wouldn't do that to us. We've got our crystals."

"They're taking them back."

Ting gasped at Jason.

"Not because they want to. But they're not prepared to send us home this way, and it'll save a lot of questions."

Ting flung her arms about Bailey's neck, almost catapulting Lacey into the air. "I don't want to forget!"

"Forget, or stay and stand."

"We can't do that!"

Trent nodded at her. "Oh, yes, we can." He leaned on his lance. "Jason has a plan."

Biting her lip, Ting said, "They'll secure all the cottages and cabins."

"We meet," Jason said firmly, "at Dead Man's Cabin. Immediately. Get your bag and leave."

The two girls nodded as they scrambled back onto the bus. Jason and Trent watched for a moment. They turned around and ran into Rich and Stefan, who'd obviously heard every word they'd exchanged.

Stefan rubbed at his stub nose. "That junk you said true? No crystal and the drink and stuff."

"Yup."

He moved his stocky body from side to side. "What happens to me then?"

"I don't know."

"I," said Rich edgily, "am probably allergic to that berry junk in the Draft."

"I can't go back like this," Stefan said. "I'll keep changing, probably. They'll put me in a circus or something. They haven't shown me enough to control it." He'd gone pale.

Jason hefted his backpack over his shoulder. "Then you heard the rest . . . Dead Man's Cabin. And I'll show you what we can do. They need us, but they don't want to ask us." Jason saw Sousa approaching, backed up, and ducked around the back of the bus, Trent at his heels.

Lightning split the sky. In an eerie flash of green and silver, Gavan and Tomaz and Jefferson came down from the sky with a boom of thunder, their hair standing on end, crystals flashing in their hands. For a moment the three stood in a blaze of shimmering color, then everything stilled.

Gavan said to the others, "The Dark Hand is closing. If I had any doubt, Tomaz, that they unleashed this, I've no doubt now."

Tomaz nodded slowly.

"Retreat?"

"We can't until everyone is safely out. We'll make a stand here, and we will let them know that this battle has just begun. Iron Gate is reflecting the mana back, and they'll feed on it if we let them. I don't intend to let them." The trio went around the corner, and Jason and Trent skittered off, out of sight.

Halfway to Dead Man's Cabin, they ran into Danno trudging up the path, his haversack on his back. He looked at them. "Where are you two going?" The wind nearly tore the words away before he could be heard.

"We're not leaving." Trent waved his lance and banner defiantly.

"Man, don't be stupid. We've gotta go. This is like a hurricane coming down on us." He stared from one to the other. "You're serious?"

"I can show you how to make the crystal shield, you and two or three others. If even a handful of us stay to help like that . . . we can shield the other Magickers while they strike. There's going to be a fight, Danno. Mano a mano, I think. We can help even if we're not trained. If we go, to protect us, they're going to take our crystals and make us drink."

"Like Henry."

"That's right."

Danno shook his head vigorously. "No way am I going out like that! I'd rather be dragged out. Poor Squibb didn't know me. Didn't know anyone but Jon." He shuddered. He fell in behind them. They made their way through the groves and underbrush to the cabin. Already abandoned, its door had not been lashed shut against the storm. They ducked inside.

"Go look for the girls," Jason told Danno. As the other went out, he took Trent by the elbow. "Okay. Now, once we get everyone set up as shields, then you and I are going to find the Gate. We're going to get it open."

"You can do that?"

"I don't know. I know I have to try."

Trent licked dry lips. "Okay. You're sure?"

"If I can get that Gate open, the storm should drain off through it. The Borderlands live off mana washes. Right now the Iron Gate is like a wall . . . the mana is coming in to pound on us and it'll just bounce off that wall and pound us some more."

"Sounds dangerous."

"Chicken?"

"Nah, but frankly, I think your plan needs some work."

"Think about it, then."

Trent nodded. "I intend to!"

Danno came in with the girls and Rich and Stefan. They dropped their bags in the corner.

"There's seven of us. I think we can make a difference, and this is how." He pulled out his crystal and lit it, then formed the shield which he had accidentally formed against Jonnard's attack. He strengthened it, extending it as he concentrated, until he had both girls behind it.

"Hit 'em, Stefan."

"Me?" The stocky boy's face reddened. "C'mon."

"Just do it."

He rocked from side to side. "Lissen. I play pranks now and then, but I never clocked a girl in the face."

Rich said calmly, "This is just for demonstration purposes. It's okay, big guy."

Stefan rubbed his nose vigorously. "Well. Okay." He lumbered over and swung halfheartedly at Bailey. He wouldn't have hit her anyway, her reflexes were too good for that, but before she could even dodge away, he bounced back with a yelp, thudding to his tailbone on the cabin floor.

He grunted. "Ow." He rubbed his face again.

Rich nodded to Jason. "That'll work. Show me?" He tugged on Stefan's ear. "Get up, you aren't hurt!"

"Just my dignity." Stefan grunted again as he shuffled to his feet.

Danno grinned. He danced on the balls of his feet. "Try again? On me?"

Jason put his shield down and said, "Everyone get their crystals out and let's do this." Trent moved to Ting, helping her Focus.

Stefan scrubbed at an itchy ear. He rolled his eyes. "Buses are all gone."

"Can't hear 'em?"

"Nope. Last one pulled out about ten minutes ago. Haven't heard one since."

The rain beat down. "We have a day, maybe two."

Rich gave Stefan an uneasy look. "I don't know if we can keep him quiet that long . . . especially if he gets hungry. . . ."

"We have to try. I want to show you all what we're doing and then, we can practice."

After what seemed hours, Ting and Stefan could manage a shield over themselves and two other people. Danno wavered, sometimes himself and two, sometimes himself and three. Bailey could shield herself and four, and Rich a surprising six people in total. Trent had been with Jason, moving back and forth, testing the crystals once they got everyone Focused.

They went to sleep, after pooling their resources and making sure Stefan ate well. Lacey even stayed quiet through the night, as if tired by all the Magick being wielded around her. They woke to a gray, misty morning, with rain glistening blackly on the ground.

Trent and Danno made a run to the mess hall and brought back leftovers from a refrigerator.

"Where is everyone?"

Trent shook his head. "In the Gathering Hall, I guess. Making a fortress out of it. Warding it, maybe?" He held out a bulging bag. "This ought to hold us for a day."

Stefan reached out and hugged the bag to himself, grunting.

"Or not." Trent looked at him thoughtfully.

They all did eat, although Stefan grudgingly passed out helpings of this and that from his grocery sack.

They practiced all day, in shifts, until Jason knew that they would be a help to the Magickers and not a burden. It was Trent, though, who said, "We have to hit the computer room."

"Why? That could get us busted."

"They called all the relatives, Jason, told them we were being sent home. We have to let them know something."

Ting made a small sound. Bailey hugged her. "A quick call each," she pleaded.

Finally, he nodded.

Perhaps it was the tone in their voices. Perhaps it was the hidden knowledge that loving parents and children share. Not one parent said no, although several said, "Do you want us there?" without even knowing what the problem was.

Bailey's mom, sounding ever so much like Bailey, choked a

little when she said, "Good-bye, hon . . . and be careful." It was heard throughout the room despite the tight hold Bailey had on the receiver. She took a deep breath as she hung up. "Jason. How are we going to get home if everything goes wrong?"

He hesitated a moment then said, "I'll show you."

And back at Dead Man's Cabin, he showed them how to open a door in their crystals and walk through. None of them dared to try it, knowing that the working of such Magick would alert Gavan and the others. Trent clutched his crystal tightly. Stefan told them when all the buses returned. They ate whatever was left for dinner and fell into fitful sleep, dreaming of tombs and howling storms.

If that first morning was eerie, the second morning was worse. The sun struggled to pierce the storm clouds that turned day into night. The strings of lights thrashed back and forth, and those on the outbuildings glared dimly, as the wind tugged and roared about them.

They were down to juice drinks and polished them off quickly. Stefan licked his mouth and drank the one remaining carton. No one begrudged him seconds. Ting looked at him in sympathy. "Not only is he a growing boy, but he's got to eat for a growing bear, too."

Stefan sighed sadly and nodded.

Jason gazed up from the cabin doorway. "It's dark and quiet. I'd say the attack is about to begin. Let's go set ourselves up." Before he could say anything else, a tremendous ker-ack and BOOM split the skies. The lights went out all over the camp.

Tomaz sensed them first or perhaps he caught wind of Stefan. He turned on the heel of his cowboy boot and then frowned heavily as he caught sight of the group.

"We had just come to the conclusion that a few of you had slipped away. We all mistakenly thought you were on another bus."

"We came to stay."

Gavan shook his head. "We cannot let you do this."

"We are all Magickers." Jason nodded to Stefan who already had his crystal curled in his big hand.

Without a word, Stefan slipped in behind him, and set his shield up over himself, Tomaz, and Hightower. Both Magickers raised eyebrows in surprise.

Each of them did the same, except for Jason and Trent. Trent shadowed Jason as he raised his shield over Gavan and Eleanora. The two of them would likely take the brunt of the attack, so they had agreed to swap shielding. When one tired, the other would take over.

Gavan considered Jason, his lips pursed in thought. "This is something you want to do?"

"This is something we have to do."

The Magicker nodded. The dark skies reflected in his eyes, making the blue irises almost black. "I cannot tell you if we'll see the Dark Hand themselves or not. They may stay behind the storm and the wolfjackals. But whether we see them or not, they'll throw everything they can at us, to break us here, and drain the mana. So if you see the line breaking, lad, take the others and flee. Promise me that?"

"Bailey has those orders," Jason said calmly. "I've shown them how to walk through their crystals."

"And you can do it?"

He nodded solemnly.

"All right." Gavan turned about, settling himself. He put his face into the wind, as the first drops of rain began to fall. "Here it comes."

If he lived to be a hundred, he would never be able to tell the wonder and horror of the storm that came sweeping down to attack them. Cloud creatures of twisted form and might rose to pound at them, swirling around into motes of sizzling energy. Rain that poured for hours and lightning that crashed around them till the very earth crackled with its discharge. Wolfjackals that came and went in howling packs, circling and attacking only to be driven away gnashing their ivory fangs.

He thought he saw forms striding through the clouds now and then. Once, he glimpsed the pale angry face of Jonnard staring at him, but of that he could not be sure. He was too busy to be frightened.

And no matter what they faced, they turned the enemy back. Again and again, until Eleanora sat in weariness, one hand bracing her wrist to hold her crystal up. Until Stefan lost his shield entirely and sat snuffling and bawling, bearlike, at failing them. Rich took over, shielding all of that group, his face dead white under his coppery head of hair. All he said was, "You done good, bro."

And they fought like that with no end in sight.

Until, hours later, when Gavan looked into the sky grimly through weary eyes and said, "Now comes the worst of it."

"It's now or never," Jason said to Trent, and signaled with a jerk of his chin. Rain fell and evaporated in sizzling drops as it spattered across the lines of Magick and wild mana and energy. The air shivered electric blue and stank of ozone and spent spells. Lake Wannameecha moved in obsidian black waves, reflecting the storm boiling over it.

They fell back from the battle line and ducked into the Gathering Hall. Jason shrugged out of his backpack and dumped its contents out quickly. Firecrackers, duct tape, and other odds and ends slid onto the varnished floor.

Trent said dryly, "Everything but garlic." He leaned over, then poked a finger at curling white cloves lying amidst the other junk. A pungent aroma drifted up. "Never mind, I stand corrected."

"You never know," Jason said. He tucked some unpeeled cloves into his pocket, and the Chinese firecrackers into his shirt. Matches went in the other pocket. The box of kitchen matches had come from FireAnn's apron and, before that, apparently an English pub. He stood up.

"What's the plan again?"

"We crystal to the Gate. The wolfjackals, some of them, will be on us almost instantly. I'm fairly sure they'll sense us right away. You'll have to hold them off while I get the Gate open." He didn't mention what he thought he would have to do to open that Gate, what Aunt Freyah had hinted to him. They had tried nearly every other way, and nothing had worked. But the Gate had to be opened. Left shut, it was damming up the mana and the storm, and the camp lay helpless in a hurricane of uncontrollable, raging Magick. Open, the mana would sweep through, into a world that not only could absorb it, but most likely needed it. Once past, the Gate's boundaries could be extended to embrace the camp. Jason had been over and over and over it in his mind. He couldn't see any other way. He left his backpack on the floor. He wanted to travel light in case he had to sprint. He touched his crystal in his pocket for the third time, just to make sure he had it. "Ready?"

Trent took a deep breath. He shook his head. "No."

"What did we forget?"

"I'm not going," Trent said.

"What—" Jason stopped in his tracks. "I can't do this without you!"

"You're going to have to."

He could not believe his ears. "You're with me. You helped me plan this. You *know* what I have to do. Look, I'm scared, too, but we've got to try this."

Trent shifted his lance in his hands. "It's not that. I'm not a Magicker. I have no Talent. I can't help you."

Jason stared, thinking he hadn't heard right, but his friend's face was serious. "You . . ."

"I'm a poser. I've been faking it. And, lately, I've been wondering when it was going to catch up with me. Well, it just did. Maybe that's why the other failures got sent home, because when you need to count on somebody, when you need them the most, you've got to know what they're made of." Trent looked up. "I'm not made of Magick, Jason. I wish to God I was, but I'm not. You know I'm telling the truth. I kept backing out on you, because I didn't want anyone to know. I didn't want anyone to catch me."

"I . . . I don't believe that."

"Have you ever seen me light my crystal?"

"Well . . . no."

"Because I can't." Trent inhaled deeply. "Ever seen me move anything through thin air? Did you see me put a shield up? No, you haven't, because I can't. You were busy with the others. I was, too. No one ever noticed I never did it myself. Henry Squibb had more Magick in his little finger than I've got in my whole body. I've been ducking out on stuff for weeks, wondering when someone was going to notice, especially you. You, with all your Talent." He smiled sadly.

Despair sank into Jason. "Come anyway. You can . . . you can use the lance. You don't have to have Magick to fight the wolfjackals."

"You don't need to be worried about protecting me. You

need to be doing what you have to do. And let me do what I
can."

"Which is . . . what?"

"I can get the backup generator hooked up, pump some
electricity into this place. I am pretty sure, with the computers
up, I can put on a sound and light show that will knock 'em
off their feet. Remember, I've been in the computer lab for
weeks. Gavan is pretty savvy, but even so . . . this is my magic. I
can use it. They depend on other means. I may even have a few
moves in me that would halt a Magicker in his tracks."

They looked into each other's faces.

Jason hardly knew what to say. "Sure?"

Trent nodded solemnly. "Pretty sure."

"I can't do this alone."

"Sure you can. All you need to do is swing that Gate
open. We're doing the tough stuff here. Give me those
firecrackers."

Jason took the long string of small crackers out of his shirt.
He could smell their sulfur and gunpowder as he handed them
over.

"No sense lighting these all at once. Three or four at a pop,"
Trent said, as he took them. "That should give the wolfjackals
something to think about, while I get to the generators." He
gave a shaky smile as he opened his prized knife and began to
cut the firecracker string up and shove the small strands inside
his shirt, the lance curled inside his elbow.

"Trent—"

His friend frowned. "What are you waiting for? It's now
or never!" He laid the lance on the table and fished around
till he grabbed the roll of duct tape. He took his Swiss army
knife and fastened it to the end of his lance, wrapping duct
tape about it tightly, then handed the lance to Jason, silk flag
rippling with the abrupt movement. The raven painted on it
seemed to snap at the air.

"What's this for?"

"That's a sharp knife. That's a long pole." Trent shrugged.
"It's the only thing I can give you to defend yourself, okay?
You do it quickly, and you get out. That's your only chance.
You hesitate, Jason, and they'll pull you down." He took Jason

by the shoulders. "Go! We can't make a stand out there much longer. I'm no Magicker, but I know everyone is dog tired."

He ducked his head and ran back into the storm, leaving Jason quite alone in the huge Hall. With a sigh, he reached for his crystal again and pictured Iron Gate.

32

Endgame

HE fell to his knees in front of the rusting gate. Jason held his hand up, setting crystal lantern light to play over its surface, and he saw the true Gate embedded around it, iron and implacable. He stood and ran his hands over it, one at a time, shifting Trent's lance back and forth. With every touch, the true Gate emerged until it was the only vision filling his sight and senses. It towered over him, and he could see the granite it had been set into. The evergreens that crowded about it were not the evergreens that grew at Camp Ravenwyng.

He pulled at it. He found the great locks that bound it shut, but they had no keyhole, and thus needed no key. He shined his crystal light onto the locks and chanted for it to open, but nothing happened.

He could feel the mana storm rolling toward him like a great tidal wave. The barricade of the lower campgrounds would not contain it much longer. Like an inexorable force, it would roll through, smashing him into the Gate's bars and battering him to pulp if he stayed. And then it would recoil with even greater force back onto the camp. Below, near the lake, he could see the lightning stabs of the fierce battle continuing. Suddenly, white light flared up. Like a beacon, it speared the mana clouds, and he saw the darkness recede abruptly, boiling around in turmoil. The light flashed off. Then on. Trent was at work. There would be sound, too, but he could not hear it.

His left hand prickled as he ran it over the lock again. His scar gave an icy, stabbing throb. They had come, sensing him. He knew it before their lupine howls cut through the sounds of the storm and Magick battle. Jason turned slowly, knowing that he had drawn them.

Five wolfjackals raced across the broken country, whipping their furred bodies through underbrush and pine branches, heedless of pain and obstruction. Jaws agape, tails like stiff banners, bodies of black and silver and dun and charcoal. Their eyes glowed reflected green and red in the night as they howled and bore down on him.

He froze.

If he'd had Trent with him, he'd have some hope.

Or anyone.

But he stood alone at the locked Gate without a clue what to do. He held his crystal with both hands, one fighting the other to throw it, to hold it. His left hand would betray his right, if it could. His hands shook. Jason clenched his jaw. He set his back to the bars.

The wolfjackals came to a halt one long jump from him, milling around, their jaws drooling, their glowing eyes slitted. They snapped and mauled at one another almost playfully, ears pricked in eagerness. They panted and eyed their leader.

The pack leader stepped forward. "It is time," it said, shuddering even as the words were forced from its throat. Its voice was hoarse and torn. What pain the language must have cost it! "I make my claim." It gave an immense convulsion on that last word, then shook itself vigorously. Hot spit flew from its jaws.

The pack behind it howled in triumph. Their eerie voices echoed off the mountains and perhaps, even the gate. They circled and paced, back and forth, forth and back. Fangs and talonlike nails flashed. He had nowhere to run.

Below, white light flared again, and he could hear a trumpet blast of sound, Sousa, amplified vastly, like Jericho from long ago, with Trent's help. Was it working? Would they stand at the camp while he fell here? Not if he could help it. He lifted the lance.

"Come get me, then."

The pack leader snarled and tensed. Muscles rippled through his furred haunches. Jason took a deep breath. He might be able to Focus and get out, but not in time.

Magicker.

Jason could hear the soft sighing, creaking word. It came from the back of his head, but he could not sense anyone there. And, if anyone was behind him, he was in more trouble than he knew, his back unprotected!

A lesser wolfjackal from the back lunged at him, hurling past the pack leader, snapping. It yelped in dismay as Jason parried with his lance, and the Swiss knife cut surprisingly deep. The beast swerved away, jowl gashed open and flapping as it tossed its head from the stinging pain. Pink foam flew from its jaws. It pawed at its face, yelping, and rubbed its wounds against the ground.

He bumped up against the Gate, recovering his balance. He gripped the lance tightly.

Magicker.

Again, that breathless, low groaning voice.

Something was calling . . . him.

Jason chanced it. He half turned and glanced, looking, despite the danger. That flinch drew the pack leader in a massive leap. Its body struck hard, hot breath in his face, and bore him down. The lance went skidding away. Jason buried his hands in the creature's ruff, holding its head back, fighting to keep the jaws from his face. It was heavier. He could not throw it off. It snapped and thrashed, coming closer and closer. In moments the others would be tearing at his feet and legs.

The mana storm hit with a boom directly overhead, and hail peppered down. He could feel the Magick turn upside down and inside out. His senses whirled.

The wolfjackal thrashed in his hold, shaking his crystal loose. It dropped and rolled. Jason gritted his teeth. He tore the fetish bag from his throat, Tomaz's charm, and shoved his fist down into the beast's mouth, as he had once before. His scar ripped open anew as it caught on the gleaming canines. He screamed with the pain, clawing at the inside of the wolfjackal's throat.

The beast spit him aside and rolled back on its haunches,

howling in its own pain, pawing at its jaws. It choked and howled and pawed madly at its muzzle. Jason scrambled to his feet, gathering the crystal, blood flowing everywhere. He got the lance, leaning heavily on it, dizzy from wrenching pain. The wolfjackal choked and spit again in an attempt to expel the fetish, then gathered itself, drooling in foamy spittles of blood. The mana storm hammered at him. Wind and rain nearly flattened him. It took the breath from his lungs. His skin stung like fire from pelting hail.

He leaned against the Iron Gate, weary and hurting. He could not stand against it. It would bring him down and leave him at the mercy of the howling beasts in front of him. He faltered and put his hand back to the Gate, trying to stay on his feet, as the wolfjackals growled and tensed to rush him.

His hand shook. Blood poured out of the gash, splashing across the metal, his crystal, the ground. As he staggered back, the Gate swung open a crack. It groaned as it did so, the metal thrilling with sound.

His body went cold. He looked into a tomb carved out of cold, gray stone. He knew this place from his worst dreams. Jason wanted to slam the Gate shut, but his body was wedged in the opening.

It was worse—and bigger—than his dreams. He could feel the icy cold of the stone. He could see the body lying on the coffin clearly. It was not dead, only nearly so, rather like a vampire at his rest. Jason slipped a hand inside his shirt, feeling the garlic cloves. He could not look away from the tall, elegant man who lay there. Fine purple veins ran just under the marblelike skin, and dark chestnut hair curled about his head. He wore clothing from long ago, but nothing seemed diminished by time.

Jason tore his gaze away. At the far end of the tomb lay another Iron Gate, also closed. He knew what he had to do.

He had to walk past the tomb between the narrow stone walls, and open the other Gate. It would be barely wide enough for him. He might even have to brush the raised coffin with its human adornment to do it.

He could not breathe. The iciness of the cave sank into his own bones, and he shook.

"I opened one Gate! Isn't it enough?"

Silence answered him. Jason gripped his crystal tightly. He Focused on it, and a golden lantern light filtered from between his fingers. It shone across the tomb floor, and pooled at the base of the faraway Gate.

He took a step forward, feeling the storm raging at his back, the dim howl of wolfjackals now in his ears, pushing the first Gate open so that he could get through entirely. It gave reluctantly, with a rusting squeal that shot and echoed through the stone chambers of the tomb.

Jason licked lips gone dry as sandpaper. His heartbeat sounded louder than his footsteps as he neared the coffin. He felt as though he were caught between two worlds, the muffled battle of one he could hear, and the other not, though his body anticipated . . . something.

Another step. He held his lance tightly, and his crystal even tighter. It kept a lot of lantern light hidden, but he could not chance dropping it again. Something snarled and tore at the back cuff of his jeans. He shook it loose.

Another step, and he stood at the foot end of the coffin. He turned sideways to sidle past. The back of his shoulders scrapped the gritty wall, and he held his breath.

Now he was nearing the head of the coffin . . . and its occupant. One last squeeze and he could bolt through to the second Iron Gate. Jason's lungs ached.

The . . . figure turned its head. One marble-white hand rose in the air, reaching for him. "Come to me," it said, in a thin voice that pierced the rising noise of the mana storm leaking in behind Jason.

"You are marked for me. Let me teach you the truth of Magick."

He wanted the truth. He always wanted the truth. But what was it? Once he thought this entombed figure was his father. Now he knew better, but what he saw and listened to was still not true. The only truth he could think of, here and now, was that he would die if he could not breathe, and he could not breathe in this tomb. His friends would die if he could not get the inner Gate opened. Beyond that, nothing he knew was true anymore.

The eyelids slowly began to open. Jason knew one more thing, and that was that he did not want to see what was in those eyes. He threw himself sideways, away from the hand, the face, the coffin, and fell onto the floor. He crawled to the Gate and put his still bleeding hand upon it. With a great roar in his ears, the second Iron Gate swung inward, and all . . . everything . . . disappeared. Jason looked down into a valley of lively green, and he lay stomach down on a road leading to it.

Suddenly— Silence. The storm gathered up and rushed past him, pushing him across the threshold, as it poured into the open valley. The wolfjackals were carried past, borne by a great tide of mana which they could not resist, and he alone was left to stand, anchored by the Gate he held onto.

He looked at his hand. The bleeding slowed, then clotted. He touched his head, wincing slightly at the tenderness. What one blooding had done, another had undone. He shuddered at the idea.

His crystal grew warm.

Faintly, he could hear . . . shouts of triumph and joy from the world beyond. The old world. His world. The sun rose somewhere, for the sky went to a thin gray-purple, and light flooded him.

Jason turned slowly to see the world he had opened the Gates to.

He stared across the vista. He stood in a pass between two rolling hills of verdant green, grasses lush from rain and sun. He didn't think civilization had ever reached into this place. A rough lane ran down the hills and into a valley, and a great, dark gray mountain towered above the scene. A waterfall pierced its side, waters tumbling down in a crystalline spray from impossible heights and foaming into a pool of darkest blue. Along the foot of the mountain, a sharp-featured rock of dark red and orange curled about half the pool, sprawling upon the landscape.

If he ran downhill, he might be at that pool in just minutes, he thought, touching that rock that looked as though molten fire itself might have poured from the iron mountain and then cooled just enough to stop at the water's edge. He paused, lance in hand, a faint breeze rippling Trent's pennant. He had no idea what lay at his back, other than his real world. He didn't want to look back to find out. He'd been there. What tugged at him now lay ahead of him, unfolding. He took a step forward.

Even as he did, he felt the real world at his back move, almost as if he wore it like a vast pair of wings or a cloak. Unseen, it billowed around him. The wind picked up, snapping the pennant flag on his lance as he leaned against it, steadying himself. And down below, a ripple ran through the dark orange-red rock. As he fastened his whole attention upon it, it moved.

An immense wedge-shaped head lifted to stare at him, and he saw then, as it stirred, its serpentine body as it pushed a paw forward and flexed long talons. The sharpness of the rock had been spines and fins that moved now, as it shook itself awake. The dragon opened eyes of orange-and-amber fire to watch him. He was too far away to see the details of its scaly form, but not too far to see the ebony sharpness of the claws it stretched out and raked into the ground. The dragon yawned, showing catlike sharp white teeth. After a very long moment, the wind carried the scent of sulfur breath to him. He wondered if he could feel the heat of its immense body if he got closer. If the eyes were cat-shaped. If it could or would speak ...

He took another slow step toward the dragon form. He gripped the lance in his hands, though it would be a poor weapon against such a beast. Jason paused.

The wingspan at his back yanked sharply at him, dragging him onto his heels. From far away, scarcely more than a whisper, he could hear Gavan Rainwater's voice.

"Not now, Jason. Do not take that journey now. Next time. ..."

Jason inhaled. He swung about sharply and just before plunging through the great Iron Gate posts, he stabbed Trent's lance into the ground. And it was marked, not only for him, but for anyone who looked for it now. The pennant snapped about as he did so.

Even Trent, who could not see the Magick, would be able to find this Gate one day. He was the Gatekeeper and had made it so, until he came back to change it.

And he would return.

Stepping past the flag, he strode across the threshold and back into his own world.

THE CURSE OF ARKADY

Dedicated to wishers and dreamers everywhere,
and especially my children,
James, Jessica, Aaron, and Maureen.

Contents

1

ALARMS

HE'D been there before. But this time, in his dreamwalk, he'd already been through the shifting sands on the beach below, and through the cemetery that wrapped about the castle ruins like a moat guarding it. He'd already tripped the dragonhead lock that held the gates shut and would spout flame if opened improperly. He had already gone into the ruins and fallen downstairs into the catacombs beneath.

He'd done all that, time and again. This once, Jason seemed to be starting where he'd always finished before. Maybe it was because now he knew how important a dreamwalk could be, as it had been explained by Tomaz Crowfeather. Maybe it was because he was different now. Trouble was, it made the dream more dangerous, not easier to escape.

A cool wind from nowhere sent chills along the back of his neck. He looked down. The cuffs of his jeans and his sneakers dripped with sea water from his trip across the beach. His toes felt like icicles and he squooshed when he took a step, but he had to keep moving down here. Silvery moonlight rayed through the broken castle roof and fell in spidery lines across the tunnel. It left behind shadows sharper than the night itself. Jason took a deep breath and strode forth. Although unsure exactly where he was going, he knew his journey led past the catacombs and he had to get there, had to get *through*.

Behind him, the wind picked up, keening, its voice beginning to howl. Jason paused, listening intently, his head tilted. No! Those *were* howls. Echoing eerily along the walls of the tunnels, faint but getting closer. Wolfjackals, racing down the stone pathways, after him! He couldn't be caught, not now, not here.

He threw caution to the wind. He put his lean body into a run, through the turning tunnels, no need to remember the way if he had to go back, because going back would lead him right into the eager jaws of the pursuers. Jason knotted his fists, pumping his arms to drive his body forward. His left hand ached as though he'd caught it on something, but it was an old injury, one he knew well. The catacomb turned sharply to the right and he with it, and then it suddenly opened into a large cavern room, dark with shadows.

He plowed to a halt, seeing no passage out of the cavern. He knew this room, too! His heart pounded heavily in his chest at the sight of the carved tomb, with the still figure resting atop it. Anyplace but here! Jason looked around wildly, but the scant moonlight filtering down from above gave little illumination. The shadows seemed to leap at him, and he swerved away instinctively, bumping into the sarcophagus itself, rapping his leg sharply and throwing his weight over it. He scrambled back, but his shirt caught on the sharp edges of the tomb, capturing him. No matter how hard he pulled, the fabric only stretched and refused to come loose.

Jason braced himself and yanked. The howling wolfjackals sounded closer, far too close. The sarcophagus refused to yield. He had two choices: remove his shirt or stay and face the wolfjackals.

The cold figure on the tomb moved. An icy hand reached out and grabbed his wrist, gripping him tightly with fingers that felt like marble.

Make that three choices!

Netted between shirt and hand, Jason froze, his heart drumming loudly in his chest. He twisted his wrist till his skin burned but the tombstone hand stayed fast around him. It pulled him down, nearer and nearer to the finely carved face with its curled dark hair. It wanted him. He could feel it . . . inhaling him. Drawing him in. He would sink into that figure until he was part of it!

In sheer panic, Jason fought, thrashing, his wrist growing bloodied and his shirt finally ripping free, though it did him no good. He remained captured, as if a steel trap held him, and he was as eager to be free as any wild animal. He fought till he couldn't struggle anymore, exhausted, shivering—and he realized the wolfjackals had stopped howling. He turned on one heel, and saw them, eager feral faces with eyes glowing green in the darkness, blocking the tunnel out.

The hand pulled him close. He bucked and battled against it, feeling the warmth being sucked right out of him by the icy fingers, his sneakers slipping and sliding against the gritty flooring. He could feel the heat in his body rushing out of him. In moments he would be as cold as the figure that gripped him!

"No!" Jason's voice echoed sharply back at him, and the wolfjackals bunched up, growling and snapping at the sound. Their eyes let out green sparks as they watched him. He braced his feet against the base of the tomb and pulled with all his might. No use!

Dream world or not, he was falling! Jason felt his body go limp and icy, unable to stand and slumping over the sarcophagus. The hand about his wrist tightened even more till he wanted to cry out in pain, the crescent scar livid and pulsing. Spread-eagled over the tomb, he knew he would never leave unless he did something desperate, and NOW. He dug his free hand into his pocket to grip his crystal tightly, focusing his thoughts into the red alarm beacon that was one of the last lessons he'd gotten from Gavan Rainwater, Magicker extraordinaire.

He could feel the very last shard of his warmth spearheading into that thought as he collapsed. In his mind's eye, he could see himself like an arrow shooting away. . . .

Gavan Rainwater's office at Ravenwyng was just as he remembered it. Cluttered, with a massive desk of scarred wood, and a huge, somewhat battered high back chair behind it. It was empty of all but a clutter of old books and papers spilling out of a corner bookcase, cascading down a dented metal file cabinet, and covering (more or less) the top of the desk. Odd lumps of quartz and semiprecious rocks, some polished and shaped and others not, were lying about haphazardly wherever they seemed to have been tossed. One massive golden topaz stood like a proud lantern, its rays catching the beams of an unseeable moon or sun and spreading the light throughout the musty office.

His shout for help came blood-red through the topaz, a single crimson ray of alarm. It pierced the quiet disorder of the office, but there was no one there to take notice of it. Jason himself saw it blearily as his eyelids began to close. A dark shadow fell across his vision, clouding the golden topaz.

Blacker than the shadows of the office, a raven hopped upon the desk. With a ker-aaack! it investigated the topaz, clacking its beak against the massive gemstone. It eyed the red beam and then, with another clack-clack of its sharp beak, spread its wings and launched into a low, lazy flight from Rainwater's office. He sensed its glide through the corridors of the empty Gathering Hall and then into the night, sailing over the lake waters, silhouetted by the low hanging moon. Was it going for help? Was there anyone at all who could help him now?

He had no more time to wonder!

The wolfjackals trotted into the cavern chamber now and raced once around the stone-and-marble tomb, then surrounded it, growling, crouched low on their paws. He could smell their heated breath and drool, like putrid steam upon the icy air. The leader paced forward, his tail making one slow wag of triumph.

He opened his sharp-toothed lined jowls, hunching his neck and shoulders in the painful effort to speak like a human. "You are *mine*," he reminded Jason, and ran his scalding raspy tongue over the throbbing hurt that Jason's left hand had become.

The pain of it jolted him. So shocking was it, that he flinched wildly, throwing himself off the tomb. He smashed onto the floor. The wolfjackals scattered as he landed, and the pain of hitting the stone with his cold brittle body shattered his dream into a thousand sharp pieces and he . . .

Came awake.

Jason lifted his face from the lined paper under his hand. A string of drool followed him, and he wiped it away quickly. His notebook lay across his desk, open, and he'd been working on homework. WHAT I DID ON MY SUMMER VACATION. Under it he had written: Found out I was a Magicker. And then he crossed that out. Learned to use crystals for Magick. Scribbled across that. Made new friends in summer camp. That had stayed. Was bitten by a wolfjackal and fought off the Dark Hand of Brennard. . . . His pencil lay over that line, as if he hadn't quite got a chance to blacken through it before he'd fallen asleep.

He lifted his other hand, stretching. From his attic bedroom, he could hear the normal, comforting sounds of the McIntires down below in the entertainment room, laughing at something on television. The hearty bellow of William "the Dozer's" big laugh, echoed by the more delicate tones of both Joanna and Alicia sounded faintly to his ears, ever so much better than the eerie wailing of wolfjackals. He took several breaths.

The porthole window of his attic bedroom stood open to the night breeze, which had grown very cold, and he leaned over, closing it. He knocked down his latest Mercedes Lackey book while doing so, and the unicorn bookmark in it fell out. Jason left it lying there on the carpeted corner near his bookcase. No one would bother it. This was his part of the world and nothing uninvited ever pulled down the trapdoor stair to come in. He liked it like that.

Jason tore the paper out of his notebook and wadded it up. With serious thoughts in mind, he pushed his dream away, and began to craft an essay that would make his Honors English teacher happy and not mark him as a candidate for a straitjacket. His room gained some warmth as he wrote of bright summer days and campfires and friends like Bailey with her twisted sayings and the pack rat she'd captured for a pet after it had pilfered many shiny items from her cabin. The words flew across the pages. Not once did he say anything that would jeopardize any of his comrades as Magickers in a world that knew nothing about them.

He came to a stop as he tried to finish the paper. What he had really done on his summer vacation was learned a lot about himself, as well as making new friends. But how much of it did he dare reveal? He tapped his pencil point on the desktop, pondering. Tap, tap. Although the time spent at Camp Ravenwyng was weeks in the past, his thoughts seemed to be stalled back there.

TAP, TAP.

Jason jumped in his chair.

TAP.

He stood up, glaring at his window. A black shape winged past it, and Jason threw himself at the pane, to catch a glimpse of it as it flew past. Raven, again!

He opened his stair and clattered down them, determined to catch a glimpse of the bird, if he could. He grabbed the trash from the kitchen as he went, it was his night anyway, and could serve as a cover. Then he headed out the back door, into the night-darkened backyard and driveway where the Dozer had the trash cans lined up like solemn soldiers. He tossed his bag in the appropriate can . . . not "Papers Only," or "Yard Cuttings!," but the one marked "Plain Old Garbage," then ducked across the yard, where he could see the yellow moon glowing through the eucalyptus and slippery elm trees.

The darker-than-night bird wheeled over him, gliding as silently through the sky as an owl. He knew it! He knew that had been no crow . . . that was a raven, and undoubtedly one of Tomaz Crowfeather's. It had been too quiet in the weeks since summer camp's abrupt ending. Far, far too quiet. He hadn't had a Tomb dream in all that time either. Something was up! But what?

He raised his hand, rather like a falconer, as he'd seen Tomaz do. The Native American had struck a far different figure than he did . . . a grown man, with a face lined by the sun, hair banded at the nape of his neck, always in comfortable blue jeans and vest and shirt, hammered silver disks and turquoise stone jewelry studding his waist, his wrists, his neck. But Jason stood there expectantly, anyway.

The raven circled above him. It dove at his hand, passing it, the wind from its wings slapping his open palm. Then, with a cry, the bird dropped something into the dewed grass and disappeared into the darkness.

He picked it out of a tangled spiderweb in the corner, strands holding it tightly for him, keeping the paper from being carried off by the faint night breeze. He tucked it into his pocket and hurried back into the house. His step on the stair caught Joanna's attention, and she called out from the TV room, "Jason?"

"Yes, Mom. I just took the trash out so I wouldn't forget it. I'm almost finished with my homework."

"Good!" Although he couldn't see her, he could hear the pleased smile in her voice.

Without further interruption, he hurried back to his attic bedroom, pulled the stair up and secured it. Then, and only then, did he take the paper out and flatten it to be readable.

Greetings, young Magicker, from Headmaster Gavan Rainwater and staff. Be diligent in your studies and beware the Curse of Arkady!

He knew it! There *was* danger lurking nearby. "What on Earth is the Curse of Arkady?"

"A thing to be feared and watched out for, it seems."

Jason whirled around in his chair. "Gavan!"

The headmaster of Camp Ravenwyng leaned against his porthole window, his unexpected presence filling the room. "You rang?"

"In my dream—"

Gavan frowned slightly. He straightened up, drawing his cape about him, and bringing his wolfhead cane up to look into the crystal held by the pewter creature's wide jaws. "You set off the alarm beacon through your dreams? That's power, Jason. Good and bad." He rubbed his palm over his cane as if communing with his crystal. "I think I'll have Tomaz visit you again, give you some more instruction on dreamwalking. Yours seem to be very potent, and yet you have to be able to read and control them."

"What more can he tell me?"

"I'm not sure." Gavan gave him a lopsided grin. "Tomaz is a man of infinite depths. His knowledge of other ways of magic is vast, and I'm still learning about it myself. But this I know." Gavan Rainwater stared into his face with eyes of crystal clear freshwater blue. "We can't afford to have you scared, Jason. A Gatekeeper has to be strong and curious, ready to explore, and wary enough to handle what he finds. I've a friend, Fizziwig, who will be training you for that, but in the meantime, we have to help you find a balance."

"I'm not scared."

Gavan reached out and put a hand on Jason's shoulder. "No?"

"Not that scared anyway."

"Good. If you were that scared, you couldn't think, and we need you to keep your wits about you. We are spread thin, Jason, watching over all of you, and there will be times when none of us can come to your aid, despite the alarm beacon."

Jason tapped his note. "Then that's why Tomaz sent this. A warning to keep us ready."

"What is that?"

Jason passed it over. Gavan scanned it, and handed it back with a sigh. "He dares what he shouldn't, and in all of our names. The Council will be furious over this, but perhaps he's right. We debated this, and the Council voted not to frighten everyone unduly. Tomaz and I disagreed, but we were out-voted. Evidently, Tomaz took the warning upon himself." Gavan rubbed his jaw. "If I can't stop the Council from bick-ering, we're not going to be able to face Brennard. You should all know there are risks out there now, of being found and attacked and not just by the Dark Hand."

"So there is a curse."

Gavan nodded slowly. "A curse that can be dark and deadly. Gather the others, and warn them if they haven't been already, and learn to guard yourselves. Take care of each other, Jason." He tapped the head of his cane, and his very body seemed to grow thin and disappear. His voice lingered after he'd van-ished, saying, "Do all that is within your power to do!"

"I will!" pledged Jason, and the Magicker was gone. It was only then that Jason realized Gavan hadn't told him what the Curse of Arkady was.

2

CURSES

"WHEN are we seven met again?" asked Bailey, her voice hollow and thready, pitched to send echoes through the air and raise the fine hairs at the back of everyone's neck.

Trent wadded up a piece of paper and threw it at her. It bounced off her freckled nose and into the pocket of her shirt. "We're in my backyard and we're only here till my dad gets home!" he snorted, unimpressed.

The pocket rippled and bumped and squeaked, and the paper wad was abruptly ejected, followed by the whiskered and curious face of the pocket's occupant. Lacey let out an indignant chirp, cleaned her pack rat face with tiny paws, and dove back into Bailey's pocket, leaving only her tufted tail hanging out. Grinning, Bailey tucked that back in, as well.

Sounded good, though!"

Ting smiled slightly as she smoothed a dark wing of hair from her oval face, her almond-shaped eyes lighting with a quiet humor. "You always sound good, Bailey. It's the mind behind the words...." Her sentence trailed off. She folded her hands in her lap and bumped her shoulder against her friend's as if to emphasize the tease.

"Yeah, yeah." Rich and Stefan had been playing cards, as usual. Stefan gathered them into his big, chunky hands as he turned his attention to the meeting. "I got football practice in thirty minutes. This had better be good."

Getting them all together at one time was no small feat, and Jason could only thank a slow Saturday morning for the timing. He'd sent a summons by crystal, but it had taken days to get them together here. He fished out the raven-delivered paper. "Anyone besides me get this from Tomaz?"

Bailey's hand shot up. Ting frowned, then shook her head. Rich grunted and both the redhead and his chunky pal nodded. Danno's answer was to pull out a similar piece of paper from inside his jacket. Trent shook his head in the negative. "What's up?"

"It's a warning."

"Trouble?" Trent's eyes lit up. "And they're worried we might get into it?"

"I think," said Danno quietly, "we've got enough problems with the Dark Hand. Fair warning against anyone or anything else is good." He wrapped his arms about his legs, darker Latino face a contrast to the cream color of his shirt.

"But no one's been bothered, have they? School's been going, days and weeks are passing. I think it's all a bunch of hooey cooked up to keep us quiet."

Stefan echoed Rich's scoff. "Yeah. Like homework."

"Homework is cooked up to help us learn," remarked Ting. She stared at her slender hands in her lap.

Jason sat down on a big rock that occupied most of the corner of Trent's small patch of yard. "I think," he offered, "that we can expect the Dark Hand, just like the Magickers, to be recovering from the battle at Ravenwyng. First we defeated their spy Jonnard, and then the others. They've probably been catching their breath, and now they're getting ready to strike again. I don't think they'll have wolfjackals to help them, but they could be anyone, anywhere, tracking us."

"Why no wolfjackals?"

Jason shrugged. "They need a lot of mana. My guess is they stay close to Havens and Gates. But members of the Hand are just like anyone."

Rich rolled his eyes. "Like they can find us. There's only how many million people in the country now?"

Trent shot him a look. "You think they couldn't?"

"I think," Rich said, tilting his head in Trent's direction, "that we're small fish to them."

"Not so small," Bailey muttered. "Remember what Jon did to Henry Squibb!"

They all sat in silence for a moment thinking of round-faced, funny, and smart Henry who'd had his newly found Magicker powers destroyed by the traitor Jonnard. The discovery that Jon had been a thief, traitor, and destroyer had shocked them all. Ting let out a little sigh. "I see Henry sometimes," she said. "At our dentist. I can't tell if he remembers me or not."

The Magickers had ways of protecting their existence, and one of them had been used on Henry after the disastrous theft of his fledgling powers. It had sent him home in a baffled, cheerful, totally clueless state. Not that Henry had been all that different, but . . . well, he *had* been magickal. "You don't think he does?"

She shook her head. "I don't think so."

Trent said quietly, "I miss Henry."

"Me, too." Danno scratched his hand through thick, dark hair. "Think we'd get in trouble with . . . them . . . if we said hi or something?"

"I don't think we'd get in trouble, but would it be fair to Henry? Seems to me, he's better off not knowing what he lost. Ignorance is bliss and all that."

Bailey glanced at Trent. "I thought it was 'Ignorance is best,' " she said. Trent nudged her. "You would!" acknowledging that Bailey seemed to have a bottomless source for her slightly twisted sayings.

"I think," Jason said slowly, "that being a Magicker—past, present, or future—is too important to forget. I won't forget Henry, and I hope someday he'll have a chance to remember just who all of us are. Ting, if you do see him, tell him I'd like to talk to him sometime. Maybe over the computer, he'd like that." Jason rolled his paper into a scroll and popped it back into a vest pocket. "We're the only ones left from camp with crystals and our full memories of what happened." Silence fell over all of them as they remembered the dreadful storm of power called mana that brought wild Magick as well as torrential rain and thunder and lightning, nearly destroying Raven-wyng. Their summer of learning the mysteries of Magick had come to a sudden ending, but Ravenwyng had survived, with their help. Jason took a deep breath. "I called us all together to . . . well, to make sure everyone was all right, and to see if we could set up a ring, to keep tabs on each other, to help out."

"We've got the alarm beacons if something goes wrong," Danno said. He watched Jason's face. "The last thing they taught us."

"What if it's not enough?" Jason looked around at all of them sprawled on Trent's back lawn. He did not want to discuss his dreams and what Gavan had said, but the foreboding it had left him with was like a bad taste in his mouth that wouldn't go away.

"What did you have in mind? We can't meet like this all the time." Trent studied the crystal in his hand, saying nothing else, but Jason knew his inner thoughts. They'd used their crystals to step through, but that ability was new and rather untried with them, not to be misused or used often. They all needed far more training. Destinations could be rocky, even dangerous without it. The elder Magickers were busy trying to ready a training program that would make up the gaps, but until then, they had to be very careful what they did.

Trent, of all of them, was in the most jeopardy. Only Jason knew his secret. Trent had no power. Not even the elder Magickers had seen through the powerful screen of wit and knowledge he'd thrown about himself. His quick mind and deep wealth of reading knowledge had kept him from being discovered, and his love of magick made him eager to be a Magicker in any way he could.

"Most of us have access to computers. I was thinking, an e-mail ring. Just a daily check on how we all are, if we've seen anything odd or felt anything."

Stefan grunted. His thick, square face reflected the bear being he could abruptly shapeshift into. "I could do that," he said.

"Me, too." Bailey and Ting answered almost at once.

"That would work for me," Danno agreed. "Getting away to meet in person is a lot trickier. Especially since my dad's company may be transferring him overseas for at least a year, and if that happens, we're all going." Rich shrugged. "Whatever," he said, as if supremely bored.

"I think it'll work. Better than phoning and trying to explain the charges." Trent crossed his arms over his lean figure.

"E-mail," Bailey added, looking about at all of them, her golden-brown ponytail bouncing as she did, "could be faked. I suggest a password. Just to identify it's really us."

"Finally something cool." Rich smiled slowly.

"How about Excalibur?" said Trent.

"How about freakazoid," countered Stefan. He clambered to his feet, shifting his weight back and forth restlessly. The backpack on his shoulder held his football gear, lumpy pads and helmet and all.

"How about something serious," said Jason. "Like what Tomaz warned us about, the curse. How about Arkady?"

Each of the seven thought about it briefly, then nodded in turn. "Done, then. Every day, when you can, send a note. We'll take down each other's addresses and we're finished."

Ting nibbled on one fingertip as she wrote out the e-mail lists for everyone, looking as if there were something she wanted to say.

"What is it, Ting?"

"Should we include Jennifer?"

Jason thought about the older girl, blonde and willowy, who had been Ting's and Bailey's cabinmate and counselor. "Well . . . I don't know . . ."

Ting fidgeted.

"What do you think?"

The pencil wobbled in Ting's hand. "I heard . . ." she said softly. "She's avoiding all of us. She has a boyfriend. She's different from last summer."

"A boyfriend? Oh, mannnnn." Trent frowned. He'd always had a kind of interest in Jennifer, Jason remembered. Not that he'd ever own up to it.

"Maybe it's best we don't, then. Till she makes up her mind and everything?"

"All right." Ting nodded, and her expression calmed as she returned to writing out copies of the lists.

It only took a few moments, and then Ting and Bailey had their crystals out. They focused and disappeared in a soft shimmer. Stefan fished his out with his great, clumsy paw of a hand, yet held his gem with a kind of tenderness as he looked into it. Rich followed him like a shadow at Stefan's heels. Danno winked at them, before focusing on his crystal and vanishing. Soon only Trent and Jason remained. Trent slapped his hand against Jason's shoulder.

"There's another reason we can't meet like this too often, besides needing more practice. We could be leaving a trail the Dark Hand might pick up on."

Jason thought. "Not if we went into the Haven."

"You're the only one who's really been there, Jason. And I couldn't get there without you."

"It's something to think about, though. The Haven is out of time and place. It could be the perfect spot for us to go to if there's trouble. I need to look into it."

"Meanwhile, how about I find out, if I can, who this Arkady is and what this curse might be? I wonder why Tomaz or Gavan couldn't just tell us what the curse is."

Jason nodded in agreement. Books and knowledge were Trent's great asset. He knew all the myths and fables, and what he didn't know, he could track down almost immediately with his expertise on the Internet and libraries. "I think," he said slowly, "we need to know as soon as possible. A warning isn't enough. We need to know what to look out for."

"Something you didn't tell us?" It was a question Trent looked like he really didn't need answered.

"Like that line from Ray Bradbury," Jason said, quoting one of his favorite books. "'By the pricking of my thumbs, something wicked this way comes.'"

Trent grinned. "Actually, I think that started with Shakespeare, but I get your meaning. And forewarned is definitely forearmed in this case. I'll let you know whatever I find."

"And I," answered Jason, "hope you don't find anything, but we both know better!" He rubbed the back of his left hand, where the scar of the wolfjackal bite looked healed and yet still remained tender. It would never go away, that mark, and there were times when it was just as fresh and painful as if newly made, despite all the months of healing. He thought of the night he'd gotten it, the very first night of summer camp, before he'd even been told he had been born with Magick in his blood. With a shudder, he recalled the snarling ambush of the beastly wolfjackal and the ripping of his skin as he'd fought it off. *You're mine!* the beast had snarled at him before slinking off into the darkness.

After a moment's hesitation, he added, "This is serious business, Trent."

"I know."

"You could be the easiest one for the Dark Hand to get to."

"Or the hardest. I can't leave a Magick trail, can I? Besides, we don't really know what Brennard is up to, if anything. Supposedly, both he and Gregory the Gray haven't been seen in a couple hundred years. His followers are pretty much on their own."

"That doesn't seem to have stopped them, and anyone who can make Gavan or Tomaz worried is gonna scare me." He thought. "I think they can move throughout our world pretty much at will. They're more organized than the others."

"It comes of *not* having a Council, I think."

That made Jason smile. "No long arguments about how to do things, right?"

"You've got the idea." Trent leaned against the back railing of the yard deck.

Jason hesitated for a long moment, but Trent seemed to be waiting for him to say something else, so he composed his words. "I still get dreams."

"Still? I thought those got pretty well squelched at camp."

"Maybe for everyone else, but not me." Jason rubbed his chin. "Why me?"

"Think you're the weak link in the chain?"

"I hope not. I don't want to, but—sometimes—I wonder."

Trent considered it, then shook his head vigorously. "Nah. It has to be more than that. If Brennard was looking for the weak ones, he'd have come after me. Or Henry. Or Rich, maybe. I think he's drawn by strong talent, and that means you, bud."

Jason shifted uneasily. He did not think of himself as being any more gifted than any other Magicker. If anything, he'd been cursed. He rubbed his scarred hand again. The only way of knowing for sure if the wolfjackal had marked him as Brennard's own was a way he did not wish to try, and that was to let Brennard tell him face-to-face. "I don't want to meet either Brennard or Jonnard again."

"One thing you have to consider is that Tomaz sent the note. I'll do all the research and digging I can, but he's the one you ought to talk to. And, with those dreams, you can't wait to do it."

"Think so?"

"I know so. Look. We're all hanging out here, and we're brand new. It's like driving in rush hour right after you get your learner's permit! You're crazy if you don't ask for help."

"You're right." Jason's head bobbed in reluctant agreement. "I'll get hold of him as soon as I can, and let you know what happens. But you've gotta let me know if anything starts happening to you!"

"Look. I'm going to worry about you, and you're going to worry about me. That's what friends are for. I promise you," and he marked his finger over his chest. "Anything weird and you'll hear about it."

"Right back at you." He cupped his crystal. "Time to bail, then."

With a wave to Trent, he looked into his crystal, focused on a doorway back to his own place with total concentration, and then stepped through.

3

CHARMED, I'M SURE

"GOD help me if I ever agree to another Council meeting," Gavan Rainwater muttered to himself, and rubbed his temple with the cool pewter wolfhead that adorned his cane. The massage failed to alleviate the dull, pounding throb of a headache as he tried to listen to the droning words of Macabiah Allenby, who was most strenuously protesting the warning Tomaz Crowfeather had sent to those new Magickers his Talents could find. At this table in the Ravenwyng meeting hall sat some of the most powerful Magickers alive—and there were few enough of those, unfortunately—and Gavan knew that they were not here because they were happy.

They should be happy. Because of the efforts of his staff, the camp had successfully been drawn beyond the borders of the Iron Gate, and now rested temporally in a Haven, a pocket of magickal mana that put it outside of the time stream of the world. Gavan was now concentrating his efforts on anchoring Ravenwyng in the small dell dominated by the Iron Mountain Range. Anchoring it and warding it against ricocheting back into place. That was why he'd agreed to a Council meeting in the hope of securing the aid of a few more Magickers in getting those wards set. But he would not get it from the six who'd come in to join his own staff. Instead, he was facing an inquisition of his actions and plans.

Tomaz, on the other hand, seemed to be amused by Allenby. The Native American was leaning forward on the long conference table, his elbows firmly planted on the table's edge and his chin resting on the steeple of his fingers. The deeply weathered lines of his face curved in an otherwise neutral expression.

Allenby, as bald as an egg except for a white fringe of hair that ran around the circle of his head, and then descended about the edges of his lower face in a wispy beard, sucked in an enormous breath and launched into what one could only hope was the summation of his speech. Gavan wove and locked his fingers together. They sounded like old women, all of them, old women gathered at the laundry vats, to argue and gossip and vent old spites. He'd come forward in time, most of them had, yet these six seemed mired in centuries long past. He sighed heavily. If anyone else at the table heard him, they made no sign, except that Tomaz looked at him briefly, with humor dancing in his dark eyes.

"And furthermore," Allenby wheezed, "the usage of such familiars as Crowfeather's ravens ought to be deplored, if not totally banned, in the future. Movement of that sort might attract the Dark Hand's attention, and put us all in jeopardy!" He stopped suddenly, as if finally out of words or breath, or both.

Tomaz waited a long moment as if making sure Allenby had finished. The Council member sat back in his chair, took out a neatly folded handkerchief and mopped first his face, and then his bald head.

"Now then," Tomaz said mildly. "The movement of natural creatures is far less likely to attract the attention of Brennard's people than any other method we could use. I also hope you don't suggest that we leave the children in the dark, uninformed. Yes, it might be said we failed in our attempt to educate so many in such a short time. We live and learn. They *lived and learned.* And a remarkable handful stayed by our sides to combat the wild Magick of a mana storm and the attack of the Dark Hand through it. I call that an amazingly successful failure." Tomaz smiled, slowly, the expression dawning on his face like the sun coming up on a desert landscape.

"Here, here!" cried Eleanora softly. Lace framed her face and the dark ringlets of hair about it, although tiny dark circles of fatigue outlined her eyes. Her musician's hands were folded gracefully upon the table.

Dr. Anita Patel, however, shook her head sadly. "We found too many. More than we can train or protect. When we disassembled the camp, we had to take their crystals and the memories of all but this handful. We had good intentions and not nearly enough resources to do what we wanted to. This is a disservice. I, for one, am not in favor of moving forward on the Academy. Not yet. It is too soon."

"What?" Her words brought Gavan leaping to his feet. "You can't mean that! I'll sit here all day and listen to bantering about quills versus ballpoint pens when writing out spells and incantations, but I will not argue about whether the Academy goes forward. It has to. There is no other way!"

"SILENCE!" roared Aunt Freyah, as she brought down her gavel sharply. "Points of order, ladies and gentlemen! You are all out of turn except for Master Crowfeather here!" Her dark eyes snapped, and the soft halo of her silvery hair fairly shimmered in her anger. "Shall we keep to parliamentary rules of procedure?" Her voice rose with every word.

Wincing, Gavan seated himself. He folded his arms across his chest and hoped he did not look as if he were sulking.

That he did not succeed was obvious when Aunt Freyah rapped the table sharply again, shattering his thoughts.

"Ow!" He sank back and looked at her reproachfully.

She twirled the gavel in her veined hands. "And we will keep to our seats at all times! We are not heathens, nor is this a brawl."

He looked at her. "It will be a brawl if it comes to a fight over the Academy, Auntie. There is not a Magicker alive who can stop me from opening its doors to take in our future and see that training is done properly." He rubbed his brow that now rang from her fervor to restore order as well as the headache he'd developed from Allenby's speech-making.

"I don't think that's really the question at the moment, Gavan," Eleanora said quietly. "We'll have a school open, but will there be any students who will be able to attend?"

"Preeeeecisely," said Allenby.

She curved her lips into a smile. "Without warnings such as Tomaz sent out, there can't be. Even with warnings, we have to face issues like Jonnard." Her face paled at the mention of the traitor who had nearly sabotaged all their efforts.

Tomaz tapped his turquoise-and-silver watch-band. "We have not been able to track him. He hasn't gone back to his home, and traces there of him seem to have vanished." He gave a rueful expression. "Computers are remarkably easy to hack, it appears."

"He was trained for nearly a year before camp opened. Anita, you recruited him, didn't you?" Soft, accented words from Isabella Ruelle who sat quietly near the table's end, her dark blonde hair pulled back from a face dominated by a hawklike nose, marring beauty into handsomeness. She wore a lacy mantilla about her shoulders, her dress of deep maroon brocade both contemporary and stylish and yet speaking of her Spanish heritage. She was seldom seen outside of Europe since the awakening, and Gavan knew he ought to be pleased by her attendance.

He was not. Despite her soft voice, Isabella trained the Leucators, the inner force of the Magickers that bore a resemblance to the Inquisition, and Gavan was prepared to swear Isabella enjoyed it.

The East Indian doctor nodded slowly. She adjusted her sari about her slender figure, and the belled anklet she wore from time to time chimed slightly. She had a tattooed bracelet of henna about one wrist that she glanced at before speaking. "Yes, myself and Hercule Fizziwig. He seemed a raw but likely candidate. He had a lot of charm. I can hardly believe . . . well, as it appears now, he recruited us."

"Where is Fizziwig anyway?" Gavan pondered.

Freyah looked about the table, waggling the gavel in her hands. "Let's see . . . he . . ." She scrunched her face up. "Ah, yes. He went off to celebrate Cinco de Mayo."

Concern ran around the conference table except for Tomaz Crowfeather, who turned in his chair to look at Aunt Freyah. "That," he said flatly, "was in early May."

"No one has heard from Fizziwig since early May?" repeated Gavan.

"Some things are provident," Freyah answered. "You don't question them, you just accept them."

Hercule Fizziwig had not been among the more trackable of the Council. Everyone was used, more or less, to his unannounced journeys and research forays. She pointed the gavel at Rainwater. "You haven't exactly been asking for him either."

"True, but—" Gavan sat back in his chair. "I can't believe no one's said, 'Where's old Fizziwig?' No one?" He glanced at each of his fellow Magickers.

"Afraid not."

"Considering Jonnard, we will have to try to find Hercule as soon as possible. If there is one traitor among us, there well may be more." Isabella tapped her fan on the tabletop. "Or I could assign a Leucator ..."

A shudder ran around the room at the thought of a shadow mage from beyond the Havens, a dark, hungry mirror image which would not stop till it found and attempted to join with the Light image who had spawned it. Yes, it would find its quarry, but if allowed to join, all would be horribly corrupted. It took an iron will to control a Leucator. She smiled, her lips outlined in brilliant crimson lipstick. "That *would* be rather drastic. Perhaps called for later."

Sousa, who'd been sitting at the far end of the table, his long tapered fingers fiddling with the battered cornet in front of him, said quietly, "More likely the Dark Hand has done him in." A man who rarely spoke out at meetings such as this, preferring to let his music speak for him, Sousa lapsed back into silence.

"Neither is beyond consideration. By his name alone, in hindsight, one might believe Jonnard to be related to Brennard. There were many rumors Antoine had a son, long before there were rumors he'd gone over to the Dark. We don't know how old such a son could have been." Eleanora put one hand to the back of her neck and rubbed slightly, as if in some pain. "An heir he had no intention of letting Gregory 'taint' with his teachings." She winced faintly again, and did not see the worried look Gavan gave her or the glances traded between Freyah and Tomaz.

"We were all fools. Too eager to find new students." Allenby took his handkerchief, and wiped his shiny pate. He then re-folded the damp cloth square many times before stowing it back in a vest pocket.

"They were all children," Anita Patel protested slightly. "How could we not trust them?"

"Most of us wouldn't be here today if we had trusted like that." Freyah tsked in emphasis, while the doctor's flush darkened her already deep complexion and she looked away. "However, if he is related to Brennard, I don't think anyone here can dispute the fact that charming, or rather, charmed, would explain how the boy managed to endear himself to us. Jonnard Albrite." She made a scoffing noise. "Albrite, the son of the Dark One. They must be laughing at us still!" The gavel whirled in her hands.

Gavan straightened in his chair. "Laughing—but defeated. And they'll stay that way, if I have anything to say about it. If we can put that aside, the one question I have has yet to be answered. Are we going to be able to get help with warding Ravenwyng?"

All eyes turned toward the massive, silent man who sat at the far end of the table, cloaked in a dark, hooded garment that hid his features uncannily well. But Gavan did not need to see him to know what the Moor looked like. Known only as Khalil, and as ancient as Brennard or Gregory, the towering man carried a presence as vast as it was aged and powerful. Had he slept through into modern times or lived it? No one knew, and Khalil was not telling.

Khalil reached up with both hands and dropped his hood. A face carved by harsh sun and sharp desert winds looked back at all of them. "At this time," he said, "the Warding of Ravenwyng is left in your hands alone."

Gavan's mouth twisted. Nicely put, to make it sound as if the elders had declined to meddle in his affairs. The two stared at one another for a long moment, but Khalil said nothing further.

"All right, then." Gavan tapped his cane on the floor, work-ing his fingers about the wolfhead handle. "Allenby, I put you in charge of tracking down old Fizziwig and seeing what he's up to, and, please, remind him what is going on. And, while we're sitting here, I will let you all know that I haven't forgotten I am neither the wisest nor the most talented among us. But I have the drive. The will. And there will be an Academy at Iron Mountain, come hell or high water. Since you all came prepared to wrangle, but not to give aid," he stood, "this Council is dismissed." He turned abruptly and strode off, leaving Freyah with her mouth open, and the gavel hanging from her fingertips.

In bursts of crystal color, most of the others left. Eleanora put out her hand and caught Freyah's wrist. "Stay for a moment."

"Of course, dear. What is it?" Freyah settled back in the chair. Her bright blue eyes sparkled with delight. She'd always been one for a spirited discussion, Eleanora thought fondly, and smiled.

"You've always been one to help, so I can't understand why you're holding back now." Eleanora gazed into those brilliant blue eyes. "Your Haven would be perfect for the Academy."

"It's too small," answered Freyah firmly.

"You know that with our help it can be enlarged. We wouldn't need much more . . . two or three acres."

Freyah shook her head so vigorously, her silver curls bounced about her face. "No. No, you'll stretch it too thin and destroy everything. Eleanora," she took Eleanora's hand in both of hers, "I worked hard for that tiny niche when it seemed no other Magickers had survived. I worked for it, and I made it. There's no great Gate to protect it. All it has is me, and it's all I've got. So I will keep it mine and I will protect it from foe or friend as fiercely as I can!"

"But . . ."

"No buts. I like it the way it is, and that's the way it shall stay. When you are ready, I'll be there for Iron Mountain Academy, but you've a long way to go, haven't you? Too many cooks spoil the broth. You don't need my energy, and my Haven does. There I'll spend it till the need is clear."

Eleanora tried to keep her mouth from curving unhappily and failed. "We need you now, Aunt Freyah."

"No, dear. You just think you do." Freyah quietly put Eleanora's hand on her knee, and stood up. "I know you think I'm a selfish old woman, but I have my reasons and my ways."

"It would save everyone so much trouble and strife . . ."

"No!" Freyah's word cracked like a whip. "Someday you may understand, but trust me now. My Haven stays as it is, or there will be nothing *but* trouble. And I'll not explain. We're both adults, and you should know to trust me."

"Oh, I do. Still . . ." Eleanora had not quite given up, and she had refrained from saying "but."

Freyah wagged an index finger at her. "No 'stills' either! Not another word." She tapped the great crystal in her necklace and disappeared in a shower of color, like a sprite into a burst of firework sparks.

Eleanora waited until she was certain the air was entirely empty, and then let out a great sigh.

4

A LITTLE ENGLISH

"YOU know," Alicia said, watching Jason, her long legs crossed in soft violet pedal pushers that matched her T-shirt, her hairbrush in hand. She perched on the edge of her rosebud-pink canopied bed. The whole room gave him the heebie-jeebies because it was so sickeningly feminine, with pink and lace everywhere. He'd had a look at Bailey's room once, cheerfully tossed and rumpled and haphazard like his own. He felt like an alien in Alicia's room, not to mention what he had to give up in privileges to come in and use her computer. "Dad would get you your own computer if you asked him to," she continued smoothly, and gave him an innocent smile.

He wasn't sure he wanted one. He said so, even as he sat over her keyboard, pecking out the letters for his e-mail.

"For one thing, it would help you with your homework. You'd learn keyboarding, and everyone has to know the computer sooner or later, for writing reports."

"Maybe."

"And you could play games on them. *Dungeons and Dragons* and stuff."

Jason stopped typing and gave her a glance. "I'd rather read books."

"Well, of course," she agreed. She ran her brush through her hair. "But you wouldn't have to borrow mine, and you could research, and your account would be private."

He stopped typing again. "Private?" She'd given him a screen name to use on her main mail account, and he had his own password and everything.

She tilted her head. "Jason, if it's on my computer, I can get to it."

"But—"

"Trust me," she said quietly. "And doesn't your camp friend Trent have a computer? He can show you all the ins and outs. There's a lot you can find on the Net much faster than in a library. I record stuff on mine, like a diary." She smiled again. "Only I know how to make sure it stays locked."

He highlighted a sentence to delete it on his mail, then sent the letter. The idea of Alicia pawing through his e-mail drove a cold shudder right through him. "Think he would?"

She shrugged, and moved past him to the desk, where she stood, waiting to sit down. "Ask him."

He couldn't get out of her room fast enough for either of them.

On the way back from the kitchen with a peanut butter and jelly sandwich and a glass of milk, he paused at the room used for the Dozer's work study. McIntire was on the phone, frowning, and tapping his heavy fingers on his desktop impatiently.

"Yes, I know the house sits on prime cliffside property. And yes, I know what it's worth as a project to all of us. But, the McHenry house is still occupied by a McHenry, and he's made it quite clear he's not selling." His fingers drummed. Jason hesitated to enter the office during a business call, one that obviously had the Dozer on edge.

"No, I'm not going to put pressure on him. That's not my job, and it's not one I want. Look, we've done some nice projects together, clean deals. Let's keep it that way. No, I don't think I misunderstood what you meant. Look, you can bring it up before the board if you want, but like I said, McHenry doesn't want to sell. All right, then. Talk to you later." His voice sounded a teensy bit calmer when he hung up and picked up a magazine, leaning back in his creaking leather chair. He spread the golfing magazine out between his two thick hands.

Jason wanted to ask, then changed his mind, but he wasn't fast enough. McIntire looked up and caught him as he started to walk past the open doorway.

"Something wrong, son?"

"Not really."

His stepfather smiled at him, his big hands practically obscuring the magazine. "Sure? How's that ankle holding up?"

"Fine! Just great, doesn't bother me at all."

"Think you'll make the first lineup?"

"I should! Another week of practice and tryouts, and the coach will post the teams." Jason hesitated, and even as the Dozer said, "Excellent, excellent!" he raised an eyebrow.

"Want to come in and have a seat? Man to man?"

"Well . . . um . . . okay."

It was not that the McIntires didn't act as if they loved and accepted him, they did. But they were equally as kind to telephone solicitors and dirty stray cats, and he often wondered if he were just a charity case. You know, the boy whose mother died and then several years after he remarried, his father died, and no one else was able to take him. He just didn't trust the cheerful good nature that William, Joanna, and Alicia flung his way every day. Were they just enduring him until he could find a better home? He never wanted to do anything that would test it. Asking for a computer might.

"What's on your mind, son? Everything all right?"

"Everything," Jason said with conviction, "is just fine."

"Good! Just a question or two, then? Something I can help you with, maybe?" William McIntire kept his booming voice down inside the house, used as he was to shouting across vast construction sites. For that, Jason could only be thankful. Someday he might want to ask a question about something personal. He fidgeted a bit on the study chair as he steadied his sandwich and milk.

"How's business?" he started. Then he wanted to kick himself for asking.

"Great, couldn't be better! Tear 'em down and build 'em up bigger and better." The Dozer's eyes twinkled with cheer at Jason's interest. "Come out to the site with me some weekend."

"I'd like that." And he would, except that his stepfather was always going just for an hour to check on something and finally trailing home a full workday later. He'd have to find a way to bail if he did go. Luckily, the McHenry thing, whatever it was, didn't seem to bother the Dozer all that much. He took a bite of his sandwich and chewed, and managed to get out, "Do you think I could get a computer of my own?"

"What?" McIntire frowned, then smiled. "Oh! Your own computer. What did you have in mind? Something fancy? Fastest speed, all the bells and whistles?"

"No. Just something basic. I'd like to be able to get on the Internet, but . . ."

His stepfather nodded. "Homework and things like that?"

"Yes, sir."

"Well." McIntire reared back in his chair. "I don't think that will be a problem. Let me look into it, see what I can find. A lot of nice bargains out there in computers right now. Good solid manufacture, at good prices." He beamed and reached for his golf magazine again.

Equally relieved, Jason blurted out, "Thank you!" grabbed his snack, and retreated from the study. Upstairs he sat for a moment or two before eating. That had almost been easy. But it wasn't easy to ask for things, it had never been, as anxious as the McIntires seemed to be to give them. Well, it wasn't a done deal yet. As Bailey would say, seeing is almost as good as holding. He'd believe it when he had a computer sitting on his desk.

Jason trotted along the soccer field lines, the grass crushing beneath his cleats with the smell of being newly mown. Far off at the main field he could hear the whistles and grunts and noise of the football team practicing, but here, on the junior varsity field, bordered by shrubbery and one warped wooden bleacher, they were all alone except for the two practice teams. He tried not to feel anxious as he jogged into position for another kickoff and glanced at the score cards being held on the sidelines. 1–1. Not good enough! No Magick. He couldn't use Magick no matter how much he wanted to. He inhaled and exhaled a few times, and dangled his arms to lose tension. Think of something besides soccer and making the team. Or Magick.

Not only was it forbidden, but could he be any more of

a freak? He didn't even want to try. It would be fun to tell Sam ... heck, he wondered if Sam had Talent or if he could get Mrs. Cowling to test Sam the way she had the others ... then they'd be a real team. Then he wouldn't be a freak, not really, 'cause he wouldn't have to keep the truth from Sam any more. Maybe she could be convinced to test him somehow. He could just talk to her after school sometime....

The coach trotted along the sidelines, whistle in his hand, watching Jason closely.

"Don't get offside," he warned, his white legs moving quickly to keep in step with the teams. Jason had only a moment to wonder how the coach managed to never get tan even though he wore shorts day in and day out, when the soccer ball came his way. The black-and-white orb shot toward him as the passer's instep met it squarely. With scarcely a pause, Jason passed it back and ran upfield. The sagging net goals waited, but he wasn't nearly close enough to catch the pass cleanly. The defender caught up with him and the two wheeled around each other, Jason breaking free.

He felt good. He'd played three quarters and he still had legs, and the breath whistling through his lungs felt clean and sharp. The old injury that had kept him out of soccer camp for the summer had long since healed.

"Coming your way!" Sam yelled, and with a grin, he passed the ball to Jason who had an almost perfect lineup for the goal.

Except for Canby, solid and mean-looking, determined to defend it.

We're on the same side, thought Jason, except, of course, for this game they weren't, and Canby didn't particularly care if Jason made it onto the first squad. It had been Canby, with a sliding tackle, who'd changed his whole plans for the summer. This time though, Jason saw him coming. He zigzagged away and heard Canby let out a faint grunt of frustration as he easily outran the other. The wind skirled about him as he dribbled the ball downfield toward the goal net. Sam kept pace with him from the other side, and as Martin Brinkford closed in, his pale blond hair flying as the older boy outran Jason with his long strides, Jason passed it off.

As he outdistanced his pursuer, Sam let out a shout and

sent the ball back his way yet again. It shot toward him, with the coach yelling, "Shoot, Jason! Cut it! Put some English on it!"

He would have to get the angle to even get close to the goal from where he'd caught the ball. Gathering himself, Jason paused a moment, breathed a faint prayer, and kicked the ball . . . *hard.* It sailed from the instep of his soccer shoe toward the net! With a grunt, and a swing of his square body, Canby lunged in defense. He and the ball collided, and the black-and-white soccer ball abruptly shot off in another direction out of bounds and deep into the wild shrubbery bordering the field's end.

Jason stopped, his mouth hanging open. He hadn't . . . heard . . . the ball cry out "Ooof!" and then, a faint "Oh, my!" as it disappeared into the greenery . . . had he? He couldn't have. Still . . . the voice sounded vaguely familiar.

"I'll get it!" he shouted and barreled into the bushes after the soccer ball. There were shouts behind him, as the coach told each and every one of the players how they'd done so far, and he felt the greenery close like a curtain behind him. The soccer ball lay in a nest of old leaves and grass. He picked it up cautiously.

"What an experience!" it said.

He almost dropped it, but instead turned the ball about till he could see a face pushing slightly out of the black-and-white leather. Jason stared. "Mrs. Cowling!" What had he done? Just by thinking about her?

"Jason! Do shut your mouth. You look like a carp at feeding time." His English teacher sounded a bit peevish.

"Yes, ma'am." His jaw snapped shut. But he could not help staring at the animated face looking back at him. Eyes snapping with vigor and soft curly hair in a halo about her aging face. "How did—are you—I mean—" He hardly knew what to say. "I'm so sorry. Are you all right?"

"How exhilarating!" Mrs. Cowling beamed at him. "As for how, well, I assume you Magicked me in here. Do Magick me out as soon as we make a goal, I've papers to grade."

"I didn't mean to. I was just thinking about errh, you know, the testing and stuff." He tried to keep his mouth firmly shut between words. "But . . . doesn't it . . . *hurt?*"

"Goodness no! I'm not the ball. I'm just a passenger, as it were."

"Oh." He held the soccer ball between his palms.

"JAAAAAson!" bellowed from the field hidden behind him.

Mrs. Cowling gave him a flashing smile. "Show time!" she said gleefully.

"Ummm . . . right." He tucked the ball under his arm and trotted back to the field. Making a goal was now not the only immediate problem he had. Getting Mrs. Cowling Magicked back where she belonged suddenly became extremely important. If only he knew how. . . . He touched the crystal pendant tucked inside his shirt. Ting had made a brass wire cage to hold his crystal loosely, and had shown him the secret way to open it and slip his focus out when he needed it. But it would do him no good if he didn't know what he'd done, and how to undo it.

The thought of Mrs. Cowling's head bouncing down the soccer field endlessly for another thirty minutes or so of practice unnerved him. Could anyone else see her? Hear her? And was she really all right? She'd always been a little . . . well . . . odd. But then, she was a Magicker, too, or at least, had come of Magicker blood. He should have asked her for help!

Sam grabbed the ball from him. "Get in there, I'll do the throw-in!" His best friend, well, one of his best friends, grinned at him, his wiry body tensed at the edge of the powdery white line.

"Right." Jason's lips felt cotton dry as he turned away and got into position, jostled by the other players, his eyes intent on the soccer ball. Sam didn't seem to notice anything unusual, his dark eyes scanning the crowd. He made a tiny movement with his chin. Jason caught it and moved to the signal as Sam threw it in. He caught it on his chest and let it drop, dead at his feet, with no one near him but the goal. He drew his foot back, then hesitated.

He only had seconds. Jason swallowed tightly, then kicked the ball as hard as he could, arcing it toward the net, and it lifted off the grass as it flew. He heard a happy "Wheeee!" as it went, then sailed past the goalee's blocking hands right square into the goal. He tapped his crystal, thinking, *Done!*

The coach fetched the ball out of the net, smiling. "Good shot, Jason."

Canby snickered as he trotted past to line up for the kick-off. "Whee!" he said mockingly, and Brinkford joined him, the two laughing as they got into position. Jason's face warmed, but he had other fish to fry. He fell in with the coach, trying to get a look at the soccer ball. He could have sworn he saw a wink, and then Mrs. Cowling's face faded into plain old black-and-white leather diamonds.

Jason let out a sigh of relief. Sam punched his shoulder. "Nice job!"

"Thanks."

It did little good, in the end. The other team got two more goals, but by the time they all left the field, tired, sore and winded, the coach looked pleased. "We're going to have a great team this year," he remarked. "Good depth in all positions. I'll be posting Monday after school."

Sam danced around Jason. "We made it, I betcha."

"Maybe." Suddenly the soccer team didn't seem quite as vital as it had. He'd worked Magick, unknowingly, and against another Magicker. That could be big trouble.

But how big?

5

GOOD NEWS AND BAD NEWS

SAM'S finger eagerly stabbed at the sheet of paper duct-taped to the gym's main door. "We made it!" He bounced once for emphasis. "First string! Well, you're first string, I'm first string alternate! How cool is that?"

Jason felt himself grinning ear to ear. "It's very cool," he said. He read the list for himself a second time, scarcely able to believe it. A heavy hand descended on his shoulder with a thump.

"Move it, Adrian. Other people want to read the list," snorted George Canby in his ear.

Other players jostled him aside. The hand on his shoulder thumped him a second time. Jason turned about, frowning as Canby gave him a grin that was anything but friendly, then added, "Made the team, too? Good."

"What's that supposed to mean?" Jason answered uneasily.

"It means," the other boy said, "I'd rather play with you than against you. And if you don't do a good job, I still get to level you." Still grinning, Canby lifted his heavy hand and moved away. The other boys scattered to let his broad body through as if he were Moses parting the Red Sea. Was it Jason's imagination or did the whole breezeway outside the gym shake as he passed through it? Jason stifled a sigh. His silver lining had a cloud named Canby.

"This means extra practice. First year first stringers and alternates go to both practices." Sam fell in with him as they headed for first bell. "I don't mind, do you?"

Jason shook his head emphatically. "Are you kidding? At least the coach is giving us a chance!"

"Yeah, and my dad can quit ragging me about the money he spent on soccer camp." Sam let out a pleased grunt punctuated by the warning bell for first class sessions.

With good news under his belt and the start of a brand new day, Jason felt ready for anything. Even as he thought it, the hairs prickled at the back of his neck.

Almost.

Was he prepared for the Curse of Arkady?

Not that he'd had any chance to be. No one had uncovered anything yet. Even Trent, with his knowledge of computers and search engines that devoured information from the Internet and spit it back out at incredible rates of speed, hadn't been able to find a reference. Truthfully, he hadn't expected there would be any. Magickers were sworn to an oath of silence about themselves and their abilities. None of the elders but Tomaz had even breathed a hint.

Jason thought he knew why, but he hadn't discussed it with anyone yet. He called it the Churchill Axiom, based on the famous quote by the World War II British leader: "The only thing we have to fear is fear itself." Grandma McIntire was good for something, he supposed. She'd taught him that one, explaining that the imagination could trap you worse than reality. The adult Magickers hadn't warned their new recruits about the curse to prevent the students from inviting it simply by worrying about it.

Tomaz Crowfeather, though, was different. Not just in that he was Native American, and dressed in comfortable faded jeans and vest over a soft white shirt that might one day be embroidered with a laughing coyote or the next day with a coal-winged raven, or that he wore hammered silver and turquoise jewelry on his wrists and belting his waist. Not in that his view of Magick was a little different from that of Gavan Rainwater or Eleanora Andarielle or any of the others. But he himself was different in his Magick. His was the longest un-broken line of Magickers since the fallout between Gregory the Gray and Brennard, which had outright killed many and sent the others, shocked, either into a deep sleep or hurtling through time. Centuries ago Crowfeather's ancestors had ab-sorbed the British Magicker blood into their own shaman line, and taught the talents accordingly. His Magick could be traced all the way back to Gregory the Gray and even earlier, if he wished to do so.

Tomaz didn't. He wasn't the type to stand on ceremony. He revered his ancestors, but he felt that he must stand on his own two feet and his own proven ability. Each man, he had told them during the summer, was responsible for his own footprint upon the earth. His Magick, strong in its own way, was a blend of Talent that the others understood, and even more power that they did not. Perhaps that was why Tomaz had answered his own conscience and sent them all a warning. Whatever the curse was, it was dangerous enough that Crow-feather had defied the Council. An involuntary shiver ran down Jason's back. If it worried Tomaz, it sure as heck would scare the beans out of him!

Sam peered at him. "You okay?"

"Yeah. I just got the creeps for a second."

"Canby is enough to give Hannibal Lechter the creeps." Sam waved as he veered away to his morning home room class, and Jason ducked his head and trotted to his own. He wouldn't let the burly boy cloud the day if he could help it. He'd made the team!

At home, the Dozer and Joanna seemed suitably impressed, although his stepmother wore a slight frown. "More tackles?" she asked, referring to the accident which had sprained his ankle badly at summer's beginning.

McIntire patted his wife's hand. "Now, Joanna," he said. "Boys need to be boys. Besides, Jason has speed and agility. He should be able to outrun most trouble. When are the games, son?" He inhaled deeply, puffing out his massive chest.

"After school most days. And practice on others."

"You'll be busy, then." He tapped the bowl of his pipe. "Make sure those homework grades don't suffer!"

"No, sir. They won't."

"Good. Good." He rumbled a bit, then cleared his throat. "Bit of a mess upstairs by your room. See you get it cleaned up before dinner!"

He hadn't been upstairs yet. Puzzled, Jason nodded and left the kitchen nook where Joanna and the Dozer were having an afternoon iced tea, he home surprisingly early. Alicia was nowhere to be seen, but she had an after-school Young Filmmakers class at the High School for the Gifted which she attended. Just as well. She wasn't the easiest stepsister in the world to get along with, almost as much of a pain as a real sister. He almost thought she couldn't help being perfect.

She'd spent her summer at a camp in Colorado aimed at the arts and had made a short film there which had promptly won an award for outstanding merit at camp's end. She returned home with an enthusiasm for moviemaking. Not that he was into competition, but the fact he had helped save Eleanora and FireAnn and Gavan and all the others from the Dark Hand of Brennard could hardly be talked about, and he'd gotten no award but the satisfaction. Finding out he had a Talent for opening Gates as well . . . well, if he so much as opened his mouth about it, his family would think he'd gone crazy. Still . . . a pennant with "Hero" stitched across it or something would have gone nicely on his attic bedroom walls!

Jason plowed to a halt in the upstairs hallway right where his trapdoor ladder could be dropped out of the ceiling. A clutter of boxes filled the corridor. He took a long, slow look, then couldn't help grinning. A computer! In box after box. . . . lying in the hallway, waiting for him to open his bedroom and take it up. And not just any computer. This was state of the art. As fast as chips could make it go, these days. Awed, he let out a whoop and then stood and stared. From down below, he could hear the pleased, rumbling laughter of the Dozer.

Alicia peeked out of her room. So she was home, after all. She wrinkled her nose. "Got it, huh?"

"Wow," was all he could manage before pulling his ladder down and eagerly beginning to haul the boxes up. His willowy blonde stepsister emerged from her own room long enough to hand boxes up to him and wish him luck.

It was even easier than it looked, and since McIntire had made sure his home was cable ready, all Jason he had to do was plug in, and he was connected to the Internet. He found himself writing Trent. His friend's name flashed on and, in surprise, messaged him.

Hey! What are you doing on-line? I thought the great Alicia wouldn't let you till after dinner! typed Trent.

She doesn't. I got a new computer. You like?

No kidding? Tell me about it.

And so Jason did, prompted by a few comments from Trent. They typed back and forth, just like talking face to face, only taking a little longer because Jason wasn't very quick at typing yet. Trent seemed impressed by his computer, but more importantly, it made communication wide open for them now. The telephone had long distance charges and people could pick up on the line. This way, they could share anything and everything they wanted. Trent showed him how to set up the computer with a password so that only Jason himself could get in. Jason found himself sitting back in his chair, still grinning broadly. He'd missed Trent and the others more than he could say. They were Magickers. They were family.

They traded news. He'd made the soccer team, Trent had made the cross-country team. Trent loved his history teacher, Jason had doubts about his math teacher. Trent told him that Stefan had made his school's first line football team, promoted from the junior varsity team. That surprised neither of them. The great hulking Magicker was a shapechanger from human to bear . . . often unpredictably. In either form, he was big and bulky. And they talked about Jennifer, slim and pretty and older than either Bailey or Ting. Trent had a thing for her which he'd kept pretty quiet all summer, but Jason could see it creeping out as they worried about where she was and why she was pulling back.

Being a Magicker is not the easiest thing in the world, he commented.

Are you kidding? Trent shot back. **It's about the only thing in the world!**

Maybe she's worried her family would never accept it.
Jason sat back, watching his computer screen for Trent's response. Heck, *he* worried about that.

Trent came back with a written shrug. They talked about other stuff, then Trent had to go, to finish chores and start dinner before his dad came home from work.

Jason took some time to set up his e-mail ring for everyone before signing off. Then he clattered down his trapdoor ladder and downstairs, bursting in on McIntire and Joanna. "Wow! It's great!"

"You have everything set up, then?"

"No problem. Thank you! It's terrific."

Dozer nodded in satisfaction. "I'm glad it worked out. I want it used sensibly, though. No late hours. Don't do anything to make me have to ground you."

"No, sir, I won't." He started out of the kitchen, paused and turned. He looked at them. "I really mean it . . . thank you!"

"We're pleased," Joanna said, smiling. She held her arms out, and he hugged her, and the Dozer slapped him on the back with his great, callused hand. The moment passed, and he tugged away. His heart was filled with warmth, but it was quickly emptied by the faint sound of Joanna's voice as he retreated.

"Do you think that's wise?"

"Wise?"

"There's so much on the Net he could be exposed to . . ."

"Ah." William McIntire grunted. "My dear, if he wanted it that badly, he'd find it anywhere. I once had a friend who underlined every dirty word in the Bible. Took so much work he lost interest."

His face red, Jason returned upstairs to collect all the empty boxes and clean his room up for dinner. She'd be watching him, he knew. She worried a lot about being a good mother. Sometimes it was a real pain. Sometimes it produced a real pain, like Alicia. With a sigh, he began to put his room in order. He'd have to be careful. Very careful.

6

DIRTY DEEDS

THE lid of the trash bin clattered down resoundingly, its BOOM echoing around them. Sam muttered, "This is getting old."

Papers and assorted trash crinkled around Jason as he got to his feet and listened for silence outside. He nudged Sam. "Yeah, but this time, it's our teammates who did it. It's an initiation!"

"Bah." Sam leaped to his feet and grunted as he tried to budge the lid over their heads. "I hate the smell. I hate being shut in!" He pounded his fists on their cell. "I hate the dark!" He pounded harder in growing panic.

Every movement drummed through the old metal bin and sent a thick, foul odor rippling through the stuffy air. Jason heard nothing further outside and put his arms up, determined to get them out before school officials noticed their being canned. "Take it easy," he said. He cupped his crystal in his hand, but the rock stayed cold instead of answering his focus. Baffled, Jason carefully pulled it partway out of his pocket. It wouldn't do to drop and lose it in all the trash around his feet!

He rubbed his fingers over it. Lantern light or maybe even a bit of levitation, he thought. The hard, faceted surface of his crystal met his fingers. The welcome flare of a bonded crystal acknowledging his touch did not happen. Jason bit his lip. Arkady's curse at work? Shoving the rock back into the deep recesses of his pocket, he decided he'd have to rely on hard work. "Help me shove," he said, as he braced himself to push.

The two of them pushed and heaved, with sweat running down their faces before they finally got the lid banged open and could clamber out. Suddenly his crystal flared out, with a bright sunlit ray, but Sam had turned away and did not see it. A golden aura settled around them as Jason choked in surprise. Quickly, he brushed his hand over it, squelching it. The warm rock settled back into its inert coolness while he stretched in relief. Welcome fresh air washed over them, and as they did a little victory dance, a cough sounded. They turned around slowly. Jason felt his face go warm.

Vice Principal Murphy stood waiting, arms crossed over his chest. "Again?"

Jason shrugged. "It happens."

"Any particular reason? Did you see who did it?"

Both boys shook their heads. Murphy sighed. He pointed a finger at Sam. "You can go, son, but you—" He pointed a finger at Jason. "You need to stay. You seem to attract trouble, Adrian. Weren't you the boy who had his clock cleaned by Canby last spring? Wound up with his leg in a splint?"

"That was me," he admitted reluctantly.

"You're on my list, then," said Murphy.

"List?"

Friday afternoon had all but cleared the school out, and so Sam hiked up his backpack, giving Jason a look of apology before heading off. Jason dusted himself off, giving the vice principal his attention. "List?" he repeated.

"My list of trouble just waiting to happen. Let's head to my office," Murphy answered. "This will be short and sweet. We all want to go home."

Jason trotted after the man, somewhat curious, and glad to be in the open air again, shedding the smell of the trash bin as he followed. Murphy was a nice enough guy, always dressed in a suit, looked like he could have been a banker or something but instead he was chief enforcer at the school. He was young, Jason supposed, and had a picture of a nice wife with freckles across her nose and two small kids, who both shared the same freckles, on his desk. This was his first year at the middle school.

"Sit down," he said, pointing in the general direction of several chairs.

"Sure." Jason settled down, feeling vaguely uneasy. Had Murphy seen anything? He gazed at the picture of his wife and two kids. Nice family. He decided to count freckles to take his mind off Murphy's expression.

"Middle school," Murphy said, "can be really demanding. It's a time in your life when you're not a child, but you're not quite a teenager yet either."

Jason throttled back a sigh. Not one of *those* lectures? He tried not to squirm in the chair.

"That's why," Murphy continued, as he steepled his hands and swung around in his chair, staring at his wall full of cheerful posters and interesting looking credentials hung in frames, "we have middle school. We have it to bridge those few years when you are in between, to help you through. As I said, you're on my list. We don't want feuds, Jason, and I'm here to intervene."

"I'm not feuding." His voice came out sulky, and he shut his mouth, deciding it was better not to talk. Jason waited. Sooner or later, Murphy was going to ask why he'd been in a cloud of golden, glowing light . . . wasn't he? How could he not have seen it? He tried to think of a logical explanation, and couldn't. The only thing he could do then, was convince the vice principal that he *hadn't* seen it. Or maybe to forget he'd seen it. He had a few options . . .

". . . and that is why I think you'll find this program beneficial."

"Program?" Jason glanced up from his tumbling thoughts, to find Murphy now staring at him. He'd obviously missed something.

"It's nothing to be embarrassed about," Murphy said. "And, of course, we'll have to discuss it formally with your parents, but since today is Mr. Finch's first day, I thought you could meet him and get things rolling. We brought him in as a kind of prevention force. Get to the problem before it really happens, you see."

It sounded to Jason as though things were already danger-ously out of control. "Ummm," he said, fishing for a useful thought.

Murphy stood. "Come on, it's just down the hall. He's waiting."

He didn't seem to have much choice, so he joined Murphy again for a short trip through the school's administration of-fice. They seemed to be heading for a tiny cubbyhole at the far end of the farthest offices. Boring beige walls led into an even more bland cubicle of an office.

"Statler," Murphy said warmly. "It was good of you to wait. Jason Adrian, this is Statler Finch. He's our new counselor, brought in for special programs. Finch, this is Jason Adrian. Excellent student, good athlete, has a bit of trouble with peer acceptance. He's on the early warning list we discussed." He put his hand on Jason's shoulder and drew him inside the doorway.

"Peer acceptance?" Jason looked at both of them warily.

"Bullying," said Finch, standing, with an expression that could be taken as a smile or a glare. "You could call it bullying."

Peer acceptance? Jason thought. This was about the bully-ing? "Then why are you hauling *me* in? I'm the victim."

"Only because you attract and allow it. But I'm here to change all that."

Statler Finch stood behind the cluttered desk which was overlaid with books and files, and boxes still half-opened, their packing leaking out onto the desktop. He was tall, thin, wore glasses perched high on a prominent nose, had pale skin, and his body teetered on the brink of clumsiness. If anyone was made to suffer smirks and bullying, it would have to be Statler Finch.

He turned, nearly pitching headfirst over the arm of his desk chair. Grabbing frantically, he righted it and himself and sat down with a thunk. Neither he nor Murphy seemed to have noticed anything, but Jason pinched his own leg, hard, to keep from laughing.

The impulse stopped dead when Finch settled his dark brown eyes on him. Eyes dark and hard as flint, without any light to them.

"Thank you, Mr. Murphy," the man said. "I'll just be a few minutes, then we can all go."

The vice principal left, with Jason quelling an urge to call out after him, not to leave him with Statler Finch. But he did not, and the two of them stared at each other.

"That name give you trouble?" Finch smiled thinly.

"Jason? No."

"Adrian. It is rather like a girl's name, isn't it?"

Jason looked over the counselor's shoulder to a single framed object hanging on the wall. There were other nails, waiting, but this was the only one that had been utilized yet. It stated that one Statler A. Finch had graduated, with honors, with his doctorate in Psychology. "People will make fun of anything," he said. "I don't worry about it."

"But you don't stop it either?"

Sitting there, with the faint reek of the trash bin still clinging to him, there wasn't much Jason could say. "It's not important."

"It isn't?"

"No."

"What is important?" Finch smiled thinly. It didn't reach his flint-hard eyes. There was no way Jason was ever going to tell him anything remotely personal or important. There was no way he'd ever admit to being a Magicker or share what was important in his life. Silence stretched between them.

"Can I go home now?" Jason finally asked.

"In a moment. You see, the school hired me to help fellows like you. Bullied around, mistreated. A lot of harm can happen. Anger driven inward. People need to know how to assert themselves, how to express that anger . . . safely. Or there can be tremendous problems later."

Great. The school thought *he* was the problem, not the idiots who did the bullying. Jason kept his silence, afraid that anything he said would be remembered and used against him.

"That's where I come in." Statler Finch leaned over his desktop, across the clutter, his thin body clenched with intensity. "I'll work with you and your family until you can handle these situations on your own. I'll . . . defuse you."

Jason had a mental image of his skull being opened from the top, his brain being defused, and his head being snapped shut again. He barely kept from shuddering. "I don't think I need a program," he said finally.

"We'll see. I'll make an appointment to talk with your parents. I am sure I can share a few insights that will help everything." Statler rustled his thin, bony hands through the paperwork on his desk. "The first evening free, I'll be there." He stood. "Thank you for stopping by, Jason."

Jason darted to his feet. Finch stopped him in the doorway. "I'll be seeing you. Soon."

Jason did not run till he hit the school's front doors. Then he bolted as if he could outrun the memory of Finch's cold stare.

Jennifer Logan frowned as the sky grew darker. Although that meant fall was coming into its prime and Halloween drawing near, she didn't like losing the sun so early. She turned the watchband on her wrist, bringing it around so the caged charm fell into her palm, and her crystal flared with a soft, welcoming light. Before homework for high school, and before a promised phone call from Matthew Douglas, before anything else, she had exercises to practice.

She stood outside in the cooling air of late afternoon, and looked about to make sure no one in the neighborhood noticed her as she walked the perimeter of her house, trying to ward it as she'd been taught. Once she'd learned it well enough, she could lend her abilities to help ward the Havens. There were other Talents, but she really had no desire to develop any yet. There were days when she wanted, more than anything, just to be invisible. Of course, if she were invisible, then Matthew Douglas would never have noticed her. If not invisible, then, just . . . normal. That was it. Normal. Normal enough to fit in with the crowd at school and not have to worry about her Magick popping out at weird times.

Stepping carefully around her home and yard, she began to gather power from the natural ley lines in the ground itself, lines of energy from the elements of the Earth, and weave it together for a protection. She could not get a ward to last longer than a night, but even that took all the will she had, and every day it grew stronger. Jennifer felt a tiny spark of pride as she walked and thought, and gathered and wove.

The last element to gather was the night itself, dark and cold in her mind as she touched it. She hesitated, as always. She'd been deathly afraid of the dark when she was little, something about having been scared one night, and although she was all grown up now . . . well, nearly, next summer she'd get her learner's permit to drive! . . . the night could still make her uneasy.

Jennifer swallowed tightly. Her fingers twitched as if she actually held ribbons in her hands to gather and braid and knot together, but it all flowed through her mind. She'd seen Aunt Freyah and Eleanora and FireAnn do this many times before. *Their* hands had never twitched. Practice! Practice makes perfect.

She needed to do this now, for herself and her family, and later she would be able to do it for all Magickers, something important, something needed.

Jennifer shuddered as the dark ribbons she held turned slimy, fighting her, fighting her will to knot them to the ley lines of bright, powerful goodness running through the earth surrounding her house. Like a snake, the ribbons seemed to want to twist and turn and writhe in her hands. Their touch made her skin crawl and her stomach turn, and her fingers twitched and danced in distaste until her crystal rattled in its cage, threatening to shake loose.

Jennifer frowned and tossed her head, shaking her long fine locks of blonde hair away from her eyes so that she could concentrate. She wanted to finish, in a hurry now, as nighttime fell and the promise of Matthew's call nagged at her. Homecoming was just around the corner, and Harvest Dance, and even though she was only a freshman and Matthew was a junior, there was a chance . . . just a glimmer of a chance, he might ask her! But if she didn't hurry and finish, she'd miss his call. She only hoped that if she did, the answering machine and not her parents would pick it up.

Impatiently, Jennifer worked at the ribbons she'd called to her, trying to force the inky lines of night into her pattern. Then, suddenly, the reluctant streams answered her, gathering and flowing around her, pouring in as though she'd broken a dam. Jennifer could hardly breathe as it began to flood around her, swirling, rising in a black cloud around her. She'd drown in it! She began to work feverishly at her wards, unknotting, letting this line drop, then that, but still the night poured in.

She looked in panic about her backyard, but there was no one around, no one she could cry out to, no one who would understand. She tried to focus for the beacon, but everything got so cloudy, she didn't know if she could get through or not.

And then it began to devour her from the inside out. Jennifer tried to scream and couldn't. She would be lost! She poured everything she had into her crystal to save herself. It flared hotly in her hands and then exploded into a thousand pieces, and rained over her like dust from a spent firework.

The night took her. Covered from head to toe, stifled, blind, numb, she fell, all thoughts gone from her head, only knowing that she fell because there was a brief jar of pain as she landed, and then the growing dampness of a night-dewed lawn beneath her.

Jennifer closed her eyes, weeping silently.

That was how Eleanora found her. She lifted Jennifer up and held her, and crooned a small bit of a song she knew from years past, and wrapped her arms around the girl tightly till the warmth came back, and Jennifer stopped weeping, and opened her eyes.

Only then did Eleanora dare ask, "What happened, lass?"

"W-w-warding, or trying to."

"Overexerted yourself and fainted?" She smoothed Jennifer's honey hair from her face, noted her pale, pale complexion, and felt the erratic pulse of her heartbeat.

"No. It turned on me. The night—" Jennifer's eyes brimmed again.

"Jennifer, dear, I don't understand. A ward is a simple thing, just a weaving of the natural elements around you, and your own strength to tie them. There is nothing evil or unnatural here. It all comes from you and your awareness, dear."

Jennifer shuddered. She said dully, "Then something in me is very, very dark and evil. I can't risk letting it out! I can't! I can't! I couldn't control it. My crystal shattered. I'm nothing anymore!"

"Now, now. I'm here. You'll be fine." Eleanora smoothed back her hair again. But her brows knit tightly as she leaned over the girl. Shattered crystals meant that Jennifer had nearly lost herself, and they her. If Jennifer could even bond to a crystal again, it might be months before she was well enough to try it. This was a dreadful setback for the young Magicker.

The girl wrapped both of her arms about Eleanora. "Save me," she begged.

"I'll try," said Eleanora quietly.

7

SEMPER FI

B AILEY'S mother leaned close and gave her a quick kiss on the forehead before pausing at the apartment door. "Now remember, if I'm late, you two take the bus. But if you miss the bus, I don't want you walking down to the next bus stop."

"I won't," Bailey agreed.

"If you're late to school this morning, just have them call me." Rebecca Landau lingered for another minute, her briefcase in one hand and purse in the other.

"I will." Bailey sat, her cereal spoon suspended in midair, waiting.

Her mother sighed. "All right, then. Everything is all set with Jiao. She'll drive Ting over to school, and then I'll see you and Ting tonight. Tomorrow we'll hit the matinee after the school festival, then home she goes."

"Great!" Bailey grinned gleefully.

Her mother waved and bolted out the door. Even as it shut, she could hear the hurried footsteps running down the corridor. Bailey waited a moment longer, then put her spoon in her mouth and crunched away. She hurried to finish her own breakfast, clear away the dishes, settle Lacey down in her pack rat habitat, and grab her backpack. Lacey wrapped her dark-tufted tail about her body, buried her face, and went to sleep in a nest of cedar shavings and toilet paper, quite unconcerned about Bailey going. She chirped reassuringly at the pack rat anyway. Lacey's tail twitched as though perturbed at being disturbed in her morning nap. Bailey wrinkled her nose.

She checked the time as she turned down the thermostat for the day, and pitched herself out the door. She was late! And, clattering down the stairs and bursting out of the apartment building, she could see the bus pulling away from the stop even as she burst into the morning sunlight.

Grumbling, she hiked her backpack on one shoulder. If she briskly walked the three blocks to the main avenue, she could catch any number of buses headed toward school. Of course, she'd been told not to. But . . . Bailey cast a look at the brisk autumn day. Blue sky, light wind, no clouds. A good day to walk. She hesitated. It wasn't the exercise that bothered her mother. It was the used car lot on the third block, where a very large and frothing dog sat inside the gates, on perpetual guard. He was heavy and mean, and the gates were wobbly. Her mother was of the opinion it was only a matter of time till Ulysses broke free and hurt someone.

Being late to school, on the other hand, was more of a problem than her mom seemed to think. Bailey broke into a trot, her ponytail bouncing in time to her stride. If she didn't look at Ulysses, perhaps he'd not notice her going by. Better safe than silly, as her grandma always said.

By the time she neared that feared last block, however, Ulysses was already at the diamond-shaped wires, barking energetically at a much older and taller passerby when he spun around to see Bailey approaching.

"GAR-woof! Woof! Woof!" he trumpeted, lunging at the fencing. It bounced and chimed as his thick brown body hit it. Spittle went flying from his flapping jowls.

"Ewwww," Bailey muttered, dodging past the flying globs. She looked at the metal signs rattling against the fence with every bounce of the madly barking dog. G & S FINE USED CARS AND MARINE Sales. Then a second sign, hanging below it. BEWARE OF DOG. And, written in marking pen under the word dog, someone had penned, Ulysses S. Grunt.

Bailey grinned. That last was her handwriting but the owners of G & S had yet to wipe it off. Maybe they liked it. There was no sign of what Ulysses thought about it, unless it was in the red curl of his tongue and the snap of his white jaws.

Ulysses launched himself at the gate, his great thick head pounding into the back of the sign. It rang like a gong. He fell to the ground, frothing and growling. Then he gathered himself and stood, panting and snarling, on sturdy if bowed legs. She did not wait to see what else he would do. She took to her heels, scurrying past, as the loosely chained gates quivered and wobbled and as he tried to thrust his massive head through the gap.

Both she and a city bus arrived at the corner at the same time. With a quick look at the routing, she climbed aboard hastily, presenting her bus pass. She sat down, slightly out of breath, as the bus pulled away and Ulysses S. Grunt bounced up and down on the other side of the car lot as if knowing she had made her getaway. She wouldn't tell her mother, but if the festival's meeting ran late, they might well miss the last bus and she might have to confront the Grunt twice in one day. And that was tempting fate!

Bailey spent the rest of her short bus ride contemplating various plans to keep herself and Ting out of trouble on the way home, but she knew there wasn't a lot she could do. Ting, as quiet and slender in her American Asian way as anyone could be, had one fault she couldn't seem to overcome. She was late. Always, continually late. And she was so quiet and unassuming that even when she arrived somewhere, she was so often not noticed that it made her seem even later!

It was glorious, though, having her summer roommate just across town. At summer camp's too quick ending, she thought they'd all be flung to the wind like autumn leaves, only to discover that Ting lived just across town from her, as did Henry Squibb. It was a big town, with a population of over 500,000 people. Still, once a month, she and Ting had an overnight. Besides having a friend who didn't think she was *totally* weird, they could share what they'd learned about their crystals in practice, talk about school, families . . . well, in Bailey's case, she only had her mom and grandmother . . . but Ting had become her best friend.

They could giggle and watch DVDs and work on the charms

that Ting had started making. She had a Talent, it seemed, for infusing small bits of crystal with a charm spell, mild and not very long lasting, but it was fun to experiment with. They both thought that, eventually, this was how the elder Magickers could make powerful warding stones. Ting seemed very pleased that she might have an ability which later would grow into something really useful. They were going to sell the charms at the All School Fall Festival tomorrow, which was one reason they were getting together tonight, to attend the last planning meeting and to get ready.

As for Bailey, well, she wasn't sure what she could do that was special. Oh, she'd disappeared for a while when she first got her crystal, but it wasn't a matter of being invisible or anything great. And she had Lacey, of course, and there was that afternoon a pondful of frogs decided to follow her around. She wasn't worried, though. Being a Magicker had been incredible so far, and she knew someday something special would trip and fall over her. She had absolutely no doubt. And it would be an adventure to discover it!

The bus came to a halt at the corner near the school. Bailey jumped up and was down the stairs almost before the doors finished opening. She just had time before the bell rang to visit her locker and switch a book or two. Today would be a great day, absolutely. It always was.

That was, of course, before she got bumped in the hallway and dropped her backpack, causing her papers to be scattered everywhere. And before the cafeteria ran out of pizza slices and she had to settle for chicken nuggets. And before they decided to play field hockey instead of getting onto the courts and playing volleyball. And before the English teacher assigned a five page essay. Of course, into every life a little rain must puddle. Nothing momentous to ruin her high spirits with a Friday night sleepover, and a Saturday movie to look forward to.

Of course, when the last bell rang, and the school parking lot cleared out, and Ting still wasn't there for the meeting, Bailey began to feel a little disgruntled. She sat on the brick planter outside the office, swinging her sneakered feet, and waited. It being the last day of the school week, no one lingered besides those who were there for the last planning

session and to get the booths set up. Not the teachers, not even
the janitor, and certainly not the students! The wind picked up
a little, with just an edge of chill to it. She wondered what the
weather would be like for Halloween next month. *Please don't
let it rain like it did last year!* she begged silently. She then wondered if Ting could make a weather charm. Now *that* would be
something to see. Imagine a Magicker strong enough to charm
away storms!

That thought brought a small sigh. She'd be happy for Ting,
of course, but . . . what lay ahead for her? Anything? Surely a
vast world of possibilities, but of what kind? Perhaps as many
possibilities as there were types of people, since the Magickers felt that all Talents came from within. So who was she, and
what could she do?

She took her crystal out from under the neckline of her
shirt and pulled it off over her head, a brilliantly purple amethyst on a pretty, twisted silver chain, and stared into it for a
moment as it rested in her palm. Some Magickers could focus
their crystals just by touching them, but she was still new at it,
and found it worked best when she held her crystal nestled in
her palm. The slant of the late afternoon sun played into the
amethyst, bringing a glow to its faceted sides. Many crystals
were common quartzes, but not all, and hers was as valuable
as it was beautiful, but that wasn't why she'd chosen it. It had
called her, somehow, to touch it and bond with it. From the
moment she'd touched it, it had warmed to her and even now
lay in her palm with a faint welcoming tingle. It was a beautiful
gem, and all hers.

Bailey crossed her legs, studying her crystal, wondering
how it was she'd managed to stare into the amethyst and get
lost in it the very first time she'd held it. Could it ever happen
again . . . ?

"Bailey! I'm here!"

Ting's soft high voice carried over the noise of a car pulling up and the door opening and shutting, yanking Bailey out
of her thoughts and putting a welcoming smile on her face.
She bounced to her feet, shoving her amethyst deep into her
pocket chain and all as Ting swung her overnight satchel over
one shoulder and they hugged.

Ting's mother leaned out. Jiao Chuu smiled although she looked faintly tired and worried. "See you tomorrow night, honey!"

"Okay!"

"Remember," Bailey added. "My mom will drive her home!"

Jiao smiled, her soft wings of shining dark hair pulled back from her round face. Ting had told Bailey that Jiao had several meanings in Chinese, charming and tender and lovely. Bailey thought Jiao was easily all of those. "Thank you, Bailey. You girls have a good time." The car pulled away slowly. Ting heaved a sigh.

"Wassamatter?"

"Grandmother isn't doing well. We may have to go up to San Francisco for a few weeks."

"You, too? What about school? You're staying tomorrow, right?"

"Mom says she can home school me for a few weeks or I can even transfer for a month or two, if we have to stay that long. My dad will take us up, then come back for work and to take care of my sisters." Ting had an older and a younger sister. Bailey sometimes thought she was so quiet because she'd been sandwiched in the middle.

Bailey looked at her in dismay. "Months?"

Ting nodded. "Mom's pretty worried about things. She won't tell me everything, but it's what she's *not* saying that bothers me." She paused. "Grandmother may be dying, I don't know."

"Oh, Ting! Don't think it."

"I can't help it. You know how you know things are really serious, but nobody will tell you? It's like that whenever they talk about my grandmother. All I catch are whispers."

The two of them fell into step, heading for the conference hall.

"They do it to protect us."

"I know, but wondering is worse. I mean, I keep wondering if she's got cancer or what." Ting shivered slightly, and Bailey hooked her arm through her friend's in warming comfort.

"If you go, what will I do? We just got the computer ring set up, too."

"We'll take my brother's laptop. She already told me that. I can't be on it long, but I can talk to you every night. She says it's easier than everyone phoning everyone. She can talk to my dad and uncles, too."

"That's not so bad, then. Maybe your grandmother just needs some help for a while?"

"I hope so. I'm going to try and make a health charm. Want to help me?"

"Sure! Two heads are better than one, if all those extra hands and feet don't get in the way!"

Ting laughed then. "Bailey!"   .

"What?"

"Oh, nothing." But Ting was still smiling widely as they ducked into the big gymnasium.

Decorators had already been at work on it, and harvest wreaths and banners hung everywhere. Piles of dried gourds and newly picked pumpkins lay by the door, and the immense hall had been cleared except for a few large round tables. Cardboard booths were being assembled as fast as the older students could get them together, and Mr. Nicholas, the music director, was orchestrating everyone as cheerfully as he did the school band. They got in line for their booth assignment, and Mrs. Nicholas, his wife, looking only slightly less cheerful and a trifle more harried, smiled at them as she sorted through a deck of cards.

"Ah. From different schools but sharing the same booth! That's the spirit! That's what we're all here for. And who are you rooting for in the big game tomorrow?"

Ting stared at Bailey and Bailey stared back at Ting. Neither of them had really wanted to stay for the football game; they were doing the matinee instead. They both shrugged.

Mrs. Nicholas laughed and hugged them both. "Just smile and pretend you like football if anyone asks."

Bailey took their placards and tucked them under one arm. "We need to finish setting up the booth," she explained.

"Of course. Oh, and your mother called, Bailey. She said she was going to be at the office for another hour, and you'll have to take the bus home. Is that going to be a problem for you girls?"

"Nah." Bailey shook her head. "I do it all the time. Working mom, you know?"

"I know," smiled Mrs. Nicholas. "Take your pick of any of the garlands and banners. Tomorrow, there should be squash for everyone, too."

"Just what I want! A squash!" Bailey laughed and waved at Mrs. Nicholas. Ting hurried after.

"You know," Ting said thoughtfully as they found their booth (already assembled!) in the corner. "Maybe we should go to the game. Isn't Stefan a tackle on the Midford team?"

"Yup, he made the Midford Bears all right." Bailey smothered a laugh. "And I think Rich is a trainer or something."

"Rich?" Without missing a beat, Ting took the placards from her and taped them neatly to the front of the booth.

"You know the most physical thing he does is trot after Stefan and hope Stef doesn't shapeshift when anyone else can see. And he'd make a great trainer, he's such a hypochondriac. He knows how to do anything for anyone who might be ill or hurt." Bailey talked quietly, although the din in the hall was so loud, it was doubtful anyone could hear them. Still, you never knew. And this was Magicker business, and had to be taken seriously.

"Think we should go to the game?"

"And miss the movie? I've been waiting months for it!"

"Well, me, too. It's settled, then. We'll stay with the movie." Ting tossed her long dark hair back over her shoulder before bending down to make sure their signs were securely fastened to the various booth sides.

Bailey went and found a harvest garland and began twining it about the wooden boards that formed the booth's window. She hurried, aware of the tick of time. It only took a few more minutes and they were all squared away. Bailey stepped back. CHARMS and TALISMANS for Luck and Fortune. She smiled. "Looks good!"

"Think we'll sell any?"

"I hope so, the school funds need it. And no one is doing anything like it, although my mom's probably right . . . food will sell the best. She says boys our age do nothing but eat." She frowned slightly. "Do you think it's right?"

"What?"

"Well." Bailey shifted her weight slightly. She lowered her voice even more. "Selling Magick."

"No one will know it's Magick. I mean, real Magick."

"They'll think it's just for fun, right?" Bailey wrinkled her nose dubiously.

Ting nodded, her dark hair swinging about her face. "Exactly! It can't be traced back to us. And besides, it fades after a week or so. I can't seem to put any strength into the charms. All they'll have left is a pretty bit of jewelry. It's only for fun, Bailey."

"Still . . ."

"Look," said Ting with a firmness not usually found in her soft voice. "Across the hall they're reading Tarot cards and they're selling fortune cookies. So . . . what could we be doing wrong?"

"It's not like anyone is going to know," repeated Bailey.

"Right."

"As long as it's not trouble. I get into enough on my own!" Bailey flashed a grin, then, tossing her head.

They went back to Mrs. Nicholas and confirmed they'd be back at ten in the morning for the festival, grabbed their things, and scurried out to the bus stop just as the bus pulled up. They settled on adjoining seats, and chattered about things in the ordinary world like school, boys, movies, and clothes. The blocks flew by and then their transfer stop came up. Both of them tumbled off the bus, looking for the next one that would head down Bailey's street. As they straightened and shouldered their bags, Bailey caught sight of the bus they wanted just pulling away. She bolted after it, shouting to Ting, "Come on!"

They sprinted down the block, sneakers thundering, backpacks and satchels bouncing, but the city bus pulled farther and farther away. Ting wobbled to a halt and bent over, catching her breath. Bailey slowed down, circled, and trotted back. "I'm sorry."

Ting giggled. "Like it's your fault. Anyway, it's not far, let's walk it."

Bailey hesitated. She dug the toe of her sneaker into the sidewalk. "Mom asked me not to walk."

Ting considered her with almond eyes. "Because of the dog?"

"Ulysses S. Grunt." Bailey nodded. "It's like tempting fate."

"Well…" A rapidly cooling afternoon wind skittered around them. Ting shivered a bit. She dug around in her satchel, then let out an exasperated sound. "I forgot my jacket!"

"You can borrow one of mine, but we have to get home first. We'll just have to walk fast. We'll keep warmer that way, and maybe Ulysses won't notice us."

Ting swung her long curtain of dark hair over her shoulder. "Maybe he just *looks* mean."

"As long as it's not one of those 'if looks could kill' situations." Bailey tossed her head. Ting matched long, hurried steps with her. "I think it's awful that someone takes a puppy and trains 'em to be mean and nasty."

"I don't see how you can train 'em to just be … well … stern if they've got to protect something. Some jobs call for nasty."

"I don't know. It just doesn't seem fair to the dog. They all start out as warm, squirmy little bundles of fur."

Ting grinned. "Only you, Bailey."

"What?"

"Nothing." Anything further she might have said was interrupted as they approached the chain-link fencing of the used car lot and marine supplies yard, and Ulysses came bounding out, in full voice. *Thieves!* he barked. *Burglars! Trespassers!* He bounced on stiff legs, hackles raised all over his neck and shoulders, jowls rippling with each bark.

He hit the fence with a clang of enthusiasm and warning. The structure trembled and rang like a gong as he slammed his thick, square body into it again and again. Bailey muttered, "Oh, shush, Ulysses. I walked by this morning and didn't touch a thing!" She put her nose in the air and walked faster, Ting scurrying to keep up. The sidewalk was broken here, in spots, with tiny clumps of wilting crab grass growing out of it, and fractured lines where the concrete mysteriously bulged up, but whatever tree roots might have caused it could no longer be seen.

Ulysses bellowed more dog warnings and curses at them. He began to sound out of breath.

"He'll huff and puff till he blows the fence down," noted Ting, almost as breathless as the dog.

Both of them shivered. They were more than halfway past the long car and boat lot now, and the dog seemed more determined than ever. The chained front gate with its signs rattled and clanged as Ulysses hit them. Bailey thought she saw the wobbly gate give way. She pushed at Ting. "Run!"

They both did, pelting across the sidewalk, but Bailey's sneaker hit a wide crack. She yelped as she fell. She went sprawling to her hands and knees, backpack flying off and skidding a few feet in front of her. Ulysses charged down the other side of the fence.

Her hands and knees burned fiercely, and her ears rang from Ulysses' loud barking. She turned her face and for a moment, was nearly nose to nose with the slobbering dog. His hot breath felt like steam across her freckled nose. His jaws opened and he charged at the bottom of the fence where it gapped.

"Oh, boy!" cried Ting. She pulled at Bailey's elbow. "Get up, get up!"

Bailey scrambled to her feet and grabbed her backpack. The outer door of the office building, a rather long trailerlike structure at the back of the car lot, opened and shut with a loud BANG!

"Ulysses!" a man bellowed. The dog paid no heed. He pawed frantically at the bottom of the fence as if he could dig a hole big enough to force his body through.

"Come on," Ting pleaded, yanking on Bailey's arm. They skittered away from the fence and down the street as Ulysses continued his tirade at the fence corner.

Bailey tried to dust herself off as they moved.

"Are you all right?"

"Yeah, yeah. What's a few scrapes and bruises if I've still got my face." Bailey grinned at her.

Ting ventured a look back. "He really is mean," she said slowly.

"He didn't start off that way," Bailey muttered. She checked the strap on her backpack. Things had started to work free, books and papers, and she shoved them back in place as they hurriedly walked along. They got to the corner and crossed quickly, before slowing down a bit. The wind nipped at their bare legs and arms.

"I can fix hot chocolate when we get home."

"That sounds great! Marshmallows?"

"Maybe. They might be a little stale."

"Stale marshmallows melt slower in hot chocolate," Ting said with delight.

By the time they got to Bailey's building, the two of them had planned a snack that included graham crackers spread with chunky peanut butter and fresh bananas on top. Bailey could hardly wait to get her key in the apartment door lock. Her mom wouldn't mind her cooking a little bit as long as they cleaned up.

Long moments later, they sat in the chairs surrounding a small table in the kitchen nook, swinging their legs and contentedly looking for a few last crumbs. Ting took out her crystal. It was a soft daffodil-yellow color.

"Did you get that polished?"

"A little. I wanted to be sure I couldn't . . . you know . . . hurt it somehow."

Bailey smiled at her. Ting's first crystal, a pinkish quartz, had gone to pieces on her. She was very careful with the second one bonded to her at summer camp. She'd kept all the shattered pieces from the first, occasionally making one of the glowing bits into a pretty piece of jewelry. Bailey eyed the quartz. "Looks cool. I wonder if I should get my amethyst polished."

She reached for her crystal. She patted her pockets.

Bailey blinked.

She pulled her backpack to her and rummaged through it. Then she held it upside down over the table and watched everything shower out of it.

Everything but her crystal.

She reached in her pocket again and finally, finally, fished out the chain. Snapped in two, the pretty twisted silver chain lay across her hand, empty.

Bailey sat back in her chair.

"What is it?" asked Ting slowly, as if afraid she already knew the answer.

"It's gone." She closed her eyes in thought a moment, remembering the dog pawing frantically at the pavement. "It's gone! And we've gotta go back and get it."

8

HOWLING LIKE a BANSHEE

TING'S face paled. "You can't mean that!"

"I have to have my crystal. I have to. You know what happened last time I lost it." She searched frantically through her backpack, coming up empty-handed. "I bet it fell out when I dropped the pack. The chain must have snapped." Bailey frowned and then rubbed between her brows, erasing the mark as she often saw her mom and grandma do. She thought the faint wrinkles made her grandmother interesting, but they seemed to feel differently. "Rub that line out," they were always lecturing her. It hadn't worked on them, but who knew? "We've got to go get it."

"It's almost dark. Your mom will be off work soon. Can't we go back with her?" Ting watched her, worry all over her slender face.

Bailey shook her head emphatically, her ponytail bouncing from side to side. "She'd never understand." The two stopped talking and looked at each other for a moment.

"That's the hardest thing, isn't it," Ting said slowly. "My mom is so cool, and I can't tell her. I can't tell her anything."

Bailey nodded, wordlessly. As close as she was to her

mother, not a word could she say about being a Magicker. If she could have, her mom would have understood about going for the crystal. As it was, there would be no excuse for what they were about to do. With a sigh, she got up from the table and went to the tiny hall closet by the apartment front door. It was crammed with jackets and coats and odds and ends. She managed to pull out two Bailey-sized jackets and gave one to Ting. "We've gotta hurry," she said finally.

With a resigned sigh, Ting nodded and followed her out the door. The shadows had lengthened and pooled under the trees, and night was very near. Bailey cast a look down the street, then took a long breath, pulling Ting along after her. Car headlights were already on as they came down the street slowly, in ever growing numbers as vast numbers of people got off work and headed home. She had to hurry before her mom showed up and caught her blatantly disobeying. They skittered down the sidewalks like fallen leaves in the evening breeze, shivering more from worry about what they were going to face, than the sudden cold.

The sidewalks, too, were crowded but suddenly, no one seemed to be nearby as they drew close to the car and boat lot. In the twilight, the looming shadowy bodies of cars, boats, and trucks looked like great, dark beasts hunkered down and waiting. The office in the back had no lights and seemed very quiet and still. The chain-link fence rattled eerily in the near dark as the wind shook it. It seemed terribly fragile. Bailey slowed and Ting stopped altogether, standing on one foot and then another.

"Maybe it's not here at all," she said.

"No." Bailey shook her head vigorously, ponytail bobbing. "I can feel it!" She reached out and took Ting's hand in hers, startled to find it was icy cold! "Hey, zip that jacket up. We can't have fun tomorrow if you're sick." She paused. "I bet I can light it up."

"Without holding it?" Ting stared at her.

"I think so. Sure would make it easier to find. I've gotta get closer, though."

They were not close enough yet for Ulysses to perceive them as a threat. Another few feet, though, and his sharp ears and nose would catch them trespassing on his sidewalk, in

ont of his yard. Both girls took a deep breath and began to
otoe closer.

A car swept past with blazing lights, dazzling them. Bailey
inked a few times, then whispered, "Okay." She squeezed
ng's hand a little to comfort her. Closing her eyes, she concen-
ated on the amethyst as if she had it in her hand, remembering
e glowing spell that would evoke a soft, sure light from it. If
worked, it would surely be visible in the twilight, wherever it
as. Thinking hard about what it felt like in her hand, Bailey
remembered its edges and ridges and rich purple color....

Bailey jumped. A soft white light flared from the corner of
e fencing, then fluttered out. "There!"

"What? I didn't see anything." Ting cast her gaze about.
lthough her hand felt warmer in Bailey's grip, she shivered.

"There!" Bailey darted forward, dragging Ting with her.
he slid into the metal fence, reaching forward into an even
arker corner of the yard, filled with old wrappers and crack-
d leaves and other debris, caught and held by the twisted
ire prongs at the fence's bottom edge.

Alarm! Ulysses bounced to his feet. WOOF! He spun
round, button nose wrinkling. WOOF! Trespassers! Rob-
ers! Another bounce and he was after them, head down,
arreling at the corner of the fence where Bailey shoved her
and through. She began to fish around wildly. The rough links
aught at her wrist and jacket. She combed her fingers through
he leaves quickly, finding pebbles and harsh sticks ... nothing.
he pushed through, leaning her shoulder into the fence, felt it
ig a little under her weight. Then ... something. She reached
or it, stretching, even as Ulysses charged down on her. Alarm!
larm! Burglars! He woofed.

The hard edge of her crystal teased her fingertips. Bailey
:aned into the fence, trying to wriggle her thin arm through
arther. "Almost ... got it," she said, with a grunt.

"Bailey!" shrieked Ting, as Ulysses tore toward them. His
owls flapped and spittle flew as he tried to growl and bark
imultaneously.

Bailey found something angular and hard. She closed her
and about it triumphantly. "Got it!"

Ting jerked on her other hand. "Come on! Run!"

She tried to pull her arm out. The fence clamped down around

her. She was stuck, and stuck fast! She could feel Ulysses' hot an
heavy breath on her as her ears rang from his loud protests.

AWOOF! Woof!

He snatched at her, sliding to a stop in a shower of grav
and dirt and leaves. His teeth clamped down on the hand hol
ing the crystal, and he froze, growling, eyes narrowed.

Ting let go of her other hand and screamed, but covere
her mouth, so it came out a strangled, thin noise.

Bailey stared into Ulysses S. Grunt's beady eyes. His ivo
teeth held her tightly, and hot drool ran over her knuckles. H
would not let go, but neither had he actually bitten her, his gre
jaws simply holding around her. She took a shaky breath.

"Let go," she whispered.

Ulysses stared at her. He braced his thick, stumpy bod
ready for tug-of-war. She had no doubt he would win.

Her crystal warmed slightly in her fingers. If she'd let go, sh
probably could have pulled her arm and hand back throug
the fence, but then—what would the point be? It was the cry
tal she needed! What to do?

It seemed as if her summer flashed by. Dark-haired Elea
nora, floating gracefully across the ground, lecturing on th
power of naming. Bailey tried to breathe. It didn't seem to b
working.

Then she got it out, her voice tight and squeaky. "Ulysses
Grunt. Let me go."

The dog flinched. His jaw worked a bit on her hand an
crystal, mouthing her. He almost let go, but then Ting starte
tugging frantically on the back of Bailey's jacket.

"Someone's coming," hissed her friend. "The office ligh
just came on!"

"You don't want to do this!" Bailey told the dog. Ulysses
Grunt made a stubborn noise and planted his thick body eve
more firmly.

He left her no choice. She'd have to bespell him. Word
rattled out of her with hardly a thought.

> *"Your life as a bad dog must end.*
> *You were born to be man's best friend.*
> *From here on out, be a happy pooch*
> *Who only wants to love and smooch!"*

Ting groaned. "Bailey, that's awful!"

"It's all I could think of on short notice."

Ulysses S. Grunt stared at her. Then, he let out a low whine. He went to his belly, jowls quivering. But he didn't let go. Instead, he seemed intent on imprisoning her hand so that he could lick it to pieces! Heavy footsteps came their way. Ting tugged on her jacket again.

"Let go!" Bailey commanded the dog.

Ulysses snuffled. He let go and rolled over onto his back, begging. She pulled her hand free, crystal still in her palm. He watched her mournfully. She took a step away from the fence, and he let out a forlorn howl. It echoed sadly about the lot.

"Good grief."

The dog rolled over, got to his feet, and lifted his head, howling again. She stuck her arm through and patted him. "Quiet down!"

He snuffled her fingers happily. Bailey pulled her hand out.

Ulysses howled.

She stuck her hand back in, and he grunted in contentment.

"You've created a monster!" Ting accused. She danced up and down in real discomfort from the cold. "I'm going to freeze out here and someone's coming. Let's go!"

Bailey pulled her hand back and straightened.

Aoooooooo!

"Hey . . . you kids! Stop teasing my dog!" Light gleamed as a flashlight snapped on, and a great, hulking man lumbered over to the dog, glaring at Bailey and Ting.

Ting froze. Bailey backed up and felt her friend as stiff as a post stuck into the sidewalk. She wasn't going anywhere unless it was in drag mode. Words ran through her mind but failed to tumble out of her mouth. "Umm . . . ummm . . . We were just making friends."

Ulysses rolled over onto the thick boot of the man. Startled, the man looked down. Ulysses drooled happily. "He was just howling up a storm."

"L–lonely, I think," Ting managed to say.

The man, who more than slightly resembled the dog, frowned heavily at them. "You do anything to him?"

"Ummm . . . no," said Bailey. She shoved her crystal into the pocket of her jacket.

The man reached down and rumpled the dog's ear. "Wow. Maybe he's beginning to come around! We got him from a rescue. He was mistreated. We've been working with him, my brother and I." A slow smile spread across the man's face. He thumped his leg. "Come on, Ulysses! Dinnertime!" The dog gave a doggy snort, bumped his muzzle against his owner's leg and, after one longing look at Bailey, trotted off happily.

"Lucky," said Ting.

"Yeah," answered Bailey, more than a little amazed at Ulysses' transformation.

"That's your Talent, Bailey, it has to be. You're . . . some kind of animal tamer."

Bailey wrinkled her nose.

"Look," said Ting earnestly. "Lacey came to you. Even the wild animals at camp would come close to you."

"You don't think . . ."

"I do."

"Wow," said Bailey, thinking. "Maybe. Or maybe not. Maybe it's just luck . . . and we're going to need a lot of that if we don't get home right away!"

They ran.

IN THE GLOOMING

FRESH from sleep, the man sat straight up in his narrow
bed. He put both hands out, palms down, to the white silken
sheets around him, and took a deep breath, remembering his
troubled dreams. One Gate open and another being rattled. The
movement in the forces of Magick troubled him. It felt like being
caught in a maelstrom unaware at first, then growing ever more
certain you were being pulled to your death by drowning.

His chamber filled with a handful of followers alerted by
his stirring. One helped him to his feet while another straightened his robes and brought him shoes and a longer, heavier
robe against the chill. Another brought him a tray holding a
carafe of dark, bitter coffee scented heavily with cinnamon,
accompanied by a small pitcher of fresh cream, and an empty
mug. He poured the coffee and liberally doused it with cream,
then took a long draft of the steaming brew. Its heat went
through him like a lightning bolt.

If he could not stop Gates from being opened, perhaps he
could find some advantage in the energies released by the
happening.

"Even in my sleep," he said to his silent followers, "I have
set in motion a plan. Your parts will require accurate and
prompt execution."

"Your will is as good as done," they answered in unison, bowing deeply. It pleased him because he knew they did not obey blindly. They obeyed because they respected his intelligence and power and foresight. He had gathered them because of that. Mindless obedience did no one any good. Here, he had the most powerful Magickers left in the lands, and their abilities and Talents were his. He smiled to himself at the thought.

"Tell us our part," said a soft, gentle voice at his elbow. "And did you rest well?"

Resting was extremely important to him right now, as he gained strength, gained stamina, returning to his old self. He shook his head slightly. "The boy invades my dreams," he said, "as I suppose I invade his." He frowned then. "In addition to what I propose we do . . . I want the boy. He must be brought to me."

"Your will is done," they answered, the chamber caught in echoes of their voices.

He smiled tightly. "Far easier said than done," he replied. "Trust me." Then he drained his coffee mug dry. "Listen well."

When he had finished detailing his plans and thoughts, he dismissed them, saying, "Send in Jonnard."

The young man came in quietly. He brought in a tray filled with two fresh mugs of coffee, cream, sugar, and biscuits, although they were far too sweet and soft for Brennard's taste. Cookies. American cookies. Something cloying with melted bits of chocolate in them. Brennard took one, leaving the others for Jonnard. The lad was not so grown up that he did not crave sweet biscuits.

Brennard sat back. He waited for the other to finish half the offering in front of him before snapping, "Progress?"

"Slow." Jonnard shifted uneasily. Dark shadows lined his cheekbones with bruises of fatigue under his eyes. "I am failing."

"Never. You took on an unknown opponent, and nearly beat him. That is not failure. The drain . . ." Brennard set down his coffee cup. "We can handle that, if and when we have to, if rest doesn't restore you."

Jonnard fisted a hand. "I should have taken him down!"

"He is more, and less, than a Gatekeeper. We had no idea of that till your encounter, and although your defeat smarts, there's no shame in it."

Jonnard stood. "He had no training!"

"True, true. But he picked it up from you almost instantly, did he not? No one could have predicted that, but now that we know it, we can and will know how to face him. How Gavan located him, I don't know, but we need to find that out, as well. Are there more of him, lost in these states of America? Around the world?" Brennard leaned forward intently. "Untrained, they will squander the mana. They endanger us all. Use them or stop them."

"I will stop Jason Adrian."

Brennard considered the other: young, so steadfast in his anger that he practically shook, his fisted hand growing white-knuckled. "Good. But first I suggest you channel that energy into recovery. I need you to be prepared."

Jonnard put his fist over his heart then, as had gladiators of old saluting their emperor, and murmured, "As you wish."

10

THE HONOR OF
YOUR PRESENCE

JASON backed away from the computer, smiling after reading his mail. Only Bailey could get into trouble like she did. He remembered the troop of frogs which had followed her around camp one day, ribbiting in worshipful chorus, while she tried in vain to drive them away. Big frogs, little ones, even tiny ones who hopped in high leaps about her, chirping had carpeted her every step. Campers had stood around making comments about kissing the right one to break the spell. She'd been mortified until Tomaz Crowfeather had taken her aside and helped.

The early Saturday morning held its misty gray chill as he slipped out, heading for the park. He'd left a note behind to remind everyone that he and Sam were going to meet and practice, then have lunch at Sam's house. He shrugged inside his sweatshirt, hunching his shoulders as if he could keep his ears warm that way, and slow jogged to the park to get his legs going. Bailey hadn't said if Ting had talked with Henry Squibb yet, but he hoped so. Friendly, klutzy, round as an owl, Henry hadn't deserved to lose his powers and, worse, to be enchanted to forget the summer they'd shared. It wasn't right, and Jason had been horrified when Gavan Rainwater and the others had insisted. His protests went unheard. Even though it was to protect him from being further harmed by the Dark Hand of Brennard, it hadn't been an easy thing to see Henry change before them. The others wouldn't talk about him after that, but Jason couldn't forget him. How could anyone?

As earnest as he was bumbling, as cheerful as he was determined, Henry had spent the summer in the cabin across from Jason and Trent. There had never been any doubt that Henry was Talented, it was his control that had always been ... well ... inept. Sometimes too much Magick, and at the end, not enough. The scary thing was, it could have happened to any of them, any that the traitorous Jon Albrite had chosen to attack with his training from the Dark Hand.

The street curved gracefully into the treed grove of the park, with its neatly groomed open grass areas beyond, the mecca of weekend soccer games and frisbee tournaments, picnics and other leisurely pursuits. A circuit of jogging and bicycle paths wrapped around the huge park, and the groves of elm, eucalyptus, and evergreens wove throughout. He and Sam liked to practice at the far end, where the field was lined by shrubbery and a little isolated from the rest of the park, and from the main fields.

There was no sign of Sam as Jason scanned the area. He slowed, and did some stretches. He wiggled out of his sweatshirt and tied it around his waist. It was Sam's turn to bring the practice ball, so he concentrated on keeping warmed up, jogging around the boundary of the area. A lone crow flew against the dark gray sky of the morning, circling overhead, coasting on unseen air currents. He took it for a good omen.

He swerved too close to a shrub, and it whipped against his hand and arm as he passed. The sting of it echoed through the small, crescent-shaped scar on the back of his left hand. It pinged as if the scar were fresh, sore and bruised, even though it had healed to a thin white line. It throbbed as he slowed to a walk and examined it. It was not tremendously imposing, as scars went. It did not reflect the great, ivory teeth that had left it, ripping at his skin. Nor the hurt of being impaled on the open jaw, with the heat of the growl rolling down his wrist, and the vicious glow of triumphant eyes in the dark. It did not show the pain underlying its supposedly healed surface, as if a thorn were pushed under his skin. Sometimes he wondered if he had a sliver of a tooth caught there.

Jason prodded his hand gingerly. Pain lanced through him as if he'd stuck himself with a needle, and he danced from one foot to the other, trying to hold back a yell. It throbbed hotly while he tried to catch his breath. It was hardly ever this painful!

Suddenly, he looked up, and around the section of park he was in. Thickly wooded, very quiet on an early Saturday morning, and far from the street.

And he seemed to be alone in it.

Jason reached for his crystal and began to trot toward the curve of the park where at least the street might be seen. Something rattled in the brush behind him. Without turning, he cupped his gemstone and began to form the spell he needed for a shield. His mind stumbled. Rushed! He couldn't remember! He'd done this every day, and now his mind was empty.

The trees and shrubbery crackled as something pushed through, running after him. He picked up speed, glancing back over his shoulder. It exploded through a hedge, crashing onto the grass and racing after him. It growled low and harshly, ivory fangs slashing at the air, huge silvery body poised to catch him. Wolfjackal!

Impossible! In the real world, here, now, and after him! He could hardly breathe at that thought. Wolfjackals came from the netherlands, borne on Magicker mana . . . how could they be so strong here, so far away from the Gates and Havens?

Jason had no doubt they would be as deadly here as they'd been at Camp Ravenwyng. He bolted.

A second unseen thing thrashed through the undergrowth as well. Jason cut back, as if defending himself on a soccer field, and the beast closing on him slipped on the still morning wet grass and went rolling. It gnashed its great jaws and leaped back onto all fours, glowering. Sun glinted in its green eyes, and it narrowed its gaze as though far more used to darkness. The wolfjackal slunk low, stalking, because Jason had halted, backing up to a great tree trunk. He could not expect to outrun it anyway. Either of them, wherever the second one was.

They would both have to face him if they wanted him now, the massive old California oak tree guarding his back.

He cupped his crystal and tried for a shield again, a cover of light, and the crystal flared. He pushed all his thoughts and hope into it. He could feel an answering warmth from the rock he held as it answered, and for a moment, an immense shield enveloped both Jason and the tree! It shimmered brightly in the thin morning light and then popped like a bubble. His ears felt the pressure as it shattered and he staggered against the rough bark of the oak as it blew. His knees went wobbly.

The beast shivered as it watched him, more jackal than wolf and yet oddly similar to a wolf with its black-and-silver coat. It might even be handsome if it were not so obviously a hunter, a tearer of flesh. His left hand ached, and sharp, jabbing pains stabbed across it as if sent by lightning. The wolf-jackal's tongue lolled, bright pink, from its toothy jaws and it crawled forward, eyes gleaming in bright anticipation. Jason gulped. Even if he could sound the alarm through his crystal, there was no time for an answer!

The wolfjackal turned its head slightly, with a welcoming growl, as the other readied to join it.

The brush rattled again, and the second of Jason's pursuers stepped out on two feet. He locked eyes with Jason and smiled slowly. Tall, with dark russet hair, and a band of freckles across his nose that belied his solemn look, he wore black pants, and a long black duster coat over a white T-shirt, dressing like someone out of the *Matrix* movie series. Pitch-black sunglasses hid the color of his eyes. He dropped a hand to the wolfjackal's ruff, and rubbed the ferocious creature gently. The wolfjackal growled and leaned against the man's knee.

"Running seems out of the question."

"Giving in definitely is." Jason looked at the other. "Who are you?"

The man's smile thinned. "Now that," he answered, "would be telling, wouldn't it? But I know who you are. Come along with me and save us both the trouble." He extended his free hand, the cuff of his sleeve falling back, revealing a bronze wrist cuff shaped like a hand gripping his arm. Jason looked at it, then quickly looked away. This was more than a simpler follower of the renegade wizard Brennard. This was a member of the Dark Hand itself, and he knew he should be afraid. They were assassins, not apprentices.

He might be if he had time to stop and think. His gaze swept the park behind the man and animal. The sounds of cars sweeping now and then along the outer border of the area could be heard but no vehicles could be seen. Sam should be along any minute now, but he'd be on foot and alone, too . . . no match for the rogue Magicker facing Jason. Still, any distraction might help.

The Dark Hand noticed his gaze and followed it before turning back quickly to Jason. "No help to be had?" he said. "What a pity." He took a step forward and the wolfjackal bounded to its feet, following. "As they say . . . we can do this the easy way or the hard way."

Jason tightened his jaw.

The other noticed, and nodded. "The hard way, then." He snapped his fingers and the wolfjackal strained forward, snarling louder. "I thought perhaps an intelligent lad like you might realize there are two sides to every story."

"Probably more than that, even," Jason responded.

"Yes. All I wish to do is extend an invitation."

"Delivered by wolfjackal?"

The man paused, then laughed faintly, coldly. The sunglasses hid his eyes, but Jason doubted if the laugh crinkled or warmed them in any way. "Got your attention, as they say." He kept his hand buried in the loose skin of the creature's ruff, holding him back but without much control if the beast decided to lunge at Jason. "Come visit with me. Give me some of your time and that intense attention you hold for Magicking, and find out the rest of the story."

He heard a car slow down beyond the edge of the park, and a car door slam. Jogger being dropped off? Sam? Anyone? "Do I have to believe what you tell me?"

That took the man aback for a moment. Then he showed his teeth, much like the beast growling and snarling at his side. "Regardless of what you think, young Jason, none of us can force you to believe anything. But there are differences, important differences. Differences urgent enough to war over. I don't expect you to make a choice in a day, but you can't make any choice at all without listening. Without *knowing*. Come with me and exercise some of that independence you think is so important." He held his hand out again.

Instinctively, Jason moved away, or tried to, but the oak held him fast. Whatever would his stepmother Joanna think about his refusing a polite invitation? She was always getting them, to one charity event or another, and she would sit at the table and read them aloud to the Dozer. "The honor of your presence is requested at this year's Gala Sunbright Dance and Auction for the ailing children at Hospital Sunflower. . . ." At which point, William McIntire would looked up, with a twinkle in his eyes, and say, "Presents? Are they asking for presents again? I thought we just gave them a bagful!" To which Jason's stepmother would respond by putting down the invitation, and giving her husband an exceedingly fond look.

Somehow, Jason didn't think this invitation was to anything nearly as fun or noble as a charity dance and auction.

"Come with me now, or regret it later." The Dark Hand looked at him, almost mournfully, in his somber dark duster and black clothing, and pale skin.

"Jaaaaaaaason!" came a faraway call.

He straightened. "It'll have to be later, then. I'm busy." He pushed himself away from the tree at a dead run, leaped over the startled wolfjackal, and took off across the green field as if the devil itself were after him. A muffled curse and snapping growl echoed after him, but he did not look back. He ran toward the faint sound of Sam's call, shouting, "Over here, Sam!"

He sprinted as if the coach's shrill whistle drove him, as if the wind itself were under his heels, as if a gold medal awaited him beyond the curve of the grass and eucalyptus trees. He thought he felt hot breath across the backs of his legs and the sound of the panting wolfjackal hounding him. The only invitation the beast had in mind was one for dinner!

Sam came trotting through the shrubs at the path's end, a wide grin across his face, and there was a snap behind him. It was as though a door opened and closed, taking the wolfjackal and the Dark Hand with it. He could feel their sudden absence. Slowing, he looked over his shoulder . . . and saw nothing.

Sam hiked up his duffel bag and paused on the jogging trail. "Hey, I'm sorry I'm late—" He looked at Jason. "What is it?"

Jason grinned. "Nothing," he said. "Just that I'm really glad to see you. Really, really glad to see you."

Sam laughed. "No kidding? Well, wait till after we do line sprints, and then tell me how glad you are!" He tugged on the referee's whistle around his neck. "Just like the coach!" He blew a sharp blast, and added, "Adrian! Give me ten!"

Jason dropped to the grass but instead of doing push-ups, toppled over to catch his breath.

"What are you waiting for?" Sam demanded, mock angry.

Jason grinned. "I'm thinking of all the different things I can tell you to do with that whistle!"

TWO WRONGS AND A WRIGHT

AN hour or so later, with the sun hotly dappling the grass and towels around their necks, Sam and Jason readied to head home. Muscles stretched and lungs full of morning air, they paced each other returning to the main areas of the boulevard park. He caught the sound of something moving through the underbrush followed them. Branches rustled heavily and gravel skittered.

"Did you hear something?"

Sam leaped over a patch of dried leaves and crashed into another, crunching and scattering them. "Hear what?"

"I don't know. Something." Jason looked back over his shoulder. He swerved along the pathway. He didn't know what Sam would do if a wolfjackal sprang on them. For that matter, he didn't know what *he* would do this time, given that his crystal had failed to shield him. How could he explain a frothing, growling, powerful beast that was neither wolf nor jackal but both, a creature not from their own dimension? But more than having to explain a wolfjackal to his buddy, he wanted to be able to tell him what *he* was. What he did. What he could do, with Magick. Who he was, a Magicker.

He could not. The Oath of Binding kept his jaws glued shut, but could not block his curiosity. How would Sam react? Would he treat Jason as he always had? And what if Sam had Talent of his own? Could Jason tell that? He'd been warned that the Binding would stop him in his tracks, that it could not be bypassed, but—was it true, or would it work that way only because he believed it would?

Could he risk their friendship and maybe even their lives by trying to show Sam the truth?

He heard no more noise but those of the thoughts wheeling around in his head. And while he thought, Sam jogged alongside him, talking about the soccer team and the schools they would be facing and making plans for defense and offense and extra training, his face intent on what he was saying, not even noticing Jason only half listened. Distracted, both of them ran onto the bicycle path without looking. There was a moment when he realized something zoomed head on at them and then they both wheeled about and dove into the bushes. A screech and clatter followed.

Jason sat up, to look at a cyclist righting himself and his bicycle. The scrawny figure seemed vaguely familiar, Jason thought, as he rose and helped Sam to his feet. The cyclist reached up to pull his helmet off, saying, "Everyone okay?"

He looked at Statler Finch. Sam picked up their gear bags, shaking dust and old leaves off them. He dusted himself off. "We're fine . . . I think."

"A lot of running. You two boys look like you're being chased. Any trouble?" Finch's cold eyes watched him. Judged him.

"No, sir," Jason said, finally. His hand itched to curl around his crystal, for comfort if nothing else, but he resisted. This was one man who must never, ever, find out what he was made of. This was a man who might believe in Magick for all the wrong reasons and try to turn Jason inside out over it. He said carefully, "We're just out getting some extra practice."

"Cross-country? Track team?" Finch's gaze stayed on him. "Exercise is as good for the mind as it is for the body."

Jason shifted uneasily. The man knew what team he was on. Why ask?

"Soccer," offered Sam. "Sorry we didn't see you. Hardly anyone bicycles here."

"It *is* a bicycle path." Finch stood, mountain cycle in hand, with scrawny legs looking as if they'd never heard of a tan, let alone had one, sticking out from his bicycle shorts and bicycling shoes on his feet.

"Yeah, I know," Sam agreed. He did a cooling off stretch.

"Everyone all right, then? You both seemed in a big hurry."

"Yes, sir, and yes, sir. Breakfast is waiting at home!" Jason put on what he hoped was a starving look. He didn't like having the fellow watching them. His left hand twitched and he put his right hand over the crescent scar for a moment. Nor did he want Statler to see him twitching.

"Hard work gets you what you want." The man smiled at both of them, but the contortion of his lips did nothing to warm his eyes. They stayed cold and dark, and Jason couldn't look at him for long. Finch made him feel like a formaldahyde frog in bio lab.

Finch put his helmet back on, distracted by having to cinch the straps down again tightly. "Well, I won't keep you boys. I remember the days when one breakfast hardly seemed enough!" He laughed, again without warmth and without caring that neither Jason nor Sam laughed with him. He straddled his gleaming vehicle, hands encased by trendy biker's gloves. He kicked off, and began to pedal away, his thin calves knotted with the effort.

Sam watched him cycle around the curve and disappear. He scratched his head. "He's creepy. Who is that?"

"The new school psych I told you about."

"Ick." Sam shuddered. "I wouldn't even tell him my name, if I could help it."

Jason stared thoughtfully after the disappearing man. "I may not have any choice," he answered. "School has decided it's not bullies who are a problem, but the victims. But I'm not telling him anything." The scar under his fingers gave a single, painful throb.

"You have to go see him?"

"Looks like. Unless my parents say no." Somehow, he

didn't think that would happen. They were very anxious he be all right ... sometimes too anxious even though he wasn't theirs. What he did need, he wasn't sure. Maybe a little more trust on their part. He sighed.

"Okay, now that's crazy. We're the bad guys 'cause we're getting trash canned?"

"Something like that." Jason's stomach growled faintly, as if the mention of food did indeed wake up hunger pangs.

"That's just wrong." Sam did another stretch before flashing a grin. "Race you home?"

"You got it!" They bolted like streaks across the pathways and out of the park, toward Sam's neighborhood.

Bailey adjusted the brilliant gold, red, and brown harvest garland at the corner of their booth. She peered across the gym. "Wow, a lot of people already. Looks like they picked a good day for this."

Ting straightened her outfit a bit nervously, flinging her black hair over her shoulder as she sat down and brought out her tray of charms and talismans. She and Bailey had been working on them all morning. Bailey perched on the stool beside her.

"Don't worry, Ting, our stuff is going to sell like hot muffins."

Ting giggled. "Hotcakes!" she corrected.

"Better than that. You can't eat hotcakes with your hands, but you can muffins." Bailey tossed her head, ponytail swinging. She looked over the tray of simple jewelry they'd made up. Small bluish crystals and quartz in the wellness area, pink for friendship, clear for studies and wisdom, hanging in simple twisted wire cages for necklaces or attached to clips for charms. The cages—free-form and pretty—were harder to make than they looked.

Ting had been very patient showing her how to twist and bend the wire after warming it a little. Ting had bought several crystals and broken them into shards, and then they were put into the settings once she had worked her Talent on them, filling them with a soft glow, giving them luck. Just like rabbit's feet, although heaven knows she'd never thought a three-legged rabbit could really be lucky!

Canned music began to play through the hall, country style and Bailey wrinkled her nose. At least it wasn't too loud. She leaned over the Lucky in Study tray and stirred the charms about a bit. In the hall's light, they didn't sparkle as much as they would outside or in stronger light, but they still had a nice glimmer to them, catching the eye. She saw a group of girls survey the hall, and then their gazes fell on the signs she and Ting had made to decorate the booth.

"Ooooh," they breathed as one and headed toward them.

"Brace yourself," Bailey said to Ting. "I think it's the Barbie clones."

Ting laughed, then she whispered, "I think they're just customers!" She offered a welcoming smile as the girls came to the booth's counter.

The tanned blonde girl with very, very short hair bounced on her toes. "Jewelry," she exclaimed, and beamed.

"Earrings? Toe rings?"

"Charms," said Ting quietly, almost shyly.

Bailey stood up. "Three kinds," she explained brightly. "One for friends, one for learning, one for happiness."

"Friends?" said the blonde's number one clone, her yellow hair done in braids. She had dark brown eyes and a nice smile and had not been born with blonde hair. She picked up one of the friendship charms. She looked at Ting. "How about . . . special friends?"

"A love potion?" chirped Barbie wannabe number three.

"Well . . . um . . ." Ting's face flushed a little and she threw an uncertain glance at Bailey.

Bailey leaned over, and lowered her voice a bit, drawing the three closer to hear her. "It can't be a Love Potion," she said, "because it's not a drink, it's a crystal. Think of it as a concentrate." And she nodded sagely.

Ting kicked her ankle under the booth counter, not hard but Bailey distinctly felt it. She paid no attention. "The charm's purpose," and she lowered her voice yet again, after looking side to side, as if revealing a great secret, "is to make sure your friend remembers and thinks of you. A lot."

All three blondes bounced. Giggles erupted, which they fought back, and looked around to see if they were getting noticed.

"I'll take one."

"And me!

"Me, too!" They all spoke nearly as one and for a few moments, she and Ting were very, very busy picking out just the
right charm for each, taking money, and bagging the jewelry.

Bailey handed the money box to Ting after they left. "See?
Was that so hard?"

"Love charms?" Ting practically stuttered.

"Well . . . not exactly . . . but kinda. Luck is mostly in the perception anyway." Bailey leaned on her elbows. She watched the
Barbie clones drifting across the hall, where they converged
into another group and disappeared in a frenzy of greetings
and hugs and bounces. "Uh-oh."

"What? What is it?"

"I think we're about to be swamped." Bailey watched the
flurry of conversation across the hall, punctuated by looks
and hands pointed in their direction. As one, the larger group
started their way.

Within moments, Ting and Bailey sold more than half the
jewelry they had made and brought. The two of them could
hardly keep up with the chattering questions and orders,
hands and fingers flying across the trays, gathering up two and
three of the various charms at a time.

"After all," said one of the last customers as she left, smiling happily, "You can't have too much luck!"

Bailey and Ting sat back exhausted on their stools. "Wow,"
remarked Ting quietly. "We may not have enough to stay the
whole afternoon." She looked at the picked-over trays, reaching under the counter to take out the lunch bags with the few
extras they had made and spread them out where they belonged. "That's all of them."

"This is going to help the benefit a lot," Bailey said with
pride. Half their proceeds went to the fund, and the other half
would just cover what Ting spent for crystals and jewelry wire
and chain, with maybe enough left for an ice cream sundae
each. Still, it was an unspoken Magicker creed, or seemed to
be, that their Talents could not be used for profit, or at least
not vast amounts of it.

A shadow fell across the gleaming charms, accompanied by

a deep snicker. "Selling Lucky Charms? Where's the marsh-mallow treats?"

She didn't have to look up to recognize Stefan and Rich. Stefan had a certain odor that, while not entirely offensive, definitely didn't come out of a cologne jar. She sat back on the stool as Ting piped up, "Hello, Rich, Hello, Stef. Ready for the game later?"

Even knowing who she was going to see, Bailey still blinked with surprise when she did look up. Stef had bulked up, standing square and big in front of her. "You could be a football team," she blurted.

He grinned. He ran his hand over his flat top haircut that made his head look like a big, mean square. "You think?"

Rich, his thin, wiry, red-haired friend, rolled his eyes. "You look like a tank," he said. "Okay?"

Stefan grinned. He hiked up his jeans and tapped his T-shirt with a big number 31 on it. "That's me."

"Cool," said Bailey. "I mean it, really. Good luck."

"You guys coming? Your team is gonna get thrashed, Bailey."

"Nah, I don't think so. We've been wanting to go to this movie for weeks, and today's our last chance, practically, before it comes out on DVD. I hear it should be a good game, though."

"I had three solo tackles last week."

"Four," corrected Rich.

Stef look at him. "Four?" Another slow grin spread across his face. "Coolio."

Rich also wore a T-shirt, but his had a zero on it. Ting tilted her head. "What do you play?"

"I'm the stats manager and I help the trainer. I get to tape wrists and ankles and stuff. And look after him." Rich gave his friend a look that was only half scornful, the other half one of genuine concern.

"Has he ever . . ." Bailey lowered her voice. "You know."

Rich shook his head quickly, a blaze of red across his pale skin. "Nope. Not without warning. Just twice since we got home."

Stef grunted. Both girls looked at him, seeing the bear he

could become in their memories. Not just any bear, but a gruff and roly-poly cub, one that listened to them like Stefan would, then went off and did whatever his own stubborn bearish mind wanted.

Ting let out a small sigh of relief. "Well, that's good."

"That's training," said Stefan. He patted his pocket, then took out his crystal and held it for a moment. "My parents don't even know."

"They'll be at the game," Rich added. "Along with mine." He tugged on Stefan's elbow. "You need to chow some lunch down now or you'll get sick." He looked at the girls. "Football stuff. Can't play on a full stomach."

"Riiiight," said Bailey. She didn't grin till the two had trudged off. Then she looked at Ting. "Who'd a thunk Rich would make a good mother hen?"

Ting chuckled. A family stopped at the booth, and Ting explained the blue wellness charms along with the clear crystal study charms to the mother who had an entire flock of small ones hanging onto her. After a few moments of consideration, the harried woman chose the most peaceful blue talisman she could find on the tray and bought it.

"Don't forget to put it to your forehead when you meditate," Ting called softly after her. The woman nodded, amidst the chatter and crying of the little ones tugging on her and begging to go to the popcorn booth.

Bailey just stared and tried to hide a shudder.

Ting nudged her. "Just 'cause you don't have brothers or sisters!"

"That was a lot, though. Like a . . . a . . . pack."

"Oh, they weren't all hers, I'm sure." Ting looked after them, a sympathetic expression on her face.

The day slowed down. They ate their tuna salad sandwiches in the booth, and customers came by occasionally, but most people were more interested in the many food booths scattered around the hall. Food was clearly the fastest way to a teenager's spending money, Bailey observed. She brightened, though, when a familiar, owl-shaped face crowned by unruly brown hair came toward them, spectacles sliding down his nose.

"Henry! Henry Squibb!" she called out, and waved her arm.

The former Magicker turned slightly, and looked at them both closely. He had his arm full of squirming toddler, a girl in a frilly dress with a matching ruffled panty, kicking her dimpled bare toes against her brother's hip. He came over to the booth, a slightly curious and anxious expression on his face, which washed away when he said, "Oh, yes. I remember you. From camp. How are you?"

Sadly, he didn't really remember them the way they had been, having washed out dramatically from Ravenwyng. Bailey smiled cheerfully at him anyway. "Fine, and you? Remember Jason and Trent? Jason has a computer now, he could use help with. He wants you to e-mail him."

"Oh. Really." Henry looked slightly baffled again, then brightened slightly. "Jason and Trent had the cabin across from me, right?"

"That's it!"

Ting took a piece of paper and wrote down the e-mail addresses for both Jason and Trent, and passed it to Henry. The owlish Henry had to grab it quickly before his sister squealed and captured it instead. A tiny piece of paper hung from the corner of her mouth already, the same color as one of the dance flyers someone had been passing out earlier.

Henry flushed slightly. "Abbie likes to eat paper," he explained.

"Don't we all?" Bailey grinned at him, and they laughed.

He bounced the toddler in his arms. "I'm just watching her for my mom . . . she's around here somewhere."

"Playing big brother, huh?"

"Trying to. It's not always much fun, but she's being good today. I guess the paper tastes great." Henry grinned then, like the old Henry who'd gone to camp with them and had a crystal and had done wondrous things. Not like the Henry who'd taken the Draft of Forgetfulness and forgotten all about having been a Magicker.

"Henry! Henry?"

He turned. "That's Mom. Gotta go. Thanks for the addresses. I'll try to write 'em, if I don't forget." Waving, he moved off across the crowd and disappeared.

Ting let out a sad sigh.

"I know," said Bailey. "I know." They finished their lunch

in silence, then each sat alone as the other took a break and came back. Selling the charms didn't seem nearly as neat as it had earlier. The day wore on.

A girl came toward them across the hall, as if homing in on a beacon, letting nothing in her way slow her down. She reached them, and gripped the counter with both hands.

"I need a love charm."

"Well, we have friendship charms," answered Ting slowly, pointing out the tray.

"Noooo. No. I was told you had love charms." The girl was older, like their friend Jennifer, probably fifteen or so. She was pretty in a natural kind of way, but her eyes looked a little red as if she might have been crying.

Ting gave her a troubled glance.

"Not exactly. I mean . . ." Bailey shifted from one foot to the other.

"You *have* to. You don't understand. She's trying to steal him from me, and . . . and . . ." The girl's voice broke. She had a tissue wrapped around the fingers of her left hand, and it looked like it couldn't take too much more damage as she brought it up to her nose.

Ting got out a pink pendant and pressed it into the girl's hand. "It's only luck. Like a reminder. That's all."

"But . . . but . . . they said . . . you said . . ." Her face began to crumple.

Ting squeezed her hand closed around the pendant. "It's just a crystal. But it'll like, absorb your feelings, and when you give it to him, he'll think of you." She smiled hopefully.

"It'll help, then?" Their customer sniffled.

"Couldn't hurt. But in the end, you're the important one. He either likes you or he doesn't. Do you see?"

"Well. All right, then."

Ting patted her hand. "Good luck," she said. A moment of concentration passed over her face, and Bailey knew instantly that she was putting extra into the crystal before it left her hand entirely.

She waited until the girl wandered off, her hands clutched together.

"That was nice of you."

Ting shook her head. "Someday," she answered, "you and I might be like that."

"I hope not!" Bailey stared across the hall in a brief moment of terror. They leaned against each other. There were days when growing up looked like it might be unbearable.

All in all, they sold out early and had time to sit and enjoy some fresh handspun cotton candy before Bailey's mom showed up to get them. She came into the hall in a crisp shirt and blue jean shorts and running shoes, looking ever so much like an adult version of Bailey that Ting was amused. She found them after just a moment of looking over the milling crowd at all the booths.

"There you are!" She waved and trotted over. "How did it go?"

"Fine," answered Ting as Bailey cried out, "Wonderful! They've already asked us back for the Spring Fling."

"Really? That's quite a compliment. Maybe you two have a future as custom jewelers." She checked her watch. "We can just make the last matinee. Ready to go?"

There was a moment of silence in the great hall, as if everyone had stopped talking. Rare, but it happens. And into that moment stumbled their desperate customer followed by a tall, rather ordinary looking boy, a silver chain dangling from his hand. It caught both Ting's and Bailey's attention, and it seemed, everyone else's.

"Caroline Wright, I adore you!"

She put her tissue up to her nose. "What were you doing in his locker? You weren't even supposed to *touch* that!" She cast her glance around, as if searching urgently for someone. Both Ting and Bailey ducked.

"I had to get Brian's books for him. But what does Brian matter? I'm the one whose heart you've captured!" The youth stopped, and pressed his hand to his chest, totally unaware of the attention he was gathering.

"Oh . . . oh . . . go away!" Caroline blew her nose on her tattered tissue. "Now, Franklin. Now!"

He looked at the floor. "As you wish." He began to move away, through the crowd, dejected. Then he thrust his fist into the air, their charm grasped tightly in it. "But I'll not give up!

Not until you see me as the one who cannot stop thinking of you!"

"Right pew," Bailey muttered. "Wrong church."

Caroline let out an annoyed shriek as he turned and left the hall, still crying out, "I adore Caroline Wright!"

Bailey bolted to her feet. "Now," she said firmly, tugging on her mom's arm, "is a really good time to go."

She and Ting beat her out to the parking lot, still looking over their shoulders fearfully for Miss Wright who seemed stuck with Mr. Wrong.

"It'll wear off," Ting repeated several times. "It'll wear off."

Bailey's mother looked at her in concern as they piled into the car. "Are you all right, dear? What will wear off?"

"Calories," answered Bailey firmly for Ting, who seemed in a bit of shock as they buckled their seat belts. "From the cotton candy. Just . . . calories."

"In that case," Bailey's mom said thoughtfully, "we'll get our popcorn unbuttered." She started the car and off they went.

12

CAN'T BEAR
THESE CHANGES

RICH looked at his friend with grudging admiration. "All suited up? Ready to go?"

Stef grunted, his helmet dangling from one hand. His uniform, which his mother had worked very hard on to launder away grass stains from the last game, sparkled, and his shoulders bulked so high with his new pads and gear that his neck nearly disappeared. He shifted from one foot to the other as the locker room cleared and everyone ran out to the field, metal door clanging shut after them. He could hear the dim sound from the bleachers, the roar of students from schools all over the city here for this game. And he was going to be in it! Varsity. Not bad for his second year in middle school. He'd worked hard for this, though, eating right, training, memorizing the playbook, waiting for his third game.

Rich pounded and tugged on his pads a little, making sure they sat exactly right. His red hair stood out under his baseball cap in unruly shocks. "Now," he repeated. "Don't be drinking the red gatorade if it's out there. It gives you headaches, all right? Just head for the water cooler."

"Right." Stef shifted his weight uneasily. "I gotta go, Rich.

My parents are in the stands and everything." He could feel the heat through his buzz cut, even with his helmet off. The backs of his ears felt itchy.

"Okay, okay." His friend stood a moment. Stef was keenly aware that Rich had tried out for football, too. He hadn't even made the lowest team, his body too thin and wiry and a little clumsy. But sharp. Rich could think circles around him. Rich pounded him into place one last time. "Okay!" He turned away and trotted out of the locker room. Stef moved to follow, then stopped, dizzy.

The feeling of something wrong swept him. Everything felt tight. His shoes hurt. Stef stared down and then gave a low groan. Oh, no. Not now. Not *now!* He patted his tight football pants down. Nothing. Nothing at all . . . his crystal was in the locker. Letting out a yell for Rich, he kicked off his athletic shoes and shuffled toward his locker. Hands going thick and clumsy, he managed to paw it open. He grabbed his crystal between his palms and held it tightly, reciting the words Tomaz had taught him, which always seemed to help.

Nothing.

He mumbled the words again, trying to focus. All he could think about was his stomach rumbling. He was hungry!

Stef threw the crystal back into the locker and began to shed his uniform as quickly as he could before it was ruined. His football dreams, his whole life, fell to the floor around him and he lifted his head and let out a bawl. It echoed through the empty locker room. A heavy metal door opened and closed.

"Hey, Stef! Coach is waiting and he's mad."

Stefan-bear dropped to all fours and bawled again, frightened and very unhappy. Rich came around the corner of the lockers and stopped dead in his tracks.

"Oh, boy," he said. Then added, "Oh, bear," unable to think of anything else.

The young bear sat down miserably on his haunches and looked at him, pawing at his nose unhappily.

Bending over, Rich quickly gathered up all the gear and thrust it back into Stef's locker which gaped open, stuff falling out of it as if it had burst. He looked at the crystal on the top shelf. Stef must have been trying to get it. Too late for that now. Too late for anything except to figure out what to do with one overgrown cub. How was he going to sneak Stef-bear out of the area without being seen? He stared at the ceiling in exasperation where the great golden bear of the school's seal stared back.

No. It couldn't be that easy . . . could it?

Rich pivoted on his heel. In the trainer's stall, extra jerseys hung. He grabbed one with a great double zero on the front and tugged it over the bear cub's head. Stef-bear licked him, long pink tongue raspy and harsh. "Cut that out. You've gotta wear this. And mind me. Really, really focus, Stef, okay?"

The bear cub stared at him, nose wrinkling. It pawed at the football jersey.

"Stef! I mean it! Listen to me. This is bad stuff. You want to be thrown in a zoo or something worse? Like a . . . a . . . a lab? So people could poke at you and try to figure out what happens? No way! Now you just focus on me and try to do what I tell you to!"

The bear cub let out a bawl, just like a frightened toddler. Rich sighed and threw his arm around the burly animal's neck.

"I won't let 'em get you. And if they do, I'm going, too. You won't be alone, okay? But I can get us out of this . . . I think. Just keep that jersey on." Rich hugged the bear cub tightly. "And . . . ermmm . . . take a bath sometime soon when this is all done. You stink." His face squinched together at the odor of the furry beast who was clumsily trying to hug him back. He pushed the cub away. "Jeez. That's enough of that."

The metal door clanged open. "Olson! Hawkins! Get out here!" The assistant coach filled the doorway as he bellowed.

Rich put both hands around the bear cub's muzzle, muffling the surprised noise from the animal. It came out like a throaty retch, sounding just awful. He called back. "That's Olson, sir! Just nervous about the game. He's ralphing. I'll have him out when he's done!"

The coach grumbled, then the door slammed shut. Rich let go as Stef-bear pulled his lips back from white teeth and shook his head uncomfortably. He made a bleating sound of protest, curled up, and went to sleep.

"Oh, man." Rich sat down on the bench. Sometimes Stef changed in his sleep. If that happened, they'd both be out of

trouble. But if it didn't . . . muffled shouts from the football
arena drifted to them. Rich sighed and pulled out a worn-out
paperback novel and began to read. He'd wait it out . . . for
now.

After fifty very long minutes, the cub rolled over and sat up,
bawling, pawing at his eyes, and making hungry noises. Rich
groaned and looked at him.

"Don't look at me like that." Rich straightened. "Okay,
here's the plan . . . we go out to the old softball field and—"

The bear reared back on his haunches, both paws waving
frantically.

"Nnnno, no, no, no. Don't worry. You're the mascot, see? If
anyone sees us, which they won't, but just in case." Rich tugged
the football jersey back into place, and pulled Stef's duffel out
of the locker. "I've got your clothes and stuff in here . . . jeez,
Stef, get some clean socks, will ya? Anyway, when you change
back, you're all set. We just duck in the bushes and wait for
you to return. Got that?"

The bear cub mournfully shook his head.

"Don't worry. I'll repeat it later. Follow me." He couldn't be
positive, but he was pretty sure the bear cub was nearsighted
with a real knack for falling into prickly bushes and scratchy
stuff. Luckily, there wasn't too much of that around the school
athletic fields. He tugged on the cub's thick neck, pulling the
shapechanger after him. He grunted as he hauled the animal's
stubborn weight behind him. He stopped and looked the bear
right in the eyes. "This is the only way. Just stay calm. They're
not looking at us, everyone will be looking at the game!"

Stef-bear rolled beady brown eyes, then began to lumber
toward the locker room door. He stopped at the end of the
locker row, and swung his head about, nose sniffing vigorously.
Rich patted his shoulder. "Come on, come on!"

The bear ignored him. He began pawing at one of the
locker doors in determination until the dented locker swung
open. Bawling in satisfaction, Stef-bear reached in and pawed
out a big package of sweet honeybuns. Wrapper and all, he
crunched contentedly.

All Rich could do was watch as the bear ate up the honey
and cinnamon pastries grunting happily and spitting out

shreds of cellophane here and there. He cleaned up the mess
but there was nothing he could do about the sprung locker. It
had been kicked shut many a time, and now had passed the
point of no return. He closed it and taped it with a few inches
of bandaging tape, and began to urge Stef-bear outside with
him again.

Having eaten and with the tantalizing flavor of honey inside rather than outside, the bear cub seemed ever so much
more willing to go along with Rich. He leaned heavily against
Rich's denim legs as they walked around the back of the roaring stadium and the sound of whistles and thuds and heavy
grunts of football battle. Rich put his hand down on his
friend's furry head. Stef was in there, somewhere, sometimes
in charge and sometimes buried under animal instinct. Tomaz
had told them both how to keep Stef in charge as much as possible through his crystal; otherwise he'd be a great danger to
himself and others. He didn't know how much either of them
was in charge right now.

He grabbed one of the cub's round ears. "Stay with me,
now," he said, as they moved into the shadow of their bleachers. A great roar went out as they did, and his friend pressed
hard against his knee. The slanted cement structure over them
rumbled with stomping and noise. "Just a little farther."

They might have made it safely, but Rich forgot two critical
factors. One . . . restrooms. Two . . . small children who had to
use the restroom frequently. Oh . . . and three . . . the restrooms
were under the bleachers.

He froze as a harried woman with a youngster in tow came
at them. "Momma, look. It's a bear in a shirt!"

Without looking, she tugged on his hand, "No, dear, it's
just someone dressed up." Like a freighter on high tide, she
plowed toward them, child in her wake.

"No, it's not! Lookie, lookie! It's real. It's a baby bear!"

"Matthew, of course it's not—" She paused. Her nose wrinkled. She turned even as Rich pulled on the bear cub's ear,
hard, to hurry him past the two. Matthew hung on his mother's hand, his own grubby fingers outstretched and reaching.
"What *is* that smell?" She frowned at Rich and Stef-bear.

Matthew grabbed a handful of fur and pulled it loose as
Rich tried to haul Stef-bear past. The cub let out a bawl of

pain and bolted, nearly knocking both mother and son on their backsides. Rich cried out and lunged after as, head down and paws churning, Stef-bear headed straight for the football arena! Rich skidded after in hot pursuit.

The crowd roared. Stef-bear bawled. As he galloped onto the field, players scattered and referees began to blow their whistles like steam engine trains.

"What the heck is that?"

"How cute! It's got a football shirt on!"

A kid leaned over the bleacher rail, waving his arm, trying to grab at them. "Mommy! I want one!"

"Now, honey . . . that's real. We can buy you a stuffed bear at half time." His mother placidly knotted her hand in his jacket and pulled him back onto the bench next to her.

Stef-bear came to a wary stop, head up and swinging about. Rich stopped, too, and tried to sneak closer. Both coaches turned and stared at Rich.

"Mascot," Rich said.

"Good lord, that's real."

The assistant coach shaded his eyes with his clipboard. "That a guy in a suit? Isn't it?"

"No, sir, it's a real bear. A cub. I can only have him here a little while, then the owners are gonna pick him up. He . . . he's an orphan and they're training him for movies and commercials and stuff." Rich stood uneasily. His friend reared on his haunches, weaving a little, pawing the air, uncertain whether to bolt again or drop to all fours and go to Rich. He held his breath. Both bleachers on both sides were filled completely and he blinked in the sunlight. It suddenly seemed like not such a good idea to have Stefan out here.

The scoreboard turned numbers, and they were behind 13–6.

The crowd roared as the other quarterback fired a long pass. Their coaches groaned, stalking up and down the sideline in frustration. And then, the pass popped out of the receiver's hand as the tackle hit him. The brown ball headed right at Rich and Stef-bear, squibbing across the grass, people diving right and left at it. The bear let out a loud bleating sound and bounded onto the field after the ball.

Darting between players and across the game line, Stef-bear went after the ball as if it were something to eat. Reflecting on it later, Rich decided it did resemble a beehive, a little. Who knew how well bears saw? All he knew was that the bear cub was off and running wild!

He pushed his way through the standing players to see Stef-bear pounce on the rolling football. He shook off two tackles as he took the ball in his jaws and munched. It deflated with a loud pop, but the bear hung on and began a field-long scramble toward the goal posts. Half the players ran from the scampering cub, the other half tried to ward him off.

By the time the whistles stopped blowing, Stef-bear sat happily in the end zone, flattened football hugged to his chest. The jersey was in shreds around him from missed grabs and tackles.

The coach turned around and bellowed at the stunned players, "By George, if the mascot can make a touchdown, so can you!"

Rich caught up with Stef-bear and took the ruined football away from him. It hung limp from his hand as the refs and equipment manager caught up with him. He handed it over, his face warm with the embarrassment of it. The equipment guy just laughed and gave it back. "Maybe he can like chew on it or something."

Coach Dumbowski waved energetically at him. "Get that critter off the field! This isn't a zoo, Hawkins. Where's Olson? I know he's in on this. Hiding in the locker room won't help!"

"He . . . he'll be out in a few, Coach. He really is sick. He . . . ah . . . he ate a bear snack!" Rich held tightly onto the bear cub's ear and it bawled in protest at his pinching fingers.

"A football field is no place for animals," the coach bellowed, although they were scant feet away. He was louder than the referees who'd just announced the touchdown was "no good!" "Get him out of here, and next time, get permission from me before pulling a stunt like that! And find me Olson!"

"Yessir. Thank you, sir!" Rich tugged on Stef-bear, *hard*.

The buzzer rang for half time and the band came marching out. Whatever nerve the bear cub had left broke as tubas and trumpets blared and drums thundered. He raced out of the stadium and Rich, gear bag in hand, took chase again, puffing and muttering.

There was no sign of the creature. Rich slapped his forehead. He cast around and shook his head.

"Oh, man." All he could do now was wander about, hoping his friend would stay hidden if he transformed back. Rich grumbled to himself as he crossed the different athletic fields, heading back to the farthest corner practice field. People would think him some kind of pervert wandering around till he found someone leaning from the bushes, going, "Psssst!"

He took out his own crystal and sat down on the ground, leaning into the sagging backstop of this little used soccer/softball field. Cupping it in his hands, he tried as hard as he could to focus on his friend and the creature he turned into. He didn't know what else he could do. Maybe in the quartz's depth, he could possibly see him or something. Feel him.

Like a magnet, the crystal whipped around in his hands, and he lost his grip. It went sailing over the backstop and into the shrubs. A moment later he heard an aggrieved bear cub grunt; it rolled over into a more irritated human grunt.

"Hey, buddy," Rich said and went to retrieve both. "You made a touchdown! And we've gotta get out of here!"

After long moments, Stefan got hold of himself and emerged, pale and shaking. He sat down and began to pull his clothes out of the gear bag. "Oh, man. Oh, man. My parents are out there, wondering what's going on. What if I turn again?"

"Just keep in control, Stef. Just do it."

Stefan finally stood, clad head to toe in Milford football splendor, but his face looked as if he could throw up any second, just as Rich had been telling the coach he'd been doing. "I can't do it."

"It's your choice." Rich listened. "Sounds like half time is over." He crossed his arms over his chest. "I'm just a trainer, but I think I'm gonna go join the team for the second half. Maybe I can be of some help or something." He picked up his gear bag.

"You can't just leave me here."

"Sure I can. Look, Stef, you wanted to be on this team. You gotta know there's gonna be moments when you turn, and you've gotta learn how to handle them, especially if there's something you want. Dumbowski is looking for you, and you're gonna blow it, big time, if you don't show. Not to mention your parents." Rich turned and started to walk back.

"Rich!"

Stefan's voice sounded high and really frightened. Rich turned back around slowly.

"You'll keep an eye on me?"

"You know it. You just keep focused. I've got your crystal here in my bag. Anytime you're on the sidelines, come by and hold it for a few."

Stef rolled his eyes, then gave an agreeing grunt and fell into step with him.

The coaches were standing by the sidelines and Dumbowski glared at Stef. "Where have you been?"

"Sick, sir."

"You look white as a sheet. You up to this?"

Stef gripped his helmet tightly, then pulled it on, to hide the paleness of his fear. "Yessir!"

Coach shook his head, stepping back. "I want no more antics like that last one. Any more and you're cut, got it? No wild animals, no getting sick on game day."

"Yessir," the two echoed.

"All right, then. Get in there." Coach pointed his pencil at the bench. "Next play, you're in the rotation. Rich, I've got one ankle somewhere needs taping. Find him and take care of it." Both nodded.

"Good." Dumbowski smiled slightly. "Only thing worse than a sick football player is a disappointed parent." He tilted his head and looked up into the stands, where Rich saw Stefan's parents stand up and bounce up and down, screaming, as he stepped onto the field's edge and sat on the players' bench.

Rich let out a sound of relief before turning away. Like a first down, they'd missed catastrophe by a bear's breadth.

13

SPOOKY OLD HOUSES

MCINTIRE came to Sam's to pick him up after lunch, which had not been planned, but the Dozer had an appointment that drove him past the neighborhood, so Jason rode with him. He liked driving with the Dozer in his business truck. It rode higher than other cars on the road, and it had a kind of solid comfort about it. It didn't matter if he was sweaty and dirty from practice either, as long as he didn't eat or spill something in the cab. Conversation with McIntire was at a minimum except for every now and then when a development he'd built got pointed out, or interesting and helpful tidbits of advice would be offered. Sometimes the advice could be deadly dull, but often it would be something interesting or offbeat. Today McIntire was quiet, and that meant he had a lot on his mind.

Jason had a lot on his mind, too. What was the Curse of Arkady and had it infected his crystal, rendering it nearly useless? If it had, would his crystal ever regain its power, or would he have to search and bond a new one? And if a curse was not the reason his crystal had not protected him in the park . . . what was?

What was it that could make him fail so terribly at something that had become as natural to him as drawing breath?

Was this how Henry Squibb had felt? Would it stay? But he wasn't empty, he could feel it inside him, filling him. He just couldn't rely on it. It was like not being able to trust himself.

Jason shivered slightly, and forced his thoughts to other things, such as their destination.

"Where are we going?"

"Place up on the bluffs. An estate, actually. I may be doing some work there."

Jason thought he knew where, remembering the talk from a few weeks ago and a few mutterings recently. "The McHenry house?"

"Mmmm," answered the Dozer. "Looks like it. Sudden death in the family leaves it available to sell. There's probate and business for them to deal with, but they want me to look at it in advance." His big hands tightened on the steering wheel till the knuckles went white, and then he forced his hands to relax. Jason decided that silence might be the way to go, so he looked out the window and enjoyed the drive.

And it was a bit of a drive, past the boundaries of town, off the main freeway onto a side road that wound into the bluffs overlooking the ocean. A little two-lane blacktop took them along a hidden coast. The homes built among the eucalyptus and California oaks were scattered, all custom, with acres between them. He wondered what kind of development someone wanted to build here. Homes? Condos? Apartments? A center of some kind? They'd gone miles without passing a grocery store or fast food stand. He rather liked that, though. This was country, and open, and although the rains hadn't come yet and it was dry, it was pretty. He liked it like this. He got the feeling the Dozer did, too. Some places, he told Jason once, need more buildings. Others don't. Men ought to be smart enough to know the difference.

They took a corner and a sparkling cove dominated by a wide, sweeping bluff came into view. The water drew his eyes naturally, the tide going out in curls of white foam, the wide Pacific beyond pulling it back into its vast steely blue depths. There was a nice spill of beach, looking private and untouched. Then Jason tilted his head to look up the bluff, and his heart nearly stopped.

The stuff of nightmares, he thought, looking at the dark,

brooding house. *His* nightmares. His blood went cold and
stayed that way, as his hand froze on the edge of the car window. His senses whirled about him as he looked up at what
could only be described as some sort of fortress, gated and
overlooking the bay like some gargoyle of an estate. He could
almost see the power tumbling about it, chaotic and wild, as if
the building were caught in its own storm of mana, and it hurt
to look at it.

"Wha–what is this place?"

"This is the McHenry estate."

He'd known it, somehow. Maybe it was the telltale fact that
the road seemed to lead right inside the coal-black gates, or
the fact that McIntire was driving right up the hillside toward
it, or even just the fact that he was here, now, and the fortress
of his nightmares yawned in front of him. He gripped the door
handle tightly. A small sound escaped his clenched lips.

"It's something, isn't it? I don't agree with his taste, and it
doesn't look like any castle I've ever seen, but word is, it was
taken from a famous old fortress in Wales. They also say he
had every board and stone shipped over to build it. Back in
the day when Huntington and other bankers and railroad men
were building their homes near Los Angeles, McHenry was
building his here. Been here over a hundred years now, and
someone wants to tear it down."

"Will they? Will you?"

"I don't know the answers, Jason. Yet. Want to come in with
me or sit and wait?"

He wanted to sit. He never wanted to set foot on the paved
driveway, but he knew he should. He should see the difference
between reality and his nightmare. The road gate, for one, was
already vastly different. No dragonhead lock, no quest to pass
this far, not even a security buzzer to press so that it might
open. It hung open as though locking it were out of the question, yet as they drove through, pain battered his skull for a
moment. His head snapped back in surprise at the sharpness
of it. Jason sank down in the seat, blinking, his ears ringing.

Gatekeeper. Of all the thoughts that used to run through
his mind when considering Magick and all its uses, that had
never been one. Yet it had been he who had found the gateway between Camp Ravenwyng and an alternate domain,

shaky though the passage might be. Now Gavan Rainwater and all the elders were working their Talents to try and make both planes steady, with an open doorway between them, so that the camp could be a sanctuary for those with Talent the real world might exploit or condemn. Efforts had not yet been successful. Jason was the only Magicker who could reliably enter the valley he'd found beyond the old rusted back gate of the summer camp. Other tries sometimes brought success, other times left Gavan or Tomaz wandering around in a blind canyon for hours, going in circles.

He was the Gatekeeper, like it or not.

He put one hand to his temple as McIntire eased his vehicle into the sweeping, circular driveway of the McHenry estate. His head felt as though it could throb hard enough to burst, and then, suddenly, all was still. He sat up on the truck seat. McIntire had parked and turned the engine off without Jason even noticing. He looked back and saw the gate swinging slightly in the wind. It wasn't a Gate, not by any means. More like a two by four to slam someone in the head with for trespassing through the real Gate.

McIntire seemed unaware of Jason's reaction. He got out and looked over an older white Mercedes already sitting in the driveway, then glanced over his shoulder at Jason.

"Getting out? This old place might be fun to look at."

He slid out gingerly as if the gate might try to bludgeon him again, but nothing happened. He could smell the sea salt spray from below, and hear the cry of gulls as they wheeled and hung in the air over the gulf for long moments of time, then plunged down to the ocean to dip and skim. He could almost feel the dizzying drop in his own gut as they fell, but they had outspread wings to catch them. Jason ran a few steps to keep up with McIntire's long stride, and they both reached the carved double front doors at the same time. Jason wasn't surprised to see that a great, bronze door knocker with a grotesquely twisted gargoyle face hung in the center of the main door.

Jason nearly winced as the Dozer grabbed the ring and thumped it, hard, three times. The noise reverberated inside the building as if he'd struck an immense Chinese gong. For a moment, he thought he caught the huge, lumpy nose of the gargoyle twitching in time with the brazen echo. The estate seemed to groan in answer, but his stepfather apparently noted none of the fuss as he released the door knocker and shifted his weight, waiting impatiently. They heard footsteps long before the door actually opened, and as it did, Jason leaned with it, to peer inside.

A huge cavernous entryway met his gaze. No wonder everything echoed. It looked like a massive concert hall, with room to hold his school's marching band. Doors at the far end stood open, leading to the north, west, and south. The individual who held the entry door, however, looked like a butler, formal suit, cravat, vest, and all, and wings of graying hair combed back into dark full hair, a strong Roman nose, and disdainful eyes as he gazed down at them.

"May I help you?"

"I am William McIntire, the builder. I have an appointment."

"Ah. Yes." The butler looked down at Jason. "Your apprentice?" One eyebrow rose in disapproval at Jason's attire and state of appearance.

"My son. He'll be fine." McIntire managed to look a bit insulted, as if the butler insinuated that Jason would be difficult to tolerate.

"Follow me, then," the tall man said quietly. He strode off, with a slight lean to his left, one shoulder a tiny bit higher than the other, as though he walked into a strong wind and had to forge his way through it. He wore a ankle boots and the heels drummed solidly on the gleaming wooden floor as he trod it, the planks creaked as they all crossed over it. For a moment, Jason stared downward, as if he could discern the hollow levels below, just waiting for the boards to give way and open up, just as in his nightmares, though these boards had not been dry-rotted by time and neglect.

Even the Dozer glanced down once as if pondering what lay under the flooring. That reassured Jason only in that it wasn't his imagination, but made him worry more about the soundness of the structure. The complaints of the boards sounded much louder under McIntire's heavier footfalls. Only the butler seemed not to notice or care as he led the way through the northern door at the foyer's far end.

While the entry had been somewhat recognizable from his dreams of the place, nothing beyond the northern door was. Understandable, as he usually fell through into the catacombs below long before getting very far in his exploration. Jason looked about warily. It was, in many ways, a very imposing fortress or castle, even in these times. It also seemed nearly empty, what furniture there was pushed to the walls, with wooden crates lying about, either nearly filled or already hammered shut and stenciled. He tried to read the wording as they were hurried past, but it seemed to be in a language other than English or something equally baffling.

McIntire let out some words of appreciation as they were led into a great library, its built-in shelves still full of books and other wonders, lined by empty crates on the floor, the wood paneling gleaming with polish and care and beauty. A great oxblood leather sofa lined one half wall, and a sprawling desk of golden oak held court in the center of the room. Three gentlemen were seated at it, two behind and one in front. His vision blurred as a fraction of the power that had hammered at him earlier, struck at him now. For a few moments, he could hardly see or stay on his feet.

Jason scrubbed at his eyes. One of the men got to his feet smoothly and left through a door in the side paneling, but not before Jason caught a blurred and fleeting glimpse of his face. He stumbled over an edge of fringed Persian carpet lining the floor and when he looked up, the man had completely disappeared from sight.

Jason righted himself quietly, and stood by McIntire in near shock. It looked like . . . but surely couldn't have been . . . the man who had attacked him in the park that morning.

14

COINKYDINKS

HE wanted to hide behind McIntire's burly frame, but he knew he couldn't. It wouldn't help any, and he'd just be that much more conspicuous. All the same, it was trouble just being here. He didn't believe in coincidences anymore. The Hand was behind this, somehow, and drawing his family in. Magick forbidden or not, he would do what he had to.

From beside McIntire's elbow, Jason watched the procedures warily.

"This is a fine old home," William McIntire said, as he leaned forward and offered one of his great hands to shake.

"It is a liability on the current market, but I agree it was made well years ago. Upkeep, however . . ." The man leaning forward to connect with McIntire was tall and thin, with graying red hair and a small sprinkling of freckles over his face. He was older but not old, slender, and held more power in his voice than in his bones. He shook swiftly and straightened, tapping a portfolio stuffed with papers that lay on the desk.

"I understand you're the one to do the work."

"I am, if it's the project I've been sent permits and drawings on. It's an ambitious project and one I think would utilize many efforts. I take it you are spearheading the holding company, and the sale on this place has gone through?"

"Yes, and nearly. We're trying to get a head start, so if we need any loans or funding, we can point out our many strengths. Having you as head of construction would certainly be an asset."

McIntire smiled only a little. He wasn't easily flattered, Jason knew. In fact, he tended to distrust flattery, preferring to earn praise after a job was done, not before it. Jason moved a little, trying to get comfortable, his legs slightly stiff after the morning's runs, and was instantly sorry as attention shifted abruptly to him.

"Brought your son along?"

"Yes, but he knows this is business. He'll keep quiet and not repeat anything."

"A good lad, then." The redheaded man studied Jason a moment, then lost interest as Jason did his best not to look noticeable.

"What do you think, McIntire? Is this a project you'd be interested in? Think you might like to come on board?"

McIntire chuckled. The deep noise reverbrated throughout his hefty frame. "We'd need to talk time, crew, and salary, of course." He looked around. "I'd hate to tear down a place like this. Maybe you could consider making it your anchor. Break it into artists' lofts upstairs and a restaurant and a few nice shops or offices down here. I know an interior decorator that would give her eyeteeth to have this room as her studio."

The other looked about, too, as if seeing the room for the first time. McIntire's finger jabbed the air. "Those are good woods, some excellent carpentry in those bookcases, the paneling."

"Yesss . . ." the other answered slowly. "We hadn't considered it really. An anchor for the development, you say?"

"A bit of class. Never hurts."

"True. We've plenty of grounds left to do what we want. Hmmm. This place is immense, you know. A good seventy-five acres."

"I think that leaves you room to be generous here. Consider it. Despite my reputation, I hate destroying to develop. This is a solid, good building with ambience and craftsmanship, and it would be a shame to pull it down."

"We have our reasons, but I'll put your ideas out. May I tell them you're interested?"

"Work up an offer to put on the table, and we'll talk again."

"Done, then." The red-haired man smiled faintly, and picked up his portfolio. "I've got a flight out, but I'll be back soon and perhaps we can do lunch then. I promise I'll have an offer to put on the table that will make it worth your while."

"Do that." They shook hands firmly and when McIntire let go, stepping back and dropping his hand to his stepson's shoulder, Jason thought he felt a creepy-crawly tingle. It had to be his imagination. Had to be.

"Can you find your way out or do I need to . . ."

"We're fine," McIntire rumbled. He turned Jason about and guided him out the library door and back down the way they'd come in. He did not say a word till they were buckled into the truck and easing out the entry gates. Then he let out a low, heavy sigh. "I don't know if it's the place or the people," he said, "but it makes me uneasy."

Jason gave a nervous laugh. "Do you really think anyone would want to have shops or stuff in there?"

"Not sure, really. The McHenry place has some historical significance, and it really shouldn't be leveled, but as far as going to a restaurant in there or anything else, I dunno. Made the hair on the back of my neck stick up."

"Me, too!" Jason put a hand back there and scratched a moment.

The Dozer laughed at him. He patted his shoulder again. "Nice thing about my job right now is that I don't have to work with people who make me feel like that! He could put all the money in the world under my nose, and I could say no if I wanted to." McIntire looked in his rearview mirror as they drove down the winding roads and could smell the ocean. "If I wanted to," he repeated slowly.

"But you're not sure yet."

"No. Not quite yet. If that bluff is developed, it ought to be done . . . how can I say it? Gently? Without disturbing the area around it, and without putting a great stucco eyesore on the face of the earth. It would be a challenge." McIntire trailed off, lost in thought. He shook himself. "Need to get you home. Showered. Homework this weekend, no doubt, and other stuff, right?"

"Right." Jason settled into the seat as the truck bumped softly over the country lane roadworks. McIntire guided the truck off a side road, and Jason realized they were leaving by a different route. They descended the cliffs and reached town in less than half the time by not following the shore but cutting straight through the bluffs.

His stepfather let out a soft sigh as they drove into town. "That's the way to cut the road," he said, as he turned down their block.

"It's much faster and shorter."

"That it is, and even though it's through the foothills, in the long run, the environmental impact on the land and the neighbors will be better. We can put in two lanes either way, do a bit of terraforming, and it'll actually be better for the watershed and wildfire danger." Then McIntire smiled at him. "Always business."

For once, Jason felt like he understood his stepfather completely. He had business at home, Magicker business.

"Jason?" Dr. Patel's soft voice sounded more in his forehead than his ears, as he gripped his crystal. "May I come in?"

He sent through a "yes," and in a moment, her petite, sari-wrapped form stepped out of nothingness and into his attic bedroom. She smiled as she removed a damp bath towel from a corner of his bed and sat down. "Trouble, you said?"

He plopped down in his desk chair facing her. His hair was still wet from his shower, and his clothes smelled fresh from the dryer. The red dot on her forehead looked like a small jewel. "Big trouble. I was chased by wolfjackals this morning."

"What? Here in your town? Tell me everything." She folded her hands in her lap, frowning, and prepared to listen. He spilled out everything he could remember, and with a gentle question or two, thought of even more, including the McHenry house and the fact his crystal had failed in either providing a shield or awakening the beacon.

"That is not good," she said quietly when he'd finished. "Our only hope in keeping you safe is that the beacon works. It did in trials. I cannot understand it, but Gavan and Tomaz need to be informed immediately. I'll handle that. I am pleased to see your wits kept you safe." She paused, tucking a strand of dark brown hair behind her ear. "Jason, may I see your hand again?"

"Well, um . . . sure." He put his left hand out and she took it in both of hers, leaning over it and peering closely at the scar along the back of it.

"I have long wondered," Dr. Patel said, "if there was a tooth splinter or something lodged beneath that marked you. It remains sore, though it appears healed, and you've told me it twinges from time to time." She looked up, into his worried expression. "Does it pull on you?"

"Pull?"

"Do you sometimes feel as if you want to do something you shouldn't do? Or . . ."

"Come over to the dark side?" he started to crack, and then stopped. Suddenly, it wasn't all that funny. He'd wondered, too, if the wolfjackal had really marked him. It said it had, but he'd decided that the beast had only been trying to psych him out.

"Yes," she answered.

He shook his head vigorously.

"Good. Well, then, I'll leave you to . . ." Her gaze swept his bedroom, and she smiled. "Clean your bedroom and work on homework?"

He blushed. The doctor nodded, still smiling. "I'll meet with Gavan and Tomaz as soon as possible. This is serious business for us." She gave him a quick hug before standing, putting a hand to her pendant, and then disappearing with a slight waver and whoosh, leaving behind only a faint aroma of sandalwood, her favorite perfume.

Jason rubbed his hand. Her probing fingers had set off a dull throb, as though the scar were freshly bruised. Again. He sighed. He hadn't told her about the Magicker at the McHenry house or any of that, and wondered if that had been a good or bad thing. But he didn't want to seem a coward or anything, and he wasn't sure how he felt about it. Had he seen the Magicker? He wasn't sure. And if he was wrong, it could bring even more trouble, which he certainly didn't need.

15

THE GAME'S AFOOT

HE checked his watch. Dinner was a good hour off, even
if his stomach was rumbling in protest. He grabbed some
emergency rations from his desk drawer (granola bar) and sat
down, munching happily, careful to eat nowhere near his keyboard. Even as he watched the screen, mail came up and he
dusted his hands off quickly so he could see who it might be.

It came from HobbitHenry, and for a second, he had no
idea who that could possibly be. Then he cried, "Henry
Squibb!" and pounced on the mail to open it. And, yes, it was
from Henry, dear owl-faced Henry with his unruly hair and
innocent eyes, and he could practically hear the voice leaping
out at him through the words.

**Dear Jason! How are you? Have any more wicked popcorn
fights? My sleeping bag still explodes every now and then in
the storage part of my closet. I can't seem to keep it tied tightly
enough. I saw Bailey and Ting, and they gave me your new
computer address. Welcome to the 21st century! I heard you
and Trent play D & D. Always wanted to try that. Well, I've
gotta babysit while Mom goes grocery shopping. C U Later!**

Jason sat back in his chair, smiling. Henry sounded nearly
like his old self, as far as Jason could tell, except that he'd no
memories of his brief time as a Magicker during their summer

together. The Henry who'd been led off after drinking the Draft of Forgetfulness had been a quiet, humble boy embarrassed at having caused trouble and being sent home early. It had broken Jason's heart to see him like that even though he knew it was necessary and Eleanora had assured him that it wouldn't hurt Henry in the long run.

He'd have to remember to tell Eleanora that Henry was back to his talkative, if bumbling self. Then he fired off a letter to Trent, in hopes that Trent would agree to let Henry into a D & D session. Not only did he want to stay close friends with Henry, but Jason had some small hope that Jonnard Albrite had not permanently damaged Henry by stealing his powers. Trent didn't come up as being on-line, and Jason squirmed in his desk chair with disappointment.

In the meantime, he opened up other e-mail that was waiting for him, and began to frown, reading in some alarm, and some amusement. Leave it to Bailey and Ting to set the rummage sale on its ear, but what had happened to Stefan, through Rich's account, could only be bad.

And, Rich added at the bottom of his mail,

It's all I can do to convince Stef not to join a circus! I don't blame him, he's afraid of being caught and taken apart to see what makes him tick.

Jason wrote back a quick, encouraging letter that the Magickers were aware of the mishaps and increased danger, and included his own stalking, and warned everyone to take care and practice their shielding. He paused as he wrote that. Even though his had failed momentarily, he had to have faith in it. Had to! His crystal was bonded to him, and as much a part of him as . . . well . . . a hand or a foot. To think of having to give it up and get another sent chills down the back of his neck.

His stomach rumbled again, reminding him that one small, crumbly sweet granola bar was hardly a whole dinner. Like it or not, he was going to have to raid the kitchen. Maybe Joanna would let him have an apple or something. He was starving!

Jason pushed away from his computer and dropped the trapdoor to his room in a hurry. No one answered his entry into the kitchen, although the oven was on and the timer ticking away. He grabbed a big shiny Red Delicious apple and bit down into it, savoring the sweet juices as he heard voices and trotted toward them in the living room. At the last possible second, he recognized oily tones and tried to swerve away, but Joanna's sharp ears heard him in the hallway.

"Jason! Come in, come in." He was backing out, but her voice hooked him and reeled him in like a gaping fish, all the way into the living room where she sat. McIntire ruled the great armchair, and the school psychologist perched at one end of the couch and smiled at him.

Of all the places in all the world, Statler had to find his way into Jason's living room.

He stopped dead in his tracks to gather his wits.

"Wasn't it nice of your counselor to stop by and visit with us?" Joanna smiled brightly at him. Statler had evidently interrupted her cooking, for she still wore her apron appliqued with big yellow sunflowers and small blue butterflies.

Jason wondered who on Earth would want to claim Statler? He looked as pasty white as ever and, even though he'd cleaned up and changed into Dockers and a soft gray shirt, he still looked unwholesome somehow. "Umm . . . well, yes. He's not exactly mine, though. I mean, he's there for the whole school, you know?"

"Ah, but, Jason. As you know well, my concern at the school is the welfare of youngsters like you who need help coping with the school yard bully. The bully is an age-old problem and not likely to go away, so we've decided to work at the other end . . . with his victims."

Joanna blinked, and her careful air of cheerfulness fell away. "Jason?" She looked at him. "Are you having trouble at school that I don't know about?"

He shifted uneasily. "Not really."

McIntire leaned his bulk back onto the armchair cushions, and the entire piece of furniture groaned and swayed a bit as he did so. "You'd know who to come to if you did, right?"

"Yes, sir."

"Actually," Statler Finch said, and he leaned forward, putting his hands on his knees, looking into Joanna McIntire's face. "Jason's already had a bit of trouble on a regular basis, and I've been asked to intervene by the vice principal. You see, it's the school of thought among administrators now, as a

result of several tragedies around the country, that it's the bullied ones who need watching, and skill coaching, or they . . ."
He paused. He turned one hand over and gestured through
the air. "Or they snap."

The only snap he felt like would have done a wolfjackal
justice. Jason clenched his jaws in case he felt himself slip.

"Oh, Jason," cried Joanna in dismay, as if she had failed him
in some fatal way. She buried one hand in her apron pocket
and knotted it.

"It's nothing, Mom, really. It happens to everyone once in
a while." He shrugged.

"Denial," murmured Statler, his dark eyes glistening as if
in sympathy.

"I can deal with it."

"I've failed you."

He kept from rolling his eyes at Joanna. "I'm fine. I can
handle it!"

"Self-delusion." The counselor's eyes brimmed.

"Look. If the vice principal who is supposed to be the enforcer can't handle him, I can," said Jason firmly, then promptly
regretted it as Statler cried out, "Shifting of blame!"

He stifled a groan away from Joanna who winced with every
proclamation of his mental instability from Statler, and looked
desperately at McIntire. His stepfather rumbled, "I think we
can work this out fairly quickly, Statler. Jason's a good lad, if
quiet. How can we help and what do you suggest we do?"

A look of triumph flashed across Statler's face, one which
he quickly squelched. "I think it would do him a lot of good
to work with me once a week, after school, say, for an hour or
two, and then monthly meetings with all of us."

Joanna seemed to relax a bit. "Oh, I think we can arrange
that!"

"Mom . . ."

McIntire frowned. "I might not always be able to make a
monthly meeting. Business is booming right now, and it looks
like I might have another development coming up. Unless
it would be all right to just meet with one parent now and
then?"

"The world is full of single parents, and they do their job
wonderfully," gushed Statler. "I'm sure we can do without

your presence now and then, just as long as we have your support in the program I'm going to lay out for Jason."

"Mom . . ." he tried again, shifting, but her attention was avidly fixed on Statler. Did mice stare at a snake before they were gobbled?

"What about my daughter? Should she be part of the family meetings?"

"She's Jason's . . . half sister?"

"Step."

"Yes. By all means . . ." Statler's eyebrows waggled in furious thought patterns before he said happily, "Yes, we can work on a number of difficulties in Jason's life. I recommend we bring her in on the second family meeting."

Joanna exhaled happily. "Oh, good."

"Mom!"

Joanna looked at him, surprised. "Yes, Jason?"

"Mom, I have soccer after school, every day, until the season ends. I can't miss practices for counseling. They'll throw me off the team for missing."

Her hand moved inside the apron pocket, clutching and unclutching whatever it was she had hidden in there. A tissue or handkerchief, no doubt. "I think," she commented slowly, "that we need to look at the whole picture, and that is dealing with your problems now. There will always be soccer later."

"But I'm on the first team *now.*" He stared incredulously. How could this be happening to him? "Next year is . . . well, it's next year! I worked hard for this. And you promised after last summer . . ." His voice trailed away. He couldn't complain too much about missing soccer camp last summer, and discovering he was a Magicker instead. Still . . . losing soccer now? How unfair could things get!

McIntire cleared his throat, sounding like approaching thunder. "I'll have a talk with your coach. Maybe something can be arranged. It's for your own good, son." He stood. "I'll make sure it's arranged. Sports and learning should be balanced, and you're right, you worked hard for this. I'll do what I can to make sure you're kept on the team. But you have to promise to work with Mr. Statler here."

A thin smile touched the counselor's lips.

That sounded like a deal, and one which he really did not

want to make. He looked from McIntire to Joanna and back to McIntire. "All right," he agreed reluctantly. The last thing he wanted was Statler poking around in his brain! He'd have to make the counselor think he'd cured him, and quickly.

If he couldn't, he was cursed. Absolutely cursed, and he was beginning to think it was no coincidence.

16

STRANGE THING IN THE NIGHT

T RENT scratched his temple for a moment. *You enter the room,* he typed, *and find ... what? What do we find? Whose perception is highest? This would be a very bad room to get killed in.*

There was a tiny lag while both Henry and Jason received and pondered his thoughts. The dungeon game room stayed on pause, tiny avatars showing the positions of their characters at the threshold of the area. Various intriguing items appeared to be awaiting them, just like chessmen on a chessboard. They could be idle but a moment or two, then they would draw monsters and the room, sought as sanctuary, would no longer be safe. Trent had his own ideas as to how they should proceed, but this was a committee decision, and so he waited to throw his suggestions out until the others spoke up.

He sat back in his chair, folding his hands behind his head, and stared for a moment at his *Lord of the Rings* wall calendar. The realization of how close it was to Halloween struck him. The days had been flying by, so busy was he in school and in trying to figure out the Magicker lore to see if there was any way, any way at all, he could catch up. If it wasn't in the blood, maybe it was in a book. Something, somewhere. So far, he hadn't found one. But then, he was the only one who hadn't been hit with the Curse yet either. Maybe there were some advantages to not being a novice magician.

The thought of not having any Talent at all ran through him like a deep wound, though. Seeing the others with their crystals doing wondrous things and hoping to learn more . . . well, it hurt. Keeping up the bluff that he was doing what they were, only they were too busy doing their own thing to catch him, or his crystal was drained, or he was joined to Jason and Jason was handling it . . . well, it was an ugly pack of lies and likely to get much, much uglier. And, sooner or later, one of the elders was bound to notice it, too. He didn't know how they hadn't, so far. Henry's misfortunes had been his good luck, he supposed. Even when a Magicker, Henry's Talent had been wild and unpredictable.

Trent grinned as he remembered how they'd been taught to fill their crystals with light, so they could act as lanterns, and Henry's had gone up in a spout of flame. For a few days after, he'd handled his focus with a big oven mitt covering his burned hand! With Henry pulling stunts like that . . . his perpetually exploding down sleeping bag and out-of-control crystal . . . who'd notice Trent?

Only Jason knew his secret and that he'd revealed only when they'd had to face down a storm of uncontrolled magical power called mana, and the fiercesome beasts of the Dark Hand as well as the dark Magickers themselves. And Jason never demanded a thing of him. Not that he tell the truth or resign or anything else. To Jason, Trent was as much a Magicker as anyone else.

If only.

Message windows began to pop up. Jason wanted to investigate the perimeter of the room cautiously. But Henry said, and Trent read it a second time to make sure . . . he wanted to use the natural thieving ability of his halfling character to scan the room and detect any traps, mechanical or magical, awaiting them. Interesting. Very interesting that in the D & D campaign they'd begun, Henry relied more and more on magical type abilities, almost as if his subconscious mind was nagging at his conscious mind to remember. Jason claimed he could see more and more signs of it; Trent had been more naturally skeptical. This game, though. Henry had been quick to choose a character with natural abilities and an affinity to magic, if perhaps a bit chaotic . . . well, maybe Jason was right.

Jason quickly sided with the other two after Trent presented the option to him, and they proceeded but not before Henry's clever character tripped an immense trap by releasing a djinn from a clay jar . . . but it all turned to the good as the djinn granted each of them a wish to be used in the future. All too soon their gaming time came to a halt and they had to stop, saving their progress in this labyrinth of adventure. Henry left after a quick, excited note, saying he had to help take care of his little sister before bedtime, but Jason lingered to talk with Trent a bit.

I think you're right. Looks like Henry's recovering some of his memory and some of his abilities!

Jason fired right back at him eagerly. **I know. This means a lot of things change. One . . . the Hand could go after Henry again, without his even knowing it, to drain those powers again. So he's gotta be protected till the elders decide if he can or should be taught again. And two . . . any of us can be drained over and over for the use of the Hand. That can't be good.**

Trent rocked back in his chair. Shades of the *Matrix!* Being used over and over to fuel the bad guys? He didn't like the sound of that at all. And it was clear that Jason had been considering all the ramifications for a few days.

He helped Jason mull over the problem of the school counselor, too. Both decided that it was best not to do anything, make it look like Jason was cooperating completely, and try to make the school officials think so, too, until Finch and the vice principal decided their idea had either 1) worked or 2) was worthless. They talked a minute or two longer about what to do, then his father knocked softly on the door, reminding him it was bedtime. Obediently, he said good night to Jason and signed off. As he was crawling under his blankets, the door swung open a crack, his father leaning in.

"Everything all right?"

"Everything is fine!" Trent punched his pillow and then

pulled his comforter up. His dad half smiled. He missed the days when his father gave his famous ear-to-ear big grins, but those times were gone. They'd left when his mother died, and he wondered if they would ever come back. He knew *he* didn't feel much like it except for those rare moments when Bailey cracked him up or Jason made him feel good about having friends and hanging out again.

His dad stepped in, which he rarely did, and tucked the comforter around him tighter. "Getting on toward winter," his father said. "And while there aren't winters here like I had back home as a kid, you still need to keep warm." He paused, his hand on Trent's head a moment. Then, without another word, he turned and left.

The bedroom door stayed open the barest of a slant, golden light from the living room raying in from the lamps there until his father turned those out, too, as he went to his bedroom. Trent waited a moment or two, then snuggled in deeper and felt himself drop off to sleep.

Jason found himself back at the mansion. Only this time, as moonlight silvered across cold and crackling sand, and he approached it with all the wariness he could, Jason knew it was the McHenry house. Naming it didn't make it feel any safer or nicer than it had before. His skin crawled. Yet he could not keep himself from entering the gate and beginning the walk across the curved driveway to the massive wooden doors. He was saved, at least, from entry through the old family cemetery with its unexpected potholes as rotting caskets and catacombed grounds gave way at the slightest step!

He put his palm upon the burnished golden oak door. The wood felt warm, almost hot to his touch, yet it continued to send shivers down his back. He didn't want to go through that door, but he had to. He was drawn as if he were a piece of metal and a powerful magnet lay beyond the door, but also his own curiosity and need to know drove him along. With hands that grew colder by the minute, he finally moved to the great door latch and lifted it. The doors swung inward with a great creaking, not of rusting hinges, but of heavy weighted wood, as if a massive barrier gave way. The knowledge and sound sent chills down his back. The McHenry house didn't have a latch, it had a knob like any other door he usually used . . . and it had opened out.

He had already known he was dreaming. But not why. He never knew why he dreamed what he did . . . if he was reliving the past or anticipating a future. Jason only knew that there were these moments in his dreams he had to endure. All he could do was watch, and remember, and hope to learn something later.

He pushed the heavy doors open with a grunt. A draft of air blasted him in the face, nearly gusting him out of the threshold . . . hot, smoldering air that stung his eyes and immediately dried his nostrils and lips. He coughed and put his hand up to shade his face.

Before he could see anything or take another step, from the dull and red glowing interior of the darkened hall, a furred shape growled and leaped at him. Jason fell back and scrambled out from under the wolfjackal, his free hand instantly wrapped around his crystal.

His shield flared to surround him, and the beast tumbled away, snarling, ivory fangs clashing angrily at empty air. Jason kicked out, catching its sleek wolfish body and sending it skidding back into the McHenry house. He slammed the doors after it.

He'd enter when he was ready, and prepared, and not before.

Jason woke, panting and sweating lightly in spite of the cooler night air, and he lay for a while until his heart stopped drumming so loudly and he thought he could sleep without wolfjackals prowling his dreams.

Bailey woke to the sound of the teakettle whistling from the kitchen. For a moment she thought of FireAnn, with her fire-red, naturally curly hair pulled back into a kerchief, her voice with a mild Irish lilt, fixing cuppas for those who wanted it while she got busy sorting herbs and recipes for the day's cooking. But it wasn't FireAnn. It was her mom, and Bailey grinned. Even better!

She threw herself out of bed, waking up Lacey who chittered sleepily from her cage before diving back into a nest of colorful bits of tissue. Bailey grabbed her robe before popping into the kitchen. Sure enough, her mom had a big china pot waiting to brew tea, and a plate of sweet rolls ready to be warmed in the microwave.

"Wow. Party?"

"Mmmmm," her mother said, not quite looking at her as she picked up the kettle from the stove and filled the teapot. Almost instantly, the smell of jasmine and oolong tea filled the kitchen as steam issued from the neck of the china pot. It had to steep for a few minutes to really taste good, so her mom straddled the kitchen stool across from the counter. She looked at Bailey. "Hon. We need to talk."

The good mood dropped from her. Bailey hadn't heard her mom sound like that since . . . well, since the divorce. As it hadn't been easy news then, she didn't think it would be anything easy now!

Her mom fixed her mug of tea with a squeeze of lemon and a heaping teaspoon of sugar just like Bailey liked it, before sliding it over. Bailey immediately wrapped her suddenly cold hands around it, and waited.

Her mom sat down, and tried to smile. "I talked to Ting's mother early this morning," she said.

Bailey's throat got very tight. "What's wrong with Ting?" The words barely squeaked out.

"Nothing, hon!" Her mom reached over, and patted her hand. "But it's not good news. Her grandmother is very ill right now, and Jiao is going up to San Francisco to be with her for the next few months while she undergoes chemo and radiation therapy, and she's taking Ting with her. Ting will be going to school up there."

"Wow. Is everything going to be all right?"

"They hope so, but the treatment can be . . . well, it's not easy. So Ting's mom thought it best she be there and that this would be an opportunity for Ting to get to know that part of her family better and to experience the culture up there. San Francisco has a very large Chinese community, you know." Her mother sipped at her mug of tea. "It's not like you're losing her, after all. There're phone calls and the Internet."

And crystal. "Yeah, I know," muttered Bailey. She picked up the spoon and clattered it around inside her mug. "I mean, she has to go, and I understand, but I'll miss her. And she's

gonna miss Thanksgiving and Christmas and New Year's . . .
we had stuff planned."

"I know, honey."

Bailey tossed her head. "We'll just have to make the best
of it, right?"

Her mother smiled. "Right."

17

ON THE OTHER HAND

"SLACKER!" said the coach, practically frothing at the mouth. "The one thing I won't have on any of my teams is a slacker!"

"Yes, sir," Jason mumbled.

The coach stabbed a finger through the air. "My office, after practice! Now get your buns out there and do drills with the rest of the team!"

"Yessir!" Jason bolted.

He joined the line for sprints, and then danced in place with Sam to keep warm on this chilly, gray afternoon while waiting for his turn.

"That went well," Sam commented dryly.

Jason nodded. The two of them had figured he'd ground Jason right then and there for even being given the note that Joanna and McIntire had sent to school. Instead, he'd studied it, turned red in the face, and ordered Jason to his office after a few well chosen words on athletics building character and commitment to the team and hard work and effort. Thirty minutes of the old, "There is no I in team" lecture.

He windmilled his arms around. The last thing he wanted was for the coach to think of him as either a troublemaker or a weasel, and the sooner he could look him in the eye and convince him of that, the better he'd feel. In the meantime, he could look forward to being worked twice as hard. He took a deep breath. Whatever Coach threw at him, it would be better than sitting in Finch's office, waiting to be dissected.

Sam dug his elbow into Jason's side. "Look who's watching."

Jason twisted about and saw a spindly figure sitting in the dilapidated bleachers that ran alongside the fields. He seemed to be taking notes. Jason groaned. Statler Finch himself.

Sam flashed him a look. "Don't worry. Coach won't let him stay."

"Hope not." Jason had no time to say anything further as he was barked at, and he lunged into movement, down the powdered white lines and withered grass, weaving a running line between bright orange cones. When he got back, sure he'd beaten his best time, Coach merely looked at the stopwatch in his hands, frowned, and made a circular motion with his hand.

"Again."

Jason inhaled. He dashed off without another sound, frowning, his arms and legs moving with controlled speed, cornering and slaloming through the cones as if he were a downhill skier. He finished, a little out of breath, and slowed going by the coach.

Coach frowned. He jerked a thumb. "Again."

Jason had it in him, but there was the rest of practice and maybe a short game ahead of them yet. He took a deep breath and set off again. This time, to save his legs, he took it slower. Because he was tired and without a break, he'd begun to wobble a bit. All he needed was five or ten minutes, but Coach wasn't giving him that. So . . . rather than touch a dreaded cone, or worse, knock one over, he had to slow down. Be careful. Treat the cones as if they were opponents to be wary of, another team to outfox. It took him minutes longer, and when he trotted back to his coach, he did so with every intention of stopping this time and gathering a few minutes' break, at least.

Coach looked him over. "A bit slower that time."

Jason nodded wordlessly. Deep breathing felt good.

"What did you learn?"

Jason, his hands on his knees to rest, looked up in surprise. "Learn?"

"Learn." Coach jabbed a thumb out to the field. "Those cones are the enemy. What did you learn?"

Puzzled, he thought about it and then warily offered, "Not to give the enemy a break, even when I'm not feeling my strongest. I took it as fast as I could and still was careful."

"Good. Take a breather, then go up and join the others." Coach turned his back on him, clipboard in hand, eyes already downfield on another player.

Surprised, Jason fell back and got a small cup of water from the big water cooler at the field's edge, washed his mouth out, and then went over to join Sam and the others. He mulled over what he had said that had pleased the coach, even if only in some small way.

The coach didn't stay pleased. By the time Jason plopped down on a spare chair in his office and waited for the man to appear, he was drenched in sweat, scratched from two falls in the bushes and brambles that cornered the practice field, and wondering if he had enough strength to walk home. He had about two seconds of peace before his coach walked in, coffee cup in hand, and muttering.

"I'll make this short. Finch and I have had a talk. If you've got problems," and he stared hard at Jason, with a piercing gaze, "I don't want to see them on the soccer field. Since this is school business, I'll allow you the one day. Once. But if you want regular counseling, then you either do it before school, in the early morning . . . or you quit the team. Got it? No slacking. None."

"But, sir, this isn't my idea."

"I don't know if it is or if it isn't. Vice Principal Murphy has been working to institute some new things here at school, most of which I support. As to this counseling . . ." Coach grunted before continuing, "All I know is that you asked to be part of a team, and that team deserves your commitment and focus. You show promise, Adrian, as an individual player, and as a team asset. I expect you to live up to it, but the team deserves to come first."

"Yes, sir." Jason stared down at the corner of the desk.

"Well? Doesn't it?"

"Yes, sir, it does. I want to play soccer more than anything!" Well, nearly. But he wasn't about to discuss Magicking with a soccer coach whose style consisted of that of a drill sergeant, even if the oath of Binding would let him. Which, thankfully, it wouldn't. Supposedly. He had no intention of putting the oath to work. The thought of sitting in front of the coach, his jaws fixed and voice frozen was, well, unthinkable!

"Then let me put it to you this way, Jason. In another year or so, you'll be in high school. An honors curriculum there means classes before and after the regular schedule. Zero hour and so forth. It's early, but students who want to get ahead work for it. If you want to stay on this soccer team, you're going to have to work for it, too. Not just on the field now, but off it. If Finch wants you to come in for counseling, tell him it's before school, not after. After school, you belong to me! Got that?"

There was no way not to get it. Jason nodded.

"All right, then. Shower and go." The coach set his coffee cup on the desk and began flipping through his clipboard.

Jason stood, then hesitated a moment. He cleared his throat. "You'll ... ah ... mention this to Mr. Finch, too? Kinda back me up?"

Coach looked up, and drilled him with his dark, unblinking eyes. Then he nodded. "I'll suggest it to him as well. But it's your job to make the arrangements."

"Yessir!" Jason bolted for the door before anything else befell him.

Absolutely cursed, no doubt about it. Not a one.

Words interrupted a tomblike silence. Brennard's hand gestured fitfully in impatience.

"I asked if all was in place."

The disciple bowed before his master, and remained quiet for a moment, staring down. "The beginnings of the trap are in motion, Brennard. The bait has been offered. I think all shall take it. And we are poised, waiting."

Brennard thoughtfully brushed his dark hair off his forehead. "We don't want any mistakes this time."

"No, sir."

He leaned back in his chair, one arm over the back of it, turned sideways for better support as if his tall, seemingly young body still needed the strength of the furniture. And, thought his disciple, perhaps it did. Brennard had nearly died, after all. "The problem is," Brennard said slowly, as if thinking aloud, "there are too many for us as well as for them. The nets are flung too far to catch all these little fishes, and so we need to concentrate on the ones who shine brightest. We will start here, and make an end here if we can. You have the teeth? The other items I prescribed?"

"I do." The disciple took out a small cloth sack and laid it on Brennard's knee.

"Excellent. Modern times are quite remarkable, actually, but also, it means that we all must take care, very very great care about what we are doing. Being revealed now would make our situation extremely precarious. Until that time when we have secured the Havens for ourselves, we are as vulnerable as Gregory's motley lot is, a fact I am not quite certain they have fully realized. If they have realized, they have not acted upon it. That becomes our advantage. I am not afraid to make use of anyone's weakness."

"And what of the dreams?"

Brennard frowned. More than an expression, the atmosphere about him seemed to fray and discharge irritably, tiny sparks zapping through the air. "They are but dreams."

"Not omens."

"Memories, at best."

"You are certain?"

Brennard stood then, looming over his disciple. He did not care to discuss the disturbing dreams he had, nor the ones he sent out. "As certain as I care to be, for the moment. Unless you would care to be divorced from your body and soul for a while, and explore that metaphysical plane?"

"N–no. No, sir. Thank you for the opportunity, but I am not prepared." The disciple bowed, quite deeply, and did not look up for a very long moment, until he heard Brennard's breathing return to normal. His glance flicked up then, and he saw Brennard sit back down, gathering up the small cloth sack he'd delivered. Then and only then, did the disciple hazard to straighten up, although he took a wary step backward. Truth be told, there was nowhere on this world he would be out of Brennard's reach. Those were the ties between them, the pledges and vows chaining him, in return for his favored disciple status. Gladly, he'd given them then. Now, he was not so certain.

"Then," remarked Brennard almost mildly, "do not question me."

"Master." He inclined his head. "I don't question you, but myself." He sighed. "It is not a matter of dedication, but confidence, I suppose."

"Working with me will dispel that. There are great things to come. Many, many great things. This is a world of vast possibilities now, with many struggling countries just waiting for strong and guiding hands. We will do well. Trust me." Brennard smiled then, drawing his cloth sack closer and cradling it for a moment against his chest. "We will do very well indeed."

Rich sat down in his backyard, almost hidden amid the long purple shadows, facing the back screen door on his porch, although he did not expect his parents to come through. They were spectacularly uninterested in him with the exception of his grades, and he made sure he always got decently high grades without having to study endlessly. Still, he didn't want anything that he, Stefan, and Tomaz Crowfeather were going to say or do to be noted. The very thought of it, or perhaps something else, sent a chill down his back. "Gad," he muttered, and shivered. "I hate that."

"What?" Stefan looked at him, dumbfounded.

"Chills down the back of my neck. Like somebody was walking on my grave."

"Ugh." Stef shuddered in disgust.

"It's just an expression," the quiet adult sitting with them said, smiling reassuringly. Tomaz Crowfeather sat cross-legged on the ground as the last shreds of the day were obscured by a pink-and-gray sunset, and he held up something in his hands, so that it caught the very last beams of sun raying through the clouds. He lowered it, and gave the small muslin bag to Stefan.

"What is it?"

"As long as you wear that," Tomaz said quietly, "you will not change skins."

"You're kidding me?" Stefan held the bag in his big, square, chubby hands and then turned the fetish bag over and over in his palms.

Rich felt the coldness in the ground through his jeans and shifted uncomfortably. "You can keep him from doing that?"

Tomaz nodded solemnly. He dropped his hands to his knees, big heavy turquoise stone bracelets rattling, and rested, watching the two of them.

"No shit." Stefan quickly tied the smallish bag to the chain he wore about his neck.

"If you could really do that," remarked Rich slowly, "why didn't you do it a lot earlier and save me . . . us . . . a lot of trouble?"

"Yeah." Stefan looked Tomaz over. "Not to mention even more trouble."

Tomaz gave a slight smile. "It is not wise."

Stef grunted and began to fidget. "I don't get it."

"Okay . . . shifting into a bear in front of a football stadium full of people is wise?" Rich put in quickly.

"Nor that." Tomaz considered Stefan calmly, then looked at Rich who'd asked the question. "But it is not good to suppress that which is meant to be. Talent needs to be trained, shaped, and nurtured, not bottled up and hidden. Tell me. Would you rather deal with a Stefan-bear you've known all along and trained with—or a full-grown, frightened, and confused beast who suddenly erupts into the world?"

Both boys rocked back slightly. Stef's thick face showed a fragment of surprise, while Rich paled at the implications.

Stefan let out a grudging exhale. "Since you put it that way."

Tomaz nodded. "I do."

"So . . . if that's my Talent . . . what happens now?"

"Until you understand the Curse, he'll stay suppressed, for a short while. And if we can't keep it under control, then . . ." Tomaz's voice trailed off.

"Then what?" Rich shifted.

Stefan rubbed his nose, grumbling.

"Well, in the old days, we'd move out where the Talent wouldn't be a problem. Now, we don't have as many options."

"So I'm stuck until I just explode?"

"Hopefully not." Tomaz got to his feet. "But, in the meantime, you won't be changing skins unless you want to."

"That's good, I guess."

Crowfeather nodded. He pulled the watch chain from the pocket of his denim vest, and an arrowhead-shaped crystal fell into his weathered hands. "Until we meet again," he said quietly, moved one hand over his crystal, and disappeared.

Stefan's hand went to his neck. He gripped the bag of herbs and magicks tightly, as if clutching a lifeline.

Rich patted his friend's shoulder and stared off into the gathering night. Magick used to seem fun. Even when it was bothersome. Now it seemed downright dangerous.

. . . And, typed Bailey quickly, **she's leaving Saturday night and I won't see her for months and months!**

Have you talked to her yet? And you can't be like that, Bailey, we've got the crystals and the computers. We'll be in touch with her constantly. She may even be better off up there, out of the Curse's reach. Jason pondered that. Did the Curse have a circle that it affected, and could it be escaped from? Like a field or area of infection?

Or she could be in worse trouble, with none of us around to help!

Jason stared at his computer screen. For a second he wondered if Bailey would be able to communicate at all if they took the exclamation key off her keyboard. The thought made him grin. **She'll be fine,** he told Bailey. **Do you think Gavan or Eleanora would let anything happen to her?** On the other hand . . . and Jason stared at his left hand splayed over the keyboard, his scar meeting his inspection. On the other hand, they hadn't prevented *that*, or the attack a few days ago. And without a beacon working reliably, could the elders help any of them?

Or were they on their own with only each other to depend upon?

Don't worry. Ting will be fine.

Bailey shot back at him—how fast did she type, anyway? Faster than she talked, which was like a bullet. **I want to get together Saturday to say good-bye. All of us, if we can.**

That might be a little risky. Crystal travel was something they hadn't quite mastered, but he didn't want Bailey any more upset than she already was. So he answered, carefully, **Sounds like fun. I'll see what I can arrange.**

She signed off after telling him a quick joke, and the computer was suddenly very still. Funny how Bailey could just fill up a place, even when she wasn't actually in it. He turned off his computer, pushed the keyboard aside, and pulled over his algebra book, his thoughts churning round and round as if he were still doing laps around a soccer field. Whatever the Curse of Arkady was, they had all better start working on a cure.

18

DRAGON MAGIC

"HOUSE of the Flower Dragon," Ting repeated slowly. Jiao Chuu smiled and teased her daughter gently. "As many times as you have visited my mother's house and you never noticed it was so named?" She took a sweater and folded it softly into the suitcase spread open on the bed as Ting sorted through keepsakes she wanted to take or leave behind.

Ting shook her head. "I only remembered the dragon along the roof. I don't think I ever bothered to look much closer." She studied the photo taken of her, her mother, and her grandmother a year ago last summer, all of them standing in front of her grandmother's San Francisco home. Behind them, a long, serpentine dragon coiled upon the roof tiles.

Chinese dragons were so different from European dragons, from the kind that Jason and Trent talked about facing in their D & D games. Far from looking like some kind of dinosaur, Chinese dragons were long and thin and incredibly agile, a source of great wisdom and knowledge, as well as fierceness and honor. She had always known their dragon was a protector and guardian, but she had never before noticed the bright chrysanthemums he carried or wore sometimes in a garland about his neck. The bronze flower petals had been cloisonne enameled a brilliant orange-red. She looked at the picture of her grandmother's home again. "Can I scan this and send it to Bailey? I want to tell her she's got Lacey, but I've got a dragon!"

Jiao laughed gently. "Perhaps when we get settled in. Your father already has the computer boxed up."

Ting nodded, and put aside the photo to pack. She looked up at her mother, who was beautiful in many ways, but who seemed tired and a little sad this day. "You had something you wanted to tell me?"

Jiao sat down next to her daughter. "Plans have changed yet again. We'll be flying up early Saturday instead of driving on Sunday."

Oh, no! Ting flinched at her words, but said nothing. All of this was hard enough on her mother without her making it worse, but she'd miss their gathering! What would Bailey think? And all the others?

"I'm sorry," continued Jiao. "I know you had plans to go for pizza with everyone, but Father thought it would be easier and safer for us to fly up and we'll be with Grandmother that much more quickly."

That was, after all, what was important. Ting nodded, soft black wings of hair tickling the sides of her face as she did. "I'll call and explain," she said. "And they'll understand. That's what friends are for."

Her mother stood without another word except to hug her quickly before moving off to finish her own packing. Her outwardly calm face, as usual, hid her true emotions, but Ting knew the worry in her eyes would not leave till Grandmother was well again.

Ting tapped the crystal on her homemade bracelet. She'd miss everyone, and especially the shenanigans Bailey had planned, but there was no helping it. Anyway, a short flight would be much easier on everyone than a long drive. Bailey and Jason would have to wait. It's not like she was going away forever or had no way to see them again. She had Magick now.

Already pulled out of school, she waited until afternoon to call Jason so he could pass the word around, not wanting to hear the disappointment in Bailey's voice.

"Hello, McIntire residence."

Ting recognized the cool tones of Jason's older stepsister Alicia. "Hello, Alicia, it's Ting. Is Jason home yet?"

"Doesn't seem to be. May I take a message?"

"Please, if you would. I won't be able to meet everyone at Trevi's Pizza tomorrow. We're flying up to San Francisco early. Tell him I'm sorry, but I'll send e-mail as soon as my computer arrives and gets all set up."

"Will do. Sorry to hear about your grandmother."

"She will be all right, I think. It's just going to take a while. Thank you," answered Ting softly before hanging up the phone.

Alicia hung up the kitchen phone and looked around. Breakfast dishes were supposed to be done by Jason before he went to school, but the kitchen looked a mess. She'd have to clean up before everyone else got home. Alicia wrinkled her forehead, then let out a huffy little snort. Funny how messages could be forgotten over kitchen messes!

Statler Finch looked at Jason over a cup holder filled with pens and pencils, all with wicked, sharp points. "Since it's been requested, I will make myself available in the early morning for our sessions, Jason, but only if you can assure me you will be here."

"Once a week."

"For now. Depending on my findings, I may need to see you more often."

Jason managed a wry grin. "Depending on how screwed up I am, huh?"

Statler did not smile back. Something cold glinted in his eyes. "Something like that." He leaned back in his office chair which let out a low squeak. "So. I understand you and your friend get trash-canned every few weeks."

"Something like that."

Statler made notes on his yellow legal pad and did not seem to notice the faint echo and irony in Jason's voice. Without looking up, he said, "Tell me how you feel about that."

"Smelly. And, you know, hassled."

"Hassled? How?"

Jason thought it should be obvious. He shrugged. "Late for class or soccer workouts. That sort of thing."

"What sort of thing?" A thin smile snaked over Statler's lips.

"Trouble."

"How does trouble make you feel? Anxious? Angry perhaps?"

"It makes me feel a little angry that guys like him get away with it, and I'm the one who gets yelled at. But it's not really all that much, so I don't think about it."

"You push it aside, then?"

Jason felt the hard chair seat under his thighs and the early morning chill of the school office and tried not to squirm. "Not really. I forget about it because it's not important."

"What do you mean by that?" Without looking up, Finch skritched lines of notes across his paper pad, the pencil lead dragging with an irritating noise over the yellow lined paper.

"I mean what I said. This time next month or the month after, it's not going to matter. It's not one of the things in life that's important." At least, that's what he tried to tell himself while he was figuring out how to peel yesterday's old hamburgers off today's book report.

"So you don't have to deal with it?"

"I didn't say that. I have to deal with it every time they do it, but . . . it's not going to matter in the long run as long as I keep my cool. Dozer says it's important to know when to pick your battles and when not to."

The counselor looked up sharply. "So this is a battle, then?" The pencil lead creaked and scratched furiously.

Jason suppressed a wince. "Not really. I think my stepdad means choosing when you're going to stand and when you're going to give way. Settle." For a second there, something had flickered in Statler Finch's eyes, and Jason didn't like the looks of it. He reminded himself to choose his words very carefully.

"Tell me about your dreams, Jason."

There was no way he was going to do that. He looked down at his shoes quickly, in case the defiance showed in his eyes. He shrugged. "Usual stuff, don't remember most of 'em."

"Any dreams about school?"

"Sometimes. You know. Forget the locker combination, or late to a test. My stepmom says not to worry, those are just anxiety dreams. She says almost everyone gets those." There was no way on Earth Statler would get him to talk about his nightmares, though. He told no one about those, because he knew that, twisted and dark as they were, they dealt with Magick.

"Perhaps," Finch responded, making another note.

Jason stared uneasily for a moment, wondering if other people really did have those kinds of dreams or if Joanna was just trying to soften life for him, as she often did.

Before he had the thought finished though, the ten minute warning buzzer sounded for late honors, and he was free, his time up. If he triple hurried, he might make the last of soccer practice. He bolted to his feet.

"Very well, then. Try to have a good weekend and week and I'll see you . . . early . . . next Friday morning."

"Yes, sir." Jason lunged for the door and as far away from Statler Finch as his quick feet would carry him.

He was right, he had missed all but the last thirty minutes of soccer and it seemed the coach had saved wind sprints and laps for last today, just for him. Sam was puffing and sweating as he joined him and grinned. Jason didn't mind.

19

WARM FUZZIES

BAILEY fidgeted on the kitchen chair, pushing her books away from her. Homework, homework. Normally she loved homework, odd as that was, but thinking about losing Ting, seeing her go so far away, and being worried about her friend's grandmother all made her very restless today. Ting had to go, there was no doubt about that; the family needed Jiao Chuu and Ting, but that also left Bailey behind. And who could she share with now? Who would understand what she meant when she worried about things? Her mother didn't, couldn't, know. She shared everything with her mom, but Magicking was one thing she couldn't. Not only did the Oath of Binding keep her jaws wired shut, but just the thought of it kept Bailey from saying anything. It was hard enough being a single mom . . . being a single mom to someone who was learning Magick and could be taken away? Locked up forever while being examined to find out why she was a freak? And what if her father found out and decided it was all her mom's fault and tried to get custody? No. She couldn't put her mom through that!

They could giggle over rock stars with torn jeans and belly buttons showing, teachers who fell asleep in class during home-work session, cars that belched blue smoke, boys who said one thing then did another while tripping over their big, sneakered feet ... but not this. Although, admittedly, Ting was more fun to talk boys with, too ... sometimes her mom would get this worried expression on her face. As if boys meant anything!

Bailey tapped her pencil on her binder and tried to concentrate on the assignment at hand. She'd actually already done this assignment once, but now that the rest of the class was catching up, she needed to go over it and make sure that she'd been correct. Boring stuff. She decided to chew on her pencil instead.

Lacey chittered from her cage. Bailey checked the kitchen clock. Late autumn meant the sky went dark early, but it was still too early for her to be up. She grinned. Why not take advantage of her usually nocturnal pet? She could use a furry snuggle.

Bailey slid her chair over to the corner bookcase that held the cage and other odds and ends pertaining to the pack rat's care. Lacey sat outside her nest, which consisted of a cardboard toilet paper roll and various fluffs of tissue and newspaper, all chewed up and about the roll inside and out for comfort and warmth. Her little black tufted tail lay curled on a wad of nose tissue, in pale yellows and pinks. Her whiskers twitched. She groomed her face, then looked up expectantly as Bailey removed the lid to reach in for her.

The room spun for a moment. Ceiling seemed to swap places with floor. Bailey had this disconcerting vision of being very small with something large reaching down for her. Everything whirled about Bailey, round and round, and she froze in place, her stomach sickened by the sudden jolting amusement park ride view of her kitchen! Sink and refrigerator and cabinets spun past in a dizzying march. Walls revolved around and around and then came to a clanking halt with a thud that made her eyeballs feel as if they were bouncing for a moment. She closed her eyes tightly, every sense revolting.

She felt a tickling in her outstretched fingers as Lacey scrambled up into her palm. Opening her eyes gingerly, she pulled her hand out of the cage, leaving the lid open as she brought Lacey out. The room seemed to have jolted back into normal gear, but she wasn't too sure it would stay that way! She rubbed her pet's head gently with her thumb. Lacey nuzzled back affectionately. They weren't exactly owner and pet; the pack rat was, after all, an animal born in the wild and hardly considered tame to anyone but Bailey.

Yet there was definitely a bond between them and there had been since they first touched, since that day when Tomaz had pried open a loose board in their summer camp floor and found the pack rat and her nest of shiny, stolen objects. Lacey chittered mournfully as if remembering that day, too, and her lost treasures.

"Awww." Bailey reached back and pulled off her hair band. It was one of twisted silvery tinsel and looked very bright and shiny. Lacey took it in her paws with a happy chirp and dove off Bailey's hand back into her cage, tissue bits flying everywhere. The inside of the cage looked like a snowstorm of color as Lacey dug, her paws sending the tissue confetti every which way, until she had finally eased the silver band into a safe spot and covered it up. Not until Lacey was done making sure the treasure was hidden, did she return and squeak up at Bailey to be picked up again.

Bailey reached inside a second time, and that awful whirling sensation hit her again, like a hammer right between the eyes. She let out a groan as her world went topsy-turvy. She clutched the edge of the kitchen table as her body threatened to slide out of the chair, unable to tell up from down, and gravity laughed at her. Lacey ran up her arm, squeaking in alarm, and buried herself in Bailey's hair and collar, her warm body burrowing against Bailey's neck. She closed her eyes until the spinning went away, and then opened them slowly.

The kitchen stayed put. She hardly dared to look at it to see if it would stay that way. Bailey put her elbows on the table and held her head in her hands, very very still for long minutes.

Click, click, click.

She listened. Something was in the hallway, in the corridor outside the apartment. Something at her apartment door.

Bailey held her breath. She thought she could hear a wet snuffling at the door. An animal. A dog? Not likely; this was pretty much a No Pets building, except for the legally blind guy who lived upstairs with his service dog, but they went to work every day.

Yet when he walked by with his dog, she would hear that

same click of the dog's nails on the tiled corridor. But surely they were still at work.

Bailey slid a hand up to her neck and stroked Lacey's silken fur, listening, thinking. Nothing. Nothing but her own breathing, her own heart beating fast. She inhaled deeply. Scaredy cat! There was nothing to fear but herself. And getting horribly dizzy again. What homework she'd done would be ruined if she threw up all over it. Bailey gulped. She reached for her pencil and decided that even boring schoolwork was better than sitting on the edge of her chair, petrified. She had barely put lead to paper when . . .

Click. Click. Click.

A muffled noise at the door as if something heavy leaned or pressed against it. A definite snuffle as if something sniffed at the bottom edge of the threshold. She couldn't be imagining this. Bailey stared out across the kitchen table and down the short hallway to the apartment door. Its deadbolts were closed as was the heavy chain lock, yet somehow she did not feel safe. Lacey gave a tiny squeak at her chin.

She thought of the wolfjackals which had pursued Jason. Could there be one here? Now? Tracking her at her door?

The wet snuffling reminded her of . . . well, Ulysses S. Grant who still eagerly greeted her at the junkyard fence every time she went by. Could he have tracked her home? She knew she had nothing to worry about if it was indeed Ulysses although she'd have to get him back to the junkyard as soon as possible. Good dog or bad wolfjackal? Who paced outside her apartment door?

There was only one way to find out, and that would be to open that door, and there was no way Bailey was going to be stupid enough to do that. She listened intently. Did she hear a snarling underlining the snuffles? A low, rumbling growl? Wolfjackal! Did she imagine it? Did she hear?

On the other hand, she wasn't about to just sit there and be terrified.

Bailey shot to her feet. She rummaged around the kitchen till she got out the cutting board, the paring knife, and the fresh garlic. Quickly she pulled off a clove of the fragrant herb and chopped it into slivers. The pungent smell filled the kitchen. Raw garlic could be very very strong. No wonder vampires didn't like it! She scooped up the slivers and tiptoed to the front door, then quickly scattered the slivers at the base of the door and its tiny crack. Then she moved back against the wall, and waited.

Click. Click.

Silence.

Then, a wet snuffle just scant feet away from her, on the other side of the door. And the low vibration of a growl. Lacey's small paws dug at her neck and hair as the frightened creature tried to hide better. Bailey stared at the door waiting.

Snuffle.

Then, a sharp sneeze. And another. Bailey put her hand over her mouth to keep from laughing.

Another sneeze, followed by a low whine. Then a rapid click click click as whatever it was trotted away.

She held her breath for a bit, to be sure. Lacey shivered against her neck. Nothing but silence.

Bailey let out a cheer. Then she wrinkled her nose. "Oh," she said to Lacey. "This is going to stink for a long time." She'd have to chop some lemon to clear away the smell. She thought of something else she had to do, right away, and pulled out her crystal.

Eleanora glided across the floor, and wrinkled her nose slightly. Ever defiant of her petite size, she had a habit of levitating a few inches, the hem of her long skirts concealing the fact that she hovered in the air. "You . . . put garlic in your tea?" she asked softly, as Bailey took the whistling pot off the stove and carefully poured very hot water into their best china teapot. The smell of lemon slices and jasmine tea wafted up from the steaming pot as Bailey blushed.

"Ummm . . . no," Bailey answered. "That's repellent."

"Very effective." Smiling, Eleanora sat down at the table, in long skirt and long-sleeved ruffled blouse, and waited for her tea to be poured. She watched Bailey. "When someone activates the alarm beacon, I would gather it's for more than tea. I expected to find trouble." She extended one slender hand from her ruffled sleeve, tapping her fingers on the table as Bailey poured out two cups and sat down.

Bailey took the chair opposite Eleanora who showed no

surprise as Lacey ran down her arm and grabbed a cookie crumb before retreating back up to a perch on Bailey's shoulder. She dunked her cookie and enjoyed the satisfying sweetness before answering. "I'm not sure if we had trouble or not. Making sure would have led to more trouble, I think. Like sending a cheese to find a cheese."

Eleanora opened a pink packet of sweetener to dose her tea. "I see. I think. There was something here but you didn't investigate what?"

"I think I had a wolfjackal at the door."

"And no way of finding out for sure unless you opened it to look?"

Bailey nodded. "The peephole wouldn't let me see something that was low and up against the door."

"So . . . you put down garlic at the threshold?"

"Something kept walking by and sniffing. At first I thought it was the guide dog upstairs, but they're usually at work now. I couldn't think of anything to do, except that."

"Ingenuous! Apparently it worked." Eleanora cupped her pendant, a distant look on her face. "There is nothing I sense in the corridor now. However . . ." She frowned, closed her eyes a moment, then opened them and looked at Bailey. "I'm afraid you might have been right. There is a taint there, and it's not raw garlic." She smiled slightly. "They were bold to have struck here, where they can be observed. They won't be back. They will try other, more shadowy methods next time. You're going to have to be awfully careful, Bailey."

Bailey shivered. The hairs on the back of her neck and along her arms stood up. She rubbed at her arms. "But I'm safe here, at least for now? They won't try to get us? My mom and I?"

"I can't guarantee that, but the Dark Hand is successful because it doesn't leave itself open to discovery. They know you know that they have located you here, and you can't be taken without a fight, a struggle they want to avoid for now." Eleanora reached over and grasped her hand. "We'll do everything we can to make sure they stay discouraged!"

Bailey shook her head slowly. "I don't know what I could have done. They had some sort of spell. It made me very, very dizzy. I could hardly sit up, let alone stand and fight, Eleanora."

"A spell? Describe it."

"It was awful. I got sick to my stomach. It was like being on one of those rides that spin you backward, then turn you upside down." Bailey paled just at the memory. "The whole kitchen just went round and round."

Eleanora looked baffled. "I don't understand, hon. There's nothing I can throw that would cause that. Which is, of course, not to say that Brennard hasn't been researching and trying to create new spells . . . but I haven't heard of that one. Tell me again exactly what happened, and don't leave anything out!" She sat back, teacup in hand, watching and sipping as Bailey began to recite the afternoon over again.

". . . and then I called for help." Bailey dunked and slurped up the next to last cookie. Lemon melts, slightly stale and gone very hard, which made them perfect for dunking. Bailey wiped her hands up very thoroughly.

Eleanora sat with an extremely thoughtful look on her face. "Tell me," she said, "what you would see if you were in Lacey's place and someone reached in for you."

"What?" Bailey felt her face wrinkle in total surprise. "But . . ."

"Just imagine. Lean back and imagine you are a wee, tiny kangaroo rat in the corner of that cage, and someone reaches in and plucks you up, turning your world upside down and around and around?"

Bailey narrowed her eyes, thinking. Then she bolted out of her chair. "Oh no! I'm turning into a shapeshifter! I'm going to be a pack rat!"

20

BUTTON, BUTTON

I'M cursed," wailed Bailey. "Cursed to become a pack rat!"

"Hmmm," murmured Eleanora in obvious amusement as she watched Bailey dart around the kitchen. "After having seen your bedroom, I'm not so sure that's incorrect, but it is. You, my dear, are not a shapeshifter."

Bailey stopped and stared. "But what, then?"

"You merely saw the world for a few moments through Lacey's eyes."

"No way!"

Eleanora nodded sagely. "Way," she countered.

"That's impossible."

"Think about it. And trust me, with your Talent, you may well find strong bonds with an animal or two. Stories of witches and cats come out of real life happenings, only distorted by those who don't understand. I know Tomaz has been wanting to work with you on this, but he's been a little busy with Stefan's problem."

"No kidding." Bailey thumped into a chair. It made a little sense, though. The impression of being reached for just before all the dizziness started. "So Lacey and I have a bond."

"Don't you think so?"

"Oh, yeah." Bailey smiled and put her hand to her shoulder

to stroke the tiny furred ball. "That was pretty awful, though. If I make her that dizzy every time I pick her up . . ."

"Once again, think about it. No doubt there was some dizziness and some problem with your mind trying to handle two sources of sensory input." Eleanora looked a little smug. "If I may retreat into the scientific for a bit."

Bailey grinned. "Well done! Pretty soon you'll believe in satellite TV and cell phones!"

"Never." Eleanora turned pink and shook her head. "Demon technology." She smiled at Bailey across the teapot. "The important thing, Bailey, is that you not let Laccy overrun your thoughts, your control. She is, after all, only a wee animal and not as smart as you are, although sometimes we may think she's terribly clever."

"Tell me what to do."

"Think of that part of your Talent as a door. It's always shut. Lacey must knock on it and get permission to enter. Use your meditation exercises on your crystal that you've been doing . . ." If Eleanora noticed the embarrassed and slightly guilty look on Bailey's face at this last, she ignored it and cruised right by. "Those exercises will help you build a framework of contact. Otherwise your mind will have a tiny creature running about in its thoughts nonstop, and that won't be good for either of you."

"No," muttered Bailey. "It certainly wouldn't be." Her hand absently reached out for the last cookie, but Eleanora beat her to it, taking it up demurely and placing it in her tea saucer.

"There are advantages, of course," the Magicker continued smoothly. "Lacey can get in and out of places very quickly that you can't. That could be very useful, if she is trained." She broke her cookie in half precisely and devoured part.

"Wow." Bailey tugged thoughtfully on her ponytail. "Can she be trained? Is she smart enough?"

The beast in question let out a tiny snort as if making fun of Bailey's words. Eleanora laughed.

"She'll do. Let me show you a training exercise that should be fun for both of you. When I was young, we used to play a game called 'Button, Button.' " She smiled slightly. "Buttons were very expensive in my youth. Rather like playing with a

silver or gold coin." Eleanora fished around in the cloth purse
attached to her slender wrist and brought out a pretty carved
bright red button. "Take this and let her see it, then hide it in
plain sight. Always reward her when she finds it." Eleanora
tapped her cookie. "I think a crumb or two of this would make
her very happy. Soon, she'll be able to find the button even
when it's well hidden!"

Bailey took the button from her. "That's it?"

"For starters, till Tomaz has time to work with you both.
Don't expect too much of her, Bailey. She is very smart in her
way, although limited, but she trusts and loves you and will
give everything she's got to please you. It is your role, as her
protector, not to abuse that devotion."

"I'll be careful," vowed Bailey.

"Good. 'Cause if you send her out to see if a wolfjackal
stands there, she'll be eaten in one gulp."

Bailey gasped.

Eleanora stood, nodding. "Don't forget that."

"I . . . won't!" Bailey had to force herself to breathe in the
middle of her words. She held the button tightly.

"In the meantime, I'll be listening for you. We also seem to
be attuned." Eleanora smiled. She glided round the kitchen
table and kissed Bailey's brow gently. "Take care and call when
you need me." She tapped Bailey's crystal. She slid her fingertips over the pendant at the hollow of her throat, nearly hidden by the ruffled neckline of her blouse, and disappeared.

Bailey cuddled Lacey gently in the palm of her hand. "Have
I got a game for you," she said softly, and pictured the cookie
reward in her thoughts.

Give a mouse a cookie! typed Trent and Jason could almost
hear the dry laugh accompanying it. Grinning, Jason typed
back, **Elephants work for peanuts, but pack rats have even
crumbier wages.**

**Hey, guys! I worked really hard and so did Lacey. In fact,
afterward she slept all day and all night!**

Jason laughed harder. The thought of a poor exhausted
Lacey curled up in her shredded paper nest with even her
tail tucked in beside her was too funny to take seriously. That,

coupled with the thought of Bailey shapeshifting into another pack rat, whiskers trembling and bright eyes looking for spar-klies, made him laugh till he nearly snorted.

Bailey must have sensed their combined mirth because she typed **Hmppph!,** added a smiley face with its tongue sticking out, and signed off the Internet messenger.

Which was too bad because Jason wanted to talk with her about the dangers of the wolfjackal lurking, but Eleanora had undoubtedly found a way to ward the Landau apartment or she wouldn't have been so certain Bailey would be safe there. Outside, however, was another matter. Bailey could be brash, but she would never be mistaken for stupid, so he had to hope for the best.

Trent sent a message to him, though, that stopped all his thoughts about Bailey. He blinked and read the screen twice to make sure he understood.

Henry wrote me and asked if I were afraid of Jon, too.

His brain stampeded. Jonnard Albrite, tall, thin, older, somewhat worldly even, a camp counselor of sorts, and cabi-nmate of Henry Squibb. Jon, a plant from the Dark Hand of Brennard, who leeched Henry's powers from him and tried to do the same to Jason! Of course they were afraid of Jon, but Henry wasn't to remember that! **When was this? How did Jonnard even get mentioned?**

He didn't. Henry just popped up with it yesterday, after our DR session. You had to leave and help Alicia with chores.

No kidding. He asked you that? What did you say?

I said that camp seemed a long time ago, and Jon was your (Henry's) roommate, not mine.

Did he drop it, then?

No. He said he had dreams, sometimes, of camp, of things that he knew were impossible. Then he stopped.

Oh, man. He couldn't be remembering . . . could he? Jason stared for long moments at his computer screen, trying to think of what to say or do. Finally, Trent sent another message.

Think about it, Jason. We shouldn't have been able to dis-cuss this with him. Not unless he were a Magicker, because of the Binding.

Jason sat back. Trent was implying that Henry was still a Magicker, even without power. Because Trent was? He couldn't be sure. There might be an even more awesome answer. Before he could respond, Trent typed again, insistently.

He might be getting his memory back. And his power. We should find a way to test this. If he is, he'll draw the Dark Hand to him, and he'll be worse off than any of us. Weak, untrained.

What about Ting's farewell party? He knows Ting.

Good idea. A party and a test.

They both signed off then.

Jason climbed into bed, but sat with his legs drawn up. He reached for a book and began to lose himself in it, in its own magic and mysteries, when he felt a familiar tingle and lifted his head. Tomaz Crowfeather appeared in a brief, rainbow shimmer. He lifted one hand in greeting, an open handshake without the shake.

"Good or bad time, Jason?"

"Good, I think." He dog-earred the corner of the page to mark it, then closed his book. "Gavan told you?"

Tomaz drew up his desk chair and straddled it, sitting backward and crossing his arms across its back. "He did. We had all hoped the dreams were gone, but it appears not. Are they frequent?"

Jason considered that. He dreamed every night, vividly, but not that dream. Every handful of weeks, perhaps. He shrugged and said as much.

Tomaz nodded. He scratched the side of his jaw with a blunt thumb, the beaten silver disks on his turquoise bracelet rattling gently as he did so. "Are you using the techniques we talked about?"

"I'm trying to. Deep breathing before I sleep, imaging, the other stuff you mentioned."

"Good. Good. Without a lodge or sweathouse, it is difficult to concentrate as you should, but there are two things you must always be keenly aware of." Tomaz leaned over the chair back. "You must always be aware of whether it is your dream you are walking in, or another's. If it is your dream, you are in control, but you must take care, for there is much for you to learn within it. If it is another's . . ." He frowned. His bronzed skin wrinkled deeply about his eyes. "It will be difficult, Jason."

"How? To leave? Will I be trapped in there?"

"Possibly, but it goes beyond that. You must tell if it is friend or foe. And, either way, there still may be something valuable to learn."

Jason felt very cold. He drew the blankets of his bed up over his pajamas for warmth. "How do I do that?"

"Again, that is difficult. Dreamwalking is not reality. We see things symbolically, and according to our own backgrounds. A coyote for me means one thing, for you, most likely another." Tomaz nodded as if to emphasize that.

"Then what do I do? How do I know?"

"You must reach even deeper within yourself and test for the truth. Even a dreamwalk meant to show or warn you of lies will ring of the truth. And you must learn to do it quickly, Jason, or else you could be trapped by another. In all other ways, your Magick and Talent can help you. In a dreamwalk, it could prove deadly."

He went icy. Even the blankets and comforters on his bed no longer helped. "Deadly?"

"You are very vulnerable to your dreams. You can be hurt both physically and mentally. So. You must think of every dreamwalk as a challenge, a race if you will, to determine what it is made of, what it can give and take away from you. You cannot hesitate either way, Jason."

"If I'm in someone else's dream, then . . . what do I do?"

"For the moment, till we've had time to train you more, you get out. Any way you can, as fast as you can." Tomaz reached out and patted Jason's knee. "Let me show you a path that works for me. Again, our dreams reflect who we are, our heritage and our culture, so your path will be different for you." He talked to Jason a while longer, his voice low and soothing. Then Tomaz reached out and covered him up as he lay down sleepily, still listening, and was still in the room talking as Jason realized he'd drifted off to sleep.

21

OOOPS

HE dreamed of the McHenry house again. As used as he was to this dream, it did not strike him as odd that it had changed, changed as he realized and grew within his knowledge of what Magick was and what being a Magicker meant. He understood the Gate now and how he opened it, and what it meant that he did. He even understood the catacombs and the deathly still figure lying on the cold stone tomb waiting for him and trying to draw him close.

What he did not understand was why he dreamed it over and over. Was he supposed to understand and vanquish every speck of it before he could move on and grow? As Tomaz had told him, it could be his dream or someone else's. He thought it was his dream. His Path. He had to learn its lessons. If not, would this specter of Brennard haunt him as long as his days in Magicking went on? Was this a war for his right to be what he was, or even more serious, a struggle for his very soul?

If it was, how could he hope to protect others like Henry and Trent who hadn't the skill? Was he meant to open a Gate where the nightmare reach of Brennard and his Dark Hand could not go? Was he the one, and the only one, who could find a way to safety?

Jason paused at the vast paneled doors to the old estate.

They stood closed, foreboding and massive. If he was intended to find a safe way, this was not it. The doors crackled with energy, sinister and draining. He hesitated to touch the entry but knew he had to, his hand resting over the dark gold wood and feeling a heat generating from it. Every hair on his body stood on end. Every fiber that he had within him told him not to do it, not to go farther, not to touch the cursed door! But he had to. He knew he had to.

He ran his palm over the door's surface, an inch or so away, without actually touching the wood. Tiny sparks of energy flared and flashed as he did. Every now and then one actually zapped his skin like static electricity. He jumped when it zapped him; he couldn't help it. Clenching his teeth, he shoved his hand out to the door and pushed it inward.

They opened soundlessly, both great doors pushing in at once. Moonlight flooded in over his shoulder, a wide silvery beam cutting through the darkness of the old estate, splaying across the interior. For a moment as he stepped inside, he almost felt as if caught in a spotlight. His shadow cut a jagged black figure within the moonbeam.

He crossed the foyer quickly, the floor creaking dangerously under him. Jason did not want to plummet downward as he often did, crashing through into the chambers below. He had a mission tonight, and it drew him, and so his movements were deft and sure. He crossed into the inner room.

As he opened that door, the moonlight gave way to golden, electrical lights, and the pleasant heat of a lit fireplace with logs burning brightly and the feeling of being in a real room somewhere, a welcoming. There were chairs and other upholstered pieces scattered about, all facing the fireplace. There were cardboard boxes against the walls, and cabinets open, their contents spilled outward and into some of the boxes. There was a sense of leaving, of packing here. Jason stopped and looked around.

"Come in, Jason. We haven't long here, as you can see." Unlike the room, the voice was cold and unfeeling.

Jason turned and saw the chair closest to the fireplace swing about slightly. There was a man sitting in it, quiet and still; brunette hair curled to his shoulders and his face had the pallor of marble. The man was dressed in a dark suit, with a soft white silken shirt. There was an unearthly aura to his entire being. He looked at Jason, unsmiling, dark eyes seeming to pierce right through him.

"Got off the tomb, I see," Jason commented. He was used to seeing this figure lying atop that cold sarcophagus.

The man laughed. None of the mirth reached his eyes or voice, or colored his skin with a pleasant blush. There was no humor in him at all as he leveled his gaze on Jason's face. "It was an effort I made," Brennard said. "No thanks to you."

Jason had no more intention of coming near Brennard now than he would have if the man were still atop his cold stone tomb below and reaching out for help. "What are you doing here?"

A thin, chill smile. "Don't you mean . . . what am *I* doing here?"

"Either way. What are either of us doing here?"

"I know," said Brennard. "I might tell you. Or I might not. It depends."

For a dizzying moment, Jason wondered if he were really in a dream or if Brennard had crafted a way to meet, to trap him. If he blinked, would he wake up, or would he lose everything by being caught? He ought to be able to wake if he had to, to escape. If this *were* a dream. And if it wasn't . . .

A shiver ran down his back, icy cold fingers trailing along his spine.

Still, given his choices, he'd rather be here facing Brennard than Statler Finch. The odd comparison ran through his thoughts, startling him for a moment, and he took a step backward because it really wouldn't do to be facing Brennard off-balance. Nor keeping half his mind, half an ear, out for his unprotected back. His left hand ached a bit, but he did not rub it. He would not touch that scar in front of his enemy. Why, he was not sure, but he thought it might not be a good thing to let Brennard know he had any edge against Jason.

"Come closer. Let me have a look at you in the light."

Jason took two steps forward, not really carrying him all that much closer, but enough to be polite. Look him over, Brennard did, the dark eyes of the Magicker examining him from head to toe.

"Strange clothes," Brennard commented dryly, "But I am

told that I should get used to them. Some things are better. Some are not. Much is greatly changed." The elder, who did not look in years to be much older than Gavan Rainwater, shifted in his chair, large slender hands moving restlessly. "You've a focus, I presume?"

"It's not what makes me a Magicker, but yes." Jason fought the need to put his hand on his crystal, to take it out and check it, make sure it was safe against this man. The more he wanted to do it, the more he felt that it was because Brennard was somehow making him want to do it, and therefore he would not.

Brennard frowned slightly. "You lack much training."

"And yet I elude you." Jason put his chin up.

"Here, yes. For the moment." Brennard gestured. "Out there, yes." He smiled thinly again. "For the moment."

"You expect things to change? I expect to get stronger."

"Do you?" Brennard leaned forward, his expression intent. "What Gregory and I fought about was nothing less than the essence of Magick itself. What if they are wrong and I am right? How can they possibly train you? How can you possibly grow into your potential and protect yourself, and your friends, from the world we have today? What if they are all wrong, and I am right? Ask yourself that."

"If you are right, why do you pursue me with nightmares and wolfjackals?"

"They are not mine. They are a . . ." Brennard sat back, and his hands made a pass through the air. "They are a negative aspect to the positive forces of the mana. A balance, if you will. For every light, there must be a dark."

Jason did not wholly believe him for a second. If the wolfjackals weren't his, he did not hesitate to use them, nor did any of his Dark Hand!

"I admit," said Brennard quietly, "what I offer is not appealing. It would be wonderful to think that Magick is unlimited, that it is flowing everywhere and we can just reach out . . . and hold it. But think, Jason. Is there any resource in your world that is unlimited? The sun? It will burn out. Perhaps a thousand thousand years, perhaps sooner, perhaps later, but it consumes itself. Our water? As we dirty it, there is less and less available. The earth itself? Wind and pollution eat away at it. What then? Nothing. Why should Magick be any different?"

The golden lights illuminating the room flickered. Brennard did not seem to notice it, but Jason did. And the one thing he desperately wanted was *not* to be left alone in the dark with this man. His words made a kind of sense, but there was a catch to them, and Jason knew he would find that catch, if he had a moment or two to himself to think. Here and now, though, was not the time to examine Brennard's teachings.

In fact, it was time to go, Jason decided. He took a step back.

"Don't go, lad. Stay. Perhaps there is something I can teach you, some little thing you will have of me, that might convince you later." Brennard looked upon Jason, and in his gaze the boy caught a glimpse of power and knowledge.

Jason didn't think staying was an option.

"Your friends aren't nearly so good at denying me," Brennard stated.

"They're as strong as I am."

"You think so? I know better. I'll have them, too, perhaps even before I have you."

He took another step back and sensed the doors right behind him. Once through those doors, he would be in the dark and hotly pursued again. Jason paused. He looked around the room. Why had he felt so much heat at the front doors?

As he looked toward Brennard, and the fireplace, he sensed a curtain of fire behind them, consuming that end of the room, like a wildfire out of control. It danced and wavered like a heat vision mirage, flames licking upon the walls and up toward the ceiling. A cold illusion, Jason thought, but not one which Brennard seemed to even be aware of. What did those flames strive to tell him?

"Good-bye," said Jason abruptly as he turned and bolted back through the doors he entered by.

Brennard snarled an oath and sprang after him, or so Jason thought because he heard the heavy chair tumble to the floor as he dove into darkness. The moon's singular beam seemed very thin and inadequate, but he'd left the front door open, and raced for it knowing that the end of his dream awaited.

He would reach it this time. He wondered if there would come a time in his nightmares when he did not—and what would happen then?

*   *   *

That worry still haunted him when Trent's dad drove by and dropped Trent off for the day. Trent shouldered his backpack as he leaped out of the car, shouting, "I'll call you when I'm ready to be picked up!"

Trent's dad grunted a reply through the rolled-up car window as he pulled away. The two boys sparred a bit, happy to actually see each other. "He doesn't mind your staying out late?"

"Nah. He's got sales projections for next year to work on, said he wouldn't be much company anyway. He doesn't mind driving back tonight, though he said I could stay over if that works out better."

"Cool. Have you got that stuff for Henry?"

"Sure do. It didn't take much time at all, with the computer and stuff." Trent tapped his backpack, grinning widely.

"Good, 'cause I need to know how much trouble Henry might be in."

"Oh? What's up?" Trent trotted up the walkway toward the back door and kitchen, matching Jason's steps.

"I think we're all under attack, in one way or another. I'm not so sure they want to do away with us . . . I think maybe he wants us corraled. Brought in. So we can be used in one way or another." Jason paused, his hand on the back doorknob. "And I don't think the Magickers can protect us."

Trent followed him in, looking about to make sure that part of the house was quiet and unoccupied, before whistling softly. "That's pretty heavy, Jason."

He went to the stove and checked the teakettle to make sure it was full before turning on the heat under it. Then he arranged two mugs and poured hot chocolate packets into each before answering, "I know. But the facts are in front of us. The beacon rarely works. Whether something is interfering with it, or they can't monitor it as they'd like, or whatever. And, face it—we won't use a beacon unless we're under attack. By then, it's too late. We're already in trouble, and we're not trained enough to be able to face all the Dark Hand can throw at us."

"So what's the solution?"

Jason shrugged. "We need a place of our own. Someplace to be safe and to study."

"Hogwarts."

Jason grinned at the fictional reference. "Well, doubt if we could find anywhere so neat, but ... yeah."

"Ravenwyng."

"They're working on that one. I've been thinking that what I need to do is find us a Gate or two, for safety. Like a shadow we can slip into, if we need to."

"Through the crystals."

"Yes."

Trent watched him solemnly. "That'll do for you guys. What about me?"

"I'm thinking I can fix a crystal with a ... a swinging door. One that anyone can push open or shut."

"Neat, if you can do it. Dangerous, too ... what if you can do it, and I drop the crystal?"

"You wouldn't."

"What if I did?"

"No one else would know how to use it."

Trent squirmed a bit on the kitchen chair. "It's tempting," he said slowly, "if you could do it."

"I'm the Gatekeeper. If anyone can, I can."

Trent watched him as he poured water into the mugs, making frothy cups of hot chocolate, plopped two big marshmallows into each, and brought them to the kitchen table. "Just because you can, doesn't mean you should."

"We have to be safe."

Jason knew Trent couldn't argue with that, and he didn't. Instead he concentrated on sinking his melting marshmallow, pushing it under with the bowl of the spoon and watching it plop! back up onto the surface. "Why can't we just pop in through the Iron Gate to Ravenwyng?"

"First of all, Gavan and the others are working in there, when they can. Council meetings and stuff. And when they're not there . . ." Jason considered. "I don't know, it worries me. Like the alarm beacon. It should work, but frequently it doesn't. I think Brennard has found a way to interfere with Ravenwyng, at least until Gavan gets it settled and locked beyond Iron Gate. Secondly, the Dark Hand knows about it just as much as we do. No, we need a Gate of our own."

"So you just open one?"

Jason rubbed the back of his neck. He looked at Trent across the table. The smell of the rich chocolate drinks in front of them scented the whole kitchen, and he pulled his mug closer and sipped at the dark froth cautiously. "Well. It's not that easy, I'll admit that. But I can feel one, close by, and it's getting . . . I dunno . . . closer?"

"Feel it?"

Jason nodded. "It's like having itchy palms and you know you're going to get unexpected money or something. It's twitching at me. I know it's there, somewhere."

"So that's what we're going to do before everything else starts happening? Find a Gate and just pop through?"

"If you'll help."

Trent looked at him, a chocolate-and-marshmallow mustache riding his upper lip, which he licked off looking quite satisfied and catlike. "What do I do?"

"I need an anchor. Someone on this side."

"I can do that." He sank his second marshmallow. "What if there's trouble?"

"Yank me back. Just like . . . just like pulling me by the arm."

Trent nodded. "I can do that, too." He lifted his mug, gulped down half his remaining drink, and sat back. "I can't let you make me a swinging door, though."

"And why not?"

"It's too dangerous. Anything could go in, or come out. Think about it, Jason. It won't work. I'm on my own, unless I'm with one of you, and I'm only as safe as you guys are. Which only means I have to do everything I can to make sure everyone else is okay, so you guys will be able to save *my* bacon when I need it!" He drummed his fingertips on the tabletop, always listening to an inner music no one else could hear. "All right then, let's rock and roll."

Jason grinned. "Soon as I'm ready."

Later, he thought he'd never be ready for this. Not really. Cupping his crystal in his hand, Jason stood with the early morning sun slanting across his back, Trent with an arm linked through his, and the tickle of a Gate growing stronger and stronger until he knew all he had to do was *Push* and it would swing open. What sort of Gate it was, he had no real idea and there was a tiny, nagging thought at the back of his mind that it could be a trap of Brennard's, but that was why he had Trent here. Like a safety ground for an electrical current, Trent would keep him tied to his own world, no matter what he found on the other side of the Gate.

He took a deep breath. "Okay," he said. "Here I go." He rubbed his crystal, looking deep into it, seeing a shadowy plane he wished to open and go through.

The Gate swung in. He stood for a moment, then swirling color hit him, and howling winds, and the stink of unbreathable ammonia, and a sense that something lay before him, all arms and tentacles, swaying and thrashing about.

The Thing lashed out, reaching for him.

"Uh-oh," said Jason.

22

ANCHORS AWAY

JASON put out a hand to steady himself, but there was nothing . . . no doorway or pass or rock or tree or anything to hold onto as the wind tore at him and threatened to knock him literally off his feet. The world seemed to be nothing but a swirl of mist and cloud and one wailing, angry *thing*.

The only solid thing, it looked like a tall and fleshy flower stalk, with a snapping jaw buried in its top and plenty of vines to catch unwary prey with. It made a noise like a high thin wailing that seemed to be almost out of Jason's hearing range. It swayed as if blindly attracted to Jason.

He jumped away from a whipping tentacle, an orange rope that smelled disgusting and left trails of slime dripping through the air as it moved. A drop touched his arm and stung like a bee! With a yelp he danced out of range and tried to peer into the heavy mists.

The air stank, and he couldn't catch his breath, couldn't breathe whatever was in the wind here. He coughed as he jerked about and knew that, wherever this Gate led, it was not to a place where people could live. He might be on an alien planet somewhere on the far side of the universe, for all he could tell. He scouted about for another moment, just to prove himself wrong, when he heard a scuttling across the rocks.

The thing came after him hungrily, hopping on its one-footed stalk. Jason rubbed his arm, the skin angry and tender, and dodged one, two, now three tentacles frantically searching through the mists for him. Time to go! He put his thoughts back to Trent, wherever he might be, and pulled, *hard*. SsssssNAP!

There was a moment when he had nothing to pull on and another moment when he firmly had Trent in his mind's grip and he boomeranged back where he belonged.

Coughing and choking, eyes tearing with the awful ammonia cleaner smell, he tumbled to the grass at Trent's feet. His friend looked down at him thoughtfully. "I take it that was a no-go."

Jason rubbed his tearing eyes as he sat up and fought for breath. He nodded wordlessly. After a few long moments of coughing and choking during which he realized he would have died inside that Gate had he stayed much longer, not as a victim of orange tentacles but poison air, he was able to take a deep breath. Trent solemnly passed him a handkerchief which Jason used thoroughly and stuffed in his pocket for laundry later.

"I think that might explain why there aren't many Gatekeepers around," Trent added thoughtfully. "Theoretically, if you're opening up doors on universal planes, most of them could be really inhospitable. In other words, it's ugly out there."

Jason snorted. "You think?" He stood, dusting himself off. There was an angry scratchlike welt on his arm where that thing had dropped slime. "If there was only a way to see through a Gate before going through."

"Maybe the other side doesn't exist till you open it. Which, of course, negates everything I just said."

Jason thought about that, then shook his head. "No, because something lived there . . . it just didn't explode out of nowhere."

Trent drummed his fingers on the side of his leg. "Don't tell me this is one of those 'if a tree falls in the forest and no one hears it, does it still make a sound' conversations? 'Cause I swore I'd never get into that."

Jason nodded. "Close, huh? But seriously, I thought I'd fallen into *Star Wars* or something. And whatever it was, it was real." He showed his arm to Trent.

"That's like a burn." Trent grimaced in sympathy.

"Hurts like it, too. I'll have to put something on it later. And I couldn't breathe for all the ammonia or whatever." He took another deep breath and it felt good, California smog or not. "Ready to go again?"

"Sure. I've got the easy part, I just sit here and wonder where you disappeared to." Trent grinned at him.

"Won't be so easy if I disappear for good. You'd have a lot of explaining to do."

Trent's smile faded, and he looked solemnly at Jason. "Just don't do that."

"Right. I won't." They both knew it might not be that easy, but it was reassuring to make it sound that way. Jason put his hand on Trent's shoulder, cupped his crystal, and found a new facet, a new angle inside its beauty to focus upon. Within a moment, he saw a threshold, and stepped through. . . .

Nighttime. Wild countryside. Late autumn chill in the frosted ground below his feet, and Jason shivered in his short-sleeved shirt. A moon overhead lay very low in the sky, just barely clearing the treetops, like a great yellow pumpkin, and he marveled at it for a moment, so large and clear. It seemed larger than any harvest moon he'd ever seen before. He took a halting breath, carefully, but it smelled only of the night, a little moist. Some faint night flower perfumed it along with the scent of the grass and trees, and there was the chill of the crackling frost on the ground. He had a sensation of dream time and shook it off. This was real. This was no dream where all he had to do was wake up to return to reality. What existed here could and would hurt him if it seemed dangerous.

Still and all, this was promising. From the brilliance of the many stars in the sky, he realized there were no city lights nearby to diffuse their strength. No traffic sounds or noise reached him. It was not quiet, by any means; he could hear the rattle of tree branches and the chirp of many crickets, and the sound of a brook flowing nearby. The nightscape was rocky and rather bare, but it was obviously nearing winter. Many of the trees were leafless, their branches shaking in a slight night breeze. He looked about, trying to imagine what it would be like to have a Haven here. They could bring a tent, perhaps, something salvaged from one of the family garages, and pitch it permanently.

It might do. It might indeed. Smiling, Jason turned around and started off over a little knoll to get a better look around. His foot hit a stone, and it rolled downhill a bit, then bounced off a boulder, and clattered noisily down a slope where he felt the brook might be. It sounded louder than it was, because there wasn't much other noise around to muffle it. He didn't hear a splash follow it, though. A few more clatters echoed as if smaller pebbles had also been dislodged and were rattling down the incline.

Then silence fell. Complete and total silence. The crickets stopped. The wind held its breath. And Jason felt a stab of fear.

A howl sounded from not very far away. Another joined it, and then a third.

Jason turned slowly. His blood went icy with recognition. It seemed he had been unlucky enough to find the world which was home to wolfjackals! He raced back to the spot at which hc'd opened the Gate, and palmed his crystal, seeking Trent's anchoring presence.

It was there, but thready, fading in and out like a cellular phone transmission with a battery going dead. He could feel his friend, and then he could not, all faint and watery feeling. He didn't know much about Gates except that they had a very real base and he couldn't run, or he'd lose this one. And if he didn't run, the wolfjackals were likely to pull him down!

The howls grew stronger in the night, and he looked across the ridge. By the light of the low, yellow moon, he could see three massive wolfish bodies racing fast across the disk's il-lumination. Another few jumps and he would be able to see their ivory fangs gleaming in their jaws, altogether way too close!

Jason rubbed his crystal. He tore his gaze from the ridge and looked down into his crystal, barely visible in the evening, his hands shaking. The scar on his left hand began to throb painfully, almost a match for the burn on his right arm. If only Trent could focus, too, from his side.

But his friend couldn't, and suddenly Jason questioned his suitability for what Jason had chosen him to do. He should have waited for Bailey. Or even Rich and Stefan. Anyone but someone with no Magick. He drew his crystal close, his breath exhaling in a white mist about it. *Just think, Trent, harder and harder—or I'm going to lose you and . . . me!*

His hands trembled, and he dropped his quartz. It bounced into the stiff and spare grasses about his feet and abruptly winked out of sight. Jason dropped to his knees, searching frantically. Nothing met his touch. He ran his hands through the brittle, frost-dried tangled grasses and found nothing. Chilled and dirty, he began to search even more desperately. Wonderful if it had bounced away and he didn't hear it.

Howls rippled nearer. He wouldn't look up. He was lost without his crystal, and it didn't matter if the wolfjackals got him or not then. Panic began to well up in him. He had to find it. It had to be here somewhere. He dug across the shale and grass tufts frantically.

Nothing. Gone. It was gone.

It couldn't be gone. He'd *feel* it if it was gone. Like . . . like a hole in himself or something. *Think, Jason, think.*

At camp when they'd been introduced to the crystals, the tables had been covered with trays. Crystals, quartzes and rocks of all kind were laid out, and they'd been told to look them over very carefully, and not touch unless very very sure of what they were doing. His had held a kind of warmth that drew him, a fuzzy kind of tingle.

He wasn't just looking for any ordinary rock in the dark. Jason took a breath to steady himself and calm his racing thoughts and put his hand out, palm down, and tried to feel for his crystal. That faint warmth that was for him and him alone.

A chorus of howls nearby shattered the air again. He could hear their hot pants, the click of their nails on the rocky slope as they bounded up. Something warm grazed his fingers, he grabbed for it.

Jason blinked in surprise. Crystal it was, but not *his* crystal. This was bigger, and absolutely transparent, with a bold lavender color to it that shone in the dark. How he'd not seen it before, he couldn't tell. Before he could stand in puzzlement, his other hand found a steady warmth and reached for his own crystal, secure, wrapped in fallen autumn leaves and damp from lying on the ground.

He turned, a crystal in each hand and made fists, as the wolf-jackals bore down on him. It was now or never for him to find Trent. Otherwise, he would have to open another Gate and just fall through.

He squeezed his hands. Trent's tuneless humming filled his mind. With a shout of relief, Jason anchored on him and pulled through just as the first wolfjackal leaped.

23

SURPRISED PARTY

TRENT blinked as Jason tumbled to the grass in front of him, pale almost beyond belief, arms stiff at his sides with his hands knotted into fists. He bent over his friend immediately and felt the icy cold radiating from him. Jason smiled stiffly up at him, teeth chattering, lips blue around the edges.

"Oh, man," Trent breathed. "That doesn't look good at all! Come on, come on, get up!" He pulled Jason to his feet, half-surprised his clothes didn't explode into frozen splinters. Jason continued to shake, jaws clattering, and he hugged himself as if trying to hold what little warmth remained inside him. "In the house. Come on." He pushed and pulled at Jason, got him upstairs—thank goodness the inquisitive sister and overachieving stepmom were out at some lesson or other—and he steered Jason up to the trapdoor ladder leading to the attic bedroom.

Once there, Jason toppled over onto the bed. Trent piled blankets and quilts on top of him. He ran downstairs and microwaved a steaming cup of hot tea, raced back up and fed it to Jason who tried to sip it, shaking so hard he spilled more of it than he drank and finally waved the mug away. Trent plunked down at the computer desk, and watched. It got worse, until Jason shook all over with helpless chills, but the color slowly came back to his face, and he finally stopped shaking. He melted into his bed, and unclenched his teeth, and drew his hands out, uncurling his fingers slowly. He sat up, and not one but two crystals fell from his fists onto the coverlet.

They both stared in astonishment.

"I . . . I . . . d–d–d–didn't imagine it," Jason got out.

"Two crystals? How'd you manage that? And what happened? You stumble onto Antarctica or something?"

"N–n–n–nothing like that." Jason stumbled onto his feet, and the two brilliant crystals tumbled to the bedroom carpet. "Did they come through with me?"

"The rocks? Yeah. We were just talking about that." Trent stared, baffled. He pushed Jason gently back onto the bed. "Just sit there till you warm up. I'm not so sure you're not in shock or something."

"N–n–no. I'm fine. I d–d–didn't know I was so c–c–cold." Jason pulled his blankets tighter around him. He reached out and picked up his own crystal, shoving it deep into his pocket, and then picked up the second. Crystalline, completely transparent, with a faint, pure lavender color throughout its many facets. He held it so that Trent could see it, too. "Look at this."

"I'm looking." Trent sighed faintly. A slight note of envy crept in, and he flushed a little.

Jason said immediately, "I'm sorry."

"Don't be. You didn't do anything. Where'd you find it? Are you Bonded, do you think? It *is* one of those rocks, isn't it?"

"I think so, and it was there, where I was. The Gate area looked like Earth this time, only out in the country, the wilderness. Nighttime, and out on the . . . the . . ." Jason tried to search for a word to fit the landscape. "Moors? Countryside. Slopes and rock and trees gone to winter. Everything very dark and still, with this huge harvest moon hanging in the sky. It looked really promising until I heard the wolfjackals. And then I dropped my crystal."

Trent looked stunned. "No way."

"I couldn't find it in the dark." Jason inspected his hands. They looked like he'd been digging in the dirt, grubby and scuffed and even bruised. "I combed the ground . . . I could hear them coming after me, howling, running across the hill."

"They knew you were there?"

"They always do." Jason shuddered. "I didn't think I'd make it back."

"What did you do?"

"I stopped trying to dig out . . . my crystal has a warmth. I decided to find that, you know? And it came to me. This strange one. I found it first, then the other, but they both just kind of answered me. One minute I had nothing, the next I had two." Jason held the lavender gem out to Trent.

He took it carefully. It hadn't been polished or faceted, but it looked like a handful of faintly purple diamond. "This could be valuable. Some gemstones are priceless, like diamonds." It held no heat for him. Disappointed, he passed it back. "You look better. Warming up?"

"Yeah." He bounced the new crystal in his hand for a moment. "I could hardly feel you. I don't think I would have made it back without this second one."

"Really?"

Jason nodded.

"Awesome."

Jason laughed then. "You're stupid."

Trent grinned. "Hey! You made it back. Don't complain!"

"Yeah, yeah. I'll have to show this to Gavan, see what he thinks of it. It could be I am bonded."

"And the problem with that is . . . ?"

Jason looked at him. "It came from the Haven where wolf-jackals roam. I've no idea what kind of energy it could hold . . . who might have had it before. Think about it, Trent. This could be big trouble."

They both looked at it in solemn silence. Trent finally broke the silence. "I don't think," he stated, "that anything about you could be evil." He cleared his throat. "Some people just have this quality about them. You're one of 'em. You can't even tell a lie to save yourself." He stopped awkwardly, then started again. "Now Bailey, on the other hand, would cheerfully kill both of us if we missed the party."

Jason's jaw dropped. "The party! I nearly forgot it. Let me get cleaned up and then go find Dozer for our ride." He shed the blankets and comforter like a cocoon, and the two of them tumbled downstairs.

*   *   *

San Francisco was hazy and cool, with a stiff wind coming in over the bay where the airport sat, far outside the city actually. Her uncle and his family came to meet them, and they rode to the city in his van, filled with his children and their conversation, mostly in English with an occasional string of Mandarin wrapped around it. Ting sat, surrounded by it all, smiling when she could. Her mother seemed cheered by her brother's presence and attitude. It was not, as Ting had feared, like going to a funeral. Grandmother might be seriously, dreadfully ill . . . but no one seemed to think they were going to be burying her soon. That made everything something to look forward to.

When the van finally neared the city and its neighborhoods, they all grew a little quieter, only her uncle and mother in the front seats talking, their voices pitched so softly that it was very hard to hear them. When they neared her grandmother's address, it was impossible not to know. Asian faces filled the streets. Chinese calligraphy lettered shop windows and billboards, even the great banks at the corners, as well as small eateries. She could smell delicious, smoky odors as they drove by . . . garlic, ginger, other spices she couldn't name. She thought of FireAnn, the Magicker cook and herbalist with the fiery red hair, and how she could probably reel off every aroma floating from restaurants and home kitchens alike.

She saw many elders walking the streets in their quilted jacket and trouser outfits, very Old World, and yet not at all strange here. Then, at last, they pulled up to the house, hidden behind its circular driveway. When Ting got out of the van, she tilted her head back and stared briefly at the bronze dragon coiled along the roof's edge. The chrysanthemums were a brilliant orange-red, like the ripest of persimmons.

Her uncle paused next to her, his arms full of baggage. "I painted the flowers for her birthday," he said. "Enameled them, actually. You like?"

Ting beamed at him. "I do!"

He nodded. "So did she. Come inside. I imagine she has lunch waiting."

They entered the house. Actually, with Uncle and all the nieces and nephews, it was more like an invasion. Her grandmother appeared in the small, very formal living room, dressed in a flowered Chinese red dress that made her appear very tiny, very pale, and very old, her formerly dark hair now almost entirely silver. Ting could not remember her grandmother's glossy black hair going gray, but it obviously had.

Pleasure spread over her grandmother's face as she opened her arms to embrace them.

And indeed, she had luncheon ready. The great, round kitchen table was spread with two kinds of rice, duck, Buddha's delight with tofu squares in vegetables and brown sauce, two green bean dishes, and one big heaping platter of chicken cooked in a gingery, garlicky sauce. Ting's stomach growled in spite of herself as she sat down, and her grandmother smiled. She sat next to Ting and hugged her shoulders.

"I am so glad you could come to help me." Little was said beyond that as everyone took out their chopsticks and practically fell on the lunch.

Ting noticed that her grandmother ate little, although she nursed a cup of egg drop soup, and a fine porcelain cup of tea throughout the meal. She looked up to meet her mother's gaze and realized Jiao had caught that as well. She shook her head slightly at Ting. Now was not the time. There would be many days ahead.

After the meal, Uncle Han took his boisterous family and left them alone. She helped her mother put away the leftovers and clear the table. Then they cleaned the kitchen. Grandmother lapsed into a silence, her lips pressed in a pained line, as if exhausted by it all. They worked around her gently, trying not to disturb her, and then Jiao fixed a pot of fragrant jasmine tea, and they gathered together again.

She took her mother's hands in hers as Ting poured them all cups.

"I am glad you came," the old woman said, her voice very thin and tired.

"I am glad you told us we could come." Jiao kissed her mother's forehead. "We will see this through."

"My fortune and house is a strong one."

Ting sat down quietly.

"As for you." Her grandmother's almond eyes turned to her. "I am sorry to take you from your school and friends."

"I'm happy to be here. And I can go to school here, and well . . . I can help here."

"But still . . ." Grandmother signaled Jiao to sit. She took up her teacup. "Ting. I have only seen you once since the summer, but I know you have changed. You have begun to walk a new path."

Ting looked into her dark, rosy tea. What did her grandmother mean? She didn't want to think. Was she going to have to sit here and listen to a lecture about growing up? She peeked at her mother. Jiao gave no sign of anything in her expression. Ting tried not to sigh, and settled on the hard rosewood chair, prepared for a lesson she was not even sure she would understand, steeped as it would be in old Chinese proverbs.

Her grandmother said firmly, "Look at me, please."

Embarrassed, Ting raised her gaze.

"We know," her grandmother said, nodding to Jiao and then looking back at her. "We know your secret."

"Know what?" Ting felt totally baffled. Then it began to creep in fearfully. Know . . . *what?*

Her grandmother stretched out a hand. It was still an elegant hand, for all the age showing in her knuckles and slightly wrinkled skin. She moved, and a fan filled her fingers, snapping open with a second graceful movement. She dropped the fan, made another gesture, and her hand filled with silk flowers. She dropped that bouquet on top of the fan. "On the mainland, my father was a magician. He was known for his talent and his wisdom, but as you know, true wizardry is not sleight of hand."

Ting thought her heart would stop. Oh, no! The Oath of Binding crept into her throat. Even if she wanted to, she could not speak! She stared at her mother desperately. *Oh, please, don't ask me anything!* she begged silently.

Her grandmother waited, watching her face. Then, after long moments in which Ting thought her heartbeat ticked as loudly as the old clock on the wall, she sat back in her chair. She reached out and took Ting's wrist in her hand, and turned it, showing plainly the bracelet with its caged bit of crystal in it. She tapped the crystal.

"We know," her grandmother repeated quietly.

Now there was no doubt about it. Ting's secret of being a Magicker was no longer secret!

Henry and Bailey were walking the mall near the pizza restaurant when McIntire dropped the two boys off. Jason and Trent bailed out of the truck, waved good-bye after a few instructions on when and where to be picked up.

"Is she here yet?"

Bailey shook her head. "Any minute now, I bet." The evening sky had begun to darken, and shoppers thinned out as dinner elsewhere called them. The atrium ceiling of the mall showed stars already, their silvery blue twinkle bright in a dark October sky. Only the costume shops were still doing a brisk business, their storefronts filled with mannequins in wizard and witch costumes, and satin cats with sequined masks. There was a werewolf in the far corner, fake fur costume bristling in gray-and-black stripes. Henry let out a shudder as they passed it, and Trent and Jason swapped glances. *Test*, mouthed Trent at Jason, and Jason nodded. If Bailey noticed, she didn't show it. She paced up and down the mall, her face scrunched up. Finally, she disappeared into the public phone kiosk.

She came out, flailing her arms in exasperation. "She's not coming."

"What?" Henry's round face collapsed in disappointment and he rubbed his nose. "Not coming?"

"She's not even in the same county any more."

"Ting?" chorused Jason and Trent together.

Bailey gave an emphatic nod. "How," she demanded, "can we have a surprise party without the honored guest?"

24

TRUTH OR DARE

"TING'S gone?"

"She's already left for San Francisco. In fact, she was up there by lunchtime." Bailey crossed her arms over her body. "I talked to her older sister, who says she called and left a message at your house yesterday, Jason, but somebody forgot to pass it along."

He winced. "I didn't get it."

"Obviously." Bailey tossed her head.

The only one he could think of who might have thoughtlessly forgotten it would have been Alicia. He made a mental note to ask her about things like that more often. Just in case. "Sorry."

Henry let out a discouraged sound, drawing Bailey's attention. Jason kept his mouth shut, happy the other distracted her.

Bailey nudged Squibb, softening. "Hey, it's not like we can't talk to her when she gets her computer set up again! After all, we've been e-mailing Danno even though he's an ocean away from us now."

His round face brightened a little. "True."

"Well, then. We're all here anyway. Let's go order a pizza and talk. You guys can tell me all about the game you've been running."

Henry fell into step with her, Jason and Trent trailing behind. "It's been great. You ought to join. Hey, guys," he threw back over one shoulder. "We can fit her in, can't we? Pick up an elf along the way or something?"

Bailey waved her hand. "No, no. My mom won't let me online that long. We have to keep the phone line clear, in case she gets a call from work or something. Sounds like fun, though. So what do you play?" and she ducked her head, listening intently, as Henry happily told her all about his halfling alter ego, filled with cheerful larceny. She laughed as they made their way to the pizza parlor.

They ordered two, because all three of the boys professed to being starving, and Bailey wanted to make sure she'd have some for herself. And a pitcher of root beer to go around for everyone but Henry. "I don't drink soft drinks any more," he apologized. "Not since I got back from camp. Something about sugary, fruity tasting things . . ." He quivered. "Water or iced tea, no sweetener, for me!"

The Draft of Forgetfulness had been a berry concoction FireAnn stewed for days at the back of Camp Ravenwyng's kitchen. No one knew what it was at first. Henry had been one of the first to drink it, and seeing him go . . . blank . . . had been devastating. Later, the other campers being sent home because of the Brennard attack would drink it, too, except for the handful Jason had rallied and hidden away. He'd had plans of his own! Jason had thought the Draft incredibly harsh, but the others had insisted it was best. He still didn't think so.

By the time the pizzas arrived, bread crust steaming on round aluminum pans dripping over with melted cheese, they had their table covered with maps and graphs and character descriptions, and lists of treasures and magic items recovered so far. They talked of orcs and dragons and enchanted swords and crafty adventurers. Curious onlookers from nearby glanced over from time to time, smiling, as tales of a fantasy world swirled around their table.

Only once did Bailey sigh and sit back, saying she wished Ting were there. Henry reached for her hand to pat it, and instead found himself holding a furry creature as it darted down Bailey's sleeve. He let out a squawk, and then shut his lips, face reddening in embarrassment.

Bailey grabbed for Lacey who had evidently decided she'd waited long enough for pizza crumbs! The little kangaroo mouse chittered in annoyance as Bailey stuffed her back in her pocket.

Henry reached for his water. He gulped down half a glass and nearly choked on an ice cube. He lowered his voice. "You picked up a rat!"

"Mouse!" hissed Bailey back. "Well, kangaroo mouse ... a pack rat. Don't you remember my pack rat from camp?"

Henry shook his head as Trent and Jason muffled their amusement and each reached for another slice of pizza.

"Well, she haunted our cottage. Stole things right and left, much like your halfling. We found her, though, and she was just too little to put back in the wild. What if something ate her? So she's mine now."

"And hungry, too, it seems." Henry scrubbed at an eyebrow. He pinched off a bit of cheesy dough and passed it to Bailey. "Maybe that'll help."

"Couldn't hurt!" Bailey said cheerfully and stuffed it down her pocket. Her shirt rumpled and rippled and there was a tiny, contented chirping sound. Henry's eyes grew a bit rounder behind his circular glass lenses.

Trent pushed aside an empty pizza tin, gathering up some of his papers. "Enough about D & D. How about some truth and dare?"

Jason leaned on his elbows. "Secrets?"

"Sure." Trent waited while everyone stored away the paperwork they had brought. "Everyone has secrets. Like Lacey."

"Well ... okay." Bailey wiped off the table in front of her carefully, poking another small bread crumb or three down into her pocket and settled down, watching Trent.

Henry took off his glasses solemnly and cleaned them. Trent nudged him, saying, "Relax! This is supposed to be fun." Henry bobbed his head, brown hair waving up and down. "Who wants to go first?" Trent looked round the table.

"Me," Bailey said with a definite nod of her head that sent her golden-brown ponytail bouncing.

"Okay. Hmm. Let me confer with my associate." Trent grinned and leaned over to Jason. They talked for a moment. Trent straightened up. He gazed at Bailey a moment before saying, "Is it true you prefer Brad Pitt over Justin Timberlake and would kiss either to death if you had the chance?"

"Trent!" Bailey gasped, her face glowing pink.

"Truth or Dare?"

She babbled for a moment, then shut her mouth and said firmly, "Dare."

"Ooooh." Trent grinned. "Gotta be a good one."

"Conference," suggested Jason, leaning over.

"Righto."

They talked for a few minutes, and then Trent pointed at Bailey. "Three times around the restaurant, making chicken noises as you go."

"We'll get thrown out!" Bailey stared at him.

"You chose the dare." Trent sat, unmoved.

"I can't do that." Bailey glanced around the parlor, which was still fairly full of diners. A sports team of boys their age reigned at two whole tables in one corner although their talk and laughter wasn't loud enough to be disturbing.

Trent just stared at her.

"All right. All right." Bailey stood slowly. She put her hands back and tightened the scrunchie on her hair, and took a deep breath. Deliberately, she walked to the center of the room. "Ladies and gentlemen," she said loudly, but not too loudly. "In praise of the barbecued chicken pizza!" And she began to trot around the room, arms bent at her elbows, begawking and clucking every few steps.

Trent rolled against Jason, laughing. Jason tried not to explode in mirth but couldn't help it. "Thank goodness we don't have live chickens in here!"

Trent turned red at that. "They'd all be following her!"

Bailey tossed her head, ponytail bobbing. "Begawk! Bock! Bock!"

Diners turned and laughed. Her face got pinker, and the cooks came out of the kitchen, watching curiously. As she drew near the end of her third circle, Bailey threw up her hands and said, "Chicken pizza so great I just had to squawk about it!"

She bowed all around to applause and chuckles, then raced back to their table amid cheers and claps. She poked Trent. "So there!"

"Well done. Your turn." Unabashed and unflinching, Trent grinned at her and gave her a tiny salute.

Henry looked at her in total awe. "That was great, Bailey. I'd have never thought of anything like that."

"I am a genius." Bailey gave another little bow. She leaned over, adding, "And I didn't get us thrown out either!"

Jason looked across the room. "I wouldn't say that." They all stopped talking as the manager began to approach them. He stopped at their table, envelope in hand.

"I don't know what brought that on, but it was one of the nicest endorsements I've ever had." He passed the envelope to Bailey and left.

She opened it slowly, then began to giggle.

"What is it?"

"A coupon for a free barbecued chicken pizza! I'll bring Ting when she gets back." Laughing, Bailey tucked it inside her backpack. "Okay. My turn!" She looked around the table. "Jason," she announced slowly.

"Rut roh," commented Trent as Jason sat up straighter.

Ignoring Trent, Bailey continued levelly, "Who would you rather kiss . . . Jennifer or Eleanora?"

Jason's jaw dropped for a moment as he tried to think of an answer. But he didn't have to give one, because he was interrupted.

Henry spluttered. "Eleanora! Jason can't kiss her!" he blurted out. "She's . . . she's . . . she's beautiful. And older. She could . . . she's got Magick . . . she could turn you into a toad if she wanted to, Jason!" He took his glasses off again and rubbed his eyes as if totally embarrassed by his outburst.

He didn't notice the looks they all exchanged round the table. "Calm down," Bailey said quietly. "It's just a game." She rolled her eyes as nearby tables looked over curiously, then looked away again and the murmur of other conversations rose around them.

"Actually," Jason said truthfully, "if I had to kiss anyone right now, it would be you, Bailey. Thank heavens I don't have to!" He grabbed Henry. "Henry, do you know what you just said? Do you?"

Henry's hands shook so his glasses fell to the table with a

clatter. His face whitened. "I . . . I . . . I . . ." His words ground to a halt, and they could all see the cords in his neck tighten.

Bailey scooted her chair over. "It's all right, Henry," she said quietly. "It's all right."

"I'm not crazy," he said finally, in a squeaky, forced, and scared voice. It was barely audible.

"No way. None of us are." Trent picked up his glasses and handed them back.

"You don't know what I mean."

"Oh, I think we do," Jason told him. He pitched his voice low so as not to be overheard, whether everyone thought they were still talking about their gaming or not. This was a public place, and they would all do well to be wary. Still, things had to be said. "We all do. We're all Magickers, Henry. And it looks like you still are, too."

"A . . . a . . . what?"

"Magicker," Jason, Bailey, and Trent all repeated to him simultaneously.

He looked very pale. Trent nudged a glass of water over to him, saying, "Drink it slowly."

He did so, every last drop, and looked much better when he set the glass down. "All of you?"

"All of us," Jason said. "Including you."

Henry made a sound of utter relief. "Thank goodness," he added. "I really thought I'd lost it." He squirmed in his chair. "I wanted to ask about it, you know . . . there are these big, blank spots about the camp which I ought to have known but didn't, even coming home early like I did. And nightmares. I've had some awful nightmares. Not about you guys, though!" He shook his head.

"About Jonnard?"

"How did you . . . well, of course you know. You remember."

"He stole your Magick, Henry," Bailey said in a rush. "No one thought you'd ever get it back, so they made you drink this juice drink, called the Draft of Forgetfulness, and they sent you home. But you were stronger than that, and Jason was right all along. He didn't want any of us to forget about you."

"What did you think?" Henry eyed Jason.

"I never thought they should send you home, and I think you're getting stronger every day. Which is good—and bad."

"Bad? How?"

Trent tapped the table, talking for Jason. "One, you're not trained well, none of us are, but you've missed a lot, and two, you're in danger because of it."

"What else could possibly go wrong?" Henry stared in disbelief at them.

Jason felt the hairs at the back of his neck prickle. The scar on his left hand gave a twinge. He moved in his chair, and looked around the mall restaurant. "Plenty," he began.

"Oh, look," someone said. "Someone's wearing that werewolf costume from the shop!"

There was a sound of chairs rattling as people moved to look.

He looked.

He stood, grabbing Henry and Bailey by their jackets and yelling for the one friend he couldn't quite reach. "Trent!"

The werewolf-looking creature peered into the windows of the pizza parlor and let out a low, rumbling growl.

"That's no costume."

25

MOONSTRUCK

"WOLFJACKAL!" Bailey's face went dead white even as she grabbed up her things.

Jason reached for his crystal as Trent joined the other two, and he searched the room for another way out as the wolfjackal sprang to the doorway, blocking it. He found one, marked Emergency Exit Only, and pulled them all that way, muttering, "If there was ever an Emergency . . ."

No one argued. Henry hit the door's big chrome bar first. His chunky body came to a halt. They piled up behind him. Jason turned and saw the wolfjackal come through the pizza parlor entrance, huge and snarling. A woman turned, looked, and screamed, her voice shrilling through the noise of other diners and the row of game machines in the corner. "It's real! George, it's real!"

The room dissolved into crashes of chairs and screams.

"Go, go, go!"

"I'm trying!" Henry grunted. He struggled to push the heavy bar with Bailey throwing her shoulder against it as well. The two suddenly plunged through, setting off loud alarms everywhere. Lacey poked her head out, squeaking in terror, her tail hanging out, black tuft jerking about. She dove back into safety, only her tuft twitching, as they all stumbled into the back street outside the pizza parlor.

"This way!" Jason spoke a word as he pushed through, and his hand filled with the golden lanternlike illumination from his crystal, and they dashed away, with a growling snarl just a leap behind. He could hear the animal grunt as it gave chase and crashed into the closing door. Above it all, the loud thin alarm of the Emergency Exit shrilled through the air.

"Run," he yelled, "as fast and hard as you can."

They didn't need his encouragement.

As golden light from his hand spilled out into the black alley, revealing dark looming shapes from huge trash bins, and skittering paper trash that the October wind swirled about as they raced through, they heard the low, haunting howl of the wolfjackal. It had gotten outside after them.

Henry managed to pant, "I don't remember that. Somehow, you'd think I would!"

They swerved around a low block wall that marked a delivery dock for the back of the big department store that took up most of the space at this part of the mall. Debris scattered about them as they ran. Trent muttered, "Hurry, hurry, hurry," while the golden light from Jason's crystal spilled out like a fountain from a Fourth of July sparkler. Cars were scattered throughout the lot, parked and empty, and great overhead lights tried to thin the darkness without much success. Their sneakers slapped the ground at a frantic pace, because they knew that no doorway or nook could be ducked into, for the sharp nose of the wolfjackal would not be easily fooled. It was a chase, a chase until someone dropped or was cornered or the wolfjackal could be attacked hard enough to frighten it away.

They swung around the lower edge of the mall and found themselves heading uphill where it was harder to run. They faced less traffic, fewer cars, as the only building they approached was a store that had gone out of business. The building was huge, dominating the whole upper end of the shopping area. It lay in front of them like some petrified giant beast.

Vast store windows were boarded over with plywood nailed securely for protection, decorated only by the trash wrappers clinging to them and the occasional spray-painted graffiti. The quiet in this section of the shopping park made the chase seem more ominous. There would be no unexpected help coming their way.

Bailey wobbled. She bumped shoulders with Henry unsteadily, then turned and threw a desperate look at Jason and Trent. "I can't run much longer . . . not on a stomach full of pizza."

"Not running is not an option!" Trent shouted back at her. He grabbed her elbow to steady her.

"I . . . can't . . . help it." She let out a belch of despair and Jason felt badly for her.

The only stand they could make was with one of them shielding and the other attacking. Trent couldn't do it, and Henry had no crystal nor training . . . if his Magick was even strong enough yet to attempt it. That left Bailey and she was good, but he feared her Magick still wouldn't be enough. Although Trent and Henry could grab something, a box or stick and whack away at it. Holding their ground seemed impossible . . . unless. . . .

The sound of tires squealing reached him. He looked out into the empty parking lot of the abandoned store and saw headlights racing closer. A vehicle careened toward them. Teens, accelerating and skidding through the open lot.

Jason swerved abruptly into the loading dock bay, pulling the others in with him. He went to one knee. "Bailey! Shield. Trent, protect Henry." He cupped his crystal, snuffing out the lantern light. Next to him, Bailey dug under her jacket and sweater, and grabbed her pendant. Its white light flared out and into an umbrella over them. She burped again, rolled her eyes, and said, "Remind me never to eat and run again." Her shield light flickered, then grew stronger.

Trent drew Henry next to him.

Jason rubbed his crystal gently, calling on the Magicker beacon. He could not feel an answering warmth. "Beacon's off again."

"It can't be."

"Well, it is! Someone's either blocking it, or it's gone out or . . ." Words failed him as the wolfjackal sprang onto the asphalt in front of them, crouching, eyes glinting, and ivory fangs gleaming from lips drawn back in a snarl. The beast put his head back in a triumphant howl.

"Yup," said Henry. "I would have definitely remembered this!"

"Good news," muttered Trent. "There's only one of 'em."

Another snarl ripped the air as a second wolfjackal padded around the corner of the building, its skulking body slinking into position next to its pack mate.

"Bad news," Trent added. "I can't count." He pulled his crystal out for Bailey's benefit. Dull and opaque even on the best days, it stayed that way now. "Even worse news, I've got the Curse. Crystal is deader than a doornail." He shoved it back into his sweatshirt pocket and reached for a length of wood, part of a splintered loading pallet, lying against the block wall of the dock. "Grab one, Henry, and make yourself useful."

Henry took up a thick piece and waved it in his hand like a club. He followed Trent's advice not a moment too soon as both wolfjackals bunched their haunches and then sprang at them!

Jason sent a beam slicing through the air, not unlike a laser sword. It sizzled as he wielded it, white-hot light cutting at the beasts. One wolfjackal yelped and curled about, biting at the beam and snarling. His pack mate hit the ground rolling and came up snapping at Henry and Trent. The creatures' hot breath steamed the cold night air. Trent fenced with one wolfjackal while Henry clubbed at its dancing feet. Bailey held steady, shielding them as well as she could, although the power of the wolfjackals slashed into her barrier again and again.

Jason turned, taking a long sweep at the beast facing him. Foam whipped from its jaws as it spun about, tracking him. His beam landed, the impulse rocking into his arm and shoulder, but the wolfjackal barely faltered. He jabbed and sliced again, his crystal sharp against the palm of his hand as he held it tightly. Jason could feel his power, holding the creature back but not really harming or driving it away. Eventually he'd weaken, and the wolfjackal would lunge through Bailey's shield. His pack mate yelped as Trent clipped it on the head, and the beast went rolling. It scrabbled for purchase on the slick, dark pavement as it did, amid the squeal of tires from outside the loading dock, and Jason got an idea.

"Drive 'em out of here and stay clear!" he said.

Trent and Henry surged forward, swinging their wooden slats and quickly fell back behind Bailey as the wolfjackal snapped, and Henry's wooden sword splintered in its jaws. The second one drove in, grabbing Trent and shaking him like a doll and not letting go till Trent beat it on the head with his jagged wooden board. He staggered back, into Henry and Bailey, with a curse, sweatshirt ripping as the beast let go. "They ain't budging."

"Try another plan," panted Henry.

Jason had one. But he wasn't at all sure it would work.

"Hold 'em here, then!" he cried out, and took a running start. He catapulted over the shoulders of the nearest beast, barely clearing it, and hit the ground in a dash. Both critters whirled with howls and scrambled after him. He knew they would, of course. Well, not knew, but hoped!

"Jason!" cried Bailey sharply in warning, and he swerved. A heavy body lunged just past him, and he could practically feel its foaming jaws as it did. It smelled of hot beast and something fearful he couldn't identify, something no natural creature smelled of. He swerved again, sharply, dodging into the parking lot.

They all collided: joyriding teens, Jason, and raiding wolfjackals. The car's headlights blinded him for a moment, the squeal of brakes filling his ears as it skimmed past him, and the heavy thud as the vehicle hit a beast, sending its limp body rolling and rolling. Wild yipes suddenly went quiet. The second wolfjackal let out a mournful howl, took a leap over its pack mate's body, and disappeared into the night.

The car skidded to a halt. Jason bent over, hands on his knees, breathing hard. The crumpled, bloody form of the remaining wolfjackal wavered as if in a mirage. Then it disappeared from sight. The asphalt where it had lain showed not a trace of its existence. Dead, yes. Gone where? Back to its own element? Or had its sender called it back?

Car doors opened and four teens piled out.

"What was that!"

He looked up. "Man, you hit my dog!" Straightening, he pointed a hand into the night.

"Oh, man. How bad is he hurt?"

"He ran off."

"Oh."

"Can't be too bad if he ran off. Come on, let's go." One of the passengers tucked at the sleeve of the stocky driver.

"What about my bumper?"

Jason stared angrily. "What about your bumper? Could have been *me* you hit! What are you doing driving out here like that, anyway?"

They sneered uncertainly. "Come on, let's get out of here." Then, almost as one, they turned and piled back into their car.

As quickly as it had spit them out, the car swallowed up the four teens. Its engines revved and it squealed away into the darkness. The upper level of the mall went pitch-black as its lights faded away.

"That was close," Trent said at his elbow.

"Yeah."

"Guys? I've gotta get back . . . it's time for my mom to pick me up," Henry said, abashed. He dropped his board and dusted his hands free of grime and splinters. Then he grinned. "And I'm even more afraid of my mom than whatever it is we just faced."

Bailey giggled, in spite of herself. She cupped her crystal, and the glow faded. Jason's felt white-hot to his hand as he put it away, wincing. "We'd better hurry," he suggested. "There's still one out there, maybe. Even one wolfjackal can do a lot of damage."

They gathered themselves to hurry Henry back to his rendezvous point.

26

GAME PLAN

THEY grouped together under a faintly shining streetlight, its amber glow nearly obscured by the evening air and a foggy mist that threatened to grow stronger. After a few deep breaths and shaky laughs between them, Jason managed, "Everyone all right?"

"I'm fine, but I think my sweatshirt is totaled."

Bailey tossed her head, cheeks apple rosy even in the dim glow of the streetlight, her golden-brown ponytail bobbing. "I'm great, but Lacey is buried in my pocket somewhere, shaking so hard she probably won't come out for two days."

"Or till she's hungry." Trent grinned at Bailey.

"Maybe a cookie." She nodded. "How about you?" She watched Jason. "They were after all of us, but I'd say you were the target."

"This thing is burning a hole in my pocket!" Jason pulled out his crystal, and it glowed in the night like a fallen star.

"Wow." Bailey leaned close. "Ever do that before?"

"It's done some odd things, but nothing quite like this."

She touched hers. "Mine is cold. Like a battery or something . . . it gets drained sometimes. Then it goes all icy." She shivered as though she shared the chill with her crystal.

"That's exactly what it is, Bailey. A battery gone dead. You have to recharge." Trent shrugged into his sweatshirt, and examined his sleeve for a moment, looking at the small, jagged tears. "That's about as close as I want to get to a wolfjackal for a long time."

Jason frowned. "He didn't break skin, did he?" He rubbed the scar on the back of his left hand absently.

"Noooo." Trent pushed his sleeve back, then shook his head emphatically. "A smack here and there, and Bailey's shield . . . I'm okay. Henry seemed to be, too, although we hustled him into his mom's car so quick it was hard to tell. A lot of good the alarm beacon did us."

"But that proves it isn't working," noted Bailey. "We've been wondering about that, and now we know. Unless that's some kind of response making your crystal glow, but I don't see what that helps and it never did that before, unless Gavan or someone is feeding you power to break the Curse."

"Maybe."

"I think we're out of range now." Trent cast his gaze around. "We can't stand out here all night, it's getting late, and we've got to get back. Focus, and see what's up, if you can."

Jason nodded absently, already cupping his crystal and beginning to look into its myriad depths. He rubbed his hands together, rolling his focus between his palms. He blinked, then looked up. "I don't know how . . ." he stopped in midsentence.

Bailey stomped her foot. "Stop that right now, Jason Adrian. How, what, when and where!"

"Someone's imprinted a message in my crystal."

Trent glanced at Bailey. "You missed Who."

"Oh, shush." She stared at Jason. "I didn't know that could be done."

Jason shook his head. "Me either. Hold on, let me see . . . I mean, I don't know how to retrieve it or anything. This is not an answering machine." He cupped his hands, looking down into his focus.

"It is now," returned Trent. He tried not to shiver as the cold, dark wind swirled around them, making it more than ever like a Halloween night. It wasn't, of course, but with wolfjackals and rogue Magickers after them, it might as well have been.

Bailey stood on one foot and then the other, hunched into

her jacket. "Who is it?" she asked several times, getting no response from Jason as he concentrated heavily on the crystal he gripped.

"Bailey!" he finally snapped.

She looked at Trent, rolled her eyes, and fell silent after muttering, "That put frost on the old pumpkin." She folded her arms over her chest and shut her mouth tightly.

Jason's lips were moving slightly as if that helped him see or concentrate on what he was revealing hidden inside the crystal, a message as slow to appear as snail tracks on a sidewalk. Tired from the long day, the chase, and the battle, Trent thought of napping while his friend worked through the message, then as quickly dismissed it. *Dark Hand,* he thought, *still trying to muddle my mind and reactions.*

Then Jason gasped! "It's from Fizziwig!"

"It is? No kidding? The guy Gavan's been looking for?" Bailey gave a bounce.

"Who?" Trent stifled a yawn.

"Yes, but it looks like he's found me." Jason frowned and gripped his crystal tightly. "He's the Magicker who's been missing, Trent. He's been on some sort of assignment for the Council and he went missing before camp even started."

Trent whistled.

"He's sent this message and engraved it inside one of the quartz walls, but it disappears as soon as I read it. All but this last word."

Bailey had uncrossed her arms. "Which is . . . ?"

Jason shook his head. "Can't say it until we're ready to go, because it'll bring us to him. It looks like some kind of hyperlink. It activates when I say it. He says he's found something of great importance to the Gatekeeper."

Bailey rubbed her nose. "Didn't you tell me he knew something about Gates?"

Jason nodded to her.

"Then let's go!"

Jason hesitated again. "Bailey, there're some urgent questions here. Like, should we tell Gavan and the others about the attack first? But if we do, are they going to rein us in?"

"And," added Trent, "how does this Fizziwig know about

you? Since he hasn't been seen since last spring. If he's been missing, I would assume he's had no contact with anybody."

Their gazes met. "True. That's a very good point, Trent."

The other bowed.

Jason looked back into his hand and crystal reluctantly. "It could be a trap."

"Something to think about anyway."

"Let's think about what Fizziwig said." Bailey peered at Jason. "What exactly did he say?"

"Desperate times mean desperate measures. I have found something of great importance for you, Gatekeeper. Speak and find me, elder Fizziwig." Jason cleared his throat. "That's about it."

"He has that flair. Victorian or something, like Eleanora. It could be a genuine message." She considered Jason's words. Trent merely shrugged.

He looked at the two of them. "Are we going, then?"

"I'm about charged up." Bailey rubbed her crystal pendant, hidden under the flap of her jacket.

Trent grinned. "I'm as charged as I'll ever be. And we've still got some time before our rides home."

"All right, then." Jason opened his hand and said, "*Come!*" His figure wavered and started to thin, like mist.

"No!" Bailey grabbed for Trent's wrist. "Jason, no! We're not joined!"

Too late, as his body disappeared altogether into fog and the wind threatened to shred even that away. Bailey gripped her pendant hard, yelling, "Follow!"

"What are you doing?" Trent gawked at her.

"Following!" Her expression was fixed in concentration as she held onto his hand tightly.

And they did. There was a moment when the night whirled around them, and they felt as cold and indistinct as a wet wisp of fog, and then with a *thump*, they appeared inside a thickly carpeted hall, well polished oak panels surrounding them, and a door just closing ahead of the two of them.

"Someone's house," Bailey murmured.

"You think? Actually, it seems to be more of a mansion. Maybe even a castle," Trent commented.

She nudged him. Her hand fell away from her pendant. "I don't like the feel of this. It stinks of wolfjackal and the others." She looked up and down the hallway uneasily.

He didn't either but wouldn't say so because his feeling came from entirely different senses than hers. "This is where your rock led us. Let's just find Jason and get out of here. *If* it worked. We could be burglars or something if it didn't." He pointed at the door. "That looks like the best bet."

She arched her neck, squinting back down the long corridor. "I know there're times when it's just not wise to go barging around. He's here somewhere, I feel it, but . . ."

"Gotta start someplace." He put his hand on the knob, turning it slowly, and pushing the door inward. It creaked with all the theatrical noise of a Hollywood horror movie. "After you."

Bailey stood in the doorway, her back to the jamb. "I think I'll keep one foot in the door, thank you."

Trent moved past her. "Well, someone has to go in."

Bailey tossed her head, ponytail swinging, and answered firmly, "It doesn't have to be me. And Jason is already in there." She looked into the amber-shadowed room, and saw the silent figure of their friend standing by the side of a great wing chair that faced an immense fireplace with brass firedogs at either side.

Trent frowned. Of course, Jason was already there! And if he'd been attuned to his crystal, he would have known that. Many more mistakes like that and the whole world would know he wasn't fit to be a Magicker. He thumbed the opaque rock hanging from its watch fob as he stopped at the center of the room. "Jason?" His voice echoed in the vast library, and sort of hung there, although he swore he could hear pages ripple as if an opened book were disturbed.

A very long moment passed during which Trent seriously wondered if he and Bailey could even be noticed by their friend. Then Jason stirred and looked up, his face pale and stricken. "I've found him," he said slowly. He put one hand on the brocaded chair. "And he's dead."

He pushed on the chair, and it swung around slowly, revealing the body of the late Fizziwig, dressed in dark suit and smoking jacket, thin white hair all tousled, with a surprised expression on his still, dead face. He'd been a spry old man from the look of him, and there wasn't a mark on him aside from his surprised expression.

A door shut with great authority. Bailey moved into the room, her face angry. "That does it." She gestured furiously. "We know it's the Dark Hand, this whole place reeks of their Magick."

"We don't know that they killed him."

Trent pointed out, "We know that they were here, and he's not alive."

Jason unclenched his left hand slowly. He looked at the two of them, first Trent, then Bailey. "We don't know what happened here. We don't even know what he thought it was important to tell me."

Trent slowly pivoted in a circle, surveying all the bookshelves built into the library walls and running from floor to ceiling on three sides, leaving only the massive fireplace and a few paintings on the fourth wall. He touched a shelf, a massive book whose spine read *Ars Magica and Secularus*. His fingers tingled, and he drew his hand back hastily. "If it's a book, we've got a long search."

"I don't intend to stay in here with a dead man long enough to look. We have to tell the elders and the authorities." Jason shifted uneasily. "We should have contacted Gavan and the others before coming."

"That's great. Not only am I out later than I should be, but I found a body." Bailey wrinkled her nose.

"We found it," Trent corrected her. "Normally, I'd vote for calling 911, but . . . this time . . . I think maybe we should get hold of an elder."

Jason nodded. "My thoughts exactly."

Bailey lifted her chin defiantly. "We've got to tell the others, warn everyone . . . and then get ready. It's us against them now, and they've given us no choice. Opposites attack."

27

THE DARK HAND CLOSES

"THE first thing we do," Tomaz said calmly, "is get you kids out of here. Then I call in Dr. Patel to get the body. We take care of our own, and no stranger will touch Fizziwig." He frowned, his weathered face showing deeply etched lines. "None of you should be here. What happened?"

"Fizziwig sent me a message." Jason tapped his crystal. "I thought it was important, so we came."

"You knew he was a Magicker?"

"Yes, I remembered the name." Jason shifted. "We wouldn't have come otherwise, Tomaz, but he etched a message inside my crystal. I've never heard of anything like that before, and it seemed important. I never thought . . . I never thought I'd find him like this." Jason gestured helplessly. "Look, we know it's dangerous now."

"Dangerous is not a strong enough word for it, and I don't want to have to be rescuing any of you from situations you shouldn't have been in, in the first place. Do I make myself clear?"

"We'll be careful!" Bailey promised.

"Good." He dropped a hand on Jason's shoulder, and squeezed slightly. "Brennard's searching for you. We cannot be sure why, but we assume it's because the handful of you seem to be the most Talented. The others are scattered to the four winds, unaware and untapped, and they'll stay that way till we have an academy to offer them safety, but you . . . all of you are at great risk. It comes with great ability." Bailey flushed, pleased, but Tomaz barely paused in his speech. "That confers extra responsibility on you. We expect many things of you. Don't disappoint us."

Jason felt the failure of Camp Ravenwyng, like a heavy burden on him. "We won't," answered Jason, with Bailey and Trent echoing him faintly.

"Good." Tomaz took a deep breath and without any of them even blinking, they were *gone,* swept away with him.

A blink of nothingness and then all stood in Gavan Rainwater's office at Camp Ravenwyng, stopping the Magicker in mid-pace, electric lights flaring in the room, and his dark cloak swirling about him. He pivoted on one heel. "Tomaz! Got them all, have you?"

Crowfeather nodded, and released his grip on Jason's shoulder. "They will tell you the tale. I have to take Anita back."

"It's true, then?" Sadness veiled Gavan's face. "You found Fizziwig?"

Tomaz nodded.

Gavan sighed before gesturing. "Better hurry, then. I don't know what the Dark Hand will make of these circumstances, but let's not give them a chance."

"It will be done." Tomaz was there, and then he was not.

"Whoa." Bailey let out her breath. "I'd like to be able to do that! He's fast . . . I have to think and think . . . it's like the hare and the snail."

Trent blinked. "You meant the tortoise and the hare."

She looked at him. "I meant what I said!" She gave an offended sniff.

Gavan smiled slightly and perched on the corner of his great desk, looking at them all. "Teleporting comes with focus and knowing exactly where you're going. The more certainty, the quicker you come and go." The beacon crystal sat on a filing cabinet in the corner, its clear crystalline facets sparkling in the light. "Practice, Bailey, practice." He rubbed his palm over the pewter wolfhead of his cane. "Are you all right? All of you?"

"That," Trent told him, "was my first dead guy."

Gavan winced. "We had no way of knowing, but we would have spared you all that if we could. I had hoped beyond hoping that Fizziwig was all right, just buried in some research of his own." He coughed. "Perhaps buried is a bad choice of words?"

Jason laughed nervously.

"It's okay. He didn't look bad or anything. Just very, very still. I mean, for a minute or two, we all wondered if he was a dummy or something." Bailey put her hand over her pocket, stilling her pet for a moment. "He was in a library, a huge one."

"Tell me what happened then," the Magicker said, and stood back as the flood of words began, prompted now and then by a question from him, until all three finally grew quiet as the last words spilled out of them and faded away.

Gavan shook his head. "To lose him, and to have you find him, is a double tragedy for us. I have to ask you to not say anything to anyone, which makes it harder. But if it bothers you at all, I want you to contact one of us, to talk, all right?"

"I'm okay with it," Trent said. Jason and Bailey quickly agreed.

Gavan nodded several times then, as if considering. "I hear there have been wolfjackals about on other occasions, as well. And Dark Hand."

"They're stalking," Jason told him. "I don't like it."

"They are getting more aggressive," Gavan agreed. "I'm not sure what we can do about it. The beacon doesn't always work. They may have found a way to circumvent us or . . ." His words trailed off. He thumped his cane on the floor smartly. "Be that as it may, it only points out the need to keep you safe. We need the Academy, a Haven where the blink of your mind can bring you to safety and give you the opportunity to learn all you need to know, but it also means we may have to reveal ourselves. I am finding much opposition. I'm bringing the Council together again in a few days. I'll gather you up then, so be prepared."

"A war council!" Bailey glowed at the thought, her cheeks apple red and her ponytail bouncing.

"Well . . . not exactly."

"I'm with Bailey, sir. I think we need to start hitting back." Trent ran a hand through his curly hair.

"We've already been through a war," said Gavan quietly. "We know the devastation, and that there can be no winners."

"They're counting on that! They're counting on no one fighting back! Can't you see?"

Gavan looked sadly at Bailey. "You have to trust us, lass. You have to trust that we know what we're doing."

She looked down at her sneakers and squeaked. Or, that is, Lacey squeaked, even though it sounded like it was coming from Bailey. She put her hand over her pocket flap.

"Any other complaints?"

No one answered.

He stood. "Away with you, then." He passed his palm over the wolfhead and first Trent disappeared, and then Bailey. Gavan aimed his brilliant blue-eyed gaze at Jason, hesitating. "You seem troubled. You're not ready to do battle?"

"There are things that could be better." Jason shoved his hands stubbornly in his pockets, as reluctant to be analyzed by Gavan as by Statler Finch. "I can handle it." He touched crystal with both hands in his jeans pockets and remembered what he'd almost forgotten.

"Of course you can. We will be asking even more of you soon." Gavan started to move his palm over his cane.

"Wait! Wait . . . there is . . . something." The weight of the second crystal reminded him, and he drew it out. "I wanted to ask about the crystals, and the bonding . . ."

"You've got a second? Already? Astounding. Where did you find it?" Gavan stepped to his side, and extended his hand, over but not touching the gemstone in Jason's palm. Its pale lavender hue shone in the office light. Fire glittered as Jason turned it, showing Gavan all its facets. "Incredible. It is a beautiful stone, my lad."

"But you can bond to more than one, right?"

"Of course, we all have and do. Sometimes a crystal fractures under stress, or burns out, and we have to replace it. Occasionally they get lost, or even stolen. Most of us have several favorites we keep on us or near us at all times. Did you worry?"

"A little."

"I won't say it's usual to get another Bond so early in your training, it's not. It can be difficult to learn your crystal, and it requires study and focus. Now your attention must be split, between this one and the other. However . . ." And Gavan looked keenly into his face. "These things are not coincidental."

"What?"

"I mean it happens for a purpose. That rock was meant to come to you, or it wouldn't have." Gavan reached out and closed Jason's fingers over it.

"No one will take it away?"

"No. Why would you think they might?"

Jason felt a keen reluctance about telling Rainwater where he'd found the crystal, and why. He just shook his head.

"None of us will. Let me put it that way." Gavan opened his hands, and then cradled them about his pewter wolfhead. "Look at this crystal closely, and tell me what you see."

Jason leaned over to look at the gemstone held in the wolf's jaws. It was brilliant, he'd noticed that the first time he and the Magicker met, but more than its diamondlike quality, he'd never really been able to see. He narrowed his eyes to look into the great, uncut gem. "It *is* a diamond," he said finally, without tearing his gaze away.

"Of a sort. It's called a Herkimer diamond, and it came from these shores to my home in England not long after the colonies were first established." Gavan scratched at his jaw absently. "It's quite flawed at the heart, if you can see it in the light. I was advised by many not to take this stone and make a focus of it as it would never allow a Bonding."

Jason peered closer. "It's like . . . it looks like a teardrop or something inside."

"Precisely. Not a teardrop, actually, but water, yes. Trapped within the heart of the gem. A bit of life, if you would, in stone."

"How did that happen?"

Gavan smiled then, and shrugged. "I am no creator, I've no idea. As the minerals came under intense heat and pressure, this bit of water became trapped and so it stayed. And it may make the stone very fragile and subject to shattering, but it's held for me. We've been through a lot, we have."

Jason straightened up. "The Bonding is really important, then, and personal."

"Yes, it is. As we learn our crystals, we learn ourselves. It's not the only important thing, but it can prove crucial. You'll have to split your studies between them. I'll consult with Eleanora. Perhaps she or Aunt Freyah can work with you on it."

Sharp-eyed Freyah might not be pleased at all when she heard where he'd found it, Jason thought. On the other hand, Gavan's disclosure had revealed a lot. It *had* come to him, even under unusual circumstances. He put the lavender stone back in his pocket. "Thanks."

"Any time. Any more surprises about you?" Sudden humor twinkled in those startling blue eyes.

"I hope not." Jason smothered a sigh, and Gavan laughed.

"The weight of the world is a heavy one, hey, my young Atlas? Just remember that you're not the only one holding it up. We're all here with you." Gavan made a face. "Come to think of it . . . it is heavy!"

Jason couldn't help laughing. He took a deep breath. It would be later than it should be, and he hoped there'd be no trouble getting his and Trent's ride home, but compared to other problems, it seemed a minor one. "I'd better go now."

"No sooner spoken, than gone." Gavan whispered in his ear, and then he was back in the mall. Lingering in his mind was the whisper: *And someday soon you'll have to tell me where you found that crystal, lad.*

Jason felt his face flush.

A few shoppers brushed past him. He looked around and saw that Trent and Bailey were both gone. He checked the large clock by the information booth and was relieved that not nearly as much time had gone as he'd feared but he was late. He called McIntire for a ride home. His stepfather did not say much till they were halfway home, then he commented, "It's a little later than we planned, Jason."

"Sorry. We had so much to talk about."

"There's a certain amount of trust in letting someone your age go off on his own." McIntire looked briefly at him before turning his attention back to the road.

"I know." What was he supposed to say? He didn't want to lie.

"I'm not accusing you of anything. I just want you to know I'm paying attention."

Jason began to nod, then said, "Okay." He added, "Ting couldn't make it, she had to fly up early this morning, but Henry Squibb was there and we were talking about camp and games and stuff. I'm sorry we ran a little over."

"I understand." And he must have, because not another word was said until they arrived home, and Alicia met them at the doorway.

His stepsister was pretty, like her blonde mother, but a lot harder to take. He frowned. "I had a phone call yesterday from Ting?"

"Did you?" Alicia looked thoughtful. "Oh, that's right. You did. I am sorry. I completely forgot. Sort of like you forgot to do the breakfast dishes."

He scowled. "I would have done them after practice."

She tossed her head, hair swinging. "By then, I would already have been in trouble. Mother likes a clean kitchen."

"Still . . . the message was important."

"Oh, all right! I won't forget again."

Jason curled his hand about the lavender crystal. It felt slightly warm and soothing in his palm. "Please try not to?" It grew hot in his hand as he talked to Alicia.

She looked at him, her face suddenly going expressionless. She blinked slowly, then said, "Whatever you want, Jason."

That surprised him. She gave him a pleasant, if blank smile, and wandered off. He let go of his crystal hastily. He hadn't done that, had he?

Upstairs, in his room, he sat down at his desk and took out the lavender gemstone to examine it more carefully. He had been, he decided, distracted by its beauty and by the fact he'd found it where he had. He had to look beyond that . . . into it. Unable to tell Gavan of his true worry over the intrinsic nature of the stone, whether it was good or evil, he realized he had to discover that himself. He rested his elbows on the desk, his chin in his hands, and looked into it. It was much clearer than his first stone and yet more complicated in its way, with more facets and planes.

He didn't know if a crystal could be good or evil, or whether it was like a pitcher that held water to be filled or poured, with no value but function. He only knew that he couldn't afford to be wrong. He cupped the gem in his hands, bringing it closer to his eyes.

Jason stared very, very deep into the pale lavender stone. Something wavered buried in its heart, an image. He held his breath, narrowing his eyes to sharpen his vision and found himself looking into dark eyes the color of rich ale, an unlined face crowned with unruly curls of silver-gray, and a clean-shaven chin that looked as if it had borne the brunt of many nicks getting that way. The image was so clear it looked as if the man might speak to him! He dropped the stone.

Bailey had been trapped in her stone once. Had he found something cursed? Panting, Jason opened his desk drawer and swept the gemstone into it. He'd have to think. He might yet have to reveal his secrets to Gavan and Eleanora and risk their anger.

28

SECRETS

THE trouble with secrets, Ting thought, is that they had to be kept that way. She sat in the atrium garden of her grandmother's house, her schoolbooks spread upon the patio table, sun pleasantly warming the back of her neck, as she read over her homework. Her grandmother napped in a chaise across the table, her voice making cheerful sleep noises as she breathed deeply. She'd had chemo that morning, and the peaceful expression on her face now hid the pain that had been there earlier from the illness. Ting's mother was in the house, quietly making chicken rice noodle soup and other delights to tempt Grandmother's fading appetite. Ting worked quietly to keep from waking her, using the calculator only when she absolutely had to. She was not to disturb her grandmother's much needed rest, but sometimes she wondered how asleep the older woman really was. An abacus lay on the table as well, but only her grandmother knew how to make the counting beads fly as rapidly as her electronic calculator.

Those sharp button eyes had already flown open once to catch Ting focusing on her charm bracelet of crystals. They had not shared more words about what had been brought up, but Ting felt more and more pressure regardless. Should she tell them? They were her family. Would it make it easier for them all, or bring them all under great danger? She'd read Bailey's excited account of what had happened Saturday, and it bothered her a lot. They had all thought that the creatures needed immense manna, or power, and stayed near Gates and storms of wild mana. What if wolfjackals came to San Francisco after her? How could she keep all of them safe, especially with her grandmother fighting cancer?

Ting found her hand on her bracelet, cupping the huge central rose quartz that made up her crystal, as if seeking comfort or answers from it. It did give her comfort, knowing it was there.

Her grandmother's eyelids flew open. Ting looked up to see her watching. Flushed for no real reason, Ting caught up her pencil again and returned to diagramming sentences.

"Secrets," her grandmother said slowly, "can be very powerful."

Had she been reading her thoughts? Ting looked back at her. "Grandmother, you know I love and honor you very much." She hesitated, unsure of what else to say.

"But you cannot tell me." Her grandmother sat up, straightening her quilted silk jacket about her. "That is the way it should be. Granddaughter, let me say this again. I understand what it is to have magic. As I grew older and saw nothing of it in my children, I became very sad for losing what was in our blood. Seeing it in you fills my heart and heals me as none of this medicine could possibly." She held her arms out. Ting went and knelt by her chaise lounge and hugged her tightly. Her grandmother was even tinier than she remembered and she held back her strength, afraid she might hurt her.

"Maybe someday I can tell you," she whispered in her grandmother's ear. "And have you meet the others."

"That would be both good and wise." Her grandmother smiled. "In the meantime, if you have a question, without revealing your secret, perhaps I have an answer or two."

"That would be wonderful. Someday." Ting pulled back reluctantly. "Now I have sentences to diagram."

Her grandmother shuddered. "English," she muttered. "An impossible language! And American is even worse."

Giggling, Ting settled back into her seat and picked up her pencil.

* * *

Despite what Gavan had promised, days dragged by without Jason hearing anything. Halloween weekend drew close. Soccer practice got harder, and Jason was afraid his ankle might start hurting, the old sprain acting up. It rained once, making the grasses slick, but the dirt stayed firm below, and he and Sam slid about the field, laughing even as they tried to take shots at the goal net. After practice they hurled insults at each other and let those of Brinkford and Canby roll off their backs as they dressed to go home. They could say anything to each other, but no one else had that right.

"What are you doing for Halloween?" Sam asked as he hoisted his backpack over one shoulder.

"Dunno yet for sure, but I think Joanna has some charity Haunted House we have to run. She's been trying to decide if I'm still too short to dress up as the Grim Reaper."

That made Sam laugh. "Better than dressing up like some wizard wannabee," he added, snickering. "They're gonna be all over the place."

"What's wrong with wanting to be a wizard?"

"Please," snorted Sam. "I want to live in the real world!" He pulled his sweatshirt jacket out of his locker and kicked it shut. "See you tomorrow!"

Jason watched him go. "Yeah. Right." He could hear the footsteps of Sam and one or two other stragglers jogging out of the P.E. building, and the clang of the metal door banging shut. He found himself holding his breath. How close he'd come to finding a way of telling Sam what he was! And what would have happened if he had? He'd have broken a vow to the Magickers, and all he would have done would be to set off his friend's scorn. Sam wouldn't have understood at all.

He got up off the wooden bench, gathered the last of his things, and closed his locker slowly. He had almost made a total fool and oath breaker of himself. It saddened him a little. It was like finding out your best friend really wasn't, and he wondered how he could have misjudged Sam that way. Not liking magic? How could he feel that way? Sam was always the one saying, "I wish" or "if only." Not that Magick worked that way, but there were possibilities Sam could only dream of, and Jason had them at hand.

There wasn't anything he could do about it, and it wasn't like he didn't have Trent, Bailey, Ting, and the others. He guessed it was that he didn't have anyone that stayed close in his life for long. No one that went all the way back to the beginning, and he missed that. He missed belonging.

If you belonged, then you could trust—no matter what. He wasn't sure how he fit into the McIntire household, and if Statler caused enough trouble, Jason wasn't sure he would even have a home. What if they decided to foster him out as some sort of troubled youth? Could they, would they, do such a thing to him? He didn't know and he never wanted to find out. His mom had been lost so long ago he had only bare memories left of her, usually ones he found in dreams. His dad . . . well, he couldn't help what happened to his dad. Car accidents took people every day, no matter how you wished that away. It had just happened, and he'd just been left behind.

Jason shouldered his gear securely before going out the gym door. They'd stayed really late, and he'd lingered, so it was nearly dark, the sky going into the deep gray-purple of dusk. Daylight savings time had gone into effect, and Halloween was just around the corner, and five-thirty in his neighborhood meant nightfall. He ought to hurry.

Outside the big gym building, he could see that the middle school campus looked deserted. The teachers' parking lot had one car left in it, and that probably belonged to one of the janitors. The cold air hit him. As he shivered slightly, he decided a slow jog home would be the best way to keep warm. He angled across the grounds. It was his own fault for thinking too much, and he had science lab and math homework waiting for him after dinner. That meant no television tonight at all, and maybe a half hour at most for the computer. If he hurried, he might be able to stretch that, because he wanted time to play with Trent and Henry, as well as time to talk with Bailey and Ting and anyone else on the network of Magickers.

His sneakers thudded rhythmically over the blacktop as he left the physical education area and neared the social studies wing where his footfalls made odd noises echoing off the breezeway. So odd that, for a moment there, he thought he heard two sets in a running tempo. Past the buildings and crossing the driveway, with only the physical plant building which provided energy for heat, lighting, cooling, pumped water, and had the trash bins lined up against its walls between him and the way home, Jason stopped dead in his tracks.

He could hear the tattoo of something racing after him. Then it stopped.

His heart thudded. Not shoes. Not sneakers. He began walking, then broke back into his steady jog, listening. After the briefest of pauses, that slightly out-of-place echo joined him. He was being followed.

By who? . . . or . . . by what?

He drew close to the physical plant. He could hear the generators and pumps inside humming away, doing whatever it was they did. The building almost radiated a comforting heat. As he swung toward it, a howl sounded sharply just behind his right shoulder. Wolfjackal! And unbearably close.

Jason swung around and grabbed his crystal from his pocket. It almost jumped into his hand as if knowing it were needed, filling his palm with a barely felt warmth. He summoned the alarm beacon. He caught a brief, mind-filling glimpse of the great crystal ball in Gavan's office, turning, scintillating with red-orange rays of alarm, and then it went dark. He blinked, his own sight and thoughts jolting back to the dusk shadowing his school.

No alarm beacon again! Yet he had triggered it . . . he'd seen it! It was as if something or someone had snuffed it almost immediately. He had no more time to consider it as a black-and-silver form came slinking across the open parking lot, growling and heading for him.

Jason backed up. Here, in the open, was no place to use his crystal. Not where he could be seen by anyone who still might be hanging around the school, despite the fact it looked abandoned.

The beast grinned, red tongue lolling from between its great ivory fangs as if it knew Jason were cornered. "Mine," it growled, shuddering and quaking as if forming a word took great effort and left it in greater pain.

"No way," Jason said. "Not today. *Not ever.*" He looked about. The janitor's car still sat in the deep purple shadows across the diagonal. He hated to do it . . . but it was the only option he could think of.

Jason turned quickly and ran to the trash bins. He spotted the least full one with a lid half open, took a running leap, and dove headfirst into the metal shape. The lid clanged shut over him not a second before it shook all over as a heavy body collided with it, growling and snarling.

Jason's nose ran and his eyes stung with the stench of the container. Trash pick up was a day or two off, which meant the thing was pretty ripe and awful. Usually when Brinkford and Canby tossed him in, it was the day after trash collection. On a scale of awfulness, it wasn't all that bad, really, except for the humiliation. And today he had jumped in on purpose!

The wolfjackal clawed at him from the outside, toenails clicking and raking down the side. It thudded against the metal again, heavily, the bin shaking from side to side on its iron wheels, and then, suddenly, he could hear the growling overhead. Something hot dripped down on him. He looked up through the gap in the lid and saw part of the wolfjackal's snarling face, dripping saliva down on him.

He had two choices. One, to use his crystal, but after the failure of the beacon he was afraid to depend on it . . . or two . . .

Jason grabbed his soccer shoes, heavy and studded, out of his gear bag. Yelling at the top of his lungs, he began to beat them against the side of the trash bin. The racket nearly deafened him, but he kept yelling and pummeled his soccer shoes till his shoulders ached. He couldn't tell what the wolfjackal was doing because the whole container rumbled and quaked all around him, rocking as if it had a life of its own.

Suddenly, yellow-white light flared in, blinding him, as someone threw the lid open, shining a flashlight in. He blinked as he stuffed his shoes back into his duffel and stood.

The janitor, flashlight in hand, peered down curiously. "What are you doing?" he demanded.

A second visage leaned in for a look. Statler Finch's nose wrinkled from the stench. "Curious behavior, Jason. I thought you hated being trash canned and yet I just saw you dive headlong into one. We'll be talking about this on Friday, I think. Oh, yes. We'll have a nice long talk about the difference between being bullied . . . and pretending to be bullied for attention."

29

THE HIDDEN

THE look of disappointment on Joanna's face was almost more than he could bear. He was used to seeing worry and concern there, for she attempted to be nothing less than a perfect parent. But this betrayal of his had stung his stepmother to the core.

"Oh, Jason," she murmured. "How could you? I thought we had everything settled with Mr. Finch."

"We did." He stared at McIntire, whose tanned, line-etched face actually seemed to be easier to look at. His stepfather had been in his offices, working on plans for the big development which had once been the McHenry estate, although the old mansion seemed to have survived demolition, and had appeared when Joanna let out a cry of dismay and called for Jason. The Dozer's wishes for a back road were even now being carved through the foothills, and his clothes were dusty with the digging of it. He looked steadily at Jason, though, and said to his wife, "Things aren't always as they seem. What's going on, Jason?"

She interrupted. "I'll tell you what's going on. Mr. Finch seems to think Jason is some kind of . . . some kind of lying psychopath! All this for attention." She put her hand to her mouth, her hand trembling, as if she might break into sobs. "I know it's hard for you, Jason, no mother and no father, but I do try. I do. And I thought talking to Mr. Finch might give you an outlet outside the family. But it appears I've failed! He says you're shamelessly manipulating all of us."

McIntire put a great arm about his wife's shoulders. "Now stop that," he said mildly. "Jason hasn't done anything wrong, that I've seen. Finch is in a new program at the school, and he strikes me as the overeager sort. The kind who might make a reputation anyway he can. I have no intention of letting him run roughshod over any of us."

She sniffled. "But . . . what happened?"

Jason exhaled at finding an unexpected ally. That put him in a spot, though, which he wasn't quite sure how to get out of. He shifted uneasily. "I can tell you it wasn't what it looked like." He bit his tongue before he could add *trust me*. There was no such emotion on Joanna's immaculately made-up face. And no tears yet, either, although they seemed just around the corner.

She sighed. "All right, then. But no Internet tonight. Do I make myself clear?"

"Yes, ma'am."

"All right then, hurry on upstairs, dinner's a little late tonight. You may have time for homework before I call you."

"Yes, ma'am." Jason turned and pitched out of the living room before anyone whatsoever could think of anything else. He took another shower and set his clothes aside to be washed after dinner, unable to bear even the faintest reminder of the garbage bin. Then he sat down, shoved the computer screen aside so he wouldn't even have to look at its darkened face, and did his science lab.

Alicia wasn't in for dinner, having gone to a friend's house after dance practice, so he was spared her knowing and accusing glances at the table. He announced he'd gotten his science lab done already and only had a page of math problems to do after dinner. Joanna's red mouth thinned to the barest of lines, and she repeated firmly, "No Internet."

"Yes, ma'am." Sometimes there was just no moving a mountain, and he knew when to not even try. He stifled a yawn and dug into the lime jello and carrot salad that also served as a kind of dessert for the evening. He cleared the table and loaded the dishwasher before heading back upstairs.

While he did his math, his mind worked on the real puzzle. How was it Statler had seen him but hadn't seen the wolf-jackal? How could that be?

Or had he seen it and not believed it? Or had he decided it was merely an overly bold coyote.

Neither option made Jason feel very comfortable. He tucked his math papers inside his workbook and stowed everything back in his backpack, ready for the next day.

And even if he were all right, that did not mean the others were. He broke his word and went on the Net long enough to send e-mail to everyone, warning them anew, especially Henry. He took his time over Henry's letter, mulling about what to say without frightening him half to death and yet urging him to be very careful.

He flipped off the computer when a floorboard creaked behind him, and he spun about in his chair guiltily. He'd been caught!

Gavan Rainwater sat down on the edge of Jason's bed, his cloak puddled about him like great, dark wings, his chin resting on the head of his wolfhead cane. He smiled as Jason gulped once or twice. "Sorry. I should have knocked, but I hate creating a fuss."

Jason pulled up his trapdoor for privacy. "I bet you do. What's wrong?"

"It's time," Gavan said simply. "Come with me?"

Of all nights to be called away from home. Jason looked at his trapdoor. It was not to be helped, he supposed. What to do?

He wrote a quick note reading "Do Not Disturb (sleeping)" and lowered it out of his room on a string, and then pulled his door up and shut tight. Just in case, he fixed his bed and Gavan stood, watching him with his mouth twitched to one side.

"The old pillow under the blanket trick?"

"I'm in a little bit of trouble," Jason told him.

"Ah. Covering your tracks, then. Let me help." Gavan gestured and the room steeped in darkness, and he could hear the very very faint sound of someone in deep sleep. Gavan dropped his voice to a whisper. "There," he said. He extended a hand to Jason. "Shall we be off?"

And they were, in what Aunt Freyah often referred to as two twitches of a lamb's tail.

Ting put the finishing touches on her English essay and printed it out. She heard the sound of the walker in the hallway, and her bedroom door eased open. "Ting," her grandmother said. "Your mother is out getting groceries, and you have a visitor. I believe you have something to do tonight."

Puzzled, Ting followed her out to the kitchen, where Fire-Ann sat with a cup of Chinese tea in her hand. "There you are, lass! I'm to bring you to a meeting."

Her grandmother hugged Ting. "We had time for a little chat," her grandmother explained, smiling widely.

She looked from the flamboyantly red-haired Magicker and cook of Camp Ravenwyng to her grandmother. "You . . . talked?"

"Indeed we did," answered FireAnn with her lively Irish accent. "Why didn't you tell me your grandmother was one of the Hidden Ones? Things could have gone a lot smoother!"

"Hidden Ones?" Ting repeated, feeling totally lost.

FireAnn bounced to her feet and took her hand. "I'll explain later. It's a good thing," she said. She hugged Ting's grandmother as if she had known her all her life, and then rubbed her crystal and *whoooosh!* Away they went.

It's a wonder, Bailey thought, they all didn't bump into each other on whatever plane it was they traveled through. She and Trent popped out of nowhere into the Council meeting room at Ravenwyng just ahead of Jason and Ting, like corks popping out of champagne bottles. Even so, it looked like the Council had been in session for a while before they got there.

Her excitement at seeing Ting so unexpectedly bubbled over in spite of everything. "Ting!" she cried out and grabbed her friend and did an excited swing. They grinned at each other. "You missed the best farewell party!"

"Without me?"

"We thought of you a lot!" Bailey teased. She hugged her friend tightly. "How is your grandmother?"

That sombered Ting's expression. She flipped her dark hair back over her shoulder. "She has a lot of healing to do, but she surprises me every day." She looked at FireAnn who gave a slight nod, before adding, "She *knows*, Bailey."

"Knows? Knows what?" Then Bailey's mouth snapped shut for a moment as thoughts tumbled. "You don't mean—"

"I do. FireAnn calls her one of the Hidden Ones."

"Wow. What's that mean?"

Eleanora put her hands on their shoulders, saying quietly, "Ladies. Shall we sit and let the Council continue?"

Ting blushed faintly as the two of them found their chairs. Bailey leaned over and whispered, "I wanna know everything!" before lapsing into dutiful silence. An empty chair with a black wreath upon it sat at one end, for dear old Fizziwig, she supposed. Eleanora tucked herself demurely into her own chair, and smiled at Gavan. She fixed her gaze on Gavan, and Bailey followed suit. She'd been at enough meetings between her mom, her dad, and the divorce lawyers, to know when something important was being discussed.

Gavan cleared his throat. "Here we are, all concerned who were asked for, and all safe."

"What about the other two . . . the skinwalker and the rather ordinary Magicker who follows him about?"

"Unable to get away without being missed." Tomaz leaned forward on the table, the beaten silver disks of his Indian jewelry gleaming. "I will fill them in later."

"All safe and accounted for," Gavan repeated firmly.

"Not good enough," snorted the one known to the children as Allenby from Gavan's wicked impersonations of him and occasional tirades. They watched him in fascination. He frustrated Gavan because of his tight-pocketed attitude, although Rainwater himself was the first to admit a good accountant could be worth his weight in gold and Magickers couldn't find a way to have money fall out of a tree. Yet.

"The fact remains that because of your actions, young Magickers are exposed and at risk. Better to have found them, one at a time, and apprenticed them, kept them close and safe, rather than to have them scattered to the four winds as they are now. The world we live in is more dangerous for all of us now, and even more so for those of Talent but without training. If found, they will be misused. Think of the days of the Inquisition, Rainwater, and you have a glimpse of what worries me." The dark, disagreeing voice issued from a man wrapped in shadows, and his words were even darker.

"Who's that?" Ting whispered into Bailey's ear. Bailey answered, "I think that's Khalil. Very mysterious."

Gavan stood at the table's end, his cloak swirling about him. He looked angry, and the flash in his eyes was echoed by a glint stabbing outward from the crystal held in the jaws of his wolfhead cane. "This is not the Old World," he said finally, and then closed his mouth tightly as if there were many, many more things he would like to have said.

Jason sat back in his chair. Trent tapped him on the arm, drawing his attention, and he looked at his worried friend. He shook his head, once, and then looked back to Gavan. Jason took a deep breath, trying to relax. Perhaps Trent was right; now was the time to listen, not to protest. It wasn't easy, though.

"The children . . . the young Magickers . . . are more at risk than ever. Surely you can see that." Khalil sat in his chair, quiet, inscrutable, his Moorish features hidden by his head-to-toe dark clothing. "This is the same argument we had but a few weeks ago. You need us to help anchor and ward this school. But you've made no progress in finding a Gated Haven to put it in. Why do you bother us? You want action, yet you hesitate to take the first step!"

"I would be a fool not to admit that I've bitten off more than I can chew. Together, we can protect them. Educate them. I need your combined wisdoms and talents. With Fizziwig's death, we know the Hand will stop at nothing. Can we survive yet another disaster? I don't think any one of us wants to find that out." Gavan put both hands on the table and leaned forward, his gaze sweeping all assembled: Council, young Magickers, and elders from all around the world. "Gregory and Brennard were masters of the arts. When they fought, they did so to destroy each other, not the world around them. They contained the havoc they wrought. I don't know about Brennard today, but I can't muster that kind of control. I don't ever want to be brought into that kind of fight. So we fight by guile, as we must."

"If, by calling this meeting, you are hoping to bring pressure to bear on us and force a hasty, perhaps unwise decision, you will fail, Rainwater." The tall, elegant woman, wrapped in dark crimson satin, sat catty-corner from the end of the table where Gavan stood and Eleanora stayed quietly, as if biding her time. The two women looked at each other, then away, as if something unspoken had passed between them. She tapped her fan, of dark watered-silk crimson that matched her gown, on the table's edge. "You will call me Isabella, children," she said imperiously, before looking to Gavan. "You have a Gate-keeper! Open Gates. Choose them wisely, and then and only then, can we work with you. You might remember that some Gates lead only to havoc and chaos."

Gavan's hands turned white around the knuckles as he leaned on them. "I need protectors for my Gatekeeper. We may well lose him, if not."

Jason went cold. He stared at Gavan. Lose? What did he mean by that?

"We've lost two candidates already," Eleanora spoke up. "Henry Squibb, fallen to betrayal by the Dark Hand, and Jennifer Logan, who was one of our more trained recruits."

"Not Jennifer!" protested both Ting and Bailey in unison before clapping their hands over their mouths and turning pink.

Eleanora smiled sadly. "Jennifer has retreated. She's renounced her Magick, and although I am working with her, her crystal has been shattered, and I'm not sure she'll ever be able to take up a new one. It happens sometimes. She won't tell me what she was attempting or what went wrong, but she is frightened. Terribly, desperately frightened. I'm doing all I can."

Both Ting and Bailey let out small breaths, and grabbed for each other's hands, and held them. Lacey poked a whiskered nose out of Bailey's pocket, then dove back in, followed by a small crunchy, munching sound.

"We'll lose more like that, too, if we don't move," Gavan finished. "If that happens, we don't have to worry about the Dark Hand. We'll be destroying them ourselves."

"We have monthly conferences," Anita Patel said in her soothing, lilting voice. "Things are not all that dire, Gavan."

He frowned briefly. "This is not the Old World," he repeated, "where we can gather them up and sweep them away and their parents will be thankful they were apprenticed somewhere. No. They may well spend their summers vacationing in different corners of the states and we may never get them all together in one group again. Not," and he took a breath, "unless we can offer them a school. An Academy of such outstanding opportunity that a parent would want nothing more than to send his child there. And we have to produce that Academy now. We can't waste any more time. Now, their powers are more open to abuse than ever, and now, when things are forever changed, their lives are even more valuable. Precious. And we Magickers are responsible for them!"

Isabella ruffled her fan. "There is no suitable Haven to hold such a school yet, Gavan. This is an old argument, one we have every time we meet. Have you trained your Gatekeeper? Does he even know what faces him? Or are you still dabbling in painting only the light side of Magick? Would you have him be caught unawares as Fizziwig was?"

Before she finished, she was interrupted by the other dissenting voice. "Open the Gates. Only then will I help establish a school. If you cannot do that, they might as well all drink the Draft and be returned to the nothingness from which they came." Khalil the Moor stood, cloaked in nightdark fabric, even his eyes unseeable. "You've a betrayer in your midst, Gavan Rainwater, but you are too blind to see it. Open your eyes! Then and only then have we any hope." With that, he raised his arm, invoked his crystal, and was gone in a heartbeat.

A moment of complete and utter silence followed. Not a soul left on the Council moved or, it seemed, even dared to breathe.

Then Bailey stirred. "He forgot to say 'Mwahahahaha,'" she commented.

Gavan stared at her, his jaw dropping slowly. Eleanora reached over and put her hand on Bailey's knee, squeezing, as she tried to contain a giggle. Then Aunt Freyah put her head back and laughed heartily, and for a very long time, before finally subsiding and saying, "Thank you, Bailey, I needed that. Khalil is nothing if not dramatic, and it doesn't take a Shakespeare to note that." She gathered her patchwork jacket about her, looking very gypsylike. "We can't let fear defeat us before the enemy has a chance."

Allenby, who had sat mostly silent, except for nervously wiping his balding head with a handkerchief from time to time, managed a few words. "Someone here has to remember this is not all fun and games."

Isabella snapped her fan and shaded her face with it. "The point remains, Council members. We've a Gatekeeper. Has he been trained? Does he know what faces him?"

"Ummm. I think I can answer that. No."

They all turned to look at Jason.

"Unless," he added apologetically, "I wasn't paying attention at the time?"

Gavan sat down. The palm of his hand rubbed the wolfhead of his cane a moment, as it did when he was thinking, before he finally said, "No, I think you would have remembered this. Fizziwig was our last and only Gatekeeper. I was hoping when we found him, he'd impart what he'd learned."

Jason looked at him, whispered words echoing in the back of his head . . . *There are secrets. Don't you think you ought to know them . . . ?* And the message etched in his crystal. Fizziwig's secrets, now lost to him forever. Was it something that could save all of them?

Eleanora glanced at Gavan as his words trailed off, before looking to Jason and adding kindly, "Fizziwig . . . Herbert was his real last name, but he liked being called something that sounded like it came from Dickens with just a little twist . . . Fizziwig was a classmate of Gavan's. They were trained together, and came forward together."

"Oh, Gavan," said Ting. "We're sorry! You must have known him well." Her brow creased in sympathy.

"We didn't know, when we found him," Bailey added.

Jason echoed with an "I'm sorry" of his own.

"That's not the point, guys," Trent cut in. "I think the point is," and he looked right at Gavan, who seemed to be studying the crystal embedded in his cane without responding to any of their kind words, "the point seems to be that they were classmates. In other words, the same age. But we found an old man."

"Not that old," snapped Freyah. Her dark eyes glared a hole through Trent.

Gavan sighed. "Old enough." He looked up. "Trent has cut

the Gordian knot again and gone right to it. Fizziwig was, or should have been, my age."

Bailey let out a small "Meep" . . . or maybe it was her pocket that squeaked. "He couldn't have been."

"Trust me, he was." Absentmindedly, Gavan pushed a shock of dark brown hair from his forehead. He did not reveal any creases by doing so, nor was there a single thread of gray in his hair. His eyes were the same, piercingly clear blue they'd always been, with only a very few fine lines at the corners.

Jason shook his head in disbelief.

Trent cracked his knuckles. "It makes sense," he said. "Magick has a price, it always does, and all the wizards and sages are old, wise. Bearded. So it takes youth, maybe even the life force itself, to use."

Aunt Freyah fastened her gaze on the back of his head, her apple cheeks blazing, her silvery hair a corona about her face. Trent didn't seem to notice.

"For all we know," he continued. "They could be the ripe old age of twenty or something."

Bailey snickered. She put her hand up to muffle it. Eleanora smiled faintly, shifting gracefully inside her lacy dark dress. "I would be hurt," she said softly. "But I know you mean well, Trent."

"Are there things you should be telling us you're not?" Jason sat forward in his chair. "Is that what killed Fizziwig? The Curse of Arkady? Do we face aging incredibly if we use any mana?" He looked at all of their faces, and no one would look back at him except Aunt Freyah.

"We don't know what killed Fizziwig," Gavan said finally. "I wish we did, but we haven't a clue. His heart just stopped. As for the Curse, well, I don't think it would have applied to Fizziwig at that point in his life." He tapped his cane lightly on the floor in a mild, uneasy rhythm, his fingers gripping the pewter wolfhead tightly. Bare glints of the massive crystal the wolf held could barely be seen.

"Will we ever know?"

"Probably not. FireAnn is working on it, but she's not found any answers yet in herbology and Dr. Patel had seen him first, of course. There doesn't really appear to have been a reason for it, despite what you think of his aged appearance.

Up till the last, he was hale and hearty, as he should have been." Gavan stood. "A lot of issues have been thrown about the table today, and I guess it's time to answer one of them." He looked at Jason. "I had hoped for you to have more time, more training, more understanding before I showed you this." He extended his hand. "Gatekeeper. Are you ready to glimpse the futures?"

30

GATES

TRENT shot him a look, but Jason shook his head slightly as he put his own hand out to meet Gavan's. Now was not the time, he thought, to be telling the others they'd done a little exploration of their own. Definitely not the time. He'd played dumb, he'd stay that way.

Trent stood, too, as Jason rose to take Gavan's hand. He asked quietly, "Do we all get to see or is this private?"

"I think we're going to need the help of all those here, who can stay to help. Jason is the Gatekeeper, but I think part of the phenomena of your Talents . . . all your Talents . . . is that you support and draw on each other." Gavan wore a wistful expression. "Perhaps if we'd been raised with that spirit of co-operation instead of competition, Brennard might never have fought Gregory. We shall never know."

Allenby pushed away from the Council table with a new sheen of nervous sweat dappling his egg-bald head. "I have appointments and work to do. We have investments we need to keep up to date and accountings to be made. I am, as always, at your disposal, Rainwater, if you need information on the finances. Good day, ladies, gentlemen." He bowed stiffly to the Magickers sitting around the table before taking out his watch from his vest, snapping open the silver cover to expose a brilliant crystal, glancing into it, and disappearing.

Trent let out a low whistle. "He makes it look easy."

Dr. Patel considered the spot which had held Allenby. "Never underestimate any of us," she said finally. She straightened her sari about her petite frame, the silver bracelet on her dusky wrist chiming as she did so.

"Ready, Jason?"

"Yeah." He slid his hand into Gavan's, aware that he was not yet full grown and his hand felt even smaller inside the other's grasp. Rainwater, like McIntire, had strong, callused hands although his stepfather's hands could be called massive. His own, while not those of a child, still had a ways to go. Gavan closed his fingers slightly around Jason's.

"I suggest that everyone else who's coming link to Eleanora. I'd like to be able to concentrate on the Gatekeeper and start with Iron Gate."

A coldness swept around the two of them. Jason had a last impression of Trent touching him, gripping his shoulder, before being drawn away from his friends and hurtling into a storm-dark nothingness, towed after Gavan.

After a long moment in which his feet did not touch anything, he could feel gravity again, and see ground below him as the nothingness they'd been in parted, and he and Gavan settled onto a rocky pass, looking down into a vale. At their flanks were the rusting iron gateposts, and a flag showing wear and tear at its edges as it fluttered in a faint breeze. Jason touched it. That banner had been made by Trent, and the flagpole was actually a crudely whittled wooden lance, to battle wolfjackals with if necessary. Instead, he had buried it into the ground to mark and claim the opening of Iron Gate.

He could feel the presence of others at his back as the gathering caught up, though they did not materialize. Gavan nodded at Jason, reading the expression on his face.

"They're here, but Eleanora is holding them back. Now, then." Gavan took a deep breath. His cloak slowly settled about him like a sail that the winds of the travel had kept unfurled, and let fall only now that he had landed completely. "These are the Four Great Gates which control the elements, that we know of. The Iron Gate, the first one, you found and opened here. We were hoping that the opening of that one Gate would lead us to what we needed, but we feel now that is probably not the case."

"Why?"

"It's not stable. The only thing we've put here, that has stayed here, has been this." Gavan tapped the flag. He smiled faintly. "We've laid a foundation twice down there, and it disappeared, shifted elsewhere, overnight."

"Wow," Jason breathed. "Where?"

"We've no idea."

"That would be cool, but I think I know what you mean. We can't have an Academy drifting in and out of realities."

"No, we can't. Think how hard it would be to assign homework." Gavan winked.

Jason laughed, though his nerves were twitching and his stomach felt a little queasy. "What about the others? Do you know?"

"We ... think we do. Mist Gate, Fire Gate, and the last is the Bone Gate." Gavan may have tried but could not conceal a shudder at the last naming. "Those are the elements that must be mastered to bring other lands into balance. There may be others, hidden, that we don't know of."

"So, even trained, I'm not fully prepared."

"No."

Jason nodded. "That's why it's so dangerous. There's no way of knowing what to expect."

It was Gavan's turn to nod. "Sometimes, it's better to be intuitive about Gates, finding them by your own best feelings, and opening them that way. There are schools of thought about doing what it is you need to do, and no one agrees. It's a very individual thing."

"How did Fizziwig do it?"

Gavan smiled sadly. "I've no idea. He usually did it alone, and he only opened one or two successfully. He helped Aunt Freyah open and maintain her small Haven, but that's not really a Gated area, that's more of a ... hmmm ... how to explain it?"

"A pocket beyond the boundaries."

"Yes. She can have incursions, though she's managed to keep them harmless and to a minimum, but she expends great energy in doing so. We can't have a school on that basis. It has to be solid, well grounded, and self-sufficient. We'll have our energy drained by many, many other things."

"No floating candlesticks?"

"Hardly. Think of the tapestry and banner liabilities alone." Gavan's expression flickered with humor.

"So what is it you can train me to do?"

"I'm not sure. I was hoping Fizziwig would be around to do it." Again that sad smile. "Jason, there are procedures. I can show you how to open a Gate or two that isn't right, and deal with what we find. I can show you how to defend yourself, and cover your tracks, and slam a Gate shut, if you need to. What I can't do is show you how to find the right ones. The Great Gates. It's a Talent, and a rare one, and although we can often describe a Talent like that later, after working with it for years and years, we can't really explain what makes it work. A Gate-keeper just . . . does."

"You don't know."

Gavan shook his head slowly.

"But didn't Fizziwig ever tell you? Even a little?"

"He tried once. He might have been speaking Mandarin Chinese for all I understood, and believe me, I tried although I had no idea how important it would become later. And, truth-fully, I can't say that it was the Gating which aged him. That seemed to happen all on its own, unrelated to anything we had done or planned to do. It was almost as if the centuries we were thrown through . . . which we skipped . . . were bound and determined to catch up with us."

Jason looked at Gavan. "Are you aging?"

"A little. Not like he did. But." Gavan pulled his cloak about him, straightening the shoulder seams and correcting its hang, a bit uneasily it seemed to Jason. "Once I was a rather shy and awkward lad, who developed a great crush on this Magicker lass, a woman really, just grown and in her prime, with a blush to her cheek and music in her hands. Then came the Happen-ing, and when I awoke and we met again, she hadn't aged at all. Not a day. But I had found a decade or so, and wore it, and had become a man. I thank the disaster for that, she could look on me as her peer and perhaps entertain my suit. When we're not bickering."

There was a noise from the misty clouds behind them rather like a snort.

"Not," Gavan added hastily, "that anything has ever come of it, thank you for grounding me, Aunt Freyah." He gave an ironic bow.

Jason, however, was not quite sure it had been Aunt Freyah who'd made the stifled noise. The cloud at their backs boiled a little bit as if a storm or wind pushed at it, but it stayed in place. He looked into it, wondering if he could make out Bailey or Trent but could not see them although he could feel their presence. It was uncanny.

He turned and looked down into the valley below, with its backdrop of dragon-spined mountains the color of red-orange spires like something out of a wind-sculpted desert rock. Once, he'd seen a dragon lying there, just like that spread of peaks, or so he'd thought. Now, he didn't know exactly what he'd seen, but surely not what he'd thought he had. The pool of water looked more blue than ever, a long thin waterfall trickling down one of the cliff faces, feeding it, its borders a luxurious and verdant green. He wanted to jog down the small pathway into the valley and taste that water . . . run through the grass and get a closer look at the spine of mountains, see how close or far away they really were, and if they could be such a thing as a petrified dragon.

He lifted his foot to take a step or two. Gavan caught him by the elbow.

He glanced up at the other. "Looks perfectly fine to me."

"Well, it's not," answered Gavan grimly. "Eleanora, might you have another brick about?"

A red clay brick came sailing out of nowhere and landed with a thud at Gavan's feet. He picked it up. A small imprint at the corner read Firehouse Station Queens 12. "An excellent vintage," remarked Gavan. Then he said firmly to Jason, "You stay here." Without explanation, he marched down the winding pathway until he reached the flat valley floor. Then he shouted back, "Here will do." With his bootheel, he scrapped out a small patch of dirt, then firmly implanted the brick there. "This will make a fine cornerstone . . . if it stays." Gavan straightened back up, dusting his hands off, and returned up the path to Jason. "Won't take long," he said confidently.

"What won't?"

"You'll see." Gavan leaned against one of the great rocks forming the pass out of Iron Gate Haven. He whipped a handkerchief out of his pocket and began to polish his cane with great care.

Jason stared downhill. The brick was so far away now, it looked little more than palm-sized as it lay in a tiny square of dirt. He watched it for a long moment, then flinched as something itchy, crawly, seemed to be going down the back of his neck. He squirmed and threw his arm up so he could scratch at it, but again Gavan caught him by the elbow.

"It's not an itch," he said.

"The heck it's not! It's a bug or something." Jason fairly danced with the need to scratch at it. "Let me go so I can get at it!"

"No," said Gavan. "It's this . . ." and he pointed downhill at the brick which lay in the sun. Jason stared as the object wavered slightly, seeming to jump and quiver upon the ground, ever so slightly and yet detectable even from where he stood. "Earthquake?"

"Confined to one tiny patch of ground? Don't be ridiculous." Gavan stared expectantly downhill now. "Wait for it."

Right elbow held tightly in Gavan's grip, Jason threw up his left arm and began to scratch furiously at the back of his neck, even as he watched the brick. It began to dance upon the dirt, vibrating, jumping up and down with enough vigor that he knew he couldn't be imagining it. "What is it doing?"

The itch wouldn't go away, the scratching wasn't helping, so he dropped both arms to his sides. He stared at the brick, which could have been a marionette on strings for all its wild activity now, standing on end and flip-flopping from side to side. Then a dull pop assaulted his ears, and the brick exploded into a chalky red cloud of dust which slowly disappeared.

Jason blinked.

He heard Bailey whisper, "Wow" out of the misty fog behind them.

Gavan sighed.

"What happened?"

"We're not quite sure. It has to do with the compatibility of the planes. Ours and this one . . . Eleanora?"

Her soft voice drifted out of nothingness. "Think of your world as a tuning fork, Jason, vibrating to a certain pitch or sound. Then think of someone else striking another tuning fork, vibrating to another note. They are not compatible, they're just pitches of noise and one will rule the other out. Everything molecular has its own pitch, its own song. If the forks are conjoined, one vibration will eventually rule the other, or both vibrations will cease to exist. In this case, the brick . . . ceased."

"But we don't belong here either." The back of Jason's neck had stopped itching but now his nose did. He rubbed it. "Could that happen to us?"

"I hope not. It is a possibility we've considered."

Jason felt itchy all over. "Worse than that can happen through other Gates?" Considering what he'd just seen, he and Trent had been incredibly lucky.

"Wrong Gates? Much, much worse."

Jason nodded. "Okay. When do we start training?"

31

TIGER, TIGER, BURNING BRIGHT

JASON woke in the middle of the night, staring at his porthole window which framed a great yellow slice of moon. For an uneasy moment, he couldn't quite remember where he'd been, other than sleeping, for it seemed he'd been somewhere, doing or thinking of something important. Then he remembered the Council meeting and sank back into his blankets, temples throbbing with a slight headache, and worry.

They had discussed Henry briefly before everyone dispersed, news the Council had not heard though Gavan had been told days ago. It seemed to hearten them a bit, to hear of a Magicker regaining lost powers since such a tragedy was often thought irreversible. The Council broke up on a positive note, each member determined to go through his or her own notes and journals for anything that might help Jason in his quest.

Afterward, all he could remember of his uneasy dream was Mrs. Cowling, Aunt Freyah's niece, both ladies so much alike with their apple cheeks and bright-eyed gazes and soft curly hair although Aunt Freyah's was definitely silver and Mrs. Cowling's a soft brown with blondish tones . . . well, all he could remember was his old English teacher reciting a poem to him. " 'Tiger, tiger, burning bright, in the forests of the night.' That's Blake, Jason. Remember it."

Burning tigers. He scrubbed at his face. Back to sleep or wake up? He was in that in between where he could easily do both, and it seemed silly to wake up in the middle of the night.

He should have been dreaming of Gates. Gavan had refused to start his lesson on the spot, saying that he had obligations to return Jason, but that lessons would and must start ... soon. In the meantime, Jason had to look within himself for that was where he would begin to find the Gate desperately needed to help anchor the Haven they wanted for the Academy.

In other words, it was all on him. Without a clue or book to help him, without a lesson or a Magicker versed in such things, it rested on his shoulders. No wonder Gavan had called him Atlas, the man in ancient mythology who carried the world on his back, and told him not to let the worry squash him. He didn't tell him not to worry, just not to be squashed.

Jason grinned at that. Rubbing his face again, he slid back down into his bed, watching the great yellow moon outside as it slowly edged past his porthole window. Once or twice, he thought he saw a crow wing across it, but that could have been his imagination. Better a crow or raven than a burning tiger, he yawned to himself sleepily, just before burrowing his head into his pillow with his eyes shut.

Earlier in the evening, however, others had been just as busy. Henry had evening chores and babysitting after dinner while his parents and all his siblings but the youngest went to a planning meeting. It took him a while to get his baby sister sleeping happily in her crib. He made sure the sides were up, for she was a toddler now and had climbed out once or twice. It was something that worried his mom, and so it worried Henry. He'd already decided he was never going to have kids when he got older, as it seemed totally not worth the hassle. Not even when his sister gave him a sloppy hug and snotty kiss.

He was taking the last sack of house trash out to the garage barrels when the shadows moved. Henry let out a stifled noise that would have been a yell except he couldn't breathe, and he threw the trash bag at whatever it was, preparing to run.

Dr. Patel emerged from the shadows. "Henry. Are you quite all right?" She bent over and picked up the plastic sack, handing it back to him. "Did I frighten you?" Her anklet chimed softly as she stepped forward, wrapped in a bronze-and-gold silken sari with a shawl folded over her arm, her smile gentle.

"Dr. Patel! N-n-no. No. I was just . . . just . . . startled." His face turned red hot as he took the trash from her and hugged it as if it could hide his embarrassment.

"It's all right, Henry, I understand the wolfjackals have been about lately. I do not blame you for jumping. Have you a moment for a visit?"

He looked back toward the house. "A quick one. Everyone's gone except me, but my sister's asleep. Would you like a . . . a cup of tea or something?" He hugged his trash sack tighter and something inside belched. He bolted into the garage, lobbed it into the trash can, and came back out, his face hotter than ever.

"Tea would be most pleasant, but I cannot stay long." Anita Patel smiled at him. Hardly taller than he was, and with soft, dark eyes, she didn't appear very intimidating. She put her hand to the crystal at her throat, worn almost like a cameo.

"R-right." Henry led the way to the kitchen's back door. He used the microwave to boil the water, and soon had two cups of his mother's most fragrant orange-and-spice tea on the table, putting out cream and sugar.

Dr. Patel made her tea like the English did, he thought, as he watched her use a lot of cream and sugar, making the cup look almost like coffee with milk, caramel colored. He almost spilled his mug watching her fix hers, and his face stayed hot just when he thought it might cool down a bit. He must look like one of his mother's garden tomatoes in August!

If his face was incredibly red, the Magicker who was also a physician did not seem to notice. She sipped at her cup a few times before settling back in her chair with a pleased sigh. "Thank you for your hospitality, Henry."

He nodded happily. "Any time."

"Do you know why I am here?"

"Well." He twisted his body about on the wooden kitchen chair, considering. "No."

"I came by to see how you were doing, and to congratulate

you. I heard the good news about your Talent returning this evening."

"Oh! That." Henry beamed, pleased. "I'm hoping I can go back to camp next summer and start lessons again."

"Oh, no. Time is too precious. Each Magicker gets a guardian of sorts, who visits and gives private lessons throughout other seasons."

"You're my guardian?"

Dr. Patel set her cup down, surrounding it with her small, neat hands. "I don't know yet, Henry, but I'll ask if you'd like. You have a great deal of potential."

"That would be terrific! I need someone calm, I think."

She laughed softly. "Couldn't hurt."

"What would we do?"

"Oh, lessons at home, mostly, perhaps a field trip now and then. Gavan is working very hard to get Ravenwyng established as the Iron Mountain Academy."

Henry felt his eyes get rounder behind his glasses. "An academy?"

"So we all hope. Anyway, I should go. You have duties here, although . . ." and Dr. Patel paused, listening. "Your sister sleeps well."

"I should hope so."

Anita stood and put her hand on his head. "This is a time when you need to be most careful, Henry. You are very vulnerable."

He looked up at her. "I know," he said, and his voice broke, to his further embarrassment.

She took off a wraparound bracelet, which he saw when she handed it to him was a snake which curled upon itself so that its own jaw clamped to its tail. Small crystals made up its eyes. "If there's trouble, break this, and I will know and come immediately to help."

"Break it?"

She showed him a tiny line. "It is meant to be undone there, by breaking it open. There is a hidden hinge inside. You're not actually breaking it. But it is a magical circle and when that is changed, I'll know it, and I'll know immediately that you did it."

"All right." Gratefully, Henry shoved it deep in his pocket, where he could feel its heavy weight against his skin even through the cloth. "Thank you."

"I expect it back when you've a new crystal and can defend yourself." Anita smiled encouragingly. "Until then, the cobra, which is also a guardian of my country, will watch you." She smoothed her sari down, and brought her shawl up about her shoulders. She raised her hand, palm out, in a kind of wave and as he blinked, she was gone.

Only the half finished tea proved she had even been there. That, and the bronze bracelet in his pocket. He finished his quickly and put everything away in the dishwasher. To his disappointment, neither Trent nor Jason were on-line for some quick game time, so he picked out a book and curled up in the old chair in his bedroom and read till everyone got home.

Jason stirred and woke again, from a dream that was really a memory of camp, from their lessons learning how to bring a lanternlike fiery glow to their crystals. Henry had set his on fire . . . twice . . . singeing his eyebrows as flames fountained upward, and the only thing protecting his hands had been a pair of FireAnn's oven mitts. It had been both funny and scary, scattering campers and adult Magickers alike. They said that in every Talent, there was a leaning toward certain elements. Obviously, Henry's had been fire.

With a sigh, Jason swung his legs over the edge of his bed. Dawn was still an hour away, school another two hours after, but it was plain the night held no more sleep for him. Too much depended on him, and he had no idea what to do or which way to go. Or perhaps he did.

He dressed quickly and as quietly as he could, although the deep rumbling snore that always accompanied McIntire's sleep thundered gently throughout the house. He left his lavender crystal behind, tucking it away in a corner of his desk drawer under a soft piece of cloth he kept for polishing his original focus.

He held up his original quartz and gently spoke a word, and it glowed with a steady golden light. He held it close with both hands, and thought of Iron Gate. In a moment, it stood before him where his bedroom wall had been, and Jason stepped through.

For all that Gavan had shown him how unstable it was, he felt good when he stepped into the dale. The sun had risen here, and although the small valley was still a bit chilled by late autumn, he could feel warming rays on his back. He put his crystal into his pocket after quenching the lantern spell, and stepped down the pathway, not exactly sure what he was here for, but knowing here was where he needed to be.

Here was where he needed to bring all the Gates to open and anchor this Haven. So . . . this was where his clues should lie. Shouldn't they? He yawned slightly, and as quickly covered his mouth. No sleepiness on the job! He needed to be keen and observant. And quick, if wolfjackals showed up again.

As he descended to the pool of water which formed from a thin veil of a waterfall issuing from the rusting mountains, a thin spray of mist dappled his face. It felt icy and left him shivering. He looked at the rim of encircling mountains which, from high up where the Gate swung open, always looked to him like a great, dark orange dragon slumbering. Once, he thought he had seen just that. But only once.

He sat on a flat slab of rock that bordered the small pond, and slid his hand into his pocket where his fingers curled comfortably about his crystal. He should not stay, in case another quake or shift struck the valley, but he liked it here. Something scampered over the toe of his sneaker, paused while he glanced down at it, and then skittered away, slithering through the grass. A small salamander, or fire lizard. His shoe even felt a trail of warmth where it had been. Jason grinned at the tiny lizard which moved so quickly and hid itself so well.

He leaned back, tilted his face skyward, and let the sun chase away the icy veil of mist. For a moment, he felt just like the salamander, basking in the sun and wondered how a dragon might have felt, if the Iron Mountains had ever once been a great winged beast.

"Why don't you ask me how I feel?"

The voice rumbled out of the very ground, its timbre deep and yet light. It was like no voice he'd ever heard before. Jason opened his eyes. Very, very slowly, he turned his head because it seemed to be all that he could move.

He wondered that he hadn't seen it before, for it was clearly visible now, its dark orange-and-rust body lying against the foot of the mountain range that mimicked it. But perhaps, like a chameleon, it could only be seen when it moved or willed itself to be seen. At any rate, a dragon rested not far from where he sat, golden amber eyes watching him. He could feel its heat and smell its coppery blood. The immense creature could only be dwarfed by the mountains themselves, and he asked himself yet again how it was he hadn't seen it!

"Sometimes one looks too hard," the dragon provided. It curled up a forepaw and considered its magnificently taloned foot. "Or so I find it."

Jason managed to inhale. "How . . . how do you feel?"

"Lazy. I am still greedily absorbing all the sunlight I can, and I am feeling drowsy with it. You?"

"Grateful. The water is very chilly."

"It will ice over in a week or so."

Jason vaguely remembered reading that one wasn't supposed to look into a dragon's eyes, but it was too late now; he was already staring directly at the great, luminous amber eyes. "I don't mean to disturb you," he said finally, feeling rather lame.

"Not at all, not at all. I rather enjoy company. Company is so much better than the stray dinner or two which often bolts past, right under my nose. Dinner, if it knows it is a repast, seldom stays to chat."

"I'm not dinner?"

"Of course not." The dragon rumbled in what must have been draconic laughter. "You're literate. Do you eat books for lunch? I think not!" He stretched his wings out, the great bones and spines in them nutmeg-colored shadows under the russet-scaled skin, and folded up again. The dragon peered at him. "You *are* literate?"

"Sometimes I wonder, myself. As a race, I mean. As people who live on the face of the Earth . . ." Jason halted. "Hard to explain." He thought of recent events, and stopped talking altogether.

"Hmmm." The sound came out as a grating rumble, heated and raspy. "This could be awkward. I think you should decide whether you are or not."

Jason winced. "Or I could be lunch?"

"That seems to be the way of the worlds." The dragon

bared its many sharp teeth in what could have been a smile or a snarl.

"I'm afraid it isn't a snap decision. I think being literate, or civilized, is something that takes a while to happen. It's realized after the fact. It might take me a whole lifetime of living to prove whether I am or not," Jason concluded sadly. "Or one awful deed could do the same."

"Weighty thoughts."

"No kidding."

The dragon stretched again, rather like a serpentine cat. "Is that why you came here?"

"No, actually, I came to think about the Gates."

A long, amber blink. "The Gates? Is that all?"

"All?" Jason twisted about on the rock slab to better look at the talkative dragon. "Seems important to me."

"Well, yes, it would. You're a Gatekeeper, but haven't they trained you? It should be as easy as roasting a sitting duck. Think of what you are, and what you need. No other Gatekeeper at all?"

Jason shook his head. "There only seems to be me at the moment."

"Hrmmm. Bad luck, that. And no wonder I've not had more company."

"Yes."

"Seems to me that finding and opening Gates would be a . . . hrmmm . . . an instinctual thing. Rather like flying, once you get a bit of strength and practice."

"Could be. Or . . . falling off a log."

"Rather like that." The dragon flexed his talons.

"Would it upset you, if I got all the Gates opened for here?"

"Not at all. This is only my sunning spot. I get here rather like you do. My own place is a Gate away. I can say this, it would be rather amusing having a bunch of you running around here. I would be asking myself constantly if you were appetizers or apprentices."

Jason grinned.

The beast got off its belly, and rested on its haunches, straightening its forelegs. Again, he was struck by the catlike quality of the dragon. "A word of advice. It is easier than you

make it. It is right in front of you, and all you have to do is look
at it. Three more Gates have you, each as elemental as it can
be. I shall repeat, think of what you are and what you need.
Think too much and you will Open that which should never
be touched!" With that, the beast reared up, roaring with a
sound that began like deep bass thunder and rose in volume
and pitch until it keened into a screech. It leaped skyward,
stretching out its wings, and was airborne in a heartbeat or
two, leaving a wake behind that rolled him about as if a giant
hand shook him, throwing him off the rock.

He flailed out to catch himself, the Haven tilted and shifted,
and his stomach wrenched as everything *changed,* and he was
thrown headlong back through Iron Gate.

32

NO I IN TEAM

"WE made a deal," Coach said, his square face creased in a heavy frown. "Three weeks ago, and this is what I get. I won't have this, Adrian. Either you're a player on my team or you're not, and this tells me you don't want to be."

The long night had turned into a long day, and Jason's baffled feeling about being called in turned into out and out worry. "I don't understand—"

"Statler wants to see you. Now." Coach tapped a piece of paper on his desk. "I thought we had this worked out. Not only does he want to see you, but he's told the vice principal he wants to see Canby, Brinkford, and your friend, Sam. He feels a need to interview them about you, and possibly add them to counseling as well."

"We did make a deal. I've been to every session. He wants to see me now?" Jason's chest felt heavy. First a home meeting, now more meetings at school. What did the man want of him?

"Now," repeated Coach flatly. His face wrinkled even more, till he reminded Jason of a thundercloud about to burst into rain and lightning.

He shifted uneasily on his chair. "I didn't have anything to do with that," he said earnestly. "Honest."

"Maybe not, but what I told you originally stands. If you can't make practice regularly, you're off the team. Your teammates deserve to play with someone who works as hard as they do, and is reliable. Not only that, but with these three, he's not leaving me with much of a team! I can't have that."

Jason tried not to clench his hands. "What does he want?"

Coach shook his head. "All I know is, I'm to send you over. This is your last chance, Adrian. Straighten these meetings out, or I will drop you from the team. Understood? You've ability, but if I have to drop you to save more players from getting caught up in your mess, I will."

Jason gulped. "Yessir." He jumped to his feet. "I'll be back as soon as I can!"

Halfway outside the P.E. building, Sam caught him by the elbow. "What's up? What was Coach so mad about?"

Jason had one tight-lipped word for him. "Finch."

"That perv."

"I have to go see him."

"I thought your appointments were Friday mornings."

"Exactly. Coach says if I miss any more time from practice, he's dropping me. And you're gonna get hauled in, too."

Sam breathed in and out indignantly. "Can he do that?"

"Yeah, he can. Listen, I've gotta go, I'll be back if I can."

Sam nodded, and watched Jason with a forlorn expression as he trotted off across campus.

Students still milled around in the hallways, going through their lockers or bunched in small groups talking, classroom doors banging open and shut as he made his way to the cubbyhole Statler Finch called an office. No one seemed to be inside as he peered cautiously through the doorway. Relief flooded Jason. He'd come back later, at his regular appointed time then....

"Ah, Jason! Go on in, I'll be right there. Just getting a cup of coffee from the staff room!"

Jason whirled. Statler stood behind him, coffee mug in hand, blocking the corridor, a most curious expression on his face. He gestured through the air with the empty cup. "Go on, go on. I'll just be a minute."

Trying not to sigh, Jason ducked his head and went into the office he'd grown to hate. He plopped down on the visitor's chair, tucked his feet around the side rungs, and waited, thinking.

His gaze swept the office. Everything was compulsively neat, what little there was of books and files. The only picture on the wall was a poster comparing a wizened chimpanzee face to an elderly Albert Einstein. Wrinkling his nose at that one, Jason turned back to the desk. He curled his fingers about his crystal, holding it close, running through his focusing exercises, feeling the anger and resentment drain away. This wasn't fair ... but then, many things weren't. He'd get through it, and once he did, it would be a small victory. Any triumph could be enjoyed later.

"Here we go." The counselor slid into his desk chair. "Thank Coach for me, for letting you out."

"I'm off the team if I miss workouts again," Jason told him.

The counselor said, without expression. "And how do you feel about that? About getting that kind of attention?"

"I feel like it's your fault, and I don't like getting into trouble for it." Jason stared back at him.

"Do you enjoy assigning blame?"

"I enjoy making a deal and sticking to it. We agreed on Friday mornings."

"As long as your behavior warranted it. But what I saw the other night convinced me that your case is a great deal more complicated than I thought." Statler wrapped spindly hands about his coffee mug and laced his fingers together. "What would you like to tell me about that? The ... trash bin ... incident."

"I saw a coyote trotting around the parking lot. It looked mean and hungry, so I dove into the can and made a lot of racket to chase it away." Jason was glad his words stayed even and did not give away the lie, and he leveled his gaze on the counselor's face.

"Did anyone else see the coyote?"

"Apparently not. But they are pretty hard to see, especially since it was nearly dark."

"Not a stray dog?"

He considered it. "Maybe. I thought it was a coyote. They come out of the hills, you know. It's been a dry year for them, and my stepdad says construction always chases them around a bit until they can resettle."

Statler drank about half his mug of coffee in one gulp. "Interesting reaction. Why didn't you try to outrun it? Or go get help?"

"Everyone seemed gone, and if you try to outrun things like that, you only attract their attention. They'll chase, if that's their gig. Chase and bring down."

Statler opened a desk drawer, reaching inside for his notepad and pencil. As he pushed through an assortment of writing instruments looking for one with a sharpened point, Jason saw deep into the drawer. Surprise hit him.

Crystals. Statler had focus crystals in his desk drawer. One, large enough to fill the man's thin hand, and two smaller ones. They glinted dully at him as the counselor pulled out what he needed and then shut the drawer tightly, and made a few notes as if deciding that Jason had finally said something worthwhile.

Jason watched. Why crystals? Why hidden? Did Finch know what they were for? Did he have an inkling of why and how they could be used? And if he did, where had he learned? An uncomfortable feeling prickled up the back of Jason's neck. He began to talk about soccer and why he loved it and why he wanted to stay on the team, not letting Statler get more than a word or two in edgewise. When he finally rambled to a halt, Statler had long since stopped scribbling whatever it was he wrote in his notebook and drained his coffee mug dry.

"And that is why," Jason finished, "I can't come to any more afternoon sessions."

Statler's eyebrows went up. "You're hardly in a position to dictate when you'll be here."

"You'll ruin everything."

"Blame again." Statler smiled thinly. "That's an interesting issue we should discuss tomorrow morning, Jason." He waggled his pencil at him. "Your usual appointment and I'll see you bright and early."

Jason took his leave, trotting back through now deserted corridors, wondering what he was going to do. A door swung open in his path. He went nose to nose with a chart covering the inside door of the science lab. "Composition of the Human

Body," it read. "Seventy percent water." Without further thought, he swung past the door, listening to the grumbles and laughs from kids who'd stayed behind to finish a lab or work on a science fair project. He got his things from his locker and headed for home, shoulders hunched against a cold, dry wind. What *were* crystals doing in Statler's desk? What were the odds he merely liked pretty rocks?

Jason didn't think it could be that simple. Brennard's forces had sent a spy deep into the camp at Ravenwyng. They could do it here, too . . . to watch and break him, if they got a chance. Or was he just beginning to think as crazily as the counselor thought him to be?

Coach grabbed Sam by the scruff of the neck as he started out of the P.E. building. Sam looked up, feeling his eyes go wide. "Come with me," the teacher said. "We have an appointment with Statler Finch."

Sam's heart sank. Just as Jason had warned. And, unlike Jason, he wasn't a stellar student and if any inkling of trouble reached home, his parents might ground him. He sighed unhappily as the coach marched him toward the offices at the front of the school. He wasn't any happier as Coach sat him down inside the office and said, his voice tight and annoyed. "I want to have a word with you, Finch."

Statler Finch got to his feet. Sam watched him, thinking all the while of Ichabod Crane. He even has a bird name like the character, he thought, as the two men went out and down the hallway. He could hear Coach's voice rising with every step.

". . . Trying to . . . ruin . . . my team?"

Sam looked around. He wasn't exactly sure why he was there or what he should say. Sure, he wanted to help Jason, but at what cost? He couldn't very well lie either till he knew what was going on!

He stood. Finch had left papers scattered across his desk. He craned his neck to look at them.

"Dear Student. This is an official notification that your loan package has been turned over for collection. As stipulated in original loan applications, all student's loans come eligible for repayment six months after leaving classes, whether graduated from a program or not. Your loans for the Masters program have been forwarded accordingly, and a payment program will be set up. . . ."

Something crashed down the hallway. Backing up guiltily from the desk, Sam jumped. His elbow hit the cubicle wall and a picture frame fell down. He almost caught it. Almost.

The frame cracked slightly, losing its tension, and the glass fell out. The diploma behind it slid out as well. Sam frantically tried to gather everything up, but as he did, the gold-embossed seal on the diploma flaked off and sailed through the air.

With muffled curses, he set the framing down on a chair seat and managed to get it back together, and the glass in place, with only a tiny nick in the corner of it. As for the diploma, Sam looked at it as he retrieved the fallen seal. It just looked . . . well . . . fake. And besides, Finch couldn't have graduated with a Masters if the letter on the desk said he'd dropped out. So how could he have the diploma?

He could hear a shout and footfalls coming back his way. Hurriedly, he licked the golden seal and managed to get it stuck back on the diploma and the whole thing back together and on the wall.

"Do what you gotta do," the coach practically bellowed. "But if you take my team apart for the sake of one kid, I will see this program of yours stopped." He paused just outside the open office door and then stomped off. A pale and shaken Statler Finch stepped inside.

He blinked at Sam as though he'd forgotten he was there. Then, he took a deep breath and sat down. "I'll make this very, very brief, Samuel."

"No, it's Sam."

"Whatever. Very brief." Hands shaking, the counselor swept his papers into his desk drawer and then drew out a notebook.

Sam appeared to be looking at Finch as the man started asking questions, and he started answering. But in reality he was looking at the diploma on the wall, and thinking about his friendship, and the team, and what everything meant.

33

OH, HENRY

HENRY got up early, readying himself for school. He always liked the last day of the week, even though it invariably meant tests in English and Math and often small quizzes in History. He liked it because he loved to sleep in on Saturdays, which his mother let them all do, because she liked to sleep in on Saturdays. If any of them did get up, they were under the strictest orders to do so quietly and stay that way, so as not to disturb the peaceful rest of anyone else. So he had only one more day to wait until Saturday, when his time was his, to be spent (in the morning anyway), any which way he could so long as it was quiet.

He'd decided to take charge of his destiny. And, although it might be just as well to wait a day or two, today was probably as good as any time to begin. There was a shop on the way home from school, a little store carrying candles and crystals and incense and stuff. He didn't intend to spend his time wondering if a wolfjackal or a terrible Magicker stood in the shadow waiting to steal his powers again. No. He'd get a crystal of his own, and he'd fight back!

The morning sun shone brightly in the backyard, and Henry took the opportunity to box his shadow around, showing it who was boss! He danced about in proper kung fu style, kicking and jabbing. It felt good to have Jason and Trent, Bailey and Ting all believing in him again. How could he have forgotten them? Well, he'd been enchanted to, but still! And to become a full-fledged Magicker again? He could hardly wait. If only he had his crystal!

He wouldn't have the summer back, but he had days of it in his mind, vivid and happy. With the exception of Jonnard, who'd betrayed all of them, the memories he had seeping back were good ones. Magick lessons and campfire sing-alongs and warm days canoeing on the lake and afternoons playing sand-lot baseball. He'd never been happier. Who'd want to forget that?

He punched and kicked at his shadowy self who deftly danced and twisted out of range. In the house and upstairs, he could hear his siblings clattering out of the house for school. One more good kick box . . .

Henry.

He halted in his tracks. The thick, unruly hair on his head stood on end. Something—someone?—hissed at him from the shadows.

He turned, straightening his glasses. The morning sun lay across his backyard in sharp contrast to the early shadows cast by corners, and fencing, and the garage. The yard almost looked black and white, rather than shades of greens and browns, edged and dotted with colorful flowers. This was his home! How could anything have got in?

But he knew better even as he thought that.

Could wolfjackals talk? And if they did, did he really want to listen? Henry pivoted cautiously and began to walk toward his back door. His sneakers swished through grass thick with dew, the bottoms of his jeans going dark purple with the wetness. Something trailed behind him. Cautious, slow, but he could hear footfalls.

Henry.

Something panted. It could be him, his chest rising and falling in gasping breaths, unable to call out, but trying to. Or it could be the something behind him, or the something in the shadows flanking him, or the something in the corner by the kitchen door waiting. . . .

He made it through the back door, lunging quickly in at the

last second and slamming it in the face of whatever pursued him. He heard a low whine, and a frantic scratch. Wood and paint splintered, by the sound of it. Still panting, he stood for a moment, then grabbed up his book bag with Henry Squibb neatly stitched across the back of it. Something bronzed and heavy fell out as he hoisted it and clattered over the kitchen floor, coming to rest under the lip of the cabinet. He bent over quickly to retrieve it.

Dr. Patel's cobra bracelet! He didn't know how he could have forgotten it so quickly, but he had. Its surface felt cool as he rubbed it between his fingers. Just break it, she'd said.

He couldn't go off and leave danger so close to home. It was up to him to make sure everyone was protected.

Taking a deep breath, Henry broke the bracelet.

His feet left the ground in a dizzying motion. His body soared upward even though his eyes appeared to be shut tight, and he had no idea where he was going or how. He moved through the air with great speed, as though a tornado had picked him up and carried him off. Everything whirled around him. He could feel his backpack straining from its strap, and his shoes tugging at his feet, laces untying and flying about like spaghetti. His ears roared so loudly that, for a few moments, he seriously wondered if it *was* a tornado.

Then everything stopped as suddenly as it had begun. He hung suspended, suddenly aware that he was no longer moving, and the roaring noise had finished, and there was nothing but the sound of silence and his own squeaking breath. Wherever he was traveling to, he'd arrived! But nothing met his feet, and it was impossible for him to stay hanging in air much longer.

"Gaaaaaah!" cried Henry and he fell.

He fell short and hard, tumbling onto an old linoleum floor that was glazed almost golden yellow with years of wax. The fall thumped the breath out of him. Henry knelt on hands and knees for a minute before getting shakily to his feet. His backpack slipped from his shoulder and fell to the floor. As he looked down, he saw that he held half a bronzed and twisted cobra in each hand. He hadn't just broken it open, he'd snapped it in two. Henry winced, hoping that Dr. Patel either wouldn't mind or could fix it.

That was probably the least of his worries, he thought, as he looked around. He was in Gavan Rainwater's camp office, and he knew that Ravenwyng was a considerable distance from anything he could even remotely call home. Furthermore, he seemed to be here alone.

"Hello?" He twisted around. The place looked as if Gavan were here often, but not this morning. No one was about this morning.

He put the pieces of jewelry in his backpack, hoping the Magicker doctor would not be angry with him. She had given it to him to use when there was trouble, and a wolfjackal at his back door meant a lot of trouble to him.

Pulsating color caught his eye. A great crystal on top of a wooden filing cabinet in the corner moved and shimmered as if alive. Amber rays shot out from it every now and then, and it revolved on a base, as if it turned about on its own. Henry hesitated. Then he licked lips gone terribly dry and moved toward it, just to look. This, he knew, belonged to Gavan. It must be the alarm beacon Jason talked about, the one that didn't always work. It seemed to be working now.

He stepped to its side and tentatively waved his hand through a ray, and amber color flowed over his hand like water, but he didn't feel it, just saw it.

"Wow." Henry dipped his hand in again. Golden waves dappled him. He grinned.

"Henry? What are you doing here? Is there a problem?"

He spun about guiltily at the voice, flinging his hands up, and backing clumsily into the file cabinet. His face lit up, though, with welcome. "Dr. Patel! We had trouble, a wolfjackal."

"Indeed? Does anyone know you're here?"

He shook his head.

"They will." Smiling, she stepped forward with a very faint chiming of the belled anklet she wore, and something snarled from the corner behind the desk, leaping over at both of them. He caught a last glimpse of the alarm beacon crystal, as he fell into the cabinet and it flew off its base, arching through the air and shattering as it hit the floor. He grabbed for a shard of it, thinking of Jason as he did. Dr. Patel was reaching for him. Then he hit his head, hard, and found only darkness.

Jason paused halfway to school. A feeling arched through him, like a shock wave of warning and dismay and terror, and it seemed to call out to him. He blinked. It was like . . . like a disturbance in the Force, corny as that sounded, but this must have been what that felt like. Something was terribly wrong somewhere. His hand went immediately to his crystal. His friends and family ran through his mind, but he found nothing but pleasant warmth when he thought of them. Except for Henry.

He found an icy cold when he thought of Henry.

Darn it! He'd known all along Henry was the most vulnerable of all of them. He didn't even have a focus he could use to help stave off the Dark Hand if they came after him.

Jason looked down the street. His early Friday morning appointment with Finch loomed. But the crystal in his hand told him Henry was in trouble, somehow, and he needed to find out why and where. He took a deep breath, turned about on the sidewalk, and headed back home.

Everyone was gone but McIntire when he came back in. He entered the study hesitantly, unwilling to disturb him, for McIntire sat with his desk covered in blueprints and sketches, and a heavy frown on his face. He looked up. "Oh. Morning, Jason. Problem?"

"Sir. You know, we talked about trust?"

"Indeed we did. Used to be, when I started out in business, you could shake a man's hand and that would be the contract, his bond. Trust. Now, you need a fleet of lawyers on both sides, and why? Because people break their trust."

Jason cleared his throat uneasily. "I know I have to see Mr. Finch and get things straightened out, but I just can't do it today. I need to . . . I need to miss my counseling appointment this morning and maybe a class or two."

"You intend to ditch some classes and you're telling me about it?" McIntire stared at him.

"Yup. Look. I need you to trust me on this. I've got to help someone out, it's this project."

"No drugs."

"No, sir." Jason swallowed tightly. "Nothing like that."

"Anything to do with Halloween?" McIntire watched his face steadily.

Tonight was Halloween night. The irony of Brennard striking out at all of them like the vampire he was hit Jason with irony. "It might, I'm not sure yet."

The Dozer put down his pencil. "You know, Jason. I never hesitated asking Joanna to marry me because of you kids. Bright, good kids, both you and Alicia. I'm proud to be your father. Stepfather." He coughed slightly. "You haven't given me any evidence otherwise, so . . . all right. Let me know when you're back then. I've got trouble with the McHenry house coming out my ears. I'll be on the cell phone. And I'll handle your mother when she gets home. But—" And McIntire pointed at him. He paused as if searching for the right word. "Be careful," he finally said.

"Yessir! I'll try!" Jason darted out of the door and upstairs to the safety of his room. He pulled his trapdoor shut after him and got first the lavender crystal out, and then his own. Cupping them closely, he summoned the alarm beacon and found no answer. Not again! Not now, not this time!

Jason closed his eyes and called on Gavan with all his might. His thoughts went ebony and then crimson with intensity, then suddenly, he conjured the image of Rainwater in his mind.

"Jason?" came a faint response. "What is it, lad?"

"Trouble."

Gavan suddenly strengthened in his thoughts as the other Magicker threw his own power into their conversation. The head and shoulders image of the man stared through Jason's mind. "What kind and where?"

"I don't know! It's Henry. He's just . . . well, he's gone cold."

"Jason, that's not enough to . . ."

"And the alarm beacon is out."

"What? I was just in my office. I had some matters to take care of, about Fizziwig. The crystal was fine. What the hell is going on?" Gavan shook his head. "Let me get some of the others. We'll follow up on Henry and let you know."

"Okay."

Then, as quickly as he'd been watching Gavan's face grow concerned and angry, the image was gone and his thoughts were empty.

Jason sat back in his chair. There was really nothing more he could do. He booted his computer and left quick messages for Bailey and Trent, not knowing if he would catch them before they left their homes. Rich and Stefan had auto-messages on their e-mail stating that the team was out of state for a middle school football tournament, and they were gone for a long weekend in Texas. He didn't even leave mail for Ting. There was no sense in frightening her.

Jason checked his watch. His session with Statler Finch was nearly half gone. Gavan would contact him, when there was anything to know. He decided to face the music and go to school anyway.

By the time he got there, the campus was crowded with students clustered around, waiting for regular morning classes to begin. He wouldn't have to deal with missing first period then, for which he could be grateful, if he wasn't so worried about Henry.

Sam caught him in the main corridor by their lockers. "Man, where have you been?"

"I got up late. I haven't missed anything yet."

"Nothing but your appointment with the psycho-ologist."

"That's not funny, Sam." Jason sighed. His friend pulled at his arm.

"It will be." Sam stuffed a folder of papers in his hand. "Listen, he was all over campus looking for you this morning. So he'll haul you out of first period soon as he finds out you've shown up. But this . . ." Sam tapped the folder. "This is your ammo, bro."

"What are you talking about?"

"I got hauled in last night to talk to him."

"Oh, man. I'm sorry, Sam. Really, really sorry."

Sam hit him in the shoulder. "Shut upppp! Let me finish. Coach brought me, and they went down to the teachers' lounge and yelled at each other for a while. So I poked around a little. Looked at the diplomas on the wall and stuff. He had mail on his desk, Jason, about repaying a student loan. Then I came home and looked everything up on the Internet." Sam shook Jason. "Jason. He didn't finish his Counseling Masters. He dropped out. The diploma is a photocopy."

Jason opened the folder. He looked at what appeared to be a list of graduates. "Doesn't exist? He's not in here?"

"Nope. That creep is a fraud. A fake. He shouldn't even be working here at the school! So when he comes after you . . . just point that folder at him and slap him down." Sam grinned. "I put copies on the principal's desk. He'll see 'em in a day or two, I'm sure."

"Wow. He's a fake? His credential is no good?" Jason tried to take in all the implications. He was free!

"Yup. I can get a better diploma from the grocery store and fill in the blanks." Sam slapped him on the shoulder as the bell rang.

"Sam . . ."

"Yeah?" Sam turned back to him.

"Thanks."

"Are you kidding? That's how friends take care of each other. Even if you are a Potter geek."

"Soccer geek!"

Sam laughed. He raised a hand as the warning bell sounded and trotted off to class.

Jason clenched his folder. He slipped into Home Room and sat through the morning's bulletins, and wasn't at all surprised when his teacher looked up, motioned him forward, and gave him a pass sending him immediately to Finch's office. Nor was he surprised at the look of cruel triumph that flashed across Statler's face.

"Breaking appointments won't do you much good, Jason." Statler practically crowed as he gestured Jason into the office.

"I'm not staying long," Jason said. "I volunteered for these sessions, and now I'm not."

Statler's thin mouth tightened until it all but disappeared. "Sit down, young man, and be quiet."

Jason stayed in the doorway. He shook his head. "No, sir. You can't hold me. I'm going back to playing soccer and making practices and doing anything else I need to, just like any other student."

Statler moved to the far side of his desk, and began to slide open a drawer. "I think," he said, "you have no idea of what you're dealing with."

Jason waved his folder. "I think you thought you were too smart for your papers to get caught. But they're fakes, and so are you. I don't have to stay here for classes with you, and I don't intend to. You're twisted, Statler, and you're caught."

"You can prove nothing."

"Copies of this are on the principal's desk right now. I don't have to prove anything. I think you're the one who needs to answer the questions."

Statler snarled. His face contorted and reshaped, and Jason could almost smell the hot spittle, just like a wolfjackal's growling snarl. He stepped back, suddenly frightened in spite of himself.

Statler reached in and grabbed a large, blood-red crystal. "You have no idea what you're dealing with!" He let out a short howl of hate.

"You're mine!" And the jaws in his face had trouble saying the word.

Jason blinked, staring into the gullet of a rapidly transforming wolfjackal. "You came after me specifically." His hand throbbed with a white-hot pain, searing through his scar. "They planted you here!"

"Cleverrrr lad," the beast managed. Its clothes disappeared as if they had only been a veil of illusion.

No wonder Statler hadn't seen the wolfjackal . . . he *was* the beast.

34

RESCUE

HE stumbled into Gavan's empty office seconds later, his heart still thudding from his escape from Statler Finch. One hand was knotted about the folder, clutching it, and the other about the crystal so tightly, it left its imprint in his palm. He slid the folder into his backpack and zipped it tightly, then looked about into chaos.

The massive desk was overturned. Amber shards were strewn everywhere . . . the alarm crystal had shattered and been rendered useless. Jason swept his gaze over the room and the destruction. Chairs, overturned. The wood filing cabinet had nearly gone, too, but it leaned heavily on a small table. Its drawers hung open, papers overflowing from it. The office looked like the aftermath of an all-out brawl, especially with broken glass lying around.

Jason shifted uneasily. Under the lip of the overturned desk, he could see Henry's backpack. Lying next to it was the prone and dead form of another wolfjackal, an amber sliver of the broken crystal through its flank. He shuddered. One close encounter too many.

"Oh, Henry," he sighed. Whatever had happened to Henry, it had begun here. He put a hand to the back of his neck, and rubbed it. He thought of Khalil's last words during the Council argument. *You have a betrayer in your midst.*

He didn't even dare think who. But he knew why. And if Gavan, Tomaz, Eleanora, and whoever else had gone after him had not yet come back, he had a lot of thinking to do about that, too.

He righted Gavan's leather chair, worn and cracked in places, and plopped down in it to wait.

After an hour, he stretched fretfully. Then, he *knew*. And knowing what he knew, he could wait all day. He scrounged around in his backpack and found the two nutritional bars he kept there for emergencies and energy. He also fished out the water bottle at the bottom and drank that, and then he napped. He got up when he woke, and left the office, wandering out of Lake Wannameecha Gathering Hall, then watched the sunset over the lake itself. It was incredibly beautiful.

An owl hooted and drifted silently over the pines. It was time. He went back to Gavan's office. Halloween Eve.

He palmed his crystal and sent for Trent, and then Bailey. Trent appeared, his jaw dropped, and then he gave a yelp as he saw where he was. He was half shrugged out of his sweatshirt and quickly pulled it back on. "What happened here?"

Bailey popped in next, blinking in astonishment, and then let out a snort. "Bachelors! Can't keep anything clean!" She put her hands on her hips. Lacey poked her head out as if to see what the commotion was about.

"Bailey!" both boys said in unison. She tossed her head. "Oh, all right, I see there's trouble and that starts with T and that rhymes with B and stands for Brennard."

Jason's jaw joined Trent's in the down position. Trent slowly shut his mouth and shrugged. "She's right. It's gotta be Brennard's doing. This is not because someone didn't get the trick or treat they wanted." He looked about at the shambles.

"And what was your final clue? The dead wolfjackal under the desk?"

Bailey's eyes got big as saucers as she looked, but Trent only frowned slightly. "What are you talking about?"

"Beast body on the floor." Jason pointed.

Trent shook his head. "I don't see a thing."

"But it's there!"

"Look. I've had enough of those things breathing down my neck! I see nothing. This one's invisible!"

Bailey sidled over and put out her foot and nudged the still form with the toe of her sneaker. "Feels like a wolfjackal," she observed. She crossed the room warily. "They can be killed, right?"

"Right. Although the bodies often don't stay here. They're not stable or something, I guess." Jason considered it. It had been there all day, remarkably unchanging. "Poke it, Trent."

"I can't even see it," Trent protested. Grumbling, he picked up a cane in the stand by Gavan's doorway. He made a show of waving it and poking it through the space under the Magicker's desk.

A ripple ran through the body, distorting it, and then it . . . disappeared. Bailey, who obviously had been able to see it, let out a shriek and jumped back against the wall.

"Very interesting." Jason took a deep breath. "Or as Alice would say, Curiouser, and curiouser."

Trent surveyed what was left of Gavan Rainwater's office. "I'd say this was really serious or you wouldn't have yanked us here. Better be, 'cause I had plans for tonight."

Jason rolled his eyes. "I know you did, 'cause they were with me!"

Bailey got in between them, her face pale under her freckles. "What happened?"

"I found it like this. They took Henry."

"Poor Henry." Bailey shuddered. "When?"

Leaving out his troubles with Statler Finch, Jason told the two of them about Henry and his probable disappearance, and what he knew of it, and his contacting Gavan. And then finding this when he hadn't heard.

Bailey whistled low. "I'd say our rescuers need a rescue."

"She has a way with words." Trent shifted uneasily.

"But she's right."

"Okay. What'll we do? What can we do that Gavan and Tomaz and whoever else was here . . . couldn't?" Trent stared at Jason, not angrily, but his eyes locked on Jason's face. "And why have you waited all day?"

"I don't know what we're going to do." Jason reached down

and picked up Henry's backpack and looked at it briefly. "I don't think we're going to have any trouble finding him," Jason replied at last. "I think Henry was bait, and I think the wrong people took it, the first time. The trap was meant for us, not the elders. Wherever he is, they are. And they're all still waiting for us. I had all the time in the world, so I took it to do a lot of thinking."

Trent let his breath out with a hiss. "Then we can get in. But we might have a lot of trouble getting out."

Bailey let out a worried sound. Then she put her shoulders back. "We might take the bait, but who says we have to go into the trap like mice?"

"Exactly. With a little planning, we can cause a lot of trouble, I think. And don't forget, if they're still alive," and Jason swallowed hard at that thought. "If they are, Gavan and Tomaz probably only need a distraction or two to break loose."

Bailey put up a second chair and set it down properly, and rested on it. "I can send Lacey in for a look around, wherever it is. She's little and she's fast."

"You can do that?"

She nodded. "I've been training her. Sometimes," and Bailey blushed at this, "sometimes I see what she does." She looked at Trent. "Remember, I said I could follow her?"

"Okay," said Trent. "That officially makes you weird, Bailey."

"I know," she huffed. "But helpful, too!"

He punched her shoulder. "Did I ever say you weren't?"

Bailey's face turned even redder.

Jason ran his hand over the backpack embroidered with Henry's name. There was a vibration, a faint path there, to be read, leading him onward. "I know where he is," he said, in sudden realization. It seemed inevitable.

"Where?" Two heads turned to look at him.

He waved the backpack. "This is an invitation to the McHenry house." And just as suddenly, just as inevitably, he desperately didn't want to have to go there.

"We're the cavalry, Jason," Trent said quietly, as if reading his reluctance. "Let's get a game plan."

So they huddled close, and made their plans and crossed their fingers. They linked arms and Jason took them to the doorstep of the McHenry house. Night had settled in, and it was dark, pitch-black with a moonless sky.

Trent looked up. "Figures," he commented. He lit one of the old camp lanterns, and handed a second to Bailey. The house looked derelict and abandoned, as if it had never even been wired for electricity.

The front door was open the tiniest crack. Bailey leaned over, fetching Lacey from her pocket, and nuzzling her gently, whispering to her. She put the little pack rat down on the porch step and Lacey cautiously went inside, her long, black tufted tail disappearing in little jerks until suddenly it was gone.

They all stood, very quiet, keeping a sharp eye out for wolf-ish figures loping over the rolling front lawns of the estate ... if any could be seen in the dark. After long moments, Bailey rubbed her temple.

"She's in," she whispered. "Lots of people in the back. Gavan! Tomaz . . . long frilly skirts . . ." She let out a sigh. "They've even got Eleanora."

"Alive?"

"Everyone, so far."

"Okay, then. We know what we have to do."

They all nodded, and Bailey started for the door.

Abruptly, Jason said, "Wait a minute." He looked at Trent. "I think we'd better tell her."

35

COME INTO MY PARLOR

"JASON, this is not a good time." Bailey put her hands on her hips, facing them. "Whatever it is you want to tell me, I think it can wait."

Jason shifted. "Ummmm. No. I don't think it can."

Trent nodded in agreement. "You're right. It can't wait."

She tossed her head, eyes rolling. "All right! Hurry up, then. Lacey is all alone in there!" She stabbed a finger at the looming McHenry house.

"This is important." Jason put a hand on each of Bailey's shoulders to still the impatient bounce. "Listen to me. Trent is a Magicker without Talent. Not an ounce of it."

Trent nodded again, solemnly. "Not a Magickal bone in my body."

She looked from one to the other. "Oh," she said slowly. Then, "This is sooooo not funny. Look, I'm sorry I ragged on you, but this is NOT funny."

"Bailey, I'm not joking, Trent isn't joking, we're not pulling your chain, this is not meant to be funny. He can't do anything you and I can."

Her jaw dropped. "How . . . what . . . how . . . ?" She stared at Trent in total amazement.

Trent shrugged, his face getting slightly red. "I'm good at

faking? I know all the moves? I've read all the magic books ever written? I know how it should go? I want it really badly? I dunno. But I'm not and Jason's been carrying me, and so have you, and . . . it might be really, really important inside there to know what we're dealing with."

"You can't go in with us."

"Oh, yes, I can. A wolfjackal can take a boot in the gut from anyone. And it's the three of us now, right? If I don't go in, who'll protect your backs while you're focusing on your crystals? You need me as much as I need you." Trent inhaled. "I hope."

Jason dropped his hands from Bailey, but not before he could feel how cold she seemed, and the slight shivers running through her. "I need you," he said quietly. "We know this is a trap. First Henry was bait, now Gavan and Eleanora and the others are bait. We're the ones Brennard wants, and so they're expecting us with whatever they can throw at us. What I'm counting on." And he halted, and looked into each of their faces. "What I'm counting on is that the traps will be aimed specifically at Magickers."

"He hasn't a chance, Jason," Bailey said earnestly, her face knotted in a frown. "I don't know if I can protect him."

"Listen to Jason," Trent pleaded. "Just listen. I belong here, if I belong anywhere!"

"I can protect him, and even more so, I think he can protect us. He won't be affected by Magicks aimed specifically at Talent. He might very well be able to get through what we can't." Jason watched Bailey closely.

"Oh. Ohhhhhhh." Bailey chewed on her lip. "Well, if he can't, it's a little late now!" She rubbed her temple as a far-away look came into her eyes and her attention was taken from them as if she was listening to something else. "Lacey says there are books everywhere, and people everywhere. She's found them! Eleanora and a round-headed boy, and Gavan and Tomaz and Dr. Patel." She gave a shaky laugh. "That's Henry."

"They're in the library, then. Figures. I've been in there before, they know I know the way. It's in the center of the house. We go in there, and we can be effectively surrounded."

"Anything else?" Trent asked as Jason's voice trailed off in thought.

"Like what?" Bailey looked at Trent, puzzled.

"Anything. Anything could be important."

Bailey got a distant look on her face again then, and again rubbed her temple slightly as if her very thoughts hurt. "Pretty things everywhere. Wax . . . cold."

"Candles?"

"Maybe. Cold, though." Bailey shrugged. "I'm not good at this yet."

"Call her back to you," Jason said. "Ask her to look at one on the way back. Soon as you scoop her up, we'll go in." He touched his first crystal, and then his second. *Armed,* he thought, *to the teeth.*

Long moments passed, and then a tiny furry creature shoved its way through the crack in the door, scampering up Bailey's jeans and into the palm of her hand. Bailey nuzzled the pack rat with her cheek before tucking Lacey away into her pocket. "Candles," she said firmly. "Everywhere. In great boxes and on every table, chair, and ledge imaginable."

"Strange." Trent scratched at the back of his neck.

"Candles burn," said Jason in an odd voice, before pulling the door open and stepping inside quickly. He didn't want to face the Fire Gate of his nightmares, yet it seemed inevitable. The itching, the nearness to a Gate waiting for him to discover and open it seemed unbearable. Not now! Not tonight, not without training. Not here. The other two tumbled after him.

At night, the old mansion seemed as cavernous and dark as any haunted house. Although electric lights burned through it in dim corners, their illumination seemed very pale and weak. Trent craned his head. "Low, low watts. Just barely enough to almost see by." He stepped around a pile of crates, reading their labels. "Someone's buying fancy floor tile. Pretty, cold things. But definitely not wax."

Jason paused at a nearby pallet of crates. "This is. Candles by the dozen. It's marked for a shop," and he read aloud, "The Flickering Flame."

"I know them!" Bailey's face brightened for an instant. "They've got the coolest shop in the county. More than candles, kind of New Age, with aromas, herbs, meditating music, that kind of thing. They said they were expanding. They must be putting a shop in here."

"Could be. Place isn't even renovated yet, though. Moving stock here is kind of jumping the gun."

"Maybe they needed storage room." Trent looked around. "Watch out for spiders."

"Spiders?" Bailey scooted to one side quickly.

He grabbed her by the sweatshirt. "Don't move."

She stood in place, eyes getting bigger.

Jason froze and looked about, carefully. "What do you see?"

"Webs. Silvery strings. Just kind of out of the corner of my eye, but the whole foyer is full of 'em."

"I don't," said Jason, even as he eyed the entryway again, "see a thing. But that doesn't mean you don't."

"What are webs for?"

"Trapping food. And the strands quiver when the prey touches and struggles in them, alerting the spider . . ." Trent stopped.

" 'Come into my parlor,' said the spider to the fly," quoted Bailey.

"The strands must be energy. An energy net, like. The minute we brush one, they know we're here."

Jason said quietly, "I think they already know we're here. I'm suspecting the webs are a lot worse than that. Take the lead, Trent, and try not to touch one." He waited for Trent's lead and wondered if Brennard had somehow gathered up and corrupted ley lines, the natural flow of the Earth's various energies.

Trent took Bailey by the hand, moving her away from the shadowed foyer wall, and began to walk to the lighted square of a door at the other end. Jason followed, but it was difficult because Trent took a very odd path through, casting right and left, ducking low, then stepping over things that Jason could not begin to see. They would have looked very peculiar, if there had been security cameras on to see them, but those awaiting them had chosen to depend on Magick for their surveillance.

Trent and Bailey stood in the golden arch and he had nearly reached them when something stung across his left arm, his bicep, as if he'd been lashed with a fiery whip. He let out a yelp of surprise and pain.

"I told you to duck!" Trent fretted as Jason wheeled

sharply to the right and then took a side step to join them. "Is it bad?"

Jason rubbed his arm gently. He pulled the sleeve of his sweatshirt around, certain it must have been ripped open, but there was nothing . . . nothing but a faint, charcoal burn mark that smelled of singed cloth, but was cold to the touch. He rubbed his hand over it and felt the powdery grit of residue.

"What did that thing do?"

"It was like . . . like a whiplash or something. Stings like crazy. It must have been the web or something. Don't touch any strands." The moment was over, but he felt a little queasy and who knew how he'd feel if he'd hit more than one of those things, whatever they were. "See any more?"

"Not as many but they're everywhere, Jason."

"I wonder if a creature makes them. Some big scary Dark Hand spider." Bailey shivered all over.

"Let's hope not. We've got enough trouble with people and· wolfjackals." Jason gestured at Trent. "We need to go that way, and through the door."

"Follow me then, and do what I do, very carefully."

They crossed the inner parlor, its room nearly empty except for alcoves with unlit candles in them, and boxes scattered about. It looked bigger, and older, and dustier than he remembered. The second-story floor overhead creaked, once, as if someone or something had taken a firm step. They all froze, and listened. Lacey stuck her head out of Bailey's pocket, whiskers trembling, but making not even a squeak as if the tiny pet sensed the danger. They all held their breath for a few long heartbeats, then Trent jerked his head.

"Old houses creak," he said. "And this one is plenty big and old."

"It must have been grand once," Bailey whispered in awe. She looked upstairs to a landing, all paneled in deep, rich wood.

Jason nodded in agreement. "Dozer calls it settling noises." He breathed in and out a few times to settle himself. His left bicep finally quit stinging. He set off after Trent and Bailey, casting glances around and behind them, wondering when the first attack would come. After that came other thoughts, wondering what kind of battle it would be, and if it would be to the finish.

Was he prepared for that? Could he even begin to do something like that? He didn't think so. But he would do what he had to in order to get his friends and the elders out of there. Even if he had to open a Gate to do it, a way through which the Dark Hand could not follow.

That thought sent a thrill right through him. The answer! He could. Yes, he could. Open a Gate, draw everyone with him through it, and snap it shut right in the faces of the Dark Hand. All he needed to do was find one, sense it, and focus on it, while Bailey and Trent distracted Brennard's efforts.

Of course, that might be a lot harder than it sounded, and it sounded impossible.

36

CHARGE!

"WE'RE going in," Jason told them. "I want you to know who you're going to grab when I say, 'Do it now!' I've got Trent. Each of you has to grab two people."

"Eleanora and Henry," Bailey claimed.

"Gavan and Tomaz."

"All right. Once I've done what I'm going to do, I can grab Dr. Patel. I'll be linking arms with Trent, so we both have our hands empty. Bailey, you'll have to stow your crystal when I yell. Everyone understand that?"

"Yeah," said Trent, and Bailey nodded. "Sorta," she answered. Then, "No. What are you going to do?"

"Something spectacular and hopefully unexpected." Jason felt excitement build in him. He could do it . . . he could! He grinned at her. "Opposites attack!"

She took a deep breath. Lacey poked her head out of the pocket, let out a tremorous squeak and dove back in, only her tail hanging outside. "I'm ready."

"You're sure."

She nodded, ponytail swinging. "Nearly sure, anyway."

"In that case . . ." Jason reared back and then kicked out hard, the doors falling open and inward under the blow. "Charge!"

The library doors slammed open with a Bang!

"JASON!" shouted Henry. His glasses sat sideways on his round face, one of the lenses broken, and a long scratch underneath it, his brown hair standing nearly straight up. One sleeve of his sweater hung in unraveled strands.

"Jason, go back!" cried Eleanora. Her pale face turned to him, dark curly hair in a disorderly mass about her face. She sat in a Victorian chair, her wrists neatly tied to the wooden arms, her long skirts tumbled about her.

"Jason, lad, think very carefully what it is you're going to do." Gavan Rainwater spoke last, bound elbow to elbow with Tomaz, who kept his silence. Even as Jason looked toward the two who stood against the bookcases, dark shadows enveloped them, and he lost sight of them. The veil, he was certain, was only illusion.

The trap was sprung.

"I can't quite see them," Trent told him in a very low whisper. "But I can see the wolfhead cane. They're still here."

Brennard stood in front of the great mahogany desk which seemed to brace him as well as set him off. Shadows held other figures which Jason could not quite see as he came to a halt in momentary dismay, then he realized it did not matter if the Magickers he hoped to rescue were tied or not. Easier, perhaps . . . a package deal!

Trent whispered behind his left ear, "Room is filled with webs. The only straight path is right for that guy."

Jason looked straight at "that guy," and said, "I believe this is the first time I've actually met you . . . Antoine Brennard."

"True. It seems our knowledge of each other has only been in dreams."

"Nightmares," Bailey snorted. "Afraid to come out in the open? Jason's not scared of you."

"Oh, but he should be." The Magicker looked at her. The expression in his dark eyes seemed to be one of amusement. When it changed, and it would, Jason thought, she would be in deadly danger.

"The Hand seems to be here, too," Jason commented.

"You can see them?" Brennard's eyebrows arched in his slender, elegant face.

He shook his head, even as Trent whispered softly to him, "One behind the desk behind Brennard, two to your left corner rear and one in the right corner rear . . . I don't see a fifth." Why show all your cards? It disturbed Brennard enough that Jason could even sense them.

Brennard relaxed slightly then, leaning back against the massive desk. He wore a dark velvet coat showing ruffles at the cuffs as he crossed his arms over his chest. "A proposition, Jason. A trade."

"I'm listening but not for long. Tell your Hand in the left corner to stop trying to flank us." Jason put his chin up and shifted his position to guard Trent, who had again relayed the enemy's movement to him. He grinned and repeated Trent's whispered comment. "Or maybe he's just a Finger?"

Total surprise flared over Brennard's face and disappeared as suddenly. He raised a hand and gestured and something Jason could almost but not quite hear ceased to happen. Anita Patel looked with concern toward Brennard. She alone seemed unbound. Bailey stared at her for a very long time, as did Henry, who seemed to have begun to twitch, and his eyeglasses now dangled even more precariously from his face. His mouth worked soundlessly.

"This need not be as unpleasant as it could," Brennard stated. "I want—"

"We know what you want," Jason interrupted. "You want the three of us. You used Henry for bait for them, and all of them as bait for us." He took a deep breath. "You're not getting any of us."

"I don't think you see the situation clearly," said Brennard. One corner of his mouth twitched, showing that he was still amused.

"I see it far better than you think I do."

"Hand moving on the right," Trent whispered quickly.

Jason looked to the right and said, "Hold it right there."

Anita Patel swung about in astonishment, and Brennard jerked an impatient thumb. "Do not force things yet," he said quietly, and again that almost noise he could almost hear stopped.

Bailey cleared her throat. "Let's play . . . Red Rover." She smiled brightly at Brennard.

The Magicker looked at her. "Red Rover?"

"Yes. Red rover, red rover, won't you please send Henry Squibb over?" And she put her hand out for Henry.

Brennard laughed. "She thinks it's a game."

"Not hardly. And you're not playing with children." Bailey held her crystal up, and a thin white light lanced across the room, smoking. It sliced across one arm of the chair Eleanora was bound to, and then she pulled on her bindings and the ropes parted with a faint *twing!* Quickly she reached over to undo her other wrist, but Brennard gestured with a harsh word that seemed to darken the room. The Magicker went limp in her chair, and Bailey went to her knees, motionless. Lacey let out a pitiful squeak.

Gavan growled from the shadows that veiled and held him. "I will kill you for that, Brennard!"

"She only sleeps. Do you think I would harm a hair on her head? And the same goes for the girl."

"No," Jason said, a little sick to his stomach, "you wouldn't hurt anyone as long as you had a use for them."

"Oh, I have uses." He held up a woven sack and scattered its contents about the room. Bones and teeth went scattering. "I need a body or two."

"What is that for?" Jason stared, not understanding that one.

"Evidence," Brennard said. "To cover your taking. Your families will grieve over these, all that will survive in the ashes." He gestured. "Get the old ones out of here. Treat them to the delight Fizziwig felt when he disobeyed me!" He stood. "Enough talk. You are well and truly mine. You are mine!" He waved his arm in a grand gesture. *"Inardesco!"* shouted Brennard.

"Burn!" whispered Trent in his ear. "It's Latin for start to burn or ignite."

What? Jason pondered. Burn? Latin? "How on earth do you know that?" He turned his head back toward Trent in total amazement.

"Harry Potter," muttered Trent, and blushed.

"Good grief." Jason turned his attention back to Brennard who had regained his cold smile.

"It is your choice, Jason. Come to me freely, and they go.

Or I will take you anyway, and they will stay here . . . to their deaths." Brennard lifted his gaze, across the library room, through the open doors at Jason's back. "Candles burn so well. The whole place will go up like tinder. An All Hallows' Eve prank. No one will prove any different, nor will anyone come after you, thinking you still alive."

Jason could smell the hot wax. Crates and crates of very flammable paraffin candles spread out downstairs and up, no doubt. His nightmare of facing Brennard and burning walls was coming true. . . .

And so was his need for a Gate. Not just any Gate. Fire Gate. He understood now, what it was all about. The McHenry house and his dreams had been trying to tell him for weeks.

He locked his eyes on Brennard's face. He curled one hand about his lavender crystal, and felt it answer to his touch, the only way a cold stone could, by warming. "Let them go."

Brennard laughed, and as in Jason's dreams, it was a sound without true joy, nor did it light his eyes. "Do you think you can coerce me? A mere boy? You don't even have chin hairs yet!" He straightened, and his voice got stronger till it roared out of him, like a banked fire awakening and leaping into roaring sound. "I am the master of anyone in this room. Anyone! Don't fool yourself into thinking you can put enough steel in your voice to make me think twice!"

While Brennard's voice boomed, Trent said in his ear, "I still have clear sight of Gavan's cane. I know where they are, I'll get them."

Bailey said nothing, but her linked arm tightened. She stayed with her head bowed, feigning unconsciousness.

Jason set himself, and began to pull forth what he knew about opening a Gate. He could smell the smoke beginning to pour into the room. By the time the flames reached them, it would be too late. They would already have suffocated. Bailey coughed once or twice harshly, as if confirming that. Smoke would kill before the heat. So the flames of his Fire Gate would have to be in his mind, a thousand thousand candles, ringing all of them.

"Let me help," said Anita Patel, moving forward to Jason, her small, slender hand outstretched. Henry went into a fit of twitches and stammers and fell over in front of her, his heels drumming on the floor.

Trent said, "She's got no ropes on her."

Eleanora, who appeared to have reawakened as Brennard's concentration was focused on Jason, tossed her head, dark eyes on Trent, and she managed a nod, going very pale then as if it took all her strength.

"Jason. Take my hand. You'll need strength for the Fire Gate!" The doctor reached for him, her voice soft as silk, her gaze intent, the bells on her anklet chiming as she drew near.

Traitor! He stared at her as she tried to step around Henry's form, and Henry thrashed back and forth attempting to block her. His glasses finally fell off completely, and Anita's heel crunched them to bits, and she didn't even stop. It might as well have been his head she stepped on, her dark eyes focused only on Jason.

Too eager for the Fire Gate. The Dark Hand wanted them, all of them, through a Gate and out of this world, so they could do with them whatever they pleased. They were driving him to it.

It hung in his head, a Gate wrought of twisting orange-red flames with blue centers, straining to open so that they might escape through it.

The fire came. He could hear the fine, old wood of the McHenry house scream as it exploded into inferno. Window glass burst outward with the heat. Smoke curled in, stinging his eyes. Deadly, it rushed toward them, and only he could lead any of them out. The Gate must be him, what he was made of, and what he needed and knew was right . . . the giant salamander had told him. Dracos infernos. Dragon. Dragon of flame-colored scales and wit and insight. The Gate must be what he was made of. Incongruously, he thought of a school lab door falling open. The human body was made of . . .

Jason *pushed*. The Gate of Flame fell open, inward, smelling like ozone and hot metal. He grabbed up Henry and wrapped his hand around Trent's wrist instead of grabbing Dr. Patel.

"Do it now!" he yelled above the din and chaos.

Trent's vision overlaid his own for a moment. That was all he needed. He pulled on his friends as they reached out for the others, and he knew in a split second when they were all connected. He looked deep into the crystal, the Herkimer Diamond, caught in the wolfhead jaws of Gavan Rainwater's cane. Water, the nemesis of Fire.

And he opened a second Gate, a Water Gate into the tiny drop held in the heart of the flawed diamond and plunged them all into cold, cold wetness . . . and life.

37

LUCKY GUESS

THEY popped up out of the pool in Jason's favorite valley like buoyant apples bobbing up in a Halloween dunking tub. Noisier, though, Bailey said later, all of them spluttering and coughing and poor Henry finally found his voice and was screaming to all who could hear that Dr. Patel was the one who'd kidnapped him and watch out!

He quieted after Trent ducked him a second time, while everyone else was hurrying to climb out, for the late October weather and water were cold, cold, cold. Gavan said a word, and his cape steamed as it dried. He wrapped it about Eleanora who forgot to levitate so she would be inches higher as she leaned quietly into his embrace. Tomaz gently made sure that little Lacey hadn't drowned while in Bailey's pocket, holding her in his hand and softly stroking the little creature's flanks until she coughed up spittles of water and finally began breathing evenly on her own.

Jason kept his arm linked with Bailey's, trying to send her reassuring feelings about Lacey and the whole mess while Trent eventually helped a much calmer if spluttering Henry out of the lake. They all straggled up the hill and through the Iron Gate, and Gavan took them home to Ravenwyng, where—after making sure that they all got messages to their families that would give them acceptable alibis for not being home—they had tea and cookies and talked while the world around them celebrated haunts and ghosts and evil running wild, only to be reined in by the morning's dawn. Jason thought he would never look at Halloween the same way again.

"How did you know?" asked Rainwater.

"I didn't. I guessed."

"Come, lad. Life and death don't ride on guesses." Gavan watched him, his cape still wrapped about Eleanora and her chair pulled very close to his.

"Well, then . . ." Jason stared down at his plate which now held nothing but crumbs and pushed the china toward Bailey. There was a pause, then a little chirp, and Lacey came out cautiously and hunkered down to steal the cookie bits. "Let's say, it came together. They wanted that Fire Gate. I realized that they'd probably already had it open once, preparing it to receive all of us . . . like a prison or concentration camp, or something."

"Why?" Tomaz rocked back in his chair, coffee mug settled deep in his hands. "How did you figure that?"

"Fizziwig. They'd got a Gate out of Fizziwig. It's probably what killed him, the strain. Even if it didn't, that's why they wanted him and took him."

Pain crossed Gavan's face. "Of course. I should have realized that." Jason stopped, and he gestured. "Go on."

"For weeks I've been pushed toward a Fire Gate. In my dreams, waking, the McHenry house, they made sure it was centered in my life. The wolfjackals were herding us toward it, and Brennard was piling the pressure on in ways you don't even know about yet, so that I would just have to discover it and open the Gate, for us all to escape." He looked around the table. "They didn't figure on all of you going after Henry, just us."

Tomaz snorted. "No credit for good sense. But it was quite a trap, and we were caught."

"That still doesn't explain why you suddenly went for water."

"The fire would have claimed or killed us. I'd been advised that Gates are within yourself, and I . . . well, it's silly . . . all I could think of, was that I'm seventy percent water. It suddenly became the only thing I could do. It had to be a Water Gate. The only drop I could find in that whole room to focus on was buried in your Herkimer diamond."

Gavan lifted his cane, smiling at the wolfhead figure with the gemstone in its jaws. "I've always been very fond of this. Now I have a reason."

Eleanora said something, muffled, and he tightened his hold about her shoulders. She quieted, smiling.

"You managed to control Brennard after all."

Jason nodded to Tomaz. "In a way. Actually, all I wanted to do was make him really angry because when you're angry, you can't think. I didn't want him following us."

"I felt a push," murmured Eleanora. She tucked some wayward hair behind one delicate ear. "What did you do, Jason?"

"I had this." He pulled the lavender stone from his pocket. "It seems to have a Talent for persuading." He grinned, thinking how nice Alicia was every time he asked her to do something while he had the stone in his hand.

"But you couldn't persuade him to let us go." Henry's voice was squeaky from too much shouting. Now he had barely said a word and looked as if he didn't want to say much more.

Jason shook his head. "I'm not strong enough for anything like that. I was standing there looking at all of you tied up like turkeys for a roasting, and I knew I couldn't outwrestle him. I persuaded him to get angry. And it worked." He kept grinning broadly.

"May I see that again, Jason?" Gavan put a hand out for it.

"Sure." He dropped the lavender crystal in Rainwater's palm.

"Where did he get that?" Eleanora stirred, sitting up straight. She put her hand over Gavan's and peered at the stone.

"I was . . . hmmm . . . well, I was practicing opening Gates."

Gavan's eyebrows went up, but he said nothing. "Were you now? I don't seem to remember you telling me." Eleanora was practically tucked under his chin, looking at the new focus, and he seemed to be enjoying her proximity, despite his concern over Jason's behavior.

"Gavan," said Eleanora quietly. "Look deep into it. Really focus."

"It's Jason's stone," he reminded her.

"Oh, I know it is! Just look."

He did. Then he looked up at Jason. "Lad . . . do you see an image inside this?"

"Sometimes."

"I cannot see it well. Describe it."

Eleanora leaned back against Gavan's chest, visibly trembling.

Jason told them of the silvery-haired gentleman, with a warm smile and humor and youth despite the color of his curled hair. He stopped as Eleanora spoke a name. "Gregory!"

Tomaz rumbled, "None other. I would say it was no accident Jason found that crystal, and even less of an accident he could use it against Brennard."

"*The* Gregory?" Trent piped up.

Bailey kept quiet, busy feeding small bits of cookie to her near-drowned Lacey.

"None other. My father," Eleanora returned. She handed the crystal back to Jason. "Use it well and wisely."

Jason stared at it as if it had become a hot potato. "He's not . . . he's not trapped in there. . . ."

"Oh, no. Nothing like that." Eleanora laughed then, a bit of color coming back into her cheeks. "Just an enchantment or two of his in there. He knew things none of the rest of us did, including, I think, what Brennard was capable of."

"It's a good thing that came into your hands, lad," Gavan said, "and we'll discuss later the appropriate discipline for trying something daft like that without a backup."

"Trent was there!"

Gavan looked at Trent, and said nothing.

"What about the others? Think they got out?" Bailey picked up Lacey and was coaxing her back into a pocket, but the pack rat seemed determined to keep an eye on everyone about the table and their cookies.

"No doubt they used their Fire Gate. I imagine the house was lost. It was meant to be. They planned a devastating fire to cover up their taking you four. They had teeth, bones . . . to scatter in the ashes." Tomaz grunted. "We underestimated them. Won't happen again."

"Well," said Bailey. "All's well that ends well."

"It's only just begun, Bailey."

She tucked Lacey back in her pocket. "I know that! We've more Gates to get open, more Magick to learn! As long as we get to that ending well part."

Trent sat back. "Since dessert is a good ending any time . . . I could use a bit more. After all, it is trick or treat." He looked about the table hopefully, and Henry hoarsely seconded him.

And as a special bonus feature,
here is a brand-new *Magickers* tale,
"Bumpity,"
created especially for this volume.

Bumpity

A Magickers Story

"**I** SUPPOSE YOU ALL WONDER why I called you here today." Gavan Rainwater watched his audience, scattered about the hotel room in various poses, taking up chairs, the small battered couch, and the rug.

"Because Colonel Mustard did it in the kitchen with a lead pipe?" Rich leaned back on one elbow as Stefan grunted in appreciation and the others gave scattered groans.

Eleanora wagged a finger at the two boys who had pulled their attention away from a football game, one of those holiday season bowl games that seemed to multiply every year and ruled the small handheld TV Rich cradled. "Pay attention or no pizza."

Burly Stefan's stomach growled in answer, and Ting blurted out, "You wouldn't dare, Eleanora! Stefan-bear really gets hungry."

"As do we all," Trent drawled. He poked a sneaker toe into the side of Jason's foot. "Besides, if you're going to tell us any of the mysteries of life, I want to know what the Curse of Arkady is, anyway."

"It's probably something profound, like, 'don't put all your bad eggs into one basket,'" Bailey said. She tossed her head, amber ponytail bouncing. "And, anyway, I bet they told us to beware of it just to keep us in line. As if."

That brought a faint blush to Ting's face and she leaned on Bailey's shoulder, all the while trying not to notice that Henry had said little and done even less except watch her whenever he thought no one else would catch him at it.

Master Magicker Gavan waited for silence, the corner of his mouth quirked just a little, his cape folded back on one shoulder. When the room got as quiet as it was going to get— meaning that even if all of them stopped talking, the TV still droned its play-by-play football in the background—he said, "I thought I'd keep one of you from blowing up the world."

That finally brought Henry's attention around. "Holy cow. One of us can do that?"

Eleanora traded a long look with Gavan before turning her lovely face toward them. "Actually, any one of you can. That's why we brought you together and, yes, Bailey, that's why we saddled you with watching out for Arkady's Curse. We thought it might make you cautious."

"But after the recent events, we've decided caution isn't what you need." Gavan paused. He hitched up his cape uneasily. "The holiday season made it easier for us to bring you all together. Your parents are already planning for the summer, and we've let them know we want you back as students. But we can't wait until the summer to educate you. You all know that."

Rich turned off his TV and put it on the small coffee table in the hotel room suite. Jason watched him before scanning the room and asking, "Where's Tomaz?"

"Tomaz is acting as a lightning rod, a decoy as it were, to distract any attention. It's just the two of us today."

"Distractions? Such as?"

"Wolfjackals, for one. And . . . others." Eleanora's curved mouth thinned a bit, and they knew they'd not get another word from her on that subject. The absence of the Native American Magic worker and favorite teacher might bother them, but if it was necessary, Tomaz knew best. "But, as for Arkady," and Gavan drew himself up as Eleanora continued, tapping his knee with her hand as she spoke, "I have this."

And she did. "Samuel Arkady was a Magicker from the olden days," she told them, leaning forward, and the group scooted nearer as she did. "He was young, talented, and quick to learn and, unfortunately, all three led to his downfall when his ego got in his way. His story was passed down to us to remember and . . . " Elenora paused, frowning, as a low rumble came from beyond the room's walls.

Gavan stood and twitched aside a curtain. The sky, which had been gray and gloomy before, had plunged into almost total darkness although it wasn't even noon. He dropped the curtain quickly but they'd all seen it. As he turned away from the window, another low rumble sounded, louder and closer. Ting and Bailey hunched together, their arms intertwined.

"Don't worry," Bailey soothed Ting. "Thunder is just when clouds go bumpity."

Ting looked at her and raised one eyebrow. "Are you serious? I'm not scared and I'm no baby." She punched Bailey's arm lightly. "I'm thinking about Tomaz. *He's* the lightning rod."

Jason felt a tingle down his arms and into his hands almost as if someone or something was opening a Gate . . . and he could feel it. "Ah, guys," he began, but the room shook as thunder rattled overhead.

Gavan swung a protective arm toward Eleanora as she jumped suddenly to her feet. "It can't be—"

BLAM!

Everything went dark.

There was a very long silence.

"Great. I'm blind and I have a terrified bear cub sitting in my lap. Or what's left of my lap. This is so not what I wanted in a best friend."

"Thank goodness! We thought we were alone!" Ting and Bailey spoke almost as one.

"Hold onto your crystals," Jason said. "It's pretty unsteady where I am. Which, as near as I can tell, is nowhere."

Henry blurted out, "Don't move, Ting!"

Rich mumbled and a wave of bear whimpers drowned out whatever else he might have said.

"So we're all here. I know Trent is holding his breath for suspense."

A noise of exhalation came, followed by: "Made you look. Sorta, anyway."

Jason continued, "All of us but Gavan and Eleanora. Everyone got your crystals? Rich, can you tell if Stefan does?"

"I tied it on a thong around his neck, after the last time. Why so worried about the rocks?"

"Because," Jason said "they may very well be the only way out of here." His voice grew stronger as he gripped his crystal, and he thought himself into a patch of light, and slowly but surely, there was one. He couldn't see the others. "I think we may be behind a shield. Maybe one Eleanora and Gavan threw up."

"If we are, this is nothing like what they've taught us." Trent's face illuminated for a moment, frowning, and then winked out.

"M . . . maybe we should consider staying here."

"Or maybe not. See if we can join hands. Hold your crystal in one hand but link up."

"Breaking out?"

Jason's image paled slightly. He didn't know if the others could see him at all or if he could only see himself. "Not sure yet, but I think we ought to have a feel for what's going on, don't you? Maybe Gavan and Eleanora put us here. And maybe they didn't."

"I don't like the sound of that." Ting's voice got a little high and uneasy.

Trent countered with, "You're not supposed to. Now link up. We're Magickers."

Almost before Trent finished, Jason added, "And quit complaining, Rich. You've got the easiest one to do, you know exactly where Stefan is and all you have to do is hold his crystal in your other hand while one of us tries to find you."

"Um. Okay."

Darkness seemed to shift and roll uneasily about Jason as he sensed his friends cautiously trying to find each other. A hand touched his elbow and then moved confidently down to his free hand and grasped it. "Well done," muttered Trent.

Jason couldn't be sure if it was well done or not. What if they were in an enemy's trap and safe only because they were separate and in the dark?

And what if they were not safe anywhere?

He decided that he was safer with friends in the dark than with no one. He felt Bailey bump his knee and dipped his crystal hand down to her, and she grasped it tightly, her fingers chilled. What was this? Bailey afraid?

"Gavan. The children are gone."

The emptiness in the hotel room had never seemed so complete until she voiced her fear. He still had his arm around her, and drew her close to him, but not too near. Just close enough to comfort. "They are hardly children."

"No. I . . . I know that. Are they taken?"

"Or just displaced? I can't tell. It's all I can do to hold a shield up."

She wrapped her hand tightly about his wrist. "Draw from me if you need to."

He might have to. He just might. He couldn't see her frown but he could feel it in her words. "I don't know who's attacking. I have never felt power like this before."

"Nor I. He . . . or she . . . is testing us." And they just might break, the two of them. Gavan set his jaw. What about Tomaz? Had he already fallen?

"We have to rescue them, Gavan. We have to."

"First, we need to rescue ourselves," he answered her grimly.

Despite the thrashing about, a semicircle had been made and Jason could hear mutters of anxiety. "Stop it."

"What would Gavan do?" Henry practically yelled at him.

"Gavan's not here. We are. And although we've moved, we haven't moved. We're still sitting in just about the same positions we were. That is, except for Rich and Stefan who seem to be mud wrestling or something."

Rich—or maybe it was Stefan-bear—growled softly, then Rich said, "Nice. Well, you try wrangling a bear cub who's scared AND hungry. Oh . . . wait!" A noise like rustling followed, and then a hearty crunching. "Score one for a nutty protein bar."

"You'd better hope there's two." Trent sounded faintly amused and he squeezed Jason's fingers.

"There are. Three more, in fact, and he's getting them. Ohhh-kay. Got it. Got him by the crystal, as it were."

"Everyone, remember where you were and try to connect. About half of us are already linked. So stretch in the direction where you remember the others were if you have a free hand. We won't get a circle, a semicircle is going to have to do it."

"Why not try for a circle?" Ting's high, melodic voice had steadied.

"Because I don't want us shifting around too much. Just in

case. I don't know what's under us, but I'm pretty sure it's not the hotel room floor."

"Ah."

A few more dark moments of grunts and mutters and then a muffled sigh, before a triumphant, "Got us. All of us."

"They taught us light. Do it," Jason reminded them.

A very long moment passed. Then another. He could feel it himself, as if something heavy weighed on him, chasing the Magick right out of him, keeping it out of his touch and control, and then, with a "POP!" he felt it where he could use it. Slowly the others lit up, Ting and Bailey as one, and then the rest. It felt good; it felt excellent.

Until Jason looked around and said, "Oh, Bailey. I think I know where we are. Do you?"

Her eyes widened. Then she answered slowly, "We're inside a crystal. But whose?"

They stared at each other across a wakening arc of illumination. Without knowing whose crystal, they might never be able to get out.

Stefan-bear let out a low, bawling cry.

"It's not mine." Trent nodded firmly. "My crystal is cloudy."

"It's not mine. No purple shading."

Jason swung about, eyes narrowing. "Mine has a fracture, like a . . . I don't know . . . a crevice." It was like falling into the darkest part of the darkest soul he could imagine, and it scared him to even think about it. But he knew it, a little, and that same fracture identified his crystal as much as the light parts of it did. He also realized he would have to explore it someday, but today was not the day! He hoped. "So we're not in my crystal."

They spoke around the circle until all eyes fastened on the bear cub, his fur ruffled and small bits of nut bar sprinkled over his muzzle, Rich's arm flung around his shoulders. Rich looked at his transformed friend. "Don't tell me."

Trent tilted his head to one side, considering the crystal that hung on a strong, braided leather tie about the bear's throat. He thought he recognized the lanyard method taught at Camp Ravenwyng. "This could be a very good thing or a very bad one."

"How so?"

"If whoever attacked is searching for us, he'd never find us in there. I mean, you'd have to go through Stefan-bear's mind to do it. Probably never suspect a thing like that could happen, so . . . " Trent shrugged. "On the other hand, if we have to decipher the cub's mind to get out, there could be some trouble there."

"Just think of honey," Ting offered. "That would probably do it."

Bailey had been oddly quiet, her brow kind of squinched up, and now she traded a look with Jason. "I think I know how to test it. Stuff I did when I was captured." Before she could get out another word, the whole nothingness in which they sat shifted abruptly, like a ledge, and they began to slide off.

"Whatever you're doing, Gavan, I think it's working."

Sweat dappled his brow and her hand had gone cold on his wrist, so he knew he was taxing her strength heavily, but it was all he could do to fight back. He couldn't push much longer and he knew he couldn't push any harder. Not without knowing specifically what sort of magic it was he fought. He let go a little. Her breathing eased as did his, but the pressure pushing down on him grew heavy again. He shook his head. "We're in a standoff."

"Yes, but he had the advantage of us and now he doesn't. That's good, isn't it?"

"Good that we're holding, but I can't find the kids, Eleanora. They're not within my senses . . . how about you?"

"I know they're alive," she answered softly. "More than that, I can't tell. Nor can I promise you they'll stay that way."

Their lights went out, but they stopped sliding. Jason took a deep breath and let it flow out through him, along with the Magick knowledge of light, and he and pushed it through the line of Magickers connected to him. He could feel it move out of him and beyond, and each Magicker was revealed just like . . . well, darned if it wasn't just like a string of holiday lights coming on, one bright bulb at a time. They all exhaled at once in relief. Henry bobbed his head once, eyes shining. "I don't like sitting in the dark," he muttered.

"I'm right here next to you," Ting told him. "In fact, we all are!"

The slide had squished them all together, shoulder-to-shoulder, and now the circle could be joined. Stefan-bear hunkered down with a mournful groan as Rich reached around him to close it.

Power surged. They could feel it.

"My hair's standing on end!" Trent gave a lopsided grin. His hair was always so tousled that Jason couldn't see any difference.

Bailey shook her head, ponytail swinging. "Mine too, or it feels like it. Like one of those static balls at the science show. You put your hands on it and wham! Your hair stands up."

"It's power. Enough power to break out of here, I think." Jason craned his neck to get a better look at his surroundings. "Rich, get your face in the bear's, look at his crystal, and tell me if you see a vein of mica and a vein of ... dunno what that is, might be like ... well, something greenish."

"Fungus?" offered Trent helpfully.

"Ew," chorused Bailey and Ting.

Rich sucked in his breath before leaning over to peer closely at Stefan's crystal. He looked at it for long minutes, his face turning redder and redder before he sat back up, and gulped down air. "Oh, his breath stinks. Why couldn't he be like a puppy dog or something with that baby animal smell?" He shuddered. Then he blinked to see they were all staring, no, glaring at him. "What? Oh. No, his crystal doesn't look like that at all."

Jason smiled thinly. "Then we've got him, whoever it is. When we bust out, we're gonna break him."

"How do you propose to manage that?"

Jason stood carefully, not letting go of his friends' hands. He straightened his shoulders. "I'm going to open a Gate, right ... about ... " His words slowed as he gathered Power and Magick still a little unfamiliar to him, but he knew he could do it. He touched a knuckle to a barely seen crystal facet behind him. "Here."

He pulled on their power. They gave it freely, trusting him, hands linked to one another, no one holding back, not even the furry essence of the bear-boy. Warmth flooded him. Warmth that turned to heat, and tingles, and ... well, he could feel a threshold etching into the crystal wall he touched, carv-

ing deeper and deeper as though his will was a cutting torch
and he drew a fiery golden-red framework. It drained him. He
could feel the strength flood out of his arms and legs until they
were like noodles and he didn't know how he could remain
standing but he had to. He needed one last punch to push the
door open. "Help me. NOW."

And they all gave him one last hard blast of their own
power, and it went through him, slamming into their prison.

The nowhere, the nothingness that held them, shattered
in a high-pitched burst of ringing, and they went sliding into
darkness. Again.

The blindness lasted only a gulp of breath or two. Jason fell to
his knees. And then light flickered on about them, the hotel
room getting power back, as they bowled into Gavan and Eleanora, knocking them head over heels.

It took a moment to sort everyone out. Gavan drew Eleanora to her feet and dusted her off, then Jason. "Well," he
said. "And here I thought I was going to come to *your* rescue.
Instead it seems you came to ours."

Rich pushed the bear cub off himself with a grunt. Or maybe
the cub grunted. Or maybe both of them did. The cub rolled
up into a ball, paws over his eyes and muzzle. "About time,"
Rich declared. "I am going to stink of bear for a week."

"Not if you remember to shower," Trent told him and then
ducked away.

Henry looked Ting and Bailey up and down. "Everyone
seems to be all right."

"Everyone," Gavan told them, "is far more than all right."
He left Eleanora to cross the room and twitch aside the cur-
tains. "The storm has cleared. Whatever you did, you broke
his power."

"And his crystal, too," Jason said. "Or we think that's what
we did."

"Really? Most interesting. We're going to have to talk
about that."

Eleanora added gently, "That was an attack and a test.
Someone is out there with a great deal of Magick and wanted
to break us."

"But he didn't. We fought back."

She smiled at Jason. "That was Arkady's Curse. He didn't have friends, he couldn't trust anyone but himself, and so when things got tough, he had to stand alone. We're always stronger together."

"We'll remember that," Jason told her, knowing he spoke for all of them. "Next time someone wants to knock heads with us, it's all of us!"

Bailey nodded. "You see? Bumpity!"